"It's a game of cat and mouse, isn't it? We try to find the evidence and he tries to make sure we don't. When is he going to give it up?"

Cam shrugged and pulled her out of the chair. "When he's tired of playing cat and mouse."

"Or when I'm dead."

"Don't say that." He placed his hands on her shoulders and massaged his thumbs into her skin.

"We both know the reason why he hasn't taken his shot at me yet."

"We do?" Cam ran his tongue over his dry teeth.

"It's because you're here, Cam. He knows I have some kind of badass bodyguard dogging me, and when you leave—" her shoulders tensed beneath his hands "—I'm a goner."

"I'm not going anywhere."

"Yet." She tucked her head beneath his chin. "How many more days until you leave?"

"Shh." He dropped his hands to her waist and pulled her body against his. "We have time. I'm gonna catch this guy, and when I do, he'll pay—for everything."

DELTA FORCE DEFENDER

CAROL ERICSON

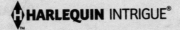

Recycling programs
for this product may
not exist in your area.

ISBN-13: 978-1-335-52673-1

Delta Force Defender

Printed in U.S.A.

Carol Ericson is a bestselling, award-winning author of more than forty books. She has an eerie fascination for true-crime stories, a love of film noir and a weakness for reality TV, all of which fuel her imagination to create her own tales of murder, mayhem and mystery. To find out more about Carol and her current projects, please visit her website at www.carolericson.com, "where romance flirts with danger."

Visit the Author Profile page at Harlequin.com.

CAST OF CHARACTERS

Martha Drake—A brainy CIA translator responsible for turning over the emails that first implicated Delta Force's Major Rex Denver in a terrorist plot. She's now having second thoughts about the veracity of those emails, but it might be too late. Now someone wants her to keep her mouth shut.

Cam Sutton—This impulsive Delta Force soldier will do anything to clear his commander's name, including confronting the CIA translator who first discovered the phony emails implicating him. He soon realizes the translator is on his side, and now he must do everything in his power to protect her.

Casey Jessup—Martha's roommate may seem like an airhead, but she may be more politically connected than Martha realizes. Those connections might not be enough to keep her out of danger.

Congressman Robert Wentworth—This politician winds up dead in Martha's town house, but his death can't be connected to the emails...can it?

Tony Battaglia—A bartender who knows too much for his own good, and doesn't know when to keep quiet.

Sebastian Forsythe—A fellow nerd, Sebastian and Martha dated a few times. He's good at fixing computers. Is he also good at planting evidence?

"Ben"—He seems to have his fingers in all the pies, but nobody can identify him and nobody knows his real name. He may be the key to absolving Major Denver or he may be the major's worst nightmare.

Major Rex Denver—Framed for working with a terrorist group, the Delta Force commander has gone AWOL and is on the run. He knows he's onto a larger plot, and he can count on his squad to have his back and help clear his name.

Prologue

A bug scuttled across his face, but Major Rex Denver didn't move one coiled, aching muscle. Twenty feet below him at the bottom of the hill, an army ranger team thrashed through the bushes, their voices loud and penetrating in the dead of the Afghan night.

Rex clenched his jaw as if willing the rangers to do the same. Didn't they realize this mountainous area was crawling with the enemy?

His eye twitched. To those rangers, Major Rex Denver *was* the enemy.

He didn't blame those boys for being out here searching for him. Hell, he'd be out here hunting down a traitor to his country, too.

He resettled his rifle and rested his finger on the trigger, not that he'd ever use it against any branch of the US Military. If the rangers found him, he'd go peacefully—but they'd never find him.

He'd started as a ranger himself, and after twenty years in Delta Force, leading his own team, he'd honed his skills at subterfuge and escape to perfection. They wouldn't catch him, but he'd die before he allowed the enemy that roamed these hills to catch those rangers.

One of the rangers yelled out. "Come out, come out, wherever you are."

Rex rolled his eyes. If that soldier was on his team, the wrath of hell would come down on him for that behavior. Rex had to bring the hammer down on Cam Sutton, one of the younger Delta team members, more than a few times for reckless behavior.

Someone issued a whispered reprimand from out of the darkness.

The young soldier answered back. "I don't care, sir, this is wrong. Major Denver's no traitor."

Rex believed he had the loyalty of most of the soldiers who knew his reputation, but the evidence against him was overwhelming. Why him? He and his Delta Force team must've stumbled on something big for someone to take them out of the picture. And he hoped to have a long time to figure it out.

A twig cracked to his right, and Rex's gaze darted toward the sound. Something glinted in the thick foliage. He flipped his night-vision goggles over his eyes and picked out the man crouched in the shadows, his focus on the team of rangers below.

Adrenaline flooded his body, and his heart hammered in his chest. Were there more? He scanned the area beyond the stealthy intruder. If this interloper wasn't solo, his companions weren't within striking distance of the rangers...at least not yet and not before the rangers could respond with their own firepower.

If Rex took out the enemy, he couldn't do it quietly. And once he made his position known, the rangers would swarm the mountainside and capture him.

He cranked his head around slowly, eyeing the steep drop-off behind him. He'd seen worse.

Rex popped up from his hiding place, and in the same motion he took the shot. It took just one. The enemy combatant pitched forward, his gun shooting impotently into the sky above him.

The rangers came to life as they fanned out and charged the hill.

Rex clutched his weapon to his chest, and rolled off the edge of the cliff into the dark unknown.

Chapter One

Martha's head pounded, and her hand trembled as she clicked open her email. Holding her breath, she scrolled past all the new emails that had come in since she'd taken lunch.

When she came to the end of the batch, she let out that breath and slumped in her chair.

The most sinister email that had come through was a reminder to submit her time sheet. She picked up her coffee cup and had to set it down as the steaming liquid sloshed over the rim onto her unsteady hand.

"Hey, Martha. Did you have a good lunch?"

Martha twisted her head around and smiled at her coworker Farah. "Errands, you?"

"Hot lunch date with the mystery man."

"I hope he's not married like the previous one."

"The previous one is still in the picture. A girl has to keep her options open." Farah winked and pushed away from Martha's cubicle almost bumping into Sebastian.

He held up his hand in an awkward wave. "Everything working okay with your computer after I dialed back that program to the previous version?"

"It's back up to speed. Thanks, Sebastian." Martha made a half turn in her chair back to her desktop, hoping he'd take the hint. They'd dated once or twice, but she wanted a relationship with some flying sparks for a change.

Sebastian took a step back, tapping the side of her cube. "Okay, then. Let me know if you need anything else."

Yeah, sparks.

Martha swung around to fully face her computer and jumped when another email came through. When would this fear go away? Those emails had started trickling into her inbox four months ago. She'd turned them over to the appropriate authorities and washed her hands of them—or tried to.

She chewed on her bottom lip. She hadn't forgotten about those emails. How could she, when they'd resulted in a huge investigation of some hotshot Delta Force commander, who'd then gone AWOL? How could she, when ever since she'd clicked on those emails, someone had been spying on her, following her?

She glanced over her shoulder at her coworkers in the CIA's translation department. Why had she been chosen for the honor of receiving those anonymous emails accusing Major Rex Denver of treason and colluding with the enemy?

What would've happened if she'd deleted those emails and never told a soul? Would she be the nervous wreck she was today?

She tapped her fingernail against her coffee cup. She couldn't have ignored those emails any more than she could jump up on her desk right now and scream in the middle of a CIA office that she had a bomb under her desk.

Maybe if she'd gotten rid of the emails like she was supposed to do, the people who'd sent them would leave her alone. But why would that matter? The senders had gotten their desired response. She reported the emails, which prompted the investigation of Denver, which then led to the discovery of his traitorous activities. The man had gone rogue. How much more guilty could you get?

But some gut instinct had compelled her to hang on to the emails. When she first received them, she'd copied them to a flash drive, which she wasn't even supposed to insert in her computer, and taken them home. She'd told everyone, including her slimy boss, Gage, that she'd deleted them. Then the IT department had come in and wiped her deleted items off the face of the earth.

She had her own suspicions about how those messages had gotten through to her email address at the Agency. It had the fingerprints of Dreadworm, a hacking group, all over it, but not even Dreadworm had claimed responsibility for forwarding those emails.

Martha had wanted to take a more careful look at the messages because of the phrasing. She spoke several languages, and she'd told Gage that the emails sounded like a foreigner had composed them.

He'd brushed her off like he always did, but she'd gotten her revenge by keeping those emails for herself.

Now she had someone stalking her.

Sighing, Martha straightened in her chair and shoved in her earbuds. She double-clicked on the file she'd been working on before lunch and began typing in the English words for the Russian ones that poured into her ears from one of the radio broadcasts the CIA monitored and recorded. After about an hour of translating, Martha plucked out the earbuds and stretched her arms over her head.

She swirled the coffee in the bottom of her cup and made a face. Then she slid open a desk drawer and grabbed a plastic bag with a toothbrush and toothpaste.

When she returned to her desk ten minutes later with a minty taste in her mouth and a bottle of water, she plopped in her chair and tucked her hair behind her ears, ready to tackle the remainder of the afternoon.

She glanced at the bottom of her computer screen, noticing a little yellow envelope on her email icon, indicating a new message. She double-clicked on it and froze. Her blood pounded in her ears as she stared at the skull and crossbones grinning at her from the computer screen, its teeth chattering.

Hunching forward, she resized the window and scrolled from the top to the bottom of it. No text accompanied the image. She scrutinized the unfamiliar email from a fake email account at the top of the window.

She glanced over her shoulder, and in a split second she forwarded the email to her home address. She deleted it and then wiped it clean from her deleted items. She knew it still existed somewhere in cyberspace, but not unless someone was looking for it. And why would anybody be checking her emails? She'd been the good little soldier she always was and turned over the others. The people up the chain of command had no reason to suspect her, and Gage thought she was a lifeless drone, so she didn't need to worry about him.

If Gage cornered her right now and asked her why she didn't tell anyone about the skull and crossbones, she wouldn't have an answer for him. Maybe because she'd been dismissed so thoroughly after turning over the first batch. Not that this message had anything to do with the others—did it?

Of course it did. The same people had just sent her a warning, but she didn't know why. She didn't know anything about those emails or what they meant—but she was determined to find out.

The rest of the afternoon passed by from one jumpy incident to the next. Her scattered focus had been worthless in her attempts to translate the recorded broadcast.

Fifteen minutes away from quitting time, Farah hung on the corner of Martha's cubicle, her dark eyes shining. "I'm meeting my guy for a drink after work tonight. Do you want to come along?"

Martha crossed her arms. "And be a third wheel? No, thanks."

"He might have a friend." Farah made her voice go all singsongy on the last word as if to heighten the temptation.

"That's even worse than being a tagalong. A blind date?"

"Oh my God, Martha. Get used to it. It's the way of the world now."

"Seems to me all online dating has gotten you is a couple of sneaky married men."

Farah pouted. "It's fun. Not every date has to be a lifetime commitment."

"Go then and have fun for me." Martha waved her hand.

Not that she'd have accepted Farah's invitation under any circumstances, but after the day Martha had just had, she'd rather be home with a good book—and those emails.

She wrapped up her work and logged out of the computer, removing her access card and slipping it into her badge holder.

Waving to the security guard at the front desk, Martha pushed out the front doors and snuggled into her jacket. Winter in DC could be mild, but this November weather was already putting a chill in her bones.

She caught the next plain-wrap CIA van that shuttled employees from Langley to Rosslyn. When the van finally lurched to a stop, Martha stashed her book in her bag, rubbed her eyes and readjusted her glasses. She stepped out of the van and into the cold night, making her way to the Metro stop on the corner.

Descending into the bowels of the city with the rest of the worker bees, she welcomed the warmth from the pressing crowd as she turned the corner for her train. She jostled for position among the crush of people, gritting her teeth against the screech of the train's wheels slowing its progress.

As the lights approached from the tunnel, a man crowded her from behind. Martha tried to take a step back, but found herself pitching forward instead as someone's elbow drove into her back.

The train screeched once more, and Martha felt herself teetering on the edge of the platform. She thrust her arms in front of her as if to break a fall... but the only thing breaking this fall was that train barreling toward her.

Chapter Two

Cam curled his arm around the waist of the woman floundering on the precipice of the platform and pulled her back against his chest. He jerked his head to the side, but the man who had been crowding Martha Drake from behind had wormed his way through the crowd, the black beanie on his head lost in a sea of commuters.

Martha's back stiffened and she tried to turn in his arms, but he tightened his hold on her until the train came to a stop in front of them.

The doors whisked open, and Cam nudged her forward, whispering in her ear. "Go on."

She squeezed into the train with a mass of other people, grabbed a pole and spun around, her eyebrows snapping over her nose. "Take your hand off me."

Cam's jaw dropped open and a rush of heat claimed his chest. He'd just saved the woman's life, and this was the thanks he got?

He wrapped his fingers around the pole above her hand and twisted his lips. "You're welcome."

"I—I..." She shoved some wispy brown bangs out of her eyes, which blinked at him from behind a pair of glasses. "Yes, you're the one who pulled me back. Thank you. But..."

Lifting his eyebrows, he asked, "Yes?"

"How do I know you're not the one who was crowding me from behind in the first place?"

"I wasn't. That guy took off."

Martha's eyes, a lighter brown than her hair, widened and her Adam's apple bobbed in her delicate throat.

His statement had scared but not surprised her, and he dipped his head to study her face for his next question. "Any reason for somebody to push you into the path of an oncoming train?"

"No." She pressed her lips together. "It was crowded. Everyone was moving forward. I don't think that was an intentional push."

"It's always crowded. Commuters don't generally fall onto the tracks."

She shifted away from him, and the odor from the sweaty guy behind him immediately replaced the fresh scent that had clung to Martha, which had been the only thing making this tight squeeze bearable.

"Well, thank you." She tilted her chin up, along with her nose, and dismissed him.

Looked like she'd perfected the art of dismissing obnoxious men, but Cam had a date with Miss Prissy-pants here, even if she didn't know it.

He left her in peace for the remainder of the ride, although her sidelong glances at him didn't go unnoticed, and the knuckles of her hand gripping the pole had turned a decided shade of white. He'd planted a seed of suspicion in fertile ground.

When the train jerked to a stop, forward and then backward, Martha peeled her hand from the pole, hitched her bag higher on her shoulder and scooted out of the car, with a brief nod in Cam's direction.

He exited the train and followed Martha up the stairs and out into the night air, its frigidity no match for Ms. Drake's.

Three blocks down from the station, she stopped in front of a crowded Georgetown bar, clutching her bag to her chest, and turned to face him.

He sauntered toward her, then wedged his shoulder against the corner of the building, crossing his arms.

"Why are you following me? I'm going to call the police." She waved her cell phone at him.

"We need to talk, Martha Drake."

She choked and pressed the phone to her heart. "Who are you? Are you the one who sent the skull and crossbones?"

Skull and crossbones? That was a new one. He filed it away for future reference.

He shrugged off the wall and straightened his spine. "I'm Sergeant Cam Sutton, US Army Delta

Force, and you discovered some bogus emails that compromised my team leader, Major Rex Denver."

Martha's expressive face went through several gyrations, and then she settled on suspicion, which seemed to be one of her favorites. "How do I know you're telling the truth?"

He pulled his wallet from his pocket and slipped out his military ID. He held it out to her between two fingers.

She wasted no time snatching it from him and holding it close to her face, peering at it through her glasses. After perusing it for at least a minute, she handed it back to him. "Bogus emails?"

"Major Denver never did any of those things in those emails—" he jabbed the corner of his ID card in the general direction of her nose "—and if you hadn't turned them over to the Agency, Denver wouldn't be in the trouble he is now."

"If I hadn't..." She stamped one booted foot. "What did you expect me to do with them?"

"We can't keep talking out here. Let's go inside." He jerked his thumb toward the bar.

Her gaze bounced to the large picture window of the bar over his shoulder and back to his face. The crowd inside must've reassured her because she dipped her head once.

Cam circled around Martha and opened the door, holding it wide for her to pass through. As she did, he got another whiff of her fresh scent, which seemed to cling to her.

DC office workers, unwinding at the end of the workweek, packed every inch of the horseshoe bar. They seemed more interested in socializing and watching the football game on the TVs over the bar than quiet conversation, leaving a few open tables toward the back of the room, near the restrooms.

Cam placed his hand on the small of Martha's back and steered her toward one of those tables. She'd twitched under his touch but didn't shrug him off. He'd take that as a good sign.

When he pulled out her chair, her eyes beneath her arched eyebrows jumped to his face, and she mumbled, "Thank you."

After he took his own seat across from her, he folded his arms and hunched over the table. "Why weren't you surprised that somebody tried to push you onto the subway tracks?"

Her nostrils flared, and then she pursed her lips. "I told you. I thought it was an accident. I still think so."

"Really?" He reached across the table so quickly she didn't have time to pull back, and smoothed his thumb over the single line between her eyebrows. "Then why are you jumpier than a long-tailed cat in a roomful of rocking chairs."

Martha's mouth hung open, and Cam didn't know if it was because he'd presumed to touch her petal-soft skin, or because he'd laid on a thick Southern accent. That slack jaw made most people look stupid, but Martha couldn't look stupid if she tried. It made her look—adorable.

"Cat?" Her soft voice trailed off.

"You know—long tails, rocking chairs going back and forth." He hit the table with his flat hand, and she jumped. "Nervous, jittery. Don't deny it."

A cocktail waitress dipped next to their table and tossed a couple of napkins in front of them. "What can I get you?"

Cam plucked a plastic drink menu from a holder at the side of the table and tapped a picture of one of the featured bottles of beer. "I'll have a bottle of this."

"I can't just point at a picture." Martha snatched the menu from his hand and flipped it over, studied it for what seemed like ten minutes and then asked about twenty questions about the chardonnays. When she finally tucked the menu back in its holder, she said, "I'll have a glass of the house chardonnay."

When the waitress dived back into the crowd, Cam drummed his fingers on the table. He needed to start at the beginning with Martha. She clearly liked to take things in order.

He took a deep breath and started again. "Can you tell me about those emails? Where they came from? What they said, exactly, or close to it?"

"I should report you." She flicked her fingers at him. "What are you doing in DC? Why aren't you on duty?"

Cam narrowed his eyes. She didn't want to report him. Her voice had quavered, and she'd broken eye contact with him. If she'd turned those emails over so quickly, there shouldn't be anything stopping her from turning him over—but she didn't want to go there.

"I'm on leave. I'm not here on any official business, just my own." He crumpled the cocktail napkin in his fist. "Look, I know Major Rex Denver, and I know he's innocent of these charges."

"He went AWOL." She sniffed. "Running indicates guilt."

"Not always." He smoothed out the napkin and traced the creases with the tip of his finger. "Not if you think there's a conspiracy against you and you're going to be railroaded."

"A conspiracy?" Her eyes widened and seemed to sparkle in the low light from the candle on the table.

"Here you go." The waitress set down their drinks and spun away before Cam could tell her to close out the tab and that he didn't need a mug.

He watched Martha over the bottle, as he tipped the beer down his throat. Maybe this night would be longer than he expected.

"We think someone is framing Denver, and it started with those emails."

"We?"

"The Delta Force team that Major Denver commanded. We were all—" he put down the bottle harder than he'd planned "—dragged in for interrogation. Do you know what that's like? You're doing your job, doing the right thing, and *bam*. They're lookin' at you like you're vermin."

She nodded and took a big gulp from her wineglass. "I do know what that's like. I turned over those emails and all of a sudden, I'm suspect. They're checking out *my* communications, *my* files."

Cam's pulse ticked faster. That's why Martha was none too anxious to report him. They'd grilled her, too.

"Exactly." He touched the neck of his bottle to her glass and the pale liquid within shimmered and reflected in Martha's eyes. *Whiskey.* Her eyes were the color of whiskey. And right now he was a little drunk just looking into them.

Cam cleared his throat and rubbed his chin. "I don't trust them, any of them. All I know is Denver is not guilty of those crimes, and I'm gonna prove it."

Martha took another sip of wine from her half-empty glass, her cheeks flushed like a rose stain on porcelain. "I'll start at the beginning with the emails."

"Did the CIA determine where they came from?" He scooted forward in his seat.

"I didn't get all the details because why would they tell *me* anything? I'm just the one who discovered them and turned them over." She cupped her glass in her two hands and rolled it between her palms. "They were looking at Dreadworm though, you know that hacking group?"

He nodded, not wanting to interrupt her flow. This stuff had been bothering her for a while, and he just became her receptacle—a very willing one.

"But I don't know if they ever determined how

my email inbox became the target, or at least they never told me. Dreadworm was just the messenger, anyway. The conduit for the message, if you will— and that message was that Major Rex Denver had been working with a terrorist group plotting against the United States."

Cam slammed his fist on the table, the tips of his ears burning.

Martha held up her index finger. "But I noticed something strange about those emails."

"Yeah, they were filled with lies."

"Well, I don't know about that, but it didn't seem as if the person who composed the emails was a native English speaker."

Cam blinked his eyes and took another swig of beer. "Go on."

"If it were a foreign entity who sent those messages, why? Why would they care to warn US Intelligence about an American serviceman?"

"Our allies would care."

"Why wouldn't our allies just use regular channels to communicate with our military or even the CIA? But an unfriendly entity might have every reason to plant those stories about Denver."

"You've been thinking about this."

"It's more than just the emails." Martha waved her hand at the passing waitress. "Another round, please."

Cam cocked his head and took in Martha's empty wineglass and flushed cheeks. She'd downed that pretty fast. Although even in low heels she stood taller than most men, she was as slim as a reed, and the booze seemed to have loosened her tongue and her attitude toward him. He'd take it.

"More than emails?" He wrapped both hands around his bottle.

She looked both ways in the crowded bar and hunched forward, wedging her chin in the palm of her hand. "I'm being followed."

"The guy on the subway platform."

"I don't know." She drew back from him...and her earlier pronouncement, and tucked a lock of silky hair behind her ear. "Nobody has ever made physical contact with me before. That push could've killed me."

The fear in her whiskey eyes plunged a knife in his gut. "Maybe it was just a warning, maybe a coincidence after all."

"You don't believe that."

"How do you know you're being followed?"

"I can feel it, sense it."

He rolled his shoulders and thanked the waitress as she brought them their drinks. Maybe Martha was just paranoid. She'd been dwelling on those emails, and he didn't blame her. They'd started a firestorm.

"And then there's the skull and crossbones."

He coughed and his beer fizzed in his nose. "You mentioned that before. Someone put a skull and crossbones on the emails?"

"Not the original messages. Someone sent me an

email, just this afternoon, with one of those animated gifs of a skull and crossbones—blinking eyes and chattering teeth." She took a gulp from her new wineglass, and Cam placed his hand over her icy cold one.

"Why is someone sending you threats? You obviously took the intended and hoped-for action. You turned over the emails and got Denver in a heap of trouble. Why the harassment?"

"I—I do have an idea."

"I'm all ears." He curled his fingers around her hand in encouragement. Why would anyone threaten Martha Drake, a by-the-book CIA translator worker bee who'd reacted exactly as the sender thought she would?

"It might be because I copied all of the emails from my work computer to a flash drive, and now I have them at home."

Chapter Three

Cam Sutton's warm hand tightened around her fingers for a second. "Whoa. I bet the emailer wasn't expecting you to do that. Why *did* you do that?"

How could she explain it? She'd never done anything against the rules in her life. "I don't know exactly. There was something about those emails that didn't sit right with me."

"You said before that they might've been written by a foreigner." Cam tapped his temple. "You're a smart woman."

"I think it was the sentence structure and the word choice. Too formal or... I don't know what." She squared her shoulders and slipped her hand from Cam's. "When I first reported the emails, I tried to tell my supervisor about my suspicions, but he brushed me off."

"I take it nobody at the CIA knows what you did with those emails?"

"N-no." She pulled her bottom teeth between

her lips and traced the stem of her wineglass. Farah didn't count, did she?

"You seem unsure. Did you tell anyone you forwarded the messages to yourself at home?"

"I didn't tell anyone anything."

"If someone's been following you and sending you poison-pen emails, somebody knows. Otherwise, they would've left you alone after verifying you'd turned over the messages."

"I don't see how someone could know I have the emails."

He hunched forward, and his energy came off him in waves and engulfed her, sweeping her up in his world. "You seemed hesitant before. Do you think your supervisor might suspect you?"

She snorted and took another swig of wine. "No way. If he did, he would've just reported me to security and gotten me fired…or worse. He wouldn't be hiring people to shove me onto the train tracks."

"You've got a point." He rubbed his hands together. "It has to be the party who sent the emails, the people who wanted to bring down Denver."

Her gaze dropped to his fingers drumming on the tabletop. "You're *glad* someone's after me."

"Wait. What?" He smacked his chest with the palm of his hand. "That's dumb. I don't want to see anyone hurt over this."

"No, but you tracked me down because I'm the one who initiated the fall of Major Denver, and you probably expected some CIA drone that you could bully and instead you've discovered a chink in the story, a new twist you weren't expecting."

He cocked his head, and a lock of hair curled over his temple. He shoved it out of the way like a man accustomed to a military cut and whistled. "Are you sure you're just a translator and not an analyst?"

"*Just* a translator? I know four languages in addition to English." She ticked off her fingers. "Russian, German, French and Spanish."

"Okay, okay." He held up his hands. "You also have a big chip on your shoulder."

"I do not." She crossed her arms, covering her shoulders with her hands. "I'm just sick of being underestimated."

"Clearly." He leveled a finger at her. "And that's why you stole those emails."

"Are you sure you're *just* a Delta Force grunt and not military intelligence?" She held her breath.

He opened his mouth, snapped it shut and hit the table with his fist. Then he laughed, and what a laugh he had. A few heads turned at the loud guffaw.

"Shush." She kicked his foot under the table.

"Did those spies pick the wrong CIA drone to mess with or what?" He shook his head. "Why *do* you think they targeted you?"

"Honestly? I think they picked me because I have a reputation for following the rules. Everyone at work knows that."

"That's kinda scary."

"What? Following rules? You're in the military. You must do a lot of that."

"Not the rule-following, but the fact that the people who sent the emails knew that about you." He rubbed his knuckles across the sandy-blond stubble on his chin. "Inside job? Some kind of bug?"

"A few minutes ago you called them spies. Do you think this is some foreign entity or worse, a foreign country?"

"I don't know." He tapped her wineglass. "Are you done? I want to see those emails."

"You mean, at my place?" Her heart fluttered. It was one thing talking to this hunky military guy in public, but bring him back to her town house?

"You still don't trust me?" He slumped in his seat and finished off his beer. "What can I do to remedy that?"

"It's not that I don't trust you...exactly. I'm just not comfortable bringing strangers to my place."

He rattled off her address and winked. "I already know where you live, Martha."

"This is all really creepy. How long have you been following me around DC? Maybe my feeling of being tailed was coming from you."

"I swear, I just started following you from the Langley bus stop today."

"How do you even know about the Langley bus stop?"

"I have friends in high places."

She rolled her eyes. "Obviously not if you're dogging a lowly translator."

"I mean it." He grabbed her hands. "I want to see those emails. I know Denver. I'd be able to detect any falsehoods in those messages. I mean it's all false, but I might be able to see something in the emails, some clue."

An edge of desperation had entered his voice, and the easygoing frat boy had morphed into this earnest man with the serious blue eyes, desperate to clear his commanding officer's name.

Despite herself, she felt a twinge of pity and then steeled herself against the emotion. Her father had always employed the same tone when trying to wheedle compassion from her.

She blinked as Cam tugged on a lock of her hair. "C'mon, Martha. I saved you from an oncoming train. If you don't want me in your personal space, you can bring your computer out to someplace neutral, if you have a laptop."

She inhaled the fresh, outdoorsy scent coming off him and counted the freckles on his nose. Cam already *was* in her personal space, and she didn't mind one bit.

"All right. I'll take you back to my town house."

Cam waved at the waitress for the bill, and as soon as she plucked it from her apron, he snatched it from her fingers. "I'll get this."

Martha didn't even hesitate as she pulled a five and a ten from her wallet and flicked them onto the table. "That's too much like paying for information. I'll get my own wine."

Out of the corner of her eye, she could see Cam raising his eyebrows at her, but she ignored him and stashed her wallet back in her purse. "Is it all there?"

"Yes, ma'am." He tucked his bills and hers beneath the candle on the table, along with the check. "Walking distance?"

"You know my address." She folded her arms, regretting her decision already.

"I know your address, not the area, but I figured you were close if you got off at the Metro stop." He pushed back from his chair and stepped to the side to let her go first.

As she shuffled past him, she noted his height again. At five foot ten, she hit eye level with most men, but her nose practically brushed the chin of this one.

When they reached the sidewalk, Cam hunched into his jacket and flipped up the collar against the wind. "It's not gonna snow, is it?"

"I hope not." She peered at the light gray sky and pulled on her gloves. "That would be pretty unusual for November."

They walked along the busy Georgetown sidewalk, occasionally bumping shoulders, which oddly reassured her, although she couldn't figure out why. Cam had the type of solid build that screamed strength and fitness. Physically, he could have his way with anyone, even a tall woman like her.

She hunched her shoulders and stuffed an errant strand of hair back under her hat. *Dream on, Martha*. Cam was the type of guy who'd wheedled homework assignments out of her. Just like in college, she had something he wanted—just not her body.

She stopped in front of the town house she owned but shared with a roommate, and grabbed the iron handrail. "I'm right here."

"Door right onto the street."

"Yeah? So what?" She fished her key from the side pocket of her purse, and for the first time in a while hoped her roommate, Casey, was on the other side of that door.

"Not that safe."

"If you haven't noticed, this is a nice area."

He looked up and down the street. "Lots of foot traffic though."

She looked up from turning the key in the lock. "I'm a very careful person."

"And yet, here I am."

She opened the door and blocked it with her body. "Are you telling me not to trust you? Because I can change my mind right here and now."

Casey yelled from the inside. "Close the door. You're letting in the cold air."

"My roommate. Protection." Martha jerked her thumb over her shoulder.

"Good thinking." He rubbed his gloved hands together. "Now can we go in? It *is* cold out here."

Martha pushed into the room, and Cam followed on her heels.

"I was just on my way…" Casey tripped to a stop in her high heels when she swung around and almost collided with Cam. "Well, hello there."

"Hey, what's up?"

"Casey, Cam. Cam, Casey, my roommate."

Casey stuck out her hand and wiggled her fingers, her long painted nails catching the light and glinting like she was casting a spell. "Nice to meet you. You're the first guy Martha's ever brought home."

The heat washed up Martha's face, and she ground her teeth together. "It's not like that. He's not a guy."

Casey fluttered her long—fake—eyelashes as she gave Cam the once-over. "You could've fooled me."

"I think what Martha means—" he hooked his arm around Martha's neck in a total buddy move and pulled her close "—is we're just friends."

"Of course you are." Casey turned toward the kitchen, giving Cam a view of her derriere in her tight dress. "Do you want a beer?"

"I thought you were going out?" Martha ducked out of Cam's hold and shed her coat.

"Just showing a little hospitality."

"Don't worry about it. He's *my* guest. I can get him a beer if he wants one."

"I'm good." Cam held out one hand as if refereeing an MMA fight. "We don't want to hold you up, Casey. Nice meeting you."

Her roommate's pretty face fell, and Martha

couldn't help the little spark of satisfaction that flared in her belly. "Have fun, Casey."

"Nice meeting you, Cam." She swept up her coat from the back of a chair. "Hope to see you again sometime."

The door slammed behind Casey in a gust of perfume and hairspray.

Cam cocked an eyebrow at her. "Not a good friend, I take it?"

"Not a friend at all, and she's a horrible roommate—messy, noisy, brings guys back here all the time."

"And you mean *guys*."

"Yeah. She's a real pain."

"Move."

"It's my place."

Cam's gaze flicked around the town house, still sporting the expensive furnishings Mom had favored and she couldn't afford to replace. "Government's paying some solid wages."

"Anyway, I can't just move." She had no intention of getting into her personal finances—or her notorious background—with Cam.

"Kick her out."

"She signed a lease."

"How long?"

"Four more months. I think she's gearing up to move out anyway."

"I'm sure you're counting the days." He clapped his hands once and she jumped. "The emails?"

"Do you want a beer? Or something else?"

"Just some water." He tipped his head at the door. "She doesn't know about the messages, does she?"

"Casey?" Martha snorted. "No. She wouldn't care, anyway. She's in DC to sleep around and maybe snag a book deal, and she has a good start on both."

"Who knew the capital was such a cesspool."

"I hope you're kidding." She strode into the kitchen and reached for a glass. As ice dispensed from the fridge, Cam joined her in the kitchen, making the space feel claustrophobic.

"I am kidding, and I'm convinced someone, somewhere in this cesspool has it out for Major Denver." He took the glass from her hand, his fingers brushing hers and giving her a jolt.

Leaning her hip against the kitchen counter, she tucked the hand behind her back. "Why would they have it out for him? Why frame him? By all accounts, he's a good soldier."

"The best and maybe that's why." He gulped down the water. "Maybe he stumbled onto something he shouldn't have."

"Again, that could point to a foreign entity."

"I agree, especially after what you told me about the emails, which are…"

"On my laptop." She brushed past him. "In my bedroom"

Leaving him in the kitchen, she jogged upstairs and pulled the door closed on Casey's messy room. She ducked into her own room, swept her laptop from the desk and tucked it under her arm. By the time she got downstairs, Cam had settled on the sofa in the living room, his long legs stretched out in front of him.

She sat next to him and opened her computer. "I put them in a folder on my hard drive."

"Where's the flash drive? You copied them to a flash drive when you stole them, right?"

She tapped the keyboard harder than she intended. "I didn't steal them. They were addressed to me."

"Addressed to your CIA address, but I'm not judging. Hey, I'm glad you did steal…take them, but where's the original flash drive?"

"It's in a safe in the office."

Raising his eyes to the ceiling, Cam asked, "This place has an office, too?"

"Yes." She zipped her lip and double-clicked on the folder holding the emails. "Is that secure enough for you?"

"I don't know if it's such a good idea to have the messages in two places. You're doubling the opportunity for someone to take them."

"Why would anyone else want them? The CIA already has them." She pointed to her screen. "This is the first of the three emails I received."

Cam moved in closer and his warm breath bathed her cheek as he read the email aloud, slowly. "'Look at Major Rex Denver, Army Delta Force, and track his actions and communications. You will understand his behavior as treason. He has many contacts in region.'"

"Sounds stilted, doesn't it?"

"Wow." Cam slumped back and kicked one foot on top of her coffee table. "That's enough to raise suspicion and get you investigated? Good thing nobody ever sent the CIA information about my activities."

"There are two more emails with more details." Her hand hovered over the keyboard. "*Your* activities?"

"Not treasonous. I'm just saying stuff happens in the field, and it's better for everyone if it stays in the field." His hand dropped to her head, and he messed up her hair with his fingers. "Don't worry. I'm not doing anything to compromise national security—and neither was Major Denver."

She jerked away from him with a scowl, smoothing her wavy hair back into place. "Do you mind?"

"Sorry. I have a younger sister, and I'm accustomed to teasing her." He tapped the keyboard. "Next email."

She huffed out a breath as she opened the second email. Great. The hottest guy she'd run into in months thought of her as a little sister. Typical.

Tipping the display toward him, she drew back and watched his profile as he digested the next message, his lips moving silently as he read it, his finger following the words. He must've read it a few times, as it took him a while to peel his eyes from the display. When he did, his jaw hardened and his eye twitched.

For all his carefree, easygoing ways, Cam really did care about Denver, and a strong desire to help him clear his commanding officer washed over her. She hated seeing anyone unfairly accused, and she'd had a feeling about these bogus emails ever since they landed in her inbox.

"Worse, huh?" She reached across him and opened the final email.

Cam took his time reading this one, as well, and when he finished, he punched the pillow next to him. "This is such garbage. All the CIA had to do was ask anyone who's ever served with the major. Even now nobody in the field believes Denver was conspiring with terrorists."

"Why'd he take off? Why didn't he just face the music and prove his innocence?"

"It's not supposed to work that way, is it? As a suspect, you don't have to prove anything. It's up to the prosecution to come up with the evidence to convict you. I'm guessing Denver recognized a setup when he saw one and figured the fix was in. There's no fighting against that when evidence is fabricated."

"He should've trusted the system." She jutted her chin.

"Really?" He bumped her knee with his own. "Like you did? C'mon, even someone like you knows there are times when the system breaks down and you have to take matters into your own hands."

"Even someone like me." She drummed her fingers on the edge of the laptop.

He cleared his throat. "You know, someone who likes to follow the rules...which is usually a good idea. I'm not knocking it."

"No offense taken. I have my reasons." She shoved the computer from her lap to the coffee table. "I'm just wondering how someone knew to target me."

"The CIA must've investigated the source of the emails. Let me guess. Fake IP address?"

"Yes, which they wrote off as coming from Dreadworm."

"So the sender got a bunch of CIA email addresses from Dreadworm, picked one at random and sent out these lies about Denver? I don't believe that for a minute, do you?"

"No, I think I was specifically targeted, but I don't know why I'm being harassed now. I did what the sender expected and wanted me to do." She shoved at her laptop with the toe of her boot.

"Because somehow they know you still have the emails, and they don't like that." He sat forward and dragged the computer to the edge of the coffee table. "You're not quite the good little soldier they anticipated."

"Serves them right." She grabbed Cam's water glass. "Do you want more water or something else?"

He held up one finger. "Does this LED light on your laptop monitor blink like this all the time?"

She squinted at the blue light at the tip of his

finger. "I don't know. I guess so. Doesn't that just mean it's on?"

"Maybe, maybe not." He pulled the computer onto his legs and started clicking around.

"What are you doing?" She wrapped her hands around the glass. "Are you some kind of computer whiz, too?"

"No, but…" He dragged an icon from a system folder onto her desktop and turned toward her, his face tight. "This is a Trojan, and someone's watching you…us, right now through your computer's camera."

Chapter Four

Martha swallowed. Her gaze darted from Cam's blue eyes to the blue eye on her laptop. She snapped shut the computer. "How do you know that?"

"Shutting it solves the problem right this second, but that Trojan's gonna have to be removed from your computer as soon as possible. It's not just computer keystrokes and actions. The person on the other side can see you as long as your laptop is open and powered on."

"Oh my God." She covered her mouth. "I wonder how long this has been going on."

"A tech can probably tell you that by looking at the program. It'll have a date on it."

"But how did you know? How did you know where to look?" The veil of her preconceived notions about Cam Sutton lifted—and she liked what she saw even more. Brawn *and* brains.

"About a year ago, my sister was being stalked." A muscle ticked in his jaw. "It became apparent that her stalker was watching her in her private moments.

One of her friends, a real computer geek, came over to inspect her computer. First she watched for the blinking LED, and then she did a search for a common Trojan used to infect the computer and allowing an outside source to gain control of it. I looked for and found that same virus on your laptop."

Martha's mind raced and reeled over the times she'd had her laptop open in her bedroom, not bothering to shut it down. She hugged herself, digging her fingers into her upper arms. "Get it off. Can you get it off?"

"I can delete it. Hell, *you* can delete it, but I don't know if that removes it from everywhere. It's probably best if you take the laptop in or call someone to do it." Cam tapped his chin with his index finger. "I wonder if they could hear us, too."

"At least we were spared that. The microphone on my laptop doesn't work. No sound in. No sound out."

"That's an unexpected bonus." He hunched forward, digging his elbows into his knees. "Whoever was watching you saw me, but at least that person won't know who I am and how I'm connected to Denver."

She handed him the glass and pushed at his solid shoulder. "Put that in the sink or get yourself more. I'm going to open this up and delete that program. Then I'll take my computer in and get the virus removed from everywhere else."

Glass in hand, Cam pushed up from the sofa while Martha flipped open the laptop, keeping her thumb over the camera lens. She gasped and nearly drove her finger through her computer as a parade of skulls and crossbones marched across her display, the word *busted* floating between the grinning teeth.

Cam clinked the glass on the countertop. "What's wrong?"

"Come and look at this. He knows I…you discovered the commandeered camera. He's admitting he's busted."

"Son of a gun." Cam hovered over her shoulder. "Cheeky bastard."

"I wish I could just communicate with him and ask him what he wants. Oh." Martha put her fingers to her lips as her email icon blinked, indicating a new message. "Maybe I can."

"If you open that email, don't click on any links. That's how your computer gets infected. He might be trying to load something even more insidious on your laptop."

"More insidious than a program to take over my camera to spy on me? That would be hard."

"Hold on." He backtracked to the kitchen. "Do you have any masking tape in here?"

"Post-its in the drawer to the right of the dishwasher."

He returned with two pink Post-it notes stuck to his fingertips. He slid a finger beneath the pad of her thumb, covering the eye of the camera with one Post-it and stuck the other on the edge of the first one to hold it in place.

"Go for it."

She opened the email and licked her dry lips.

"'Do you want to…play?'" Cam read the message out loud, which took off its sinister edge and made it sound almost sexy.

Of course, Cam could make anything sound, or look, sexy.

Dragging in a breath, she put her fingers on the keys.

"Wait." He cinched her wrist with his fingers. "What are you going to write back?"

"I'm going to write 'Hell, yes.' What do you think?"

"Shouldn't you ask him what he means? Ask him what he wants? That's what he'd expect out of you. If you agree too quickly, he's going to wonder if he picked the right person for the job."

His thumb pressed against her pulse. Could he feel it throbbing with excitement? She couldn't tell if the buzz claiming her body was coming from the email or Cam's warm touch. Did it matter? The two had mingled in her scattered brain.

Rotating her wrist out of his grasp, she said, "You're right. I'll take it slowly."

She voiced the words as she replied to the email. "'Play what? What do you want? Who are you?'"

She clicked Send and held her breath.

Her heart stuttered when the quick reply came through. She clicked on the email and read it aloud to Cam. "'I'm a patriot.'"

Cam snorted and she continued. "'I'm a patriot. That's all you need to know. You did the right thing. Leave it alone, or you might not like the game.'"

She whipped her head around to face Cam. "He's threatening me."

This time her hands trembled as she held them poised over the keyboard.

Lacing his fingers through hers, Cam pulled her hand away from the computer. "Ask this patriot why he's so nervous if the information he revealed in the emails about Major Denver is true."

"Shouldn't I ask him about his threats? If he's the one who pushed me at the Metro?" She untwined her fingers from his.

"He's not going to give you a direct answer or admit that he tried to harm you, but I'm interested to see his lies about why he wants you to stop digging."

"I haven't even started digging." She puffed at a strand of hair that had floated across her face, and Cam caught it and tucked it behind her ear.

"He knows you saved the emails and shared them with me." He flicked his finger at the Post-its. "And he knows you're on to him."

"If you say so." As long as he kept finding excuses to touch her, she'd do just about anything he asked. She cleared her throat and her mind, and then typed in Cam's question.

They both jumped when a message showed up in her inbox, but it was an ad for ink cartridges.

"Come on, patriot." She flexed her fingers over the keys. "I think we scared him off."

"Or he's thinking up a good story." Cam stretched his arms over his head before standing up. "I'm going to get more water. Do you want something from the kitchen?"

"No, thanks." She wedged the toes of her boots against the coffee table. "We lost him."

"Do you think my question was too direct?" He called back at her over the running water from the kitchen faucet. "We must've hit a nerve. He wants you to stop because he doesn't want the truth revealed—that the claims in those emails were all bogus."

Instead of an answer, grinning skulls danced across her screen, giving her the chills. "Ugh. He really is just playing games."

Cam returned to the living room and hung over the back of the sofa. "Idiot. I don't think he plans to tell you anything. He does want you to stop snooping though, and he's trying to scare you off."

"All the more reason to continue." She rolled her shoulders in an effort to release the tension bunching her muscles. "Maybe I should turn all this stuff over to the CIA."

"Martha, you committed a crime by making a copy of those emails. Even if you're not prosecuted, you'll lose your job." He reached past her and closed the lid of her laptop on the skulls. "It's not worth it. Do you want to wind up in federal prison?"

"No!" She dumped her computer from her lap to the sofa cushion. "You're right. I'm not telling the CIA a thing."

He drew back at the violence of her exclamation, but she didn't have to explain herself as the key turned in the door.

"Casey's home early." Her eyes wide, Martha watched the door handle turn and released a sigh when Casey crept into the room on tiptoes.

"Oh, you're still up…and *you're* still here."

The reason for Casey's dismay followed her into the room wearing an expensive suit and a sheepish grin. "Sorry to intrude."

"Join the party." Cam spread out his arms and then dropped them to his sides as his invitation was met with silence. "Just kidding. We were just wrapping up."

"Take your time." Casey circled one finger in the air. "Bob and I will be upstairs. Bob, this is my roommate Martha and her friend Cam."

They all managed awkward hellos and goodbyes as Casey led Bob up the stairs of the town house.

When she heard the door click above, Martha made a face. "She usually doesn't bring them home this early. I never have to meet them."

Cam whistled. "I can see why she doesn't."

"Why?"

Jerking his thumb at the ceiling, Cam whispered. "Old Bob up there is Congressman Robert Wentworth from some district down in Florida."

"What? Are you serious? How do you know that?"

"He's on the House Intelligence Committee—and he's married, as far as I remember."

"That makes it doubly worse that they're up there…" She waved a hand toward the staircase and heated up to the roots of her hair. "Why do women go for these married men?"

Martha flicked a glance at Cam's bare left ring finger and let out a little breath. Of course, lots of men didn't wear wedding rings.

"Imprudent of him at the very least." Cam leaned forward and lifted the laptop lid. "Still no communication from the patriot, so I'm going to head back to my hotel. Are you going to be okay?"

"I will be once I power down my computer and stick it in the office tonight."

"How many rooms does this place have?" He raised his eyes to the ceiling.

"Just three bedrooms. I could sublet the other room, but I'd probably go crazy with another roommate." She tucked the laptop under her arm. "Should I…should I call you tomorrow or something?"

"I'll go with you to cleanse your computer. Is that okay?"

More than okay. "Sure."

Cam strode to the kitchen and ripped a Post-it from the pad. He scribbled something on the pink square and then stuck it to the edge of the counter. "My number. Call me when you're ready to roll."

He grabbed his jacket from the back of the chair

and hunched into it. "I'm sure I don't have to tell you to lock your door."

"Nope. I've got that one down. Besides, I have a US congressman upstairs for protection."

"All right, then." Cam stood in the entryway and thrust his hand forward for a shake. "Take care and thanks for trusting me."

She tucked her laptop against her side and took his hand in a firm grip—no nonsense. "Thanks for... rescuing me on the platform and discovering I'd been hacked."

They both released at the same time, and Cam saluted. "All right, then. See ya later."

Martha shut the door behind him and then rested her back against it, hugging her computer to her chest. Had Cam been nervous? Maybe he thought she'd expected a hug or a kiss or something. Did she appear that desperate?

She spun around and threw the locks into place and then launched herself up the stairs. Cam probably hadn't given her much thought at all.

Martha crept past Casey's bedroom door and the low voices murmuring within, and slipped into her own room. At least her master bedroom had a bathroom attached.

Tripping to a stop, she glanced at the laptop in her hands. She didn't want to go into the hallway again, so she made an abrupt turn and stuffed the computer on the floor of her closet under some folded clothes.

She got ready for bed. Several minutes later as

she slipped between the covers, her mind was still racing with the day's events.

Casey squealed from somewhere beyond the walls, and Martha burrowed beneath the covers. Her roommate and her lovers always made a lot of noise.

Martha reached into the top drawer of her night-stand for her earplugs and cupped them in her hand as the congressman let out a growl.

Shutting her eyes, Martha closed her fingers around the earplugs. What would Cam sound like in the throes of passion?

Casey yelped, and Martha stuffed the earplugs into her ears as she buried her face in the pillow. One thing she *did* know is that she wouldn't be squeaking and squealing like Casey if she ever did get a chance with Cam.

And with that delicious thought making her shiver, Martha closed her eyes.

What seemed like moments later, Casey's scream punctured Martha's dream state...and her earplugs. She groaned and rolled onto her side.

Didn't the woman have any shame—or self-control?

Casey screamed again, and Martha pulled the pillow over her head, gritting her teeth.

"Martha! Martha!"

The bedroom door burst open, and Martha sat up, the pillow falling from her face. She blinked her eyes at Casey standing in the doorway, a filmy nightgown clutched to her chest. Was she dreaming?

"Martha, wake up. We're in terrible trouble."

"What?" Martha flicked on the light above her bed, and Casey's face looked whiter than it had in the darkness. "What's wrong? What's going on?"

"Oh, Martha." Casey stumbled across the room and tottered before she dropped to the edge of Martha's bed. "Bob, Congressman Wentworth, is dead in my bed…in your town house."

Chapter Five

Cam glanced at his phone for about the hundredth time that morning. Maybe Martha had decided to get her computer wiped on her own. It's not like she needed him to do it. He didn't know that much about technical stuff, and she probably figured that out about him in a hot minute. She seemed like the self-sufficient type, anyway.

In fact, Martha Drake had a surprising rebellious streak. He never would've guessed she'd be the type to sneak out those emails. The woman had gone rogue—and he was glad she'd decided to do so.

And maybe she was going rogue again by handling the patriot herself. Cam wouldn't put it past her, but he didn't think it was a good idea. What if she'd fallen in front of that train last night? She needed a right-hand man, even if she didn't realize it yet.

He tossed his phone onto the cushion next to him and snatched up the remote. Propping one bare foot on the table in front of him, he clicked over to one of the cable news shows.

He studied the reporters and news vans with a crease forming between his eyebrows. Someone had died, and the street where the buzzing media had gathered looked familiar with all those rows of town houses with shutters and arched windows.

When the words scrolled across the bottom of the screen, Cam choked and his foot slipped from the table. His thumb drilled into the remote to increase the sound.

The reporter breathlessly gushed into the mic. "All we know so far, Carrie, is that Congressman Robert Wentworth, from the Second Congressional District in Florida, died in this town house behind me sometime last night or this morning. There was a 911 call and the DC Metro Police responded. The body has not yet been removed."

Carrie put on a concerned face, but Cam could see the speculative light in her eyes. "Have the police said whether they're looking at foul play here, Stacie?"

"They haven't released any statement yet or talked to reporters."

Cam curled his fingers around the remote and hardly noticed the edges digging into his flesh. The reporter hadn't mentioned anything about anyone else being hurt…or arrested. What the hell had gone down in that town house after he'd left last night?

Cam muted the TV and reached for his phone. Damn that Casey for dragging Martha into her messy life. He stopped, his thumb hovering over the screen. Or was it the other way around?

Could this really be just a coincidence after what Martha had gone through yesterday? What possible connection could Wentworth have to Martha and the emails?

Cam dropped his phone when it hit him that he didn't even have Martha's number. He'd given her his number with the understanding that she'd call him to go with her to fix the laptop. Some understanding. Seemed like he didn't know Martha at all.

He paced the room, juggling his phone from hand to hand, occasionally turning up the TV for more news on the congressman's death. The stiff muscles across his shoulders began to unwind when he didn't see anything about any other injuries or anyone getting taken in for questioning, and then seized up again as Martha had been identified as the owner of the town house.

More than an agonizing hour later, Cam's phone buzzed with a DC number. "Hello?"

"Cam, it's Martha… Martha Drake."

"Yeah, I know. You're kind of famous right now, or at least your town house is. What the hell happened over there?"

"My name's out there, isn't it?"

"Are you worried about your job?"

"I'm worried about a lot of things right now." She sighed. "It looks like the congressman had a heart attack. Casey didn't even realize it until this morning. His body was slumped halfway out of the bed when she woke up."

"A heart attack? Of course, they're gonna do an autopsy before they rule on the cause of death." He wiped a hand across his mouth. "How are you holding up? How's Casey?"

"Casey is hysterical. I'm…nervous."

"Why, Martha?"

"Why do you think?"

"Are you linking this to the emails?"

"Aren't you?" Her voice rose, and for a second she sounded close to hysteria herself.

"Crossed my mind, but I can't see how this can be related to the emails or how it affects you." He wedged a shoulder against the window and watched one bare branch from a tree scrape against the edge of the balcony. "Heart attack, right?"

"Right." She cleared her throat. "We need to talk."

"And clean that computer."

"Don't come anywhere near here. It's a madhouse. I'll slip out the back and head over to your hotel. The police are still questioning Casey, poor girl."

He gave her the name of the hotel and the address before turning up the volume on the TV again. Several reporters were still camped out in front of Martha's town house, and the speculation had begun. Since Martha owned the town house, the reporters had her name on their lips.

It wouldn't be long before they dug up the fact that Martha worked for the CIA, and he hoped it wouldn't be long before they discovered she hadn't been the one who'd invited Congressman Wentworth to an after-hours meeting.

His blood percolated as he listened to the innuendo linking Martha to Wentworth, but he still couldn't figure out how this had anything to do with the threats from the patriot.

With the TV still droning in the background, Cam straightened his hotel room, stuffing clothes back into his suitcase and shoving toiletries into the plastic bag hanging from a hook on the bathroom door. He hadn't needed to see Martha's place last night to figure she'd be a neat freak, and for some reason he wanted to assure her he wasn't a slob.

He went a few steps further and got a couple cans of soda from the vending machine down the hall and stuck them in the mini-fridge. The woman must've had a rough morning.

By the time Martha tapped on his door, Cam had rendered the room acceptable to the neatest of neat freaks.

He opened the door and she barreled past him without even a hello, striding to the sliding door to the balcony.

She turned to face him, twisting her fingers in front of her. "This is bad."

"Tell me what happened." He gestured toward the sofa facing the TV. "Not many details on the news, except that you own the town house where Wentworth croaked."

She perched on the edge of the sofa. "Casey's name will come out. The police are still talking to her."

"At least you won't be portrayed as the other woman for much longer." He yanked the chair back from the desk and straddled it, resting his arms across the back. "Give me all the details."

"After you left, I went to bed and I could hear those two…whooping it up." Two bright spots of red formed on her cheeks. "I have earplugs for just those occasions, and I was able to fall asleep."

"Damn, you need earplugs?" Noticing Martha's pursed lips, he wiped the grin off his face. "Go on. You fell asleep during noisy sex."

"I…" She ran her fingers through her messy hair, dragging it back from her face. "Yes, I fell asleep, and the next thing I knew Casey was in my room hysterical and crying, saying Bob had died sometime during the night."

"What time did she discover him?"

"About six. I ran into her room and felt his neck for a pulse. He seemed dead to me, but I have no experience in medicine. I called 911 right away."

"The news said possible heart attack, so I'm assuming no blood or visible injuries."

"No." Martha crossed her arms, cupping her elbows. "He was half out of the bed, as if he'd tried to get up but didn't make it."

"Did Casey have anything to say?"

"Not much to me, but the cops were grilling her.

They'd met for a drink at a quiet place. Bob wasn't feeling great, and they decided to head back here."

"You'd never met him before? It didn't seem like you had last night."

"No. I'm not saying she's never brought him back to our place, but I usually make myself scarce when she brings guys home, so I'd never met him before."

Cam tugged on his earlobe. "I don't understand why you think some congressman's heart attack is related to you and the emails."

"Who says it's a heart attack?" She jumped up from the sofa and twitched back the drapes at the sliding door, peeked out the window and yanked the drapes back together.

"It could be something else. Poison. He didn't feel well. Or there are drugs out there that mimic heart attacks. Nobody would know the difference and *poof*—" she tried snapping her fingers, failed miserably and flicked them in the air instead "—you're gone."

Cam flattened the smile from his lips and drew his brows together to look concerned instead. He couldn't help it. Even when he listened to Martha talking about murder, he found her irresistibly cute.

"Wait, wait." He held up his hands. "How does that impact you, unless the patriot plans to frame you for Wentworth's so-called murder…and that's a long shot. How exactly does Casey's illicit affair with a politician affect you and your investigation of the emails?"

"It brings everything back up. It tarnishes me and anything I might have to say about these emails. It's a warning that he can get to me if he wants to." She pulled her bottom lip between her teeth.

"Yeah, okay. It shows he's powerful, although this is a risky way to do that. But—" he frowned for real this time "—what do you mean by bringing everything back up? Finding the emails?"

Her gaze darted to the TV, still humming in the background, and she took two steps toward the coffee table, picked up the remote and aimed it at the TV.

The reporter mentioned Martha's name, and Cam jerked his head toward the TV. A picture of a young Martha with thick glasses and braces stared back at him next to a picture of a gray-haired man, who looked vaguely familiar. He tuned into the reporter's words.

"In a bizarre twist to this story, the owner of the town house is none other than the daughter of convicted stock trader Steven 'Skip' Brockridge, who's currently serving twenty-five years in federal prison for his role in a Ponzi scheme that bilked investors out of millions."

He twisted his head back toward Martha, her arms crossed and shoulders hunched. She raised one hand.

"That's me, Martha Brockridge, daughter of a convicted felon."

Cam swallowed. "That's your father, not you. Obviously the CIA already knows about your background. A name change isn't going to throw off the Agency."

"I never tried to throw them off. I was up front about my father. They knew. I think they even believed that my father's criminal behavior had influenced me to follow the straight and narrow path, and they were right...until now."

Her voice broke at the end, and he jumped up from the chair and took her by the shoulders. He dug his fingers into her tight muscles. "This situation is completely different."

"Maybe, but do you think anyone's going to believe me about the emails now? A convicted felon's daughter?" She shook her head, and the ends of her hair tickled the backs of his hands.

"I doubt the patriot went through all this trouble to discredit or warn you, and the CIA already knows about your father. It didn't stop them from believing you the first time you turned over those emails."

"I don't know what to think. It's hard for me to believe there's no connection between my online conversation with the patriot and the death of Congressman Wentworth."

He blew out a breath. "I don't believe that, either. I don't believe in coincidences, but I can't wrap my mind around his motives."

"You think there might be another reason?"

He smoothed his hands down her arms and released her, stepping back. "How long has Casey been living with you?"

Martha blinked her long lashes. "About eight months."

"You received the emails four months ago, right?"

"You're not implying Casey is involved? That ditz?"

"It could've all been an act. The people who sent you the emails needed someone on the inside, and it would've been too hard to get one of your coworkers to cooperate. How'd that virus get on your laptop? I'm sure the CIA must drill computer security measures into your head and you didn't just click on some random link in an email. Who does that anymore?"

Martha chewed on the edge of her thumb. "I thought maybe he'd used Dreadworm again to get to me."

"How'd you meet Casey?"

"Through one of those roommate finders. She had the money up front—first, last and insisted on a larger security deposit than I'd asked for." She smacked her knee. "I should've trusted my instincts. I thought she was a little too eager."

"Something else about her choice in boyfriends." He straddled the desk chair again just to keep from touching Martha. It felt…manipulative to use her distress to get close to her. She didn't need any more distractions in her life right now, and neither did he.

"Congressman Wentworth?"

"Remember I told you last night I knew him from the House Intelligence Committee? He must have a lot of information on Denver."

She lowered herself to the bed as if in slow motion. "So, this is a twofer for Casey. She moves in to keep an eye on me, and she dates Wentworth to keep an eye on him and Major Denver."

"It makes sense that a lot of that stuff about Denver came from an inside source." Cam's anger at the injustice of Denver's situation burned in his gut. He crouched to grab the sodas from the fridge, cracked one open and took a long swig from the can. He held the other out to Martha, and she shook her head.

Tucking one leg beneath her on the bed, she said, "We're just guessing. How are we going to prove any of this?"

"Let's start with Casey. Where was she when you left?"

"She was still with the police."

"She'd admitted to the affair?"

"Of course. What other explanation could she give?"

"It's odd." Cam smoothed a hand across his freshly shaved jaw. "Why risk such public exposure? If Wentworth had served his purpose and they wanted to get rid of him, and maybe scare you in the process, why do it so publicly? They could've killed him without dragging Casey into the picture."

"You're asking me?" She jabbed a finger at her

chest. "I still don't even know what the patriot wants of me, and I hate calling him that since he's clearly not one."

"I think he wants you to stop thinking about those emails for one thing and delete them. He wants you to drop your investigation."

"It's hardly an investigation, but I'm not dropping anything. People can't just get away with things." She pointed to her laptop case propped up against the wall by the door. "I called a computer repair place, and the guy told me to bring the laptop in today."

"You know this tech guy?" Cam stood up and stretched.

He didn't know how much longer he could be cooped up with Martha in this small room, anyway. He always had these instant attractions to women, and those never ended well, although Martha wasn't his usual type so maybe he'd learned a few lessons.

Her gaze flicked over his body as he reached for the ceiling, and then she took off her glasses and wiped the lenses with a corner of the bedspread. "He's worked on my computer before. He's good."

When she'd been checking him out, he'd had the crazy idea to flex and show off for her, but a woman like Martha would probably laugh at that. All the smart girls in school had him pegged as a meathead jock who couldn't even read. So he'd gravitated toward the pretty cheerleaders who only cared if he could read their flirtatious signals. He'd gotten good at that.

Coughing, he loped toward her laptop and hooked the case over his shoulder. "Have you checked your messages this morning for anything from the patriot?"

"It's one of the first things I did this morning after checking on Wentworth and calling 911—nothing."

He hunched the shoulder with the strap over it. "I'd find it hard to believe, but maybe this really is all a coincidence."

"You're right. Too hard to believe." She bounded off the bed. "My car's valet parked. We'll take that."

MARTHA DROVE HER hybrid like she did everything else—carefully and precisely. Cam felt like he'd wandered into the middle of a drivers' training video.

When she'd lined up the car perfectly between the white lines of a parking space in a mini-mall, she cut the engine and glanced at his profile. "What?"

"What, what?"

"Why are you grinning like that?"

"Nice parking job."

She huffed through her nose and swung open her car door.

The computer tech in the store didn't blink an eye when Martha walked up to the counter. He either hadn't seen the news yet about Congressman Wentworth croaking in Martha's town house, or he was trying to be polite.

Martha plunked her laptop on the counter and spun it around to face the techie. "Hi, Marcel. I've been hacked, invaded, compromised, whatever you want to call it."

"Ooh, a Trojan?" Marcel flipped up the lid and widened his eyes when he saw the Post-its blocking the camera. "Dude got to your camera?"

"Yes, he's been watching me." Martha wrinkled her nose. "So creepy."

"And pretty sophisticated." Marcel stuck some tape over the camera lens and plucked off the Post-its. "Any idea who your stalker is?"

"No. Just get rid of it." Martha gripped the edge of the counter. "You can, can't you?"

"Oh, yeah." He nodded toward a computer in the corner humming through some diagnostics. "I'm working on that one, but I can get yours started. You can wait. There's a pretty good Thai place two doors down."

"That sounds good. I'm starving." Martha's gaze darted to Cam's face. "I mean, if you want to get something to eat while we wait."

"Absolutely." Cam peeked out the window through the blinds. "It's already getting dark. I had breakfast at the hotel but completely skipped lunch."

"I guess that's settled." She turned to Marcel, waving a slip of paper. "Do you need my password?"

"Honestly, I can get past it, but I'll do it on the up-and-up." He took the paper from her between his two fingers and lifted the laptop from the counter to take it to a station in the back of the shop.

Cam beat Martha to the door and opened it for

her. "The restaurant is to the right. I noticed it when we drove into the parking lot. I already knew I was hungry."

She stuffed her hands into her pockets as she headed into the blustery wind, listing to the side.

"Are you going to get swept off your feet?" Cam placed a hand on her arm.

"No." She dropped her eyes to his hand, and he released her.

"For a minute there I thought you were going to take off with the wind." He felt like he needed some kind of excuse for touching her again.

When they entered the empty restaurant, the waitress on the phone behind the counter waved them into one of a dozen tables scattered around the room.

"I guess we're too late for lunch and too early for dinner." Martha shed her coat and folded it onto a chair at a table by the window.

Ten minutes later, they waited for their food while Martha blew on her hot tea and Cam tipped his beer into a glass. "That must've been rough on you when your father was arrested. You were a teenager?"

"Yes. It couldn't have happened at a worse time."

"Yeah, those awkward teen years, and then you have to deal with notoriety on top of it all."

Her eyes met his briefly and then seemed to search his face before moving in a slow inventory down his neck, chest, across his shoulders and down his arms.

Her study of him felt like a caress, exploratory and featherlight.

Then her brows snapped over her nose. "*You* had awkward teen years? Not likely."

He smiled and his jaw ached with the effort. "We all have our issues. What was your father's crime? Securities fraud?"

"Something like that." She waved her hand. "It's confusing, but it boiled down to cheating and scamming. He was always good at that."

"How long is he in for?"

"He's been in for ten, and he's eligible for parole in about five more."

"Do you see him?"

"Occasionally."

"He must've made good money—legitimately—at one time."

"He did quite well for a number of years. I did the whole private school thing, and when I started showing an aptitude for languages, he arranged for language schools and tutoring."

"He must've been proud of you."

"The feeling was not mutual." She rubbed the back of her hand across her nose. "What about you? Where are you from? How long have you been in the military?"

"I enlisted when I was nineteen, after one year in college playing football." He tapped his glass and watched the bubbles rise and try to break through the thick head of foam blocking their escape.

One disastrous year when he couldn't keep up academically, no matter how many tutors the coaches sent his way, and flunked out, losing his football scholarship. "Yeah, the military was a good fit, and it didn't take long before Delta Force started looking my way."

"You must be something special. That's an elite unit."

"It suits me."

The waitress interrupted them with several plates of steaming food, and as Martha removed her glasses, Cam raised his eyebrows.

"The food is fogging up my lenses."

Martha looked cute in glasses, but without them her eyes mesmerized him as they seemed to shift in color and glow like a cat's in the low light.

The soft pink that crept into her cheeks gave him a jolt. He was staring at her like an idiot. She probably dated educated guys with multiple degrees and witty conversation.

"Do you want some rice?" He held up the round container of sticky white rice. *Real witty, Cam.*

For the rest of the meal, they danced around each other, sharing little bits of information about themselves. Cam took his cues from Martha, skimming across the surface of his life and allowing her to fill in the blanks.

He tried to fill in her blanks, too, but she'd perfected the art of the dodge. Maybe she'd learned that from her old man, even though she seemed to reject everything he stood for.

Her cell phone buzzed on the table beside her plate, and she flicked a grain of rice from its display before she tapped it. Her lips pursed as she read the text. "You're not going to believe this."

Cam's pulse jumped. "What? It's not the patriot, is it?"

"No, it's Casey. She wants to meet me—away from the town house. She has a lot of nerve."

"You're not meeting her alone." Cam pushed his empty plate to the middle of the table. "She might be involved in Wentworth's death up to her eyeballs."

"She says she wants to apologize and discuss moving out. She doesn't want to go back to the town house now that she's been outed as Wentworth's mistress."

"Where is she?"

"At a hotel not far from yours." Martha tapped her phone to reply to Casey's text.

"She wants to see you now?"

"As soon as I can get over there."

Cam checked the time on his own phone. "Let's pick up your computer before the shop closes, and then we'll head over there—together."

"I told her to give me an hour." She grabbed her glasses and put them on, peering at him through the lenses. "You're serious? You're coming with me?"

"Like I said—" he reached for his wallet "—I

don't trust that woman. And don't tell her I'm coming along. We'll surprise her."

"I didn't mention you, but I still think you're wrong. Casey is too flakey to be some international spy." She plunged her hand into her purse and withdrew her wallet.

Cam's gaze dipped to Martha's hand, pulling out some cash, and he swallowed. No woman he ever dated expected to pay, not that he'd allow it, but this really wasn't a date, and a woman like Martha might be offended if he insisted on paying.

He waved the check. "Uh, fifteen bucks each, but I'll throw in twenty since I had the beer and you had tea."

"Whatever." She tossed a ten and a five onto the table. "I'll pitch in for your beer in exchange for your protection…from Casey. She might poke me with her stiletto or shoot me in the face with hairspray."

"Go ahead and scoff. Congressman Wentworth trusted her and look where that got *him*."

They walked back to the computer store and picked up Martha's newly cleansed laptop. She did a quick check of her emails before putting it away.

As Cam stashed the computer case in the trunk of her car, Martha said, "Now if the patriot wants to contact me about Wentworth's death, he'll have to find another method."

"If he really wants to contact you again, he will.

He already has your email address. He doesn't need to watch you."

Martha drove back into DC toward a hotel a few blocks away from his own. She paid for guest parking in the structure beneath the hotel, and they rode up in the elevator to the fifth floor.

As the doors opened and they stepped onto the thick carpet, Martha whispered, "Maybe she wants to tell me what really happened to Wentworth."

"If she didn't tell you in the time you two were waiting for the ambulance, why would she be coming clean now?"

She shrugged, and they turned the corner in the direction of Casey's room. Cam trailed behind Martha just in case his appearance in the peephole scared off the woman.

But he didn't have to worry about a peephole. Casey had propped open the hotel door with the latch, wedging it between the door and the jamb.

Martha raised her brows at him as she knocked on the door and called out. "Casey?"

No response.

"Maybe she stepped out and wanted to leave the door open for me." Martha placed her hand flat against the door. "Casey? It's Martha."

A tingle raced across the back of Cam's neck, and he pulled his gun from his pocket.

Martha jerked back when she saw it. "What are you doing? Where'd that come from?"

"My pocket." He put a finger to his lips. "Shh."

As Martha pushed open the hotel door, Cam followed closely on her heels. Nothing about this felt right. He flicked the lever back and pulled the door closed.

A lamp in the corner illuminated the empty space, a suitcase open on the bed, a curtain billowing into the room from the open door to the balcony.

"Casey?" Martha crept to the closed bathroom door and pushed down on the handle, swinging it open.

Cam hovered behind her.

Martha gasped and choked. She stumbled against him.

He caught her around the waist and peered over her shoulder.

His gut churned as he took in the sight of Casey in a tub of red-tinted water, one hand hanging over the side, pointing at the pool of blood on the tile floor.

Chapter Six

All at once, the smell flooded Martha's nostrils, the metallic taste filling her mouth. She gagged.

Cam dragged her backward out of the bathroom and propped her against the wall while he dashed toward the sliding glass door, his weapon raised.

She blinked and slid down the wall, her legs crumpling beneath her. Where was he going? Was he cold? She was cold. A ferocious shiver had gripped her body, making her teeth chatter and her hands shake.

The cold had crept into her limbs and she couldn't move them, couldn't get up. Cam had left her, had disappeared out the sliding glass door, had left her alone with... Casey.

Oh, God. Maybe Casey wasn't dead.

It took all Martha's concentration to hunch forward onto her hands and knees and turn toward the open bathroom door, but she remained rooted to the carpet, rocking back and forth like a baby learning to crawl.

"Martha!" Cam scooped her up as easily as if she

were a baby and wrapped his arms around her, holding her back against his front.

"You don't need to go back in there. Casey's dead."

"H-how can you know?"

"The blood, the…" He walked backward, towing her along with him, and settled her on the edge of the bed. "Stay here. I'll check."

As Cam left her again, her knees began bouncing up and down. She clasped her hands over them and pressed down, digging her heels into the carpet.

Cam returned and crouched in front of her, taking her stiff hands in his. "She's gone."

"Did she drown? I don't understand. Did she slip and fall? Where did all that blood come from?" Her voice began to rise, and she clamped a hand over her mouth to stop the panic burgeoning in her chest.

Cam brought her hands to his lips and kissed her knuckles. "She slit her wrists, Martha."

"No. Oh, no." She shook her head back and forth so hard, her glasses slipped down her nose.

"We have to call 911 and the hotel." Cam pocketed his gun, pulled his sleeve over his hand and picked up the room's telephone.

He murmured into the receiver, hung up and placed another call. Then he walked to the door of the room and wedged it open the same way Casey had left it for her.

Martha watched all his actions, the fog starting

to lift from her brain. Casey was dead in the bath-tub—a suicide.

Minutes later, a hotel security guard and a hotel manager burst through the door.

Cam pointed to the bathroom. "She's in there. I already called 911."

The two hotel employees crowded at the bathroom door, and the manager screamed, "Oh my God!"

Cam pulled Martha up from the bed and wrapped her in a hug. He whispered in her ear, "Are you okay? Still in shock?"

Her lips moved against the rough material of his shirt, but she didn't make a sound. She cleared her throat and tried again. "Why would she do that?"

He squeezed her tighter and she closed her eyes, breathing in the scent of him. She never wanted to leave this safe place.

All too soon, the police and EMTs surged into the room and the questions started.

Of course the police had heard of Casey Jessup, the DC intern who'd been too hot for the congress-man to handle.

They questioned Martha about her presence here at the hotel, Casey's demeanor, her motives. They hauled some booze and pills out of the bathroom, items Martha hadn't even noticed.

Cam handled everything calmly and confidently, subtly protecting her by moving closer whenever the cop's questioning veered toward the intrusive.

After what seemed like hours, the nightmare finally wound down. Casey's body was still in the bathroom, but the police were letting them leave. The officer had her number and would call if they had any more questions or needed to visit the town house and search Casey's things.

She and Cam said nothing as they walked out of the room, but he entwined his fingers with hers on the way to the elevator. When the doors of the car closed behind them, he let out a long breath.

"I'm sorry you had to go through all that, sorry you had to stay in that room. I would've hustled you out of there and made an anonymous 911 call, but I'm sure the hotel has cameras that would've caught our arrival and departure, and the cops may even be checking Casey's cell and would've identified that text going to your phone number."

He'd released her hand, and she threw it out now to brace against the mirrored back of the elevator car. "We couldn't have left. We found her. Th-that's like leaving the scene of a crime."

"A crime?" He stabbed at the elevator button again.

"Technically, suicide is a crime, isn't it?" She sagged against the elevator wall and twitched when it landed in the parking garage.

As they exited onto their level, Cam held out his hand, palm up. "I'll drive. You're still shaken up."

Biting her bottom lip, Martha rummaged through her purse and pulled out her key chain. She dropped the keys into his hand, and he opened the passenger door for her.

She plopped onto the seat and snapped her seat belt, keeping a tight hold on the shoulder strap. When Cam slid behind the wheel and started the engine, she turned to him. "Why did you go outside to the balcony? What were you doing out there?"

"Why'd she leave that door open?"

"Maybe she was enjoying a last breath of fresh air."

"The police think she may have taken an overdose of pills with some alcohol for good measure. Did she think slicing her wrists in the bathtub wasn't going to do the trick?"

"What did you see on the balcony?" Martha trapped her hands between her knees and trapped the air in her lungs as she held her breath.

"A way out."

"Do you think someone else was in that room?"

"Why did Casey text you? We were there an hour later. You're telling me she drank that vodka, took those pills, climbed into the bath and slit her wrists all before we got there?"

Martha spoke up over the roar building in her head. "She drank the booze and popped the pills before she contacted me. She thought maybe I'd get here before she was dead, so she decided to speed up the process."

"Why would she do that, notify you, I mean? The two of you weren't even close." He hunched over the steering wheel, crossing his arms on top of it. "I could see that original text. She didn't want to go back to the town house and wanted to give you some kind of notice that she was moving out. Maybe she even wanted you to help her out by packing up her stuff and shipping it to her. But why would she want you here at her death?"

Martha lifted her shoulders to her ears and held them there. "She didn't want a loved one or a close friend to find her, but she wanted *someone* to find her."

"Do you really believe Casey was so distraught over Wentworth's death that she offed herself in commiseration? If anything, a girl like that would've relished the attention, gotten a book deal, landed on reality TV. You told me that's what she was all about."

Martha rested her head against the cool glass of the window. "You think she had help. You think she was murdered."

"C'mon, Martha. Use that logical mind of yours—emails, threats, a dead congressman in your place and now Casey's so-called suicide. All coincidence?"

"It all seems so random."

"It does, but I guarantee you, it's not. This is all connected somehow."

"Do you think the police will figure it out? What about those hotel cameras? If they would've caught us, they would've caught Casey's…killer."

"Unless he snuck over that balcony or disabled the cameras."

"I'm scared, Cam."

He reached over and squeezed her knee. "Get rid of those emails. Forget this whole thing."

"What about Major Denver?"

"We'll figure out a way to help him. Hell, he's probably helping himself."

"Oh, no." Martha pressed her nose to the window and took in the reporters still hovering on the sidewalk outside her place. Her breath fogged the glass. "I can't go through that. Wait until they find out this latest news."

Cam ducked his head and swore. "Vultures. Don't they have more important stories to report on? Is there a back way into your place?"

"They discovered it already." She tucked her hands beneath her thighs. She didn't want to be alone in that town house. Didn't want to leave Cam.

"You should stay in a hotel tonight." Cam flexed his fingers on the steering wheel. "If you want, you can stay in my room."

"That would be great…if you really don't mind." Had she just guilted him into that invitation? Did he see her as the poor, little friendless nerd? "I mean, I can call a friend if it's too much trouble."

The car lurched forward, and he squealed away from the curb. "I think it's better if you stay with someone who knows what's going on right now—someone with a gun."

She twisted her head to the side. "You really think I'm in danger."

"Martha, I don't want to freak you out right now, but I have my doubts that Casey killed herself. I have my doubts she even texted you."

"That balcony. You think someone was waiting for me out there?"

"I think he heard us talking at the door. He wasn't expecting you to have company, so he took off." Cam flicked on the wipers and rubbed the inside of the windshield with his fist.

"He could've shot me...us as soon as we walked into the room." She watched a drip of water on the outside of the window join up with another one and then another to form a little stream.

"Who said he had a gun? Who said he wanted to kill you? We don't know what the patriot wants."

"According to you, he killed Casey. Why would he do that?"

"She knew too much."

"I know more than she does."

"She knew the right things." He swung into the driveway in front of his hotel and left the keys with the valet.

As they entered the lobby, Cam pointed to the gift shop next to the elevators. "Do you want to pick up a toothbrush and whatever else you might need?"

After her shopping spree, Martha dangled the plastic bag from her fingers as she and Cam made their way to his room. She'd rushed here this afternoon convinced Wentworth's death had something to do with the emails about Denver. Now another death had been added to the mix, and she wasn't sure about anything anymore—except Cam.

He had her back—whether from pity or his strong desire to use those emails to clear Major Denver, she didn't know and she didn't care. She'd bask in the safety of the protective aura that wafted around him.

He opened the hotel door for her and gestured her through. "Sorry it's not a suite, just the one room. You can take the bed and I'll camp out on the sofa."

Her gaze swept the length of the truncated sofa— almost a love seat—and then scanned Cam head to toe. "You're not going to fit on that thing. I'll sleep there."

"I've slept on worse than that." He held up one finger. "Don't argue with me."

She raised her eyebrows. "I hadn't planned on it. I'll take the bed, and you don't have to twist my arm. And I'll even lay claim to the bathroom first."

"Be my guest." He dragged a pillow from the bed. "I will take one of these."

"Be *my* guest." She twirled the plastic bag of toiletries around her finger and tripped to a stop at the bathroom door. "Do you have a T-shirt or something I can wear to bed?"

"The ones in the closet are all clean. Help yourself."

Martha reached into the closet and yanked a gray T-shirt from a hanger. She made for the bathroom and closed and locked the door behind her—not that she expected Cam to make a raid on the bathroom while she was in here undressing.

Bracing her hands on the vanity, she hunched toward the mirror. Her flushed cheeks and bright eyes were signals of the adrenaline that had been pumping through her system nonstop all day as she bounced from one crazy event to the next.

At the end of it all she'd wound up in the hotel room of this hot Delta Force D-Boy, who had zero expectations of her. And why would he? She'd helped guys like this with their homework and papers many times in college, and they'd never demanded anything from her except the guarantee that she'd help them again.

She let out a long breath and brushed her teeth. She took off all her clothes except for her bra and underwear, and pulled the T-shirt over her head.

Cam's extra-large T-shirt billowed around her tall, thin frame, hitting her midthigh. It would sweep a tinier woman's knees, but she'd never been a tiny person. Tall, gawky and awkward had marked her teen years.

She folded her clothes into a neat pile. Clutching the bundle to her chest, she crept back into the room.

Cam jerked his head up and jabbed at the TV remote, but not before she heard Congressman Wentworth's and Casey's names.

She placed her clothes on a vacant chair. "They're on that like a pack of dogs on a rabbit's scent."

"Until the next scandal breaks." He tossed the remote onto the bed. "Did you have everything you needed in there?"

"I did. Your turn."

As Cam disappeared into the bathroom, Martha turned on the TV but skipped all the news channels. She *was* the news for the second time in her life. She didn't have to watch it. Settling on a nature show, she bunched the pillows behind her and settled back.

Ten minutes into the program, Cam eased open the bathroom door and poked his head around the corner. "Are you still awake?"

"After the day I just had, I'm wired. I'm going to need a few more hours of watching plants grow in fast-motion before I can even think about sleeping."

He stopped in front of the TV and shook his head. "That would put anyone to sleep."

He turned off the lone light in the room, the tall lamp next to the sofa, and grabbed the hem of the white T-shirt he'd been wearing beneath his denim shirt, pulling it up.

Martha got a quick glimpse of his six-pack, illuminated by the blue light from the flickering images on TV, before he pulled the T-shirt over his head and she averted her eyes.

As he unbuckled his belt, she shoved her glasses up the bridge of her nose and studied the insects hatching on the screen. And she hated insects.

Yanking down his jeans, Cam turned his back to her and she turned her gaze onto him. His pants dropped down his powerful thighs, and Martha swallowed at the sight of his muscled buttocks in the black briefs.

He kicked his jeans into a corner and then shot her a look over his shoulder.

She cleared her throat and pulled a pillow into her lap. Had he caught her watching him undress?

"Guess I should try to keep the room neater with two people in here."

She waved her hand. "Do whatever you'd normally do."

He walked to the discarded jeans and picked them up. As he draped them over the back of a chair, he said, "I don't think you mean that."

"Sure I do. I don't want to upset your routine."

He cocked his head. "Really? 'Cause I usually bunk in the buff."

A flood of warmth washed into her cheeks. "I—I mean, if that's what you…"

He held up his hands and flashed that boyish grin that pretty much did her in. "Don't worry. I'm not a perv."

What if she admitted she wouldn't mind one bit if he stripped down completely?

"And I'm not a complete prude, you know."

"Prude? I never thought you were." He crawled into the bed he'd made from the sofa, propping his head on the arm of it. "What did I miss?

"We don't have to watch this if you don't want."

She held out the remote into the space between bed and sofa. "Just no news."

"As long as we're both awake, how about you mute this fascinating look at mating insects and we talk instead?"

She squinted at the image on the TV. "Is that what they're doing? I think they're just eating."

"Whatever. Can we talk about what happened today? I know you think Casey was too stupid to be involved, but I think you're wrong."

"Stupid? I didn't mean to imply that Casey was stupid. She's flakey. *Was* flakey." Martha pulled her knees to her chest with one arm.

"Maybe flakey Casey was putting on an act, or maybe they used her, used her flakiness."

"You mean perhaps she was a legit roommate and they got to her *because* she was my roommate, instead setting her up to be my roommate?" Martha rolled her head to the side to face Cam, resting her cheek on her knee.

"That's exactly what I mean." He curled one arm behind his head, bunching up his biceps. "She moved in with you, and they approached her with an offer."

"And Congressman Wentworth? How does he fit into the picture?"

"Maybe once they had her hooked, they told her to target him. She was a beautiful woman. Wentworth already had a rep for inappropriate sexting. It wouldn't have taken much for a girl like Casey to get her claws into him."

Of course, he'd noticed Casey's attractiveness. Had he compared her to her sexy roommate and found her wanting? Her sexy, *dead* roommate.

Martha drew her bottom lip between her teeth. "Do you think they killed her to tie up loose ends? To keep her from talking?"

"Those would be a couple of reasons."

"Why would they, or *he* if we're just talking about the patriot, want to lure me to Casey's hotel room to discover her body?" Martha stretched out her legs, pulling the pillow up to her chin. "Another warning? They got what they wanted from me originally. I turned over those emails to the proper authorities. Now they want me to leave well enough alone. That's the only motive I can figure out."

"It's a strong motive." Cam yawned and slid farther beneath his blanket. "So, why don't you?"

"Leave it alone?" She clicked off the TV and rolled to her side. "Maybe I will."

Of course, if she deleted the emails and let the patriot know what she'd done and put all her efforts back into her job at the Agency, she'd never see Cam Sutton again.

And she didn't know if she could give him up just yet, danger or not.

THE FOLLOWING MORNING, Martha sat up and squinted against the weak wintry light slipping through the drapes.

Cam yanked them closed. "Sorry."

"That's okay. What time is it?"

"Almost seven. You can go back to sleep if you want. You had a long day yesterday that turned into a longer night."

"I'm awake." She eyed his fully dressed form by the window and rubbed her eyes. And her dream had ended. "It might actually be a good time to drop by my town house and collect a few things. The press might still be sleeping, or maybe some celebrity couple got a divorce overnight and Wentworth and Casey are no longer the hot news."

"Collect your things?"

Cam's gaze darted wildly around the room as if assessing how all her stuff was going to fit in here.

"Don't worry." She whipped back the bedcovers and swung her legs over the side of the bed, tugging on the T-shirt with one hand. "I'm not moving in here. I can relocate to my mom's place."

"Where's that?"

"Maryland."

"She lives here, and you haven't called her yet with all this going on?"

"Her house is here. She's in Florida with her new husband."

"Has she called you? She must've heard about Wentworth dying in your town house—even in Florida."

"She texted me, asked if I was okay and went on with her life."

"She's all right with you relocating to her house?"

"She suggested it." Martha jerked her thumb over her shoulder. "I'm going to shower here."

"Do you want breakfast before we leave?"

"No." Her head jerked up. "We?"

"I'm not letting you back into that lion's den by yourself. You can collect your stuff, drop me off here and hole up in your mother's house." He whipped open the drapes. "And think about letting this go."

She nodded before ensconcing herself in the bathroom. She showered and dressed in record time. The sooner she got away from Cam, the easier it would be to forget about him whether she wanted to or not. And she didn't want to.

She snorted softly as she turned her back to the warm spray from the showerhead. There was going to be nothing easy about getting Cam out of her mind.

An hour later, she drove up to her place, Cam in the passenger seat beside her. One news truck had taken up residence across the street, but the hordes of reporters and cameras had taken a break.

"We're in luck." She parallel parked half a block down from her place. She kept her head down as Cam took her hand and pulled her along quickly to her front door.

As she used her key to open the door, she sucked in a breath. "I need to get Casey's extra key from its hiding place before I leave."

Cam followed her closely into the town house.

"That's risky, keeping a key like that. I hope it's not under the welcome mat."

"No. It's a good hiding place." She dropped her key chain into her purse and hung it on a peg by the front door. "Casey was always forgetting her keys or losing them, so I stashed an extra for her just in case."

Cam surveyed the room. "At least the police didn't designate this as a crime scene."

"They did search Casey's bedroom and bathroom, but there were no injuries on Wentworth's body, no evidence of foul play. Looked like a heart attack, but we both know there are ways to mimic that with a drug."

"We'll let the police figure that out. Pack up and let's get out of here before the hyenas gather."

"I thought they were vultures…" She put her foot on the bottom step of the staircase and turned. "You can help yourself to whatever if you're hungry."

"I plan to buy you breakfast." He nodded toward the TV. "I am going to take a look at the news though."

"Knock yourself out. I won't be long."

Once in her room, Martha rolled a suitcase from the closet and started packing for her workweek. What would Gage have to say to her about this weekend?

She hadn't done anything to jeopardize her security clearance—at least nothing Gage knew about.

She finished up with her toiletries from the bathroom and even threw in a couple pairs of disposable contacts. She wore them occasionally, even though they dried out her eyes by the end of the day. Wanting to wear contacts had nothing to do with Cam.

She'd dragged her suitcase into the hall and rolled it to the top of the staircase when Cam came bounding up the stairs.

"I'll help you with that." He picked it up by the handle and carried it down as if it were empty. "Is that everything?"

"What I don't have, I can come back for or buy. Mom has more than enough at her place."

She plucked her purse from the peg and balanced it on top of her suitcase. "I'm just going to get that key, and I'll be ready. Have the vultures started circling yet?"

Standing to the side of the bay window in the front, Cam peeked through a gap in the drapes. "Nope. I'll come with you to get the key."

"It's out back in the garden." She crossed through the kitchen and turned the dead bolt on the back door.

She stepped onto the pavers, kept dry from the recent rains by an awning over the patio. Then she crouched next to a patio chair with a plastic cover and pulled back the zipper on the cover about an inch. She shoved two fingers inside, probing.

When she found the key, it had some paper wrapped around it. "This is weird. Maybe it's the tag from the chair cover."

Cam kneeled beside her. "Did you find the key?"

"I did, but there's some paper wrapped around it." She pinched the key and the paper between two fingers and pulled it out.

She tipped the key into her palm and unwrapped the scrap of paper. Her heart flipped in her chest and she gasped. "She knew. She left me a note. Casey left me a note."

"What does it say?"

Martha read the words from the slip of paper that shook in her hand. "'If anything happens to me, talk to Tony.'"

Chapter Seven

Cam caught Martha's shoulder as she started to tip over. She'd almost been clear of this mess.

"Who the hell is Tony?"

Martha pressed her fingertips to her temples. "I'm not sure. There have so many men since Casey moved in. Tony. Tony."

The rain started up again, pinging the fiberglass awning above them. He took Martha's arm. "Put that away and let's get out of here."

Martha shoved the note and key in her pocket and turned toward the town house.

While she locked up, Cam flicked the edge of the drapes aside and peered out. "They're back. Get ready to do the duck and dodge."

She grabbed her purse from the top of her suitcase and slung it over her shoulder. "Maybe I can use my suitcase as a battering ram through the crowd."

"Don't worry about your bag. I'll handle that. Just put your head down and make a beeline to the car."

They faced the front door, and as he grabbed the

handle Martha put a hand on his wrist. "Thanks for helping me out, Cam."

"Since I kinda got you into this mess, it's the least I can do."

"Even if you hadn't shown up when you did, this patriot person would've still taken these actions. Maybe I would've been dead beneath the wheels of that oncoming train two nights ago."

"I'm glad you're not." He pressed a kiss on her forehead and opened the front door.

The media sensed movement, smelled blood and swarmed around the front porch. They shouted Martha's name, Casey's name, Wentworth's name. Cam couldn't make out any of the questions—not that Martha would be answering them anyway.

He put his arm around her shoulders and charged down the sidewalk to her car, dragging the suitcase behind him. He breathed into her ear, "Get in the driver's seat and start the engine. As soon as I get in the car, take off."

Martha hurried to the car, ten feet away, and unlocked the doors. She scurried around to the driver's side, and Cam lifted the lid of the trunk and swung the suitcase inside. As he slammed it shut, she started the car.

He strode to the front passenger door, and someone touched his back. "Who are you? Martha's boyfriend?"

Cam growled, "I wish," and slammed the door in the reporter's face.

"Hit it."

She peeled away from the curb, her eyes on the rearview mirror. "Don't they ever get tired? What do they hope to gain from sitting in front of a building?"

"They just got it—a shot of you hauling your suitcase out of there." He clicked his seat belt in place. "What about Casey's family. Do you know if they've been notified?"

"The police contacted her mother and sister last night. I've never met them. Casey never talked about her family, but I told the police to give them my contact information when they get to town and I'll let them into the house." She hunched her shoulders. "What awful news."

"And now we know it's murder."

"We should tell the police, give them the note."

"Do you think Tony's going to be willing to talk to the police? Do you think he wants to expose Casey if she'd been doing something illegal?" He rubbed his eyes. "That's if we can even figure out who he is."

"I know who Tony is."

"You do?"

"I remembered when we were running down the sidewalk. He's a bartender. Through all the guys, he's pretty much been a constant fixture."

"Last name?"

"I don't know, but he works at a bar in Georgetown. I'd just need to call to see if he's working tonight."

Her phone buzzed in the cupholder where she'd

stashed it, and Cam glanced at the display. "It's the DC Metro Police. Do you want to answer it?"

"Yeah. Speaker."

He tapped the phone for her and put it on Speaker. "Hello?"

"Ms. Drake, this is Detective Merchant with DC Metro. I have a couple of questions for you about Ms. Jessup."

"Go ahead. I'll try to help." She raised her brows at Cam.

"Have you been back to the town house you shared with Ms. Jessup?"

"I have."

"Did she leave a suicide note there or any indication what she was planning? We didn't find any notes at the hotel."

"No notes."

Her jaw tightened, and Cam knew what it cost her to lie to the police.

"Also, do you know what keys she had on her key chain?"

"No. Why do you ask?"

"We didn't find a key chain or any keys at all in her personal belongings or in her purse—just her wallet, some makeup, her cell phone. Did she have a car?"

"No car, but that seems weird she didn't have her house key, at least." Martha turned her head to meet Cam's gaze.

The officer cleared his throat. "Not so strange if she wasn't planning to return to the town house."

"Y-you're right. Do you know if her family is coming to DC to collect her personal items?"

"They'll be in touch and so will we. That's all for now, Ms. Drake."

"Okay, thanks."

Cam ended the call for her. "That's not good, Martha."

"The keys?"

"Exactly. Who has them? Maybe those attack reporters staking out your place saved you from an unwanted visitor last night. If the person who killed Casey took her key, he now has easy access to your place…and you."

"I'll get the locks changed."

"Good idea." He patted his growling stomach. "How about that breakfast I promised you?"

"I don't feel like going out. We can eat at my mom's place if we stop for some groceries on the way. Is that okay with you?"

He tipped his head. "Are you worried about being followed by the patriot, or you're afraid people will recognize you from TV?"

"Do you think he's following me?" She grabbed the rearview mirror and adjusted it.

"I've been watching." He rapped his knuckle on the window toward his own mirror. "Nobody has been following us, not even the press."

Slumping back in her seat, she said, "I just don't

want people staring at me. I had enough of that when my dad was arrested."

"I'm more than happy to eat a home-cooked breakfast at your mom's, but I don't think you have to worry about people recognizing you. That picture the reporters keep flashing of you on TV must've been from a while ago." His gaze lingered on her face and hair. "You look different."

"That picture was from my late teenage years, years I just wanted to disappear."

"I can see that from the picture. You wore bigger glasses, baggy clothes and your hair practically covered your face." He reached out and tucked a loose strand of hair behind her ear, his fingers hovering at her earlobe. "I like it this way better—where I can see your face...your eyes."

She coughed and pinned her shoulders against the seat. "Maybe my appearance won't inspire a paparazzi frenzy, but I'd still rather eat in."

"You got it." He dropped his hand. "I'll even cook, if you like something simple like bacon and eggs."

"Simple? Bagels and toast are about the most complex I get in the morning. You know how to cook?"

"I know the basics."

"I'm impressed."

Cam lifted his chin and smiled. He couldn't help it if Martha's praise stoked his ego. Somehow meeting this woman's approval had become a priority for him.

After a stop at a grocery store, Martha headed east until she hit the coast and then turned north, where Cam caught glimpses of the bay between big houses and rolling lawns. Guess the government hadn't forced Skip Brockridge to give back all the money he swindled.

Martha wheeled her car into the circular driveway and pulled up in front of the double doors.

Cam whistled. "Nice digs. Does she have a bay in her backyard?"

"A bay and a boat dock." She threw the gear into Park. "But no boat."

"Cutting costs?"

"The boats were always my dad's thing—his and mine." She rubbed the end of her nose and exited the car.

He followed her to the trunk and hoisted her suitcase out. He balanced one of the grocery bags on top while Martha snagged the other two. "Did you grow up in this house?"

"This dump?" She swept her arm across the expansive, light blue clapboard front with the wraparound porch. "Mom did have to readjust when Dad was sent to prison, downsize. I don't even know why she bought on the bay. It was never her thing."

"Is there someone here? It doesn't look abandoned."

Martha plucked a key from her key chain and swung it back and forth. "Not right now, but Mom's housekeeper comes in once a week to dust mostly, and the gardeners keep up their weekly schedule."

"You said your mother was in Florida?"

"For the winter—like a bird." She unlocked the dead bolt and shoved the key into the handle to finish the job.

Cam followed her inside, dragging her suitcase behind him, his head swiveling from side to side. "Do you share a decorator with your mother? Looks similar to your place."

"The town house was my mother's, from my grandmother. I can afford to live there—with a roommate—but I can't afford to redecorate."

"Do you want this upstairs?" Cam rolled the suitcase to the foot of a curved staircase.

"You can leave it for now." She held out the two grocery bags. "Let's put you to work in the kitchen."

Cam widened his eyes as he stepped into the kitchen, the copper pots hanging above a center island catching the light and reflecting off the shiny granite counters, lined with enough appliances and gadgets to stock a cooking show. "This is way beyond my capabilities."

"If it's beyond yours, you can imagine how I feel walking in here and pouring my cereal in a bowl." She placed the groceries on the island and then rolled up the sleeves of her sweater. "Tell me what to do."

He held up a finger. "You always wash your hands first. That's what my mama taught me."

"Did your mother teach you how to cook, or did she and your sister baby you and you had to learn on your own later?"

"My mom baby me?" He snorted. "She was a

single parent, worked nights a lot so I had to fend for myself."

"Oh." She paused, hugging the carton of eggs to her chest. "What happened to your father?"

He bumped her hip so he could wash his hands at the sink. "My dad took off when my sister Lexie was a baby and I wasn't much older. We never saw him again."

"I'm sorry."

"I'm not. From all accounts he was a bastard, and we were better off without him."

"Funny, I thought..." She shook her head. "Bowls are in that cupboard. I'll leave the egg mixing to you, and I'll start cutting some veggies and grating the cheese."

He lodged his tongue in the corner of his mouth as he cracked several eggs into a bowl. What had she thought about him? At least she'd given him some thought.

"Milk?"

She opened the fridge and pulled out the carton she'd just put away. Looking over his shoulder, she asked, "Do you want me to pour it in? Just tell me when to stop."

He continued whisking. "Okay, pour, little more, little more. Stop."

She put away the milk and tipped her head back to survey the pots swinging above them. "I don't even know which one would work for an omelet."

He reached over her head to grab a pan. "This one will do."

"Is this enough for the filling?" She held up the cutting board for his inspection.

"I've never heard omelet ingredients called filling before, but that'll work."

"I told you I didn't know my way around a kitchen."

"Let me guess. You had a cook."

"We did." Her mouth tightened. "All bought and paid for with ill-gotten gains, but my mother liked to cook. She must've been thrilled when she had a daughter because Mom enjoyed all those typically feminine pursuits, but I was interested in…other things."

"Boating?" The butter sizzled in the pan as Cam swirled it around and up the sides. "I figured you must've spent most of your time holed up with books and studying."

"Oh, the boating." She shrugged. "I did that because *he* liked it."

"Your father."

"Uh-huh." She sniffled. "Too much onion, I think."

"It's fine." Her sniffling had nothing to do with onions. She'd acted like she hated her father before, but that couldn't be further from the truth.

He finished off the first omelet and tipped it onto a plate. Then he constructed the second, messing up the corner when he flipped up the one side.

"I'll take the defective one."

She twisted off the cap of the orange juice bottle and poured two glasses. "They both look perfect to me."

"We didn't get coffee." He slid the damaged omelet onto the second plate with a flourish.

"I'm okay without it."

She carried the glasses to the center island and placed them at the corner of the place mats. He followed her with the plates and centered them on the mats, trying to match her perfection.

"I don't need coffee. I think I'm too wired as it is." She pointed to her laptop case on the coffee table. "I haven't even checked my messages today. What if my friend has some news for me?"

"Unless he can tell you he's going to leave you alone or tell you what he wants from you, his news is worthless." He shook out the cloth napkin next to his plate and draped it over one knee. Martha had brought them back to reality, so he might as well jump in with both feet. "Are you going to call Tony's workplace later to see if he's on tonight?"

"Yes, but I wonder what he knows. Why wouldn't he tell the police or why wouldn't Casey have warned *him* to call the cops if anything happened to her?"

"Maybe she didn't want to involve him." He cut off a corner of his omelet and waved it at Martha. "She warned you instead because you're already involved."

"Great." She poked at her eggs. "This looks really

good. I'm sorry I brought up the other stuff. I don't want to ruin your appetite."

"Mine?" He stabbed a mushroom. "Not possible."

They continued chatting, avoiding the issues front and center, and Martha told him about growing up in the Chesapeake Bay area. Her upbringing couldn't have been more different from his on the hardscrabble streets of Atlanta, but the most glaring difference involved father issues. He had no desire to even find out where his was, and Martha had clearly idolized hers—until he'd disappointed her.

No wonder she didn't have a boyfriend on the scene. She must've set her standards high after the fiasco with her father.

They finished breakfast, and Martha insisted on cleaning up since he'd done the cooking.

"You can do the dishes, but I have to help. My mom ingrained that into me, and she'd smack me upside the head if she found out I let someone else do all the cleaning."

"Your mother still lives in Georgia?"

"Yeah, and I can't get her to leave the old neighborhood." He shook his head. "I keep trying to get her to find another job and move, but she claims she doesn't do the physical work like she used to."

"What does she do?"

"For years she worked as a maid at a hotel. She's still at the same damned place, but now she's the housekeeping supervisor." He shrugged. "She won't give up that job."

Martha dried the plate in her hands and then folded her arms around it, clutching it to her chest. "She worked hard to support you and your sister."

"That she did."

"She must be proud of you now."

"She says she is."

As she stacked the plate in the cupboard, Martha twisted around to stare at him. "She *says* she is. You don't believe her?"

A knot twisted in Cam's gut. "She didn't go to college, so she really wanted me to go. I had a football scholarship to pay for it and everything, but I just couldn't hack it. Couldn't get through those classes."

She turned away from the cupboard and leaned her back against the counter. "Ah, the good-looking jock couldn't find someone to do his homework for him?"

His gaze darted to her face and she flinched, blinking her eyes behind her glasses. Was that what she thought of him? Easy for her to make judgments with all this privilege and the brains to go with it.

"I wouldn't know." He slammed the dishwasher door. "I never tried to get someone to do my work for me. Just tried to do it myself—and failed miserably."

Curling her fingers around the edge of the counter behind her, she said, "I-I'm sorry. I didn't mean…"

"Sure you did." He ground out a laugh. "Girls like you, so superior."

She shoved off the counter and grabbed his hand

with both of hers. "It's not even about you, Cam. It's all about me and my shortcomings."

"*Your* shortcomings." He rolled his eyes, but her hands, warm and soft from washing the dishes, squeezed his, and his tight jaw started to relax.

"It's just that you reminded me of all the hot guys in high school and college who used me to do their homework and write their papers, and then completely ignored me in every social setting. Guys I'd studied with all semester would look right through me at the next frat party, and I kept telling myself I wouldn't help them anymore, but I always did. It was one small way to fit in, and I desperately wanted to fit in."

He licked his lips and searched her face for any sign of deception. Her incredible eyes shimmered with tears, and he saw a woman who trusted him enough to be honest and open.

"Those guys were idiots, but even if I'd had a girl like you helping me every night, I still would've flunked out of school."

"I don't know about that. I was a pretty mean tutor back in the day."

"I'm sure you were, but I wouldn't have been able to concentrate with you sitting across from me."

Her eyebrows shot up, and now it seemed to be her turn to study his face. "You're serious."

"Damn straight."

Red flags flew in her cheeks, and she wrinkled her nose. "I'm still sure I could've gotten you through."

"Naw, and it's no reflection on your talents." He twisted his hands out of her grasp and placed them on her shoulders. "I couldn't handle school because I'm dyslexic. I thought you'd noticed before. I can barely read."

Chapter Eight

Martha put a hand to her heart, which Cam's words had just pierced. "I'm the idiot."

He rubbed his thumbs against her collarbone. "You didn't know."

"Yes, but the assumptions I made about you." Her hand crept to her throat. "I feel like such a fool, and I'm so sorry for stereotyping you as the dumb jock. Like I said, I'd been humiliated by plenty of them. And honestly? It probably wasn't even their fault. They didn't twist my arm to help them. I gladly did it to bask in their...hotness."

Cam tipped back his head and laughed at the ceiling, breaking the tension between them although she wasn't sure she wanted it broken. That tension had been building for a while, and she'd assumed it was all one-sided...hers, but he'd called her a distraction. She'd never been someone's distraction before.

"Take it from the dumb jock. You intimidated those dudes. They're used to admiration not admonitions."

"When you say things like that, you don't sound

dumb at all. You need to stop calling yourself that."
She pressed both hands against his chest. "You have
to know that you wouldn't be a member of one of the
most elite special ops teams in the military if you
were all brawn and no brain."

"I'll make you a deal."

Her fingers curled against his shirt. If she could
keep standing this close to him forever, she'd be willing to make a deal with the devil himself. "What
kind of deal?"

"I'll stop referring to myself as a dumb jock if you
stop referring to yourself as a geek, especially with
that tone of voice you use when you do it."

"Do I?" She dropped her eyelashes. "Have a tone
of voice when I call myself a geek?"

"You do." He brushed his knuckles across her
cheek. "And I don't like it."

"Should we shake on it?" She made no move to
remove her hands from his chest, and he hadn't released her shoulder yet.

His gaze dropped to her mouth, and a pulse
throbbed in her lower lip. So much better to seal it
with a kiss.

Her phone went off, and she almost sobbed with
frustration when Cam jerked his head to the side.

"You'd better see who that is. Whoever used
Casey's phone to text you yesterday now has your
number, and I'm sure he's going to take advantage
of that."

She broke away from the already broken spell and

lunged for her phone, ready to scream at the person on the other end. She drew her brows over her nose when she recognized Gage's number from the office. "My boss is calling me on a Sunday?"

"Do you mind if I listen in? It might have something to do with the emails."

She tapped the phone to engage the speaker. "Hello? Gage?"

"Martha, I'm here with the section chief, Rand Proffit."

She swallowed the lump in her throat. "Hello, Mr. Proffit."

"How are you, Martha? Pretty rough weekend."

"Yes, it's been crazy. I had no idea my roommate was…dating Congressman Wentworth. If I had, I would've reported it."

She drove a fist into her belly. Would she have reported it? Was that any of the Agency's business? Did she owe them anything?

Proffit's voice reassured her over the phone, like some creepy, condescending uncle. "I'm sure you would have, Martha. I know we can count on you to always do the right thing, but this whole situation has put us in an interesting and unfortunate position. One of our employees, someone with a questionable past of her own caught up in a sex scandal involving a ranking member of the House Intelligence Committee. Doesn't look good."

"Sex scandal?" She ground her back teeth. "I'm not involved in any sex scandal."

Cam had been moving closer to her and now he hunched over the counter, a scowl marring his handsome features.

"Of course you're not, but all that was taking place in your town house...under your nose."

"Hardly under my nose. They were in another room with the door closed." Heat flared in her cheeks as she recalled eavesdropping on the sounds of their lovemaking through the walls and across the hall.

Proffit clicked his tongue, or was that her moronic boss?

"We're not blaming you in any way, Martha, nor are we holding you accountable." He cleared his throat and she held her breath. "However, we're putting you on a leave of absence for the time being—just until the whole situation dies down—and it will be paid leave. So, think of it as a vacation."

"I have work to do."

"Farah can take over." Gage couldn't hide the glee in his voice.

"Farah doesn't speak Russian."

Gage had a ready answer. "We'll get someone in the department to handle your work, Martha. Don't worry about that."

She gripped the phone so hard she thought the screen would crack. "When this...situation dies down, my job had better be waiting for me when I come back, or you'll answer to my attorney."

"Are you going to use your father's attorney?" Gage snorted.

"Damn straight." She ended the call and tossed the phone across the counter.

Cam whistled. "That's the way to handle 'em. They're so sure of you, aren't they? I'd like to see the looks on their faces if they ever discovered you took charge of those emails."

Her anger backtracked to fear, prompting her to worry her bottom lip with her teeth. "They can't ever find out. I'd lose my job and probably wind up in a cell next to my father's."

"They're not gonna find out from me." Cam walked around to her side of the counter and patted the stool between them. "Sit down. You look ready to collapse."

She perched on the stool and folded her hands in front of her. "Gage would like nothing better than to get rid of me."

"I noticed. What's that guy's problem?"

"He's afraid I'm going to take the job he wants." She twisted her fingers. "He probably doesn't have to worry about that anymore."

"If we can get enough proof that those emails were lies, you'll be right in line for that promotion." He patted her back and then strode toward her laptop abandoned on the coffee table. "Are you ready to take a look at your cleaned-up computer?"

"At least my cleaned-up computer won't be looking at me anymore, although now that the patriot and I are like this—" she crossed her fingers "—he'll probably feel free to email me. I'm sure he got my home email address, thanks to Casey the unlikely spy."

"Maybe he'll be kind enough to tell you what the hell he wants." Cam slipped her laptop out of its case, brushed a few crumbs from the place mat and set it down in front of her.

She wiggled her fingers before powering up the computer and entering her password. "If he admits to killing Casey or Wentworth, I'm turning him in. I don't care what the ramifications are for me."

"Even if he admits it, we don't know who he is. Is he one person? A group? Is he the same person who pushed you at the Metro station?"

Her shoulders stiff, she launched her email and watched the messages populate on the screen. She eked out a breath with each email she scanned and discarded. "Nothing from him."

"Maybe he's done with you. Showed you the reach of his power, got rid of a few loose ends and figures you've been adequately warned to let the emails implicating Major Denver drop."

She shoved the laptop away from her. "We're still going to see Tony tonight if he's working, aren't we?"

"Of course."

"Then he figured wrong."

As LUCK WOULD have it, Tony Battaglia still worked at the Insider in Georgetown, and he had a shift that night.

Cam insisted on babysitting her at her mom's

house the rest of the day, and she didn't put up much of a fight. She made sandwiches for lunch, her one culinary accomplishment, and they both worked on their laptops until she took him out back for a walk along the shore of the bay.

She'd had an online conversational Russian class that afternoon, but she couldn't tell what Cam's work involved, and she didn't want to ask. He'd requested a quiet place to listen on some headphones and speak into a mic, so she invited him into her mother's library, which was really her father's library since all the books had belonged to him.

She'd shown Cam where to plug in and then had gotten out of there as fast as she could. The sight and the musty smell of her dad's books served as a reminder of all she'd lost when he decided to play fast and loose with the rules.

Like she was doing now.

When they'd come in from their walk, the cold had reddened Cam's cheeks and the breeze had ruffled his light brown hair, giving him the appearance of a model for a men's magazine on the great outdoors. She had a hard time reconciling his Adonis good looks with the insecurities he'd shared about his dyslexia.

Her heart ached for that part of him, while her body ached for the other part. She couldn't have ordered a more perfect hero than if he'd come special delivery from central casting.

As he removed his coat, he said, "No more of this

eating in. We'll go to out to dinner on our way to the Insider—and I'm paying. You've had to put up with me hanging around all day."

The only negative to having him hang around all day was that he was in a different room from her.

She shrugged out of her coat and dropped it on the sofa. "That works for me. I'm going to shower and change. Do we need to stop by your hotel on the way so that you can do the same?"

He brushed his hands over his faded jeans and stomped his work-style boots. "Yeah, I definitely need to clean up."

"Help yourself to anything in the kitchen." She waved her hand in the general direction. "And you can carry on with...whatever you were working on before."

"Reading."

"What?"

"I was working with a reading program. I try to keep at it whenever I'm on leave. If I'd had this program when I was younger, it would've helped a lot."

"That's admirable."

He ducked his head and his cheeks got redder. "I wasn't fishing for praise."

"I know that." She spun around not wanting to embarrass him anymore. "Well, get to work then, and I'll get ready for dinner."

Several minutes later as Martha stepped into the shower, a smile played about her lips. She hadn't felt this connected to a man ever.

She stepped beneath the warm spray and by the time she emerged, she'd lost the smile. What she and Cam had didn't come close to real life. She felt close to him because he'd become her protector, her lifeline in a crazy sequence of events that had just spun out of control. He felt close to her because he liked playing the protector.

If he hadn't come on the scene and all this stuff had gone down, she'd probably be sitting in a police station right now confessing everything. He'd naturally assumed she wouldn't go to the police, and she'd gone along with him on this roller-coaster ride—just like she'd gone along with her father even though she'd discovered his crimes long before the FBI had come knocking on their door.

She ended her shower far from the dreamy state she'd been in at the time she cranked on the water. She yanked her towel from the rack and gave her skin a harsh rubbing. She'd fallen into her old patterns. Some hot guy with a boyish grin crooked his finger at her, and she'd been ready to do his bidding.

But it wasn't exactly his bidding. Cam had saved her, had been there for her, protected her. That all made this a different experience completely.

Buoyed by her renewed justification of events, Martha leaned close to the mirror and popped in her contact lenses, blinking rapidly after she inserted each lens. Nothing out of the ordinary about wearing contacts. She usually chucked the glasses when she went on dates.

She finished getting ready, and then slipped out of the bathroom into the connecting bedroom. She'd already laid out a pair of black skinny jeans and some tall black boots. Pulling a teal sweater over her head, she tugged it into place and resisted the urge to pull at the shoulders to bring up the V-neck. She patted the neckline, which was a long way from plunging.

She put on the finishing touches with a blow-out of her hair and a heavier than usual application of makeup. She wanted to present a different appearance from the one plastered all over the news—at least that was her story and she was sticking to it.

She rested her hand on the bannister as she took one step at a time in her high-heeled boots. By the time she reached the bottom, Cam was there to meet her, his eyes as wide as his grin.

"You look…great." He held out his hand to help her off the last step.

"Thanks." She fluffed the ends of her wavy hair. "I figured I should disguise myself a little just to keep a low profile."

"Uh-huh." He lifted one eyebrow. "Good idea, but I'd hardly call that look low profile. You're gonna have all eyes on you in that getup."

"Too much?" She placed a hand flat against her tummy.

"For a night out in Georgetown? Nope. For me? Not at all."

She moistened her lip-sticked mouth. She hadn't fooled Cam at all with this supposed disguise. She'd dressed for him and had gotten exactly the reaction she'd craved—and she didn't feel silly or nervous or uncertain at all.

She felt beautiful because he made her feel that way.

"Are you ready?" She held up a small black bag. "I'm just going to switch purses."

"I'm ready. My laptop is all packed up." He pointed to the front door. "I took the liberty of making sure everything was locked up down here. How come that security system wasn't engaged when we got here?"

"Mom's housekeeper leaves it off because she keeps forgetting the code."

"Do you know it?"

"Yes."

"Engage it tonight and leave it activated for as long as you're staying here. You can always call the housekeeper and give her the code."

She looked up from shuffling things from one purse to another. "Is that why you stayed all day? You're afraid I'm vulnerable here?"

"The guy, or guys, killed a congressman and his mistress. I'm not taking that lightly even though we still don't know what he wants from you."

"I agree. Give me two minutes."

While Cam waited by the door, Martha set the alarm system for the house. When she joined him, she said, "All done."

"Better safe than, well…you know."

When they got to his hotel, she insisted on waiting at the bar while he went up and changed to spare them both the awkwardness of having her watch over him while he showered and changed.

"I need a glass of wine anyway."

"Okay, I won't be long." He wagged a finger at her. "Don't talk to strangers."

His warning gave her a little chill, but she laughed it off. "I'll be here when you come back down."

She slid onto a stool at the bar and barely glanced at the scattered couples at the tables. She ordered a glass of red wine from the bartender and took a deep sip, closing her eyes as the warmth spread to her muscles.

"Long day?"

Her eyelids flew open, and she turned her head in the direction of the male voice beside her. "You could say that."

"Same for me." He raised his glass of whiskey. "Travel day. Those are the worst."

"Let's see." She held up her hand and ticked off her fingers. "Lobbyist, congressman back from a home district visit, attorney. Shall I keep guessing?"

"You do know this town." He swirled the amber liquid in his glass. "Lobbyist."

She laughed and fluttered her eyelashes, which seemed to act as some kind of invitation to the stranger. They spent the next half hour exchanging witty repartee. She didn't even know where half the stuff out of her mouth was coming from.

"You know, Martha, you've already made my travel day one hundred percent better. Can I buy you dinner?"

"Oh, I'm sorry." And just like that she'd led someone on even though she hadn't meant to. "I'm meeting a…friend for dinner. In fact, here he is. Nice talking to you, Alan. Have a good week."

Alan cranked his head over his shoulder in time to see Cam making his way through the bar and muttered, "Lucky bastard. Have a nice dinner, Martha."

She met Cam halfway through the bar and nodded. "You clean up nicely."

Cam jutted his chin and glared over her head. "Was that guy trying to pick you up?"

"Just passing time." She took his hand. "Until the main event."

"I don't blame him." Cam interlaced his fingers with hers and did a U-turn to exit the bar. "I figured you wouldn't be flying under the radar looking like a million bucks."

Martha lengthened her stride to keep up with him, noticing a few other admiring glances thrown her way. She flipped back her hair and straightened her spine. Cam could go on about her looks all night, but she understood the difference.

Cam's attentions had given her confidence, and even the plainest girl in the room could command the spotlight exuding confidence.

Even with her newfound assurance, Martha rejected a trendy Georgetown restaurant for a quieter place serving Italian food in a homey atmosphere.

Once they each had a glass of red wine and a basket of bread between them, Cam hunched forward, crossing his arms on the table. "What's our strategy with Tony? Have you ever met him?"

"He's probably the one guy Casey *didn't* bring home, not that I saw much of the others. I swear, running into Congressman Wentworth that night was a rare occurrence." She tapped a fingernail against her glass. "But if Tony's some kind of confidante of Casey's, I'm sure he knows about me or at least knows my name. Why would she blab secrets to a bartender?"

"Are you kidding? Most bartenders probably hear more of people's problems than therapists do." He tore off a piece of garlic bread and pointed it at her. "You're just going to march in and introduce yourself?"

"I'll start slowly and then hit him with the note I found. Who knows? Maybe he's expecting it because Casey told him she'd be calling him out as some kind of witness if anything happened to her."

"I hope he doesn't plead the Fifth. If it's not crowded in the bar, maybe we'll have a chance to talk to him while he's on the job, or at least make arrangements to talk to him later."

When the waitress arrived with their food, Cam pointed to Martha's glass. "Do you want another?"

"No. I want to have my wits about me tonight, and I already had half a glass at the hotel. That first night after the incident on the Metro platform? Those two glasses of wine were my limit. You wouldn't want to see me after a third."

"Wanna bet? Don't get me wrong. I admire your... restraint, but I can't help wondering what an out-of-control Martha would look like."

"I don't—" she cut off a corner of her spinach lasagna "—let myself go."

"You should try it sometime. It's good for the soul." He broke off another piece of garlic bread. "You should also try some of this bread before I eat it all."

She watched his fingers as he brushed them together, dislodging crumbs into the napkin on his lap and wondered what it would be like to let go with Cam. She was no virgin, but all of her sexual encounters had been very measured and controlled. Probably her fault.

For the rest of the meal they didn't talk any more about losing control or Tony or Casey or the congressman. It was as if this dinner represented a deep breath, a chance to step away from the crazy before plunging back into it headfirst.

They finished their food and, true to his word, Cam picked up the check. As he placed some bills on the tray, he said, "Are you okay to drive?"

"I think so, although I usually don't drive at all after I've imbibed."

"When it comes to drinking and driving, you can never be too careful." He held out his hand. "I'll take the wheel."

"You've had a glass of wine, too."

"I'm twice your size and drank half as much."

"You have a point." She fished her keys from her purse and dropped them into his cupped palm. "You know where you're going?"

"It's not far from here, right? You can be my navigator."

When they reached the bar, Cam pulled up to the valet parking attendant and left him the keys. As they walked in, Cam ducked to whisper in her ear, "Do you have any idea what Tony looks like?"

She nodded to the bar where a man and a woman were mixing and pouring drinks. "Easy. He's the man."

"At least it's not crowded." He tipped his head toward one of the TVs over the bar displaying photos of Wentworth and Casey. "I wonder how Tony feels about that playing 24-7 in here."

"I guess we're going to find out soon enough."

They claimed two empty seats at the bar, the nearest customer three stools down.

The female bartender got to them first. "What would you like?"

"I'll have one of these." Cam held up a cardboard coaster printed with the name of a bottled beer.

"Club soda with lime for me, please."

Martha tilted her head back and followed the muted images parading across the TV screen. Even without the sound she could piece together the story—or maybe that was just because it was *her* story.

When the bartender set their drinks in front of them, Cam handed her a folded ten and asked, "Is that Tony Battaglia?"

The bartender's gaze flicked from Cam to Martha, two small lines forming between her eyebrows. "Yes. Do you have business with him?"

"Business?" Cam's hand jerked and a dab of foam leaped over the edge of his mug and rolled down the side. "We have mutual friends."

The woman's scowl deepened.

Martha added, "Just when he has a minute."

"I'll let him know." She snatched up Cam's bill and spun away.

Cam lifted one shoulder. "Weird."

"Okay, so that wasn't just me?"

"Definitely an odd reaction. Maybe the media made the connection between Casey and Tony and have already swooped in for a comment or reaction."

"That's probably it." Martha swirled the straw in her glass, clinking the ice against the sides.

From the corner of her eye, she saw the bartender

say something to Tony. He glanced their way, but his face didn't change expression. They waited another ten minutes and three customers before Tony meandered over to them.

He whipped a towel from his waistband and wiped the clean counter next to them. "We have a mutual friend?"

"Casey Jessup. She was my roommate."

Tony choked and bunched up the towel in his fist. Whatever he'd been expecting from them—that was not it.

"You're Martha?"

Martha's heart fluttered in her chest. "Yes. Casey mentioned me?"

"Uh-huh." He swept his head from side to side, and then he focused on Cam. "Who's he? The po-po?"

"I'm not the police. I'm Martha's friend." Cam narrowed his eyes. "Why are you worried about the police?"

"They don't know about me, do they?"

Martha shrugged. "Not that I know of. I didn't tell them anything about you. Why do you care? Shouldn't one of Casey's friends want to talk to the police about her suicide?"

"Friend? Yeah, I guess we were friends. I told her." He stopped and shook his head.

"Told her what? If you two weren't friends, how did you know her?"

"You really don't know, do you?"

"If I knew, I wouldn't be asking you."

"Casey was a paid girlfriend. You know, an escort."

Chapter Nine

She gaped at him like an idiot and then snapped her jaw closed.

Folding his hands around his glass, Cam leaned in. "She wasn't an intern for some congresswoman?"

"Oh, yeah. She was all that, but she made the big money working as an escort—a professional girl-friend." Tony cranked his head to the side to take in two men in suits talking at the end of the bar. "And I was her facilitator."

"Her pimp, you mean." Cam's voice had rough-ened around the edges.

"That's a harsh word for what I did. This is an upscale place, and when I ran into someone who was looking for that special girl, I referred that person to Casey. Sure, I got a cut of the action, but Casey was her own boss. She'd tried working for an agency, didn't like it and struck out on her own. She just felt safe having me on her side, and man—"

Dear Reader,

Since you are a lover of our books, your opinions are important to us... and so is your time.

That's why we made sure your **"FAST FIVE" READER SURVEY** can be completed in just a few minutes. Your answers to the five questions will help us remain at the forefront of women's fiction.

And, as a thank-you for participating, we'd like to send you **4 FREE THANK-YOU GIFTS!**

Enjoy your gifts with our appreciation,

Pam Powers

Tony wiped the corner of his eye with his towel "—I loved that girl."

"Tony!" The other bartender called out to her co-worker and then held up one hand. "Never mind. You can take a break. It's slowing down."

"Do you want to join us at a table?" Cam jerked his thumb over his shoulder. "We have a few more questions for you, if you don't mind."

"I don't mind. Better you than the police. God, I hope they don't get suspicious about the suicide story and start digging into Casey's finances."

"Suicide *story*?" Cam lifted one eyebrow.

"C'mon. We all know it was murder. That's why you're here, isn't it?"

Martha's eyes met Cam's as Tony tossed his towel on the edge of the sink. He met them on the other side of the bar, and they crowded around a small cocktail table.

"Before we get started, I want you to know why we're here." Martha dragged the slip of paper with Casey's handwriting from her purse and flattened it in front of Tony. "Casey left this for me where we kept our extra key."

Tony smoothed his thumb over the words. "Inside the chair cover."

"She told you about that?"

"Casey told me everything." He picked up the note and pressed his lips against the paper. "That's why she left this for you."

Having left his beer on the bar, Cam took a sip of Martha's club soda. "Start from the beginning. Are you the one who set her up with Congressman Wentworth?"

"I am, but the setup was a setup." Tony's gaze darted around the room, and he rubbed his upper lip. "Some guy who already knew about Casey's line of work approached me. Wentworth had been in here a few times—they all make it to this bar eventually."

"This guy wanted you to make sure Casey and Wentworth hooked up?" Martha crossed one leg over the other and kicked her foot back and forth.

"Exactly."

"He targeted Casey, didn't he? This man wanted Casey and only Casey for Wentworth. He already knew about her, knew she was an escort…knew she lived with Martha."

Cam's intensity had Tony shrinking back. "Y-yeah. It was all about reaching out to Casey and getting her to spy on her roommate, but Wentworth was definitely part of the equation, too. It had to be Wentworth for some reason."

Martha rubbed the goose bumps forming on her forearms. "It was a plan to get to me."

"I'm sorry. It was." Tony scratched the scruff on his lean jaw. "But I don't know the details about that, and neither did Casey. He instructed her to steal your computer password, stuff like that."

"That's how he hacked into my laptop, how he

took over my camera." She smacked her hand on the table, and her ice tinkled in protest.

"Look, Casey never got the impression this guy wanted to hurt you...or her. She wouldn't have done it, otherwise."

"Did she have a choice?" Cam's jaw formed a hard line. "Did he threaten to expose her? Expose her lifestyle? Yours?"

"Maybe there was a little of that, but no way would Casey, or me, be down with violence."

Martha folded the four corners of her cocktail napkin. "What about Wentworth? What was the plan with him?"

"Information. He wanted information from Wentworth." Tony chewed on the edge of his thumb. "The night Wentworth died at your place? Casey had been ordered to bring him back there that night once he started feeling sick. Usually they went to the apartment he kept in town. Casey had access to all his stuff there."

Cam tapped her thigh. "The emails, intel about Denver."

Tony looked from Cam to Martha, a deep crease between his eyebrows.

"Once he started feeling sick?" Martha ran her tongue around her dry mouth. "Did Casey do something to make Wentworth sick?"

"She didn't. No! She wouldn't do that." Tony dug his fingers into his spiky black hair, making it stand on end even more. "But she thinks someone slipped him something because her contact knew Wentworth would become ill that night and she had those orders to bring him back to her place when he did."

"So he'd die in my town house."

"Casey never thought that would be the endgame. She thought it was just a little information, some spy game that wouldn't affect anyone."

"Spy games always affect someone…including the spy." A dangerous light sparked in Cam's eyes. "Now you're going to tell us about this guy. What does he look like? What does he call himself? How does he contact you? Has he been in touch since Casey's murder?"

Tony spread his hands out on the table, his thumbs touching. "He introduced himself as Ben, but I'm sure we can all agree that's bogus. He's average, average everything except his beard. He wears a bushy beard and glasses. Without that stuff, I probably wouldn't recognize him on the street."

Martha glanced at Cam. "Disguise."

"Yeah, probably." Tony rubbed his brow. "Always wore a hat, too. He comes in here when he wants to make contact."

Martha asked, "Does Ben show up at the bar when he wants to communicate with Casey or just you?"

"Both. He told her to get a temporary phone. They exchange messages that way."

Cam's eyebrows collided over his nose. "Did the cops mention anything to you about Casey having two phones, Martha?"

"No, and I had no idea she had two phones."

"If Ben was in that hotel room with Casey, I'm sure he took the burner phone with him when he left." Tony pinched the bridge of his nose, squeezing his eyes closed. "I can't believe she's gone."

"Why would Ben do it? Why kill Wentworth and Casey unless he got all he wanted from them and decided to tie up loose ends?" Cam drummed his fingers on the table.

"He had gotten what he wanted from them, and everything would've been status quo until he found out I kept those emails." Martha's bottom lip quivered. "I'm the one who caused all of this."

"Emails?" Tony's eyes flew open.

Cam drew his finger across his throat. "Need to know basis. Martha, none of this is your fault. If Casey hadn't been so greedy, she wouldn't have set you up and involved you in all this. If Wentworth had been able to keep it in his pants, he never would've been targeted."

Tony twirled the earring in his lobe. "And let's not leave out Ben himself. What information *did* he have Casey get from Wentworth, and how did it relate to you? Casey told me you were CIA."

"Like I said—need to know, and you don't," Cam growled. "What kind of man is a pimp anyway?"

"Hey, man. It wasn't like that. I protected Casey. I loved her."

"Dude, that's not love."

"A-are you going to tell the cops any of this? I'll deny everything."

"We're not ready to do that yet. We have no proof, but I'm not ruling it out when we do. Don't you want to see Casey's killer brought to justice?"

"I do, but it'll sacrifice her reputation."

"And yours." Cam rolled his eyes at Martha.

"If you're not a cop—" Tony waved at his co-worker behind the bar "—why do you care about Ben? Whatever damage he caused has been done."

"I wanna know who he is and who he works for. The damage he did had a huge impact on a friend of mine, someone I admire and look up to. I'm not gonna let that slide. I'm not gonna let him get away with it."

Martha tapped on the table. "I have an idea. Doesn't this bar have security cameras? Would it be possible for us to see Ben?"

"I suppose I can offer to close up on my own, and you can meet me back here at closing. I'd have to disable the cameras or erase the footage so nobody sees you coming back here."

"I can take care of the camera. What time?"

"We close up at two."

Cam tapped his phone. "Almost three hours."

"We can go back to my place for a few hours."

Tony glanced over his shoulder and held up one finger at the other bartender. "I'll let you in the back door. Now I gotta go back to work."

As Tony walked away, Cam slumped back in his chair. "What do you think?"

"I can't believe I was so naive I didn't figure out Casey's real profession." Martha scooped her hair back from her face. "Is everyone in this town scamming?"

"It seems like it."

"Maybe it *is* time to call in the police."

He snorted. "Right. If we do that, you'll have to admit you stole those emails, and then it won't be just the police, it'll be the FBI. Your family doesn't have a great track record with the Fibbies."

"If everyone didn't have something to hide, including me, maybe we could actually get to the bottom of this." She sighed and stirred the melting ice in her glass.

"Maybe it is over for you, Martha." He took her hand and traced over her knuckles with his fingertip. "Ben or the patriot or whatever else he calls himself knows you have the emails, but you already sent them up the chain of command. His work is done. He showed his power and reach by killing Wentworth and Casey, and figures you're not going to do any more investigating. You can leave it now."

"But you're not going to."

He grabbed his coat from the back of the chair. "Let's go to your place."

"I'm going to use this time to pack up Casey's things for her family. Maybe we'll find this phone… or something else."

With one last look at Tony behind the bar and a nod, they slipped outside. Cam took the wheel of her car again and drove back to her place.

As they pulled up to the front, Cam said, "Let's not forget. Ben could've been in possession of Casey's house key since last night."

Martha glanced up at the glow from the front window. She'd left a lamp on in the living room, so the light didn't surprise her or make her nervous—but Cam's words did.

She peeled her tongue from the roof of her dry mouth. "What if someone's in there?"

"I have my gun." He patted the pocket of his jacket. "Let me go in first."

He parked the car and then led the way up the steps to her town house. After she unlocked the door, he eased it open with his foot. He swung his weapon in front of him and stepped inside.

"Stay back, Martha."

She ducked behind his solid frame, but peeked around his body and surveyed the empty room. She let out a slow breath as Cam crept forward.

He waved his hand behind him, so she hovered in the entryway while he continued farther into the room. He poked his head around the corner to check out the kitchen. "Nobody in here."

He threw open the door to the half bathroom and then checked the lock on the back door. Pointing the barrel of his gun at the ceiling, he said, "I'll take a look upstairs."

"I'm coming with you." She turned and locked the front door although if Ben had Casey's key, that wouldn't do much good.

"Just stay behind me."

Martha followed Cam up the stairs and stayed back as he checked the second bathroom. When he pushed open her bedroom door, she held her breath and then released it when nothing but the silence of the room greeted them.

Cam turned, putting his finger to his lips, and yanked open the door of the master bathroom connected to the room. He shook his head. *"Nada."*

She crossed the hall to Casey's room, but Cam beat her there and pulled her back.

"One more."

He turned the handle and bumped the door with his shoulder. The door swung open and Cam crouched, clutching his weapon in front of him.

Martha gasped and pulled back, flattening herself against the opposite wall. Her fingers clawed against the smooth surface and she squeezed her eyes closed, waiting for…whatever.

Cam swore. "He was here. The bastard was here."

Martha peeled herself from the wall and stumbled forward. Hanging on to the doorjamb, she leaned into Casey's bedroom and a chill zigzagged up her spine.

Someone had torn apart Casey's room looking for something, and Martha hoped to God he'd found it because if he hadn't, she had a feeling he'd come after her next.

CAM SHOVED HIS gun into the waistband of his pants. Whoever was responsible for tossing Casey's room had come and gone. He turned in a slow circle, surveying the damage. "What the hell is he looking for?"

"I don't know." Martha gulped in a breath and hiccupped. "But I hope he found it."

"You do?" Came drew his brows together. "I don't."

"Easy for you to say. It's not your place he's searching."

Cam smacked his fist into his palm. "You should've had your locks changed as soon as the police told you Casey's keys were missing. It's too late now."

Chewing on her bottom lip, Martha picked up one of Casey's T-shirts with two fingers and dropped it on the bed. "That's an understatement."

"I mean time-wise it's too late. You'll never get a locksmith out here at midnight."

"Luckily, I'm not staying here tonight. I'll get someone out first thing tomorrow morning." She ran her hands over a bunched-up pillow. "I'm sure as heck not going to work."

"What could Casey have that this guy wants?"

"And why didn't he ask her for it before he killed her?"

"Maybe he did and that's why he killed her. She wouldn't give it up."

Tilting her head to one side, Martha put a fist on

her hip. "You met Casey. Tony told you what she did. Do you really think she's the kind of person who would die for her country? I'm pretty sure Casey would've given Ben whatever he wanted, especially if she thought it would save her life."

"You knew her better than I did." Cam rubbed his chin. "If Ben didn't ask her nicely for what he wanted or even threaten her if she didn't give it up, why? What is he looking for now? He has the emails."

"That's what I don't get." Martha collapsed on the foot of Casey's disheveled bed. "Ben sent me those emails, knowing I'd send them up the chain of command, and I did. Those messages launched the investigation into Major Denver, which then caused him to go AWOL. Mission accomplished."

"Not quite." Cam leveled a finger at Martha. "Nobody was expecting you to hold on to the emails yourself."

"It shouldn't matter to him. The emails reached their intended target and did the intended damage. So what if I have the emails on an external storage device? The only thing that does is open me up to charges within the Agency."

"It also proves you're suspicious about the emails. You said your superiors didn't take your concerns seriously or at least felt they'd done their due diligence in investigating them. For old Ben, case closed— until you messed things up. He tried warning you. He tried tying up his loose ends by killing both Wentworth and Casey."

"As far as he knows, those actions worked. I'm so terrified, I left my home. Why would he think I'd pursue it further?"

"Maybe he believes case is closed on you, too, but now he has another problem. Casey."

"And whatever evidence she left behind, perhaps linking Ben to the emails."

"He should be worried." Cam joined Martha on the bed. "Because if we find that evidence before he does, we might have some proof that the emails were all a scam."

"Maybe we don't need the evidence if we can ID the guy tonight on the bar's security video."

Cam pushed off the bed and spread his arms wide. "You wanted to start packing up Casey's things for her family. Now you have the incentive. I'll help you clean up this mess."

"Thanks. I'll get some garbage bags in case there isn't enough room in her suitcase for her clothes." Martha headed for the door and stopped. "Ben would've expected Casey to have the burner phone on her, wouldn't he?"

"Probably, if that's the way he contacted her."

"I mean, Tony told us she had a burner phone, but the cop didn't say anything to me about two phones. He mentioned her purse, her wallet and her cell phone. Wouldn't he have said two phones or maybe even asked me about two phones?"

Cam dragged a suitcase from the closet, which

had also been thoroughly ransacked. "So, Ben took it, or that's what he's looking for."

"Maybe he found it in here, and now he'll leave me alone."

"If he did, that's one less thread of proof for us to tie him to Casey and the planting of the emails."

"C-can you blame me for wanting to back out of this mess? I know. I started out so full of myself, and now I'm just a coward."

"I wouldn't blame you at all, and you're far from a coward." He flipped open the suitcase. "Let's see what we can find out tonight, and if the video doesn't show us anything, you can call it a night…and forget the whole thing."

She dipped her chin to her chest and pivoted out of the room.

Cam started shoveling the clothes strewn about the room into the open suitcase. At least he had the emails. Martha would turn them over to him, and he could get someone else to look at them. Maybe he could convince someone in intelligence to look at the emails—if there were a way to leave Martha's name out of it.

Then his leave would be over, and he'd get sent on his next Delta deployment, and Martha could get back to doing what she did best—translating and following CIA rules. And their paths would never cross again.

His heart did a strange twist, and he thumped his fist against his chest.

"Playing Tarzan?" Martha leaned against the doorjamb, a garbage bag clutched in each hand.

"Just trying to clear my lungs. Dust." He gestured to the suitcase, half-full with jumbled clothes. "Should I be folding up this stuff neatly?"

"I'll tell you what. You take a bag and fill it with the stuff from this desk." She thrust a plastic bag at him. "I'll pack her clothes."

They worked side by side, the silence broken by the occasional theory or rhetorical question.

Cam thumbed through Casey's papers before tossing them in the bag, but didn't find anything suspicious or out of the ordinary. He looked up when he'd cleared out the desk. "So, I guess professional girlfriends don't keep receipts or records. I've never even heard that term before. Where I come from, we have another name for it."

"I can't believe how naive I am." She dropped the lid on the suitcase and flattened one hand on the top while she zipped it. "I honestly just thought Casey had a lot of boyfriends and dates."

"How were you supposed to know? She hardly fits the profile of a hooker."

Martha raised one finger. "Professional girlfriend, and I guess she *is* the profile."

Cam slid his phone from his pocket and glanced at the time. "It's almost two. We should be heading back to the bar. I hope Tony has something to show us."

Martha followed Cam out of Casey's room and

stopped at the door, turning around to look at their handiwork. "Her family hasn't even contacted me to pick up Casey's things. Maybe that's why she did it, the girlfriend thing."

"Why?"

"She just wanted some love, even if it was pretend."

BY THE TIME they got back to the Insider, the traffic on the street had thinned out but not disappeared. Martha parked on a side street, and they slipped into the alley behind the bar.

They reached the door, and Cam pointed to a wedge jammed beneath the bottom of the door to prop it open.

Martha tipped her head back and tugged on Cam's sleeve. "Looks like he already disabled the camera."

Cam looked up and his brow creased. "He sprayed the lens. I guess that way it doesn't look like the camera has been tampered with, as long as it cleans off."

"We'll have to remind him to wipe it off."

Cam used his foot to push open the door, and Martha stepped inside the back hallway of the bar.

She whispered Tony's name.

"He's probably in the office." Cam nudged her back, and she veered toward a closed door past the restrooms.

"Tony?" She knocked, pressing her ear against the door.

Cam stepped around her and opened the door, pushing it wide.

The computer on the desk glowed, and Cam hunched over it. "Looks like he's already been checking the security camera footage."

Martha backed up a step, one arm wrapped around her midsection. "Where is he? He should've heard us come in by now."

Cam reached into his pocket and Martha's heart skipped a beat, knowing that's where he'd stashed his gun.

Cam waved her away from the door and he crept through it, squeezing past her.

She followed him down the hallway to the bar... and then wished she hadn't.

Tony was still here all right—slumped at a table, his head resting in a pool of blood.

Chapter Ten

The floorboards creaked behind him, and Cam whipped around from Tony's dead body, clutching his weapon.

Martha gaped back at him, her face white and her mouth wide.

"Get back. He's dead."

"What happened to him?"

Cam launched forward and ran down the hallway toward the back door, which they'd left propped open. He pulled it closed and locked it.

When he returned to the bar, Martha was leaning over Tony, both hands over her mouth. If she got sick all over the body, they'd have more explaining to do than he was prepared for.

"Martha, what are you doing?"

"He left us a message."

"Tony?" He joined her at the table and then jerked back. Someone had written on the table in Tony's blood: "Back off."

Martha stumbled back from the table, as if obeying the order written on it. "That's for us. He knew. He knew about this meeting, or suspected it and was watching Tony."

Cam backtracked to the mahogany bar and peered over it at the register, gaping open. "He staged this as a burglary. Cleaned out the cash. He took care of the security cameras, too."

"And probably deleted the rest of the footage showing his meetings with Tony."

"We're done here." Cam leaned over the bar and grabbed a clean bar towel. "Did you touch anything at the table?"

"God, no." She shoved her hands in her pockets.

"Then we need to clean off our prints in the office—on the door and the computer keyboard—and at the back door. At least our images won't be on security footage, either."

As he made for the office, Martha grabbed his back pocket. "You mean we're going to just leave him here without calling the police?"

He glanced over his shoulder at her. "And how would that story go? We came here after hours to meet with Tony and get a look at security footage of his meeting with a man who knows you stole classified emails from your employer—the CIA?"

She sagged against the wall outside the office. "That's the problem with lying, isn't it? It never stops. You have to tell more and more lies to cover up the previous lies."

"I'd lie to hell and back to protect you, Martha.

You don't need to get in trouble for something you did that felt right at the time."

"I guess that's what my father would've said. It felt right at the time. Your father, too."

He ran the towel across the computer's keyboard. "What we're doing doesn't compare to what our fathers did. Not even close. You sensed something was off about those emails—and you were right—but nobody believed you. You just took matters into your own hands."

"And made a mess of things."

Cam wiped down the front of the door and then, with the towel in his hand, closed it and finished off with the doorknob. "By keeping those emails, you forced Ben out into the open. He's running scared. If you hadn't stored those messages on a flash drive, Ben would've been home free."

"He might not have killed Wentworth, Casey and Tony though."

"Really?" Cam got to work on the back door, deleting their after-hours visit. "I think he would have. He didn't want to leave any witnesses."

"So we just leave Tony like this?"

"Nothing we can do for him now. He was playing with fire, and he knew it."

She tipped her head down the hallway. "What about the message on the table? Should we wipe that off?"

"Let the cops puzzle it out. If we wipe it up, the police are going to be able to tell something was there. Why would a killer wipe up his victim's blood?"

Cam shoved the block of wood beneath the door with his foot to prop it open again, leaving everything as they'd found it when they arrived. "Now we just have to hope nobody saw us go in here."

"I was watching." Martha pulled her keys from her purse. "Nobody saw us."

They slipped into the alley, and Cam did a quick survey of the surrounding businesses. "I'm pretty sure Tony's killer took care of the other cameras in this alley that would have a shot at the Insider's back door."

"He's protecting us at the same time he's protecting himself." Martha sidled along the back wall of the building for good measure.

When they got to the street with the car, they ducked inside, just a couple of late-night bar-hoppers along with other stragglers on the sidewalk "This is going to be all over the news tomorrow. Do you think the police will make the connection between Casey and Tony?"

"They're going to look at him more closely because of that message, but I don't know why they'd connect him to Casey. As far as the cops are concerned, Casey's death is a suicide and they don't seem to be going through her contacts." Martha put the car in gear and eased away from the curb.

"They might be going through the contacts of her burner phone—if they had it."

She pulled around the corner, checking the rearview mirror. "And you're thinking if Ben had that phone, he wouldn't be running around murdering people and sending me warnings?"

"Oh, he still would've murdered Tony because he had access to that footage showing Ben meeting with him and Casey in the Insider."

"He obviously didn't think that footage was important enough to kill for—until we showed up. He must be following us. He knew we'd paid a visit to Tony."

"He could've been watching Tony. Where are you going?"

"To drop you off at your hotel."

"If you think I'm letting you go back to your mother's place alone tonight, you're crazy. I'm camping out on that ritzy sofa in the living room."

Cam could just make out the pink tint to Martha's cheek. She wanted him there. Maybe she even wanted *him*.

"Okay. Th-that actually makes me feel better, safer. If he thinks I have something he wants, who knows what lengths he's willing to go to get it?"

"And if it's that phone, it could blow his cover if Casey has texts with him on there."

"If his phone is a temp, too, how is Casey's phone going to incriminate him?"

"There could be ways to track those phones. Just the fact that Casey might have texts giving her instructions on what to do about Wentworth would be huge, especially if those instructions mention Denver and our assignments."

Her hand slid from the steering wheel and dropped to his thigh. "That might not be enough to clear his name. There's more evidence against him than what was uncovered as a result of those damned messages."

"I know that, but it's a start. If bogus, planted emails initiated the entire investigation, it'll cast suspicions over the rest of the so-called evidence."

"You'll never give it up, will you? Major Denver means that much to you?"

"Everything." Cam closed his eyes as a sharp pain pierced his gut.

The pressure of Martha's hand on his leg soothed his hurt and frustration.

"I understand." Her whispered words floated toward him. "When my father first came under investigation, I believed with all my heart that he was innocent. I was willing to do anything to prove it. I think that's why he finally admitted his guilt."

"Why?"

"He couldn't stand to see my vehemence in his defense when he knew it was all a lie."

Her voice broke, and he covered her hand with his—the soothed become the soother.

"He loved you though, despite his shortcomings." He traced the tips of her fingers, outlining her hand. "And you love him, despite your disappointment in him."

She sniffled. "I tried to hate him, but I didn't have it in me."

"He made a big, big mistake and he's paying for it. Don't charge him an even bigger price by withdrawing your love from him."

Her head jerked toward him and then back to the road. "You wouldn't be so forgiving of your father, would you?"

"Two different situations." He rubbed a circle in the condensation on the window with his fist. "Your father did what he did out of greed. Sure, he wasn't thinking of the consequences to his family, but he never stopped loving or caring for that family. My father didn't give a damn about my mother or me and my sister."

"I guess." She slid her hand from beneath his and wrapped her fingers around the steering wheel. "Totally different situation between my father and Major Denver, too. You're convinced he's innocent."

"Absolutely." He smacked a hand against his thigh. "He's being set up, and we're going to figure out by who and why."

"We?"

"The rest of our Delta Force team. Most of us don't believe the charges against him, and we've made a pact to clear his name."

"Then I'm glad to be part of that. If my father isn't deserving of my efforts, I believe you when you say Major Denver is."

They drove the rest of the way back to Martha's

mother's house in silence, his thoughts on his good-for-nothing father and hers probably on her own father—two men who couldn't be more dissimilar, from two different sides of the tracks, but who'd both made bad choices that ultimately hurt their families.

If he ever got the opportunity to be a father, he'd do things differently, but he'd need a partner who could tame him. He slid a sidelong glance at Martha's profile, her pert nose and wide mouth, giving her a look of innocence. Maybe her sweet expression gave people the impression they could take advantage of her.

She pulled into her mother's driveway and cut the engine. "We should've stopped by your hotel so you could pick up some of your things. My mom has plenty of extra toothbrushes and toiletries, but I'm pretty sure you don't want to wear any of my dad's clothes now that orange is his new black."

"Probably not, but I'll take the toothbrush."

While she disarmed the alarm system and unlocked the door, Cam faced outward, his muscles tense. He'd made sure they weren't followed from the bar, but he'd bet Ben knew about Martha's mom's house out here on the bay.

Martha pushed open the door, and Cam followed her inside, close on her heels. She locked up from the inside and entered the alarm's code.

She tossed her purse and coat onto the nearest chair and covered her face with both hands.

"You okay?" Cam stroked her back, which arched slightly like a satisfied cat's.

"It's been a long, long day." Her hands moved from her face through the coffee-colored strands of her hair. "I can't believe we were so close to getting a look at Casey's contact and to have it all end in Tony's gruesome murder. I'd never seen a dead body before in my life, and I just chalked up three. How is that possible?"

"I know." He touched her arm. In fact, he couldn't seem to stop touching her. "I'm sorry you had to see any of it, but I'm glad you're still safe."

She turned wide eyes on him. "For how much longer? He's looking for something of Casey's, and he wants to find it before I do. If he doesn't, he may just be satisfied with making sure I never find it either, and the only way to do that is by making sure I meet the same fate as Wentworth, Casey and Tony."

"Do you think I'm gonna let that happen?" He gripped her shoulders.

"You do have a life, a job, outside of saving Major Denver." She dropped her gaze. "Saving me."

"Not yet. We have time. We're going to find what this guy's looking for, and we're going to implicate him. I'll be here for you, Martha."

Tipping her head to the side, she rubbed her cheek against the back of his hand. "Are you saving me because you can't save him, Cam? Or is saving me mixed up in your mind with saving him?"

"What does that mean?" He stepped back. "Do you think you're some sort of substitute for Denver?"

She raised her shoulders, rolling them at the same time, dislodging his hands. "If you could prove his innocence tomorrow in some other place, with someone else's help, wouldn't you?"

His brows shot up. "And leave you? Leave you in this situation without protection?"

Her chin began to dip, and he pinched it and tilted her head back.

"I want to help Denver. That's why I came out here in the first place, but you're my first priority now, Martha."

A tear danced on the ends of her long lashes. "I don't think I've ever been someone's first priority before."

His hand slid along her jaw, and he captured her earlobe between his fingers. "I may not be the brightest guy in the world, but I know a precious gem when I see it."

She blinked, dislodging the tear, which splashed on the back of his hand. "Some of the brightest guys in the world don't have kind hearts like yours."

The side of his mouth twitched into a half smile. "I've never heard that one before."

Crossing one hand over the other, she pressed them against his chest. "That's because you've never bothered to let anyone in before. Too busy being the big, macho lug."

His heart thundered under the pressure of her hands, and he expanded his chest. "You found me out."

She looked around, as if aware of her surroundings for the first time. "Why are we still standing here in the entryway? It's almost dawn."

"Good thing neither of us has a job to go to." A slow pulse beat in his throat as he looked down into Martha's face. He just needed some sign from her. Anything they did had to originate from her desire. He had to avoid even a hint of coercion or persuasion.

Her gaze meandered to his mouth, as her own lips parted and her fingertips curled into the material of his shirt.

He brushed a kiss across her forehead, and she sighed, dropping her shoulders. His next kiss landed on her cheekbone.

This time she shifted from one foot to the other, moving closer so that the tips of her breasts made contact with his chest.

He swallowed. "Do you want to sit down?"

She rested her forehead on his collarbone. "I want to go to bed—with you."

Her simple request lit a fire in his belly, and he pulled her against his body, wrapping his arms around her waist and resting his cheek against the top of her head.

"I want that, too." As he spoke, the stubble on his chin caught the wavy strands of her hair. This slow burn between them made him harder than if she'd ripped his clothes off.

"Shouldn't we make a move upstairs?" She pulled away from him, but they were still connected through her wisps of hair that clung to his chin.

That's how he felt with Martha—connected—as if she always had some hold on a part of him.

MARTHA'S STOMACH DROPPED. Cam didn't really want her. He was being polite...too damned polite. She turned away from him quickly and stumbled on the first step of the staircase, grabbing the bannister.

He caught her around the waist, more to steady her than make a move on her. "H-have you changed your mind?"

"No, but I think you have." She broke away from him and charged up the stairs.

His footsteps pounded behind her. She felt the air at her back as he made a swipe at her blouse, and she took the next set of steps two at a time.

"Martha, wait." This time he grabbed her swinging arm and pulled her down one step. "What did I do wrong?"

Her whiskey eyes flashed at him. "I just told you I wanted to go to bed with you. Maybe it was clumsy or whatever. Maybe I should've batted my lashes and swiveled my nonexistent hips, but I thought it was pretty direct."

A slow flush crawled up his neck. "And I thought my answer was direct. It's what I want, too."

"But then you—" she wrinkled her nose "—you hugged me, put your cheek on my hair. Comforted me."

"So." He spread his hands and hunched his shoulders. "What does that mean? We just came from a murder scene. I figured you needed some comfort."

She bit her bottom lip. What did it mean? It had felt…brotherly. She was done being everyone's favorite little sister.

"It's just not the reaction I expected after telling you I wanted to sleep with you."

"What did you expect?" Cam leaned against the bannister as if waiting for a long, drawn-out explanation.

"I expected you to j-jump my bones. Rip my clothes off." A hurt little bark escaped from her throat. "I guess I just don't inspire that kind of passion."

A slow smile crept across his mouth, and before she had time to ask him what it meant, he had her against the wall, pressing the full length of his body against hers.

He captured her wrists in one hand, dragged her arms above her head and pinned them to the wall. He growled, his lips one hot breath away from hers. "You talk too much."

The kiss he planted on her mouth heated her blood. Her knees wobbled. Her skin tingled. Her lashes fluttered closed and as his tongue invaded her mouth, she wrapped one leg around his in an attempt to stay upright.

When he finished draining her with that one kiss, he unbuttoned her pants. To allow him to pull them down easily, she arched her back. Instead, with her pants still around her hips, Cam plunged his hand inside her panties, and she gasped at the sweet invasion.

He toyed with the swollen folds of her flesh, and she closed around his fingers as she rocked against him.

She couldn't just let him do all the work, but his other hand still held her wrists captive. She rested her head on his shoulder and pressed her lips against his neck.

As she got closer to her release, she bared her teeth against his skin and nipped at it.

And then it happened. Her orgasm clawed through her body, and her head fell back against the wall, banging it.

Cam tucked his hand beneath her bottom, his fingers still toying with her, as she rocked against him.

He released her wrists, and she grabbed the front of his shirt. With shaking fingers she unbuttoned it, fanned it out and slipped it from his arms.

His broad chest looked chiseled from granite. With a fever burning in her veins, she trailed her fingers from his throat to the waistband of his jeans.

As she worked on the fly, Cam braced his hands

against the wall on either side of her and kept dipping his head to tease her with kisses.

"I thought you were supposed to be ripping my clothes off. You're kinda slow."

She yanked his fly open and skimmed her palm over the bulge in his briefs. "Oh, I want you."

He toed off his shoes and kicked them down the stairs. Then he shed his jeans and his underwear at the same time and kicked them off the side of the staircase.

He tugged at her clothing, not quite ripping it off, and dropped each piece over the bannister to the floor below to join his clothes.

For a brief moment she thought he'd taken her hand to lead her up the rest of the staircase to her bedroom. Instead, he urged her down to the step directly beneath her.

She sat with her legs extended down the stairs, as he crouched beside her. Looked like she'd have to wait to have him because he seemed intent on having her again.

He spread her legs, and the toes of her left foot curled around the wooden balusters that drilled into each step. He positioned himself between her thighs a few steps below her.

When his tongue touched her aching flesh, her bottom bounced from the step.

"You're not going anywhere." He flattened his palms against her inner thighs and dipped his head to renew his tender assault.

She didn't even last as long as the previous time, and the heat surged through her body and into her cheeks as her orgasm raced through every cell of her body.

He came up for air and rested his chin on her mound as she still writhed beneath him. "That didn't take long. Either you haven't had sex in a while, or I'm the greatest lover known to womankind."

"It's been years."

Cam's eyes popped open, and Martha giggled as she ran one foot up the back of his leg and planted it against his muscled buttocks. "I'm just kidding."

"You're cruel." He reached up and cupped one of her breasts. "And who knew Martha Drake giggled?"

"Only when she's with the greatest lover known to womankind."

He rose above her, as if doing a push-up over her body, and skimmed the tip of his erection along her belly. "I haven't even gotten started yet."

He grabbed the bannister and pulled himself up, hooking one arm around her waist. He pressed his naked body against hers and kissed her hard and long.

"Where the hell is your bedroom in this dump?"

She traced his perfect form with her hands on either side of his body and trailed her fingertips across his smooth, tight skin. "I thought you'd never ask."

"I could take you right here on the staircase if you want." He tapped the hard wood of the bannister. "Lean you right over and claim you from behind."

"But my bed is so soft and warm."

"Just like you." He swept her up in his arms, cradling her five-foot-ten-inch frame against his chest like she was a teddy bear.

Her head fell into the hollow of his shoulder, fitting perfectly, and her mouth watered as she anticipated the other perfect fit between their bodies.

She directed him to her bedroom, and he kicked open the half-closed door, which gave her a thrill. As he dropped her on the bed, she reached for him with greedy hands.

Grabbing those hands, he kissed her fingertips. "You're so beautiful. I watched your face during your first orgasm, and it was like witnessing the birth of a butterfly."

A wash of red immediately claimed Cam's cheeks. "Was that the stupidest comparison ever?"

A tear leaked out of the corner of her eye. "That was the sweetest thing anyone has ever said to me. The best bit of poetry I've ever heard."

"You're just saying that." He stretched out beside her and caressed every inch of her body as he rained kisses all over her face.

She wanted to pleasure him, too, but he wouldn't allow it.

He whispered in her ear, "This is all about you tonight. I want you to feel pampered, desired…"

Loved. She wanted to feel loved, but what right did she have to expect that from Cam? She'd practically dragged him into bed. What was he going to do, turn her down? Cam Sutton was a hot-blooded, all-American male. Men like Cam didn't turn down invitations to sex—ever.

As he began moving against her, spreading her open, entering her, all her insecurities slipped away in breathless wanting. He filled her up, seemed to find every deficit in her soul and had an answer for it.

This time, she got to watch him as he experienced his release, and the sheer pleasure that spasmed across his face gave her a sense of power and tenderness at the same time. For several moments, she held his joy cupped within her.

As he shifted off her body, he nuzzled her neck. "I don't know if that just made the situation between us better or worse."

She froze, her fingers ceasing their combing his hair back from his forehead. "What does that mean? How can what we just experienced make anything worse? Unless I just misread everything that happened."

"You didn't misread a damned thing, Martha." He rolled to his side and propped up his head with his hand, his elbow digging into the pillow. "That was incredible and we both know it, but I still have to protect you. I don't know how I can do that job with a clear head now."

"It'll be better." She traced his bottom lip with her thumb. "Now that we've gotten the sex part out of the way, we'll be able to focus better on the issues in front of us."

His eyebrows shot up. "The sex part?"

"You know, all that tension between us, or at least on my side?" She tried to keep the insecure questioning out of her voice but failed miserably.

"I know exactly what you mean." He kissed the pad of her thumb.

She cupped his jaw briefly with her hand. "I'm going to pick up our clothes downstairs."

He grabbed her hand as she rolled from the bed. "I can do that if it's driving you crazy knowing they're in heaps on the floor."

"That's okay. I'm going to get some water, too."

Yawning, he settled back against the pillow. "Hurry back."

From the edge of the bed, she surveyed his heavy lids and slow, steady breathing. She rolled her eyes. Even if she hurried, he'd probably be sleeping by the time she came back.

She tiptoed from the room and crept down the stairs, picking up items of clothing as she went. She gathered up the rest of their things where Cam had dropped them over the bannister, and her lips twitched. He'd really shown her a night of passion.

She bundled the clothes on a chair and flicked on the lights beneath the kitchen cabinets. She grabbed a glass from the cupboard and turned toward the fridge.

A quick movement caught her eye, and she glanced at the sliding glass doors to the back. She let out a scream and dropped the glass on the floor where it shattered.

But she still couldn't tear her gaze away from a pair of gleaming eyes that had caught her in their malevolent stare.

Chapter Eleven

A crash and a scream from Martha yanked Cam to full consciousness. He bolted upright and reached for his gun...which he'd left downstairs in his jacket.

"Martha!" Scrambling from the bed, he scanned the floor for his briefs and remembered he'd dropped them over the stairs. "Just great."

He stumbled for the door and charged down the stairs, calling Martha's name again. He followed the glow of the low light emanating from the kitchen.

He almost plowed into Martha's back as he launched into the kitchen.

She stumbled forward, and he caught her around the waist as she raised her arm, pointing toward the sliding door to the back of the house.

He peered at the darkness beyond the glass, beyond the reflection of the two of them naked and entwined in some other kind of dance from the one they'd left upstairs. Martha's body was stiff and unyielding, and she hadn't said one word to him since that scream had echoed throughout the house.

Giving her a little shake, he asked, "What's wrong? What happened, Martha? Did you see something outside?"

She cranked her head to the side and worked her mouth for a few seconds before she finally found her voice. "A man. A man with a black ski mask covering his whole face was looking in at me."

Adrenaline ripped through Cam's body and he lunged for the door, but Martha grabbed his arm.

"Wait. There's glass on the floor and…and you don't have any clothes on."

"More importantly, I don't have my weapon." He spun around and strode to the chair where he'd left his jacket. He plunged his hand in the pocket and grabbed his gun. He swiped his jeans from the same chair and struggled into them on his way back to the kitchen.

This time he nearly tripped over Martha, on her hands and knees, sweeping a towel across the kitchen floor.

"You need shoes. I think I pushed most of the glass aside, but it's freezing out there. Your shoes are under the chair where I put our clothes."

With the intruder most likely putting more and more distance between himself and the house—and Cam's gun—Cam turned and stuffed his bare feet into his shoes. Finally, he charged outside.

Martha had turned on the outdoor lights, and Cam scanned the small patio and the lawn beyond it, which tumbled down to the boat dock and the bay.

He took the corner of the house and ran in a crouched position to the front.

He peered around the corner to the driveway, but if the masked man had arrived in a car and driven up to the front of the house, he was gone now. It made sense that Ben would know about this place. He seemed to know everything else about Martha.

The cold night air seeped into his bare flesh as he made his way to the circular driveway. He cocked his head, listening for—anything, a receding car, the squeal of a tire. He heard nothing but his own heart slamming against his chest.

He returned to the back patio where Martha hovered at the sliding door, his jacket clasped to her chest.

"Nothing out front?"

"No."

She thrust the jacket at him when he got close. "Put this on. It's freezing out here."

Poking his arms through the sleeves, he asked, "What was he doing at the door? What did you see?"

"Not much." She hugged herself. "I glanced up and saw his face at the door, except it wasn't really his face. His face was completely covered by a ski mask."

"Did he try to get in?"

"I-I'm not sure. He didn't run away until you got down here."

"Close the door. I want to check something."

Martha stepped onto the patio next to him and slid the door closed.

Cam ran his hand over the window closest to the door handle, skimming his palm over the chilly glass. Then he felt it. His fingertips traced over a rough edge in the glass.

"Did you find anything?"

"I did. Feel this." He took her hand and guided her fingers over the damaged window.

She snatched her hand back and wrinkled her nose. "It's cut."

"He used some glass-cutting tool. He was going to slice out a part of the window and reach in to unlock the door."

She jerked upright. "He knows about this house."

"Of course he does, Martha."

Flicking her fingers at the window, she jerked upright. "That's what he was doing when I discovered him. He stopped because you came onto the scene. I guess he wasn't expecting anyone else to be here."

"Too bad I wasn't prepared for him." He snapped his fingers. "The camera system. I noticed the house has cameras on all corners. Can you pull that up on the computer?"

"Yes." She sighed. "The sun's going to be coming up soon anyway. Who needs sleep?"

He caught a strand of her hair and wrapped it around his finger. "I'd rather do what we did instead of sleep any day of the week."

"Me, too."

He tugged her forward by her hair and kissed her sweet lips. "Video."

"Maybe you could put on the rest of your clothes, so I won't get distracted." She wiggled her fingers in the air over his bare chest, and his skin tingled as if she'd actually touched him.

"Yeah, distractions." He yanked open the sliding glass door and stalked to the chair where a lone shirt hung. Martha had already put on all her clothes from last night.

At the entrance to a door off the main hallway, Martha crooked her finger at him. "The office. My mom's desktop computer is in here, and we can look up the footage."

Martha stationed herself behind the big desk and clicked on a lamp. "Let me see if I can remember how to retrieve it."

"It's all pretty standard." He leaned over her shoulder as she clicked through the files on the computer's desktop.

The monitor displayed four squares, and Martha poked at each one as she identified it. "Driveway, front door and porch, back door, boat dock."

"Time?" He swirled his finger around the date and time stamp in the lower-right corner of each panel.

Martha enlarged the driveway display and moved the cursor to the menu. She adjusted the time to just about thirty minutes before she went downstairs.

Cam squinted at the video. "Is it motion-activated?"

"I honestly don't know that much about it, but I think so. It's just dark, isn't it?"

"Do you know for sure if it works?"

She slumped against the deep, leather chair. "No."

"Maybe he didn't come up the driveway. He wouldn't be that obvious, would he? I didn't see or hear any evidence that he had a car out front. Switch to another view. We know for sure he was at the back door."

Martha switched to the video panel showing the back door and made it bigger. She set the time back, and they both stared at the murky display again.

The image came to life and Cam let out a breath. "There he is."

A figure moved into the frame, a ski mask pulled low over his face, dark, baggy clothing loose around his body.

Martha bolted upright. "That's our guy."

"Unfortunately, that could be any guy. That could be me or even you. Just like using a disguise at the Insider, he's covering up."

The man came in from the side and crowded the door for several seconds, hunching over.

"He's probably working on the window."

The man stood still, placing gloved hands against the door, staring into the house.

"Ugh, that's probably when I noticed him."

The intruder sprang back from the door, stumbling over a potted plant. He dashed toward the lawn and out of the camera's view.

"He's heading toward the boat dock." Martha pulled up that panel, but the camera recorded nothing, no movement at all. "That one might be broken."

"We wouldn't have been able to identify him anyway, not with that ski mask."

Martha shoved back from the desk. "I wish I knew what he wanted. He must've come here to break in and do a search."

"If all he wanted to do was search your place for whatever he thinks Casey left you, he would've taken off when you appeared in the kitchen and caught him red-handed."

Slowly turning the chair to face him, Martha asked, "Do you think he wanted to harm me this time?"

"You said he didn't leave until I stumbled onto the scene. You'd already noticed him, and that didn't make him go away."

"So, he's reached the point where he doesn't want to take a chance that I'll discover his identity from something Casey might have left behind." Martha's fingers clawed into the arms of the chair.

Cam bent forward and smoothed his hands down her arms. "Maybe he just wanted to question you."

"Question?" She tilted her head back to meet his eyes. "Is that a nice way of saying interrogate under a single bright light? The man's a killer, Cam. He's proven that three times now."

"He *is* desperate to protect his identity. He probably never figured you'd find Tony and never figured Tony would fess up to being Casey's pimp."

"But I did, and Tony did and now we have a chance to discover who this guy is and why he set me up with those emails about Major Denver."

"And who's giving him orders." Cam's jaw tightened. "I'd like to get *him* under a single bright light to find that out."

"He must know we don't have this super-secret thing he's searching for because he's still after it—and us. I don't understand why he doesn't just disappear." She cupped his jaw with her hand. "Even if we get a good look at him and we're able to convince the FBI or the CIA to investigate him for those emails, it's not going to change anything for Denver, is it? There's still the rest of the evidence against the major that these emails brought to light."

"It's a start. It's a connection. Right now, we don't know who set him up or why. If this Ben can give us some insight, maybe we can unravel the rest of it."

"Then it's a game of cat and mouse, isn't it? We try to find the evidence, and he tries to make sure we don't. When is he going to give it up?"

Cam shrugged and pulled her out of the chair. "When he's tired of playing cat and mouse."

"Or when I'm dead."

"Don't say that." He placed his hands on her shoulders and drove his thumbs into her skin.

"We both know the reason why he hasn't taken his shot at me yet."

"We do?" Cam ran his tongue over his dry lips.

"It's because you're here, Cam. He knows I have some kind of badass bodyguard dogging me, and when you leave—" her shoulders tensed beneath his hands "—I'm a goner."

"I'm not going anywhere."

"Yet." She tucked her head beneath his chin. "How many more days until you leave?"

"Shh." He dropped his hands to her waist and pulled her body against his. "We have time. I'm gonna catch this guy and when I do, he'll pay—for everything."

LATER THAT MORNING, Martha, still sleepy-eyed, greeted him in the kitchen, holding up a plate of eggs. "Scrambled. Is that okay with you?"

"You didn't have to make breakfast...but I'm glad you did." He straddled the stool at the island counter. "I'd like to have a look out back now that it's light and see if Ben left anything. Would also be interesting to figure out how he got here. Unless that camera out front is broken like the one at the boat dock, he didn't come up the driveway."

She dropped two slices of toast on his plate and put it on the place mat in front of him. "I wanted to show you the boat dock, anyway. It's not as big as the one we had when my dad was a free man, but it's similar."

"Must've been an idyllic childhood."

"It was lonely. I didn't make friends easily, and my

mother insisted on sending me to a private school, miles away from our house. My parents' home wasn't exactly part of a neighborhood." She waved her fork around. "Kind of like this place. I couldn't run down the block to play with friends. That's one of the reasons why I read a lot—and hung out with my dad."

"At least you had a dad you could hang out with... and at least you could read." Cam shook his head as soon as the words left his lips. "I sound like a self-pitying idiot."

She smiled, and his world got brighter by several shades.

"A little, but it's safe to do that with me. At least you had godlike good looks and athletic abilities. You must've been Mr. Popularity growing up."

"Yeah, but that can get kind of lonely too in its own way."

She sat on the stool next to him and bumped his shoulder with hers. "Two lonely kids and now here we are."

"No place I'd rather be." He dabbed a crumb from the corner of her mouth. "When I discovered the identity of the CIA translator who turned over the emails that upended Denver's life, I was ready to give you the third degree. I thought you might've even been involved in the setup—until I met you. Then I knew exactly why you'd been the conduit for those emails."

"Because of my rigid adherence to protocol."

"But you surprised me, and you sure as hell surprised Ben."

She twirled her fork on her plate. "Do you think the patriot and Ben are the same person? We've been assuming they are, but maybe we're dealing with two different people—the computer geek and the killer."

"Could be." He brushed the toast crumbs from his fingers into the napkin on his lap. "The patriot warned you the night before Wentworth's death. That's for sure. He knew that was coming."

"Just seems like we're dealing with someone who has two very different sets of skills."

"A computer nerd can't be a killer? Or an assassin can't also be well versed in computer programming?"

"Anything's possible, but I dated a tech whiz and I couldn't see him taking out Tony like that."

So, Martha did date. Cam stirred the eggs around his plate, intently studying the pattern they made. "What happened to that relationship?"

"Bad idea all around. We were too much alike, and I worked with him or at least near him."

"CIA analyst?"

"Not nearly that exciting. CIA tech guy."

"Who broke it off?"

"I sort of did. It wasn't that serious to even be called a breakup. We talked a lot. We were friends first, and then he got the bright idea to ask me out. He never even saw the inside of my bedroom."

Cam raised his eyebrows. Was that Martha's way of telling him she hadn't slept with the guy? "Still friends?"

"We chat when we see each other at work." She picked up her plate and held it out toward him. "Are you done?"

He stacked his plate on top of hers. "That hit the spot. Now let's bundle up and take a look around outside."

Martha left their plates in the sink, and they grabbed their jackets. When they slipped through the back door that had been compromised the previous night, Cam stepped back and looked at the scratches on the window.

He rubbed the rough patch of glass. "You should get this fixed. It wouldn't take much to punch that out. He was probably minutes away from doing that."

"Add it to my list, which includes getting my Georgetown locks changed."

Cam crouched and searched the ground in front of the door. The mat seemed undisturbed, and the brick beneath didn't show any marks or footprints, not even theirs from last night.

He took two steps back, grazed the edge of the planter with his leg and squatted beside the container to study the plant for threads.

"You're retracing his steps?" Martha tilted her head.

"Yeah. It looked like he ran straight back to the boat dock and the bay."

Martha turned and faced the water. The brisk breeze blew her hair back from her face. "He must have, unless he circled back to the front, but we didn't see anything on the camera footage. Maybe he came up by water."

"You did want to show me the boat dock."

She stuck her hand out behind her. "Let's go."

In two strides he joined her and grabbed her hand. Their footsteps crunched on the gravel path leading toward the dock.

Cam stopped and dropped to one knee. "If he took this path, he would've left footprints."

Martha crouched beside him and poked at the gravel with her finger. "Looks like he may have even smoothed this over by shuffling his feet."

"Maybe, or the wind covered his tracks." Cam cupped her elbow and helped her rise. "I think we're on the right track here."

When they reached the dock, Cam stomped on it. "Sturdier than it looks."

"It has to hold up to the weather, especially this time of year." She pounded on the side of the shed that was designed to hold a small boat. "This, too, even though my mom doesn't have a boat."

Cam peered around the corner at the water stirring inside the empty boat shed. "Maybe he parked his own boat here when he came up."

Martha placed her hands on her hips and stared at the gray water lapping at the shore. "He could've come from the public dock, moored here and then attempted his break-in. When you showed up, he hightailed it back to his boat and took off, probably knowing you'd look for a car out front."

"I probably could've caught him if I'd come straight back here instead of wasting time putting clothes on and going to the front of the house." He fired a pebble into the water.

"You couldn't have come out here without your clothes." Martha moseyed to the edge of the dock and kicked at the mooring.

"Don't fall in." Cam leaned over to gather a few more stones for skipping, and a half-smoked cigarette on the shore. He pinched it between his thumb and forefinger and held it up. "Look at this. Does your mother smoke?"

"No."

He cupped it in his palm and bounced it in his hand. "This looks hand rolled. Would anyone else be down here? It's dry. Looks like someone meant to toss it in the water and missed—maybe because it was dark."

"My mom's handyman smokes. He's married to the housekeeper, and he comes down here sometimes when MayBeth is working, but I don't think he rolls his own."

"When was the last time he was here? If this had been tossed here any earlier than last night, it would be wet by now or swept into the bay."

"I don't know for sure, but MayBeth usually comes on Fridays. Maybe Ben smokes."

"I'm hanging on to this." He slipped the cigarette into his pocket. "He knows you're staying at your mom's. He knows how to get here, and he tried to break in."

"And he knows you're here too—for now."

"You've been checking your texts? We know he has your number from Casey's phone."

She patted her jacket pocket. "All the time. He's gone quiet after weeks of harassing me."

"Then he was just trying to intimidate you into keeping quiet about your suspicions."

"Now he's afraid I'm going to find him out and report him. If he hadn't started murdering people, I wouldn't have had a clue to his identity."

"Those murders were always in his playbook— maybe not Tony's—but he wanted to cover his tracks and get rid of Wentworth and Casey. She could tie him to both Wentworth and the emails, and he wanted to erase that link. The only loose end left was you holding on to those emails for some reason he can't figure out."

"Believe me. I couldn't figure it out at first either, but now I know it was instinct that led me to hold on to them." She tucked her hand in his pocket. "And that instinct led you to me. It all happened for a reason."

He inserted his hand and folded it around hers. "I feel it, too. We're like puzzle pieces, and we both fill a part in this mosaic."

She pressed her arm against his as she hunched

her shoulder. "I'm cold. Let's go inside, and I'll find someone to fix that window."

A phone buzzed and Cam dipped his hand into his other pocket. "That's yours."

Martha pulled out her phone and cupped a hand around the display to read the text. "It's my friend Farah. She's a translator who works with me."

"I'm assuming everyone at work knows what's going on with you."

"Yeah." She looked up from the phone. "Farah wants to meet for drinks tonight to tell me what's going on, what people are saying."

"Can she be trusted?"

"Farah? Absolutely."

"Then I think it's a good idea. Get the pulse of what's going on there."

"I think you're right." Martha cupped the phone with one hand and texted with her thumb.

She had two more exchanges with Farah and then pocketed the phone. "We're all set for eight o'clock tonight."

Cam took her hand. "Plenty of time to replace the glass in the window, get your locks changed and make a trip to and from my hotel."

"To and from?"

"To pick up my stuff and bring it here." He pressed a kiss against her temple. "After what happened here this morning, you don't think I'm going to allow you to stay on your own, do you?"

Cam pulled her close on their walk back to the

house, inhaling the crisp scent of the bay that clung to her hair. He didn't know how he was ever going to leave Martha on her own as long as this killer had her in his sights.

SECURITY BUSINESS AND errands ate up the rest of the afternoon. Martha had a locksmith change the locks to her town house, got the glass replaced in the sliding glass door and Cam moved from his hotel to Mom's house.

Too tired to cook and too frazzled to go out, they picked up a pizza on the way back to Mom's. Martha patted her full tummy and curled one leg beneath her on the sofa. "I was relieved to see that our friend hadn't made a return visit to my town house."

"Not that we know of, anyway. You should've followed your mother's example and wired that place with a security system."

"He probably would've disabled that like he did the one at the bar." She nudged the pizza box with the toe of her shoe. "There are two pieces left. Do you want them, or should I wrap them up and put them in the fridge?"

"People actually wrap and refrigerate leftover pizza instead of just eating it in the morning?"

"Ugh." She wrinkled her nose as she eyed the gooey cheese congealing on top of the slices.

Reaching forward and ripping the pieces apart, Cam said, "I'd better do them justice now."

As a shot of the Insider flashed on the muted TV

screen, Martha lunged for the remote and turned up the volume. "I wonder if they have any suspects yet."

"You and I both know the police will never find the real killer."

They listened to the story for a minute, and then Martha muted the sound again. "They're still putting out the burglary story. Maybe they don't want to reveal the message on the table to the general public."

"Well, he did clean out the cash drawer and the safe to make it look good."

"And destroyed the security system."

"Good thing he did that or we'd be on it, front and center." Cam dragged a napkin across his mouth. "I haven't heard anything yet about Tony's extracurricular activities."

"Or his connection to Casey."

"Just another vicious murder in DC."

"Georgetown, and that's why it's getting so much air play."

"Is this bar we're going to tonight near the Insider?"

"Not far." Martha sniffed the air. "What is that smell? Tobacco? I've been smelling it on and off all day."

Cam reached across her and plucked his jacket from the arm of the sofa. "It's that cigarette I picked up by the boat dock. The tobacco is kind of sweet, isn't it?"

"And strong." She pushed up from the sofa. "I'll get you a plastic bag from the kitchen."

As she made a grab for the pizza box, Cam snatched up the last piece of pizza. "I'm saving this piece from the fate of being wrapped and stored."

She snorted. "A great sacrifice for you, I'm sure."

An hour later, they were on their way to another bar in Georgetown, and Martha hoped for a better outcome than last night.

She yawned as she pulled into a public parking lot on the crowded street. "I'm not sure I should have a drink tonight. I'm ready to fall asleep as it is."

"I wouldn't make any promises you can't keep." Cam tapped on the window to point out an empty parking space. "You may need a drink after listening to what your friend has to say."

They walked the two blocks to the waterfront bar hand in hand, and Martha could almost imagine they were on a regular date. She couldn't help noticing the admiring glances women threw at Cam, and she was just superficial enough that the attention to her date brought a smile to her face.

She tugged on Cam's hand as the bar came into view. "This is a date, right? You're not in Delta Force, you didn't track me down to interrogate me about the Denver emails, you never met Casey or saw Wentworth at my place."

"Just like we discussed." He opened the door for her and put his hand on her back as he whispered in her ear, "Do you see Farah?"

Martha swept the bar with her gaze and spotted Farah at a table with the guy she'd met on a dating website a few months ago—the married guy. "She's over there, and..."

Cam didn't give her a chance to finish her sentence. He crooked an arm around her neck and pulled her around for a kiss on the mouth.

For a few seconds Martha forgot she was standing in a crowded bar, forgot she had a three-time killer stalking her, forgot she was going to lose Cam in a week.

Her arm curled around his waist, and she sagged against him as a pool of heat ached between her legs.

He ended the long kiss, punctuated by another peck on the lips. "There. That should put any doubt about this being date night to rest."

Martha blinked and adjusted her glasses. She cleared her throat. "Right."

She yanked on his sleeve. "What I was going to say before you ambushed me is that Farah is here with her scumbag boyfriend."

"He's a scumbag?"

"He's married."

"Oh, that kind of scumbag." He rubbed her back. "You weren't planning to get top secret with Farah anyway, were you?"

"No."

"Then let's see if she can tell you what they're saying about you in the office." He nudged her back, and she led him to Farah's table.

Farah rose from her chair, her wide, dark eyes darting from Martha to Cam. She gave Martha a one-armed hug and said, "You take a day off work and collect a boyfriend along the way?"

Martha kissed her friend's cheek. "Farah, this is Cam. Cam, this is Farah and Scott."

Everyone shook hands, and Martha and Cam crowded around the small table, as Cam craned his neck. "Waiters coming by?"

"Not often enough." Scott raised his almost empty bottle of beer. "I need to hit the men's room. I'll swing by the bar on the way and get us a round. Farah?"

She covered her wineglass with her hand. "I'm good."

Cam tapped Scott's bottle. "I'll have one of these."

Martha pointed to Farah's glass of wine. "And I'll make it easy and have a glass of white wine, thanks."

Scott kissed Farah on the top of the head. "Be right back."

"Thanks, babe." Wiggling her fingers over her shoulder, Farah flicked back her hair. "I'm glad you came out, Martha. I just wanted to give you a heads-up about work. First of all, are you okay? My God, to find Wentworth dead in your town house and then Casey the next day. I can't even imagine what you're going through."

And Farah didn't even know about Tony. Martha shot a look beneath her lashes at Cam. "It's been a pretty rough few days. What are they saying at the office? What's *Gage* saying?"

"Just, you know." Farah swirled her wine in the

glass. "Lots of gossip about the congressman and your roommate."

Martha narrowed her eyes. "What's the real reason Proffit asked me to take a few days off?"

"I don't know." Farah hunched forward and twisted her head toward Cam. "Is he okay?"

"You can say anything in front of Cam."

Farah's tongue darted out of her mouth in a quick sweep of her lips. "Martha, they're looking at your computer."

Martha's jaw dropped, and a tickle of fear crept up her neck. "D-did they remove it from my cubicle."

Cam pressed his knee against hers and she welcomed the contact, although it did nothing to alleviate the panic galloping through her veins.

"No, but they've been in your cubicle a few times—all hush-hush. What else would they be doing in there?"

Cam asked, "Who's they? Who's been in Martha's cube?"

"Gage, Proffit and that tech guy." Farah tapped a fingernail against her glass. "Sebastian Forsythe, the one you dated a few times."

"That's not good." Martha grabbed Farah's glass and took a gulp of wine.

"You don't have anything to hide, do you, Martha? No, of course you don't, but if the Agency is looking at your work computer that may not matter."

"You're right. It may not matter. Thanks for clueing me in, Farah."

She nodded and then put a finger to her lips as she glanced to the side. "Zip it."

Martha looked up to see Scott with three drinks gathered in his hands.

"Success." He placed the drinks on the table in a huddle, and then slid them to their owners. "Wine, beer, beer. I can go for another round if you need me to."

Farah squeezed his hand. "Thanks, babe. Maybe later. Let's toast."

"To Mondays." Scott leaned in and clinked his bottle to Martha's glass, and she instinctively drew away.

She'd never liked Farah's taste in men. She'd met Scott just a few times, but any guy who claimed to have an arrangement with his wife raised a red flag with her. She gave Scott a weak smile and took a sip of her wine. Cam had been right. She might need the whole glass to get through this get-together.

"Oh my God, did you hear about that bartender who was murdered during a robbery? It happened not far from here." Farah twisted the gold chain around her neck with her fingers. "Terrible."

"I did see that on the news." Martha shook her head. "Why'd the guy have to kill the bartender?"

"Maybe he didn't expect the bartender to be there, and he didn't want the bartender to ID him." Scott ran a thumbnail through the damp label on his bottle.

"Well, it was probably all for nothing anyway. I know that area, and there are CCTVs in all the bars."

Farah pointed to a corner of the ceiling. "Probably in here, too."

"The robber took care of the cameras." Martha picked up her glass for another sip of wine, and someone kicked her under the table.

She choked on her wine and ended up taking a deeper gulp. She avoided looking at Cam. Who else would kick her?

"Took care of the cameras?" Farah tilted her head to one side.

Scott asked, "You mean disabled them? We didn't hear that."

Martha could've kicked herself—in the same spot Cam had kicked her. She'd better stick to translating because she clearly didn't have the makings of a spy.

"I think we heard something like that on the news before we left." Cam dragged his napkin over a few drops of wine on the table in front of Martha. "Do you follow football, Scott?"

The men talked football while Farah filled Martha in on other office gossip.

Several minutes later, Scott patted his front shirt pocket. "I'm going to head out to the deck for a smoke. Join me, Cam?"

"I don't smoke, but I do need to hit the men's room." Cam scooted back from the table and winked. "We'll leave you ladies to exchange secrets if you want."

Cam and Scott walked several feet together until

Scott peeled off for the deck on the side of the bar, and Cam continued to the back and the restrooms.

Farah bent her head to Martha's and whispered, "Is it those emails, Martha? I didn't want to say anything in front of Cam, but do you think Proffit knows you copied those emails onto a flash drive?"

"I don't know how he could…unless someone told him."

"Not me, I swear." Farah drew a cross over her heart with one long fingernail. "Did you tell someone else?"

"No, but…" She snapped her mouth shut as she saw Scott coming in from the patio. "That was fast."

"Oh, he's trying to quit, so he doesn't smoke his cig all the way down. Screwy method if you ask me." Farah rolled her eyes and touched her glass to Martha's.

Martha cupped her wineglass with one hand and swirled another sip of the oaky chardonnay in her mouth, her eyebrows knitting over her nose as she followed Scott's progress back to their table.

Even as Cam appeared several feet behind Scott with a bottle of beer in each hand, Martha pinned her gaze to Scott, tracking his every movement. He stuffed something, a pouch, in the pocket of his jacket.

Martha jerked her head once and allowed the wine to run down the back of her throat. That pouch could be anything. Maybe it wasn't even a pouch. It didn't have to be loose tobacco, and plenty of people didn't smoke their cigarettes all the way down to the butt. He probably wanted to get back to Farah.

Eyeing her half-empty wineglass, Martha pushed it away from her as Scott reached their table.

He leaned in to kiss Farah on the mouth, and she shooed him away with both hands. "You know I can't stand smoking. I grew up with just about every member of my family lighting up, and I can't stand it—especially that tobacco and especially those roll-your-own cancer sticks."

Martha froze. This time when Scott sat down and pulled his chair up to the table, instead of moving away from him, she moved closer and inhaled deeply.

Her heart slammed against her rib cage. The odor of the tobacco from his breath caused a cold dread to snake up her spine.

Chapter Twelve

Cam placed the beers on the table and nodded to Scott. He didn't want to stay much longer, but he owed Scott a round. Unless Farah had dropped a bombshell in the past ten minutes, she'd told Martha everything she knew about the office. Wasn't much Martha could do about it now.

Someone kicked his shin under the table, and he shifted his leg to the side. Then Martha scooted her chair toward him and dug her fingernails into his thigh—at least he hoped those were Martha's fingers so close to his crotch.

Picking up his beer, he met her gaze above the bottle and almost choked on the liquid running down his throat. Her pale face and her lips pressed together in a thin line made his stomach drop. Had Farah delivered more bad news?

Martha made a grab for her wineglass and knocked it over. She jerked back from the table. "Sorry."

Scott tossed his napkin on top of the spreading pool of wine. "Do you want another?"

"No!" Martha shoved her chair back from the table. "No, thank you. I think we'd better be going. I—I have to let my mom's dog out."

"Your mom has a dog?"

As Farah tilted her head, Cam drew his eyebrows together. What had lit a fire under Martha? Farah didn't seem to know.

Martha jumped up from the table. "Thanks so much for the heads-up, Farah. If anything else happens, let me know. Hopefully, I'll be back at work next week once the Agency realizes I wasn't at all involved in Casey and the Congressman's relationship."

"Sounds like a movie of the week, Casey and the Congressman." Farah stood up and gave Martha a one-armed hug and shook Cam's hand. "Nice to meet you."

Scott stood up, as well, and everyone said their goodbyes, which couldn't happen fast enough for Cam. Something had obviously happened to spook Martha when he'd been absent, but that something hadn't come from Farah.

Cam slid Martha's coat and purse from the back of her chair. "We'll have to do this again."

As he handed Martha's purse to her, she elbowed him in the ribs, and he sucked in a breath. He helped her into her coat and she grabbed his arm, practically dragging him out of the bar.

When they hit the sidewalk, Martha folded her arms and continued her quick pace.

He bumped her shoulder. "What's going on?

Where are we going? Your mother doesn't even have a dog."

She didn't say one word until they got into the car and closed the doors. Then she turned to him and grabbed his sleeve.

"Farah's boyfriend? Scott?"

He nodded. "Yeah?"

"He's our guy."

"Our guy? The one who hacked you?"

"The one who killed three people."

"How do you know that?" His gaze darted to the side mirror.

"Did you smell him when he came back to the table?"

"I don't usually make a habit out of sniffing other dudes."

She slugged his shoulder. "I'm serious, Cam. He smelled sweetish, just like that cigarette you picked up on the boat dock."

"Same tobacco?"

She licked her lips. "It's more than that. He rolls his own cigarettes, and when he came back from his smoke after just a few minutes, Farah told me he's trying to quit and smokes only half his cigarette."

"The one on the dock was only half smoked." He rubbed his knuckles against his jaw. "Maybe you're onto something."

She closed her eyes and pressed her fingers against her temples. "I think I am. It's too coincidental."

"When did Farah start dating him?"

"About four months ago. Met him online, and he told her he was married right away. She's not looking for something permanent, so that didn't bother her."

"He told her he was married to explain why he didn't bring her to his place or introduce her to his friends."

Martha started the car but didn't make a move. "He started dating her to get close to me. Just like he ordered Casey to keep an eye on me. Everyone around me is proving to be false."

He grabbed her hand. "Not me. Do you think Farah's in on it? She could've been the one who identified you to be the conduit of those emails."

"No way. Farah wouldn't do that."

"That's what you thought about Casey, too." He entwined his fingers with hers. "It's like they're forming a snare around you, Martha. They wanted people on the inside, watching you—from work and from home."

"That doesn't make sense." The chattering of her teeth swallowed up her last word.

"Sure it does." He turned up the heat in the car. "On some level you know it. You recognized the smell of that cigarette when it had been in my pocket. It struck a chord with you because you'd smelled it before—on him."

"If it's all true, if Scott's the killer, we can't leave Farah to him. I'm not going to allow her to be alone with a killer."

He reached over and cut the engine, and then

grabbed the door handle. "I wish you would've told me this sooner, right outside the bar. I could've confronted him then."

"What are you doing?"

He cranked his head over his shoulder. "I'm going back. He's right under our noses. I'm not going to let him slip through my grasp now after trying to ID him for days."

"Wait." She put her hand on his back. "Do we really want him to know we're onto him? What do you think he was planning in there? He *did* get us our drinks."

Cam ran his tongue around the inside of his mouth. "What would be the point in drugging us in a public place, in front of his supposed girlfriend?"

"Maybe he wanted to drug us for later. Knock us out at my mom's house and break in without disturbing us."

"That's some long-acting drug."

"I don't know." She flattened her palm against her chest. "You do know that he arranged this meeting tonight, don't you? Somehow, someway, he got Farah to invite me out."

"I agree. None of this is coincidence." He pushed open the door. "And I'm going to find out why. I'm going to find out who put him up to this, and why they want to bring down Major Denver."

"Cam!"

The urgency burned in his gut. On some logical level he knew Martha was right. Why show their hand now? But he might never get a crack at this guy again. He was two blocks away. He had to make a move.

Cam broke into a jog, even as he heard Martha calling behind him. He dodged a couple of cars to cross the street to the restaurant and burst through the doors.

The chairs where the four of them had sat were empty, the table still littered with their glasses and bottles. He threaded his way through the bar and loomed over the table.

"Forget something?"

He spun around and almost knocked into the waitress. "The other couple, they left?"

"Right after you did." She balanced her tray on her hip and repeated her question. "Forget something?"

"It's all right. I'll call them later." Cam backed up to the table and wrapped his fingers around the neck of Scott's beer bottle. He shuffled around the waitress, keeping the bottle behind him. "Thanks."

Outside the bar when he reached the street corner, Martha pounced on him. "What were you doing? How could confronting him in public possibly work?"

"Don't worry. They'd left." He presented the beer bottle with a flourish and held it in front of Martha's face. "And I snagged this."

"His fingerprints."

"Exactly. I have a buddy with the PD in Virginia who can help out with the prints."

She slipped her fingers in the back pocket of his jeans as they walked to the car. "Scott's playing with fire. How did he know we wouldn't be able to ID him?"

"He probably felt secure since he was obviously wearing a disguise when he met with Casey and Tony, and he had a mask on this morning at your mom's house. When Tony described him with the beard and glasses, we already figured he'd donned a disguise."

"We can't prove anything based on a tobacco brand, Cam."

"Who knows? We could even be wrong about him, but I doubt it."

When they reached the car, Martha leaned against it, shoving her hands in her pockets. "Farah. We can't leave her alone with him."

"Would they go back to her place?"

"They never go to his place. He's conveniently married, remember?"

"We can't go charging into Farah's place. We need a plan." Cam rubbed his hands together against the chill of the night. "But let's do it in the car with the engine running and the heat blasting."

Once in the car, Cam turned to Martha. "Do you know where Farah lives?"

"A town house not far from here."

"We could drop by on some pretext—you left your phone at the bar, or something work related. If Scott's still there, you could get Farah alone. Maybe you could warn her against him."

She worried her bottom lip. "If he's at her place and you see him again, will you be able to control yourself? You charged back to the bar, ready to get some answers from him."

"If he is there, it might be the perfect opportunity to get some answers." Cam drummed his thumbs against the dashboard. "He'd be in a private place. I could let him know we have his prints and are going to the police with our suspicions."

"Like you said before, we have nothing to tie him to the three murders. Heck, the cops aren't even calling Congressman Wentworth's death a murder." She rolled her eyes. "I don't think a cigarette is going to do the trick, do you? We never even reported his attempted break-in to the police."

"We know that, but he doesn't. It might give us a little leverage with him. He's gonna realize he dropped a cigarette at your place, so that'll ring true." He slapped his hand against the dashboard. "It's worth a try. I'm not letting this guy slip away."

Martha threw the car into gear. "I agree, but I don't want anyone getting hurt."

"Nobody's going to get hurt." He ran a hand down her thigh. "Especially not you."

"Or Farah."

"Or Farah."

"Or you."

"Got it."

Ten minutes later, Martha parallel parked at the curb and pointed to a row of town houses. "Farah's is on the end."

Cam twisted around and peered out the back window. "Quiet street."

"Well, it is all residential and it's a weeknight." She turned off the engine and blew out a breath. "Ready?"

"We're ready." He patted his jacket pocket, feeling the hard outline of his weapon.

Martha's gaze followed the gesture. "Nobody's getting hurt, right?"

"Would you really care if Scott-Ben-Patriot got hurt? He murdered three people—that we know of— and he's after you and using Farah, putting her in danger."

"I know you're right, but you can't just run around shooting people based on a half-smoked cigarette— even if you are a hotshot D-Boy." She touched his face. "I'm more worried about you than him. I don't want you getting into any trouble."

He captured her fingers and kissed the tips. "And I don't want you getting into any trouble. Nobody's going to know you took those emails."

"My hand may be forced in the end if we want to put a stop to this guy." Closing her eyes, she sighed.

"You're not going to end up like your father." He squeezed her fingers before releasing them. "Let's go."

When Cam slammed the passenger door, a dog

popped up at a window of a town house and barked. "At least someone's on guard around here."

"Let me do the talking." Martha pocketed her keys and took the lead to Farah's place on the corner.

This neighborhood lacked the understated elegance of Martha's with the fronts of the town houses closer to the edge of the sidewalk, but still nobody glanced out their windows at them as they passed by.

The area didn't scream high crime, but Cam shoved his hand in his jacket pocket and caressed the handle of his gun anyway. The silence of the street had him coiling his muscles in expectation of…something.

Martha drew up to the steps of Farah's town house and pulled back her shoulders. "This is it."

Cam looked over Martha's head at the glow from the front window, the drapes tugged close, keeping the warmth and light from spilling onto the sidewalk. No light gleamed from the window to the left of this one, and the town house seemed draped in silence like the rest of the block.

Martha breezed up the steps and rang the doorbell. Shifting to the side, she said, "I want her to see me from the peephole."

Cam kept his eye in the square of light that was the front window, searching for movement or shadows.

He swallowed. "I don't think she's home, Martha."

"Not home?" Martha jabbed at the doorbell again. "Where would they be?"

Cam lifted a stiff shoulder. "Don't know."

Martha stepped back, tilting her head to scan the windows of the second story. "No lights on up there. Maybe they're in bed."

"Farah and Scott?"

Martha stuck her finger in her open mouth to mimic gagging. "I know. It makes me sick to think about it."

"Maybe you should call her." Cam's jaw ached with the insidious tension that had crawled through him ever since he stepped from the car. "Call her."

Martha shot him a sharp glance and then fumbled with her phone. She tapped the screen and listened for several seconds. "It's Martha. I'm on your front porch. Something I need to ask you, so give me a call when you get this or let me in if you're home."

"This place has a side door and a back door?"

"Back door, I think." Martha folded her arms, clutching her purse to her side. "Why?"

"I want you to go back to the car, Martha. Just sit inside and wait for me. I'm going to do a quick check."

Her eyes got round behind her glasses. "Why?"

"Just want to make sure."

"Make sure about what, that Farah's not dead behind those doors? Like Casey? Like Tony?"

Her voice had risen to a squeal, and Cam put a finger to her soft lips. "We came here to check on Farah, didn't we? To make sure she was okay. I'm gonna do that now, and you're gonna go back to the car and wait for me."

He put his hands around her waist and twirled her toward the car as if they were on the dance floor. "It's just a precaution. I'm sure she's fine."

She cranked her head over her shoulder and covered her mouth. "What if we endangered Farah's life by taking off like that? Maybe Scott realized we'd made the connection. I said my mom had a dog. If Scott was the one prowling around this morning, he's going to know there's no dog at that house."

He stroked her back. "That's not a given. Could be a lapdog, one of those little fur balls. Don't think that way. I won't be long."

He watched as she stumbled toward the car, and then he slipped around the side of the town house. If something had happened to Farah, Martha didn't need to bear witness to it.

He crept up to the first window and touched the glass with his nose, squinting to see through the gap in the curtains. He saw a slice of neat, undisturbed kitchen, and the threshold of the living room beyond.

He tried raising the window, but it didn't budge. If he did break in and discovered Farah and Scott in bed, he'd have a lot of explaining to do—especially if Scott really was just some cheatin' dog and not a killer.

Hunching forward, he made his way to the back of the town house where a short gate blocked his path. As he reached over the top to feel for the latch, he froze.

The eerie silence of the neighborhood had been broken by something much worse—Martha's scream.

Chapter Thirteen

About five feet from the car, Martha aimed the remote to unlock the doors. A sick feeling had been gnawing at her gut ever since Cam's true purpose for searching Farah's place and sending her to the car had dawned on her.

If anything happened to Farah, she'd never forgive herself. How many people had to pay the price for her stupidity of snagging those emails for herself?

A pair of headlights flooded the street, and Martha caught her breath. Maybe Scott and Farah had come back and if so, she'd have to waylay them out here until Cam finished his search—and then somehow explain where Cam had gone and why.

The car slowed down, and Martha ran her tongue along her bottom lip as she recognized Farah's vehicle. She whispered, "C'mon, Cam."

The car double-parked next to her own, and just as Martha pasted a fake smile on her face, the driver's door sprang open.

"Hey, Farah, we—"

Martha broke off as the figure moved toward her, the black ski mask covering his face. She tripped backward, throwing her arms out to her sides to recover her balance.

The man circled behind her and took advantage of her unsteadiness. One strong arm curled around her chest, dragging her to the street and the idling car—Farah's car.

She used her last burst of air to scream. She dug her heels into the pavement. They scraped against it as her attacker pulled her to the street. When he reached Farah's car, he pulled open the passenger door and scrambled in backward, pulling her along with him even as she clawed at his arm and kicked at his legs.

"Hey, hey!"

Martha sobbed as Cam's shouts echoed in the night.

The man holding her grunted as he landed behind the wheel, and he threw the car into gear. As the car jerked into motion, he growled, "Stay out of this, or I'll be forced to kill you."

He'd released his hold on her, but the car was now in motion and her body was half in and half out, one foot inches off the ground.

She felt rather than saw Cam launch himself at the moving car. With one hand, he grasped onto the door as it swung wide, his other hand clutching his weapon pointed futilely at the ground. His legs scrambled beneath him, as they tried to keep pace with the moving vehicle.

Martha screamed again as the car veered toward a pole. The masked man would crush Cam if he could.

Through his panting, Cam said, "Get out, Martha. You have to get out. Fall on me."

The driver punched the gas pedal, and the car leaped forward. The car door swung back again.

Martha braced her foot against the seat as her attacker made a grab for her leg. She twisted and kicked him in the side.

Her new position gave her a view of the back seat, and she choked. "Cam, Cam."

"Out now!"

Cam yanked her by the arm, and she felt suspended in air for a second before landing on top of Cam's solid body. His arms wrapped around her, and they rolled together for several feet along a stretch of foliage.

They came to rest against a rise that broke their momentum, and Martha squeezed a painful breath from her lungs.

"Are you all right?" Cam's hands brushed across her face.

"I—I think so." She heaved a strangled sob.

"My God. He was trying to get you into the car." He smoothed the hair back from her face. "I should've never left you."

"Cam." She bunched fistfuls of his jacket in her hands. "He had Farah."

"What do you mean? That was her car?"

"He had her in the back seat. She was knocked out or…" She buried her face against his chest.

Cam struggled to sit up, brushing bits of leaves and twigs from his sleeves. "We have to call the police now. We'll stick as close to the truth as possible, but we need to report Farah's kidnapping and his attempted kidnapping of you."

"He warned me again. When it became clear he wasn't going to succeed in his abduction, he told me to back off. He said something weird."

Cam curled his arm beneath her back, and she winced as she sat up. When a car drove by, they both hunched toward the ground, but the driver rolled by without even noticing them.

"What was weird?"

"He told me to stay out of this or he'd be forced to kill me." Martha combed her fingers through her tangled hair. "Forced to kill me. He doesn't want to, but why? If he took me out now, he wouldn't have to worry about my finding anything else that Casey left behind for me."

"How would that look?" Cam rose to his knees, and cupped her elbow to help her up along with him. "A CIA translator is the conduit for a batch of emails implicating a Delta Force commander in colluding with the enemy. That translator's roommate kills herself after her congressman lover dies, and then the translator accidentally dies? Disappears? Is murdered? If Wentworth's death wasn't on the FBI's radar, your death and Casey's would definitely put it there."

"This is all blowing up for him and his plans to make the emails seem like some concerned patriot looking out for the good of the country."

"You're blowing it up for him. You and your out of left field decision to keep those emails." Cam touched her nose. "What happened to your glasses?"

"I don't know. I can't even remember if I had them when he pulled me into Farah's car." She bunched a fist against her midsection. "What are we going to do about Farah? He can't kill her, either. Even though she didn't receive the emails, she's a CIA translator."

"With no connection to Casey or Wentworth or as you just mentioned, the emails. He could make her death look like an accident."

"But we're friends." Martha clung to Cam as if she were clinging to hope about Farah's safety. "That would look suspicious."

"If he doesn't kill her, she's going to report him."

"Maybe not." Martha took a wobbling step and grabbed Cam's arm for support. "If he drugged her wine and took her to the car where she passed out, she's not going to know any of this happened."

"Unless we call the police right now and tell them what we witnessed."

"Maybe that's not the way to go right now. We'd force his hand if he we do that."

"We have to go to the authorities at some point with what we know, Martha, or what would've been the whole point in all this? We have to let them know the emails were a plant to discredit Major Denver."

She slipped her hand in his pocket as they limped back to her car parked down the block from Farah's place. "What happened to your gun?"

"Dropped it." He pointed to the ground. "That's why I'm walking with my head down."

"What a pair we are." She leaned her head against his shoulder. "I guess Scott knew I realized his identity in the bar."

"Yeah, well, don't beat yourself up over that. If I'd put two and two together about those cigarettes, I probably would've assaulted him right then and there, and that wouldn't have been smart."

"It probably would've saved Farah."

Cam stopped suddenly and she bumped into him.

"Found it." He stooped to pick up his weapon, which had landed in the gutter of the street.

"You haven't seen a pair of glasses down there, have you?"

"I've been looking."

They reached the car, and Martha shivered when she saw the black skid marks in the street. If Cam hadn't come to her rescue, she'd be God knew where right now with a killer and a comatose Farah in the back seat of her car.

Cam swooped down and snatched up the keys she'd dropped during the attack. He dangled them from his fingers. "Are you okay to drive?"

She tapped her temple. "No glasses. You take the

wheel." She looked up and down the empty street. "I can't believe all that commotion didn't prompt someone to call the police. Didn't anyone hear me scream?"

"I did." He opened the passenger door and helped her in. "That's all that matters."

As Cam walked around to the driver's side, two more cars drove by and Martha slid down in her seat.

He slammed the door and gripped the top of the steering wheel, stretching his arms in front of him. "We need to make a decision about Farah. She's incapacitated in the clutches of a killer."

"On the other hand..." She put one hand over her mouth. "Did I really say that after what you stated as the obvious?"

"This is me you're talking to, Martha." He thumped his chest with his fist. "I understand the gray areas. Let me finish your thought. On the other hand, if Farah's in the dark about being drugged, or kidnapped or Scott's wild ride with us clinging to an open car door, she's still safe and maybe we don't have to do anything at all right now to help her."

Martha nodded, happy that Cam had understood her coldhearted statement. "That's what I mean. Scott could take her to a hotel and tell her she passed out, got sick, whatever. He wouldn't have to harm her at that point because she never would even know she'd been in danger—except for us and if we call the police..."

Cam squeezed the bridge of his nose. "That's our dilemma."

"Cam." Martha spread her hands in front of her and inspected an abrasion on her knuckle. "I think it might be time for me to call an attorney. Gage at work was joking, but I *should* call my father's attorney. He's a family friend."

"Are you thinking of coming clean about the emails?" He traced a scratch on the back of her hand to her wrist.

"I think it's the only way now to protect Farah and tell the police and the FBI everything about Wentworth, Casey and Tony. I haven't heard any news about an autopsy for Wentworth, but they're still calling it a heart attack and Casey's still a suicide. The police haven't asked me anything else about her death or friends or state of mind."

"I don't want you to get in trouble, Martha."

"I did that all by myself." Her nose tingled, and she swiped the back of her hand across it.

"You tried to go through the right channels about your suspicions, but it didn't work. Nobody would listen to you."

"Coming clean would also help your cause. This guy, these people, have gone to great lengths, even murder, to set this all up and then deal with the loose ends. It will prompt an investigation of the emails and Major Denver."

"Like you said before. It still won't clear his name."

"But the doubt will be out there. What other evidence was fabricated against him? The CIA will have to take a second look." She dragged her purse from the floor of the back seat and fished her phone from the side pocket. Scanning through her contacts, she said, "I'm not sure I have Sam Prescott's number on my phone, but it will be on my mom's computer."

"Whoa. You're going too fast." Cam splayed his hands across the steering wheel. "Don't you think you should talk to someone first? Get some advice?"

"That's why I'm going to call Sam." She pointed the corner of her phone at Cam.

"I suppose there's no point in waiting for Scott to bring Farah back home." Cam pulled away from the curb and made a U-turn in the middle of the street.

Martha's phone buzzed in her hand and she jerked it in front of her face. "I-it's Farah. It must be him."

"Answer it and put it on speaker."

"Farah?" Martha pressed a hand against her chest and her thundering heart.

"What's up? What's so urgent?" Hearing Farah's voice, clear if slow, sent a rush of relief flowing through Martha's body.

"You're okay?"

Cam put a hand on her arm and shook his head.

He was right. If Farah didn't know she was in danger, that just might save her. Her captor wouldn't have to kill her.

"Kinda woozy, but yeah. What's wrong? I got your voice mail from earlier. What was so urgent that you had to come out to my place?"

Martha cleared her throat. "Cam thought he left his cell phone at the bar and figured you and…Scott might've picked it up."

"I didn't notice any phone. We left pretty soon after you did. Are you going to tell me about Cam? He's a hot hunk of man, girl."

Martha snuck a peak at Cam, who rolled his eyes. He'd probably heard that line a million times.

"Where are you, Farah?" Cam poked her in her sore ribs. "A-Are you home now?"

"No. Scott treated me to a hotel suite. I was so out of it, he thought a nice spa day tomorrow would make me feel better. Isn't that sweet?"

Martha gritted her teeth. "He's still married, Farah. You need to get out of that relationship."

Farah giggled. "Shh. You're on speakerphone and Scott just heard that. That's just Martha, baby. You know this suits me just fine."

A chill snaked up Martha's back. She knew whose idea it was for Farah to broadcast this call.

Scott shouted from the background. "You're totally right, Martha. Maybe Farah and I should end this relationship—for good, but we'll enjoy ourselves for now. I'm not going to hurt Farah, and she's free to leave me whenever she wants—after I pamper her for a few days."

"Aww, see what you did, Martha? You let me worry about my own affairs…and you can concentrate on that handful of man you have. By the way, did Cam ever find his phone?"

"He did, thanks."

"Okay, then. I'll see you later."

"Be…have fun."

"We will." Farah ended the call on another giggle.

Martha cupped the dead phone in her hands. "That call was a message to us. Farah is safe…for now, as long as she doesn't discover his true motives."

"He can't keep her at that hotel forever."

"Two days. I think she's taking a few days off this week for Thanksgiving, and as long as he has her there, we can't call the police." She tucked her hands between her bouncing knees. "He as good as threatened her."

"Do you still want to consult that attorney?"

"I have to." Her voice shook, and she shot a sideways glance at Cam to see if he noticed.

He reached over and pinched her chin. "I'm sorry you lost your glasses."

"I have contacts at my mom's."

By the time they reached her mother's house, it was past midnight. Martha's knees trembled as Cam opened the front door for her, and it wasn't due to the aches and pains racking her body from the tumble out of the car.

Would she and Cam share a bed again tonight? Would they make love? The clicking clock on their time together echoed in her head, marked her every breath.

Once she contacted Sam and came clean, she might lose her job, she might go to jail, but none of that mattered as much as the looming threat of losing Cam.

Could a member of Delta Force ever be involved with a spy, a federal criminal?

Cam tapped the alarm system. "Arm it, even though our guy will be spending the night somewhere else."

"Unless he drugs Farah again and sneaks out." She punched in the code for the alarm system and tossed her purse into a chair. "How long does he expect to buy my silence by holding a threat over Farah's head? Once I go to the authorities and tell all, Farah will know everything."

Cam walked to the kitchen with a hitch in his step and reached for a glass.

"I didn't even ask if you were okay." She followed him into the kitchen and wrapped her arms around his waist from behind. "You took the brunt of that tumble from the car."

He lifted his broad shoulders. "I took it like a football tackle. I know how to fall and roll."

"With a gangly woman attached to your body?"

He threw back the water and kissed her mouth with wet lips. "That was the best part. Should we undress each other slowly and inspect our bodies for injuries?"

"Is that a new line?"

"I don't know. Will it work?"

"You don't need any lines to get me into bed, Cam Sutton." She skimmed her hands across his face and flicked his earlobe, which sported a spot of dried blood. "But I do think we need a soak in the bathtub first to clean all our boo-boos."

"Is *that* a new line, 'cause I gotta tell you, discussing my...boo-boos is a total turnoff."

She rested her head against his chest. Her lips formed a smile, but a tear leaked from the corner of her eye and she sniffled.

Drawing away, he wedged a knuckle beneath her chin and tilted back her head. "I'm sorry. Boos-boos are a turn on. Gives me a chance to take care of you."

She sniffed, but he coaxed a bigger smile from her. "When I'm in federal prison sharing a cell block with my dad, will the army forbid you from fraternizing with an enemy of the state?"

He snorted. "I just might be in the next cell block over."

"What do you mean?" She wrinkled her nose. "You haven't done anything wrong?"

He lifted one eyebrow. "Really? I have knowledge about your theft of those emails and failed to disclose that intelligence. I helped you clean evidence off your computer. I stumbled upon a murder scene and didn't report it. I could go on, but I'm sure your attorney can fill you in."

Her chest tightened as she dug her fingernails into Cam's biceps. "I can't do it. I can't do that to you."

He scooped his hands through her hair. "You do what you have to do to stay safe, Martha."

"Not if it's going to put you in jeopardy."

He pulled her head down and kissed the top. "Let's talk to that lawyer first…but not before we take a bath and check out each other's bodies."

She took the glass from his hand and drank the rest of the water. "Deal."

Just in case Cam thought she was kidding about the bath, she threw open the door of the master bathroom and cranked on the faucets for the sunken, oval tub while he prowled around downstairs, securing every door and window in the place.

By the time he joined her upstairs, Martha had a tub full of steaming, scented bubbles and candles.

He hung on the doorjamb and whistled. "I should've brought up two glasses of wine."

"That would probably put me to sleep, and I'm still trying to get the taste of that other wine out of my mouth."

Two steps took him into the room, and he slid his hands beneath her robe and squeezed her shoulders. "Do you still think he put something in your wine?"

"He sure put something in Farah's."

"But you feel okay? No strange aftereffects?"

"I'll feel better once I crawl into that warm water." She dropped her phone on top of a basket full of rolled-up towels and dipped her toe past the bubbles and into the water. "It's perfect."

He slipped the robe from her shoulders and kissed the side of her neck. "You're perfect."

Cam shrugged off his clothes, they shared a long kiss before sliding into the tub together. Despite

Cam's size, the cavernous bathtub allowed him to stretch out. He settled her between his legs and ran his hands gingerly across her back.

"You're going to have a few bruises back here."

"I'm glad that's all. I expected some broken bones." She scooped up a handful of bubbles and scattered them with a breath from her pursed lips. "Do you think Farah's okay?"

"He doesn't want to harm her. He doesn't want to harm you."

"Cam, why do you think he's still here? He planted the emails with me, or an associate did, he took care of his loose ends by killing Wentworth, Casey and Tony. What more does he want? He knows, or at least he thinks he knows, that I'm not going anywhere with the info I have. Where would I go? Implicating him implicates me."

"He's still looking for whatever Casey left behind." Cam's hands made waves in the water pooling over her belly. "He knows you don't have it, and he wants to find it before you do."

"We searched through her stuff. There's nothing there that implicates him or anyone else. What could it be?"

"Maybe it was just his identity, and now that we have that—or at least who he's pretending to be—he has Farah. I guess he believes that will stop us from turning him in."

"Well, he's right, but how long can he keep her? Like you said before, he can't make her stay in that hotel forever. She'll have her spa day tomorrow, and another few days, but what then?"

His hands floated toward her breasts, and he cupped them. "You're safe. Farah's somewhat safe, and you're going to talk to your father's attorney tomorrow. There's nothing left for us to do tonight. Let me make you feel better."

She succumbed to the sweet kisses and gentle caresses that slowly stoked the embers of her passion, so different from the fiery explosions of last night.

By the time they returned to her bedroom, Cam had to pour her limp body onto the sheets. He whispered in her ear, "You're still going to need some ibuprofen tomorrow."

She burrowed under the covers. "Bring it on. I feel ready for anything right now."

The bed dipped as Cam snuggled in behind her. His arm draped heavily across her midsection, and his leg hitched over her hip. She felt engulfed by him, and she soaked up the feeling, trying to drown out the thought of his departure that echoed in her head like a hollow drumbeat.

The buzzing of her cell replaced the dirge, and her lids flew open. "It has to be him."

Cam bolted upright and made a grab for her phone. He squinted at the display. "It's not Farah. Unknown number."

"It's him." She snapped her fingers, and Cam held out the phone to her. She tapped in her password and swiped open the text.

"Is it Scott?"

Tilting her head to the side, Martha blew a wisp of hair from her eyes as she read the text. A cold fist squeezed her heart, and she dropped the phone with a gasp.

Cam snatched it up. "Is it him? Is it that bastard?"

"No. It's a text from a dead woman."

Chapter Fourteen

Martha's pale face stood out in the darkness of the room. Cam fumbled with the light switch on the wall to turn on the ceiling fans above the bed, and brought the phone close to his face.

"Casey? Is it from Casey?"

"H-how can that be?"

The letters on the display swam before Cam's eyes, the words they formed, nothing but gibberish to his brain. "What did she write? What does it say?"

"Read it." Martha had folded her hands together, her knuckles as white as the sheets beneath them, seemingly incapable or unwilling to take the phone from him.

He made another pass at the jumbled words on the screen, and then shoved the phone between her wrists. "I can't, damn it. I can't read it, Martha."

His words shocked her out of her stupor, and she picked up the cell and read aloud the words from Casey. "'Martha, it's me, Casey. If you get this message after I've disappeared, I locked myself out. I'm sorry.'"

"Locked herself out?" Cam tipped his head back against the headboard and stared at the ceiling. "If she locked herself out, she'd get the key from the zippered cover of the lawn chair, but we already looked there. She must be referring to the message she left you about Tony."

"Did she even send that message, Cam? How? How do we know it came from her?"

"She scheduled the text to be delivered at a later date. She obviously knew she'd taken a step too far, knew her life was in danger." He folded one arm behind his head. "Why wouldn't it be from her? You and she are the only ones who know about the hiding place for the key, right?"

"I never told anyone, and as flakey as she was, I don't think Casey did, either, well, except Tony."

"Another reason is that Scott would have no need to send you a message like that. Why would he want to further pique your curiosity or provide you with any more evidence to bring to the authorities that Casey was anything more than a suicide?"

Martha had been panting, sipping in short spurts of air. Filling her lungs, she closed her eyes. "I guess Casey really wanted me to talk to Tony."

"Do you think that's it?"

"What do you mean?" Martha asked.

"Maybe there's something more. Maybe this is

what we've been waiting for, what Scott has been looking for."

"We looked in the cushion and found the key with the note. Are you saying there's something more?"

"It's a big, square cushion. You shoved your fingers into the zippered opening, found the key and the note. We didn't look for anything else. We didn't know there was anything else."

"The phone?"

"If we found that phone and it contained instructions from Scott, aka Ben, regarding Congressman Wentworth and the emails, we'd have some real proof against this guy. You wouldn't even have to admit to taking the emails. Your roommate died, you got this message from the grave and you found the phone. It all smelled like yesterday's fish, and you did your duty as a citizen and CIA employee and turned it over."

"You're making a lot of assumptions. Maybe she did just want me to contact Tony. It could be nothing more than that."

Cam flicked off the light and slid back beneath the covers. "Or a whole lot more."

The following morning while they ate breakfast, Martha called Farah. When she ended the call, she picked up her fork and poked at the eggs on her plate. "She sounds fine, happy."

"Was she suspicious that you were calling her?"

"A little. I don't know if you heard, but I told her I wanted to check on her because she didn't sound well last night."

"As long as you didn't spook her and didn't spook Scott." Cam rinsed off his plate and stacked it in the sink. "He's keeping your silence today by holding on to Farah, but what about tomorrow and the days to follow?"

"Maybe he plans to leave the capital and isn't worried even if I do report him. Is Farah ever going to believe Scott drugged and kidnapped her? As far as she's concerned, he's treating her to a spa day. What about your friend on the police force?"

"I called him this morning, but I can't get the glass to him until tomorrow. I could just hold on to it and turn it over to the FBI once we report our suspicions about Farah's boyfriend. And your father's attorney? Have you called him?"

"While you were in the shower. He wants a video conference with us later this afternoon." She held up her plate to him and he took it.

"Everything has to wait until we go back to your place and search that cushion for further evidence." He loaded the rest of their breakfast dishes from the sink into the dishwasher.

"You got a text." Martha held up his phone.

Cam dried his hands on a towel and hunched over the counter, holding out his hand for the phone. Martha dropped it in his palm and he opened the text.

"D-do you need any help reading it?"

He glanced up, a warm flush creeping up his neck to the roots of his hair. "Last night was just because of the stress of the situation. I'm okay."

"I'm sorry."

"Don't be. It's all right. I'm glad you asked." He held his phone under the light and read the text. "It's from one of my teammates, Joe. He's asking about my progress."

"Is he in the States?"

"Just arrived. He's taking leave for Christmas."

"What are you going to tell him?"

"The truth. That we're onto something and the emails were a setup, just as we suspected—not that we ever believed anything else."

"We'd better get going. If we find further evidence in that seat cushion linking Scott to the murders, we'll have something more to discuss with Sam."

On the drive to Martha's town house, Cam texted back and forth with Joe. He wanted to warn him, just as Martha kept pointing out to him, that even if they could prove some foreign entity planted the emails implicating Denver, there was still the rest of the evidence against him. They wouldn't be able to clear his name right away, but this had to be a start.

The reporters had cleared out from the front of Martha's town house. Another Washington scandal had already diverted their attention, and Martha hadn't been around for days.

She pulled her car up to the curb. "I might as well collect my mail while I'm here and water some plants."

"First things first." Cam looked up and down the street. A few pedestrians walked to and from their cars. One with a dog waved to Martha and she waved back. Nobody looked suspicious, but then Scott was guarding his pampered captive.

Martha unlocked the front door, and Cam nudged her aside to walk in first. "Anything out of place?"

"Not this time, but I'm going to check Casey's room again." She bounded up the stairs ahead of him, and his heart pounded as he followed on her heels.

"Wait." He stopped her before she opened Casey's door. Holding his breath, he pushed it open.

The neat row of bags and the suitcase they'd packed up the other day greeted him, and he blew out a gust of air. "At least nobody's been back."

"I'm sure changing the locks helped." Martha placed her hands on her hips and surveyed the room. "Incredible I haven't even heard from Casey's mom yet."

"Do you know if they've made arrangements for her body?"

"I couldn't tell you." Martha wandered to the window and pressed her nose against the glass. "The patio furniture's still where we left it."

"Let's go take it apart."

They went downstairs and out the back door. Martha crouched beside the same chair.

"It wouldn't be in the other one?"

"We always used the same cushion for the key." She pulled the zipper back. This time she shoved her whole hand into the cover, wrinkling her nose. When most of her arm disappeared into the cushion, she squeaked. "I got it. Cam, it's a phone."

His pulse jumped. "It must be the phone she used for contact with Ben."

Martha pulled out the type of phone typically sold as temp phones, and framed it in her hand. She pressed and held a button. "It's dead."

"Maybe she has a charger in her room. Did you see something?"

"I think just her regular smartphone charger." She pressed the phone to her chest. "This is huge, Cam. This is what Scott was looking for, what he was afraid I'd find."

"He must've thought Casey would have the phone on her when he lured her to that hotel room to kill her. When he couldn't find it, he took her keys instead and searched her room for it."

"It must have evidence pointing to him, or he wouldn't have wanted it so badly." A dog barked and Martha jumped.

Cam grabbed her arm. "Let's go inside and find the charger. I cleaned out her desk and dumped a bunch of items in a plastic bag. It could be in there."

Once inside, Cam took the stairs two at a time, clutching the phone in his fist. If the FBI could use the evidence on this phone to tie Scott to the murders and implicate him in the faked emails, Martha could completely avoid scrutiny for stealing the messages.

He pounced on the plastic bag containing the

items from Casey's desk and dumped the contents onto the floor.

Martha dropped beside him and pawed through the papers, pens and business cards. She grabbed a black cord, pulled it free from the mess and dangled it from her fingers. "This could be it."

He grabbed the swinging end and compared it to the outlet on Casey's phone. "I think it is."

He inserted the USB into the phone and it clicked into place. "That's it."

Martha sprang to her feet in one movement. "Let's charge it downstairs. I take back every bad thing I said about Casey. Would a flake think to hide her cell phone where she knew I'd find it?"

"Not so fast. She's still a spy who stole secrets from a US congressman and worse...put her roommate's life in danger."

They traipsed down the stairs, and Martha pointed him to an outlet in the kitchen.

"Let's get this going. I can't wait to see what's on this phone."

Cam plugged the power cord into the outlet. "I suppose we can sit here and stare at it until it juices up."

The doorbell echoed through the house, and Martha gripped the edge of the counter. "Scott wouldn't be ringing my bell, would he?"

Cam pulled his gun from his jacket pocket and jerked his thumb at the door. "Check it out."

Martha crept to the door, crouching below the

fan-shaped window at the top so the visitor couldn't see her coming. Cam stayed to the side, his gun at the ready.

She ducked her head and peered through the peep-hole. She whispered. "It's Sebastian."

"That guy you dated from work?" Cam rolled his eyes. "What does he want, a date? You don't have to answer the door."

"Martha? It's just Sebastian. I know you're home because I saw your car on the street. No press out here if you're worried."

Martha shrugged and slipped back the dead bolt. She opened the door wide enough so that Sebastian could see Cam hovering behind her.

He'd pocketed his weapon.

"This is a surprise."

"Is it?" Sebastian's eyes behind his glasses darted from Martha's face to Cam's. "I've been worried about you. First the congressman, then Casey and now the suspension from work."

"Speaking of work, why aren't you there?"

"I'm taking the whole week off for Thanksgiving. Aren't you going to visit your mother?"

"With all this going on—" she swept her arm behind her to encompass Cam "—I completely forgot about Thanksgiving."

Sebastian smiled and seemed to dig his Oxfords into the mat on Martha's porch. If Martha thought she was getting rid of this guy, she wasn't reading his signals.

"D-do you want to come in for a few minutes? We were just on our way out. I'm not staying here."

"At your mom's?" Sebastian stepped across the threshold, and a muscle ticked in Cam's jaw. This guy seemed to know a lot about Martha's family, but she *did* date him. Probably had a genius IQ.

Martha nodded toward Cam. "Sebastian, this is Cam. Cam, Sebastian."

Cam gave him a handshake that could've brought him to his knees if he'd kept it up, but he released his grip just as a grimace started to twist the other man's lips.

Sebastian put his hand behind his back. "Nice to meet you. Friend of Martha's?"

"Uh-huh." Cam wandered back to the charging phone and perched on the stool next to it while Martha and Sebastian talked.

She offered him a soda and he accepted. She couldn't be rude and kick the guy out?

As she walked toward the kitchen, her back to Sebastian, she rolled her eyes at Cam and pointed at the phone.

He shook his head.

She returned to Sebastian with a can in each hand and joined him on the sofa, where he'd made himself comfortable.

Cam ground his back teeth. Why was Sebastian here, anyway? Martha had made it clear they were over.

Cam kept one eye on the phone, and one ear on

the conversation between Martha and Sebastian. He couldn't help it. Since his reading skills had been so poor in school, he'd honed his listening comprehension skills to an art.

Sebastian knew a lot about Martha's family, her father's situation, her mother's house. Her likes and dislikes. Their conversation had turned to art, and Cam felt a little bit of panic. Did he know enough about art to converse with Martha about it?

Martha said, "I'm not sure I know that artist."

"His work is similar to the print you have in your room."

"The Gaspar?"

Cam snorted softly. What the hell was a Gaspar?

Then something clicked in his brain, and his head twisted slowly to the side. Her room? The print in Martha's bedroom? Unless she'd been lying, Martha had told him she'd never slept with Sebastian, that he'd been to her place just twice and had never made it past the entryway.

How could he know what was in her bedroom—unless he'd seen it from her laptop camera, which he'd hacked into as the patriot?

Chapter Fifteen

Martha swallowed. "The Gaspar? In my bedroom?"

Sebastian licked his lips, his tongue flicking out of his mouth like a snake's. "The one you told me about."

Martha's eye twitched. Two seconds later, Cam barreled across the room and grabbed Sebastian by the neck.

Martha shouted, "What are you doing?"

"He's the patriot, Martha. He's the one who hacked your computer. He's the one who IDed you as the CIA employee to set up. He sent Scott to your mother's house, and Scott probably sent him here to watch your place while he's with Farah."

Martha's mouth dropped open, but every word Cam said she knew to be true. Sebastian had set her up, and he'd probably set up Farah, too.

Sebastian gagged and choked as his face turned blue above Cam's powerful hand clutching his throat.

"Let him go, Cam. You're choking him."

He uncurled his fingers, and Sebastian slumped to the sofa, coughing.

Cam got in his face. "Start spilling."

Sebastian rubbed his throat. "You're crazy. I don't know what you're talking about."

"You can choose that route if you want." Cam pushed away from the sofa and held up the charging phone. "But we have Casey's burner phone. Is that what Scott sent you here to find?"

Sebastian dropped his head in his hands. "I—I didn't know it would go this far. It started with information. I was approached on an overseas trip. It was the money. They offered me so much money. You wouldn't know what it's like, Martha. You, with your privileged background. I had so much student loan debt, it was suffocating me."

"Oh, I thought you were doing it because you were such a *patriot*." Martha jumped up and took a turn around the room.

"How did this email plan start and why?" Cam slammed his fist in his palm. "Why Major Denver?"

Sebastian held up his hands as if deflecting physical blows. "I don't know anything about any of that. I was just asked to identify someone at Langley who would turn over a set of emails, no questions asked. I knew Martha would do it. I knew how she felt about her father's crimes."

"Oh my God. You used our conversations against me."

"It was nothing, Martha. You didn't have to be

involved any more than turning over those emails—
and then you broke bad."

"Ha!" She tossed her head. "That's quite a charge
coming from someone involved in espionage against
the government."

"It was more than just the emails. You helped
Scott set up the liaison between Casey and Congress-
men Wentworth, putting Martha in further danger."

"Martha was never supposed to be in danger."

"But she was." Cam smacked his hand against the
wall, and Sebastian's eyes widened as his Adam's
apple bobbed in his skinny neck.

How had she ever been remotely interested in
him?

"I wanna know why Scott is still here. Why didn't
he murder those people and get out of town?"

"I-I'm not sure."

Cam stalked toward him, and Sebastian shrank
against the sofa cushion. "I swear. I don't know.
Maybe it's the phone. He wants to make sure we secure Casey's phone first."

His fist clenched, Cam loomed over Sebastian.
"Who's he with? Who is Scott working with?"

"I swear. I don't know any of that."

All three heads swiveled toward a buzzing noise
from the phone.

"It's operational." Cam stepped away from Sebastian, flexing his fingers as if he'd gone through
with the hit.

As Cam strode toward the counter, Sebastian half rose from the sofa, and Martha said, "Cam!"

He swung around and leveled a finger at Sebastian, who'd stopped in midrise. "Sit."

Cam grabbed the phone and tapped it awake. "No password."

"Check the texts." Martha cast a nervous glance at Sebastian, who looked ready to bolt at any minute.

Cam's eyebrows collided over his nose, and he thrust the phone out to Martha. "You look through it, while I watch our spy here."

She took the phone from him.

Martha saw just two sets of texts, and one was the single text to her phone. The other was to a number, no name attached to it. It had to be the man Casey knew as Ben and they knew as Scott, but Martha would bet her town house that both names were false.

"The most recent text is the one directing Casey to the hotel for a meeting. She must've received that text, scheduled her text to me and then hid the phone in the hiding place for our key." Martha held up the phone. "This is enough to cast suspicion on Ben, even if this is a temp phone for him."

"Ben? Who the hell is Ben?" Sebastian shoved his glasses up the bridge of his nose.

Cam growled. "Ben is your buddy Scott. You know, the guy you set up with your coworker Farah. The guy who murdered three people."

"Ben?" Sebastian emitted a high-pitched, hysterical laugh. "He got that from when I told him I felt like a regular Benedict Arnold, and I had to explain who he was."

"He didn't know Benedict Arnold?"

"I don't think so."

"You were right about those emails, Martha. They came from a foreign entity, a non-native speaker." Cam twirled his finger in the air. "What else? What other texts are between the two of them."

Martha backtracked through the conversation between Casey and Ben. "There's not a lot of substance here. It's mostly Ben setting up meetings. He must've been very careful about committing anything to text or probably even telephone conversations. I don't know why he was so worried about our finding this phone."

"Those texts are going to cast suspicion on Casey's death and Wentworth's. Maybe that's all we need."

Cam dragged a chair from the dining area, placed it in front of Sebastian and straddled it. "Here's what you're gonna do. We're gonna contact the FBI, and you're gonna confess to your crimes. You're gonna tell them about those faked emails and give them everything you know about Ben or Scott or whatever he calls himself. I have his fingerprints on a glass, and maybe we can get his real identity from his prints—even if it has to come from Interpol."

"We have to wait the rest of the day, Cam. He still has Farah, and if he finds out Sebastian went to the FBI, he could harm her."

"I—I can't stay here the rest of the day." Sebastian looked wildly from Martha to Cam. "I have plans for Thanksgiving."

Martha tapped Casey's phone against her chin. "What are we going to do with him? If we let him leave, he might disappear. If we call the FBI now, we put Farah in danger."

"If we let him leave, he just might go back to the office and try to destroy the evidence that points to him as the one who got those emails to your computer."

"Wait. You can't keep me a prisoner." Sebastian shook his finger at Martha. "You're in a lot of trouble, Martha *Brockridge*."

"That makes two of us."

"We'll keep him here until Farah is safe. Maybe—" Cam drummed his fingers on the chair back "—we'll have him contact Ben and let him know he got Casey's phone."

"What? No!" Sebastian had turned even whiter. "He'd expect me to bring it to him right away."

"I still don't understand why tomorrow is some magic date for Ben. He releases Farah tomorrow, and we go through with our plans to report him once she's safe."

"He obviously plans to leave tomorrow."

"But why not leave today?"

Sebastian's eyebrows jumped to his hairline. "Why are you two looking at me? I told you. I don't know any of his plans. I'm paid for my contacts within the Agency and my access to and knowledge of its computers. That's it. When Wentworth died and then Casey, I knew everything had exploded."

Martha smoothed her thumb along the curve of Casey's phone. "If he's willing to give up Farah to-morrow and take off, let him. I suppose he figures once he's out of the country, the FBI won't be able to track him down. But at least he'll be out of my life, and Sebastian can testify to the falsity of the emails."

"I won't know the why or who behind the setup of Major Denver though."

"Maybe once the FBI and CIA get a handle on Ben, it'll give them a good idea." She came up be-hind Cam and rubbed his shoulders. She couldn't help that Sebastian's bug eyes at the gesture gave her a thrill of satisfaction.

Casey's phone slipped from her hand and landed at Cam's foot. He bent forward to pick it up. "I'm not looking forward to spending the night with this guy, but... What's this?"

"What?" She leaned over his shoulder and looked at the phone cupped in his hand.

"Pictures. You didn't check the phone's photos, did you?"

"No." She knelt beside him, and even Sebastian hunched forward.

Cam's finger brushed across the display. "They're documents. Security plans and diagrams."

"For what?"

"I'm not sure yet. Casey must've gotten these

from Wentworth. Tony told us she would get info from the congressman and pass it along to Ben. This must be part of that."

"Why would Ben want this type of information?"

"To gain knowledge of the security plans for a building or place…and bypass it."

Sebastian exhaled a noisy breath. "A terrorist attack. You'd want intel like that to plan a terrorist attack."

"He's right." Cam's lips formed a thin line. "And this is what Ben doesn't want us to see. He knows these pictures are on this phone."

When Cam swiped to the next picture, his body jolted. "It's the Mall, the monuments on the National Mall."

Martha crossed her arms over her chest. "And it's going down tomorrow."

Chapter Sixteen

"Answer it." Cam handed Sebastian his ringing phone, pressing the button on the side to activate the speaker.

They'd forced Sebastian to text Ben from Casey's phone to let him know he'd found it at Martha's town house. The response from Ben had been instantaneous.

Sebastian cleared his throat. "Scott."

"So you found it. How?"

"I—I remembered when I was dating Martha she told me Casey was always losing or forgetting her key, so they had a hiding place. I found the phone there."

"Did you look at anything on the phone?"

"Just the texts." Sebastian licked his lips. "Did you want me to look for something?"

"No, just bring it to me in two hours."

"Where are you?"

Cam dug his fingers into his biceps as they waited a beat for Ben's response.

"I took Farah to the St. Regis to get her out of the way while all this was happening. I didn't want her questioning Martha too closely about anything."

"Good idea."

"I don't need your approval, geek. Just bring me the phone."

Sebastian turned bright red. "Sure, sure. Am I supposed to see Farah while I'm there?"

"No need for that. We're ordering dinner up to our room tonight. I'll make an excuse to get ice or something, and you can meet me at the vending machines down the hall. Text me from the phone when you get here, so I know you still have it."

"Is this going to get me a bonus?" Sebastian wiped his upper lip with the back of his hand.

"Bonus?" Ben chuckled. "Sure, I'll give you a bonus."

When Sebastian ended the call, he gagged. "He's going to kill me."

Cam snatched the phone from his hand. "I'll try to save you...after I take care of Ben."

"And after I get Farah out of that room."

"Don't worry, Sebastian." Cam smacked him on the back. "This will all look better for you when you make your confession."

After a few informative hours at Martha's town house where Sebastian spilled his guts on video, Cam wiped Casey's phone clean and handed it to Sebastian.

"No tricks."

"Tricks? I don't have any tricks. I just want this to be over. I never imagined Ben would be planning a terrorist attack on our soil."

"So, it's okay on someone else's soil?" Martha yanked her coat from a hook by the door. "Your actions endangered so many lives."

"I didn't think."

"For a smart guy like you, that's quite an admission." Cam shoved his gun in his pocket. "Let's go."

With Sebastian in the back seat and Cam in the passenger seat beside her, Martha drove to the St. Regis near the Mall. "I guess he wanted to stay close to the site of his attack."

A valet took Martha's car, but they walked around to a side entrance. Their whole plan would blow up in their faces if Ben or Farah saw them in the lobby of the hotel.

They slipped through a side door and once inside, Cam prodded Sebastian in front of him until they reached an empty hallway leading to some restrooms. He slammed Casey's phone against Sebastian's chest. "Send the text."

He watched over Sebastian's shoulder as he texted the words, I'm here. Cam could read those words clear as day.

Less than a minute later, Ben called Sebastian on his own phone. Cam bent close to Sebastian's ear so he could hear the conversation.

"Where are you?"

"Lobby."

"I'm on the tenth floor. On one end of that floor, around the corner from the elevators, there's an alcove with vending and ice machines. Meet me there, hand over the phone and take your money. We're done."

"Will you be contacting me for further assignments?"

"We're done."

Ben ended the call.

Cam held out his hand. "I'll take that."

Sebastian dropped his phone into Cam's palm. "I just hope he doesn't call me again on my phone."

"Why would he?" He slipped Casey's phone into Sebastian's front pocket. "If you use that phone to double-cross me, I'll make sure I kill you both."

A bead of sweat ran down the side of Sebastian's face. "I'll follow the plan."

Cam turned to Martha. "As soon as I give you the signal from the stairwell, you text Farah and tell her to get out of that room as soon as she can. Once she's safe, call that number I gave you for the FBI. I'll surprise Ben in the vending room."

"Be careful." Martha grabbed his hand and pressed her lips against his cheekbone. "I may be losing you in a week, but I'm not going to lose you forever."

"I'm not gonna let that happen. Who's going to help me read my texts?" He kissed her mouth as Sebastian watched their exchange with round eyes.

"And you." He poked his finger in Sebastian's

chest. "Give us a few minutes to climb ten flights of stairs before you even punch that elevator button."

"Got it."

They edged around the corner of the hallway and started to cross the lobby for the bank of elevators and the stairwell across from it. Their path took them past the crowded lobby bar.

"Martha?"

The voice sent a surge of adrenaline through Cam's veins, and he spun around. He made a grab for Martha's hand, but Farah had moved between them.

His gaze met Ben's above the women's heads, and his gut twisted.

Sebastian made a strange gulping sound beside him.

"Go, Martha!" His shout barely made it above the music and conversation spilling out of the bar. He'd reacted too late, anyway.

Ben had Martha's arm and was pulling her back toward him.

Farah's dark eyebrows formed a V over her nose. "What's going on? What are you doing here? Sebastian? What are *you* doing here?"

Cam saw the flash of the blade in Ben's hand as he pressed it against Martha's side.

"Now I have a bigger prize." Ben smiled through his words as if they were all part of the convivial bar scene behind them.

"I—I don't understand." Farah's head was snapping back and forth between Ben and Martha, and Cam and Sebastian.

Cam took Farah's hand and pulled her toward him. "You're safe now."

"Safe?" Farah sobbed and stretched her hand out. "Martha?"

Martha drew back her shoulders and straightened her spine, standing taller than the man who held her at knifepoint. "The man you know as Scott is planning a terrorist attack."

"No, I..."

"Shh." Ben put his finger to his lips. "Quiet, Farah, unless you want to see your friend hurt. I at least had some feelings for you. Her? I don't care about her at all."

Farah's shoulders slumped and she dropped her head.

Cam pulled Farah behind him. "What are you going to do with Martha?"

"Just like Farah, Martha stays with me until I can conduct my business tomorrow."

Cam ground his words through his teeth. "Your business is terror, mayhem, murder of innocents."

"So is yours, Sergeant Sutton."

A lash of heat whipped through Cam's body, and he curled his fists. "You'll have to kill all of us to carry out your plan. We all know."

"I think I just need Martha. Do you want to see her die right here and now to save a bunch of strangers on the Mall tomorrow? And how do you know I don't have others to take my place?"

"Oh, we'll be prepared for you and others like you. Planning a truck or van attack, aren't you? Planning to mow down some civilians? Once I outline your plans to the FBI and DC Metro Police, they'll be ready for you."

That got him.

Ben's eyes, which had been focused on Cam the entire time, widened, and his arm slipped an inch from Martha's waist.

Cam would have to act here and now in the hotel lobby. He'd never allow this man to take Martha away from him—not now, not ever.

A muscle in his jaw twitched as he sensed movement behind him from Sebastian, who'd remained speechless and frozen up until this point.

Sebastian took a deep breath and shouted. "Help! Help!"

Ben's head jerked up, and Martha wrenched away from him, creating just enough space for Cam to make a move.

Cam lunged forward and grabbed the wrist of the hand that held the knife, and twisted. A woman in the bar screamed.

Ben made a thrusting motion to the side, and Cam slammed his body against Ben's, knocking him over, his hand still grappling for the knife.

They landed with a thud, and people began shouting around them. Hands grabbed at the back of Cam's jacket as moisture began seeping into the front of his shirt.

Ben released the knife, and Cam found himself in sole possession of it. He pushed himself off Ben, and the wound beneath Ben's heart began gushing blood.

"Cam?" Martha dropped to the floor, her hand on the back of his neck.

"I'm fine. It's not me." Cam looked into the dying man's eyes and grabbed the front of his shirt. "Not yet, you bastard. Who sent you? Why'd you set up Denver?"

A trickle of blood seeped from Ben's mouth as his lips curled into a smile.

Epilogue

Martha stretched out on the huge bed in the penthouse suite of the St. Regis and curled her toes. "It's a shame we have this big bed and end up crowding together in one corner of it every night."

"A shame?" Cam grabbed her foot and kissed her arch. "We can just crowd together on another corner of the bed if you want to make good use of it."

She sat up and wrapped her arms around Cam, burying her head against his chest. "Promise me you'll come back to me safe and sound after this deployment."

"That's the easy part." He ran his knuckles down her spine. "Promise me you won't engage in any more illegal activities."

"I'm done breaking bad, as Sebastian put it, although he's the one who's going to be spending time in federal prison."

"His actions after we confronted him went a long way toward reducing his sentence."

"And his sheer cowardice when he screamed and

started scrambling for his own safety allowed you to take down Ben." Martha suppressed a shiver. "I can't believe we wound up uncovering a terrorist attack. He had the van already rented and everything. There would've been plenty of people on the Mall the day before Thanksgiving."

Cam's muscles tensed beneath her touch. "He died before I could get any answers out of him, although we know he killed Tony and Casey and made sure Casey got together with Wentworth to get info from him about Denver."

"He must've killed Wentworth too after Casey got the info about Denver out of him, even though the authorities are still calling Wentworth's death a heart attack. Maybe they'll take a second look at that now that Interpol identified him as Alain Dumont, a Frenchman of Algerian descent, a man involved in petty crimes but with no known terrorist ties…but we know he's not working alone."

She rubbed his back. "His involvement with the emails is forcing the CIA to take a closer look at the evidence against Major Denver."

"A closer look is not clearing him."

"I know. I'm sorry." She flattened her hands against his chest and pushed away from him. "If you say he's innocent, I believe you and others will, too."

"Even Asher, one of our own teammates…" He shook his head. "I don't want to get into all that when we have just a few days left together. How's Farah holding up?"

"She's fine. Feels humiliated, but maybe this whole thing cured her of her propensity for unavailable men."

"No way she's going to top that guy for unavailability." Cam ran his hand up her thigh. "And you? Looks like you wound up with someone unavailable yourself."

"I'm willing to wait."

"Good, because I fell in love with the smartest girl in class, and I'm not about to let her slip through my hands." He scooped her into his lap and tore off her robe.

"Oh, I like where this is going, D-Boy." She reached for her glasses, and he grabbed her hand.

"Nope, I wanna make love to you wearing nothing but your glasses."

And then he did and the sparks flew.

* * * * *

*Look for the next book in
award-winning author Carol Ericson's new
Red, White and Built: Pumped Up miniseries,
Delta Force Daddy, available next month.*

*And don't miss the titles in her
Red, White and Built miniseries,
which introduced us to some sexy,
powerful Navy SEALs:*

Locked, Loaded and SEALed
Alpha Bravo SEAL
Bullseye: SEAL
Point Blank SEAL
Secured by the SEAL
Bulletproof SEAL

Available now from Harlequin Intrigue!

#1821 UNDERCOVER CONNECTION
by Heather Graham
FBI agent Jacob Wolff and Miami detective Jasmine Adair are frustrated when they discover they're both undercover to take down the same crime group. After their main informant is killed, can they find a way to work together to stop the ring before anyone else dies?

#1822 FIVE WAYS TO SURRENDER
Mission: Six • by Elle James
Navy SEAL Jake Schuler rescues Alexandria Parker, a teacher, from a group of terrorists in Niger. Will their teamwork be enough to save the other captives?

#1823 BULLETPROOF CHRISTMAS
Crisis: Cattle Barge • by Barb Han
Rory Scott returns to Cattle Barge on business, but his trip turns personal when he sees that Cadence Butler, a woman with whom he had an unforgettable fling, is pregnant. He will do anything to keep Cadence safe, especially since his unborn twins are in danger.

#1824 DELTA FORCE DADDY
Red, White and Built: Pumped Up • by Carol Ericson
Delta Force lieutenant Asher Knight has amnesia after a botched mission. When Paige Sterling claims she's his fiancée, he starts questioning everything around him, including whether the doctors at the rehabilitation center are helping him recover—or keeping him from remembering his past.

#1825 RENEGADE PROTECTOR
by Nico Rosso
Someone will do anything to get Mariana Balducci to sell her family orchard. Ty Morrison, a San Francisco cop and a member of a secret organization known as Frontier Justice, is Mariana's only hope...if she can trust him.

#1826 WYOMING CHRISTMAS RANSOM
Carsons & Delaneys • by Nicole Helm
Coroner Gracie Delaney has never believed Will Cooper's theory that the car accident that killed his wife two years ago was actually a murder. When Will's car is tampered with, causing a near-fatal crash, Gracie must accept that Will may be right. If so, a seasoned killer is now targeting Will.

An absolute melee had begun.

Jasmine helped up a young man, a white-faced rising star in a new television series. He tried to thank her.

"Get out, go—walk quickly," she said.

There were no more gunshots. But would they begin again?

She made her way to Josef Smirnoff, ducking beneath the notice of his distracted bodyguards. She knelt by him as people raced around her. "Josef?" she said, reaching for his shoulder, turning him over.

Blood covered his chest. Covered him. There was no hope for the man; he was already dead, his eyes open in shock. There was blood on her now, blood on the designer gown she'd been wearing, everywhere.

She looked up; Jorge had to be somewhere nearby.

That's when she knew she was about to be attacked herself.

There was a man coming after her, reaching for her.

She rolled quickly, avoiding him once. But as she prepared to fight back, she felt as if she had been taken down by a linebacker. She stared up into the eyes of the shaggy-haired newcomer. Bright blue eyes, startling against his face and dark hair. She felt his hands on her, felt the strength in his hold.

No. She was going to take him down.

She jack-knifed her body, letting him use his own weight against himself, causing him to crash into the floor.

He was obviously surprised; it took him a second—but only a second—to spin himself. He was back on his feet in a hunched position, ready to spring at her.

HIEXP1118

Where the hell was Jorge?

She feinted, as if she would dive down to the left, dove to the right instead, and caught the man with a hard chop to the abdomen that should have stolen his breath.

He didn't give; she was suddenly tackled again, down on the ground, feeling the full power of the man's strength atop her. She stared up into his eyes, blue eyes, glistening ice at the moment.

She realized the crowd was gone; she could hear the bustle at the doorway, hear the police as they poured in at the entrance.

But right there, at that moment Josef Smirnoff lay dead in an ungodly pool of blood—blood she wore—just feet away.

And there was this man.

And herself.

"Hey!" Thank God, Jorge had found her.

He dove down beside them, as if joining the fight.

But he didn't help Jasmine; he made no move against the man. He lay by Jasmine, as if he'd just been floored himself.

He whispered urgently, "Stop! FBI, meet MDPD. Jasmine, he's undercover. Jacob… Jasmine is a cop. My partner."

The man couldn't have looked more surprised. Then he made a play of socking Jorge, and Jorge lay still.

Jacob stood and dragged Jasmine to her feet. For a long moment he looked into her eyes, and then he wrenched her elbow behind her back.

"Play it out," he said, "nothing else to do."

"Sure," Jasmine told him.

And as he led her out—toward Victor Kozak, who now stood in the front, ready to take charge, Jasmine managed to twist and deliver a hard right to his jaw.

He swirled her around again, staring at her, and rubbing his jaw with his free hand.

"Play it out," she said softly.

Don't miss
Undercover Connection
by New York Times *bestselling author Heather Graham,
available November 20, 2018, wherever
Harlequin® Intrigue books and ebooks are sold.*

www.Harlequin.com

HIEXP1118

THE SEAGULL BOOK OF

Plays

Fourth Edition

THE SEAGULL BOOK OF

Plays

Fourth Edition

edited by Joseph Kelly

College of Charleston

W. W. Norton & Company · New York · London

To Spencer Jones

W. W. Norton & Company has been independent since its founding in 1923, when William Warder Norton and Mary D. Herter Norton first published lectures delivered at the People's Institute, the adult education division of New York City's Cooper Union. The Nortons soon expanded their program beyond the Institute, publishing books by celebrated academics from America and abroad. By mid-century, the two major pillars of Norton's publishing program—trade books and college texts—were firmly established. In the 1950s, the Norton family transferred control of the company to its employees, and today—with a staff of four hundred and a comparable number of trade, college, and professional titles published each year—W. W. Norton & Company stands as the largest and oldest publishing house owned wholly by its employees.

Composition by Cenveo.
Manufacturing by LSC Harrisonburg.
Book design by Chris Welch.
Production Managers: Lisa Kraege and Stephen Sajdak.

Library of Congress Cataloging-in-Publication Data

Names: Kelly, Joseph, 1962- editor.
Title: The seagull book of plays / edited by Joseph Kelly, College of Charleston.
Other titles: Seagull reader. Plays.
Description: Fourth edition. | New York : W. W. Norton & Company, 2017. |
    Includes bibliographical references and index.
Identifiers: LCCN 2017041601 | **ISBN 9780393631616 (pbk.)**
Subjects: LCSH: Drama—Collections. | Drama—History and criticism. | College readers.
Classification: LCC PN6112 .S36 2017 | DDC 808.82—dc23 LC record available at https://
lccn.loc.gov/2017041601

W. W. Norton & Company, Inc., 500 Fifth Avenue, New York, NY, 10110-0017
wwnorton.com

W. W. Norton & Company Ltd., 15 Carlisle Street,
London W1D 3BS

1 2 3 4 5 6 7 8 9 0

Contents

Acknowledgments

I would like to thank Susan Farrell, whose support throughout the production of this volume was invaluable. And I thank John Alvarez, whose student I was long ago: encouragement that he must have considered unremarkable was not.

Thanks also to Troy Appling of Florida Gateway College for authoring the Instructor's Guide and helping create the thematic index for this edition.

Along with the publisher, I am happy to thank the following for their valuable feedback during various stages of editing this edition:

Megan Anderson (Limestone College), Lena Andersson (Fulton-Montgomery Community College), Nancy Applegate (Georgia Highlands College), Troy Appling (Florida Gateway College), Michael J. Beilfuss (Oklahoma State University), Belle Boggs (North Carolina State University), J. T. Bushnell (Oregon State University), David Eugene Clark (Suffolk County Community College), Bonnie Dowd (Montclair State University), Claire Englehart (Glendale Community College), Sophie Freestone (Hartnell College), Evan Gottlieb (Oregon State University), James M. Hilgartner (Huntingdon College), Shawn Iden (Harper College), Timothy Jackson (Rosemont College), Ashley Kniss (Stevenson University), Barbara Krasner (William Paterson University), Stephanie Miller (Oklahoma State University), Cate Nelson (Dos Pueblos High School), Steven Nelson (Springfield Technical Community College), Susan Pelle (University of West Florida), Carissa Pokorny-Golden (Kutztown University), Haleh Risdana (Moorpark College), Theresa Scott (Hillsborough Community College–Southshore),

Scott Smith (Art Institute of San Antonio), Charmaine Vannimwegen (Riverside City College), Joshua Weiner (University of Maryland, College Park), and K. Siobhan Wright (Carroll Community College).

Note on Dates

After each play, we cite the date of first book publication on the right, and in a few instances (when the information may be relevant to the reading of a play), we cite the date of composition on the left.

*

What Is Drama?

Even if you have never read a play before, you have probably spent your life absorbing the skills necessary to read one. Anyone who has grown up going to the movies and watching television learned the common language of drama long ago. When your pulse races during a tense scene in a movie, or when you laugh at a pratfall in a sitcom, you're responding as you should when you read a play: exercising your best judgment of character, following and reacting to the manipulations of plot, and staying alert to underlying meanings.

Purely by instinct, you most likely react to drama with the "correct" emotions. These reactions don't happen accidentally, of course. Directors, scriptwriters, and playwrights avidly study human nature, and they use their knowledge of instinctual responses to push your emotional buttons. For example, they count on your responding in a particular way when you see a child in danger, in a different way when you see an attractive person disrobing by candlelight. But instinct is only half the story; many of your responses are shaped not by your instincts but by **dramatic conventions**—devices, phrases, or actions that have, over time, become so common that their meaning is immediately apparent. Without knowing it, you've internalized dozens of dramatic conventions. When you hear a violin playing in a minor key on a movie soundtrack, you, like most people, probably feel melancholy. That's not so much instinct as a learned response, even if you are not consciously aware of it. You don't need to *know* you've been conditioned to feel sad when you hear a violin in the background for your emotions to respond "correctly." The process has become automatic.

Dramatic Conventions Then and Now

While familiar dramatic conventions produce responses automatically (or nearly so), unfamiliar ones can seem strange and can elicit "incorrect" emotional responses. If you've ever struggled through Shakespeare or puzzled over Sophocles, your confusion might have resulted from unfamiliar conventions. The use of a **chorus** in ancient Greek theater—a group of singers and dancers who participate in or comment on the action—is a good example. When you first read Greek tragedy, the chorus's pronouncements can seem odd—unrealistic and alienating. Once you absorb the rules of this particular dramatic convention, however, the strangeness disappears.

Contemporary dramas don't use choruses (unless they're self-consciously, perhaps ironically, borrowing the ancient device) but the conventions of long-ago theater have modern counterparts. What these now-strange conventions accomplished for their audiences are accomplished today by other means, other conventions that contemporary audiences feel perfectly comfortable with and interpret without even noticing. One such convention is the "voiceover" narration common in movies. The voiceover would no doubt strike someone completely unfamiliar with film or television as very odd. Where, after all, is that voice *coming from*? Whose voice is it? And where, exactly, is the speaking supposed to be occurring? To the person asking questions such as these, the voiceover would be just as strange as the Greek chorus is to you today.

By learning about some of the older conventions of drama, and keeping in mind that contemporary forms of cultural expression have their own particular conventions, you should be able to overcome many of the difficulties inherent in reading plays written for past societies, even ones that have long since perished.

Cultural Context

Another possible confusion when reading plays written in the past has to do with cultural differences between you—the reader (or theatergoer)—and the characters inhabiting the play (and the playwright who created those characters). In all the plays reprinted in this book, the characters struggle with questions that remain pertinent: What is the meaning of existence? What constitutes a good life? How can men and women get along? Why must children contest their parents? Why is there suffering and injustice? As universal as these questions may be, however, the ways they are presented, and the assumptions that guide the characters' actions and words as they seek to answer them, are often rooted in a specific time and place—in a **cultural context**—that can seem unfamiliar and confusing now. But just as frequent exposure to dramatic conventions can make them seem familiar, learning about the time and place in which a play was written can help you respond to the work in a more direct and meaningful way.

Take an example from Shakespeare's *Hamlet* (page 45). Near the end of act 2, his fellow students Rosencrantz and Guildenstern inform Prince Hamlet about the late difficulties of a traveling group of tragic actors. In subsequent scenes, Hamlet digresses on the proper way to perform a play. Though the whole issue of acting troupes occupies hundreds of lines, it is so tangential to the main line of the play's action that modern directors, looking for places to cut this long play, often dispense with them altogether. To modern readers, Hamlet's long speeches on acting may prove confusing or, worse, intrusive and boring. But to Shakespeare's contemporaries, the lines made perfect sense, as a reference to a particular theatrical controversy going on at the time.

Theaters like the Globe, which Shakespeare co-owned and where most of his plays were performed, dominated theatrical London until about 1600, when a more exclusive type of theater developed. The Globe was an open-air structure where people from different social classes took in popular entertainments that mixed verbiage with physicality and were performed entirely by men and boys. In the alternative, private type of theater, the venues were smaller and enclosed. Admission was expensive, so the clientele tended to exclude the lower orders. Because the actors were children, the plays tended to be less raucous and bawdy (a company of boys could hardly have acted many scenes in a play like *Hamlet*); and they were seen as more erudite than the lowbrow affairs Shakespeare wrote.

So the strange digressions about theater in the second and third acts of *Hamlet* can be seen as Shakespeare's contribution to the bitter dispute among competing acting companies.

Henrik Ibsen's *A Doll's House* (page 173) provides another type of cultural dissonance between an older play—this one from nineteenth-century Europe—and contemporary readers. The plot hinges on a bit of contractual fraud that most readers today find fairly trivial. Whenever I teach the play, my students wonder why the characters make such a fuss about a course of events that would pretty well meet their own ethical standards. To feel any of the tension Ibsen meant you to feel, you have to understand how important public reputation was to a business career at the time, and how even a small slip could ruin a reputation.

Throughout this book, I keep footnotes to a minimum, but I use them to explain cultural differences like these that would otherwise make the plays harder to understand.

Page Versus Stage

Unlike a short story or a novel, a play is written not primarily for *reading*, but instead as the guiding text for *performing* a story onstage. When reciting lines, actors provide all sorts of physical cues—facial expressions and body language and tone of voice—that make the words more understandable, that deliver to their audience a thousand subtleties latent in the written words. For example:

> MAN: I'm through with everything here. I want peace. I want to see if somewhere there is something left in life with charm and grace. Do you know what I'm talking about?
> WOMAN: No. I only know that I love you.
> MAN: That's your misfortune.
> WOMAN: If you go, where shall I go? What shall I do?
> MAN: Frankly, my dear, I don't give a damn.

Once you reached the last line, you might have realized that this dialogue comes from the last scene of Victor Fleming's film *Gone With the Wind* (1939), in which Rhett Butler (Clark Gable) abandons a sobbing Scarlett O'Hara (Vivien Leigh) on the staircase of their mansion. If you've seen the film, you can probably conjure images of Gable and Leigh, he delivering his lines with cold disdain, she delivering hers with panicked desperation. But if you *haven't* seen the movie, you might wonder, reading the lines above, what all the fuss is about—why some people claim that the final scene of *Gone With the Wind* is one of the most powerful and memorable movie endings they've ever seen. Without the actors' intonations and gestures, without the sets and lighting, without dozens of contextual cues, the dialogue can seem dry.

Although plays can be enjoyed and studied as texts, fundamentally they are meant to be performed by a whole team of artists—directors, actors, set designers, and many others. When you read a play on the page, those artists are not present to help you imagine all aspects of the performance, as they would be if you saw the play performed. Therefore, your imagination needs to be fully engaged when you read—at every turn, you essentially decide how you would stage the play if you were the director.

After you've read a play once, you should try to see it performed—not as a *substitute* for your reading, of course, but as a *supplement*. It is not likely that you will have the chance to see a live performance of one of these plays during the time that you're studying it, but if you do, be sure to go. Probably, your library will have recordings of some productions, and you will find it very helpful to watch them. Watching the lines being brought to life often reveals subtleties of meaning that are barely perceptible in the text. This is especially true of Shakespeare. I often show my students scenes from Franco Zeffirelli's 1990 film adaptation of *Hamlet* and only then do they realize that Polonius is something of a fool, understand how betrayed Hamlet feels by Ophelia, and recognize the barely submerged sexual tension between Hamlet and his mother. But even more recent plays—plays with characters whose speech patterns are closer to our own, or with detailed stage directions—become more accessible when experienced in performance.

Perhaps more important, a performance helps you see that the very act of putting a play into action involves interpretation and analysis on the part of the director, the actors, and every other artist involved in the production—activities very similar to the interpretative and analytical work you do when you read the play on the page and form a version in your mind's eye. Each production of a play, even one that follows the text to the letter, differs from every other production, and the differences among productions reveal interesting differences of opinions about the play's meanings.

Before you can fully appreciate the differences among performances though, you need to understand the elements common to all drama. Let's turn to those elements now.

The Parts of a Play

Analysis means "a breaking down into parts." You do this whenever you come out of a movie arguing with your friends about one thing or another—did the main character deserve what he got? did you like or dislike so-and-so? and other questions of that nature. To answer those questions, you analyze the film, meaning you break it into parts and scrutinize these parts in some detail.

People have been breaking plays down into parts for over two thousand years. Aristotle, a Greek philosopher of the fourth century B.C.E., wrote the first great work of literary criticism, *Poetics*, not long after Sophocles wrote his tragedies. In fact, the *Poetics* drew on one of those plays, *Oedipus the King,* for most of its examples. Aristotle invented the first list of parts to drama: plot, (moral) character, spectacle, diction, melody, and thought. Over the centuries, these have been modified somewhat, but most discussions of dramatic form owe a debt to Aristotle's acute analysis of Greek theater.

Plot

The **plot** is the sequence of events that happen in a play. Generally, a play acts out a story before its audience, so that people in the audience feel as though they were witnessing the events. (Some specialized forms of drama, such as Samuel Beckett's extremely minimal monologues, do not work this way, but those genres are beyond the scope of this book.) And so a play includes all the elements you expect of a story:

1. It begins in some state of **equilibrium**, which is stable and often (though not necessarily) more or less pleasant.
2. A **conflict** is introduced into this state of equilibrium by some event (the **complication**).
3. Over the course of the play, the conflict grows (**rising action**).
4. The conflict comes to a head at the **climax**, which ends the conflict.
5. The climactic event brings about a sequence of consequences (**falling action**).
6. Finally, the plot reaches its **resolution**, a concluding situation that rests in another state of equilibrium, though the condition of the characters is probably different from what it was at the story's beginning.

These elements constitute just about any plot. The story in nearly every mainstream movie, television drama, short story, novel, narrative poem, or play can be broken down into these parts.

Let's take a simple fairy tale for an example, say the story of the Three Little Pigs. An initial state of equilibrium exists when the story begins, with the three pigs building and moving into their houses of straw, sticks, and brick. Everything is stable at this point in the story. But this initial condition of stability is disrupted by the arrival of a wolf, who threatens to eat the pigs. This event is the complication, because it introduces into the story a conflict: pig versus wolf.

Conflict can always be expressed as one force struggling against another. Sometimes these forces are people: in *Hamlet*, Hamlet struggles against Claudius; in *A Doll's House*, Nora opposes Helmer. Sometimes the "forces" battle within one character: Hamlet fights against his own tendency to overanalyze the situation and procrastinate rather than act; Nora fights against her own motherly instincts. And, as the preceding examples make clear, typically several conflicts occur in any play.

Most plays don't devote much time to the original state of things before the complication. They tend to begin **in media res** (literally, "in the midst of things"), after the action has started, the complication has occurred, and the conflict is in its beginning stages. Typically, a dramatist will provide some sort of background information in the opening scene to give viewers an understanding of the early stages of the plot. This information is called **exposition.**

The rising action depicts the escalating struggle of the conflict. In our example, the rising action plays out in the huffs and puffs of the wolf. He threatens the first pig, then blows down the house of straw; but this pig escapes to the house of sticks, and the wolf renews his threats and blows down that house too. The rising action is often compared to the uphill slope of a mountain, and you've probably seen graphs of plots in that shape:

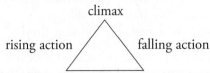

climax

rising action   falling action

This metaphor is apt. As the play moves toward the climax, the conflict grows more and more acute, and so the audience tends to feel more and more anxiety about the outcome.

The climax of the Three Little Pigs is that scene in which the wolf fails to blow down the brick house and resorts to climbing down the chimney. The clever pigs, of course, have a hot cauldron on the fire, and the wolf gets cooked or, in less gruesome versions, runs away. No matter the version, the wolf clearly won't come back any time soon; the pigs have won the struggle. The climax has resolved the conflict. One side wins, so to speak, and the other side loses. You can speak in terms of a contest even when the conflict happens within one character, as if two impulses or sides within that character are fighting for control. At the climax, one impulse or side "wins" and the other "loses."

The falling action is the sequence of events that cascade in consequence of the climax. In movies and television dramas, the falling action tends to be very brief, but in plays it often occupies a fairly substantial portion of the drama. The Three Little Pigs contains practically no falling action. Once the pigs win, the wolf disappears without further incident. You're launched immediately into the resolution: that final situation in which order and stability are restored. Usually, the fairy tale ends with a scene depicting the "happy ever after" of the pigs as they dance around, feast, and live the high life in their brick house.

In most of the plays in this book, the resolution is a state considerably less attractive than the original state of equilibrium. The characters enjoy no happy ever after. That's because most of these plays either are tragedies, which tend to depict the fall of the main character, or owe a debt to tragedy. We'll talk more about tragedy a little later.

Character

A **character**, of course, is a person on the stage, a personage being acted for the audience. Time has proven character to be the element of drama that distinguishes great plays from the rest. Plays that rely on interesting plots but superficial characters are often popular for a short time, but they burn out quickly and are then forgotten. An entire genre of drama, the **well-made play** of the nineteenth century, exploited the crowd-pleasing elements of plot, like surprise revelations and dramatic climaxes, while purposely neglecting to develop memorable characters. The formulaic nature of Hollywood **genre** movies—westerns, crime films, horror, superhero movies, and so on—makes them the modern versions of plot-driven drama. Some movies made in these genres rise above the others and join the ranks of classic films, but they always do so by adding depth of character to their exciting plots. In fact, fascinating characters enable even plays, television shows, and films with straightforward or simple plots to live beyond their first seasons or initial releases. Obviously, the best works have both interesting plots and interesting characters, but of the two, character seems more important.

You analyze characters in a play much the same way you analyze people in life. At first, you react to them spontaneously. Gradually, as each character acts, speaks, and develops (or doesn't develop), you modify your first impression to create a more complex sense of each character's nature. At every stage, you should trust your instincts, but be open to new information and new impressions. Be cautious about personal likes and dislikes—you might hate redheads, for instance, for no good (or a very personal) reason, and thus fail to sympathize with a character with whom the playwright intends you to sympathize. As long as you're mindful of your prejudices and idiosyncrasies, you'll probably have little trouble judging characters. Of all parts of analysis, analyzing characters will come most naturally.

At the most basic level, you should determine which characters you like and which you dislike. As in real life, characters tend to be a mixture of good and bad, but, typically, the play will lead you to sympathize with some over others—to wish them well and feel sorry for them when they suffer. Such characters are called **sympathetic characters**. Characters with whom you are not meant to sympathize are called **unsympathetic characters**. Sometimes, a play will ask you to do more than sympathize. In fact, according to Aristotle, tragedy works only if the play gets you to **identify** with the protagonist, to imagine yourself in the character's place.

No one can call your responses to characters wrong, but you should cultivate an ability to justify your spontaneous reactions. Rather than merely saying you like this person or dislike that one, try to explain why you have made these judgments. Again, your reasons may be the same as they would be in real life. As you watch a play, all sorts of things influence your spontaneous impressions: the costumes, the actors' body language, the way a character talks (his or her **diction**), and so on. If you're reading the play, you have fewer cues. You will be able to judge the characters mostly by what they say and do, and also by how the other characters react to them. So the process of analyzing characters, while fairly easy, might require you to slow down and become conscious of how your affinities have been manipulated by the writer. You might keep in mind these very simple questions: *Why do I like so-and-so? What is it about so-and-so that rubs me the wrong way?* Simple questions like these will lead to sophisticated answers about character.

You should also note certain roles played by characters. Every play, if it has a conflict, will have a **protagonist.** The protagonist is the character that the play focuses on—logically enough, it is Hamlet in *Hamlet* and Antigone in *Antigone*. Though the protagonist is usually a good person, it does not have to be. It is not sufficient to define *protagonist* as "the good guy." For example, some critics say that the unsympathetic character Creon is the real protagonist of *Antigone*. In most plays, the protagonist faces some physical or psychological challenge, and the play dramatizes his or her grappling with that challenge. If the protagonist struggles against another character, that character is called the **antagonist.**

Generally, the struggle (or conflict) causes some change in the protagonist. Any character who changes through the course of the play is called a **dynamic character**. A character who does not change is called a **static character**. A static character may be so two-dimensional, even one-dimensional, that it is called a **stock character**, as if the playwright just rummaged around in the stockroom to find a character to perform a particular function. The gravediggers in *Hamlet* might be called stock characters—in this case, witty stereotypes of the working class, often found in Elizabethan plays.

Spectacle

Spectacle was Aristotle's term for what the audience sees—the play as a physical reality. We might amplify this category to include all the material aspects of the play, including the **set**, costumes, **props**, music, sound effects, and so on. These elements contribute much to your experience of a play. Think, for example, of **scenery**. The lights come up on a deserted stage. You see nothing but the setting—*Before is the Salesman's house. We are aware of towering, angular shapes behind it, surrounding it on all sides. . . . As more light appears, we see a solid vault of apartment houses around the small, fragile-seeming home.* Thus Arthur Miller describes the set of *Death of a Salesman* (page 352). The set is designed to make you feel constricted, even claustrophobic, almost as if the characters were living inside prison walls. You might not even realize this intellectually, but the set can have this emotional effect on you.

Thus the spectacle establishes the **atmosphere** for the play. The production manipulates your attitude and mood. Essentially, as a viewer, you are told how to regard the action you are about to see. A good production uses spectacle to communicate to you on a non-verbal level, and you begin "interpreting" the spectacle before you even hear any words. Your gut reacts to it.

This is another way that *reading* a play rather than *viewing* it puts you at a disadvantage. When you read a play, of course, you have to picture the scene in your mind, so the process is somewhat lengthened. For plays as old as those of Sophocles and Shakespeare, that imaginative work puts you on a level playing field with the original audiences. The older playwrights don't provide elaborate directions for how to set the scenes because their theaters didn't use much scenery or costuming. You have to pay careful attention to the dialogue, which is often encumbered by descriptions of the setting and the weather. These verbal cues enable you, like the plays' original audiences, to visualize the spectacle.

Contemporary plays often use fairly elaborate scenery, which you won't see if you just read the plays. But the play texts tend to give detailed descriptions of that scenery, usually at the very beginning. In fact, by reading contemporary plays you might have an advantage over theatergoers, because playwrights often go beyond mere description and actually interpret sets for you. For example, Lorraine Hansberry describes the set of *A Raisin in the Sun* (page 263) like this:

> *[The] furnishings . . . have clearly had to accommodate the living of too many people for too many years—and they are tired. Still, we can see that at some time, a time probably no longer remembered by the family (except perhaps for* MAMA*), the furnishings of this room were actually selected with care and love and even hope—and brought to this apartment and arranged with taste and pride. That was a long time ago. Now . . . [w]eariness has, in fact, won in this room.*

No matter how talented the set designer is, audiences can hardly see all that Hansberry says "we can see." In this case, the *reader* of the play has a much sharper understanding than the *theatergoer*.

Music can help to create atmosphere in the theater and a mood in the viewer. Reading a text cannot re-create in you the physical reaction you might have to music, but usually you can approximate the experience intellectually. And sometimes the playwright will tell you flat out how the sound should affect you, as Arthur Miller does.

The spectacle necessarily raises another important element in drama: symbolism.

Symbolism

A **symbol** is a thing that represents something else. It might represent an object or objects, or it might represent an idea or a set of ideas. Some things, usually things in the natural world, seem to carry the same symbolic meaning in just about any culture. The sunrise will probably call to mind birth or beginning no matter where you go, just as the sunset seems to naturally represent death or ending. The general meaning is the same in Bali as it is in Belgium. Ferocious predators might symbolize evil in many different cultures. A dense forest might symbolize the unknown. Having such broad applicability makes something a **universal symbol**. For example, Hamlet contemplates a skull in act 5; for many cultures (Hamlet's included), a human skull is a natural reminder of human mortality.

Other things and objects carry meaning only in a particular culture. In any culture acquainted with Christianity, for example, the cross represents Jesus's crucifixion, his redemption of humanity, and all the religious sects that believe in his divinity. But if you erected a cross in some distant town whose inhabitants had never heard of the Christian Gospels, the villagers might hang their laundry from it, never thinking they were dishonoring someone's god. A cross would have no symbolic meaning for them; it carries meaning only within the context of cultures familiar with Christianity. Rather than being universal, the symbol has a meaning that is agreed on by a particular group of people. It is a **conventional symbol**.

Sometimes, the symbolic meanings of conventional symbols have obviously been contrived by particular people. The regalia of clubs and political organizations are good examples. A new baseball franchise in Arizona chooses "Diamondbacks" for its name, and suddenly this Major League team is symbolized by a rattlesnake. A committee adopts the flag sewn by Betsy Ross, and thereafter the stars and stripes symbolize a nation.

But most conventional symbols have anonymous genealogies. It is impossible to say who created them, as though they simply arose out of their cultures. Who can say when apple pie came to symbolize the values of Middle America? Who decided that the American Midwest would represent wholesomeness and honesty, while the West would symbolize rugged individualism? Show anyone who grew up in American culture a picture of John Wayne on a horse in a Texas landscape, and that person will understand the symbolism. In fact, many people around the globe would recognize it too, for the icon of the cowboy, with the notions of self-reliance and freedom (and violence) that he represents, is one of America's cultural exports, courtesy of Hollywood. But show the same picture to a farmer in rural China, and he might see just a man on a horse. Richard Nixon's face represents, to a great many Americans, the personification of political dishonesty, but to a Latvian it might be just another face. No one person or committee decided that these images would convey symbolic meaning in American culture; nevertheless, they do. And outside that culture and its global ripple effects they are meaningless.

A **literary symbol** is a thing that represents something else only within a particular work of literature. Outside the work, the thing does not mean what it does inside the work. A literary symbol, then, is authored neither by nature nor by a culture, but by a writer. As with a conventional symbol, when you take a literary symbol out of its original context, it stops being a symbol. For example, you will see that a bird in *Trifles* (page 245) symbolizes something, but only within the context of the play. Its significance was invented by Susan Glaspell, and outside the play a bird would not carry the same meaning.

How do you recognize that an object in a play is not just its literal self but also represents something else? Identifying literary symbols is an art, but a few tricks will help you hone your interpretive skills. If a play title refers to an object, for example, you can be pretty sure the object symbolizes something. Pay careful attention, then, to the fence in *Fences* (page 444). By calling attention to the fence through his title, Wilson tips us off to its importance. On your first reading of the play you should be asking yourself, *What could the fence represent?* Meanwhile, watch for textual references to it. Repeated references are another good indication that something has symbolic significance.

No foolproof way exists, though, to recognize immediately which objects are symbolic and which are not. Trust your instincts. If you find your attention drawn to an object, if you suspect that something might have more than literal significance, you're probably right. The text will guide you to its literary symbols. Even if Wilson had called his play *The Tragedy of Troy Maxson*, you still could figure out that the fence is symbolic, because the characters draw your attention to it.

After you've identified a potential symbol, you still have the tougher task of figuring out what the symbol represents. You might have to read scenes or passages a few times until an idea comes to you. Usually, a symbol represents an abstraction: love, death, dreams, hope, and so on.

Trust your gut, but be prepared to revise your interpretation. If you try to interpret an object symbolically and it doesn't seem to work, maybe you were wrong. As Sigmund Freud reportedly put it, "Sometimes a cigar is just a cigar." Maybe the object is not a symbol. Or maybe you were wrong about what the object represents. Keep revising and refining your idea until you have it right—until your interpretation of the symbol's meaning and importance fits your sense of the play as a whole.

Tragedy

Everything we've considered so far applies to plays in general. But now we need to focus on one particular genre of plays: **tragedy**. *Antigone, Hamlet, Death of a Salesman*, and *Fences* are tragedies, and many other plays in this collection share some elements of tragedy. So an understanding of how tragedy affects plot and character will prove useful in much of your reading here.

The plot of tragedy follows the general pattern of all plots, but there are some aspects of plot unique to tragedy. Tragedy always begins with the protagonist in a state of **prosperity.** Sometimes, you can take this term literally—the character is rich, well liked, and admired, a figure of some prominence in the community. Other times, especially in modern plays, the character displays a metaphoric "prosperity" based on a different measure of success. For example, at the beginning of *Fences*, Troy Maxson, despite his modest economic status, enjoys stature among his friends and relations. He is a success in their eyes, even a leader among them.

The conflict in a tragedy usually occurs between the protagonist and some larger force, like the gods or fate in Greek tragedy, or a social imperative in modern plays. This force is so powerful that it overwhelms the protagonist, who nonetheless gains nobility in the struggle. For example, in *Fences*, Troy defies the insults and indignities that segregation imposed on African Americans. He is doomed to fail, but in his determined attempt he anticipates the civil rights activists of the 1960s.

The conflict reaches its breaking point at the climax, and in tragedy the climax always enacts a **reversal**. In the plainest terms, the hero's original prosperity turns into poverty. In Greek tragedy, this is a literal reversal. But for works from other ages, these terms apply figuratively: after the reversal, the protagonist somehow falls from his or her metaphorical prosperity. At the play's end, the protagonist has a lower status than at the beginning, having lost something crucial to that earlier success and happiness.

The falling action of tragedy typically reveals that the protagonist has gained some self-understanding. Aristotle called this element **recognition** and considered it crucial to tragedy. Tragic heroes must face up to their own complicity in reversal. They have to take responsibility for the events that bring them to the point of poverty.

The term **tragic hero** merits some explanation. The protagonist in a tragedy is, by definition, a tragic hero. But over the ages such protagonists have tended to share certain character traits. For example, tragic heroes generally have been drawn from the higher classes—even from royalty, as in *Antigone* and *Hamlet*. This exalted status ensures that audiences view the heroes as, in some ways, larger, even better, than themselves, and their fates as more important than ordinary people's fates. In the modern world, especially in democratic societies, this imbalance seems anachronistic, even offensive, so dramatists convey largeness of character in other ways. In *Fences*, for example, Troy transcends his job as a sanitation worker by carrying himself like the sports hero he once was. He fills the stage when he walks onto it.

The audience must admire the hero to some extent, whatever his or her faults, for a tragedy to work properly. Viewers must feel **pity** as they watch the hero go from a position above them to a position below them. They must feel sorry for the hero. And so the character's final state of poverty must appear out of proportion. The punishment cannot fit the crime. If the plot depicted a wicked person (someone visibly worse than the audience) receiving just deserts, viewers probably would feel satisfaction rather than pity or sorrow.

Still, the protagonist must have earned some punishment. The tragic hero cannot be a saint, someone too good and exalted to make a mistake. High school textbooks often label this aspect of the hero a tragic "flaw," and they typically identify overweening pride (or **hubris**) as the most common tragic flaw. These ideas derive from Aristotle's *Poetics*, but they are a bit too loosely translated and are too reductive to describe complex heroes. It would be a mistake, for example, to try to figure out Hamlet's "flaw" merely because a tragic hero "must" have one. Instead, think of the proverb "To err is human." The tragic hero must be as imperfect, perhaps as full of contradictions, as any human being.

If the hero were a god or good beyond reason, the audience would not be able to identify with the hero, and this sense of identification lies at the heart of tragedy. Viewers must be able to see themselves in the hero, to think that they are not all that different from the hero, to recognize shared human traits in even a large or exalted character. Not many people will identify with a saint; but most people will identify with a character who is mostly but not entirely good, because that is how they think of themselves. Once people put themselves in the hero's shoes, they can experience the second of the tragic emotions, what Aristotle somewhat grandly called **terror**.

After first pitying the hero, viewers realize that they, who are not fundamentally different from the hero, can or do share the character's fate; that they are, in fact, pitying themselves. And it should be a bit terrifying to contemplate suffering the same fate as the hero, to realize that the hero's struggle could be your own and to conclude that a massive reversal of fortune may be part of the human condition.

You might wonder why anyone would go to a tragedy if seeing one just leads to feelings of pity and terror. Who would pay money to experience those emotions? The answer is a bit elusive. Aristotle thought tragedies were valuable, even popular, because they not only make people feel pity and terror, but they ultimately flush those emotions out of people. It is almost as if tragedies inoculate viewers against the effects of those emotions in real life. This purgation is sometimes called **catharsis**. But whatever the reason, throughout history audiences have enjoyed watching, and vicariously experiencing, tragic events onstage.

Comedy

Comedy's popularity presents no such mystery. As a genre or sub-genre, however, comedy is much more difficult to describe and define than tragedy (Aristotle's thoughts on the subject are lost to the ages). Everyone can recognize a comedy when they see one, and perhaps the common understanding of the term is the best: a comedy is a play that makes people laugh a lot. Just as tragedy elicits feelings of pity and terror in viewers, so comedy must make viewers happy. And just as tragedy makes viewers experience (at least vicariously) the difficulties and frailties of the human condition, so comedy celebrates humanity in all its sloppy, raucous, robust fertility.

The comedic plot is generally the reverse of the tragic plot: the protagonist begins in a state of relative poverty and ends in a state of prosperity. But these terms must be taken even more metaphorically than they are in tragedy, because the "poverty" often consists of nothing more than the protagonist's feelings of loneliness or emptiness in not having a mate. That is certainly the case in the thousands of **romantic comedies** that have been forever popular. You might describe the standard plot reductively but pretty accurately as *Boy is alone; boy meets girl; boy is separated from girl; boy and girl reunite.* (For many contemporary examples, substitute *boy* for *girl* or *girl* for *boy* as necessary.) While tragedies often end in death, romantic comedies usually end in betrothal or marriage, a symbol of human renewal and fecundity.

This description is not meant to trivialize comedy. The most famous comedies of all time, including Shakespeare's, basically tell boy-meets-girl stories. The genius of such plays resides never in the plot itself, but in the playwright's handling of the characters. Ingenuity enables comedians to still delight and entertain audiences as they tell the same basic story time and time again.

Major Moments in the History of Theater

I mentioned earlier that the conventions of theater have changed throughout the ages, and that the strange conventions of long-past civilizations might make it harder to enjoy reading plays from those eras. What follows here is a very brief discussion of the types of theater represented in this volume. You should not take it as a comprehensive history—nor even an outline of theater history. I focus only on the contexts of the plays in this book: eight nearly discrete points in a timeline. I've skipped everything between those points, even the evolutionary connections between the different epochs. But this sketch should help you appreciate the plays that follow. I recommend that you read it through from beginning to end now, then return to an individual section when (before, after, while) you read the corresponding play.

Greek Theater

The Greeks invented drama. Johnny Depp and Angelina Jolie and Will Smith earn millions today because of what the Greeks did twenty-five centuries ago. This is not to say Greek theater much resembled movies. Drama grew out of religious festivals devoted to the worship of Dionysus, the god of wine. Raised to the pantheon of gods fairly late in Greek history, Dionysus was a social leveler. His rites first became popular in Athens during the antiaristocratic reign of Peisistratus (d. 527 B.C.E.), so drama, from its very beginnings, was linked to democratic traditions. In ecstatic dances and songs, choruses took on the identities of historical figures (soldiers of Argos, for example) and satyrs. They sometimes retold traditional epic stories in song, but they did not dramatize the events.

Spoken dialogue became possible after a man named Thespis (sixth century B.C.E.), from whose name comes the word *thespian*, added an actor to these choral dances and songs. The earliest tragedy (by Aeschylus, 525–456 B.C.E.) includes three choruses, who dance and sing for 603 of 1,073 lines. In performances, an actor playing a character would give speeches that interacted with the chorus's songs. When Aeschylus added a second actor to subsequent plays, the songs and speeches began to dramatize stories. Having two actors enabled Aeschylus to introduce conflicts between people, and conflict is the essential element of plot. So drama as the playing out of a story really began with Aeschylus. Sophocles (c. 496–406 B.C.E.) added a third actor and was thus able to increase the complexities of the stories. He retained the chorus, but diminished its role to a supporting function, such as representing the people (the citizens of Thebes, in *Antigone*); and he used its songs to punctuate the action, commenting on and sometimes interpreting for the audience what the characters do and say. The performance focuses not on the lyric songs, but on the story unfolded by the characters.

Greek plays were performed during daytime in immense, outdoor amphitheaters, with semicircular rows of stone bleachers rising up hillsides. These theaters could seat up to fifteen thousand spectators—as many people as can fit into sports arenas today. At the base of the bleachers was a circular floor, the **orchestra**, where the chorus danced and sang its odes. Behind this level space stood a slightly raised, uncurtained stage area, where the actors performed in front of a wooden facade. The actors could change costumes in a backstage area behind the facade. They made their entrances through doors in this structure—a door might represent, for example, the entrance to a palace, as it does in *Antigone*. Sophocles introduced painted scenery to the stage, but otherwise these productions employed no sets.

The actors could use their voices expressively thanks to the theaters' incredible acoustics. Even in the largest theaters, whispers could project into the audience. As an undergraduate, I went on a school trip to Greece, where we visited the theater at Epidarus, one of the best-preserved Greek amphitheaters. I sat in the very back row and looked down on my teacher, who stood on a stone that marked the exact center of the theater. I could barely see his face. He removed from his pocket a bus ticket, a flimsy thing about as thick as the tissue paper we stuff in gift boxes. When he tore this little piece of paper in half, I could barely see the thing in his fingers, but I could hear it rip. Such subtleties, of volume and vocal tone, will of course be lost when you read a play, so you'll have to imagine how each speech should be delivered.

The size of the Greek theaters made it impossible for actors to use anything but the grandest gestures. Actors today—on television, in movies, and even in smaller theaters—can communicate through facial expressions, like raised eyebrows or slight frowns, but these expressions would be lost in theaters the size of sports arenas. So Greek actors wore large masks, carved and painted with realistic faces, that could be seen even from the back rows of the theaters. These masks provided one way for the audience to distinguish one character from another (remember, only three actors played all the roles in Sophocles's plays; Sophocles expanded the repertoire of dramatic masks). Because these masks were stiff, the actors had to rely on their voices and the words themselves to convey subtleties of emotion and attitude. And because the playwrights couldn't rely on the actors' facial expressions to convey emotions, they put a lot of emotional cues into the texts. So a *reader* (as opposed to a *viewer*) might find it relatively easy to imagine the characters' emotions. Contemporary plays sometimes read much flatter than ancient Greek plays, because actors now perform the work of those cues.

Even so, contemporary audiences tend to find Greek drama a bit stiff, even boring. That's because contemporary culture is dominated by the visual. If something dramatic happens, people want to *see* it. They're much more interested in watching people *do* something than in listening to them *talk* about something. Even when they read fiction—consuming through the eyes, but not in the same visual way movies are consumed—the text must involve them vicariously in the action, to make them feel as though they were part of what's happening.

Greek culture was much more aural. Greek drama, then, unfolds in verbal exchanges. Not much *happens*. While a lot of blood spills in *Antigone*, it spills offstage, away from the audience's eyes, and is reported by messengers. And the real drama of the play doesn't reside in the bloody scenes anyway—it's in the verbal battles between Antigone and Creon and Teiresias. This convention can be a barrier to modern readers, but because you come to the play prepared, you should be able to bypass the problem.

No doubt some conventions of ancient Greek drama have been lost forever. But the ones I've discussed should help you approximate in your imagination what Sophocles wanted his audience to experience when they saw *Antigone* performed.

Elizabethan Theater

The term *Elizabethan* refers to the first Queen Elizabeth of England, who ruled from 1558 to 1603. During her reign, England rose to the level of superpower among the nations of Europe, and London was the continent's largest city, a sprawling, gangly octopus of narrow, filthy streets, bustling docksides, grand palaces, lively bars, spectacular churches, and a vibrant mix of European tongues and English dialects.

Some of Shakespeare's contemporaries—more learned men like Ben Jonson—were influenced by Roman drama (itself indebted to Greek theater), but for the most part early Elizabethan theater was a homegrown phenomenon. Entertainers performed modest scenes from wagons at fairs or, sometimes, in the banquet halls of the rich. But those dramatists hardly seem related to the energetic, industrious, and glamorous London play companies in Shakespeare's time. Theater struck London in the 1580s as suddenly as movies hit America in the 1920s and television did in the 1950s. Coming out of nowhere, it completely reshaped the cultural landscape.

The theaters and the life surrounding them were seen as disreputable. Onstage and offstage, actors and playwrights excited the public with the prospect of love affairs, villainy, and swordplay. People from all social levels came together in audiences to witness murder, mayhem, and sex. (Because women were not allowed to act, boys in drag played all the female roles.) The phenomenon seemed uncontrollable, and governmental figures feared the effects on the people. When the Puritans came to power, in 1642, they closed the theaters outright rather than try to moralize them. You might think of the theatrical explosion in Elizabethan England as the Internet revolution of its day. In each case, a new medium becomes immensely popular and seems able to democratically influence politics and, perhaps, undermine morals. In Shakespeare's chaotic, raucous world, theater companies were every bit as entrepreneurial as today's startups. They schemed against each other, stole each other's talent, and jealously guarded their material. Fortunes were made nearly overnight, especially by those who built the theater buildings. (Fortunes were also lost nearly overnight, especially when the Puritans closed the theaters.)

Shakespeare's Globe theater was built on the south side of the River Thames in 1599. *Hamlet* most likely was first played in this theater, probably around 1600. The theater was shaped like a doughnut. Its empty center was open to the sky and contained no seats; like the Greeks, the Elizabethans performed plays only during the daytime. The common people, or **groundlings**, each paid a penny, or about a day's wage, to enter this yard, where they stood and chewed their sausages and watched the action onstage. The stage, uncurtained though canopied with an elaborate roof, stood on five-foot-high trestles and jutted into this open-air space, so the players would have been acting practically in the midst of the groundlings, their feet in the faces of the poor. People who could afford more expensive tickets (about three pence) sat in the tiers of roofed seats that made up the outside of the doughnut. All together, these audiences represented a broad range of London's one hundred thousand citizens, from nobility down to artisans and shopkeepers. As many as three thousand people could fit in the theater at once, making it large by contemporary standards but much more intimate than the Greek theaters.

At the back of the stage stood a facade with, perhaps, three curtained doors that led into the backstage area, or **tiring-house**. Above these doors were box seats for wealthy spectators, making the stage almost a "theater-in-the-round." The actors also appeared in these boxes during some rare scenes, like the famous balcony scene in *Romeo and Juliet*. A trapdoor in the stage enabled actors to suddenly appear or disappear, as, for example, when playing the ghost in the first act of *Hamlet*.

The Elizabethans used few props and, like the Greeks, little to no scenery, so audiences had to imagine the setting from clues given in the dialogue. Despite similarities like this, Elizabethans experienced the theater very differently from the Greeks. The Elizabethan actors' physical proximity to the groundlings more than likely led to a fair amount of give-and-take between the two. The play texts sometimes call for characters to whisper confidences to the audience about the other characters, and playwrights seem to have expected actors to interact with the audience almost the way stand-up comics "play to" their audiences today. In the last act of *Hamlet*, for example, the gravediggers certainly played to the groundlings, who must have delighted in watching their counterparts onstage outwit their betters.

You will probably find *Hamlet* more immediately interesting than *Antigone*, because it employs nearly contemporary plot conventions. The action might seem a bit tame to a reader conditioned by superhero films and kung-fu movies, but the play is still fairly busy. In fact, the multiple scene changes and time shifts, the swords drawn and people killed onstage would all have seemed quite dizzying to an ancient Athenian.

But you will also find more speeches than you are used to. Contemporary dialogue tends to sound close to natural speech—with informal vocabulary, rough grammar, clipped sentences—to provide the illusion of reality. In real life, people generally don't talk to each other in paragraphs; one interlocutor hardly completes a sentence before the other speaker responds. Some dialogue in *Hamlet* doesn't work this way. Even in the midst of informal exchanges, like Hamlet's famous harangue of Ophelia, the characters go on much longer than people would in real life. This is not to say Shakespeare had a bad ear for real conversation (the dialogue in the opening scene will sound remarkably "real" even to contemporary ears). It is just that Elizabethan audiences tolerated much longer exchanges without any insult to their sense of reality. Indeed, Elizabethan audiences tolerated much longer stretches of sustained drama, for the actors didn't pause between scenes and acts. Scene and act numbers were added by later editors, not by Shakespeare.

Nineteenth-Century Middle-Class Theater

Henrik Ibsen's *A Doll's House* was staged in a new type of theater that corresponded (more or less) to what most people today think of when they hear the word *theater*. With the advent of good artificial lighting, first gas and later electric, the theater became a decidedly indoor activity. People attended the theater at night, to fill their leisure hours.

Actors no longer performed in the midst of the audience—they acted in a space removed from the theater seats, as if an invisible fourth wall separated them from the audience. Curtains could be drawn to close the stage from view, enabling theater companies to divide one scene from another and change sets. The sets became far more elaborate and important than in Shakespeare's day, and set designers took full advantage of innovations in engineering to create special effects. In general, the *spectacle* of the theater became nearly as important as the actors. Sometimes, it even overwhelmed the actors, as when, for example, in productions of *Ben Hur*, an epic set in ancient Rome, live horses on treadmills recreated chariot races on stage.

The nineteenth-century theater also sharply divided audiences according to economic status. The music hall variety show catered to the lower classes, who watched, cheered, and heckled these performances in penny theaters—cheap, no-frills playhouses with tables and chairs that ran perpendicular to the stage. People could drink, facing each other, with the show going on over their shoulders. Other theaters—the ones we are concerned with here—catered to the middle class. They used the auditorium seating still in use today: rows of individual seats facing a stage, which was usually crowned by what came to be known as the **proscenium arch**. The seats sported cushions, which encouraged audiences to be more passive than those in the music halls were (or than the groundlings in Shakespeare's Globe theater had been). Going to a play began to resemble your experience today—you pay for your ticket, find your seat, settle back in the darkness, then quietly witness what happens on the lighted stage.

The new style of theater separated audiences from the actors decisively. Actors no longer confided in the audience with knowing winks or clever asides. Watching scenes played out in elaborate sets and with authentic costumes, audiences began to feel like flies on the wall, eavesdropping on real life. They lost themselves in the drama—forgot they were in a theater at all. Thus the current custom of studied silence in the audience established itself in these theaters. To make noise was considered impolite. It disturbed the illusion of reality.

In general, nineteenth-century theater demanded a much higher degree of realism than had been present in either Greek or Elizabethan drama. In plays like *A Doll's House* theatergoers expected to see people like themselves moving about in rooms that resembled their own houses. And the style of acting grew progressively less exaggerated, quieter, and more subtle.

Audiences still demanded to be entertained, however, and most of the plays that thrilled the middle class then would probably be called "melodramatic" today. Most popular of all were the well-made plays, a tradition that Ibsen reacted against with his serious social dramas and that others made fun of in highly unserious social comedies.

The Provincetown Players

By the early twentieth century, Broadway in New York City had become the established center of theater in America, and most of the productions there could be described as well-made plays. These plays often made a lot of money, but they seemed superficial and lightweight to a coterie of disaffected intellectuals, many of whom lived in New York's Greenwich Village. It was a heady time for radical thinkers, and the Village was full of revolutionaries who challenged the inherited social institutions (like monogamous marriage) and the inherited economic structures and political structures of American society. These progressives firmly opposed, for example, the exclusion of women from politics (women still could not vote in America) and the near-exclusion of women from higher education and the professions. From the art of painting to the art of politics, these bohemian artists and activists were ready to remake the world.

They came largely from the middle and upper-middle classes, but repudiated the paths provided for them by their social status—jobs as lawyers or stockbrokers or doctors for the men, roles as socialites for the women—to pursue what they saw as more vital and meaningful lives. As one member of the group, Susan Glaspell, put it, "Most of us were from families who had other ideas—who wanted to make money, played bridge, voted the Republican ticket, went to church, thinking one should be like everyone else." Glaspell's husband, George Cook, came from a wealthy, stolid Iowa family, whom he shocked by divorcing two wives; the second divorce freed him to marry Glaspell.

Cook and Glaspell (among others) established a new kind of theater that was decidedly uncommercial. They didn't care whether the typical Broadway audience was interested. They set about writing and staging plays they were interested in seeing: theater that would examine and interpret the national character and present to audiences intelligent plays regardless of commercial concerns.

In summers, Glaspell, Cook, and a number of their friends would escape the heat of New York City and gather in the fishing village of Provincetown, Massachusetts, where they could rent cheap cottages and discuss their ideas late into the night. In 1915, Cook converted a small warehouse on a fishing wharf into a crude theater, and the group of New Yorkers wrote some short plays to present to themselves—a fairly informal and certainly uncommercial beginning for what would blossom into the Provincetown Players, an amateur troupe of actors with a bona fide theater in New York City. Their notion of theater was purposely stripped down: gone were the elaborate sets and the spectacle of nineteenth-century tradition. The focus was on character. This serious, intellectual theater scorned easy entertainment, and it helped produce America's first acknowledged great dramatist: Eugene O'Neill.

Because the Provincetown Players scorned spectacle, you won't be missing too much visually by reading rather than viewing Glaspell's play *Trifles*. You will lose, of course, the actors' interpretations of their lines (which you should try to imagine). Glaspell wrote her play for an intimate theater in which the slightest gesture on stage could be seen by the audience. Consequently, a fair amount of subtlety was conveyed by the actors. The trend toward realistic dialogue and gesture that dominated the nineteenth century was extended even further.

Contemporary American Theater

Unsurprisingly, theater companies like the Provincetown Players never became hugely popular. They cultivated a sophisticated, perhaps even elite, audience. Meanwhile, Broadway chugged merrily along. In the 1920s, the kind of theater that Glaspell was reacting against grew even more successful. Nevertheless, its days were numbered, because live theater faced the challenge of a new medium—movies—that easily outdid the best spectacles and well-made plots that the commercial theaters produced. After the 1920s, plays would never again occupy the central cultural role they enjoyed in previous centuries, because they could never hope to compete with the popularity of movies—which drew audiences from not only the lower classes but also the middle classes. After the stock market crash of 1929, live theater declined.

The stories and characters on the American stage during the Great Depression exposed and diagnosed problems in modern society, much the way that Henrik Ibsen did in *A Doll's House*, which examines the limitations of the domestic role assigned women by the expanding middle class. Glaspell's *Trifles* helped bring this tradition of serious, realistic drama to America, where it reached its peak of importance in the 1930s.

Going into the 1940s, serious American theater was still influenced by old traditions, and plays tended toward the style popularized by Ibsen. Arthur Miller cut against this tradition, experimenting with new techniques, some of which he borrowed from the film industry, which in turn had borrowed from the melodramatic drama vilified by Ibsen and Glaspell. For example, the music in *Death of a Salesman* resembles a movie soundtrack, with different instruments and themes complementing the action on the stage. And while the scenes with Ben are not exactly **flashbacks**, they do seem to be influenced by the narrative technique of film.

One important change that Miller participated in had to do with the actors. The new style of acting was called **method acting**. In 1947, Elia Kazan established the Actors Studio to train actors in "the method," which relied less on stock gestures and more on subtleties like facial and tonal expression. This style encouraged actors to draw on their own emotional memories in embodying their roles, to *become* their characters and let their bodies act in a natural, almost unconscious manner. Some of the most successful actors to come out of the 1940s and 1950s, such as Marlon Brando and Paul Newman, made their names in conjunction with Kazan. When Miller's play debuted on Broadway in 1949, Kazan was the director.

Nevertheless, Miller never drifted too far from the realism pioneered by Ibsen, and both his and Lorraine Hansberry's (and later Margaret Edson's) successes on Broadway probably demonstrate more continuity than change in the history of drama. Someone who watched Ibsen's plays in the 1870s would probably feel pretty much at home going to a New York theater in the 1950s or even the early 2000s. The position of the audience, for example, had changed hardly at all in eighty years. Theatergoers still sat in the dark in comfortable, ticketed seats, politely quiet and passive, witnessing the events as if looking through an invisible fourth wall.

Regional Theaters

Though August Wilson has certainly found success on Broadway, it might be more appropriate to associate him with the regional theater movement. Regional theaters have grown in cities all across North America, and they vary so widely that it is difficult to generalize about them. Often, they're subsidized by cadres of patrons—private individuals who donate money to keep the theaters afloat. So they typically do not depend on developing a viable commercial market for live theater.

This type of funding would seem to make theater the domain of the wealthier classes of society. But the regional theaters tend to customize their repertoires to the needs and interests of their local populations, and they usually cut against the economic grain—bringing theater to groups excluded by the highbrow nature of most contemporary theater. Many regional theaters have specific missions, like the Kuntu Repertory Theater at the University of Pittsburgh, which is committed to educating audiences about the black experience and moving them to social action.

Because they are uncommercial, regional theaters do not often produce theatrical spectaculars. Typically, their plays take place in single settings, so that only one set has to be built for each production. Contemporary works derived from that world, like *Fences*, employ no difficult or arcane theatrical conventions.

How Do You Write about Plays?

Your instructor might ask you to write one of several different types of papers—for instance, a response paper, a character analysis, a research paper, an interpretation. This section guides you through only one of these: an interpretive essay. But interpretation is the core of just about any critical essay, even research papers, so the advice here will probably serve you no matter what your specific assignment.

An interpretive essay asserts your opinion about the meaning of a play or of a part of a play. You might consider only a scene or a character or a recurring motif, or you might interpret the entire play (this is more likely if you're writing about a one-act play). When we talk about *meaning* in this context, we're talking about what the play intends to do to readers: What emotional reactions does it elicit? What sympathies or antipathies does it generate? What ideas does it raise in the audience's mind? What does the play want us to think about those ideas? You'll notice I'm anthropomorphizing plays, as if the selections in this book were people each with his or her own notions about the world, each with his or her own political or social agenda and intentions about how to move the audience. If you were writing a research paper, you might actually read some biographical material about the playwright or do some historical sleuthing, trying to reconstruct the writer's intentions or the way the play's original audience might have reacted to a scene. But in an interpretive essay, you rely on your sensitivities and cues you find in the play itself. Thus, it's helpful to think about the *play's* intentions.

However large or small the scope of your interpretation, the bulk of your essay will consist of arguments persuading your readers to agree with your opinion. These arguments will point to evidence from the play itself, evidence produced by what critics sometimes call **close reading**. Close reading is not so different from the casual reading or the reading for pleasure that most people do, except that the close reader is more conscious of how he or she is reacting to the play and to those things in the play that cause those reactions. As you'll see later, close reading means very careful scrutiny of those elements discussed in "The Parts of a Play."

In the beginning of this book, I said that you've become fluent in the language of plays by viewing dramas like movies and television shows. You've internalized much of their grammar, so to speak, so you can understand plays almost instinctively. You get their meaning. I also discussed how the script of a play is just part of a production. If you've ever seen two different productions of the same play you know how important the director, the actors, the set designer, lighting, and sound are to the play's meaning. Each production offers its own interpretation of the script. When you read a play, you yourself become director, actor, and set designer. Your own imagination provides the staging and adds intonation and emotion to the lines. One might be tempted, then, to claim that any and all interpretations are equally valid. "Hamlet's clearly an idiot," one might say. "That's just how I see him."

But when you write an interpretive paper you're adding a crucial new dimension to your claim. Not only are you asserting what the play means to you but you're also claiming that your reader ought to agree with you. In other words, you're trying to persuade people that the meaning you take from the play is probably the meaning that the play intended you to get. "I think Hamlet's an idiot," you might say, but then you must add, "and you should think he's an idiot too." When you're trying to persuade people to agree with you, it becomes clear that some interpretations are more plausible than others, and some are so implausible we might as well say they're wrong.

This section will explain how to develop your own interpretations and, once you've done that, how best to persuade others to agree with you.

Theme, Meaning, and Interpretation

If you're writing about a one-act play, your assignment might ask you to interpret the entire thing. But if you're writing about something longer, like *Antigone* or *Death of a Salesman,* your assignment probably allows you to narrow your area of inquiry. Are you writing about one character? A particular speech—one of Hamlet's soliloquies, for instance? Does the assignment specify your focus, or does it let you choose for yourself? No matter the assignment, your first task is to gauge its scope.

Once you've defined the scope of your inquiry, you want to decide what you think that particular part of the play is *about.* Sometimes, you can take that question literally. For instance, if you're asked to interpret Hamlet's famous "To be or not to be" soliloquy, you might say the speech is about *suicide*. (By the way, someone else might say that it's about *human suffering*, and yet a third might say it's about *indecision*. That's OK. In fact, this kind of multiplicity of themes is a good thing.) Sometimes deciding what the element is about is not quite so literal. Say you've set out to interpret the character Dr. Kelekian in *Wit*. A person is not really "about" anything. Nevertheless, that character might illustrate certain traits or attitudes, so you might say that *figuratively* Kelekian represents a scientific way of looking at the world. In that case, the theme you identify would be a scientific attitude or ideology. Through Kelekian, the play has something to say about science and the attitude it produces in people. That's one of its themes.

So **theme** is what the play is about on an abstract level, those generalized issues dramatized in or embodied by the dialogue, action, and spectacle. Theme distinguishes plays from most of the stories you read in newspapers. A newspaper will tell a story merely because it happened: a plane crashed, and everyone on board died; the president gave a speech in a nearby city; a famous actor got married; the Red Sox beat the Yankees in extra innings. These stories usually don't have any larger thematic importance. Sometimes they do. For example, when the "unsinkable" *Titanic* sank on its maiden voyage, many saw the event as an enormous reminder of the puniness of humans as compared to nature or God and as a rebuke for our pride. When the Twin Towers were attacked, everyone wanted to interpret the event. What did it mean? Was this about religion? Was it about democracy? Was it about America's role in the world? But most stories in the newspapers don't explore abstract themes. They are "news," and we read them because they tell us what happened. Once the news is stale, we don't read the stories again: they have nothing more to say to us. Plays last longer because their themes broaden the scope of the events they relate. They are about more than the individual characters and events they dramatize.

Imagine the events in *Hamlet* as they might be reported in a newspaper. The article would have the same characters and the same events. On a literal level, it would be about the changes in the ruling class of Denmark, the political intrigues that raise one person and topple another. But as told on stage, the play is also about ambition in general, revenge, family, sin, and forgiveness. Those are some of its themes. Henrik Ibsen's *A Doll's House* is about marriage, domestic duties, life in the middle class, and probably half a dozen other things you might name. Six readers of the same play might be interested in six different themes.

A play's **meaning** is what it has to say about one of its themes. Ask yourself the further question, *What does* Hamlet *have to say about revenge?* or *What does* A Doll's House *tell us about marriage?* In this sense, we can almost think of a play like a political argument, an editorial, an academic essay, or any other persuasive speech or piece of expository writing. In fact, one of the most influential studies of literature (a book that has a pretty big influence on this volume) is Wayne Booth's *The Rhetoric of Fiction.* That word, *rhetoric,* implies that what a play does to readers is a kind of persuasion. Just as an essay might try to persuade readers to believe something about, say, patriotism or friendship, so do plays.

But literature has this big difference from most persuasive writing: it mainly moves through the imagination. Political speeches and thesis-driven essays (such as the one you might be writing) mainly use logic, what English teachers call "argumentation," to influence opinions. Arguments touch you more superficially, like wind on the surface of a lake. Imaginative literature moves like deep ocean currents, where your heart swims. Reading or seeing a play can be like entering a virtual reality: you *see* the scene, you *hear* the words and sounds, you *feel* the whirl of dresses in a dance and the grief in the lowering tone of an actor's voice. And as you read plays, you get to *know* the characters the way you know people in real life—and sometimes more intimately than you know real-life people.

Because it is so tied up in imagination, the meaning of a play can be hard to pin down, almost as hard as interpreting the meaning of life itself. We don't read plays to extract some sort of moral, as we would read a fable. Plays do not offer some universally applicable lesson that can be easily paraphrased, such as "Slow and steady wins the race," which is the meaning of Aesop's fable of the tortoise and the hare. It's pretty hard work to put into your own clear prose what a play does to you on a deep level. Meaning involves how a play makes readers *feel,* what it makes them *think* about, where it *directs* their sympathies, all sorts of things you don't expect from expository prose.

Your interpretation is what you think the play means. Your **thesis** is a brief statement—a sentence or two—that sums up that interpretation. Just as a play might have several different themes, it can also support several different, sometimes even contradictory, interpretations. And while meaning might be tough to pin down, the following sections offer some practical advice for developing your interpretation and give you strategies for persuading other people to agree with it.

The Writing Process

No one, not even the cleverest literary critic, can write an effective interpretive essay completely off the top of their head. *Thinking* takes you only so far. It is by *writing* that we generate ideas, test those ideas with evidence, try out arguments, rethink our initial notions, revise our strategies of persuasion.

Rhetoricians describe the writing process as **recursive.** In other words, writing a paper rarely follows step-by-step instructions like a recipe in a cookbook, even if it sometimes is represented that way in textbooks like this one. When you're cooking, you might have to melt the butter before you toss the onions in the pan, and you might have to sauté the onions before you put them in the soup. Steps go in a necessary order.

Writing doesn't work that way. You'll find yourself constantly circling back to earlier steps. Don't worry if it seems more natural for you to do step four before you've finished step two, and don't worry about going back to step three after you've finished step five. Follow your instincts. The writing process is not linear. It spirals back on itself all the time.

Nor should you worry about completing each and every step in the first place. Writing is a lot messier than cooking, and you should violate these instructions whenever going your own way is more productive. Skip a step if it helps you write. Add your own step. Writing is very individual: no two people go through the process exactly the same way. One of the most important things you can do in a writing class is to figure out what's *your* most productive writing process. You might find that you can't generate your ideas unless you're already writing a rough draft of your paper: then you should skip discovery and begin by drafting. Or you might find that you can't think of anything to say when you're at the keyboard: that you need a cup of coffee, a pen, and your literature book open to the play. Begin by filling the margins of your book with notes. Everybody does it a little differently, and you've got to figure out what's your own most productive process.

But the one universal is this: writing is a *process*. It takes several stages to produce an effective paper, and each of those stages takes time and energy. Your hard work will be rewarded with several intellectual pleasures, and one of those is the pleasure that comes from working hard. If you don't work hard, you won't write an effective essay.

1. Discovery

Discovery simply means finding things to say: you discover ideas and evidence. Discovery is a collaboration between you and the play. You bring to the play all sorts of advantages—your knowledge of how the world works and how people behave, your sense of right and wrong, your own personal set of things that you tend to notice and things you tend to overlook—that individualize your experience of the text. In discovery, you explore your own interaction with the play. You slow it down and observe it.

Reading the play, and then reading it again is the first stage of discovery. You might think that reading goes without saying, but my experience teaching literature courses tells me it's worth a few words, because there's reading and then there's close reading.

The first time you read a play, let it work on your imagination. Don't worry about anything other than entering the world of the play and enjoying it. Let the play do things to you. Then read it a second time in order to begin analyzing it. That means consciously thinking about the parts of plays: character, plot, symbolism, etc. This is the close reading I mentioned earlier. You're reading the text with a more specific purpose than the general reader. You're not just letting it do things to you: you're trying to figure out *how* it does things to you. How does it get you to like this character? Where does it make your heart race and how did it do it? You're looking more closely, looking for specific things, using examination tools almost the way a scientist will use a microscope or a spectrometer. Your toolbox is chock-full with all of those instruments I discussed in "The Parts of the Play."

Write in your book! Fill up the margins of the play with your notes. Record your reactions to characters. Mark where you see the complication introduced and where the climax occurs. Put question marks where you don't understand something. Mark anything and everything. Get into dialogue with the play. Where do you disagree with what it seems to be telling you? Where are you pleased? Clutter the white spaces with your own handwriting. If the pages are clean, you probably haven't analyzed the play enough. You need to do some more close reading.

You also might use some deliberate strategies to generate ideas. These are tried-and-true methods of discovery, some of them going back to Aristotle and the ancient Greeks. You'll see that most of them involve asking and answering questions. The technical term for using questions this way is **heuristics**, but of course that's not the only way to generate ideas. As an academic writer, you want to find out what works best for you, given your own strengths and weaknesses. Here are some strategies to help you start to generate ideas.

Talk. Find someone who has read the same play, and talk about it, argue, agree, explore your thoughts together. If you're interested in a particular issue that arises in the play, talk about that issue with other people. Take for instance Ibsen's *A Doll's House.* You might begin with some basic questions, like which characters appeal to you and why. Talk about your own experiences with romance. Was the relationship unequal in power? Have you ever felt the same kind of need for deceit that Nora feels? Let the conversation go where your interests take it

Class discussion. Classroom analysis is talk extraordinaire. What did your colleagues in class have to say about the play? Did you discover any angles that did not occur to you before? Did anyone react differently from you? Which passages did you discuss? What was said about those passages?

Brainstorm. That's just talking with a little more direction or formality. With pen and paper in hand, talk with a classmate about the play, jotting down everything that you think might be useful to you. Let one idea lead you to the next, and write everything down, both promising and unpromising ideas. You can sort them out later.

Free writing. I've found that this can be the best way to develop ideas and arguments. Give yourself a small stretch of time—say fifteen or twenty minutes—and write down everything you can think of about the play. What attracts you to it? What do you find interesting? Don't police your thoughts. Write it all down. You'll mine all of those sentences later, finding the nuggets among the dross.

View a production of the play. If you have the rare chance to see a live production of the play, be sure to go. You can find a movie version of most of the plays in this volume—if you can, watch that movie. See if you agree with the director's interpretation of the play. Does the film emphasize the same themes you would if you directed it? Do the actors play the characters the way you imagined them? Are any parts of the play changed or left out? If so, why? What is lost? What is gained? Essentially, you're using someone else's interpretation of the play to discover your own.

The proverbial shower. You might have that eureka moment of discovery in the shower, where so many brilliant ideas have hatched. Or is it a cup of coffee and a blank computer screen that help you think? Does your mind grow fruit while you're sitting on the bus? Listening to classical music? Figure out for yourself what makes *your* intellect productive, and *do it.*

2. Planning

When planning, review all of those discovery notes, whether they're in the margins of your book, in a notebook, in a computer document, or on sticky notes stuck on the edges of your desk. Try to identify the theme that emerges out of the discovery stage.

What it is it you most want to talk about? What issue raised in the play interests you the most? Remember, themes tend to be abstractions, like "friendship" or "war" or "gender roles." Perhaps there's a cluster of ideas that are all related to each other. Try to identify them. Write them down. Even if you're writing down only one or two words, write them down. Writing cements them in your mind.

Ultimately, your goal is to offer an assertion concerning this theme, to claim that the play has this or that to say about the theme. At this point, you could be very far along in your thinking. You might be able to venture a pretty complex assertion. Go ahead if you're ready. That statement will be your first draft of a thesis statement, a short statement that encapsulates your interpretation. The purpose of your paper is to persuade readers to agree with that statement, so this is the most important part of your paper. That's your destination. It will guide you as you construct your arguments: every paragraph should be one stage in the journey toward accepting that thesis.

If you're not ready to draft a thesis statement, don't worry about it. Use your theme as a guide for now.

Either way, at this stage, you're dealing mostly with arrangement. Sift through your discovery notes, identify those ideas that you want to use, and arrange them in some order. Which idea comes first after stating the theme or thesis? What seems to come logically after that? What's the third thing you want to talk about? What idea does that logically set up? It should seem to you that *X* logically precedes *Y*; that you have to dispense with *Y* before you can proceed to *Z*. If your organization mirrors the chronology of the play, that's a red flag. It might mean that you're not really constructing an argument, but instead you are summarizing the plot. Perhaps you're making a few observations as you go along, but you're not really proving a point. Ask yourself, *What do I want my readers to believe when they finish reading my paper?* and start again.

You might be able to keep your arrangement in your head, but I recommend that at the very least you jot down a sketchy outline. Probably, you don't want to get more detailed than a few bullet points. But at this stage, you should be thinking that each of the items in your outline is a potential paragraph. The paragraph is your main unit of organization, and you'll use paragraphing to help your reader recognize the stages in your argument.

Don't forget that writing is recursive. As you are arranging your thoughts, you might discover new ideas; and almost surely, as you begin drafting your paper, you'll realize you need to rearrange your paragraphs.

3. Drafting

In the drafting stage, you actually write what resembles a paper. Consequently, students often find this point the most challenging: you've got something to say, but the words don't come; you stare at a blank screen; the fingers on the keyboard are uninspired.

This advice might help: because this is a rough draft, don't worry about writing an introduction. Most writers find that to write an effective introduction, they have to wait to the very last stage of the process. Fretting about an introduction at this early stage is probably wasted energy. All you need at the head of your paper right now is your first version of your thesis.

Then consult your sketchy outline. You don't have to write from beginning to end. Pick a section that you feel most confident about. Maybe it's your third point, but you already have a couple of passages in the text that you know support that idea. Begin where you're most sure of yourself. Then, once the ball is rolling, go back to the other parts.

Many writers try too hard on their first draft. They'll work on one paragraph, realize that it's not quite right, and so they'll tinker with it, rewrite it, improve it, revise it again. Resist the temptation to perfect one paragraph before you move on to the next. Your main goal in drafting is to get all of your ideas and evidence down for the first time in paragraph format. You're in conversation with yourself, so there's no need for perfection. No one else is going to see what you've written. If you tend toward this kind of perfectionism, you should train yourself to be comfortable with a poorly argued train of thought or an awkwardly stated complex idea. You'll have plenty of time to improve things later, so just keep moving on from one point in your outline to another.

You might even time yourself: allow ten minutes to write your second paragraph. After ten minutes, move on to paragraph three, no matter what stage paragraph two is in—even if you've put nothing on paper but a couple of broken sentences. When I assign a rough draft for homework, I tell my students to give themselves a circumscribed amount of time: an hour perhaps; no more than two. Don't waste time polishing anything: just write.

When you're done writing your arguments, you should draft a full conclusion. Sum up your arguments and restate your thesis, probably in different words. Now that you've drafted your first version of your arguments, you can ask yourself again, *What is it that I want my readers to believe about the play?* You might discover that your answer to that question is different—perhaps even very different—from what it was in the discovery stage. That's OK. In fact, it's a good sign, as you'll see in the revising section that follows.

4. Revising

Revising is a lot more important than many writers realize. This stage will probably require most of your effort and time. If writing the entire paper, from discovery to proofreading, takes you ten hours, you could easily spend five or more hours on this stage.

Take a hard look at your rough draft. It's best to take a day off after writing your rough draft, so you can come to it cold, so to speak, reading it with a more objective eye. *Rough* draft is probably the wrong metaphor because it implies that your draft is a gemstone that just needs a little judicious cutting and polish before you turn it in. Instead, think of drafts like mountains that you're going to mine to find veins or seams of argument imbedded in the paragraphs. I really think of that first draft as a type of discovery: by writing it, you discover your arguments.

Finding Your Thesis

The first thing you want to dig out of your rough draft is your thesis. What is it that you really want to prove about the play? What do you think the play means? Take some real care here. This statement must be something debatable. For example, let's consider again Shakespeare's *Hamlet*. It takes place in Elsinore, the royal castle of Denmark, and in the opening act we discover some intrigue about how the king, Claudius, came to power. Here's a statement that does not quite pass muster as a thesis:

> In Shakespeare's *Hamlet,* the central character, the younger Hamlet, is confronted with the notion that his uncle usurped the throne from his father. He is charged with the task of taking revenge, and throughout the play we see him struggle with indecision, with his inability to take action.

This statement does a good job of naming a few themes: the play is about the impulse to revenge and the fear of action. But very few readers, if any, would disagree with that statement, so it's not really debatable. If it's not debatable, there's no point to writing a paper about it, because the purpose of an interpretive paper is to persuade skeptical readers to agree with your interpretation. Your thesis has got to go further than identifying themes.

You could take your interpretation one step further by asking and answering the question, *What does the play say about the fear of taking action?* One answer to that question might read like this:

> According to Shakespeare's play, failing to take swift and decisive action leads one to ruin and can harm many innocents as well.

Some readers might disagree with that interpretation. They might think the play is about how hard it is to ever discern the right thing to do and that we're sometimes fooled by our impulses to act. As you write your interpretive essay, you should imagine that your own readers are those who disagree with you. Your job in writing the paper would be to convince them to change their minds.

Usually, you'll find that you best articulated your thesis in that concluding paragraph of your rough draft. That's because it is often in the act of writing that first draft that you figure out what it is you want to prove to readers. Look at that conclusion. Does it offer a debatable point? Does it assert a statement that some people will disagree with? Is it worth writing a whole paper to prove that point? If not, then you need to work on your thesis some more. At this stage, you *must have a solid thesis statement*. Put that thesis statement at the head of a new outline.

Outlining

Now ask yourself, *What do I need to do to prove that I'm probably right?* You're trying to map out the steps in your argument. Remember that the thesis governs all. For example, let's consider again that thesis about *Hamlet: According to Shakespeare's play, failing to take*

swift and decisive action leads one to ruin and can harm many inno-
cents as well. Your outline might look like this:

- prove that Hamlet keenly feels the impulse to avenge
- demonstrate that revenge dictates a course of decisive action
- discuss why Hamlet feels the need to test the truth of the ghost's accusation
    - how that stratagem requires him to pretend to lose his sanity
    - explain how that decision affects first Ophelia and then Laertes
- discuss why Hamlet wants to persuade his mother to reform
    - explain how that delay affects Polonius and Gertrude

Each of those bullet points relates back to the thesis. And just as importantly, you can see how each stage in this argument has its logical place in the overall order: it makes sense to prove Hamlet feels the impulse to avenge his father's death before you prove that revenge dictates a course of decisive action; it makes sense to prove that revenge gives Hamlet a decisive course of action before you begin considering the various ways he rationalizes delay.

Now you need to gather evidence to support each one of those main points. Your evidence mostly will come from the text of the play itself. Let's imagine you're thinking about how to prove the first part of the third bullet point: how Hamlet pretends to be insane in order to test the truth of the ghost's accusation. To prove that point, you would draw on your close reading of the play. You might discuss how Hamlet's supposedly unstable mind allows him to say things aloud that would not otherwise be tolerated. And you might show how his mental instability allows him the opportunity to have the players stage *The Mousetrap.* In other words, you'd be analyzing Hamlet's motivation, and in each of these instances, you'd either quote from or paraphrase the text of the play. That's your evidence.

Remember, of course, that many readers would disagree with the main point in this stage of the argument: in fact, many readers think Hamlet really is insane or at least highly unstable. It's those readers you'd need to convince. Each paragraph in your paper—each stage of your argument—should point to specific details in the play. Perhaps several times in each paragraph you'll cite the text.

Only through the evidence of close reading will you ever be able to change someone's mind.

Redrafting

Now you're ready to write your second draft. Open an entirely new word processing document: a completely blank page. This will prevent you from merely tinkering with or polishing that first draft, adding a few sentences, moving paragraphs around, editing for grammar and usage, polishing the style. Though the work you put into the rough draft was absolutely essential—only through *writing* that draft could you discover what you have to say—the purpose of that first draft was to help you develop your ideas. *You* were the audience. You wrote it in order to communicate something to yourself. Your second draft is a public document. Your audience is someone else, perhaps your classmates; the general public; your teacher; an imaginary, thoughtful literary critic. Above all, imagine that your readers are people who disagree with your thesis. In revision, you start making rhetorical decisions based on how you want to affect that audience, which calls for a fresh start.

Using your new outline, write the second draft of your paper on this blank page. Each of your bullet points might serve as the main point of a body paragraph. You might end up cutting-and-pasting significant portions of your rough draft. That's perfectly fine. But I think you'll find that, while you're using ideas from the first draft, there are very few complete sentences and practically no paragraphs that can be cut-and-pasted wholesale into the second draft. The second draft is a true *rewriting:* you're writing the paper a second time. All the while, you need to be thinking about your audience: *Will this idea be clear to my reader or do I need to explain it a little more fully? Is my argument convincing to a skeptical reader? What do I need to do to improve it?*

Writing an Introduction

Only at this point do I recommend you write your introduction. Now you know *exactly* what you want to prove to your readers, and you know *exactly* how you're going to do it. So only now are you ready to craft an introduction that sets all of that up for your readers.

Think of the introduction as having three purposes: (1) to grab your reader's interest, (2) to introduce the relevant theme you're discussing, (3) to deliver your thesis. More often than not, the best way to accomplish these is to open with a vivid scene, something that engages your reader's imagination. For example, in the paper we've been discussing, which deals with the theme of indecision in *Hamlet,* you might begin by painting the picture of act 3, scene 3, where

> Hamlet finds Claudius at prayer. He holds the sword over the king's head and is ready to kill. He could "do it pat," as he tells himself, but just before he strikes, Hamlet persuades himself to delay (3.3.73). He lowers his sword, he sneaks out of the chamber, and Claudius lives another day. I am not so interested in why Hamlet hesitates as I am in the consequences. What happens when "the native hue of resolution / Is sicklied o'er with the pale cast of thought" (3.1.84–85)? The play suggests that when decisive action is clear, one should act without delay. Hamlet's failing to take swift, decisive action leads him to ruin and the ruin of many innocents as well.

5. Editing

Editing means polishing your arguments. Read through your revision, trying to imagine you're someone who disagrees with the thesis. Go from beginning to end, marking up the revision. Don't stop to fix anything yet—just identify all of the problems. Look for places in your logic that are weak or unconvincing. Do you need more evidence someplace? Does it seem odd that paragraph three leads into paragraph four? Do several sentences within one paragraph seem to be unrelated to that paragraph's main purpose?

After you've marked the entire paper, correct these problems.

Don't be afraid to change things pretty significantly in the editing phase. You might find yourself moving several sentences from one paragraph to another. You might cut out chunks of the paper that are unrelated to your thesis. You might even tweak your thesis, in which case you need to reassess everything else to make sure the paper still relates to your new thesis. Maybe you'll realize that before you get to point *X* you have to write a whole new paragraph proving point *Y*. Editing can be pretty labor-intensive, even if it does not rise to the level of a full revision.

6. Citation

You need to cite your references to the play, whether you're paraphrasing, summarizing, or quoting. That's so your readers can go back to the source of your evidence and check things out for themselves. Don't forget also that precision in **citations** has its own rhetorical effect. You look like an expert when you cite with perfect competence, and readers—including the teacher grading your essay—are more likely to believe your arguments.

You'll find a few references to online citation guides a little later, which will give you more detail. But take a second look now at my model introductory paragraph on the previous page. The citation (3.3.73) means you'll find these words in act 3, scene 3, line 73. This is standard practice when referencing Shakespeare, and often people writing about other plays will use the same method of documentation. Other times, the parenthetical citations instead would include page numbers. Ask your instructor which method she prefers. Your general rule of thumb should follow this practical advice: *Have I told my readers where to find each piece of evidence I take from the play?* If you have, then your citations are sufficient. You can find a complete guide to citation at this book's companion site, wwnorton .com/write.

7. Proofreading

Read your edited revision. At this stage, you're fine-tuning your sentences rather than working on your arguments. Read through the entire paper. I often tell my students to read the paper backward, sentence by sentence. That way, you get out of the flow of your argument and can see each sentence as a sentence. When proofreading you're looking for sentences that sound confusing or even ungrammatical. You're looking for spelling and punctuation errors. Have you documented your quotations and paraphrases correctly? Mark anything that's suspicious. If it sounds slightly unclear to you, you can be sure the sentence is very unclear to your readers. Go through the entire paper, pausing only long enough to mark where there's a problem.

When you've marked the entire paper, go back and start fixing the problems.

Some of those problems will be easy to fix because they're mere typos, either mistyped words or simple errors that derive from haste or inattention, like an *it's* for an *its*. But other problems might take more work, especially those sentences that sound confusing to you. If you've got a sentence that seems tangled, whose sense is not clear and you're not quite sure why, try this easy trick of the trade: ask yourself, *What was I trying to say here?* Then write down the answer as it comes to you. Probably, your answer to that question will be clearer, the grammar will be correct, and you can just plug it into your paper, replacing the problem sentence. Usually, your correction will be longer than the original, and sometimes you might find that you use two or three sentences to explain what you were trying to say. That's not surprising, because often the problem with tangled sentences is that you're trying to do too much all at once.

Once all of the problems you noted in your proofreading have been corrected, you're ready to turn in your essay.

Conclusion

After all of this prefatory material, it would be easy to lose sight of an important goal in reading these plays: to have fun. Ultimately, increasing your reading pleasure is the purpose of this introduction. You should enjoy reading these plays (your level of enjoyment being a good index of your level of understanding), just as your teacher and I delight in introducing you to plays that we continue to enjoy reading.

THE SEAGULL BOOK OF

Plays

Fourth Edition

Sophocles

496?–406? B.C.E

ANTIGONE

The backstory to this play, the tragic history of several generations of rulers in Thebes, was well-known to every Athenian who saw it first performed in the theater in 442 B.C.E. King Laïus and Queen Jocasta had a son, Oedipus, whom the oracles prophesied would kill his father and marry his mother. The parents gave orders to have the baby killed, but a kindly servant brought the boy to the frontier of Theban territory, where he gave the infant to a shepherd from neighboring Corinth. The king and queen of Corinth adopted the child for their own. When Oedipus was a young man, another oracle delivered to him the same prophecy his birth parents had heard years earlier. Not knowing who his true parents were, he exiled himself from Corinth, unwittingly setting his fate in motion. He met Laïus on the road to Thebes, they quarreled, fought, and the son killed his father, not knowing who he was. When Oedipus reached Thebes, he defeated the monstrous Sphinx and was rewarded with the crown; he married the widowed queen, his own mother, and they had four children: the two girls, Antigone and Ismene, and the two boys, Eteocles and Polyneices. Later, when his relation to Jocasta was revealed, Oedipus gouged out his own eyes to expiate the sin, and he gave up the crown. (These events are the subject of Sophocles' play Oedipus the King, *which he wrote about a dozen years after* Antigone.*)*

Eteocles and Polyneices were supposed to rule in cycles, each occupying the throne for a year before his brother succeeded him for the next year. But after the first year, Eteocles refused to give Polyneices his turn. Polyneices went to Argos, where he raised an army to attack Thebes and secure his crown by force. Both brothers were killed in the fighting, leaving the crown to their uncle, Creon. Aeschylus's famous play Seven Against Thebes, *which was performed about twenty-five years before* Antigone, *tells the story of the Theban civil war. Sophocles picks up where Aeschylus left off, as if this play were a sequel to the other.*

As I discussed in the Introduction, Aristotle based his theory of tragedy on the plays of Sophocles. With that in mind, a good way to begin analyzing this play is to think about the tragic hero: Is it Antigone or Creon? Which character has the flaw that sets in motion the conflict? Who undergoes a change from (figurative) prosperity to poverty? Whose punishment is disproportionate to his or her tragic mistake? Who achieves a self-understanding by the play's end? And perhaps most importantly, with whom do you think Sophocles wants you to identify?

Sophocles' treatment of Antigone's story has long inspired philosophers, political theorists, artists, and especially dissidents. The German philosopher Hegel praised her heroism, as did the English radical poet Percy Bysshe Shelley and the early feminist writer, Virginia Woolf. In the modern age, Antigone has become a potent symbol to those who resist unjust laws of state. For example, Jean Anouilh retold her story in a play that debuted in Nazi-occupied France in 1944, and the heroine inspired men and women in the French Resistance to endeavor what Antigone herself enacted: civil disobedience. As Martin Luther King Jr. explained so eloquently in his "Letter from Birmingham Jail," the civil disobedient does not only refuse to obey unjust laws, she does so openly without trying to avoid the penalty for such violations. The act is meant to inspire social change: the example of the righteous law-breaker suffering the unjust hand of the law-enforcer should move people to outrage. This theme, the conflict between personal conscience and duty to the state, is relevant to every age.

Antigone*

CHARACTERS

ANTIGONE	HAEMON
ISMENE	TEIRESIAS
CHORUS OF THEBAN ELDERS	A MESSENGER
CREON	EURYDICE
A SENTRY	SECOND MESSENGER
SERVANTS	

The two sisters ANTIGONE *and* ISMENE *meet in front of the palace gates in Thebes.*

* Translated by David Grene.

ANTIGONE: Ismene, my dear sister,
   whose father was my father, can you think of any
   of all the evils that stem from Oedipus
   that Zeus does not bring to pass for us, while we yet live?
   No pain, no ruin, no shame, and no dishonor   5
   but I have seen it in our mischiefs,
   yours and mine.
   And now what is the proclamation that they tell of
   made lately by the commander, publicly,
   to all the people? Do you know it? Have you heard it?   10
   Don't you notice when the evils due to enemies
   are headed towards those we love?
ISMENE: Not a word, Antigone, of those we love,
   either sweet or bitter, has come to me since the moment
   when we lost our two brothers,
   on one day, by their hands dealing mutual death.   15
   Since the Argive army[1] fled in this past night,
   I know of nothing further, nothing
   of better fortune or of more destruction.
ANTIGONE: I knew it well; that is why I sent for you   20
   to come outside the palace gates
   to listen to me, privately.
ISMENE: What is it? Certainly your words
   come of dark thoughts.
ANTIGONE: Yes, indeed; for those two brothers of ours, in burial 25
   has not Creon honored the one, dishonored the other?
   Eteocles, they say he has used justly
   with lawful rites and hid him in the earth
   to have his honor among the dead men there.
   But the unhappy corpse of Polyneices   30
   he has proclaimed to all the citizens,
   they say, no man may hide
   in a grave nor mourn in funeral,
   but leave unwept, unburied, a dainty treasure

---

1. Polyneices married the daughter of the King of Argos, another Greek city-state, and raised an army
there to attack Thebes.

for the birds that see him, for their feast's delight.   35
That is what, they say, the worthy Creon
has proclaimed for you and me—for me, I tell you—
and he comes here to clarify to the unknowing
his proclamation; he takes it seriously;
for whoever breaks the edict death is prescribed,   40
and death by stoning publicly.
There you have it; soon you will show yourself
as noble both in your nature and your birth,
or yourself as base, although of noble parents.

ISMENE: If things are as you say, poor sister, how   45
    can I better them? how loose or tie the knot?

ANTIGONE: Decide if you will share the work, the deed.

ISMENE: What kind of danger is there? How far have your thoughts
    gone?

ANTIGONE: Here is this hand. Will you help it to lift the dead man?

ISMENE: Would you bury him, when it is forbidden the city?   50

ANTIGONE: At least he is my brother—and yours, too,
    though you deny him. I will not prove false to him.

ISMENE: You are so headstrong. Creon has forbidden it.

ANTIGONE: It is not for him to keep me from my own.

ISMENE: O God!   55
    Consider, sister, how our father died,
    hated and infamous[2]; how he brought to light
    his own offenses; how he himself struck out
    the sight of his two eyes;
    his own hand was their executioner.   60
    Then, mother and wife, two names in one, did shame
    violently on her life, with twisted cords.
    Third, our two brothers, on a single day,
    poor wretches, themselves worked out their mutual doom.
    Each killed the other, hand against brother's hand.   65
    Now there are only the two of us, left behind,
    and see how miserable our end shall be
    if in the teeth of law we shall transgress
    against the sovereign's decree and power.

2. Oedipus. See the headnote to this play.

You ought to realize we are only women, 70
not meant in nature to fight against men,
and that we are ruled, by those who are stronger,
to obedience in this and even more painful matters.
I do indeed beg those beneath the earth
to give me their forgiveness, 75
since force constrains me,
that I shall yield in this to the authorities.
Extravagant action is not sensible.

ANTIGONE: I would not urge you now; nor if you wanted
to act would I be glad to have you with me. 80
Be as you choose to be; but for myself
I myself will bury him. It will be good
to die, so doing. I shall lie by his side,
loving him as he loved me; I shall be
a criminal—but a religious one. 85
The time in which I must please those that are dead
is longer than I must please those of this world.
For there I shall lie forever. You, if you like,
can cast dishonor on what the gods have honored.

ISMENE: I will not put dishonor on them, but 90
to act in defiance of the citizenry,
my nature does not give me means for that.

ANTIGONE: Let that be your excuse. But I will go
to heap the earth on the grave of my loved brother.

ISMENE: How I fear for you, my poor sister! 95

ANTIGONE: Do not fear for me. Make straight your own path to
destiny.

ISMENE: At least do not speak of this act to anyone else;
bury him in secret; I will be silent, too.

ANTIGONE: Oh, oh, no! shout it out. I will hate you still worse
for silence—should you not proclaim it, 100
to everyone.

ISMENE: You have a warm heart for such chilly deeds.

ANTIGONE: I know I am pleasing those I should please most.

ISMENE: If you can do it. But you are in love
with the impossible. 105

ANTIGONE: No. When I can no more, then I will stop.

ISMENE: It is better not to hunt the impossible
   at all.
ANTIGONE: If you will talk like this I will loathe you,
   and you will be adjudged an enemy—   110
   justly—by the dead's decision. Let me alone
   and my folly with me, to endure this terror.
   No suffering of mine will be enough
   to make me die ignobly.
ISMENE: Well, if you will, go on.   115
   Know this; that though you are wrong to go, your friends
   are right to love you.
CHORUS: Sun's beam, fairest of all
      that ever till now shone
      on seven-gated Thebes;   120
      O golden eye of day, you shone
      coming over Dirce's stream;[3]
      You drove in headlong rout
      the whiteshielded man from Argos,
      complete in arms;   125
      his bits rang sharper
      under your urging.

      Polyneices brought him here
      against our land, Polyneices,
      roused by contentious quarrel;   130
      like an eagle he flew into our country,
      with many men-at-arms,
      with many a helmet crowned with horsehair.

      He stood above the halls, gaping with murderous lances,
      encompassing the city's   135
      seven-gated mouth
      But before his jaws would be sated
      with our blood, before the fire,
      pine fed, should capture our crown of towers,
      he went hence—   140

---

3. Dirce, the wife of an ancient Theban ruler, was a devotee of the god Dionysus. When she died, he made a spring flow from her tomb.

such clamor of war stretched behind his back,
from his dragon foe, a thing he could not overcome.

For Zeus, who hates the most
the boasts of a great tongue,
saw them coming in a great tide,   145
insolent in the clang of golden armor.
The god struck him down with hurled fire,
as he strove to raise the victory cry,
now at the very winning post.

The earth rose to strike him as he fell swinging.   150
In his frantic onslaught, possessed, he breathed upon us
with blasting winds of hate.
Sometimes the great god of war was on one side,
and sometimes he struck a staggering blow on the other;
the god was a very wheel horse on the right trace. 155

At seven gates stood seven captains,
ranged equals against equals, and there left
their brazen suits of armor
to Zeus, the god of trophies.
Only those two wretches born of one father
    and mother   160
set their spears to win a victory on both sides;
they worked out their share in a common death.

Now Victory, whose name is great, has come
to Thebes of many chariots
with joy to answer her joy,   165
to bring forgetfulness of these wars;
let us go to all the shrines of the gods
and dance all night long.
Let Bacchus[4] lead the dance,
shaking Thebes to trembling.   170

---

4. Alternative name for Dionysus, one of the twelve Olympian gods. He was linked to fertility and religious and sexual ecstasy, and was associated with communication between the worlds of the living and the dead. His father was Zeus and his mother, Semele, was the daughter of the Theban king Cadmus.

But here is the king of our land,
Creon, son of Menoeceus;
in our new contingencies with the gods,
he is our new ruler.
He comes to set in motion some design—   175
what design is it? Because he has proposed
the convocation of the elders.
He sent a public summons for our discussion.

CREON: Gentlemen: as for our city's fortune,
the gods have shaken her, when the great waves broke,   180
but the gods have brought her through again to safety.
For yourselves, I chose you out of all and summoned you
to come to me, partly because I knew you
as always loyal to the throne—at first,
when Laïus was king, and then again   185
when Oedipus saved our city and then again
when he died and you remained with steadfast truth
to their descendants,
until they met their double fate upon one day,
striking and stricken, defiled each by a brother's murder. 190
Now here I am, holding all authority
and the throne, in virtue of kinship with the dead.
It is impossible to know any man—
I mean his soul, intelligence, and judgment—
until he shows his skill in rule and law.   195
I think that a man supreme ruler of a whole city,
if he does not reach for the best counsel for her,
but through some fear, keeps his tongue under lock and key,
him I judge the worst of any;
I have always judged so; and anyone thinking   200
another man more a friend than his own country,
I rate him nowhere. For my part, God is my witness,
who sees all, always, I would not be silent
if I saw ruin, not safety, on the way
towards my fellow citizens. I would not count   205
any enemy of my country as a friend—
because of what I know, that she it is
which gives us our security. If she sails upright

and we sail on her, friends will be ours for the making.
In the light of rules like these, I will make her greater still. 210

In consonance with this, I here proclaim
to the citizens about Oedipus' sons.
For Eteocles, who died this city's champion,
showing his valor's supremacy everywhere,
he shall be buried in his grave with every rite 215
of sanctity given to heroes under earth.
However, his brother, Polyneices, a returned exile,
who sought to burn with fire from top to bottom
his native city, and the gods of his own people;
who sought to taste the blood he shared with us, 220
and lead the rest of us to slavery—
I here proclaim to the city that this man
shall no one honor with a grave and none shall mourn.
You shall leave him without burial; you shall watch him
chewed up by birds and dogs and violated. 225
Such is my mind in the matter; never by me
shall the wicked man have precedence in honor
over the just. But he that is loyal to the state
in death, in life alike, shall have my honor.
CHORUS: Son of Menoeceus, so it is your pleasure 230
to deal with foe and friend of this our city.
To use any legal means lies in your power,
both about the dead and those of us who live.
CREON: I understand, then, you will do my bidding.
CHORUS: Please lay this burden on some younger man. 235
CREON: Oh, watchers of the corpse I have already.
CHORUS: What else, then, do your commands entail?
CREON: That you should not side with those who disagree.
CHORUS: There is none so foolish as to love his own death.
CREON: Yes, indeed those are the wages, but often greed 240
has with its hopes brought men to ruin.
SENTRY: My lord, I will never claim my shortness of breath
is due to hurrying, nor were there wings in my feet.
I stopped at many a lay-by in my thinking;
I circled myself till I met myself coming back. 245

My soul accosted me with different speeches.
"Poor fool, yourself, why are you going somewhere
when once you get there you will pay the piper?"
"Well, aren't you the daring fellow! stopping again?
and suppose Creon hears the news from someone else— 250
don't you realize that you will smart for that?"
I turned the whole matter over. I suppose I may say
"I made haste slowly" and the short road became long.
However, at last I came to a resolve:
I must go to you; even if what I say 255
is nothing, really, still I shall say it.
I come here, a man with a firm clutch on the hope
that nothing can betide him save what is fated.
CREON: What is it then that makes you so afraid?
SENTRY: No, I want first of all to tell you my side of it. 260
I didn't do the thing; I never saw who did it.
It would not be fair for me to get into trouble.
CREON: You hedge, and barricade the thing itself.
Clearly you have some ugly news for me.
SENTRY: Well, you know how disasters make a man 265
hesitate to be their messenger.
CREON: For God's sake, tell me and get out of here!
SENTRY: Yes, I will tell you. Someone just now
buried the corpse and vanished. He scattered on the skin
some thirsty dust; he did the ritual, 270
duly, to purge the body of desecration.
CREON: What! Now who on earth could have done that?
SENTRY: I do not know. For there was there no mark
of axe's stroke nor casting up of earth
of any mattock; the ground was hard and dry, 275
unbroken; there were no signs of wagon wheels.
The doer of the deed had left no trace.
But when the first sentry of the day pointed it out,
there was for all of us a disagreeable
wonder. For the body had disappeared; 280
not in a grave, of course; but there lay upon him
a little dust as of a hand avoiding
the curse of violating the dead body's sanctity.

There were no signs of any beast nor dog
that came there; he had clearly not been torn.   285
There was a tide of bad words at one another,
guard taunting guard, and it might well have ended
in blows, for there was no one there to stop it.
Each one of us was the criminal but no one
manifestly so; all denied knowledge of it.   290
We were ready to take hot bars in our hands
or walk through fire, and call on the gods with oaths
that we had neither done it nor were privy
to a plot with anyone, neither in planning
nor yet in execution.   295
At last when nothing came of all our searching,
there was one man who spoke, made every head
bow to the ground in fear. For we could not
either contradict him nor yet could we see how
if we did what he said we would come out all right.   300
His word was that we must lay information
about the matter to yourself; we could not cover it.
This view prevailed and the lot of the draw chose me,
unlucky me, to win that prize. So here
I am. I did not want to come,   305
and you don't want to have me. I know that.
For no one likes the messenger of bad news.
CHORUS: My lord: I wonder, could this be God's doing?
 This is the thought that keeps on haunting me.
CREON: Stop, before your words fill even me with rage,   310
 that you should be exposed as a fool, and you so old.
 For what you say is surely insupportable
 when you say the gods took forethought for this corpse.
 Is it out of excess of honor for the man,
 for the favors that he did them, they should cover him?   315
 This man who came to burn their pillared temples,
 their dedicated offerings—and this land
 and laws he would have scattered to the winds?
 Or do you see the gods as honoring
 criminals? This is not so. But what I am doing   320
 now, and other things before this, some men disliked,

within this very city, and muttered against me,
secretly shaking their heads; they would not bow
justly beneath the yoke to submit to me.
I am very sure that these men hired others   325
to do this thing. I tell you the worse currency
that ever grew among mankind is money. This
sacks cities, this drives people from their homes,
this teaches and corrupts the minds of the loyal
to acts of shame. This displays   330
all kinds of evil for the use of men,
instructs in the knowledge of every impious act.
Those that have done this deed have been paid to do it,
but in the end they will pay for what they have done.

It is as sure as I still reverence Zeus—   335
know this right well—and I speak under oath—
if you and your fellows do not find this man
who with his own hand did the burial
and bring him here before me face to face,
your death alone will not be enough for me.   340
You will hang alive till you open up this outrage.
That will teach you in the days to come from what
you may draw profit—safely—from your plundering.
It's not from anything and everything
you can grow rich. You will find out   345
that ill-gotten gains ruin more than they save.
SENTRY: Have I your leave to say something—or should
    I just turn and go?
CREON: Don't you know your talk is painful enough already?
SENTRY: Is the ache in your ears or in your mind?   350
CREON: Why do you dissect the whereabouts of my pain?
SENTRY: Because it is he who did the deed who hurts your
    mind. I only hurt your ears that listen.
CREON: I am sure you have been a chatterbox since you were born.
SENTRY: All the same, I did not do this thing.   355
CREON: You might have done this, too, if you sold your soul.
SENTRY: It's a bad thing if one judges and judges wrongly.

CREON: You may talk as wittily as you like of judgment.
　　Only, if you don't bring to light those men
　　who have done this, you will yet come to say　　　　360
　　that your wretched gains have brought bad consequences.
SENTRY: [*Aside.*] It were best that he were found, but whether
　　the criminal is taken or he isn't——
　　for that chance will decide—one thing is certain,
　　you'll never see me coming here again.　　　　365
　　I never hoped to escape, never thought I could.
　　But now I have come off safe, I thank God heartily.
CHORUS: Many are the wonders, none
　　　　is more wonderful than what is man.
　　　　　This it is that crosses the sea　　　　370
　　　　with the south winds storming and the waves swelling,
　　　　breaking around him in roaring surf.
　　　　He it is again who wears away
　　　　the Earth, oldest of gods, immortal, unwearied,
　　　　as the ploughs wind across her from year to year　　375
　　　　when he works her with the breed that comes from horses.

　　　　The tribe of the lighthearted birds he snares
　　　　and takes prisoner the races of savage beasts
　　　　and the brood of the fish of the sea,
　　　　with the close-spun web of nets.　　　　380
　　　　A cunning fellow is man. His contrivances
　　　　make him master of beasts of the field
　　　　and those that move in the mountains.
　　　　So he brings the horse with the shaggy neck
　　　　to bend underneath the yoke;　　　　385
　　　　and also the untamed mountain bull;
　　　　and speech and windswift thought
　　　　and the tempers that go with city living
　　　　he has taught himself, and how to avoid
　　　　the sharp frost, when lodging is cold　　　　390
　　　　under the open sky
　　　　and pelting strokes of the rain.
　　　　He has a way against everything,

and he faces nothing that is to come
without contrivance.   395
Only against death
can he call on no means of escape;
but escape from hopeless diseases
he has found in the depths of his mind.
With some sort of cunning, inventive   400
beyond all expectation
he reaches sometimes evil,
and sometimes good.

If he honors the laws of earth,
and the justice of the gods he has confirmed by oath,   405
high is his city; no city
has he with whom dwells dishonor
prompted by recklessness.
He who is so, may he never
share my hearth!   410
may he never think my thoughts!

Is this a portent sent by God?
I cannot tell.
I know her. How can I say
that this is not Antigone?   415
Unhappy girl, child of unhappy Oedipus,
what is this?
Surely it is not you they bring here
as disobedient to the royal edict,
surely not you, taken in such folly.   420

SENTRY: She is the one who did the deed;
   we took her burying him. But where is Creon?
CHORUS: He is just coming from the house, when you most need him.
CREON: What is this? What has happened that I come
   so opportunely?   425
SENTRY: My lord, there is nothing
   that a man should swear he would never do.
   Second thoughts make liars of the first resolution.
   I would have vowed it would be long enough
   before I came again, lashed hence by your threats.   430
   But since the joy that comes past hope, and against all hope,

is like no other pleasure in extent,
I have come here, though I break my oath in coming.
I bring this girl here who has been captured
giving the grace of burial to the dead man.   435
This time no lot chose me; this was my jackpot,
and no one else's. Now, my lord, take her
and as you please judge her and test her; I
am justly free and clear of all this trouble.
CREON: This girl—how did you take her and from where?   440
SENTRY: She was burying the man. Now you know all.
CREON: Do you know what you are saying? Do you mean it?
SENTRY: She is the one; I saw her burying
  the dead man you forbade the burial of.
  Now, do I speak plainly and clearly enough?   445
CREON: How was she seen? How was she caught in the act?
SENTRY: This is how it was. When we came there,
  with those dreadful threats of yours upon us,
  we brushed off all the dust that lay upon
  the dead man's body, heedfully   450
  leaving it moist and naked.
  We sat on the brow of the hill, to windward,
  that we might shun the smell of the corpse upon us.
  Each of us wakefully urged his fellow
  with torrents of abuse, not to be careless   455
  in this work of ours. So it went on,
  until in the midst of the sky the sun's bright circle
  stood still; the heat was burning. Suddenly
  a squall lifted out of the earth a storm of dust,
  a trouble in the sky. It filled the plain,   460
  ruining all the foliage of the wood
  that was around it. The great empty air
  was filled with it. We closed our eyes, enduring
  this plague sent by the gods. When at long last
  we were quit of it, why, then we saw the girl.   465

She was crying out with the shrill cry
of an embittered bird
that sees its nest robbed of its nestlings
and the bed empty. So, too, when she saw

the body stripped of its cover, she burst out in groans,   470
calling terrible curses on those that had done that deed;
and with her hands immediately
brought thirsty dust to the body; from a shapely brazen
urn, held high over it, poured a triple stream
of funeral offerings; and crowned the corpse.   475
When we saw that, we rushed upon her and
caught our quarry then and there, not a bit disturbed.
We charged her with what she had done, then and
the first time.
She did not deny a word of it—to my joy,
but to my pain as well. It is most pleasant   480
to have escaped oneself out of such troubles
but painful to bring into it those whom we love.
However, it is but natural for me
to count all this less than my own escape.

CREON: You there, that turn your eyes upon the ground,   485
    do you confess or deny what you have done?
ANTIGONE: Yes, I confess; I will not deny my deed.
CREON: [*To the* SENTRY.] You take yourself off where you like.
    You are free of a heavy charge.
    Now, Antigone, tell me shortly and to the point,   490
    did you know the proclamation against your action?
ANTIGONE: I knew it; of course I did. For it was public.
CREON: And did you dare to disobey that law?
ANTIGONE: Yes, it was not Zeus that made the proclamation;
    nor did Justice, which lives with those below, enact   495
    such laws as that, for mankind. I did not believe
    your proclamation had such power to enable
    one who will someday die to override
    God's ordinances, unwritten and secure.
    They are not of today and yesterday;   500
    they live forever; none knows when first they were.
    These are the laws whose penalties I would not
    incur from the gods, through fear of any man's temper.

    I know that I will die—of course I do—
    even if you had not doomed me by proclamation.   505

If I shall die before my time, I count that
a profit. How can such as I, that live
among such troubles, not find a profit in death?
So for such as me, to face such a fate as this
is pain that does not count. But if I dared to leave 510
the dead man, my mother's son, dead and unburied,
that would have been real pain. The other is not.
Now, if you think me a fool to act like this,
perhaps it is a fool that judges so.
CHORUS: The savage spirit of a savage father 515
 shows itself in this girl. She does not know
 how to yield to trouble.
CREON: I would have you know the most fanatic spirits
 fall most of all. It is the toughest iron,
 baked in the fire to hardness, you may see 520
 most shattered, twisted, shivered to fragments.
 I know hot horses are restrained
 by a small curb. For he that is his neighbor's slave cannot
 be high in spirit. This girl had learned her insolence
 before this, when she broke the established laws. 525
 But here is still another insolence
 in that she boasts of it, laughs at what she did.
 I swear I am no man and she the man
 if she can win this and not pay for it.
 No; though she were my sister's child or closer 530
 in blood than all that my hearth god acknowledges
 as mine, neither she nor her sister should escape
 the utmost sentence—death. For indeed I accuse her,
 the sister, equally of plotting the burial.
 Summon her. I saw her inside, just now, 535
 crazy, distraught. When people plot
 mischief in the dark, it is the mind which first
 is convicted of deceit. But surely I hate indeed
 the one that is caught in evil and then makes
 that evil look like good. 540
ANTIGONE: Do you want anything
 beyond my taking and my execution?
CREON: Oh, nothing! Once I have that I have everything.

ANTIGONE: Why do you wait, then? Nothing that you say
    pleases me; God forbid it ever should. 545
    So my words, too, naturally offend you.
    Yet how could I win a greater share of glory
    than putting my own brother in his grave?
    All that are here would surely say that's true,
    if fear did not lock their tongues up. A prince's power 550
    is blessed in many things, not least in this,
    that he can say and do whatever he likes.

CREON: You are alone among the people of Thebes
    to see things in that way.

ANTIGONE: No, these do, too, 555
    but keep their mouths shut for the fear of you.

CREON: Are you not ashamed to think so differently
    from them?

ANTIGONE: There is nothing shameful in honoring my brother.

CREON: Was not he that died on the other side your brother? 560

ANTIGONE: Yes, indeed, of my own blood from father
    and mother.

CREON: Why then do you show a grace that must be impious
    in *his* sight?

ANTIGONE: *That* other dead man
    would never bear you witness in what you say. 565

CREON: Yes he would, if you put him only on equality
    with one that was a desecrator.

ANTIGONE: It was his brother, not his slave, that died.

CREON: He died destroying the country the other defended.

ANTIGONE: The god of death demands these rites for both. 570

CREON: But the good man does not seek an *equal* share only,
    with the bad.

ANTIGONE: Who knows
    if in that other world this is true piety?

CREON: My enemy is still my enemy, even in death.

ANTIGONE: My nature is to join in love, not hate. 575

CREON: Go then to the world below, yourself, if you
    must love. Love *them*. When I am alive no woman shall rule.

CHORUS: Here before the gates comes Ismene
    shedding tears for the love of a brother.

A cloud over her brow casts shame 580
on her flushed face, as the tears wet
her fair cheeks.

CREON: You there, who lurked in my house, viper-like—
secretly drawing its lifeblood; I never thought
that I was raising two sources of destruction, 585
two rebels against my throne. Come tell me now,
will you, too, say you bore a hand in the burial
or will you swear that you know nothing of it?

ISMENE: I did it, yes—if she will say I did it
I bear my share in it, bear the guilt, too. 590

ANTIGONE: Justice will not allow you what you refused
and I will have none of your partnership.

ISMENE: But in your troubles I am not ashamed
to sail with you the sea of suffering.

ANTIGONE: Where the act was death, the dead are witnesses. 595
I do not love a friend who loves in words.

ISMENE: Sister, do not dishonor me, denying me
a common death with you, a common honoring
of the dead man.

ANTIGONE: Don't die with me, nor make your own 600
what you have never touched. I that die am enough.

ISMENE: What life is there for me, once I have lost you?

ANTIGONE: Ask Creon; all your care was on his behalf.

ISMENE: Why do you hurt me, when you gain nothing by it?

ANTIGONE: I am hurt by my own mockery—if I mock you. 605

ISMENE: Even now—what can I do to help you still?

ANTIGONE: Save yourself; I do not grudge you your escape.

ISMENE: I cannot bear it! Not even to share your death!

ANTIGONE: Life was your choice, and death was mine.

ISMENE: You cannot say I accepted that choice in silence. 610

ANTIGONE: You were right in the eyes of one party, I in the other.

ISMENE: Well then, the fault is equally between us.

ANTIGONE: Take heart; you are alive, but my life died
long ago, to serve the dead.

CREON: Here are two girls; I think that one of them 615
has suddenly lost her wits—the other was always so.

ISMENE: Yes, for, my lord, the wits that they are born with
  do not stay firm for the unfortunate.
  They go astray.
CREON: Certainly yours do,
  when you share troubles with the troublemaker.   620
ISMENE: What life can be mine alone without her?
CREON: Do not
  speak of *her*. She isn't, anymore.
ISMENE: Will you kill your son's wife to be?
CREON: Yes, there are other fields for him to plough.
ISMENE: Not with the mutual love of him and her.   625
CREON: I hate a bad wife for a son of mine.
ANTIGONE: Dear Haemon, how your father dishonors you.
CREON: There is too much of you—and of your marriage!
CHORUS: Will you rob your son of this girl?
CREON: Death—it is death that will stop the marriage for me. 630
CHORUS: Your decision it seems is taken: she shall die.
CREON: Both you and I have decided it. No more delay.

    [*He turns to the* SERVANTS.]

  Bring her inside, you. From this time forth,
  these must be women, and not free to roam.
  For even the stout of heart shrink when they see   635
  the approach of death close to their lives.
CHORUS: Lucky are those whose lives
      know no taste of sorrow.
      But for those whose house has been shaken by God
      there is never cessation of ruin;   640
      it steals on generation after generation
      within a breed. Even as the swell
      is driven over the dark deep
      by the fierce Thracian winds
      I see the ancient evils of Labdacus' house   645
      are heaped on the evils of the dead.[5]

5. Thrace is a region constituted today by eastern Greece, western Turkey, and southeastern Bulgaria; the wind originating in the Thracian mountains was called Boreas, the northern wind that brings winter.

Labdacus' house: Oedipus, Polyneices, and Eteocles were all descendants of Labdacus, the grandson of Cadmus, who founded Thebes. Their "house" is the ruling family of the city.

No generation frees another, some god
strikes them down; there is no deliverance.
Here was the light of hope stretched
over the last roots of Oedipus' house,   650
and the bloody dust due to the gods below
has mowed it down—that and the folly of speech
and ruin's enchantment of the mind.

Your power, O Zeus, what sin of man can limit?
All-aging sleep does not overtake it,   655
nor the unwearied months of the gods; and you,
for whom time brings no age,
you hold the glowing brightness of Olympus.[6]

For the future near and far,
and the past, this law holds good: 660
nothing very great
comes to the life of mortal man
without ruin to accompany it.
For Hope, widely wandering, comes to many of mankind
as a blessing,   665
but to many as the deceiver,
using light-minded lusts;
she comes to him that knows nothing
till he burns his foot in the glowing fire.
With wisdom has someone declared   670
a word of distinction:
that evil seems good to one whose mind
the god leads to ruin,
and but for the briefest moment of time
is his life outside of calamity.   675
Here is Haemon, youngest of your sons.
Does he come grieving
for the fate of his bride to be,
in agony at being cheated of his marriage?

---

6. Mount Olympus, Greece's highest mountain, was home to the main pantheon of gods in Greek mythology.

CREON: Soon we will know that better than the prophets. 680
　My son, can it be that you have not heard
　of my final decision on your betrothed?
　Can you have come here in your fury against your father?
　Or have I your love still, no matter what I do?
HAEMON: Father, I am yours; with your excellent judgment 685
　you lay the right before me, and I shall follow it.
　No marriage will ever be so valued by me
　as to override the goodness of your leadership.
CREON: Yes, my son, this should always be
　in your very heart, that everything else 690
　shall be second to your father's decision.
　It is for this that fathers pray to have
　obedient sons begotten in their halls,
　that they may requite with ill their father's enemy
　and honor his friend no less than he would himself. 695
　If a man have sons that are no use to him,
　what can one say of him but that he has bred
　so many sorrows to himself, laughter to his enemies?
　Do not, my son, banish your good sense
　through pleasure in a woman, since you know 700
　that the embrace grows cold
　when an evil woman shares your bed and home.
　What greater wound can there be than a false friend?
　No. Spit on her, throw her out like an enemy,
　this girl, to marry someone in Death's house. 705
　I caught her openly in disobedience
　alone out of all this city and I shall not make
　myself a liar in the city's sight. No, I will kill her.
　So let her cry if she will on the Zeus of kinship;
　for if I rear those of my race and breeding 710
　to be rebels, surely I will do so with those outside it.
　For he who is in his household a good man
　will be found a just man, too, in the city.
　But he that breaches the law or does it violence
　or thinks to dictate to those who govern him 715
　shall never have my good word.

The man the city sets up in authority
must be obeyed in small things and in just
but also in their opposites.
I am confident such a man of whom I speak   720
will be a good ruler, and willing to be well ruled.
He will stand on his country's side, faithful and just,
in the storm of battle. There is nothing worse
than disobedience to authority.
It destroys cities, it demolishes homes;   725
it breaks and routs one's allies. Of successful lives
the most of them are saved by discipline.
So we must stand on the side of what is orderly;
we cannot give victory to a woman.
If we must accept defeat, let it be from a man;   730
we must not let people say that a woman beat us.
CHORUS: We think, if we are not victims of Time the Thief,
that you speak intelligently of what you speak.
HAEMON: Father, the natural sense that the gods breed
in men is surely the best of their possessions.   735
I certainly could not declare you wrong—
may I never know how to do so!—Still there might
be something useful that some other than you might think.
It is natural for me to be watchful on your behalf
concerning what all men say or do or find to blame.   740
Your face is terrible to a simple citizen;
it frightens him from words you dislike to hear.
But what *I* can hear, in the dark, are things like these:
the city mourns for this girl; they think she is dying
most wrongly and most undeservedly   745
of all womenkind, for the most glorious acts.
Here is one who would not leave her brother unburied,
a brother who had fallen in bloody conflict,
to meet his end by greedy dogs or by
the bird that chanced that way. Surely what she merits   750
is golden honor, isn't it? That's the dark rumor
that spreads in secret. Nothing I own
I value more highly, father, than your success.

What greater distinction can a son have than the glory
of a successful father, and for a father   755
the distinction of successful children?
Do not bear this single habit of mind, to think
that what you say and nothing else is true.
A man who thinks that he alone is right,
or what he says, or what he *is* himself,   760
unique, such men, when opened up, are seen
to be quite empty. For a man, though he be wise,
it is no shame to learn—learn many things,
and not maintain his views too rigidly.
You notice how by streams in wintertime   765
the trees that yield preserve their branches safely,
but those that fight the tempest perish utterly.
The man who keeps the sheet of his sail tight
and never slackens capsizes his boat
and makes the rest of his trip keel uppermost.   770
Yield something of your anger, give way a little.
If a much younger man, like me, may have
a judgment, I would say it were far better
to be one altogether wise by nature, but,
as things incline not to be so, then it is good   775
also to learn from those who advise well.
CHORUS: My lord, if he says anything to the point,
    you should learn from him, and you, too, Haemon,
    learn from your father. Both of you
    have spoken well.   780
CREON: Should we that are my age learn wisdom
    from young men such as he is?
HAEMON: Not learn injustice, certainly. If I am young,
    do not look at my years but what I do.
CREON: Is what you do to have respect for rebels?
HAEMON: I   785
    would not urge you to be scrupulous
    towards the wicked.
CREON: Is she not tainted by the disease of wickedness?
HAEMON: The entire people of Thebes says no to that.

CREON: Should the city tell me how I am to rule them?   790
HAEMON: Do you see what a young man's words these are of yours?
CREON: Must I rule the land by someone else's judgment
    rather than my own?
HAEMON: There is no city
    possessed by one man only.
CREON: Is not the city thought to be the ruler's?   795
HAEMON: You would be a fine dictator of a desert.
CREON: It seems this boy is on the woman's side.
HAEMON: If you are a woman—my care is all for you.
CREON: You villain, to bandy words with your own father!
HAEMON: I see your acts as mistaken and unjust.   800
CREON: Am I mistaken, reverencing my own office?
HAEMON: There is no reverence in trampling on God's honor.
CREON: Your nature is vile, in yielding to a woman.
HAEMON: You will not find me yield to what is shameful.
CREON: At least, your argument is all for her.   805
HAEMON: Yes, and for you and me—and for the gods below.
CREON: You will never marry her while her life lasts.
HAEMON: Then she must die—and dying destroy another.
CREON: Has your daring gone so far, to threaten me?
HAEMON: What threat is it to speak against empty judgments?   810
CREON: Empty of sense yourself, you will regret
    your schooling of me in sense.
HAEMON: If you were not
    my father, I would say you are insane.
CREON: You woman's slave, do not try to wheedle me.
HAEMON: You want to talk but never to hear and listen.   815
CREON: Is that so? By the heavens above you will not—
    be sure of that—get off scot-free, insulting,
    abusing me.

    [*He speaks to the* SERVANTS.]

                        You people bring out this creature,
    this hated creature, that she may die before
    his very eyes, right now, next her would-be husband.   820
HAEMON: Not at my side! Never think that! She will not

die by my side. But you will never again
set eyes upon my face. Go then and rage
with such of your friends as are willing to endure it.
CHORUS: The man is gone, my lord, quick in his anger. 825
    A young man's mind is fierce when he is hurt.
CREON: Let him go, and do and think things superhuman.
    But these two girls he shall not save from death.
CHORUS: Both of them? Do you mean to kill them both?
CREON: No, not the one that didn't do anything. 830
    You are quite right there.
CHORUS: And by what form of death do you mean to kill her?
CREON: I will bring her where the path is loneliest,
    and hide her alive in a rocky cavern there.
    I'll give just enough of food as shall suffice 835
    for a bare expiation, that the city may avoid pollution.
    In that place she shall call on Hades, god of death,
    in her prayers. That god only she reveres.
    Perhaps she will win from him escape from death
    or at least in that last moment will recognize 840
    her honoring of the dead is labor lost.
CHORUS: Love undefeated in the fight,
        Love that makes havoc of possessions,
        Love who lives at night in a young girl's soft cheeks,
        Who travels over sea, or in huts in the countryside— 845
        there is no god able to escape you
        nor anyone of men, whose life is a day only,
        and whom you possess is mad.
        You wrench the minds of just men to injustice,
        to their disgrace; this conflict among kinsmen 850
        it is you who stirred to turmoil.
        The winner is desire. She gleaming kindles
        from the eyes of the girl good to bed.
        Love shares the throne with the great powers that rule.
        For the golden Aphrodite[7] holds her play there 855
        and then no one can overcome her.

---

7. Olympian goddess associated with beauty and love.

Here I too am borne out of the course of lawfulness
when I see these things, and I cannot control
the springs of my tears
when I see Antigone making her way   860
to her bed—but the bed
that is rest for everyone.

ANTIGONE: You see me, you people of my country,
as I set out on my last road of all,
looking for the last time on this light of this sun—   865
never again. I am alive but Hades who gives sleep to everyone
is leading me to the shores of Acheron,[8]
though I have known nothing of marriage songs
nor the chant that brings the bride to bed.
My husband is to be the Lord of Death.   870

CHORUS: Yes, you go to the place where the dead are hidden,
but you go with distinction and praise.
You have not been stricken by wasting sickness;
you have not earned the wages of the sword;
it was your own choice and alone among mankind   875
you will descend, alive,
to that world of death.

ANTIGONE: But indeed I have heard of the saddest of deaths—
of the Phrygian stranger, daughter of Tantalus,
whom the rocky growth subdued, like clinging ivy.   880
The rains never leave her, the snow never fails,
as she wastes away.[9] That is how men tell the story.
From streaming eyes her tears wet the crags;
most like to her the god brings me to rest.

CHORUS: Yes, but she was a god, and god born,   885
and you are mortal and mortal born.
Surely it is great renown
for a woman that dies, that in life and death
her lot is a lot shared with demigods.

---

8. The border between life and death. The newly dead were ferried across the river Acheron to the underworld.

9. Niobe, a queen of Thebes, whose boasting led Artemis and Apollo to kill all her children. In grief, she fled to her childhood home on Mount Sipylus. She was turned to stone, an outcropping on the mountain, and her continual tears made a spring.

ANTIGONE: You mock me. In the name of our fathers' gods   890
   why do you not wait till I am gone to insult me?
   Must you do it face to face?
   My city! Rich citizens of my city!
   You springs of Dirce, you holy groves of Thebes,
   famed for its chariots! I would still have you as my witnesses,   895
   with what dry-eyed friends, under what laws
   I make my way to my prison sealed like a tomb.
   Pity me. Neither among the living nor the dead
   do I have a home in common—
   neither with the living nor the dead.   900

CHORUS: You went to the extreme of daring
   and against the high throne of Justice
   you fell, my daughter, grievously.
   But perhaps it was for some ordeal of your father
   that you are paying requital.   905

ANTIGONE: You have touched the most painful of my cares—
   the pity for my father, ever reawakened,
   and the fate of all of our race, the famous Labdacids;
   the doomed self-destruction of my mother's bed
   when she slept with her own son,   910
   my father.
   What parents I was born of, God help me!
   To them I am going to share their home,
   the curse on me, too, and unmarried.
   Brother, it was a luckless marriage you made,   915
   and dying killed my life.

CHORUS: There *is* a certain reverence for piety.
   But for him in authority,
   he cannot see that authority defied;
   it is your own self-willed temper   920
   that has destroyed you.

ANTIGONE: No tears for me, no friends, no marriage. Brokenhearted
   I am led along the road ready before me.
   I shall never again be suffered
   to look on the holy eye of the day.   925

But my fate claims no tears—
no friend cries for me.

CREON: [*To the* SERVANTS.] Don't you know that weeping and wail-
    ing before death
would never stop if one is allowed to weep and wail?
Lead her away at once. Enfold her   930
in that rocky tomb of hers—as I told you to.
There leave her alone, solitary,
to die if she so wishes
or live a buried life in such a home;
we are guiltless in respect of her, this girl.   935
But living above, among the rest of us, this life
she shall certainly lose.

ANTIGONE: Tomb, bridal chamber, prison forever
dug in rock, it is to you I am going
to join my people, that great number that have died,   940
whom in their death Persephone[1] received.
I am the last of them and I go down
in the worst death of all—for I have not lived
the due term of my life. But when I come
to that other world my hope is strong   945
that my coming will be welcome to my father,
and dear to you, my mother, and dear to you,
my brother deeply loved. For when you died,
with my own hands I washed and dressed you all,
and poured the lustral offerings on your graves.   950
And now, Polyneices, it was for such care of your body
that I have earned these wages.
Yet those who think rightly will think I did right
in honoring you. Had I been a mother
of children, and my husband been dead and rotten,   955
I would not have taken this weary task upon me

---

1. The daughter of Demeter, the goddess of the harvest, and wife of Hades, king of the underworld. When Persephone first was abducted by Hades and brought to the underworld, Demeter's grief caused all the crops to die. In a compromise, Zeus ruled that Persephone would dwell with Hades half the year and with her mother the other half: hence our seasons.

against the will of the city. What law backs me
when I say this? I will tell you:
If my husband were dead, I might have had another,
and child from another man, if I lost the first.   960
But when father and mother both were hidden in death
no brother's life would bloom for me again.
That is the law under which I gave you precedence,
my dearest brother, and that is why Creon thinks me
wrong, even a criminal, and now takes me   965
by the hand and leads me away,
unbedded, without bridal, without share
in marriage and in nurturing of children;
as lonely as you see me; without friends;
with fate against me I go to the vault of death   970
while still alive. What law of God have I broken?
Why should I still look to the gods in my misery?
Whom should I summon as ally? For indeed
because of piety I was called impious.
If this proceeding is good in the gods' eyes   975
I shall know my sin, once I have suffered.
But if Creon and his people are the wrongdoers
let their suffering be no worse than the injustice
they are meting out to me.

CHORUS: It is the same blasts, the tempests of the soul,   980
     possess her.
CREON: Then for this her guards,
     who are so slow, will find themselves in trouble.
ANTIGONE: [*Cries out.*] Oh, that word has come
     very close to death.
CREON: I will not comfort you   985
     with hope that the sentence will not be accomplished.
ANTIGONE: O my father's city, in Theban land,
     O gods that sired my race,
     I am led away, I have no more stay.
     Look on me, princes of Thebes,   990
     the last remnant of the old royal line;
     see what I suffer and who makes me suffer
     because I gave reverence to what claims reverence.

CHORUS: Danae[2] suffered, too, when, her beauty lost, she gave
    the light of heaven in exchange for brassbound walls,   995
    and in the tomb-like cell was she hidden and held;
    yet she was honored in her breeding, child,
    and she kept, as guardian, the seed of Zeus
    that came to her in a golden shower.
    But there is some terrible power in destiny   1000
    and neither wealth nor war
    nor tower nor black ships, beaten by the sea,
    can give escape from it.

    The hot-tempered son of Dryas, the Edonian king,[3]
    in fury mocked Dionysus,   1005
    who then held him in restraint
    in a rocky dungeon.
    So the terrible force and flower of his madness
    drained away. He came to know the god
    whom in frenzy he had touched with his
    mocking tongue,   1010
    when he would have checked the inspired women
    and the fire of Dionysus,
    when he provoked the Muses[4] that love the lyre.
    By the black rocks, dividing the sea in two,
    are the shores of the Bosporus, Thracian Salmydessus.   1015
    There the god of war who lives near the city
    saw the terrible blinding wound
    dealt by his savage wife
    on Phineus' two sons.
    She blinded and tore with the points of her shuttle,   1020
    and her bloodied hands, those eyes

2. Because a prophecy told that Danae's son would kill her father, she was imprisoned in a chamber and kept away from all men. Zeus came to her as a golden rain that impregnated her with a child, Perseus, who fulfilled the prophecy and performed many heroic deeds.

3. Lycurgus in other versions of the myth, locked up Dionysus. Struck with a homicidal mania, Lycurgus then killed his wife, his children, and finally himself.

4. Terpsichore, one of the nine muses, was the patron of dance and was associated symbolically with the lyre.

that else would have looked on her vengefully.[5]
As they wasted away, they lamented
their unhappy fate that they were doomed
to be born of a mother cursed in her marriage.   1025
She traced her descent from the seed
of the ancient Erechtheidae.
In far-distant caves she was raised
among her father's storms, that child of Boreas
quick as a horse, over the steep hills,   1030
a daughter of the gods.
But, my child, the long-lived Fates
bore hard upon her, too.

[*Enter* TEIRESIAS, *the blind prophet, led by a* BOY.]

TEIRESIAS: My lords of Thebes, we have come here together,
one pair of eyes serving us both. For the blind   1035
such must be the way of going, by a guide's leading.
CREON: What is the news, my old Teiresias?
TEIRESIAS: I will tell you; and you, listen to the prophet.
CREON: Never in the past have I turned from your advice.
TEIRESIAS: And so you have steered well the ship of state.   1040
CREON: I have benefited and can testify to that.
TEIRESIAS: Then realize you are on the razor edge
of danger.
CREON: What can that be? I shudder to hear those words.
TEIRESIAS: When you learn the signs recognized by my art   1045
you will understand.
I sat at my ancient place of divination
for watching the birds, where every bird finds shelter;
and I heard an unwonted voice among them;
they were horribly distressed, and screamed unmeaningly.   1050
I knew they were tearing each other murderously;
the beating of their wings was a clear sign.
I was full of fear; at once on all the altars,

---

5. The chorus refers in this verse to a complex myth. Phineas, the king of Salmydassus in Thrace, had two sons by Cleopatra, a descendant of King Erechtheus of Athens and daughter of Boreas. Phineas shunned Cleopatra in favor of a second wife. In jealousy, the new wife poked out the eyes of these sons.

as they were fully kindled, I tasted the offerings,
but the god of fire refused to burn from the sacrifice,   1055
and from the thighbones a dark stream of moisture
oozed from the embers, smoked and sputtered.
The gall bladder burst and scattered to the air
and the streaming thighbones lay exposed
from the fat wrapped round them—   1060
so much I learned from this boy here,
the fading prophecies of a rite that failed.
This boy here is my guide, as I am others'.
This is the city's sickness—and your plans are the cause of it.
For our altars and our sacrificial hearths   1065
are filled with the carrion meat of birds and dogs,
torn from the flesh of Oedipus' poor son.
So the gods will not take our prayers or sacrifice
nor yet the flame from the thighbones, and no bird
cries shrill and clear, so glutted   1070
are they with fat of the blood of the killed man.
Reflect on these things, son. All men
can make mistakes; but, once mistaken,
a man is no longer stupid nor accursed
who, having fallen on ill, tries to cure that ill,   1075
not taking a fine undeviating stand.
It is obstinacy that convicts of folly.
Yield to the dead man; do not stab him—
now he is gone—what bravery is this,
to inflict another death upon the dead?   1080
I mean you well and speak well for your good.
It is never sweeter to learn from a good counselor
than when he counsels to your benefit.

CREON: Old man, you are all archers, and I am your mark.
I must be tried by your prophecies as well.   1085
By the breed of you I have been bought and sold
and made a merchandise, for ages now.
But I tell you: make your profit from silver-gold
from Sardis[6] and the gold from India

---

6. A city in western Turkey, a source of silver and gold in the ancient world.

if you will. But this dead man you shall not hide   1090
in a grave, not though the eagles of Zeus should bear
the carrion, snatching it to the throne of Zeus itself.
Even so, I shall not so tremble at the pollution
to let you bury him.
                No, I am certain
no human has the power to pollute the gods.   1095
They fall, you old Teiresias, those men,
—so very clever—in a bad fall whenever
they eloquently speak vile words for profit.

TEIRESIAS: I wonder if there's a man who dares consider—

CREON: What do you mean? What sort of generalization   1100
   is this talk of yours?

TEIRESIAS: How much the best of possessions is the ability
   to listen to wise advice?

CREON: As I should imagine that the worst
   injury must be native stupidity.   1105

TEIRESIAS: Now that is exactly where your mind is sick.

CREON: I do not like to answer a seer with insults.

TEIRESIAS: But you do, when you say my prophecies are lies.

CREON: Well,
   the whole breed of prophets certainly loves money.   1110

TEIRESIAS: And the breed that comes from princes loves to take
   advantage—base advantage.

CREON: Do you realize
   you are speaking in such terms of your own prince?

TEIRESIAS: I know. But it is through me you have saved the city.

CREON: You are a wise prophet, but what you love is wrong.   1115

TEIRESIAS: You will force me to declare what should be hidden
   in my own heart.

CREON: Out with it—
   but only if your words are not for gain.

TEIRESIAS: They won't be for *your* gain—that I am sure of.

CREON: But realize you will not make a merchandise   1120
   of my decisions.

TEIRESIAS: And you must realize
   that you will not outlive many cycles more
   of this swift sun before you give in exchange

one of your own loins bred, a corpse for a corpse,
for you have thrust one that belongs above   1125
below the earth, and bitterly dishonored
a living soul by lodging her in the grave;
while one that belonged indeed to the underworld
gods you have kept on this earth without due share
of rites of burial, of due funeral offerings,   1130
a corpse unhallowed. With all of this you, Creon,
have nothing to do, nor have the gods above.
These acts of yours are violence, on your part.
And in requital the avenging Spirits
of Death itself and the gods' Furies⁷ shall   1135
after *your* deeds, lie in ambush for you, and
in their hands you shall be taken cruelly.
Now, look at this and tell me I was bribed
to say it! The delay will not be long
before the cries of mourning in your house,   1140
of men and women. All the cities will stir in hatred
against you, because their sons in mangled shreds
received their burial rites from dogs, from wild beasts
or when some bird of the air brought a vile stink
to each city that contained the hearths of the dead.   1145
These are the arrows that archer-like I launched—
you vexed me so to anger—at your heart.
You shall not escape their sting. You, boy,
lead me away to my house, so he may discharge
his anger on younger men; so may he come to know   1150
to bear a quieter tongue in his head and a better
mind than that now he carries in him.
CHORUS: That was a terrible prophecy, my lord.
The man has gone. Since these hairs of mine grew white
from the black they once were, he has never spoken   1155
a word of a lie to our city.
CREON: I know, I know.
My mind is all bewildered. To yield is terrible.

---

7. The Furies are goddesses, somewhat primordial and vague in their origin, who wreak vengeance
upon transgressors; sometimes invoked by curses.

But by opposition to destroy my very being
with a self-destructive curse must also be reckoned   1160
in what is terrible.
CHORUS: You need good counsel, son of Menoeceus,
and need to take it.
CREON: What must I do, then? Tell me; I shall agree.
CHORUS: The girl—go now and bring her up from her cave,   1165
and for the exposed dead man, give him his burial.
CREON: That is really your advice? You would have me yield.
CHORUS: And quickly as you may, my lord. Swift harms
sent by the gods cut off the paths of the foolish.
CREON: Oh, it is hard; I must give up what my heart   1170
would have me do. But it is ill to fight
against what must be.
CHORUS: Go now, and do this;
do not give the task to others.
CREON: I will go,   1175
just as I am. Come, servants, all of you;
take axes in your hands; away with you
to the place you see, there.
For my part, since my intention is so changed,
as I bound her myself, myself will free her.   1180
I am afraid it may be best, in the end
of life, to have kept the old accepted laws.
CHORUS: You of many names, glory of the Cadmeian
bride, breed of loud thundering Zeus;
you who watch over famous Italy;   1185
you who rule where all are welcome in Eleusis;
in the sheltered plains of Deo—
O Bacchus that dwells in Thebes,
the mother city of Bacchanals,
by the flowing stream of Ismenus,   1190
in the ground sown by the fierce dragon's teeth.

You are he on whom the murky gleam of torches glares,
above the twin peaks of the crag
where come the Corycean nymphs
to worship you, the Bacchanals;   1195
and the stream of Castalia has seen you, too;

and you are he that the ivy-clad
slopes of Nisaean hills,
and the green shore ivy-clustered,
sent to watch over the roads of Thebes,   1200
where the immortal Evoe chant[8] rings out.

It is Thebes which you honor most of all cities,
you and your mother both,
she who died by the blast of Zeus' thunderbolt.
And now when the city, with all its folk,   1205
is gripped by a violent plague,
come with healing foot, over the slopes of Parnassus,[9]
over the moaning strait.
You lead the dance of the fire-breathing stars,
you are master of the voices of the night.   1210
True-born child of Zeus, appear,
my lord, with your Thyiad attendants,[1]
who in frenzy all night long
dance in your house, Iacchus,
dispenser of gifts.   1215

MESSENGER: You who live by the house of Cadmus and Amphion,[2]
hear me. There is no condition of man's life
that stands secure. As such I would not
praise it or blame. It is chance that sets upright;
it is chance that brings down the lucky and the unlucky,   1220
each in his turn. For men, that belong to death,
there is no prophet of established things.
Once Creon was a man worthy of envy—
of my envy, at least. For he saved this city
of Thebes from her enemies, and attained   1225
the throne of the land, with all a king's power.
He guided it right. His race bloomed
with good children. But when a man forfeits joy
I do not count his life as life, but only

---

8. A frenzied chant in Bacchanalian rites. These places and names are associated with Dionysus.

9. One of the highest mountains in Greece and associated with Dionysus.

1. Female devotees associated with Dionysian rites. The goddess Thyia's shrine was on Parnassus.

2. Ruling family of Thebes.

a life trapped in a corpse.   1230
Be rich within your house, yes greatly rich,
if so you will, and live in a prince's style.
If the gladness of these things is gone, I would not
give the shadow of smoke for the rest,
as against joy.   1235
CHORUS: What is the sorrow of our princes
    of which you are the messenger?
MESSENGER: Death; and the living are guilty of their deaths.
CHORUS: But who is the murderer? Who the murdered? Tell us.
MESSENGER: Haemon is dead; the hand that shed his blood   1240
    was his very own.
CHORUS: Truly his own hand? Or his father's?
MESSENGER: His own hand, in his anger
    against his father for a murder.
CHORUS: Prophet, how truly you have made good your word!   1245
MESSENGER: These things are so; you may debate the rest.
    Here I see Creon's wife Eurydice
    approaching. Unhappy woman!
    Does she come from the house as hearing about her son
    or has she come by chance?   1250
EURYDICE: I heard your words, all you men of Thebes, as I
    was going out to greet Pallas with my prayers.
    I was just drawing back the bolts of the gate
    to open it when a cry struck through my ears
    telling of my household's ruin. I fell backward   1255
    in terror into the arms of my servants; I fainted.
    But tell me again, what is the story? I
    will hear it as one who is no stranger to sorrow.
MESSENGER: Dear mistress, I will tell you, for I was there,
    and I will leave out no word of the truth.   1260
    Why should I comfort you and then tomorrow
    be proved a liar? The truth is always best.
    I followed your husband, at his heels, to the end of the plain
    where Polyneices' body still lay unpitied,
    and torn by dogs. We prayed to Hecate, goddess   1265
    of the crossroads, and also to Pluto[3]

3. Alternative name for Hades, god of the underworld.

that they might restrain their anger and turn kind.
And him we washed with sacred lustral water
and with fresh-cut boughs we burned what was left of him
and raised a high mound of his native earth;   1270
then we set out again for the hollowed rock,
death's stone bridal chamber for the girl.
Someone then heard a voice of bitter weeping
while we were still far off, coming from that unblest room.
The man came to tell our master Creon of it.   1275
As the king drew nearer, there swarmed about him
a cry of misery but no clear words.
He groaned and in an anguished mourning voice
cried "Oh, am I a true prophet? Is this the road
that I must travel, saddest of all my wayfaring?   1280
It is my son's voice that haunts my ear. Servants,
get closer, quickly. Stand around the tomb
and look. There is a gap there where the stones
have been wrenched away; enter there, by the very mouth,
and see whether I recognize the voice of Haemon   1285
or if the gods deceive me." On the command
of our despairing master we went to look.
In the furthest part of the tomb we saw her, hanging
by her neck. She had tied a noose of muslin on it.
Haemon's hands were about her waist embracing her,   1290
while he cried for the loss of his bride gone to the dead,
and for all his father had done, and his own sad love.
When Creon saw him he gave a bitter cry,
went in and called to him with a groan: "Poor son!
what have you done? What can you have meant?   1295
What happened to destroy you? Come out, I pray you!"
The boy glared at him with savage eyes, and then
spat in his face, without a word of answer.
He drew his double-hilted sword. As his father
ran to escape him, Haemon failed to strike him,   1300
and the poor wretch in anger at himself
leaned on his sword and drove it halfway in,
into his ribs. Then he folded the girl to him,
in his arms, while he was conscious still,

and gasping poured a sharp stream of bloody drops   1305
on her white cheeks. There they lie,
the dead upon the dead. So he has won
the pitiful fulfillment of his marriage
within death's house. In this human world he has shown
how the wrong choice in plans is for a man   1310
his greatest evil.

CHORUS: What do you make of this? My lady is gone,
without a word of good or bad.

MESSENGER: I, too,
am lost in wonder. I am inclined to hope
that hearing of her son's death she could not   1315
open her sorrow to the city, but chose rather
within her house to lay upon her maids
the mourning for the household grief. Her judgment
is good; she will not make any false step.

CHORUS: I do not know. To me this over-heavy silence   1320
seems just as dangerous as much empty wailing.

MESSENGER: I will go in and learn if in her passionate
heart she keeps hidden some secret purpose.
You are right; there is sometimes danger in too much silence.

CHORUS: Here comes our king himself. He bears in his hands   1325
a memorial all too clear;
it is a ruin of none other's making,
purely his own if one dare to say that.

CREON: The mistakes of a blinded man
are themselves rigid and laden with death.   1330
You look at us the killer and the killed
of the one blood. Oh, the awful blindness
of those plans of mine. My son, you were so young,
so young to die. You were freed from the bonds of life
through no folly of your own—only through mine.   1335

CHORUS: I think you have learned justice—but too late.

CREON: Yes, I have learned it to my bitterness. At this moment
God has sprung on my head with a vast weight
and struck me down. He shook me in my savage ways;
he has overturned my joy, has trampled it,   1340

underfoot. The pains men suffer
are pains indeed.

SECOND MESSENGER: My lord, you have troubles and a store besides;
some are there in your hands, but there are others
you will surely see when you come to your house.   1345

CREON: What trouble can there be beside these troubles?

SECOND MESSENGER: The queen is dead. She was indeed true mother
of the dead son. She died, poor lady,
by recent violence upon herself.

CREON: Haven of death, you can never have enough.   1350
Why, why do you destroy me?
You messenger, who have brought me bitter news,
what is this tale you tell?
It is a dead man that you kill again—
what new message of yours is this, boy?   1355
Is this new slaughter of a woman
a doom to lie on the pile of the dead?

CHORUS: You can see. It is no longer
hidden in a corner.

[*By some stage device, perhaps the so-called eccyclema,*[4] *the inside
of the palace is shown, with the body of the dead* QUEEN.]

CREON: Here is yet another horror   1360
for my unhappy eyes to see.
What doom still waits for me?
I have but now taken in my arms my son,
and again I look upon another dead face.
Poor mother and poor son!   1365

SECOND MESSENGER: She stood at the altar, and with keen whetted knife
she suffered her darkening eyes to close.
First she cried in agony recalling the noble fate of Megareus,[5]
who died before all this,
and then for the fate of this son; and in the end   1370
she cursed you for the evil you had done
in killing her sons.

---

4. Wheeled platform rolled forward onto the
stage to depict interior scenes; often used in tragedies to reveal dead bodies.

5. Creon's son who, like Eteocles, died fighting
against Polyneices.

CREON: I am distracted with fear. Why does not someone
strike a two-edged sword right through me?
I am dissolved in an agony of misery.   1375
SECOND MESSENGER: You were indeed accused
by her that is dead
of Haemon's and of Megareus' death.
CREON: By what kind of violence did she find her end?
SECOND MESSENGER: Her own hand struck
her to the entrails   1380
when she heard of her son's lamentable death.
CREON: These acts can never be made to fit another
to free me from the guilt. It was I that killed her.
Poor wretch that I am, I say it is true!
Servants, lead me away, quickly, quickly.   1385
I am no more a live man than one dead.
CHORUS: What you say is for the best—if there be a best
in evil such as this. For the shortest way
is best with troubles that lie at our feet.
CREON: O, let it come, let it come,   1390
that best of fates that waits on my last day.
Surely best fate of all. Let it come, let it come!
That I may never see one more day's light!
CHORUS: These things are for the future. We must deal
with what impends. What in the future is to care for   1395
rests with those whose duty it is
to care for them.
CREON: At least, all that *I* want
is in that prayer of mine.
CHORUS: Pray for no more at all. For what is destined   1400
for us, men mortal, there is no escape.
CREON: Lead me away, a vain silly man
who killed you, son, and you, too, lady.
I did not mean to, but I did.
I do not know where to turn my eyes   1405
to look to, for support.
Everything in my hands is crossed. A most unwelcome fate
has leaped upon me.
CHORUS: Wisdom is far the chief element in happiness

and, secondly, no irreverence towards the gods.   1410
But great words of haughty men exact
in retribution blows as great
and in old age teach wisdom.

c. 441 B.C.E.

William Shakespeare
1564–1616

HAMLET

Sometime in the late 1580s, William Shakespeare, then in his early twenties, traveled the muddy roads that connected the picturesque country town of Stratford-on-Avon to England's metropolis, the London of Queen Elizabeth. No one knows how Shakespeare made his living in Stratford, nor why he left. But most Shakespeare scholars believe he joined an acting company in London and learned the business of theater from the bottom up. When he started writing plays, Shakespeare broke the mold—playwrights were typically men of much higher education. His plays were undeniably popular, but to those in polite English society, Shakespeare and his fans were somewhat lowbrow.

As he did for many of his plays, Shakespeare borrowed the story for Hamlet. *At least four hundred years old when Shakespeare adapted it, the story of* Hamlet *had its roots in Norse legend. Its earliest written version was nearly a hundred years old by 1600, when Shakespeare based his play on another Elizabethan* Hamlet, *perhaps by John Kyd. Staged in the late 1580s, this first version had helped popularize the genre known as* **revenge tragedy**, *which is roughly equivalent to today's action thriller. In the typical revenge tragedy, the main character commits acts of terrible violence to avenge some murdered relative. Catering to unsophisticated tastes, the revenge tragedy fills the stage with bloody bodies.*

Shakespeare's Hamlet, *too, ends in carnage, but in other respects it differs from its immediate predecessor and from the earlier versions of the Hamlet story. In the previous incarnations, for example, Claudius's regicide is well known, not a secret, and Ophelia is indubitably Hamlet's mistress. This organic quality to the Hamlet story—its changing and growing in each new telling—probably accounts for the many inconsistencies in Shakespeare's version. In act 3, for example, Hamlet spies on Claudius and leaves him praying, then goes directly to Gertrude's chamber, where he thinks he finds Claudius hiding. The play presents dozens of such problems, which seem to derive from Shakespeare's rewriting of an existing tale for his own purposes, purposes that in some ways contradict the conventions of the revenge tragedy.*

The most important of these changes involves Hamlet's character—and audiences' responses to it. Shakespeare's audience would have known Hamlet's basic story, and they would have expected Hamlet to be a swashbuckling hothead. They would have been surprised by the brooding, introspective character Shakespeare gave them. Even so, Hamlet's long delays, apparently, did not much affect them. Not until the Romantic period, in the early 1800s, did critics remark on Hamlet's slow execution of revenge. The Romantics, perhaps seeing themselves in Shakespeare's hero, attributed his procrastinating to a fatal introspection, which drains his will of energy for action. In the twentieth century, after the advent of Freud's theories of human psychology, critics added an Oedipal complex to Hamlet's problems. Some contemporary readers hear in Hamlet's ravings what would become the angst of the existential philosophers. You should consider for yourself why Hamlet takes so long to act and what his delays mean.

How the play is staged can radically change your interpretation of such issues. For example, is Hamlet's madness real or fake? Of course, he tells Horatio in the first act that he will pretend to be mad, but this plot device might have been one of those awkward holdovers from Shakespeare's sources. There, the feigned madness protects Hamlet from Claudius's suspicions; it doesn't seem to have that effect here, nor does Hamlet seem too careful to hide his enmity for Claudius. Consider his treatment of Ophelia in act 3: does he rave so angrily because her sudden, inexplicable coldness has driven him to the edge of sanity, or because he knows she's a pawn in a plot against him? Franco Zeffirelli's 1990 film adaptation of Hamlet *presents the second version: Hamlet secretly watches Polonius manipulate Ophelia, and so he knows she's in league with her father and the king. Mel Gibson's Hamlet in this film, though distraught, is clearly sane.*

In making the story of Hamlet his own, Shakespeare created a huge, linguistically rich drama, one that addresses themes too complex and varied to fit within a conventional telling of the same story. He crafted a protagonist large enough—spiritually, intellectually, emotionally—to continue fascinating audiences four hundred years later. Whether you see yourself in that character, become engrossed in his predicament and his contradictory responses to it, or find some other route into the play's many inner chambers, Hamlet should leave you feeling as though you've witnessed an expansion of the theater's possibilities. When the Danish prince tells his friend Horatio that "There are more things in heaven and earth . . . / Than are dreamt of in your philosophy" (1.5.165–66), his wisdom about life could easily apply to the work in which he appears.

Hamlet

CHARACTERS

CLAUDIUS, *King of Denmark*

HAMLET, *son of the former and nephew to the present King*

POLONIUS, *Lord Chamberlain*

HORATIO, *friend of Hamlet*

LAERTES, *son of Polonius*

VOLTEMAND
CORNELIUS
ROSENCRANTZ } *courtiers*
GUILDENSTERN
OSRIC
A GENTLEMAN

A PRIEST

MARCELLUS } *officers*
BERNARDO

FRANCISCO, *a soldier*

REYNALDO, *servant to Polonius*

PLAYERS

TWO CLOWNS, *gravediggers*

FORTINBRAS, *Prince of Norway*

A NORWEGIAN CAPTAIN

ENGLISH AMBASSADORS

GERTRUDE, *Queen of Denmark, and mother of Hamlet*

OPHELIA, *daughter of Polonius*

GHOST OF HAMLET'S FATHER

LORDS, LADIES, OFFICERS, SOLDIERS, SAILORS, MESSENGERS, AND ATTENDANTS

SCENE: *The action takes place in or near the royal castle of Denmark at Elsinore.*

ACT I
SCENE 1

A guard station atop the castle. Enter BERNARDO *and* FRANCISCO, *two sentinels.*

BERNARDO: Who's there?

FRANCISCO: Nay, answer me. Stand and unfold yourself.

BERNARDO: Long live the king!

FRANCISCO: Bernardo?

BERNARDO: He.   5

FRANCISCO: You come most carefully upon your hour.

BERNARDO: 'Tis now struck twelve. Get thee to bed, Francisco.

FRANCISCO: For this relief much thanks. 'Tis bitter cold,
    And I am sick at heart.

BERNARDO: Have you had quiet guard?

FRANCISCO: Not a mouse stirring.   10

BERNARDO: Well, good night.
    If you do meet Horatio and Marcellus,
    The rivals[1] of my watch, bid them make haste.

        [*Enter* HORATIO *and* MARCELLUS.]

FRANCISCO: I think I hear them. Stand, ho! Who is there?

HORATIO: Friends to this ground.

MARCELLUS: And liegemen to the Dane.[2]   15

FRANCISCO: Give you good night.

MARCELLUS: O, farewell, honest soldier!
    Who hath relieved you?

FRANCISCO: Bernardo hath my place.
    Give you good night.   [*Exit* FRANCISCO.]

MARCELLUS: Holla, Bernardo!

BERNARDO: Say—
    What, is Horatio there?

HORATIO: A piece of him.

BERNARDO: Welcome, Horatio. Welcome, good Marcellus.   20

HORATIO: What, has this thing appeared again tonight?

BERNARDO: I have seen nothing.

MARCELLUS: Horatio says 'tis but our fantasy,

---

1. Companions.

2. The king of Denmark, also called "Denmark," as in line 48 of this scene.

And will not let belief take hold of him
Touching this dreaded sight twice seen of us. 25
Therefore I have entreated him along
With us to watch the minutes of this night,
That if again this apparition come,
He may approve[3] our eyes and speak to it.
HORATIO: Tush, tush, 'twill not appear.
BERNARDO: Sit down awhile, 30
And let us once again assail your ears,
That are so fortified against our story,
What we have two nights seen.
HORATIO: Well, sit we down.
And let us hear Bernardo speak of this.
BERNARDO: Last night of all, 35
When yond same star that's westward from the pole[4]
Had made his course t' illume that part of heaven
Where now it burns, Marcellus and myself,
The bell then beating one—
    [*Enter* GHOST.]
MARCELLUS: Peace, break thee off. Look where it comes again. 40
BERNARDO: In the same figure like the king that's dead.
MARCELLUS: Thou art a scholar; speak to it, Horatio.
BERNARDO: Looks 'a[5] not like the king? Mark it, Horatio.
HORATIO: Most like. It harrows me with fear and wonder.
BERNARDO: It would be spoke to.
MARCELLUS: Speak to it, Horatio. 45
HORATIO: What art thou that usurp'st this time of night
Together with that fair and warlike form
In which the majesty of buried Denmark
Did sometimes march? By heaven I charge thee, speak.
MARCELLUS: It is offended.
BERNARDO: See, it stalks away. 50
HORATIO: Stay. Speak, speak. I charge thee, speak.
        [*Exit* GHOST.]
MARCELLUS: 'Tis gone and will not answer.
BERNARDO: How now, Horatio! You tremble and look pale.

3. Confirm the testimony of.   5. He.
4. Polestar.

Is not this something more than fantasy?
What think you on't?   55

HORATIO: Before my God, I might not this believe
  Without the sensible[6] and true avouch
  Of mine own eyes.

MARCELLUS: Is it not like the king?

HORATIO: As thou art to thyself.
  Such was the very armor he had on   60
  When he the ambitious Norway combated.
  So frowned he once when, in an angry parle,[7]
  He smote the sledded Polacks on the ice.
  'Tis strange.

MARCELLUS: Thus twice before, and jump[8] at this dead hour,
  With martial stalk hath he gone by our watch.   65

HORATIO: In what particular thought to work I know not,
  But in the gross and scope of mine opinion,
  This bodes some strange eruption to our state.

MARCELLUS: Good now, sit down, and tell me he that knows,
  Why this same strict and most observant watch   70
  So nightly toils the subject[9] of the land,
  And why such daily cast of brazen cannon
  And foreign mart for implements of war;
  Why such impress of shipwrights, whose sore task
  Does not divide the Sunday from the week.   75
  What might be toward that this sweaty haste
  Doth make the night joint-laborer with the day?
  Who is't that can inform me?

HORATIO: That can I.
  At last, the whisper goes so. Our last king,
  Whose image even but now appeared to us,   80
  Was as you know by Fortinbras of Norway,
  Thereto pricked on by a most emulate pride,
  Dared to the combat; in which our valiant Hamlet
  (For so this side of our known world esteemed him)
  Did slay this Fortinbras; who by a sealed compact   85

6. Perceptible.   8. Precisely.
7. Parley, debate.   9. People.

Well ratified by law and heraldry,
Did forfeit, with his life, all those his lands
Which he stood seized of,[1] to the conqueror;
Against the which a moiety competent[2]
Was gagéd[3] by our king; which had returned   90
To the inheritance of Fortinbras,
Had he been vanquisher; as, by the same covenant
And carriage of the article designed,
His fell to Hamlet. Now, sir, young Fortinbras,
Of unimprovéd[4] mettle hot and full,   95
Hath in the skirts of Norway here and there
Sharked up a list of lawless resolutes
For food and diet to some enterprise
That hath a stomach in't; which is no other,
As it doth well appear unto our state,   100
But to recover of us by strong hand
And terms compulsatory, those foresaid lands
So by his father lost; and this, I take it,
Is the main motive of our preparations,
The source of this our watch, and the chief head   105
Of this post-haste and romage[5] in the land.
BERNARDO: I think it be no other but e'en so.
  Well may it sort[6] that this portentous figure
  Comes arméd through our watch so like the king
  That was and is the question of these wars.   110
HORATIO: A mote[7] it is to trouble the mind's eye.
  In the most high and palmy state of Rome,
  A little ere the mightiest Julius fell,
  The graves stood tenantless, and the sheeted dead
  Did squeak and gibber in the Roman streets;   115
  As stars with trains of fire, and dews of blood,
  Disasters in the sun; and the moist star,[8]
  Upon whose influence Neptune's empire stands,

1. Possessed.
2. Portion of similar value.
3. Pledged.
4. Unproved.
5. Stir.
6. Chance.
7. Speck of dust.
8. The moon.

Was sick almost to doomsday with eclipse.
And even the like precurse[9] of feared events,   120
As harbingers preceding still the fates
And prologue to the omen coming on,
Have heaven and earth together demonstrated
Unto our climatures[1] and countrymen.
　　[*Enter* GHOST.]
But soft, behold, lo where it comes again!   125
I'll cross it though it blast me.—Stay, illusion.
　　[*It spreads (its) arms.*]
If thou hast any sound or use of voice,
Speak to me.
If there be any good thing to be done,
That may to thee do ease, and grace to me,   130
Speak to me.
If thou art privy to thy country's fate,
Which happily foreknowing may avoid,
O, speak!
Or if thou hast uphoarded in thy life   135
Extorted treasure in the womb of earth,
For which, they say, you spirits oft walk in death,
　　[*The cock crows.*]
Speak of it. Stay, and speak. Stop it, Marcellus.
MARCELLUS: Shall I strike at it with my partisan?[2]
HORATIO: Do, if it will not stand.
BERNARDO:　　　　　　　　　　'Tis here.
HORATIO:　　　　　　　　　　　　　'Tis here.   140
MARCELLUS: 'Tis gone.　　　　　　　　[*Exit* GHOST.]
　　We do it wrong, being so majestical,
　　To offer it the show of violence;
　　For it is as the air, invulnerable,
　　And our vain blows malicious mockery.   145
BERNARDO: It was about to speak when the cock crew.
HORATIO: And then it started like a guilty thing
　　Upon a fearful summons. I have heard

9. Precursor.　　　　　　　　　　2. Halberd.
1. Regions.

The cock, that is the trumpet to the morn;
Doth with his lofty and shrill-sounding throat   150
Awake the god of day, and at his warning,
Whether in sea or fire, in earth or air,
Th' extravagant and erring[3] spirit hies
To his confine; and of the truth herein
This present object made probation.[4]   155
MARCELLUS: It faded on the crowing of the cock.
Some say that ever 'gainst that season comes
Wherein our Savior's birth is celebrated,
This bird of dawning singeth all night long,
And then, they say, no spirit dare stir abroad,   160
The nights are wholesome, then no planets strike,
No fairy takes,[5] nor witch hath power to charm,
So hallowed and so gracious is that time.
HORATIO: So have I heard and do in part believe it.
But look, the morn in russet mantle clad   165
Walks o'er the dew of yon high eastward hill.
Break we our watch up, and by my advice
Let us impart what we have seen tonight
Unto young Hamlet, for upon my life
This spirit, dumb to us, will speak to him.   170
Do you consent we shall acquaint him with it,
As needful in our loves, fitting our duty?
MARCELLUS: Let's do't, I pray, and I this morning know
Where we shall find him most conveniently. [*Exeunt.*]

SCENE 2

A chamber of state. Enter KING CLAUDIUS, QUEEN GERTRUDE, HAMLET, POLONIUS, LAERTES, VOLTEMAND, CORNELIUS *and other members of the court.*

KING: Though yet of Hamlet our dear brother's death
The memory be green, and that it us befitted
To bear our hearts in grief, and our whole kingdom

---

3. Wandering out of bounds.   5. Enchants.
4. Proof.

To be contracted in one brow of woe,
Yet so far hath discretion fought with nature   5
That we with wisest sorrow think on him,
Together with remembrance of ourselves.
Therefore our sometime sister, now our queen,
Th' imperial jointress[6] to this warlike state,
Have we, as 'twere with a defeated joy,   10
With an auspicious and a dropping eye,
With mirth in funeral, and with dirge in marriage,
In equal scale weighing delight and dole,
Taken to wife; nor have we herein barred
Your better wisdoms, which have freely gone   15
With this affair along. For all, our thanks.
Now follows that you know young Fortinbras,
Holding a weak supposal of our worth,
Or thinking by our late dear brother's death
Our state to be disjoint and out of frame,   20
Colleaguéd with this dream of his advantage,
He hath not failed to pester us with message
Importing the surrender of those lands
Lost by his father, with all bonds of law,
To our most valiant brother. So much for him.   25
Now for ourself, and for this time of meeting,
Thus much the business is: we have here writ
To Norway, uncle of young Fortinbras—
Who, impotent and bedrid, scarcely hears
Of this his nephew's purpose—to suppress   30
His further gait[7] herein, in that the levies,
The lists, and full proportions are all made
Out of his subject; and we here dispatch
You, good Cornelius, and you, Voltemand,
For bearers of this greeting to old Norway,   35
Giving to you no further personal power
To business with the king, more than the scope

6. A widow who holds a *jointure*, or life inter-   7. Progress.
est, in the estate of her deceased husband.

Of these dilated[8] articles allow.
Farewell, and let your haste commend your duty.
CORNELIUS: ⎫
VOLTEMAND: ⎭ In that, and all things will we show our duty.   40
KING: We doubt it nothing, heartily farewell.
              [*Exeunt* VOLTEMAND *and* CORNELIUS.]
And now, Laertes, what's the news with you?
You told us of some suit. What is't, Laertes?
You cannot speak of reason to the Dane
And lose your voice. What wouldst thou beg, Laertes,   45
That shall not be my offer, not thy asking?
The head is not more native to the heart,
The hand more instrumental[9] to the mouth,
Than is the throne of Denmark to thy father.
What wouldst thou have, Laertes?
LAERTES: My dread lord,   50
Your leave and favor to return to France,
From whence, though willingly, I came to Denmark
To show my duty in your coronation,
Yet now I must confess, that duty done,
My thoughts and wishes bend again toward France,   55
And bow them to your gracious leave and pardon.
KING: Have you your father's leave? What says Polonius?
POLONIUS: He hath, my lord, wrung from me my slow leave
By laborsome petition, and at last
Upon his will I sealed my hard consent.   60
I do beseech you give him leave to go.
KING: Take thy fair hour, Laertes. Time be thine,
And thy best graces spend it at thy will.
But now, my cousin[1] Hamlet, and my son—
HAMLET: [*Aside.*] A little more than kin, and less than kind.   65
KING: How is it that the clouds still hang on you?
HAMLET: Not so, my lord. I am too much in the sun.
QUEEN: Good Hamlet, cast thy nighted color off,
And let thine eye look like a friend on Denmark.

8. Fully expressed.   1. Used here as a general term of kinship.
9. Serviceable.

Do not for ever with thy vailéd lids[2]   70
Seek for thy noble father in the dust.
Thou know'st 'tis common—all that lives must die,
Passing through nature to eternity.

HAMLET: Ay, madam, it is common.

QUEEN: If it be,
Why seems it so particular with thee?   75

HAMLET: Seems, madam? Nay, it is. I know not "seems."
'Tis not alone my inky cloak, good mother,
Nor customary suits of solemn black,
Nor windy suspiration of forced breath,
No, nor the fruitful river in the eye,   80
Nor the dejected havior[3] of the visage,
Together with all forms, moods, shapes of grief,
That can denote me truly. These indeed seem,
For they are actions that a man might play,
But I have that within which passes show—   85
These but the trappings and the suits of woe.

KING: 'Tis sweet and commendable in your nature, Hamlet,
To give these mourning duties to your father,
But you must know your father lost a father,
That father lost, lost his, and the survivor bound   90
In filial obligation for some term
To do obsequious sorrow. But to persever[4]
In obstinate condolement is a course
Of impious stubbornness. 'Tis unmanly grief.
It shows a will most incorrect to heaven,   95
A heart unfortified, a mind impatient,
An understanding simple and unschooled.
For what we know must be, and is as common
As any the most vulgar thing to sense,
Why should we in our peevish opposition   100
Take it to heart? Fie, 'tis a fault[5] to heaven,
A fault against the dead, a fault to nature,

---

2. Lowered eyes.
3. Appearance.

4. Persevere. *Obsequious:* suited for funeral obsequies, or ceremonies.
5. Insult.

To reason most absurd, whose common theme
Is death of fathers, and who still hath cried,
From the first corse[6] till he that died today,   105
"This must be so." We pray you throw to earth
This unprevailing woe and think of us
As of a father, for let the world take note
You are the most immediate[7] to our throne,
And with no less nobility of love   110
Than that which dearest father hears his son
Do I impart toward you. For your intent
In going back to school in Wittenberg,
It is most retrograde[8] to out desire,
And we beseech you, bend you to remain   115
Here in the cheer and comfort of our eye,
Our chiefest courtier, cousin, and our son
QUEEN: Let not thy mother lose her prayers, Hamlet.
    I pray thee stay with us, go not to Wittenberg.
HAMLET: I shall in all my best obey you, madam.   120
KING: Why, 'tis a loving and a fair reply.
    Be as ourself in Denmark. Madam, come.
    This gentle and unforced accord of Hamlet
    Sits smiling to my heart, in grace whereof,
    No jocund health that Denmark drinks today   125
    But the great cannon to the clouds shall tell,
    And the king's rouse the heaven shall bruit[9] again,
    Respeaking earthly thunder. Come away.
                    [*Flourish. Exeunt all but* HAMLET.]
HAMLET: O, that this too too solid flesh would melt,
    Thaw, and resolve itself into a dew,   130
    Or that the Everlasting had not fixed
    His canon[1] 'gainst self-slaughter. O God, God,
    How weary, stale, flat, and unprofitable
    Seem to me all the uses of this world!
    Fie on't, ah, fie, 'tis an unweeded garden   135

---

6. Corpse.   9. Echo. *Rouse:* carousal.
7. Next in line.   1. Law.
8. Contrary.

That grows to seed. Things rank and gross in nature
Possess it merely.[2] That it should come to this,
But two months dead, nay, not so much, not two.
So excellent a king, that was to this
Hyperion to a satyr,[3] so loving to my mother,   140
That he might not beteem[4] the winds of heaven
Visit her face too roughly. Heaven and earth,
Must I remember? Why, she would hang on him
As if increase of appetite had grown
By what it fed on, and yet, within a month—   145
Let me not think on't. Frailty, thy name is woman—
A little month, or ere those shoes were old
With which she followed my poor father's body
Like Niobe,[5] all tears, why she, even she—
O God, a beast that wants discourse of reason   150
Would have mourned longer—married with my uncle,
My father's brother, but no more like my father
Than I to Hercules.[6] Within a month,
Ere yet the salt of most unrighteous tears
Had left the flushing in her gallèd eyes,   155
She married. O, most wicked speed, to post
With such dexterity to incestuous sheets!
It is not, nor it cannot come to good.
But break my heart, for I must hold my tongue.
        [*Enter* HORATIO, MARCELLUS, *and* BERNARDO.]
HORATIO: Hail to your lordship!
HAMLET: I am glad to see you well.   160
     Horatio—or I do forget myself.
HORATIO: The same, my lord, and your poor servant ever.
HAMLET: Sir, my good friend, I'll change[7] that name with you.
     And what make you from Wittenberg, Horatio?
     Marcellus?   165

2. Entirely.
3. In Greek mythology, a lecherous creature, half man and half goat, in contrast to Hyperion, a god.
4. Permit.
5. In Greek mythology, Niobe was turned to stone while weeping over the death of her fourteen children.
6. The demigod Hercules was noted for his strength and a series of spectacular labors.
7. Exchange.

MARCELLUS: My good lord!

HAMLET: I am very glad to see you. [*To* BERNARDO.] Good
    even, sir.——

    But what, in faith, make you from Wittenberg?

HORATIO: A truant disposition, good my lord.

HAMLET: I would not hear your enemy say so,   170
    Nor shall you do my ear that violence
    To make it truster of your own report
    Against yourself. I know you are no truant.
    But what is your affair in Elsinore?
    We'll teach you to drink deep ere you depart.   175

HORATIO: My lord, I came to see your father's funeral.

HAMLET: I prithee do not mock me, fellow-student,
    I think it was to see my mother's wedding.

HORATIO: Indeed, my lord, it followed hard upon.

HAMLET: Thrift, thrift, Horatio. The funeral-baked meats   180
    Did coldly furnish forth the marriage tables.
    Would I had met my dearest[8] foe in heaven
    Or ever I had seen that day, Horatio!
    My father—methinks I see my father.

HORATIO: Where, my lord?

HAMLET: In my mind's eye, Horatio.   185

HORATIO: I saw him once, 'a was a goodly king.

HAMLET: 'A was a man, take him for all in all,
    I shall not look upon his like again.

HORATIO: My lord, I think I saw him yesternight.

HAMLET: Saw who?   190

HORATIO: My lord, the king your father.

HAMLET: The king my father?

HORATIO: Season your admiration[9] for a while
    With an attent ear till I may deliver[1]
    Upon the witness of these gentlemen
    This marvel to you.

---

8. Bitterest.

9. Moderate your wonder.

1. Relent. *Attent*: attentive.

HAMLET: For God's love, let me hear!   195
HORATIO: Two nights together had these gentlemen,
    Marcellus and Bernardo, on their watch
    In the dead waste and middle of the night
    Been thus encountered. A figure like your father,
    Arméd at point exactly, cap-a-pe,²   200
    Appears before them, and with solemn march
    Goes slow and stately by them. Thrice he walked
    By their oppressed and fear-surpriséd eyes
    Within his truncheon's³ length, whilst they, distilled
    Almost to jelly with the act of fear,   205
    Stand dumb and speak not to him. This to me
    In dreadful secrecy impart they did,
    And I with them the third night kept the watch,
    Where, as they had delivered, both in time,
    Form of the thing, each word made true and good,   210
    The apparition comes. I knew your father.
    These hands are not more like.
HAMLET: But where was this?
MARCELLUS: My lord, upon the platform where we watch.
HAMLET: Did you not speak to it?
HORATIO: My lord, I did,
    But answer made it none. Yet once methought   215
    It lifted up its head and did address
    Itself to motion, like as it would speak;
    But even then the morning cock crew loud,
    And at the sound it shrunk in haste away
    And vanished from our sight.
HAMLET: 'Tis very strange.   220
HORATIO: As I do live, my honored lord, 'tis true,
    And we did think it writ down in our duty
    To let you know of it.
HAMLET: Indeed, sirs, but
    This troubles me. Hold you the watch tonight?
ALL: We do, my lord.
HAMLET: Armed, say you?

2. From head to toe. *Exactly:* completely.   3. His baton of office.

ALL: Armed, my lord.   225
HAMLET: From top to toe?
ALL: My lord, from head to foot.
HAMLET: Then saw you not his face.
HORATIO: O yes, my lord, he wore his beaver[4] up.
HAMLET: What, looked he frowningly?
HORATIO: A countenance more in sorrow than in anger.   230
HAMLET: Pale or red?
HORATIO: Nay, very pale.
HAMLET: And fixed his eyes upon you?
HORATIO: Most constantly.
HAMLET: I would I had been there.
HORATIO: It would have much amazed you.
HAMLET: Very like.
    Stayed it long?   235
HORATIO: While one with moderate haste might tell a hundred.
BOTH: Longer, longer.
HORATIO: Not when I saw't.
HAMLET: His beard was grizzled, no?
HORATIO: It was as I have seen it in his life,
    A sable silvered.
HAMLET: I will watch tonight.   240
    Perchance 'twill walk again.
HORATIO: I warr'nt it will.
HAMLET: If it assume my noble father's person,
    I'll speak to it though hell itself should gape[5]
    And bid me hold my peace. I pray you all,
    If you have hitherto concealed this sight,   245
    Let it be tenable[6] in your silence still,
    And whatsomever else shall hap tonight,
    Give it an understanding but no tongue.
    I will requite your loves. So fare you well.
    Upon the platform 'twixt eleven and twelve   250
    I'll visit you.
ALL: Our duty to your honor.

4. His helmet's visor.   6. Held.
5. Open (its mouth) wide.

HAMLET: Your loves, as mine to you. Farewell.

                           [Exeunt all but HAMLET.]

My father's spirit in arms? All is not well.
I doubt[7] some foul play. Would the night were come!
Till then sit still, my soul. Foul deeds will rise,   250
Though all the earth o'erwhelm them, to men's eyes.

                                     [Exit.]

SCENE 3

The dwelling of POLONIUS. *Enter* LAERTES *and* OPHELIA.

LAERTES: My necessaries are embarked. Farewell.
  And, sister, as the winds give benefit
  And convoy is assistant,[8] do not sleep,
  But let me hear from you.

OPHELIA: Do you doubt that?

LAERTES: For Hamlet, and the trifling of his favor,   5
  Hold it a fashion and a toy in blood,
  A violet in the youth of primy[9] nature,
  Forward, not permanent, sweet, not lasting,
  The perfume and suppliance of a minute,
  No more.

OPHELIA: No more but so?

LAERTES: Think it no more.   10
  For nature crescent[1] does not grow alone
  In thews and bulk, but as this temple[2] waxes
  The inward service of the mind and soul
  Grows wide withal. Perhaps he loves you now,
  And now no soil nor cautel[3] doth besmirch   15
  The virtue of his will, but you must fear,
  His greatness weighted,[4] his will is not his own,
  For he himself is subject to his birth.
  He may not, as unvalued persons do,

---

7. Suspect.
8. Means of transport is available.
9. Of the spring.
1. Growing.

2. Body.
3. Deceit.
4. Rank considered.

Carve for himself, for on his choice depends   20
The safety and health of this whole state,
And therefore must his choice be circumscribed
Unto the voice[5] and yielding of that body
Whereof he is the head. Then if he says he loves you,
It fits your wisdom so far to believe it   25
As he in his particular act and place
May give his saying deed,[6] which is no further
Than the main voice of Denmark goes withal.
Then weigh what loss your honor may sustain
If with too credent ear you list[7] his songs,   30
Or lose your heart, or your chaste treasure open
To his unmastered importunity.
Fear it, Ophelia, fear it, my dear sister,
And keep you in the rear of your affection,
Out of the shot and danger of desire.   35
The chariest[8] maid is prodigal enough
If she unmask her beauty to the moon.
Virtue itself scapes not calumnious strokes.
The canker galls the infants[9] of the spring
Too oft before their buttons be disclosed,[1]   40
And in the morn and liquid dew of youth
Contagious blastments[2] are most imminent.
Be wary then; best safety lies in fear.
Youth to itself rebels, though none else near.
OPHELIA: I shall the effect of this good lesson keep   45
　　As watchman to my heart. But, good my brother,
　　Do not as some ungracious pastors do,
　　Show me the steep and thorny way to heaven,
　　Whiles like a puffed and reckless libertine
　　Himself the primrose path of dalliance treads
　　And recks not his own rede.[3]   50

5. Assent.
6. *May give . . . deed:* can do what he promises
(i.e., marry Ophelia).
7. Too credulous an ear you listen to.
8. Most circumspect.

9. The rose caterpillar injures the shoots.
1. Before the buds blossom.
2. Blights.
3. Heeds not his own advice.

LAERTES: O, fear me not.

[*Enter* POLONIUS.]

I stay too long. But here my father comes.
A double blessing is a double grace;
Occasion smiles upon a second leave.

POLONIUS: Yet here, Laertes? Aboard, aboard, for shame!   55
The wind sits in the shoulder of your sail,
And you are stayed for. There—my blessing with thee,
And these few precepts in thy memory
Look thou character.[4] Give thy thoughts no tongue,
Nor any unproportioned thought his act.   60
Be thou familiar, but by no means vulgar.
Those friends thou hast, and their adoption tried,
Grapple them unto thy soul with hoops of steel;
But do not dull[5] thy palm with entertainment
Of each new-hatched, unfledged comrade. Beware   65
Of entrance to a quarrel, but being in,
Bear't that th' opposéd[6] may beware of thee.
Give every man thy ear, but few thy voice;[7]
Take each man's censure, but reserve thy judgment.
Costly thy habit as thy purse can buy,   70
But not expressed in fancy; rich not gaudy,
For the apparel oft proclaims the man,
And they in France of the best rank and station
Are of a most select and generous chief[8] in that.
Neither a borrower nor a lender be,   75
For loan oft loses both itself and friend,
And borrowing dulls th' edge of husbandry.
This above all, to thine own self be true,
And it must follow as the night the day
Thou canst not then be false to any man.   80
Farewell. My blessing season this in thee!

LAERTES: Most humbly do I take my leave, my lord.

POLONIUS: The time invests you. Go, your servants tend.[9]

---

4. Write.   7. Approval.
5. Make callous.   8. Eminence.
6. Conduct it so that the opponent.   9. Await.

LAERTES: Farewell, Ophelia, and remember well
   What I have said to you.
OPHELIA: 'Tis in my memory locked,   85
   And you yourself shall keep the key of it.
LAERTES: Farewell.   [*Exit.*]
POLONIUS: What is't, Ophelia, he hath said to you?
OPHELIA: So please you, something touching the Lord Hamlet.
POLONIUS: Marry, well bethought.   90
   'Tis told me he hath very oft of late
   Given private time to you, and you yourself
   Have of your audience been most free and bounteous.
   If it be so—as so 'tis put on me,
   And that in way of caution—I must tell you,   95
   You do not understand yourself so clearly
   As it behooves my daughter and your honor.
   What is between you? Give me up the truth.
OPHELIA: He hath, my lord, of late made many tenders
   Of his affection to me.   100
POLONIUS: Affection? Pooh! You speak like a green girl,
   Unsifted in such perilous circumstance.
   Do you believe his tenders, as you call them?
OPHELIA: I do not know, my lord, what I should think.
POLONIUS: Marry, I will teach you. Think yourself a baby   105
   That you have ta'en these tenders for true pay
   Which are not sterling. Tender yourself more dearly,
   Or (not to crack the wind of the poor phrase,
   Running it thus) you'll tender me a fool.
OPHELIA: My lord, he hath importuned me with love   110
   In honorable fashion.
POLONIUS: Ay, fashion you may call it. Go to, go to.
OPHELIA: And hath given countenance[1] to his speech, my lord,
   With almost all the holy vows of heaven.
POLONIUS: Ay, springes to catch woodcocks.[2] I do know,   115
   When the blood burns, how prodigal the soul
   Lends the tongue vows. These blazes, daughter,
   Giving more light than heat, extinct in both

---

1. Confirmation.   2. Snares to catch gullible birds.

Even in their promise, as it is a-making,
You must not take for fire. From this time   120
Be something scanter of your maiden presence.
Set your entreatments[3] at a higher rate
Than a command to parle. For Lord Hamlet,
Believe so much in him that he is young,
And with a larger tether may he walk   125
Than may be given you. In few, Ophelia,
Do not believe his vows, for they are brokers,[4]
Not of that dye which their investments[5] show,
But mere implorators[6] of unholy suits,
Breathing like sanctified and pious bawds,   130
The better to beguile. This is for all:
I would not, in plain terms, from this time forth
Have you so slander any moment leisure
As to give words or talk with the Lord Hamlet.
Look to't, I charge you. Come your ways.   135
OPHELIA: I shall obey, my lord. [*Exeunt.*]

SCENE 4
  The guard station. Enter HAMLET, HORATIO *and* MARCELLUS.

HAMLET: The air bites shrewdly;[7] it is very cold.
HORATIO: It is a nipping and an eager[8] air.
HAMLET: What hour now?
HORATIO: I think it lacks of twelve.
MARCELLUS: No, it is struck.
HORATIO: Indeed? I heard it not.
  It then draws near the season   5
  Wherein the spirit held his wont to walk.
    [*A flourish of trumpets, and two pieces go off.*]
  What does this mean, my lord?
HAMLET: The king doth wake tonight and takes his rouse,
  Keeps wassail, and the swagg'ring up-spring[9] reels,

---

3. Negotiations before a surrender.   7. Sharply.
4. Panderers.   8. Keen.
5. Garments.   9. A German dance.
6. Solicitors.

And as he drains his draughts of Rhenish[1] down,   10
The kettledrum and trumpet thus bray out
The triumph of his pledge.
HORATIO: Is it a custom?
HAMLET: Ay, marry, is't,
But to my mind, though I am native here
And to the manner born, it is a custom   15
More honored in the breach than the observance.
This heavy-headed revel east and west
Makes us traduced and taxed of other nations.
They clepe[2] us drunkards, and with swinish phrase
Soil our addition,[3] and indeed it takes   20
From our achievements, though performed at height,
The pith and marrow of our attribute.[4]
So oft it chances in particular men,
That for some vicious mole of nature[5] in them,
As in their birth, wherein they are not guilty   25
(Since nature cannot choose his origin),
By their o'ergrowth of some complexion,
Oft breaking down the pales[6] and forts of reason,
Or by some habit that too much o'er-leavens
The form of plausive[7] manners—that these men,   30
Carrying, I say, the stamp of one defect,
Being nature's livery or fortune's star,
His virtues else, be they as pure as grace,
As infinite as man may undergo,
Shall in the general censure take corruption   35
From that particular fault. The dram of evil
Doth all the noble substance often doubt[8]
To his own scandal.
        [*Enter* GHOST.]
HORATIO: Look, my lord, it comes.
HAMLET: Angels and ministers of grace defend us!
Be thou a spirit of health or goblin damned,   40

---

1. Rhine wine.   5. Some natural, vice-related blemish.
2. Call.   6. Defensive palisade or fence.
3. Reputation.   7. Pleasing.
4. Honor.   8. Extinguish.

Bring with thee airs from heaven or blasts from hell,
Be thy intents wicked or charitable,
Thou com'st in such a questionable⁹ shape
That I will speak to thee. I'll call thee Hamlet,
King, father, royal Dane. O, answer me!   45
Let me not burst in ignorance, but tell
Why thy canonized¹ bones, hearséd in death,
Have burst their cerements;² why the sepulcher
Wherein we saw thee quietly inurned
Hath oped his ponderous and marble jaws   50
To cast thee up again. What may this mean
That thou, dead corse, again in complete steel³
Revisits thus the glimpses of the moon,
Making night hideous, and we fools of nature
So horridly to shake our disposition   55
With thoughts beyond the reaches of our souls?
Say, why is this? wherefore? What should we do?
    [GHOST *beckons.*]
HORATIO: It beckons you to go away with it,
  As if it some impartment⁴ did desire
  To you alone.
MARCELLUS: Look with what courteous action   60
  It waves you to a more removéd⁵ ground.
  But do not go with it.
HORATIO: No, by no means.
HAMLET: It will not speak; then I will follow it.
HORATIO: Do not, my lord.
HAMLET: Why, what should be the fear?
  I do not set my life at a pin's fee,⁶   65
  And for my soul, what can it do to that,
  Being a thing immortal as itself?
  It waves me forth again. I'll follow it.
HORATIO: What if it tempt you toward the flood, my lord,
  Or to the dreadful summit of the cliff   70

9. Prompting question.
1. Buried in accordance with church canons.
2. Burial cloths.
3. Armor.

4. Communication.
5. Beckons you to a more distant.
6. Price.

That beetles[7] o'er his base into the sea,
And there assume some other horrible form,
Which might deprive your sovereignty of reason
And draw you into madness? Think of it.
The very place puts toys of desperation,[8]   75
Without more motive, into every brain
That looks so many fathoms to the sea
And hears it roar beneath.
HAMLET: It wafts me still.
    Go on. I'll follow thee.
MARCELLUS: You shall not go, my lord.
HAMLET: Hold off your hands.   80
HORATIO: Be ruled. You shall not go.
HAMLET: My fate cries out
    And makes each petty artere[9] in this body
    As hardy as the Nemean lion's[1] nerve.
    Still am I called. Unhand me, gentlemen.
    By heaven, I'll make a ghost of him that lets[2] me.   85
    I say, away! Go on. I'll follow thee.
                              [*Exeunt* GHOST *and* HAMLET.]
HORATIO: He waxes desperate with imagination.
MARCELLUS: Let's follow. 'Tis not fit thus to obey him.
HORATIO: Have after. To what issue will this come?
MARCELLUS: Something is rotten in the state of Denmark.   90
HORATIO: Heaven will direct it.
MARCELLUS: Nay, let's follow him.
                                                      [*Exeunt.*]

SCENE 5
Near the guard station. Enter GHOST *and* HAMLET.

HAMLET: Whither wilt thou lead me? Speak. I'll go no further.
GHOST: Mark me.

---

7. Juts out.
8. Desperate fancies.
9. Artery.

1. A mythological lion slain by Hercules.
2. Hinders.

HAMLET: I will.

GHOST: My hour is almost come,
  When I to sulph'rous and tormenting flames
  Must render up myself.

HAMLET: Alas, poor ghost!

GHOST: Pity me not, but lend thy serious hearing   5
  To what I shall unfold.

  HAMLET: Speak. I am bound to hear.

  GHOST: So art thou to revenge, when thou shalt hear.

HAMLET: What?

GHOST: I am thy father's spirit,
  Doomed for a certain term to walk the night,
  And for the day confined to fast³ in fires,   10
  Till the foul crimes done in my days of nature⁴
  Are burnt and purged away. But that I am forbid
  To tell the secrets of my prison house,
  I could a tale unfold whose lightest word   15
  Would harrow up thy soul, freeze thy young blood,
  Make thy two eyes like stars start from their spheres,
  Thy knotted and combinéd⁵ locks to part,
  And each particular hair to stand an end,
  Like quills upon the fretful porpentine.⁶   20
  But this eternal blazon⁷ must not be
  To ears of flesh and blood. List, list, O, list!
  If thou didst every thy dear father love—

HAMLET: O God!

GHOST: Revenge his foul and most unnatural murder.   25

HAMLET: Murder!

GHOST: Murder most foul, as in the best it is,
  But this most foul, strange, and unnatural.

HAMLET: Haste me to know't, that I, with wings as swift
  As meditation or the thoughts of love,   30
  May sweep to my revenge.

GHOST: I find thee apt.

---

3. Do penance.   6. Porcupine.
4. That is, while I was alive.   7. Description of eternity.
5. Tangled.

And duller shouldst thou be than the fat weed
That rots itself in ease on Lethe wharf,—[8]
Wouldst thou not stir in this. Now, Hamlet, hear.
'Tis given out that, sleeping in my orchard,   35
A serpent stung me. So the whole ear of Denmark
Is by a forgéd process[9] of my death
Rankly abused. But know, thou noble youth,
The serpent that did sting thy father's life
Now wears his crown.

HAMLET: O my prophetic soul!   40
  My uncle!

GHOST: Ay, that incestuous, that adulterate beast,
  With witchcraft of his wits, with traitorous gifts—
  O wicked wit and gifts that have the power
  So to seduce!—won to his shameful lust   45
  The will of my most seeming virtuous queen.
  O Hamlet, what a falling off was there,
  From me, whose love was of that dignity
  That it went hand in hand even with the vow
  I made to her in marriage, and to decline[1]   50
  Upon a wretch whose natural gifts were poor
  To those of mine!
  But virtue as it never will be moved,
  Though lewdness court it in a shape of heaven,
  So lust, though to a radiant angel linked,   55
  Will sate itself in a celestial bed
  And prey on garbage.
  But soft, methinks I scent the morning air.
  Brief let me be. Sleeping within my orchard,
  My custom always of the afternoon,   60
  Upon my secure hour thy uncle stole,
  With juice of cursed hebona[2] in a vial,
  And in the porches of my ears did pour
  The leperous distilment, whose effect

---

8. The asphodel that rots on the bank of Lethe, the river of forgetfulness in the classical underworld.

9. False report.
1. Sink.
2. A poison.

Holds such an enmity with blood of man   65
That swift as quicksilver it courses through
The natural gates and alleys of the body,
And with a sudden vigor it doth posset[3]
And curd, like eager[4] droppings into milk,
The thin and wholesome blood. So did it mine,   70
And a most instant tetter barked about[5]
Most lazar-like[6] with vile and loathsome crust
All my smooth body.
Thus was I sleeping by a brother's hand
Of life, of crown, of queen at once dispatched,   75
Cut off even in the blossoms of my sin,
Unhouseled, disappointed, unaneled,[7]
No reck'ning made, but sent to my account
With all my imperfections on my head.
O, horrible! O, horrible! most horrible!   80
If thou hast nature in thee, bear it not.
Let not the royal bed of Denmark be
A couch of luxury[8] and damnèd incest.
But howsomever thou pursues this act,
Taint not thy mind, nor let thy soul contrive   85
Against thy mother aught. Leave her to heaven,
And to those thorns that in her bosom lodge
To prick and sting her. Fare thee well at once.
The glowworm shows the matin[9] to be near,
And gins to pale his uneffectual fire.   90
Adieu, adieu, adieu. Remember me.   [*Exit.*]
HAMLET: O all you host of heaven! O earth! What else?
And shall I couple hell? O, fie! Hold, hold, my heart,
And you, my sinews, grow not instant old,
But bear me stiffly up. Remember thee?   95
Ay, thou poor ghost, whiles memory holds a seat
In this distracted globe.[1] Remember thee?

---

3. Coagulate.   8. Lust.
4. Acid. *Curd:* curdle.   9. Morning.
5. Covered like bark. *Tetter:* a skin disease.   1. Skull.
6. Leperlike.
7. Without having received the Eucharist, made a
final confession, or been given last rites.

Yea, from the table[2] of my memory
I'll wipe away all trivial fond[3] records,
All saws of books, all forms, all pressures past   100
That youth and observation copied there,
And thy commandment all alone shall live
Within the book and volume of my brain,
Unmixed with baser matter. Yes, by heaven!
O most pernicious woman!   105
O villain, villain, smiling, damnéd villain!
My tables—meet it is I set it down
That one may smile, and smile, and be a villain.
At least I am sure it may be so in Denmark.
So, uncle, there you are. Now to my word:[4]   110
It is "Adieu, adieu. Remember me."
I have sworn't.

    [*Enter* HORATIO *and* MARCELLUS.]

HORATIO: My lord, my lord!

MARCELLUS: Lord Hamlet!

HORATIO: Heavens secure him!

HAMLET: So be it!

MARCELLUS: Illo, ho, ho, my lord!   115

HAMLET: Hillo, ho, ho, boy![5] Come, bird, come.

MARCELLUS: How is't, my noble lord?

HORATIO: What news, my lord?

HAMLET: O, wonderful!

HORATIO: Good my lord, tell it.

HAMLET: No, you will reveal it.

HORATIO: Not I, my lord, by heaven.

MARCELLUS: Nor I, my lord.   120

HAMLET: How say you then, would heart of man once think it?
  But you'll be secret?

BOTH: Ay, by heaven, my lord.

HAMLET: There's never a villain dwelling in all Denmark
  But he's an arrant knave.

HORATIO: There needs no ghost, my lord, come from the grave   125
  To tell us this.

---

2. Writing tablet.
3. Foolish.

4. For my motto.
5. A falconer's cry.

HAMLET: Why, right, you are in the right,
    And so without more circumstance at all
    I hold it fit that we shake hands and part,
    You, as your business and desire shall point you,
    For every man hath business and desire   130
    Such as it is, and for my own poor part,
    Look you, I'll go pray.
HORATIO: These are but wild and whirling words, my lord.
HAMLET: I am sorry they offend you, heartily;
    Yes, faith, heartily.
HORATIO: There's no offence, my lord.
HAMLET: Yes, by Saint Patrick, but there is, Horatio,
    And much offence too. Touching this vision here,
    It is an honest ghost, that let me tell you.
    For your desire to know what is between us,
    O'ermaster't as you may. And now, good friends,   140
    As you are friends, scholars, and soldiers,
    Give me one poor request.
HORATIO: What is't, my lord? We will.
HAMLET: Never make known what you have seen tonight.
BOTH: My lord, we will not.
HAMLET: Nay, but swear't.
HORATIO: In faith,   145
    My lord, not I.
MARCELLUS: Nor I, my lord, in faith.
HAMLET: Upon my sword.
MARCELLUS: We have sworn, my lord, already.
HAMLET: Indeed, upon my sword, indeed.
        [GHOST *cries under the stage.*]
GHOST: Swear.
HAMLET: Ha, ha, boy, say'st thou so? Art thou there, truepenny?[6]
    Come on. You hear this fellow in the cellarage.[7]   150
    Consent to swear.
HORATIO: Propose the oath, my lord.
HAMLET: Never to speak of this that you have seen,
    Swear by my sword.

6. Trusty fellow.   7. Below.

GHOST: [*Beneath.*] Swear.

HAMLET: Hic et ubique?[8] Then we'll shift our ground.   155
   Come hither, gentlemen,
   And lay your hands again upon my sword.
   Swear by my sword
   Never to speak of this that you have heard.

GHOST: [*Beneath.*] Swear by his sword.   160

HAMLET: Well said, old mole! Canst work i' th' earth so fast?
   A worthy pioneer![9] Once more remove, good friends.

HORATIO: O day and night, but this is wondrous strange!

HAMLET: And therefore as a stranger give it welcome.
   There are more things in heaven and earth, Horatio,   165
   Than are dreamt of in your philosophy.
   But come.
   Here as before, never, so help you mercy,
   How strange or odd some'er I bear myself
   (As I perchance hereafter shall think meet   170
   To put an antic[1] disposition on),
   That you, at such times, seeing me, never shall,
   With arms encumbered[2] thus, or this head-shake,
   Or by pronouncing of some doubtful phrase,
   As "Well, we know," or "We could, and if we would"   175
   Or "If we list to speak," or "There be, and if they might"
   Or such ambiguous giving out, to note
   That you know aught of me—this do swear,
   So grace and mercy at your most need help you.

GHOST: [*Beneath.*] Swear.   180

   [*They swear.*]

HAMLET: Rest, rest, perturbéd spirit! So, gentlemen,
   With all my love I do commend me to you,
   And what so poor a man as Hamlet is
   May do t'express his love and friending[3] to you,
   God willing, shall not lack. Let us go in together,   185
   And still your fingers on your lips, I pray.

8. Here and everywhere?
9. Soldier who digs trenches.
1. Mad.

2. Folded.
3. Friendship.

The time is out of joint. O cursèd spite
That ever I was born to set it right!
Nay, come, let's go together.   [*Exeunt.*]

ACT II
SCENE 1
The dwelling of POLONIUS. *Enter* POLONIUS *and* REYNALDO.

POLONIUS: Give him this money and these notes, Reynaldo.
REYNALDO: I will, my lord.
POLONIUS: You shall do marvellous wisely, good Reynaldo,
    Before you visit him, to make inquire[4]
    Of his behavior.
REYNALDO: My lord, I did intend it.
POLONIUS: Marry, well said, very well said. Look you, sir.   5
    Enquire me first what Danskers[5] are in Paris,
    And how, and who, what means, and where they keep,[6]
    What company, at what expense; and finding
    By this encompassment[7] and drift of question   10
    That they do know my son, come you more nearer
    Than your particular demands[8] will touch it.
    Take you as 'twere some distant knowledge of him,
    As thus, "I know his father and his friends,
    And in part him." Do you mark this, Reynaldo?   15
REYNALDO: Ay, very well, my lord.
POLONIUS: "And in part him, but," you may say, "not well,
    But if't be he I mean, he's very wild,
    Addicted so and so." And there put on him
    What forgeries you please; marry, none so rank[9]   20
    As may dishonor him. Take heed of that.
    But, sir, such wanton, wild, and usual slips
    As are companions noted and most known
    To youth and liberty.

4. Inquiry.
5. Danes.
6. Live.

7. Indirect means.
8. Direct questions.
9. Foul. *Forgeries:* lies.

REYNALDO: As gaming, my lord.
POLONIUS: Ay, or drinking, fencing, swearing,   25
    Quarrelling, drabbing[1]—you may go so far.
REYNALDO: My lord, that would dishonor him.
POLONIUS: Faith, no, as you may season it in the charge.[2]
    You must not put another scandal on him,
    That he is open to incontinency.[3]   30
    That's not my meaning. But breathe his faults so quaintly[4]
    That they may seem the taints of liberty,[5]
    The flash and outbreak of a fiery mind,
    A savageness in unreclaiméd[6] blood,
    Of general assault.[7]
REYNALDO: But, my good lord—   35
POLONIUS: Wherefore should you do this?
REYNALDO: Ay, my lord,
    I would know that.
POLONIUS: Marry, sir, here's my drift,
    And I believe it is a fetch of warrant.[8]
    You laying these slight sullies on my son,
    As 'twere a thing a little soiled wi' th' working,   40
    Mark you,
    Your party in converse,[9] him you would sound,
    Having ever seen in the prenominate[1] crimes
    The youth you breathe[2] of guilty, be assured
    He closes with you in this consequence,   45
    "Good sir," or so, or "friend," or "gentleman,"
    According to the phrase or the addition
    Of man and country.
REYNALDO: Very good, my lord.
POLONIUS: And then, sir, does 'a this—'a does—What was I
    about to say?
    By the mass, I was about to say something.   50
    Where did I leave?

---

1. Whoring.
2. Soften the accusation.
3. Sexual excess.
4. With delicacy.
5. Faults of freedom.
6. Untamed.

7. Touching everyone.
8. Permissible trick.
9. Conversation.
1. Already named.
2. Speak.

REYNALDO: At "closes in the consequence."

POLONIUS: At "closes in the consequence"—ay, marry,
    He closes thus: "I know the gentleman.
    I saw him yesterday, or th' other day,   55
    Or then, or then, with such, or such, and as you say,
    There was 'a gaming, there o'ertook in's rouse,[3]
    There falling out at tennis," or perchance
    "I saw him enter such a house of sale,"
    Videlicet,[4] a brothel, or so forth.   60
    See you, now—
    Your bait of falsehood takes this carp of truth,
    And thus do we of wisdom and of reach,[5]
    With windlasses and with assays of bias,[6]
    By indirections find directions out;   65
    So by my former lecture and advice
    Shall you my son. You have me, have you not?

REYNALDO: My lord, I have.

POLONIUS: God b'wi' ye; fare ye well.

REYNALDO: Good my lord.

POLONIUS: Observe his inclination in yourself.   70

REYNALDO: I shall, my lord.

POLONIUS: And let him ply[7] his music.

REYNALDO: Well, my lord.

POLONIUS: Farewell.   [*Exit* REYNALDO.]
      [*Enter* OPHELIA.]
               How now, Ophelia, what's the matter?

OPHELIA: O my lord, my lord, I have been so affrighted!

POLONIUS: With what, i' th' name of God?   75

OPHELIA: My lord, as I was sewing in my closet,[8]
    Lord Hamlet with his doublet all unbraced,[9]
    No hat upon his head, his stockings fouled,
    Ungartered and down-gyvéd[1] to his ankle,
    Pale as his shirt, his knees knocking each other,   80
    And with a look so piteous in purport

---

3. Carousing.
4. Namely.
5. Ability.
6. Indirect tests.

7. Practice.
8. Chamber.
9. Jacket all unlaced.
1. Fallen down like fetters.

As if he had been loosèd out of hell
 To speak of horrors—he comes before me.
POLONIUS: Mad for thy love?
OPHELIA: My lord, I do not know,
 But truly I do fear it.
POLONIUS: What said he?   85
OPHELIA: He took me by the wrist, and held me hard,
 Then goes he to the length of all his arm,
 And with his other hand thus o'er his brow,
 He falls to such perusal of my face
 As 'a would draw it. Long stayed he so.   90
 At last, a little shaking of mine arm,
 And thrice his head thus waving up and down,
 He raised a sigh so piteous and profound
 As it did seem to shatter all his bulk,[2]
 And end his being. That done, he lets me go,   95
 And with his head over his shoulder turned
 He seemed to find his way without his eyes,
 For out adoors he went without their helps,
 And to the last bended[3] their light on me.
POLONIUS: Come, go with me. I will go seek the king. 100
 This is the very ecstasy of love,
 Whose violent property fordoes[4] itself,
 And leads the will to desperate undertakings
 As oft as any passion under heaven
 That does afflict our natures. I am sorry.   105
 What, have you given him any hard words of late?
OPHELIA: No, my good lord, but as you did command
 I did repel[5] his letters, and denied
 His access to me.
POLONIUS: That hath made him mad.
 I am sorry that with better heed and judgment 110
 I had not quoted[6] him. I feared he did but trifle,
 And meant to wrack[7] thee; but beshrew my jealousy.

---

2. Body.
3. Directed.
4. Character destroys.

5. Refuse.
6. Observed.
7. Harm.

By heaven, it is as proper to our age
To cast beyond ourselves in our opinions
As it is common for the younger sort   115
To lack discretion. Come, go we to the king.
This must be known,[8] which being kept close, might move
More grief to hide than hate to utter love.
Come.   [*Exeunt.*]

SCENE 2
A public room. Enter KING, QUEEN, ROSENCRANTZ *and*
GUILDENSTERN.

KING: Welcome, dear Rosencrantz and Guildenstern.
   Moreover that[9] we much did long to see you,
   The need we have to use you did provoke
   Our hasty sending. Something have you heard
   Of Hamlet's transformation—so call it,   5
   Sith[1] nor th' exterior nor the inward man
   Resembles that it was. What it should be,
   More than his father's death, that thus hath put him
   So much from th' understanding of himself,
   I cannot deem of, I entreat you both   10
   That, being of so young days[2] brought up with him,
   And sith so neighbored to his youth and havior,[3]
   That you vouchsafe your rest here in our court
   Some little time, so by your companies
   To draw him on to pleasures, and to gather   15
   So much as from occasion you may glean,
   Whether aught to us unknown afflicts him thus,
   That opened lies within our remedy.
QUEEN: Good gentlemen, he hath much talked of you,
   And sure I am two men there are not living   20
   To whom he more adheres. If it will please you
   To show us so much gentry[4] and good will

---

8. Revealed (to the king).   2. From childhood.
9. In addition to the fact that.   3. Behavior. *Neighbored:* closely allied.
1. Since.   4. Courtesy.

As to expend your time with us awhile
For the supply and profit of our hope,
Your visitation shall receive such thanks   25
As fits a king's remembrance.

ROSENCRANTZ: Both your majesties
Might, by the sovereign power you have of us,
Put your dread pleasures more into command
Than to entreaty.

GUILDENSTERN: But we both obey,
And here give up ourselves in the full bent⁵   30
To lay our service freely at your feet,
To be commanded.

KING: Thanks, Rosencrantz and gentle Guildenstern.

QUEEN: Thanks, Guildenstern and gentle Rosencrantz.
And I beseech you instantly to visit   35
My too much changed son. Go, some of you,
And bring these gentlemen where Hamlet is.

GUILDENSTERN: Heavens make our presence and our practices
Pleasant and helpful to him!

QUEEN: Ay, amen!
            [*Exeunt* ROSENCRANTZ *and* GUILDENSTERN.]
        [*Enter* POLONIUS.]

POLONIUS: Th' ambassadors from Norway, my good lord,   40
Are joyfully returned.

KING: Thou still⁶ hast been the father of good news.

POLONIUS: Have I, my lord? I assure you, my good liege,
I hold my duty as I hold my soul,
Both to my God and to my gracious king;   45
And I do think—or else this brain of mine
Hunts not the trail of policy⁷ so sure
As it hath used to do—that I have found
The very cause of Hamlet's lunacy.

KING: O, speak of that, that do I long to hear.   50

POLONIUS: Give first admittance to th' ambassadors.
My news shall be the fruit⁸ to that great feast.

5. Completely.   7. Statecraft.
6. Ever.   8. Dessert.

KING: Thyself do grace to them, and bring them in.

> [*Exit* POLONIUS.]

He tells me, my dear Gertrude, he hath found
The head and source of all your son's distemper.   55
QUEEN: I doubt it is no other but the main,
His father's death and our o'erhasty marriage.
KING: Well, we shall sift[9] him.

> [*Enter Ambassadors* (VOLTEMAND *and* CORNELIUS) *with*
> POLONIUS.]

>   Welcome, my good friends,
Say, Voltemand, what from our brother Norway?
VOLTEMAND: Most fair return of greetings and desires.   60
Upon our first,[1] he sent out to suppress
His nephew's levies, which to him appeared
To be a preparation 'gainst the Polack,[2]
But better looked into, he truly found
It was against your highness, whereat grieved,   65
That so his sickness, age, and impotence
Was falsely borne in hand, sends out arrests[3]
On Fortinbras, which he in brief obeys,
Receives rebuke from Norway, and in fine,
Makes vow before his uncle never more   70
To give th' assay[4] of arms against your majesty.
Whereon old Norway, overcome with joy,
Gives him three thousand crowns in annual fee,
And his commission to employ those soldiers,
So levied as before, against the Polack,   75
With an entreaty, herein further shown, [*Gives* CLAUDIUS
    a paper.]
That it might please you to give quiet pass[5]
Through your dominions for this enterprise,
On such regards of safety and allowance

---

9. Examine.
1. I.e., first appearance.
2. King of Poland.
3. Orders to stop. *Falsely borne in hand:* deceived.

4. Trial.
5. Safe conduct.

As therein are set down.

KING: It likes[6] us well,   80
And at our more considered time[7] we'll read,
Answer, and think upon this business.
Meantime we thank you for your well-took[8] labor.
Go to your rest; at night we'll feast together.
Most welcome home!   [*Exeunt* AMBASSADORS.]

POLONIUS: This business is well ended.   85
My liege and madam, to expostulate[9]
What majesty should be, what duty is,
Why day is day, night night, and time is time,
Were nothing but to waste night, day, and time.
Therefore, since brevity is the soul of wit,   90
And tediousness the limbs and outward flourishes,[1]
I will be brief. Your noble son is mad.
Mad call I it, for to define true madness,
What is't but to be nothing else but mad?
But let that go.

QUEEN: More matter with less art.   95

POLONIUS: Madam, I swear I use no art at all.
That he is mad, 'tis true: 'tis true 'tis pity,
And pity 'tis 'tis true. A foolish figure,
But farewell it, for I will use no art.
Mad let us grant him, then, and now remains   100
That we find out the cause of this effect,
Or rather say the cause of this defect,
For this effect defective comes by cause.
Thus it remains, and the remainder thus.
Perpend.[2]   105
I have a daughter—have while she is mine—
Who in her duty and obedience, mark,
Hath given me this. Now gather, and surmise.
"To the celestial, and my soul's idol, the most beautified
    Ophelia."—That's an ill phrase, a vile phrase, "beautified"   110

6. Pleases.
7. Time for more consideration.
8. Successful.

9. Discuss.
1. Adornments.
2. Consider.

is a vile phrase. But you shall hear. Thus:
"In her excellent white bosom, these, etc."

QUEEN: Came this from Hamlet to her?

POLONIUS: Good madam, stay awhile. I will be faithful.

> "Doubt thou the stars are fire, 115
> Doubt that the sun doth move;
> Doubt truth to be a liar;
> But never doubt I love.

"O dear Ophelia, I am ill at these numbers.[3] I have not art to
reckon my groans, but that I love thee best, O most 120
best, believe it. Adieu.

"Thine evermore, most dear lady, whilst this machine[4] is to
him, Hamlet."

This in obedience hath my daughter shown me,
And more above, hath his solicitings, 125
As they fell out by time, by means, and place,
All given to mine ear.

KING: But how hath she
Received his love?

POLONIUS: What do you think of me?

KING: As of a man faithful and honorable.

POLONIUS: I would fain prove so. But what might you think, 130
When I had seen this hot love on the wing.
(As I perceived it, I must tell you that,
Before my daughter told me), what might you,
Or my dear majesty your queen here, think,
If I had played the desk or table-book, 135
Or given my heart a winking, mute and dumb,
Or looked upon this love with idle sight,[5]
What might you think? No, I went round[6] to work,
And my young mistress thus I did bespeak:
"Lord Hamlet is a prince out of thy star.[7] 140
This must not be." And then I prescripts[8] gave her,
That she should lock herself from his resort,

3. Verses.
4. Body.
5. If he had remained silent and kept the information to himself.

6. Directly.
7. Beyond your sphere.
8. Orders.

Admit no messengers, receive no tokens.
Which done, she took[9] the fruits of my advice;
And he repelled, a short tale to make,   145
Fell into a sadness, then into a fast,
Thence to a watch,[1] thence into a weakness,
Thence to a lightness, and by this declension,
Into the madness wherein now he raves,
And all we mourn for.

KING: Do you think 'tis this?   150

QUEEN: It may be, very like.

POLONIUS: Hath there been such a time—I would fain know that—
   That I have positively said "Tis so,"
   When it proved otherwise?

KING: Not that I know.

POLONIUS: [*Pointing to his head and shoulder.*] Take this from
   this, if this be otherwise.   155
   If circumstances lead me, I will find
   Where truth is hid, though it were hid indeed
   Within the centre.[2]

KING: How may we try it further?

POLONIUS: You know sometimes he walks four hours together
   Here in the lobby.

QUEEN: So he does, indeed.   160

POLONIUS: At such a time I'll loose[3] my daughter to him.
   Be you and I behind an arras[4] then.
   Mark the encounter. If he love her not,
   And be not from his reason fall'n thereon,
   Let me be no assistant for a state,   165
   But keep a farm and carters.

KING: We will try it.

   [*Enter* HAMLET *reading a book.*]

QUEEN: But look where sadly the poor wretch comes reading.

POLONIUS: Away, I do beseech you both away,
   I'll board[5] him presently.   [*Exeunt* KING *and* QUEEN.]
                 O, give me leave.

9. Followed.
1. An insomnia.
2. Of the earth.

3. Let loose.
4. Tapestry.
5. Accost.

How does my good Lord Hamlet? 170

HAMLET: Well, God-a-mercy.

POLONIUS: Do you know me, my lord?

HAMLET: Excellent well, you are a fishmonger.

POLONIUS: Not I, my lord.

HAMLET: Then I would you were so honest a man. 175

POLONIUS: Honest, my lord?

HAMLET: Ay, sir, to be honest as this world goes, is to be one man picked out of ten thousand.

POLONIUS: That's very true, my lord.

HAMLET: For if the sun breed maggots in a dead dog, being a 180 god kissing carrion[6]—Have you a daughter?

POLONIUS: I have, my lord.

HAMLET: Let her not walk i' th' sun. Conception is a blessing, but as your daughter may conceive—friend, look to't.

POLONIUS: How say you by that? [*Aside*.] Still harping on my 185 daughter. Yet he knew me not at first. 'A said I was a fishmonger. 'A is far gone. And truly in my youth I suffered much extremity for love. Very near this. I'll speak to him again.—What do you read, my lord?

HAMLET: Words, words, words. 190

POLONIUS: What is the matter, my lord?

HAMLET: Between who?

POLONIUS: I mean the matter that you read, my lord.

HAMLET: Slanders, sir; for the satirical rogue says here that old men have grey beards, that their faces are wrinkled, 195 their eyes purging thick amber and plum-tree gum, and that they have a plentiful lack of wit, together with most weak hams[7]—all which, sir, though I most powerfully and potently believe, yet I hold it not honesty to have it thus set down, for yourself, sir shall grow old as I am, if like a crab 200 you could go backward.

POLONIUS: [*Aside*.] Though this be madness, yet there is method in't.—Will you walk out of the air, my lord?

HAMLET: Into my grave?

---

6. The Elizabethans believed that sunshine on dead flesh produced maggots.

7. Limbs.

POLONIUS: [*Aside.*] Indeed, that's out of the air. How pregnant 205
sometime his replies are! a happiness that often madness
hits on, which reason and sanity could not so prosperously
be delivered of. I will leave him, and suddenly contrive the
means of meeting between him and my daughter.—My
honorable lord. I will most humbly take my leave of you. 210

HAMLET: You cannot take from me anything that I will more
willingly part withal—except my life, except my life, except
my life.

    [*Enter* GUILDENSTERN *and* ROSENCRANTZ.]

POLONIUS: Fare you well, my lord.

HAMLET: These tedious old fools! 215

POLONIUS: You go to seek the Lord Hamlet. There he is.

ROSENCRANTZ: [*To* POLONIUS.] God save you, sir!

                    [*Exit* POLONIUS.]

GUILDENSTERN: My honored lord!

ROSENCRANTZ: My most dear lord!

HAMLET: My excellent good friends! How dost thou,
Guildenstern? 220
    Ah, Rosencrantz! Good lads, how do you both?

ROSENCRANTZ: As the indifferent[8] children of the earth.

GUILDENSTERN: Happy in that we are not over-happy;
On Fortune's cap we are not the very button.[9]

HAMLET: Not the soles of her shoe? 225

ROSENCRANTZ: Neither, my lord.

HAMLET: Then you live about her waist, or in the middle of
her favors?

GUILDENSTERN: Faith, her privates[1] we.

HAMLET: In the secret parts of Fortune? O, most true, she is a 230
strumpet.[2] What news?

ROSENCRANTZ: None, my lord, but that the world's grown
honest.

HAMLET: Then is doomsday near. But your news is not true.
Let me question more in particular. What have you, my 235

---

8. Ordinary.
9. I.e., on top.

1. Ordinary citizens, but also private parts (sexual organs).
2. Prostitute.

good friends, deserved at the hands of Fortune, that she sends you to prison hither?

GUILDENSTERN: Prison, my lord?

HAMLET: Denmark's a prison.

ROSENCRANTZ: Then is the world one. 240

HAMLET: A goodly one, in which there are many confines, wards[3] and dungeons. Denmark being one o' th' worst.

ROSENCRANTZ: We think not so, my lord.

HAMLET: Why then 'tis none to you; for there is nothing either good or bad, but thinking makes it so. To me it is 245 a prison.

ROSENCRANTZ: Why then your ambition makes it one. 'Tis too narrow for your mind.

HAMLET: O God, I could be bounded in a nutshell and count myself a king of infinite space, were it not that I have bad 250 dreams.

GUILDENSTERN: Which dreams indeed are ambition; for the very substance of the ambitious is merely the shadow of a dream.

HAMLET: A dream itself is but a shadow.

ROSENCRANTZ: Truly, and I hold ambition of so airy and light 255 a quality that it is but a shadow's shadow.

HAMLET: Then are our beggars bodies, and our monarchs and outstretched heroes the beggars' shadows. Shall we to th' court? for, by my fay,[4] I cannot reason.

BOTH: We'll wait upon you. 260

HAMLET: No such matter. I will not sort[5] you with the rest of my servants; for to speak to you like an honest man, I am most dreadfully attended. But in the beaten way of friendship, what make you at Elsinore?

ROSENCRANTZ: To visit you, my lord; no other occasion. 265

HAMLET: Beggar that I am, I am even poor in thanks, but I thank you; and sure, dear friends, my thanks are too dear a halfpenny.[6] Were you not sent for? Is it your own inclining? Is it a free visitation? Come, come, deal justly with me. Come, come, nay speak. 270

---

3. Cells.
4. Faith.

5. Include.
6. Not worth a halfpenny.

GUILDENSTERN: What should we say, my lord?

HAMLET: Anything but to th' purpose. You were sent for, and there is a kind of confession in your looks, which your modesties have not craft enough to color. I know the good king and queen have sent for you.   275

ROSENCRANTZ: To what end, my lord?

HAMLET: That you must teach me. But let me conjure you by the rights of our fellowship, by the consonancy of our youth, by the obligation of our ever-preserved love, and by what more dear a better proposer can charge you withal, be   280 even and direct with me whether you were sent for or no.

ROSENCRANTZ: [*Aside to* GUILDENSTERN.] What say you?

HAMLET: [*Aside.*] Nay, then, I have an eye of you.—If you love me, hold not off.

GUILDENSTERN: My lord, we were sent for.   285

HAMLET: I will tell you why; so shall my anticipation prevent your discovery,[7] and your secrecy to the king and queen moult no feather. I have of late—but wherefore I know not—lost all my mirth, forgone all custom of exercises; and indeed it goes so heavily with my disposition, that this   290 goodly frame the earth seems to me a sterile promontory, this most excellent canopy the air, look you, this brave o'er-hanging firmament, this majestical roof fretted[8] with golden fire, why it appeareth nothing to me but a foul and pestilent congregation of vapors. What a piece of work is   295 a man, how noble in reason, how infinite in faculty, in form and moving how express[9] and admirable, in action how like an angel, in apprehension how like a god: the beauty of the world, the paragon of animals. And yet to me; what is this quintessence of dust? Man delights not   300 me, nor woman neither, though by your smiling you seem to say so.

ROSENCRANTZ: My lord, there was no such stuff in my thoughts.

HAMLET: Why did ye laugh, then, when I said "Man delights not me"?   305

7. Disclosure.   9. Well built.
8. Ornamented with fretwork.

ROSENCRANTZ: To think, my lord, if you delight not in man, what lenten entertainment[1] the players shall receive from you. We coted[2] them on the way, and hither are they coming to offer you service.

HAMLET: He that plays the king shall be welcome—his majesty shall have tribute of me; the adventurous knight shall use his foil and target; the lover shall not sigh gratis; the humorous[3] man shall end his part in peace; the clown shall make those laugh whose lungs are tickle o' th' sere;[4] and the lady shall say her mind freely, or the blank verse shall halt for't. What players are they? 310 315

ROSENCRANTZ: Even those you were wont to take such delight in, the tragedians of the city.

HAMLET: How chances it they travel? Their residence,[5] both in reputation and profit, was better both ways. 320

ROSENCRANTZ: I think their inhibition comes by the means of the late innovation.

HAMLET: Do they hold the same estimation they did when I was in the city? Are they so followed?

ROSENCRANTZ: No, indeed, are they not. 325

HAMLET: How comes it? Do they grow rusty?

ROSENCRANTZ: Nay, their endeavor keeps in the wonted pace; but there is, sir, an eyrie of children, little eyases,[6] that cry out on the top of question,[7] and are most tyrannically clapped for't. These are now the fashion, and so berattle the common stages (so they call them) that many wearing rapiers are afraid of goose quills[8] and dare scarce come thither. 330

HAMLET: What, are they children? Who maintains 'em? How are they escoted?[9] Will they pursue the quality no longer than they can sing? Will they not say afterwards, if they 335

---

1. Scanty reception.
2. Passed.
3. Eccentric. *Foil and target:* sword and shield.
4. Easily set off.
5. Permanent or home theater.

6. Little hawks; an allusion to the boy-actor companies that rivaled the Globe theater.
7. With a loud, high delivery.
8. Many noblemen fear the pens of satirical writers.
9. Supported.

should grow themselves to common players (as it is most like, if their means are no better), their writers do them wrong to make them exclaim against their own succession?[1]

ROSENCRANTZ: Faith, there has been much todo on both sides; and the nation holds it no sin to tarre[2] them to controversy. There was for a while no money bid for argument,[3] unless the poet and the player went to cuffs[4] in the question.

HAMLET: Is't possible?

GUILDENSTERN: O, there has been much throwing about of brains.

HAMLET: Do the boys carry it away?

ROSENCRANTZ: Ay, that they do, my lord. Hercules and his load too.[5]

HAMLET: It is not very strange, for my uncle is King of Denmark, and those that would make mouths at him while my father lived give twenty, forty, fifty, a hundred ducats apiece for his picture in little.[6] 'Sblood,[7] there is something in this more than natural, if philosophy could find it out.
[A flourish.]

GUILDENSTERN: There are the players.

HAMLET: Gentlemen, you are welcome to Elsinore. Your hands. Come then, th' appurtenance of welcome is fashion and ceremony. Let me comply with you in this garb, lest my extent[8] to the players, which I tell you must show fairly outwards should more appear like entertainment[9] than yours. You are welcome. But my uncle-father and aunt-mother are deceived.

GUILDENSTERN: In what, my dear lord?

HAMLET: I am but mad north-north-west; when the wind is southerly I know a hawk from a handsaw.[1]
[Enter POLONIUS.]

---

1. Future careers.
2. Urge.
3. Paid for a play plot.
4. Blows.
5. During one of his labors, Hercules assumed for a time the burden of the Titan Atlas, who supported the heavens on his shoulders. Also a

reference to the effect on business at Shakespeare's theater, the Globe.
6. Miniature. *Make mouths*: sneer.
7. By God's blood.
8. Fashion. *Comply with:* welcome.
9. Cordiality.
1. I.e., I know a plasterer's tool from (perhaps) a hernshaw, or heron.

POLONIUS: Well be with you, gentlemen.

HAMLET: Hark you, Guildenstern—and you too—at each ear
a hearer. That great baby you see there is not yet out of his
swaddling clouts.[2]

ROSENCRANTZ: Happily he is the second time come to them,   370
for they say an old man is twice a child.

HAMLET: I will prophesy he comes to tell me of the players.
Mark it.
—You say right, sir, a Monday morning, 'twas then indeed.

POLONIUS: My lord, I have news to tell you.

HAMLET: My lord, I have news to tell you.   375
When Roscius was an actor in Rome[3]—

POLONIUS: The actors are come hither, my lord.

HAMLET: Buzz, buzz.

POLONIUS: Upon my honor—

HAMLET: Then came each actor on his ass—   380

POLONIUS: The best actors in the world, either for tragedy,
comedy, history, pastoral, pastoral-comical, historical-
pastoral, tragical-historical, tragical-comical-historical-
pastoral, scene individable, or poem unlimited. Seneca
cannot be too heavy nor Plautus[4] too light. For the law of   385
writ and the liberty,[5] these are the only men.

HAMLET: O Jephtha, judge of Israel, what a treasure hadst
thou![6]

POLONIUS: What a treasure had he, my lord?

HAMLET: Why—
"One fair daughter, and no more,   390
The which he loved passing well."

POLONIUS: [Aside.] Still on my daughter.

HAMLET: Am I not i' th' right, old Jephtha?

2. Wrappings for an infant.

3. Roscius was the most famous actor of classical Rome.

4. Roman writers of tragedy and comedy,
respectively.

5. The *law of writ* refers to plays written

according to classical rules; the *liberty*, to those
written otherwise.

6. In the Bible, Jephtha asked God for victory
and vowed to sacrifice the first creature he encountered upon his return. His only daughter became
the victim of his vow.

POLONIUS: If you call me Jephtha, my lord, I have a daughter
    that I love passing well. 395
HAMLET: Nay, that follows not.
POLONIUS: What follows then, my lord?
HAMLET: Why—
    "As by lot, God wot"
    and then, you know, 400
    "It came to pass, as most like it was."
    The first row of the pious chanson[7] will show you more,
    for look where my abridgement comes.

       [*Enter* the PLAYERS.]

    You are welcome, masters; welcome, all—I am glad to see
    thee well.—Welcome, good friends.—O, old friend! Why 405
    thy face is valanced[8] since I saw thee last. Com'st thou to
    beard[9] me in Denmark?—What, my young lady and mis-
    tress? By'r lady, your ladyship is nearer to heaven than when
    I saw you last by the altitude of a chopine.[1] Pray God your
    voice, like a piece of uncurrent gold, be not cracked within 410
    the ring.[2]—Masters, you are all welcome. We'll e'en to't
    like French falconers, fly at any-thing we see. We'll have a
    speech straight. Come give us a taste of your quality,[3] come
    a passionate speech.
FIRST PLAYER: What speech, my good lord? 415
HAMLET: I heard thee speak me a speech once, but it was never
    acted, or if it was, not above once, for the play, I remem-
    ber, pleased not the million; 'twas caviary to the general.[4]
    But it was—as I received it, and others whose judgments in
    such matters cried in the top of mine—an excellent play, 420
    well digested[5] in the scenes, set down with as much mod-
    esty as cunning. I remember one said there were no sallets[6]
    in the lines to make the matter savory, nor no matter in

---

7. Song. *Row:* stanza.
8. Fringed (with a beard).
9. Defy.
1. The height of a woman's thick-soled shoe.
2. A reference to the Elizabethan theatrical practice of using boys to play women's roles; Hamlet
hopes that this boy has not matured to the point at
which his voice might change.
3. Trade.
4. Caviar to the masses.
5. Arranged. *Cried in the top of:* were weightier
than.
6. Spicy passages.

the phrase that might indict the author of affectation, but
called it an honest method, as wholesome as sweet, and by   425
very much more handsome than fine. One speech in't I
chiefly loved. 'Twas Æneas' tale to Dido, and thereabout of
it especially where he speaks of Priam's slaughter.[7] If it live
in your memory, begin at this line—let me see, let me see:
   "The rugged Pyrrhus, like th' Hyrcanian beast"[8]—   430
'tis not so; it begins with Pyrrhus—
   "The rugged Pyrrhus, he whose sable arms,
Black as his purpose, did the night resemble
When he lay couchéd in th' ominous horse,[9]
Hath now this dread and black complexion smeared   435
With heraldry more dismal; head to foot
Now is he total gules, horridly tricked[1]
With blood of fathers, mothers, daughters, sons,
Baked and impasted with the parching[2] streets,
That lend a tyrannous and a damnéd light   440
To their lord's murder. Roasted in wrath and fire,
And thus o'er-sizéd with coagulate[3] gore,
With eyes like carbuncles, the hellish Pyrrhus
Old grandsire Priam seeks."
So proceed you.   445

POLONIUS: Fore God, my lord, well spoken, with good
   accent and good discretion.

FIRST player: "Anon he finds him[4]
Striking too short at Greeks. His antique[5] sword,
Rebellious[6] to his arm, lies where it falls,   450
Repugnant to command. Unequal matched,
Pyrrhus at Priam drives, in rage strikes wide.
But with the whiff and wind of his fell sword
Th' unnervéd father falls. Then senseless[7] Ilium,

---

7. In Virgil's *Aeneid*, Aeneas tells Dido, the queen of Carthage, about the fall of Troy. Here he describes Pyrrhus's killing of Priam, the aged king of Troy, also known (like his city) as Ilium.
8. Tiger.
9. I.e., the Trojan horse.
1. Adorned. *Total gules:* completely red.

2. Burning. *Impasted:* crusted.
3. Clotted. *O'er-sizéd:* glued over.
4. I.e., Pyrrhus finds Priam.
5. Which he used when young.
6. Unmanageable.
7. Without feeling.

Seeming to feel this blow, with flaming top   455
Stoops[8] to his base, and with a hideous crash
Takes prisoner Pyrrhus' ear. For, lo! his sword,
Which was declining[9] on the milky head
Of reverend Priam, seemed i' th' air to stick.
So as a painted tyrant Pyrrhus stood,   460
And like a neutral to his will and matter,[1]
Did nothing.
But as we often see, against some storm,
A silence in the heavens, the rack[2] stand still,
The bold winds speechless, and the orb below   465
As hush as death, anon the dreadful thunder
Doth rend the region; so, after Pyrrhus' pause,
A rouséd vengeance sets him new awork,[3]
And never did the Cyclops' hammers fall
On Mars's armor, forged for proof eterne,[4]   470
With less remorse than Pyrrhus' bleeding sword
Now falls on Priam.
Out, out, thou strumpet, Fortune! All you gods,
In general synod take away her power,
Break all the spokes and fellies[5] from her wheel,   475
And bowl the round nave[6] down the hill of heaven
As low as to the fiends."

POLONIUS: This is too long.

HAMLET: It shall to the barber's with your beard.—Prithee
say on. He's for a jig,[7] or a tale of bawdry, or he sleeps.   480
Say on; come to Hecuba.[8]

FIRST PLAYER: "But who, ah woe! had seen the mobléd[9]
queen—"

---

8. Falls.
9. About to fall.
1. Between his will and the fulfillment of it.
2. Clouds.
3. To work.
4. Mars, the Roman war god, had impenetrable armor made for him by the blacksmith god, Vulcan, and his assistants, the Cyclopes.

5. Parts of the rim.
6. Roll the round hub.
7. A comic act.
8. Wife of Priam and queen of Troy. Her "loins" are described below as "o'erteemed" because of her celebrated fertility.
9. Muffled (in a hood).

HAMLET: "The mobléd queen"?

POLONIUS: That's good. "Mobléd queen" is good.

FIRST PLAYER: "Run barefoot up and down, threat'ning the
    flames   485
  With bisson rheum, a clout[1] upon that head
  Where late the diadem stood, and for a robe,
  About her lank and all o'er-teeméd loins
  A blanket, in the alarm of fear caught up—
  Who this had seen, with tongue in venom steeped,   490
  'Gainst Fortune's state[2] would treason have pronounced.
  But if the gods themselves did see her then,
  When she saw Pyrrhus make malicious sport
  In mincing[3] with his sword her husband's limbs,
  The instant burst of clamor that she made,   495
  Unless things mortal move them not at all,
  Would have made milch[4] the burning eyes of heaven,
  And passion in the gods."

POLONIUS: Look whe'r[5] he has not turned his color, and has
  tears in's eyes. Prithee no more.   500

HAMLET: 'Tis well. I'll have thee speak out the rest of this
  soon.—Good my lord, will you see the players well
  bestowed?[6] Do you hear, let them be well used, for they
  are the abstract[7] and brief chronicles of the time; after your
  death you were better have a bad epitaph than their ill   505
  report while you live.

POLONIUS: My lord, I will use them according to their desert.

HAMLET: God's bodkin,[8] man, much better. Use every man
  after his desert, and who shall 'scape whipping? Use them
  after your own honor and dignity. The less they deserve,   510
  the more merit is in your bounty. Take them in.

POLONIUS: Come, sirs.

HAMLET: Follow him, friends. We'll hear a play tomorrow.
  [*Aside to* FIRST PLAYER.] Dost thou hear me, old friend, can
  you play "The Murder of Gonzago"?   515

---

1. With blinding tears, a cloth.
2. Government.
3. Cutting up.
4. Tearful (literally, milk-giving).

5. Whether.
6. Provided for.
7. Summary.
8. Dear body.

FIRST PLAYER: Ay, my lord.   520

HAMLET: We'll ha't tomorrow night. You could for a need
   study a speech of some dozen or sixteen lines which I
   would set down and insert in't, could you not?

FIRST PLAYER: Ay, my lord.

HAMLET: Very well. Follow that lord, and look you mock him
   not.   [*Exeunt* POLONIUS *and* PLAYERS.]
   My good friends, I'll leave you till night. You are welcome
   to Elsinore.

ROSENCRANTZ: Good my lord.   525

                    [*Exeunt* ROSENCRANTZ *and* GUILDENSTERN.]

HAMLET: Ay, so God b'wi'ye. Now I am alone.
   O, what a rogue and peasant slave am I!
   Is it not monstrous that this player here,
   But in a fiction, in a dream of passion,
   Could force his soul so to his own conceit⁹   530
   That from her working all his visage wanned;¹
   Tears in his eyes, distraction in his aspect²
   A broken voice, and his whole function suiting
   With forms to his conceit? And all for nothing,
   For Hecuba!   535
   What's Hecuba to him or he to Hecuba,
   That he should weep for her? What would he do
   Had he the motive and the cue for passion
   That I have? He would drown the stage with tears,
   And cleave the general ear with horrid speech,   540
   Make mad the guilty, and appal the free,
   Confound the ignorant, and amaze indeed
   The very faculties of eyes and ears.
   Yet I,
   A dull and muddy-mettled rascal, peak³   545
   Like John-a-dreams, unpregnant of ⁴ my cause,
   And can say nothing; no, not for a king
   Upon whose property and most dear life

9. Imagination.   3. Mope. *Muddy-mettled:* dull-spirited.
1. Grew pale.   4. Unenlivened by. *John-a-dreams:* a loafer.
2. Face.

A damned defeat was made. Am I a coward?
Who calls me villain, breaks my pate across,   550
Plucks off my beard and blows it in my face,
Tweaks me by the nose, gives me the lie i' th' throat
As deep as to the lungs? Who does me this?
Ha, 'swounds,[5] I should take it; for it cannot be
But I am pigeon-livered and lack gall[6]   555
To make oppression bitter, or ere this
I should 'a fatted all the region kites[7]
With this slave's offal. Bloody, bawdy villain!
Remorseless, treacherous, lecherous, kindless[8] villain!
O, vengeance!   560
Why, what an ass am I! This is most brave,
That I, the son of a dear father murdered,
Prompted to my revenge by heaven and hell,
Must like a whore unpack[9] my heart with words,
And fall a-cursing like a very drab,   565
A scullion! Fie upon't! foh!
About, my brains. Hum—I have heard
That guilty creatures sitting at a play,
Have by the very cunning of the scene
Been struck so to the soul that presently   570
They have proclaimed[1] their malefactions;
For murder, though it have no tongue, will speak
With most miraculous organ. I'll have these players
Play something like the murder of my father
Before mine uncle. I'll observe his looks.   575
I'll tent him to the quick. If 'a do blench,[2]
I know my course. The spirit that I have seen
May be a devil, and the devil hath power
T' assume a pleasing shape, yea, and perhaps
Out of my weakness and my melancholy,   580
As he is very potent with such spirits,
Abuses me to damn me. I'll have grounds

5. By God's wounds.
6. Bitterness.
7. Vultures of the area.
8. Unnatural.
9. Relieve.
1. Admitted.
2. Turn pale. *Tent:* try.

More relative[3] than this. The play's the thing
Wherein I'll catch the conscience of the king.   [*Exit.*]

ACT III
SCENE 1

A room in the castle. Enter KING, QUEEN, POLONIUS, OPHELIA,
ROSENCRANTZ *and* GUILDENSTERN.

KING: And can you by no drift of conference[4]
　　Get from him why he puts on this confusion,
　　Grating so harshly all his days of quiet
　　With turbulent and dangerous lunacy?
ROSENCRANTZ: He does confess he feels himself distracted,　5
　　But from what cause 'a will by no means speak.
GUILDENSTERN: Nor do we find him forward to be sounded,[5]
　　But with a crafty madness keeps aloof
　　When we would bring him on to some confession
　　Of his true state.
QUEEN:　　　　　　Did he receive you well?　10
ROSENCRANTZ: Most like a gentleman.
GUILDENSTERN: But with much forcing of his disposition.[6]
ROSENCRANTZ: Niggard of question, but of our demands[7]
　　Most free in his reply.
QUEEN:　　　　　　Did you assay[8] him
　　To any pastime?　15
ROSENCRANTZ: Madam, it so fell out that certain players
　　We o'er-raught[9] on the way. Of these we told him,
　　And there did seem in him a kind of joy
　　To hear of it. They are here about the court,
　　And as I think, they have already order　20
　　This night to play before him.
POLONIUS:　　　　　　　　'Tis most true,
　　And he beseeched me to entreat your majesties
　　To hear and see the matter.[1]

3. Conclusive.
4. Line of conversation.
5. Eager to be questioned.
6. Mood.

7. To our questions.
8. Tempt.
9. Passed.
1. Performance.

KING: With all my heart, and it doth much content me
    To hear him so inclined.   25
    Good gentlemen, give him a further edge,[2]
    And drive his purpose into these delights.
ROSENCRANTZ: We shall, my lord.
                  [*Exeunt* ROSENCRANTZ *and* GUILDENSTERN.]
KING: Sweet Gertrude, leave us too,
    For we have closely sent for Hamlet hither,
    That he, as 'twere by accident, may here   30
    Affront[3] Ophelia.
    Her father and myself (lawful espials[4])
    Will so bestow ourselves that, seeing unseen,
    We may of their encounter frankly judge,
    And gather by him, as he is behaved,   35
    If 't be th' affliction of his love or no
    That thus he suffers for.
QUEEN: I shall obey you.—
    And for your part, Ophelia, I do wish
    That your good beauties be the happy cause
    Of Hamlet's wildness. So shall I hope your virtues   40
    Will bring him to his wonted[5] way again,
    To both your honors.
OPHELIA: Madam, I wish it may.
                          [*Exit* QUEEN.]
POLONIUS: Ophelia, walk you here—Gracious,[6] so please you,
    We will bestow ourselves.—[*To* OPHELIA.] Read on this
    book,[7]
    That show of such an exercise may color[8]   45
    Your loneliness.—We are oft to blame in this,
    'Tis too much proved, that with devotion's visage
    And pious action we do sugar o'er
    The devil himself.
KING: [*Aside.*]   O, 'tis too true.

---

2. Sharpen his intention.
3. Confront.
4. Justified spies.
5. Usual.

6. Majesty.
7. Prayer book or devotional text.
8. Act of devotion may explain.

How smart a lash that speech doth give my conscience!   50
The harlot's cheek, beautied with plast'ring⁹ art,
Is not more ugly to the thing that helps it
Than is my deed to my most painted word.
O heavy burden!
POLONIUS: I hear him coming. Let's withdraw, my lord.   55

[*Exeunt* KING *and* POLONIUS.]
[*Enter* HAMLET.]

HAMLET: To be, or not to be, that is the question:
Whether 'tis nobler in the mind to suffer
The slings and arrows of outrageous fortune,
Or to take arms against a sea of troubles,
And by opposing end them. To die, to sleep—   60
No more; and by a sleep to say we end
The heartache, and the thousand natural shocks
That flesh is heir to. 'Tis a consummation
Devoutly to be wished—to die, to sleep—
To sleep, perchance to dream, ay there's the rub;   65
For in that sleep of death what dreams may come
When we have shuffled off this mortal coil¹
Must give us pause—there's the respect²
That makes calamity of so long life.
For who would bear the whips and scorns of time,   70
Th' oppressor's wrong, the proud man's contumely,³
The pangs of despised love, the law's delay,
The insolence of office, and the spurns⁴
That patient merit of th' unworthy takes,
When he himself might his quietus⁵ make   75
With a bare bodkin? Who would fardels⁶ bear,
To grunt and sweat under a weary life,
But that the dread of something after death,
The undiscovered country, from whose bourn⁷
No traveller returns, puzzles the will,   80

---

9. Thickly painted.
1. Turmoil.
2. Consideration.
3. Insulting behavior.

4. Rejections.
5. Settlement, as in the paying off of a debt.
6. Burdens. *Bare bodkin:* an unsheathed dagger.
7. Boundary.

And makes us rather bear those ills we have
Than fly to others that we know not of ?
Thus conscience does make cowards of us all;
And thus the native[8] hue of resolution
Is sicklied o'er with the pale cast of thought,   85
And enterprises of great pitch and moment[9]
With this regard their currents turn awry
And lose the name of action.—Soft you now,
The fair Ophelia.—Nymph, in thy orisons[1]
Be all my sins remembered.

OPHELIA: Good my lord,   90
  How does your honor for this many a day?
HAMLET: I humbly thank you, well, well, well.
OPHELIA: My lord, I have remembrances of yours
  That I have longéd long to re-deliver.
  I pray you now receive them.
HAMLET: No, not I,   95
  I never gave you aught.
OPHELIA: My honored lord, you know right well you did,
  And with them words of so sweet breath composed
  As made the things more rich. Their perfume lost,
  Take these again, for to the noble mind   100
  Rich gifts wax[2] poor when givers prove unkind.
  There, my lord.
HAMLET: Ha, ha! are you honest?[3]
OPHELIA: My lord?
HAMLET: Are you fair?   105
OPHELIA: What means your lordship?
HAMLET: That if you be honest and fair, your honesty
  should admit no discourse to your beauty.
OPHELIA: Could beauty, my lord, have better commerce[4] than
  with honesty?   110
HAMLET: Ay, truly, for the power of beauty will sooner trans-
  form honesty from what it is to a bawd than the force of

---

8. Natural.   2. Become.
9. Great height and importance.   3. Chaste.
1. Prayers.   4. Dealings.

honesty can translate beauty into his likeness. This was
sometimes a paradox, but now the time gives it proof. I did
love you once. 115

OPHELIA: Indeed, my lord, you made me believe so.

HAMLET: You should not have believed me, for virtue cannot
so inoculate[5] our old stock but we shall relish of it. I loved
you not.

OPHELIA: I was the more deceived. 120

HAMLET: Get thee to a nunnery.[6] Why wouldst thou be a
breeder of sinners? I am myself indifferent honest, but yet
I could accuse me of such things that it were better my
mother had not borne me: I am very proud, revengeful,
ambitious, with more offences at my beck[7] than I have 125
thoughts to put them in, imagination to give them shape,
or time to act them in. What should such fellows as I do
crawling between earth and heaven? We are arrant[8] knaves
all; believe none of us. Go thy ways to a nunnery. Where's
your father? 130

OPHELIA: At home, my lord.

HAMLET: Let the doors be shut upon him, that he may play
the fool nowhere but in's own house. Farewell.

OPHELIA: O, help him, you sweet heavens!

HAMLET: If thou dost marry, I'll give thee this plague for thy 135
dowry: be thou as chaste as ice, as pure as snow, thou shalt
not escape calumny. Get thee to a nunnery, farewell. Or
if thou wilt needs marry, marry a fool, for wise men know
well enough what monsters[9] you make of them. To a nunnery, go, and quickly too. Farewell. 140

OPHELIA: Heavenly powers, restore him!

HAMLET: I have heard of your paintings, too, well enough. God
hath given you one face, and you make yourselves another.
You jig, you amble, and you lisp; you nickname God's
creatures, and make your wantonness your ignorance.[1] 145

5. Change by grafting.

6. Both a convent of nuns and, in Elizabethan slang, a brothel.

7. Command. *Indifferent*: moderately.

8. Thorough.

9. Horned because cuckolded.

1. Call things by pet names and then blame the affectation on ignorance. *Jig . . . lips*: walk and talk affectedly.

Go to, I'll no more on't, it hath made me mad. I say we
will have no more marriage. Those that are married already,
all but one, shall live. The rest shall keep as they are.
To a nunnery, go.   [*Exit.*]

OPHELIA: O, what a noble mind is here o'erthrown!   150
  The courtier's, soldier's, scholar's, eye, tongue, sword,
  Th' expectancy and rose[2] of the fair state,
  The glass of fashion and the mould[3] of form,
  Th' observed of all observers, quite quite down!
  And I of ladies most deject and wretched,   155
  That sucked the honey of his music[4] vows,
  Now see that noble and most sovereign reason
  Like sweet bells jangled, out of time and harsh;
  That unmatched form and feature of blown[5] youth
  Blasted with ecstasy. O, woe is me   160
  T' have seen what I have seen, see what I see!
      [*Enter* KING *and* POLONIUS.]
KING: Love! His affections do not that way tend,
  Nor what he spake, though it lacked form a little,
  Was not like madness. There's something in his soul
  O'er which his melancholy sits on brood,[6]   165
  And I do doubt the hatch and the disclose[7]
  Will be some danger; which to prevent,
  I have in quick determination
  Thus set it down: he shall with speed to England
  For the demand of our neglected tribute.   170
  Haply the seas and countries different,
  With variable objects, shall expel
  This something-settled matter in his heart
  Whereon his brains still beating puts him thus
  From fashion of himself. What think you on't?   175
POLONIUS: It shall do well. But yet do I believe
  The origin and commencement of his grief
  Sprung from neglected love.—How now, Ophelia?
  You need not tell us what Lord Hamlet said,

---

2. The hope and ornament.
3. Model. *Glass:* mirror.
4. Musical.

5. Full-blown.
6. I.e., like a hen.
7. Result. *Doubt:* fear.

We heard it all.—My lord, do as you please,   180
But if you hold it fit, after the play
Let his queen-mother all alone entreat him
To show his grief. Let her be round⁸ with him,
And I'll be placed, so please you, in the ear⁹
Of all their conference. If she find him not,¹   185
To England send him; or confine him where
Your wisdom best shall think.

KING: It shall be so.
Madness in great ones must not unwatched go.

                                         [*Exeunt.*]

SCENE 2

A public room in the castle. Enter HAMLET *and three of the*
PLAYERS.

HAMLET: Speak the speech, I pray you, as I pronounced it to
  you, trippingly on the tongue; but if you mouth it as many
  of our players do, I had as lief the town-crier spoke my
  lines. Nor do not saw the air too much with your hand
  thus, but use all gently, for in the very torrent, tempest, and   305
  as I may say, whirlwind of your passion, you must acquire
  and beget a temperance that may give it smoothness. O, it
  offends me to the soul to hear a robustious periwig-pated²
  fellow tear a passion to tatters, to very rags, to split the ears
  of the groundlings, who for the most part are capable of³   310
  nothing but inexplicable dumb shows and noise. I would
  have such a fellow whipped for o'erdoing Termagant. It
  out-herods Herod.⁴ Pray you avoid it.

FIRST PLAYER: I warrant your honor.

HAMLET: Be not too tame neither, but let your own discretion   315
  be your tutor. Suit the action to the word, the word to the
  action, with this special observance, that you o'erstep not

---

8. Direct.
9. Hearing.
1. Does not discover the cause of his behavior.
2. A noisy bewigged.
3. I.e., capable of understanding. *Groundlings:*

the spectators in the cheapest area.
  4. Termagant, an imaginary deity, and the biblical Herod were violent and loud stock characters
in popular drama.

the modesty of nature; for anything so o'erdone is from
the purpose of playing, whose end both at the first, and
now, was and is, to hold as 'twere the mirror up to nature,   320
to show virtue her own feature, scorn her own image,
and the very age and body of the time his form and pressure.[5] Now this overdone, or come tardy off, though it
makes the unskilful laugh, cannot but make the judi-
cious grieve, the censure[6] of the which one must in your   325
allowance o'erweigh a whole theatre of others. O, there
be players that I have seen play—and heard others praise,
and that highly—not to speak it profanely, that neither
having th' accent of Christians, nor the gait of Christian,
pagan, nor man, have so strutted and bellowed that I   330
have thought some of nature's journeymen[7] had made
men, and not made them well, they imitated humanity so
abominably.

FIRST PLAYER: I hope we have reformed that indifferently[8] with
us, sir.   335

HAMLET: O, reform it altogether. And let those that play
your clowns speak no more than is set down for them, for
there be of them that will themselves laugh, to set on some
quantity of barren[9] spectators to laugh too, though in the
meantime some necessary question of the play be then to   340
be considered. That's villainous, and shows a most pitiful
ambition in the fool that uses it. Go, make you ready.

[*Exeunt* PLAYERS.]

[*Enter* POLONIUS, GUILDENSTERN, *and* ROSENCRANTZ.]

How now my lord? Will the king hear this piece of work?

POLONIUS: And the queen too, and that presently.   345

HAMLET: Bid the players make haste.   [*Exit* POLONIUS.]

Will you two help to hasten them?

ROSENCRANTZ: Ay, my lord.   [*Exeunt they two.*]

HAMLET: What, ho, Horatio!

[*Enter* HORATIO.]

---

5. His shape and likeness. *From*: contrary to.   8. Somewhat.
6. Judgment. *Unskilful*: ignorant.   9. Dull-witted.
7. Inferior craftsmen.

HORATIO: Here, sweet lord, at your service.   350
HAMLET: Horatio, thou art e'en as just a man
  As e'er my conversation coped[1] withal.
HORATIO: O my dear lord!
HAMLET: Nay, do not think I flatter,
  For what advancement may I hope from thee,
  That no revenue hast but thy good spirits   355
  To feed and clothe thee? Why should the poor be flattered?
  No, let the candied tongue lick absurd pomp,
  And crook the pregnant[2] hinges of the knee
  Where thrift[3] may follow fawning. Dost thou hear?
  Since my dear soul was mistress of her choice   360
  And could of men distinguish her election,
  S'hath sealed thee for herself, for thou hast been
  As one in suff'ring all that suffers nothing,
  A man that Fortune's buffets and rewards
  Hast ta'en with equal thanks; and blest are those   365
  Whose blood and judgment are so well commingled
  That they are not a pipe[4] for Fortune's finger
  To sound what stop[5] she please. Give me that man
  That is not passion's slave, and I will wear him
  In my heart's core, ay, in my heart of heart,   370
  As I do thee. Something too much of this.
  There is a play tonight before the king.
  One scene of it comes near the circumstance
  Which I have told thee of my father's death.
  I prithee, when thou seest that act afoot,   375
  Even with the very comment[6] of thy soul
  Observe my uncle. If his occulted[7] guilt
  Do not itself unkennel[8] in one speech,
  It is a damnéd ghost that we have seen,
  And my imaginations are as foul   380
  As Vulcan's stithy. Give him heedful note,[9]

1. Encountered.
2. Quick to bend.
3. Profit.
4. Musical instrument.
5. To play what note.

6. Keenest observation.
7. Hidden.
8. Break loose.
9. Careful attention. *Stithy:* smithy, forge.

For I mine eyes will rivet to his face,
And after we will both our judgments join
In censure of his seeming.[1]

HORATIO: Well, my lord.
If 'a[2] steal aught the whilst this play in playing,   385
And 'scape detecting, I will pay[3] the theft.

[*Enter Trumpets and Kettledrums,* KING, QUEEN, POLONIUS,
OPHELIA, ROSENCRANTZ, GUILDENSTERN, *and other*
LORDS *attendant.*]

HAMLET: They are coming to the play. I must be idle.
Get you a place.

KING: How fares our cousin Hamlet?

HAMLET: Excellent, i' faith, of the chameleon's dish.[4] I eat the   390
air, promise-crammed. You cannot feed capons so.

KING: I have nothing with this answer, Hamlet. These words
are not mine.

HAMLET: No, nor mine now. [*To* POLONIUS.] My lord, you
played once i' th' university, you say?   395

POLONIUS: That did I, my lord, and was accounted a good
actor.

HAMLET: What did you enact?

POLONIUS: I did enact Julius Cæsar. I was killed i' th' Capitol;
Brutus killed me.[5]   400

HAMLET: It was a brute part of him to kill so capital a calf
there. Be the players ready?

ROSENCRANTZ: Ay, my lord, they stay upon your patience.[6]

QUEEN: Come hither, my dear Hamlet, sit by me.

HAMLET: No, good mother, here's metal more attractive.   405

POLONIUS: [*To the* KING.] O, ho! do you mark that?

HAMLET: Lady, shall I lie in your lap? [*Lying down at* OPHELIA'*s
feet.*]

OPHELIA: No, my lord.

HAMLET: I mean, my head upon your lap?

---

1. Manner.
2. He.
3. Repay.
4. Chameleons were popularly believed to eat
nothing but air.

5. Perhaps an allusion to Shakespeare's *Julius
Caesar,* which dramatizes the assassination of Julius
Caesar by Brutus and others.
6. Leisure. *Stay:* wait.

OPHELIA: Ay, my lord.   410

HAMLET: Do you think I meant country matters?[7]

OPHELIA: I think nothing, my lord.

HAMLET: That's a fair thought to lie between maids' legs.

OPHELIA: What is, my lord?

HAMLET: Nothing.   415

OPHELIA: You are merry, my lord.

HAMLET: Who, I?

OPHELIA: Ay, my lord.

HAMLET: O God, your only jig-maker![8] What should a man
   do but be merry? For look you how cheerfully my mother   420
   looks, and my father died within's two hours.

OPHELIA: Nay, 'tis twice two months, my lord.

HAMLET: So long? Nay then, let the devil wear black, for I'll
   have a suit of sables.[9] O heavens! die two months ago, and
   not forgotten yet? Then there's hope a great man's mem-   425
   ory may outlive his life half a year, but by'r lady 'a must
   build churches then, or else shall 'a suffer not thinking on,
   with the hobby-horse, whose epitaph is "For O, for O, the
   hobby-horse is forgot!"[1]

   [*The trumpets sound. Dumb Show follows. Enter a* KING
   and a QUEEN *very lovingly; the* QUEEN *embracing him and
   he her. She kneels, and makes show of protestation unto
   him. He takes her up, and declines[2] his head upon her neck.
   He lies him down upon a bank of flowers; she, seeing him
   asleep, leaves him. Anon come in another man, takes off his
   crown, kisses it, pours poison in the sleeper's ears, and leaves
   him. The* QUEEN *returns, finds the* KING *dead, makes passionate action. The* POISONER *with some three or four come
   in again, seem to condole with her. The dead body is carried
   away. The* POISONER *woos the* QUEEN *with gifts; she seems
   harsh awhile, but in the end accepts love.*]

                                                              [*Exeunt.*]

---

7. Here and elsewhere in this exchange Hamlet
intends some ribald double meanings.

8. Writer of comic scenes.

9. Fur; also, black.

1. An Elizabethan ballad refrain. In traditional
games and dances one of the characters was a man
represented as riding a horse.

2. Lays.

OPHELIA: What means this, my lord?   430

HAMLET: Marry, this is miching mallecho;³ it means mischief.

OPHELIA: Belike this show imports the argument⁴ of the play.

    [*Enter* PROLOGUE.]

HAMLET: We shall know by this fellow. The players cannot
    keep counsel; they'll tell all.

OPHELIA: Will 'a tell us what this show meant?   435

HAMLET: Ay, or any show that you will show him. Be not
    you ashamed to show, he'll not shame to tell you what it
    means.

OPHELIA: You are naught, you are naught. I'll mark⁵ the play.

PROLOGUE: *For us, and for our tragedy,*   440
    Here stooping to your clemency,
    We beg your hearing patiently.   [*Exit.*]

HAMLET: Is this a prologue, or the posy⁶ of a ring?

OPHELIA: 'Tis brief, my lord.

HAMLET: As woman's love.   445

    [*Enter the* PLAYER KING *and* QUEEN.]

PLAYER KING: *Full thirty times hath Phoebus' cart gone round*
    Neptune's salt wash and Tellus' orbéd ground,
    And thirty dozen moons with borrowed sheen⁷
    About the world have times twelve thirties been,
    Since love our hearts and Hymen⁸ did our hands   450
    Unite comutual⁹ in most sacred bands.

PLAYER QUEEN: *So many journeys may the sun and moon*
    Make us again count o'er ere love be done!
    But woe is me, you are so sick of late,
    So far from cheer and from your former state,   455
    That I distrust¹ you. Yet though I distrust,
    Discomfort you, my lord, it nothing must.
    For women's fear and love hold quantity,²

---

3. Sneaking crime.
4. Explains the plot.
5. Attend to. *Naught:* obscene.
6. Motto engraved inside.
7. Light.
8. The speech contains several references to Greek and Roman mythology. Phoebus was the

sun god; his chariot, or "cart," is the sun. Neptune was the sea god; his "salt wash" is the ocean. Tellus was an earth goddess; her "orbed ground" is Earth, or the globe. Hymen was the god of marriage.
9. Mutually.
1. Fear for.
2. Agree in weight.

In neither aught, or in extremity.[3]
Now what my love is proof hath made you know,   460
And as my love is sized,[4] *my fear is so.*
Where love is great, the littlest doubts are fear;
Where little fears grow great, great love grows there.

PLAYER KING: *Faith, I must leave thee, love, and shortly too;*
  My operant powers their functions leave[5] *to do.*   465
  And thou shalt live in this fair world behind,
  Honored, beloved, and haply one as kind
  For husband shalt thou—

PLAYER QUEEN: *O, confound the rest!*
  Such love must needs be treason in my breast.
  In second husband let me be accurst!   470
  None wed the second but who killed the first.

HAMLET: That's wormwood.

PLAYER QUEEN: *The instances*[6] *that second marriage move*
  Are base respects[7] *of thrift, but none of love.*
  A second time I kill my husband dead,   475
  When second husband kisses me in bed.

PLAYER KING: *I do believe you think what now you speak,*
  But what we do determine oft we break.
  Purpose is but the slave to memory,
  Of violent birth, but poor validity;   480
  Which now, like fruit unripe, sticks on the tree,
  But fall unshaken when they mellow be.
  Most necessary 'tis that we forget
  To pay ourselves what to ourselves is debt.
  What to ourselves in passion we propose,   485
  The passion ending, doth the purpose lose.
  The violence of either grief or joy
  Their own enactures[8] *with themselves destroy.*
  Where joy most revels, grief doth most lament;
  Grief joys, joy grieves, on slender accident.   490
  This world is not for aye,[9] *nor 'tis not strange*

3. Without regard to too much or too little.
4. In size.
5. Cease. *Operant powers:* active forces.
6. Causes.

7. Concerns.
8. Actions.
9. Eternal.

That even our loves should with our fortunes change;
For 'tis a question left us yet to prove,
Whether love lead fortune, or else fortune love.
The great man down, you mark his favorite flies; 495
The poor advanced makes friends of enemies;
And hitherto doth love on fortune tend,
For who not needs shall never lack a friend,
And who in want a hollow¹ friend doth try,
Directly seasons him² his enemy. 500
But orderly to end where I begun,
Our wills and fates do so contrary run
That our devices³ still are overthrown;
Our thoughts are ours, their ends none of our own.
So think thou wilt no second husband wed, 505
But die thy thoughts when thy first lord is dead.

PLAYER QUEEN: *Nor earth to me give food, nor heaven light,*
Sport and repose lock from me day and night,
To desperation turn my trust and hope,
An anchor's cheer⁴ in prison be my scope, 510
Each opposite that blanks⁵ the face of joy
Meet what I would have well, and it destroy,
Both here and hence⁶ pursue me lasting strife,
If once a widow, ever I be wife! 515

HAMLET: If she should break it now!

PLAYER KING: *'Tis deeply sworn. Sweet, leave me here awhile.*
My spirits grow dull, and fain I would beguile
The tedious day with sleep. [Sleeps.]

PLAYER QUEEN: *Sleep rock thy brain,*
And never come mischance between us twain! [Exit.]

HAMLET: Madam, how like you this play? 520

QUEEN: The lady doth protest too much, methinks.

HAMLET: O, but she'll keep her word.

KING: Have you heard the argument? Is there no offence in't?

HAMLET: No, no, they do but jest, poison in jest; no offence 525
i' th' world.

---

1. False.
2. Ripens him into.
3. Plans.

4. Anchorite's food.
5. Blanches.
6. In the next world.

KING: What do you call the play?

HAMLET: "The Mouse-trap." Marry, how? Tropically.[7] This
play is the image of a murder done in Vienna. Gonzago is
the duke's name; his wife, Baptista. You shall see anon. 'Tis
a knavish piece of work, but what of that? Your majesty,   530
and we that have free souls, it touches us not. Let the galled
jade wince, our withers are unwrung.[8]

   [*Enter* LUCIANUS.]

This is one Lucianus, nephew to the king.

OPHELIA: You are as good as a chorus, my lord.

HAMLET: I could interpret between you and your love, if   535
I could see the puppets dallying.

OPHELIA: You are keen, my lord, you are keen.

HAMLET: It would cost you a groaning to take off mine edge.

OPHELIA: Still better, and worse.

HAMLET: So you mistake your husbands.—Begin, murderer.   540
Leave thy damnable faces and begin. Come, the croaking
raven doth bellow for revenge.

LUCIANUS: *Thoughts black, hands apt, drugs fit, and time agreeing,*
Confederate season,[9] else no creature seeing,
Thou mixture rank, of midnight weeds collected,   545
With Hecate's[1] ban thrice blasted, thrice infected,
Thy natural magic[2] and dire property
On wholesome life usurp immediately.

        [*Pours the poison in his ears.*]

HAMLET: 'A poisons him i' th' garden for his estate. His name's
Gonzago. The story is extant, and written in very choice   550
Italian. You shall see anon how the murderer gets the love
of Gonzago's wife.

OPHELIA: The king rises.

HAMLET: What, frighted with false fire?

QUEEN: How fares my lord?   555

POLONIUS: Give o'er the play.

KING: Give me some light. Away!

---

7. Figuratively.

8. Let the horse with the sore back wince. Our
shoulders are not chafed by the harness.

9. Helpful time for the crime.

1. Classical goddess of witchcraft.

2. Native power.

POLONIUS: Lights, lights, lights!

[*Exeunt all but* HAMLET *and* HORATIO.]

HAMLET: Why; let the strucken deer go weep,

The hart ungalléd[3] play.   560

For some must watch while some must sleep;

Thus runs the world away.

Would not this, sir, and a forest of feathers—if the rest

of my fortunes turn Turk with me[4]—with two Provincial

roses on my razed shoes, get me a fellowship in a cry of   565

players?

HORATIO: Half a share.

HAMLET: A whole one, I.

For thou dost know, O Damon dear,[5]

This realm dismantled was   570

Of Jove[6] himself, and now reigns here

A very, very—peacock.

HORATIO: You might have rhymed.[7]

HAMLET: O good Horatio, I'll take the ghost's word for a

thousand pound. Didst perceive?   575

HORATIO: Very well, my lord.

HAMLET: Upon the talk of the poisoning.

HORATIO: I did very well note him.

HAMLET: Ah, ha! Come, some music. Come, the recorders.

For if the king like not the comedy.   580

Why then, belike he likes it not, perdy.[8]

Come, some music.

[*Enter* ROSENCRANTZ *and* GUILDENSTERN.]

GUILDENSTERN: Good my lord, vouchsafe me a word with

you.

HAMLET: Sir, a whole history.   585

GUILDENSTERN: The king, sir—

HAMLET: Ay, sir, what of him?

GUILDENSTERN: Is in his retirement marvellous distempered.

HAMLET: With drink, sir?

---

3. Uninjured.

4. Turn against. *Feathers*: plumes.

5. A common name in ancient lyric poetry. Also, a legendary friend.

6. Chief Roman god.

7. "Ass," for example, would have completed the rhyme.

8. *Par Dieu* (by God).

GUILDENSTERN: No, my lord, with choler.[9]   590

HAMLET: Your wisdom should show itself more richer
to signify this to the doctor, for for me to put him to
his purgation[1] would perhaps plunge him into more
choler.

GUILDENSTERN: Good my lord, put your discourse into some   595
frame,[2] and start not so wildly from my affair.

HAMLET: I am tame, sir. Pronounce.

GUILDENSTERN: The queen your mother, in most great
affliction of spirit, hath sent me to you.

HAMLET: You are welcome.   600

GUILDENSTERN: Nay, good my lord, this courtesy is not of the
right breed. If it shall please you to make me a wholesome[3]
answer, I will do your mother's commandment. If not, your
pardon and my return[4] shall be the end of my business.

HAMLET: Sir, I cannot.   605

ROSENCRANTZ: What, my lord?

HAMLET: Make you a wholesome answer; my wit's diseased.
But, sir, such answer as I can make, you shall command, or
rather, as you say, my mother. Therefore no more, but to
the matter. My mother, you say—   610

ROSENCRANTZ: Then thus she says: your behavior hath struck
her into amazement and admiration.[5]

HAMLET: O wonderful son, that can so stonish[6] a mother! But
is there no sequel at the heels of his mother's admiration?
Impart.   615

ROSENCRANTZ: She desires to speak with you in her closet[7] ere
you go to bed.

HAMLET: We shall obey, were she ten times our mother.
Have you any further trade with us?

ROSENCRANTZ: My lord, you once did love me.   620

HAMLET: And do still, by these pickers and stealers.[8]

9. Bile.
1. Treatment with a laxative.
2. Speech into some order.
3. Reasonable.
4. That is, to the queen.

5. Wonder.
6. Astonish.
7. Bedroom.
8. These hands.

ROSENCRANTZ: Good my lord, what is your cause of distemper? You do surely bar the door upon your own liberty, if you deny your griefs to your friend.

HAMLET: Sir, I lack advancement. 625

ROSENCRANTZ: How can that be, when you have the voice of the king himself for your succession in Denmark?

HAMLET: Ay, sir, but "while the grass grows"—the proverb[9] is something musty.

[*Enter the* PLAYERS *with recorders.*]

O, the recorders! Let me see one. To withdraw with you[1]— 630 why do you go about to recover the wind of me, as if you would drive me into a toil?[2]

GUILDENSTERN: O my lord, if my duty be too bold, my love is too unmannerly.

HAMLET: I do not well understand that. Will you play upon 635 this pipe?[3]

GUILDENSTERN: My lord, I cannot.

HAMLET: I pray you.

GUILDENSTERN: Believe me, I cannot.

HAMLET: I do beseech you. 640

GUILDENSTERN: I know no touch of it,[4] my lord.

HAMLET: It is as easy as lying. Govern these ventages[5] with your fingers and thumb, give it breath with your mouth, and it will discourse most eloquent music. Look you, these are the stops. 645

GUILDENSTERN: But these cannot I command to any utt'rance of harmony. I have not the skill.

HAMLET: Why, look you now, how unworthy a thing you make of me! You would play upon me, you would seem to know my stops, you would pluck out the heart of my mys- 650 tery, you would sound me from my lowest note to the top of my compass;[6] and there is much music, excellent voice,

---

9. The proverb ends "the horse starves."

1. Let me step aside.

2. The figure is from hunting. Hamlet asks why Guildenstern is attempting to get windward of him, as if he would drive him into a net.

3. Recorder.

4. Have no ability.

5. Cover and uncover these holes, or stops.

6. Range. *Sound*: play.

in this little organ, yet cannot you make it speak. 'Sblood,
do you think I am easier to be played on than a pipe? Call
me what instrument you will, though you can fret⁷ me, you   655
cannot play upon me.

    [*Enter* POLONIUS.]

God bless you, sir!

POLONIUS: My lord, the queen would speak with you, and
    presently.

HAMLET: Do you see yonder cloud that's almost in shape of a   660
    camel?

POLONIUS: By th' mass, and 'tis like a camel indeed.

HAMLET: Methinks it is like a weasel.

POLONIUS: It is backed like a weasel.

HAMLET: Or like a whale.   665

POLONIUS: Very like a whale.

HAMLET: Then I will come to my mother by and by. [*Aside.*]
    They fool me to the top of my bent.⁸—I will come by and
    by.

POLONIUS: I will say so.   [*Exit.*]   670

HAMLET: "By and by" is easily said. Leave me, friends.

                       [*Exeunt all but* HAMLET.]

    'Tis now the very witching time of night,
    When churchyards yawn, and hell itself breathes out
    Contagion to this world. Now could I drink hot blood,
    And do such bitter business as the day   675
    Would quake to look on. Soft, now to my mother.
    O heart, lose not thy nature; let not ever
    The soul of Nero⁹ enter this firm bosom.
    Let me be cruel, not unnatural;
    I will speak daggers to her, but use none.   680
    My tongue and soul in this be hypocrites—
    How in my words somever she be shent,¹
    To give them seals² never, my soul, consent!   [*Exit.*]

---

7. To annoy; also, to play a guitar or similar
instrument using the "frets," or small bars on the
neck.

8. Treat me as an utter fool.

9. Roman emperor who reputedly murdered
his mother.

1. However much by my words she is shamed.

2. Fulfillment in action.

SCENE 3

A room in the castle. Enter KING, ROSENCRANTZ *and* GUILDENSTERN.

KING: I like him not, nor stands it safe with us
    To let his madness range. Therefore prepare you.
    I your commission will forthwith dispatch,
    And he to England shall along with you.
    The terms of our estate[3] may not endure   5
    Hazard so near 's as doth hourly grow
    Out of his brows.
GUILDENSTERN: We will ourselves provide,[4]
    Most holy and religious fear[5] it is
    To keep those many many bodies safe
    That live and feed upon your majesty.   10
ROSENCRANTZ: The single and peculiar[6] life is bound
    With all the strength and armor of the mind
    To keep itself from noyance,[7] but much more
    That spirit upon whose weal[8] depends and rests
    The lives of many. The cess[9] of majesty   15
    Dies not alone, but like a gulf [1] doth draw
    What's near it with it. It is a massy[2] wheel
    Fixed on the summit of the highest mount,
    To whose huge spokes ten thousand lesser things
    Are mortised and adjoined,[3] which when it falls,   20
    Each small annexment, petty consequence,
    Attends[4] the boist'rous ruin. Never alone
    Did the king sigh, but with a general groan.
KING: Arm[5] you, I pray you, to this speedy voyage,
    For we will fetters put about this fear,   25
    Which now goes too free-footed.
ROSENCRANTZ: We will haste us.
      [Exeunt ROSENCRANTZ *and* GUILDENSTERN.]
     [*Enter* POLONIUS.]

---

3. Condition of the state.
4. Equip (for the journey).
5. Care.
6. The individual and private.
7. Harm.
8. Welfare.

9. Cessation.
1. Whirlpool.
2. Massive.
3. Are attached.
4. Joins in.
5. Prepare.

POLONIUS: My lord, he's going to his mother's closet.
　Behind the arras I'll convey myself
　To hear the process. I'll warrant she'll tax him home,[6]
　And as you said, and wisely was it said,　　　　　　　　　30
　'Tis meet that some more audience than a mother,
　Since nature makes them partial, should o'erhear
　The speech, of vantage.[7] Fare you well, my liege.
　I'll call upon you ere you go to bed,
　And tell you what I know.
KING:　　　　　　　　　　　　Thanks, dear my lord.　　　　35

[*Exit* POLONIUS.]

　O, my offence is rank, it smells to heaven;
　It hath the primal eldest curse[8] upon't,
　A brother's murder. Pray can I not,
　Though inclination be as sharp as will.
　My stronger guilt defeats my strong intent,　　　　　　40
　And like a man to double business[9] bound,
　I stand in pause where I shall first begin,
　And both neglect. What if this cursèd hand
　Were thicker than itself with brother's blood,
　Is there not rain enough in the sweet heavens　　　　　45
　To wash it white as snow? Whereto serves mercy
　But to confront the visage of offence?
　And what's in prayer but this twofold force,
　To be forestallèd[1] ere we come to fall,
　Or pardoned being down?[2] Then I'll look up.　　　　　50
　My fault is past. But, O, what form of prayer
　Can serve my turn? "Forgive me my foul murder"?
　That cannot be, since I am still possessed
　Of those effects[3] for which I did the murder—
　My crown, mine own ambition, and my queen.　　　　　55
　May one be pardoned and retain th' offence?[4]
　In the corrupted currents of this world
　Offence's gilded[5] hand may shove by justice,

6. Sharply. *Process:* proceedings.
7. From a position of vantage.
8. I.e., of Cain (the biblical figure who murdered his brother, Abel).
9. Two mutually opposed interests.

1. Prevented (from sin).
2. Having sinned.
3. Gains.
4. That is, benefits of the offense.
5. Bearing gold as a bribe.

And oft 'tis seen the wicked prize itself
Buys out the law. But 'tis not so above.   60
There is no shuffling; there the action[6] lies
In his true nature, and we ourselves compelled,
Even to the teeth and forehead of [7] our faults,
To give in evidence. What then? What rests?[8]
Try what repentance can. What can it not?   65
Yet what can it when one cannot repent?
O wretched state! O bosom black as death!
O liméd[9] soul, that struggling to be free
Art more engaged! Help, angels! Make assay.
Bow, stubborn knees, and heart with strings of steel,   70
Be soft as sinews of the new-born babe.
All may be well. [*He kneels.*]
    [*Enter* HAMLET.]
HAMLET: Now might I do it pat,[1] now 'a is a-praying,
And now I'll do't—and so 'a goes to heaven,
And so am I revenged. That would be scanned.[2]   75
A villain kills my father, and for that,
I, his sole son, do this same villain send
To heaven.
Why, this is hire and salary, not revenge.
'A took my father grossly, full of bread,[3]   80
With all his crimes broad blown, as flush[4] as May;
And how his audit stands who knows save heaven?
But in our circumstance and course of thought
'Tis heavy with him; and am I then revenged
To take him in the purging of his soul,   85
When he is fit and seasoned[5] for his passage?
No.
Up, sword, and know thou a more horrid hent.[6]
When he is drunk, asleep, or in his rage,
Or in th' incestuous pleasure of his bed,   90

6. Legal case.
7. Face-to-face with.
8. Remains.
9. Caught as with birdlime.
1. Easily.

2. Calls for evaluation.
3. In a state of sin and without fasting.
4. Full-blown, as vigorous.
5. Ready.
6. Opportunity.

At game a-swearing, or about some act
That has no relish⁷ of salvation in't—
Then trip him, that his heels may kick at heaven,
And that his soul may be as damned and black
As hell, whereto it goes. My mother stays. 95
This physic⁸ but prolongs thy sickly days. [*Exit.*]
KING: [*Rising.*] My words fly up, my thoughts remain below.
Words without thoughts never to heaven go. [*Exit.*]

SCENE 4

The Queen's chamber. Enter QUEEN *and* POLONIUS.

POLONIUS: 'A will come straight. Look you lay home to⁹ him.
Tell him his pranks have been too broad¹ to bear with,
And that your grace hath screen'd and stood between
Much heat and him. I'll silence me even here.
Pray you be round² with him. 5
HAMLET: [*Within.*] Mother, mother, mother!
QUEEN: I'll warrant you. Fear³ me not.
Withdraw, I hear him coming.
[POLONIUS *goes behind the arras. Enter* HAMLET.]
HAMLET: Now, mother, what's the matter?
QUEEN: Hamlet, thou hast thy father much offended. 10
HAMLET: Mother, you have my father much offended.
QUEEN: Come, come, you answer with an idle tongue.
HAMLET: Go, go, you question with a wicked tongue.
QUEEN: Why, how now, Hamlet?
HAMLET: What's the matter now?
QUEEN: Have you forgot me?
HAMLET: No, by the rood,⁴ not so. 15
You are the queen, your husband's brother's wife,
And would it were not so, you are my mother.
QUEEN: Nay, then I'll set those to you that can speak.
HAMLET: Come, come, and sit you down. You shall not budge.

7. Flavor.
8. Medicine.
9. Be sharp with.
1. Outrageous.

2. Direct, forthright.
3. Doubt.
4. Cross.

You go not till I set you up a glass[5]   20
Where you may see the inmost part of you.

QUEEN: What wilt thou do? Thou wilt not murder me?
Help, ho!

POLONIUS: [*Behind.*] What, ho! help!

HAMLET: [*Draws.*] How now, a rat?   25
Dead for a ducat, dead![6] [*Kills* POLONIUS *with a pass
through the arras.*]

POLONIUS: [*Behind.*] O, I am slain!

QUEEN: O me, what hast thou done?

HAMLET: Nay, I know not.
Is it the king?

QUEEN: O, what a rash and bloody deed is this!   30

HAMLET: A bloody deed!—almost as bad, good mother,
As kill a king and marry with his brother.

QUEEN: As kill a king?

HAMLET: Ay, lady, it was my word.
[*Parting the arras.*] Thou wretched, rash, intruding fool,
farewell!
I took thee for thy better. Take thy fortune.   35
Thou find'st to be too busy[7] is some danger.—
Leave wringing of your hands. Peace, sit you down
And let me wring your heart, for so I shall
If it be made of penetrable stuff,
If damnéd custom have not brazed it[8] so   40
That it be proof and bulwark against sense.[9]

QUEEN: What have I done that thou dar'st wag thy tongue
In noise so rude against me?

HAMLET: Such an act
That blurs the grace and blush of modesty,
Calls virtue hypocrite, takes off the rose   45
From the fair forehead of an innocent love
And sets a blister[1] there, makes marriage-vows
As false as dicers' oaths. O, such a deed

---

5. Mirror.
6. I bet a gold coin he's dead.
7. Officious.

8. Plated it with brass.
9. Feeling. *Proof:* armor.
1. Brand.

As from the body of contraction[2] plucks
The very soul, and sweet religion makes   50
A rhapsody of words. Heaven's face does glow
O'er this solidity and compound mass[3]
With heated visage, as against the doom[4]—
Is thought-sick at the act.

QUEEN: Ay me, what act
    That roars so loud and thunders in the index?[5]   55

HAMLET: Look here upon this picture and on this,
    The counterfeit presentment[6] of two brothers.
    See what a grace was seated on this brow:
    Hyperion's curls, the front[7] of Jove himself,
    An eye like Mars, to threaten and command,   60
    A station like the herald Mercury[8]
    New lighted[9] on a heaven-kissing hill—
    A combination and a form indeed
    Where every god did seem to set his seal,
    To give the world assurance of a man.   65
    This was your husband. Look you now what follows.
    Here is your husband, like a mildewed ear[1]
    Blasting[2] his wholesome brother. Have you eyes?
    Could you on this fair mountain leave to feed,
    And batten[3] on this moor? Ha! have you eyes?   70
    You cannot call it love, for at your age
    The heyday in the blood is tame, it's humble,
    And waits upon the judgment, and what judgment
    Would step from this to this? Sense sure you have
    Else could you not have motion, but sure that sense   75
    Is apoplexed[4] for madness would not err,
    Nor sense to ecstacy was ne'er so thralled
    But it reserved some quantity of choice

2. The marriage contract.
3. Meaningless mass (Earth).
4. Judgment Day.
5. Table of contents.
6. Portrait.
7. Forehead.
8. A bearing like that of the messenger of the gods.
9. Newly alighted.
1. Of corn.
2. Infecting.
3. Fatten.
4. Paralyzed.

To serve in such a difference.[5] What devil was't
That thus hath cozened you at hoodman-blind?[6]   80
Eyes without feeling, feeling without sight,
Ears without hands or eyes, smelling sans[7] all,
Or but a sickly part of one true sense
Could not so mope.[8] O shame! where is thy blush?
Rebellious hell,   85
If thou canst mutine[9] in a matron's bones,
To flaming youth let virtue be as wax
And melt in her own fire. Proclaim no shame
When the compulsive ardor gives the charge,[1]
Since frost itself as actively doth burn,   90
And reason panders[2] will.

QUEEN: O Hamlet, speak no more!
Thou turn'st my eyes into my very soul;
And there I see such black and grainéd[3] spots
As will not leave their tinct.[4]

HAMLET: Nay, but to live
In the rank sweat of an enseaméd[5] bed,   95
Stewed in curruption, honeying and making love
Over the nasty sty—

QUEEN: O, speak to me no more!
These words like daggers enter in my ears;
No more, sweet Hamlet.

HAMLET: A murderer and a villain,
A slave that is not twentieth part the tithe[6]   100
Of your precedent lord, a vice[7] of kings,
A cutpurse[8] of the empire and the rule,
That from a shelf the precious diadem stole
And put it in his pocket—

---

5. The power to choose between such different
men.
6. Blindman's buff. *Cozened:* cheated.
7. Without.
8. Be stupid.
9. Commit mutiny.
1. Attacks.
2. Pimps for.

3. Ingrained.
4. Lose their color.
5. Greasy.
6. One-tenth.
7. The "Vice" was a clown or buffoon in moral-
ity plays. *Precedent lord:* first husband.
8. Pickpocket.

QUEEN: No more.   105
    [*Enter* GHOST.]
HAMLET: A king of shreds and patches—
    Save me and hover o'er me with your wings,
    You heavenly guards! What would your gracious figure?
QUEEN: Alas, he's mad.
HAMLET: Do you not come your tardy[9] son to chide,   110
    That lapsed in time and passion lets go by
    Th' important acting of your dread command?
    O, say!
GHOST: Do not forget. This visitation
    Is but to whet thy almost blunted purpose.   115
    But look, amazement on thy mother sits.
    O, step between her and her fighting soul!
    Conceit[1] in weakest bodies strongest works.
    Speak to her, Hamlet.
HAMLET: How is it with you, lady?
QUEEN: Alas, how is't with you,   120
    That you do bend[2] your eye on vacancy,
    And with th' incorporal[3] air do hold discourse?
    Forth at your eyes your spirits wildly peep,
    And as the sleeping soldiers in th' alarm,
    Your bedded hairs like life in excrements[4]   125
    Start up and stand an end. O gentle son,
    Upon the heat and flame of thy distemper
    Sprinkle cool patience. Whereon do you look?
HAMLET: On him, on him! Look you how pale he glares.
    His form and cause conjoined,[5] preaching to stones,   130
    Would make them capable.[6]—Do not look upon me,
    Lest with this piteous action you convert
    My stern effects.[7] Then what I have to do
    Will want true color—tears perchance for blood.
QUEEN: To whom do you speak this?   135
HAMLET: Do you see nothing there?

---

9. Slow to act.
1. Imagination.
2. Turn.
3. Incorporeal.

4. Nails and hair.
5. Working together.
6. Of responding.
7. Deeds.

QUEEN: Nothing at all, yet all that is I see.

HAMLET: Nor did you nothing hear?

QUEEN: No, nothing but ourselves.

HAMLET: Why, look you there. Look how it steals away.   140
    My father, in his habit[8] as he lived!
    Look where he goes even now out at the portal.

                                   [*Exit* GHOST.]

QUEEN: This is the very coinage[9] of your brain.
    The bodiless creation ecstasy[1]
    Is very cunning[2] in.

HAMLET: Ecstasy?   145
    My pulse as yours doth temperately keep time,
    And makes as healthful music. It is not madness
    That I have uttered. Bring me to the test,
    And I the matter will re-word, which madness
    Would gambol[3] from. Mother, for love of grace,   150
    Lay not that flattering unction[4] to your soul,
    That not your trespass but my madness speaks.
    It will but skin and film the ulcerous place
    Whiles rank corruption, mining[5] all within,
    Infects unseen. Confess yourself to heaven,   155
    Repent what's past, avoid what is to come.
    And do not spread the compost on the weeds,
    To make them ranker. Forgive me this my virtue,
    For in the fatness of these pursy[6] times
    Virtue itself of vice must pardon beg,   160
    Yea, curb[7] and woo for leave to do him good.

QUEEN: O Hamlet, thou hast cleft my heart in twain.

HAMLET: O, throw away the worser part of it,
    And live the purer with the other half.
    Good night—but go not to my uncle's bed.   165
    Assume a virtue, if you have it not.
    That monster custom[8] who all sense doth eat,

---

8. Costume.
9. Invention.
1. Madness.
2. Skilled.
3. Shy away.

4. Ointment.
5. Undermining.
6. Bloated.
7. Bow.
8. Habit.

Of habits devil, is angel yet in this,
That to the use of actions fair and good
He likewise gives a frock or livery   170
That aptly⁹ is put on. Refrain tonight,
And that shall lend a kind of easiness
To the next abstinence; the next more easy;
For use almost can change the stamp of nature,
And either curb the devil, or throw him out   175
With wondrous potency. Once more, good night,
And when you are desirous to be blest,
I'll blessing beg of you. For this same lord
I do repent; but heaven hath pleased it so,
To punish me with this, and this with me,   180
That I must be their scourge and minister.
I will bestow¹ him and will answer well
The death I gave him. So, again, good night.
I must be cruel only to be kind.
Thus bad begins and worse remains behind.   185
One word more, good lady.
QUEEN: What shall I do?
HAMLET: Not this, by no means, that I bid you do:
    Let the bloat² king tempt you again to bed,
    Pinch wanton³ on your cheek, call you his mouse,
    And let him, for a pair of reechy⁴ kisses,   190
    Or paddling in your neck with his damned fingers,
    Make you to ravel⁵ all this matter out,
    That I essentially am not in madness,
    But mad in craft. 'Twere good you let him know,
    For who that's but a queen, fair, sober, wise,   195
    Would from a paddock, from a bat, a gib,⁶
    Such dear concernings hide? Who would so do?
    No, in despite of sense and secrecy,
    Unpeg the basket on the house's top,
    Let the birds fly, and like the famous ape,   200

9. Easily.
1. Dispose of.
2. Bloated.
3. Lewdly.

4. Foul.
5. Reveal.
6. Tomcat. *Paddock:* toad.

To try conclusions, in the basket creep
And break your own neck down.[7]
QUEEN: Be thou assured, if words be made of breath
And breath of life, I have no life to breathe
What thou hast said to me.   205
HAMLET: I must to England; you know that?
QUEEN: Alack,
I had forgot. 'Tis so concluded on.
HAMLET: There's letters sealed, and my two school-fellows,
Whom I will trust as I will adders fanged,
They bear the mandate; they must sweep[8] my way   210
And marshal me to knavery. Let it work,
For 'tis the sport to have the enginer
Hoist with his own petard;[9] and't shall go hard
But I will delve[1] one yard below their mines
And blow them at the moon. O, 'tis most sweet   215
When in one line two crafts directly meet.
This man shall set me packing.
I'll lug the guts into the neighbor room.
Mother, good night. Indeed, this counsellor
Is now most still, most secret, and most grave,   220
Who was in life a foolish prating knave.
Come sir, to draw toward an end with you.
Good night, mother.
    [*Exit the* QUEEN. *Then exit* HAMLET *tugging* POLONIUS.]

ACT IV
SCENE 1
A room in the castle. Enter KING, QUEEN, ROSENCRANTZ *and*
GUILDENSTERN.

KING: There's matter in these sighs, these profound heaves,
You must translate;[2] 'tis fit we understand them.

---

7. Apparently a reference to a now-lost fable in
which an ape, finding a basket containing a cage of
birds on a housetop, opens the cage. The birds fly
away. The ape, thinking that if he were in the basket he too could fly, enters, jumps out, and breaks
his neck.

8. Prepare. *Mandate:* command.
9. Blown up by his own bomb.
1. Dig.
2. Explain.

Where is your son?

QUEEN: Bestow this place on us a little while.

              [*Exeunt* ROSENCRANTZ *and* GUILDENSTERN.]

  Ah, mine own lord, what have I seen tonight!   5

KING: What, Gertrude? How does Hamlet?

QUEEN: Mad as the sea and wind when both contend

  Which is the mightier. In his lawless fit,

  Behind the arras hearing something stir,

  Whips out his rapier, cries "A rat, a rat!"   10

  And in this brainish apprehension[3] kills

  The unseen good old man.

KING: O heavy deed!

  It had been so with us had we been there.

  His liberty is full of threats to all—

  To you yourself, to us, to every one.   15

  Alas, how shall this bloody deed be answered?

  It will be laid to us, whose providence[4]

  Should have kept short, restrained, and out of haunt,[5]

  This mad young man. But so much was our love,

  We would not understand what was most fit;   20

  But, like the owner of a foul disease,

  To keep it from divulging, let it feed

  Even on the pith of life. Where is he gone?

QUEEN: To draw apart the body he hath killed,

  O'er whom his very madness, like some ore   25

  Among a mineral of metals base,

  Shows itself pure: 'a weeps for what is done.

KING: O Gertrude, come away!

  The sun no sooner shall the mountains touch

  But we will ship him hence, and this vile deed   30

  We must with all our majesty and skill

  Both countenance and excuse. Ho, Guildenstern!

        [*Enter* ROSENCRANTZ *and* GUILDENSTERN.]

  Friends both, go join you with some further aid.

  Hamlet in madness hath Polonius slain,

---

3. Insane notion.
4. Prudence.

5. Away from court.

And from his mother's closet hath he dragged him.   35
Go seek him out; speak fair, and bring the body
Into the chapel. I pray you haste in this.
        [*Exeunt* ROSENCRANTZ *and* GUILDENSTERN.]
Come, Gertrude, we'll call up our wisest friends
And let them know both what we mean to do
And what's untimely done;   40
Whose whisper o'er the world's diameter,
As level as the cannon to his blank,[6]
Transports his poisoned shot—may miss our name,
And hit the woundless air. O, come away!
My soul is full of discord and dismay.   45
                       [*Exeunt.*]

SCENE 2

A passageway. Enter HAMLET.

HAMLET: Safely stowed.

ROSENCRANTZ *and* GUILDENSTERN: [*Within.*] Hamlet! Lord Hamlet!

HAMLET: But soft, what noise? Who calls on Hamlet? O, here they come.   5
        [*Enter* ROSENCRANTZ, GUILDENSTERN, *and* OTHERS.]

ROSENCRANTZ: What have you done, my lord, with the dead body?

HAMLET: Compounded it with dust, whereto 'tis kin.

ROSENCRANTZ: Tell us where 'tis, that we may take it thence And bear it to the chapel.   10

HAMLET: Do not believe it.

ROSENCRANTZ: Believe what?

HAMLET: That I can keep your counsel and not mine own. Besides, to be demanded of a sponge—what replication[7] should be made by the son of a king?   15

ROSENCRANTZ: Take you me for a sponge, my lord?

HAMLET: Ay, sir, that soaks up the king's countenance,[8] his rewards, his authorities. But such officers do the king best

6. Mark. *Level:* direct.   8. Favor.
7. Answer. *Demanded of:* questioned by.

service in the end. He keeps them like an apple in the corner of his jaw, first mouthed to be last swallowed. When he needs what you have gleaned, it is but squeezing you and, sponge, you shall be dry again. 20

ROSENCRANTZ: I understand you not, my lord.

HAMLET: I am glad of it. A knavish speech sleeps in a foolish ear.

ROSENCRANTZ: My lord, you must tell us where the body is, and go with us to the king. 25

HAMLET: The body is with the king, but the king is not with the body.

The king is a thing—

GUILDENSTERN: A thing, my lord!

HAMLET: Of nothing. Bring me to him. Hide fox, and all after.[9]   [*Exeunt.*] 25

Scene 3

A room in the castle. Enter KING.

KING: I have sent to seek him, and to find the body.
How dangerous is it that this man goes loose!
Yet must not we put the strong law on him.
He's loved of the distracted[1] multitude,
Who like not in their judgment but their eyes, 5
And where 'tis so, th' offender's scourge[2] is weighed,
But never the offence. To bear all smooth and even,
This sudden sending him away must seem
Deliberate pause.[3] Diseases desperate grown
By desperate appliance are relieved, 10
Or not at all.
    [*Enter* ROSENCRANTZ, GUILDENSTERN, *and all the rest.*]
        How now! what hath befall'n?

ROSENCRANTZ: Where the dead body is bestowed, my lord,
We cannot get from him.

KING: But where is he?

9. Apparently a reference to a children's game like hide-and-seek.
1. Confused.
2. Punishment.
3. That is, not an impulse.

ROSENCRANTZ: Without, my lord; guarded, to know[4] your
    pleasure.
KING: Bring him before us.
ROSENCRANTZ: Ho! bring in the lord.   15
    [*They enter with* HAMLET.]
KING: Now, Hamlet, where's Polonius?
HAMLET: At supper.
KING: At supper? Where?
HAMLET: Not where he eats, but where 'a is eaten. A certain
    convocation of politic worms are e'en[5] at him. Your worm   20
    is your only emperor for diet. We fat all creatures else to
    fat us, and we fat ourselves for maggots. Your fat king and
    your lean beggar is but variable service—two dishes, but to
    one table. That's the end.
KING: Alas, alas!   25
HAMLET: A man may fish with the worm that hath eat of a
    king, and eat of the fish that hath fed of that worm.
KING: What dost thou mean by this?
HAMLET: Nothing but to show you how a king may go a prog-
    ress through the guts of a beggar.   30
KING: Where is Polonius?
HAMLET: In heaven. Send thither to see. If your messenger
    find him not there, seek him i' th' other place yourself. But
    if, indeed, you find him not within this month, you shall
    nose[6] him as you go up the stairs into the lobby.   35
KING: [*To* ATTENDANTS.] Go seek him there.
HAMLET: 'A will stay till you come.
                                [*Exeunt* ATTENDANTS.]
KING: Hamlet, this deed, for thine especial safety—
    Which we do tender, as we dearly[7] grieve
    For that which thou hast done—must send thee hence   40
    With fiery quickness. Therefore prepare thyself.
    The bark is ready, and the wind at help,
    Th' associates tend, and everything is bent
    For England.

---

4. Await.
5. Now. *Convocation of politic:* gathering of
scheming (or cunning).

6. Smell.
7. Deeply. *Tender:* consider.

HAMLET: For England?

KING: Ay, Hamlet.

HAMLET: Good.

KING: So it is, if thou knew'st our purposes.   45

HAMLET: I see a cherub that sees them. But come, for England!
    Farewell, dear mother.

KING: Thy loving father, Hamlet.

HAMLET: My mother. Father and mother is man and wife,
    man and wife is one flesh. So, my mother. Come, for   50
    England.   *[Exit.]*

KING: Follow him at foot;[8] tempt him with speed aboard.
    Delay it not; I'll have him hence tonight.
    Away! for everything is sealed and done
    That else leans on th' affair. Pray you make haste.   55
                      [Exeunt all but the KING.]
    And, England, if my love thou hold'st at aught—
    As my great power thereof may give thee sense,[9]
    Since yet thy cicatrice[1] looks raw and red
    After the Danish sword, and thy free awe   60
    Pays homage to us—thou mayst not coldly set[2]
    Our sovereign process,[3] which imports at full
    By letters congruing[4] to that effect
    The present death of Hamlet. Do it, England,
    For like the hectic[5] in my blood he rages,   65
    And thou must cure me. Till I know 'tis done,
    Howe'er my haps, my joys were ne'er begun. *[Exit.]*

SCENE 4

Near Elsinore. Enter FORTINBRAS *with his army.*

FORTINBRAS: Go, captain, from me greet the Danish king.
    Tell him that by his license Fortinbras
    Craves the conveyance[6] of a promised march
    Over his kingdom. You know the rendezvous.

---

8. Closely.
9. Of its value.
1. Scar.
2. Set aside.

3. Mandate.
4. Agreeing.
5. Chronic fever.
6. Escort.

If that his majesty would aught with us,   5
We shall express our duty in his eye,[7]
And let him know so.
CAPTAIN: I will do't, my lord.
FORTINBRAS: Go softly on.   [*Exeunt all but the* CAPTAIN.]
        [*Enter* HAMLET, ROSENCRANTZ, GUILDENSTERN, *and* OTHERS.]
HAMLET: Good sir, whose powers are these?
CAPTAIN: They are of Norway, sir.   10
HAMLET: How purposed, sir, I pray you?
CAPTAIN: Against some part of Poland.
HAMLET: Who commands them, sir?
CAPTAIN: The nephew to old Norway, Fortinbras.
HAMLET: Goes it against the main[8] of Poland, sir,   15
    Or for some frontier?
CAPTAIN: Truly to speak, and with no addition,[9]
    We go to gain a little patch of ground
    That hath in it no profit but the name.
    To pay five ducats,[1] five, I would not farm it;   20
    Nor will it yield to Norway or the Pole
    A ranker rate should it be sold in fee.[2]
HAMLET: Why, then the Polack never will defend it.
CAPTAIN: Yes, it is already garrisoned.
HAMLET: Two thousand souls and twenty thousand ducats   25
    Will not debate the question of this straw.
    This is th' imposthume[3] of much wealth and peace,
    That inward breaks, and shows no cause without
    Why the man dies. I humbly thank you, sir.
CAPTAIN: God b'wi'ye, sir.   [*Exit.*]
ROSENCRANTZ: Will't please you go, my lord?   30
HAMLET: I'll be with you straight. Go a little before.
                            [*Exeunt all but* HAMLET.]
    How all occasions do inform against me,
    And spur my dull revenge! What is a man,
    If his chief good and market[4] of his time

7. Presence.   2. Outright. *Ranker:* higher.
8. Central part.   3. Abscess.
9. Exaggeration.   4. Occupation.
1. That is, in rent.

Be but to sleep and feed? A beast, no more.   35
Sure he that made us with such large discourse,[5]
Looking before and after, gave us not
That capability and godlike reason
To fust[6] in us unused. Now, whether it be
Bestial oblivion, or some craven scruple   40
Of thinking too precisely on th' event[7]—
A thought which, quartered, hath but one part wisdom
And ever three parts coward—I do not know
Why yet I live to say "This thing's to do,"
Sith[8] I have cause, and will, and strength, and means,   45
To do't. Examples gross as earth exhort me.
Witness this army of such mass and charge,[9]
Led by a delicate and tender prince,
Whose spirit, with divine ambition puffed,
Makes mouths at[1] the invisible event,   50
Exposing what is mortal and unsure
To all that fortune, death, and danger dare,
Even for an eggshell. Rightly to be great
Is not to stir without great argument,
But greatly to find quarrel in a straw   55
When honor's at the stake. How stand I then,
That have a father killed, a mother stained,
Excitements of my reason and my blood,
And let all sleep, while to my shame I see
The imminent death of twenty thousand men   60
That for a fantasy and trick of fame
Go to their graves like beds, fight for a plot
Whereon the numbers cannot try the cause,
Which is not tomb enough and continent
To hide the slain?[2] O, from this time forth,   65
My thoughts be bloody, or be nothing worth!   [*Exit.*]

---

5. Ample reasoning power.   1. Scorns.
6. Grow musty.   2. The plot of ground involved is so small that
7. Outcome.   it cannot contain the number of men involved in
8. Since.   fighting or furnish burial space for the number of
9. Expense.   those who will die.

SCENE 5

A room in the castle. Enter QUEEN, HORATIO *and a* GENTLEMAN.

QUEEN: I will not speak with her.

GENTLEMAN: She is importunate, indeed distract.
Her mood will needs to be pitied.

QUEEN: What would she have?

GENTLEMAN: She speaks much of her father, says she hears
There's tricks i' th' world, and hems, and beats her heart,   5
Spurns enviously at straws,[3] speaks things in doubt
That carry but half sense. Her speech is nothing,
Yet the unshapéd use of it doth move
The hearers to collection;[4] they yawn at it,
And botch the words up fit to their own thoughts,   10
Which, as her winks and nods and gestures yield them,
Indeed would make one think there might be thought,
Though nothing sure, yet much unhappily.

HORATIO: 'Twere good she were spoken with, for she may strew
Dangerous conjectures in ill-breeding minds.   15

QUEEN: Let her come in.   [*Exit* GENTLEMAN.]
[*Aside.*] To my sick soul, as sin's true nature is,
Each toy seems prologue to some great amiss.[5]
So full of artless jealousy is guilt,
It spills itself in fearing to be spilt.   20
[*Enter* OPHELIA *distracted.*]

OPHELIA: Where is the beauteous majesty of Denmark?

QUEEN: How now, Ophelia!

OPHELIA: [*Sings.*]
How should I your true love know
From another one?
By his cockle hat and staff,[6]   25
And his sandal shoon.[7]

QUEEN: Alas, sweet lady, what imports this song?

---

3. Takes offense at trifles.
4. To decipher her meaning.
5. Catastrophe. *Toy:* trifle.

6. Things associated with a pilgrimage.
7. Shoes.

OPHELIA: Say you? Nay, pray you mark. [*Sings.*]
>He is dead and gone, lady,
>>He is dead and gone;
>At his head a grass-green turf,
>>At his heels a stone.
>O, ho!

QUEEN: Nay, but Ophelia—

OPHELIA: Pray you mark. [*Sings.*]
>White his shroud as the mountain snow—
>[*Enter* KING.]

QUEEN: Alas, look here, my lord.

OPHELIA: [*Sings.*]
>Larded all with sweet flowers;
>Which bewept to the grave did not go
>>With true-love showers.

KING: How do you, pretty lady?

OPHELIA: Well, God dild[8] you! They say the owl was a baker's daughter. Lord, we know what we are, but know not what we may be. God be at your table!

KING: Conceit[9] upon her father.

OPHELIA: Pray let's have no words of this, but when they ask you what it means, say you this: [*Sings.*]
>Tomorrow is Saint Valentine's day,
>>All in the morning betime,
>And I a maid at your window,
>>To be your Valentine.

>Then up he rose, and donn'd his clo'es,
>>And dupped[1] the chamber-door,
>Let in the maid, that out a maid[2]
>>Never departed more.

KING: Pretty Ophelia!

OPHELIA: Indeed, without an oath, I'll make an end on't.
>[*Sings.*]
>By Gis[3] and by Saint Charity,
>>Alack, and fie for shame!

30

35

40

45

50

55

8. Yield.
9. Thought.
1. Opened

2. Virgin.
3. Jesus.

Young men will do't, if they come to't;
   By Cock,[4] they are to blame.
Quoth she "before you tumbled me,   60
   You promised me to wed."
He answers:
  "So would I'a done, by yonder sun,
   An thou hadst not come to my bed."

KING: How long hath she been thus?   65

OPHELIA: I hope all will be well. We must be patient, but I cannot choose but weep to think they would lay him i' th' cold ground. My brother shall know of it, and so I thank you for your good counsel. Come, my coach! Good night, ladies, good night. Sweet ladies, good night, good   70 night.

                             [Exit.]

KING: Follow her close; give her good watch, I pray you.
               [Exeunt HORATIO *and* GENTLEMAN.]
O, this is the poison of deep grief; it springs
All from her father's death, and now behold!
O Gertrude, Gertrude!   75
When sorrows come, they come not single spies,
But in battalions: first, her father slain;
Next, your son gone, and he most violent author
Of his own just remove; the people muddied,[5]
Thick and unwholesome in their thoughts and whispers   80
For good Polonius' death; and we have done but greenly[6]
In hugger-mugger[7] to inter him; poor Ophelia
Divided from herself and her fair judgment,
Without the which we are pictures, or mere beasts;
Last, and as much containing as all these,   85
Her brother is in secret come from France,
Feeds on his wonder, keeps himself in clouds,[8]
And wants not buzzers[9] to infect his ear
With pestilent speeches of his father's death,

---

4. God.
5. Disturbed.
6. Without judgment.

7. Haste.
8. Rumors, suspicions.
9. And doesn't lack scandal mongers.

Wherein necessity, of matter beggared,[1]   90
Will nothing stick our person to arraign[2]
In ear and ear.[3] O my dear Gertrude, this,
Like to a murd'ring piece,[4] in many places
Gives me superfluous death.
    [*A noise within.*]
QUEEN: Alack, what noise is this?   95
KING: Attend!
    Where are my Switzers?[5] Let them guard the door.
    What is the matter?
MESSENGER: Save yourself, my lord.
    The ocean, overpeering of his list,[6]
    Eats not the flats with more impiteous[7] haste   100
    Then young Laertes, in a riotous head,[8]
    O'erbears your officers. The rabble call him lord,
    And as the world were now but to begin,
    Antiquity forgot, custom not known,
    The ratifiers and props of every word,   105
    They cry "Choose we, Laertes shall be king."
    Caps, hands, and tongues, applaud it to the clouds,
    "Laertes shall be king, Laertes king."
QUEEN: How cheerfully on the false trail they cry![9]
    [*A noise within.*]
    O, this is counter,[1] you false Danish dogs!   110
KING: The doors are broke.
    [*Enter* LAERTES, *with* OTHERS.]
LAERTES: Where is this king?—Sirs, stand you all without.
ALL: No, let's come in.
LAERTES: I pray you give me leave.
ALL: We will, we will.
LAERTES: I thank you. Keep[2] the door.

                      [*Exeunt his followers.*]

---

1. Short on facts.
2. Accuse. *Stick:* hesitate.
3. From both sides.
4. A cannon that fires grapeshot so as to kill as many soldiers as possible.
5. Swiss guards.
6. Towering above its limits.
7. Pitiless.
8. With an armed band.
9. As if following the scent.
1. Backward.
2. Guard.

O thou vile king, 115

Give me my father!

QUEEN: Calmly, good Laertes.

LAERTES: That drop of blood that's calm proclaims me bastard,
Cries cuckold to my father, brands the harlot
Even here between the chaste unsmirchéd brow
Of my true mother.

KING: What is the cause, Laertes, 120
That thy rebellion looks so giant-like?
Let him go, Gertrude. Do not fear[3] our person.
There's such divinity doth hedge a king
That treason can but peep to[4] what it would,
Acts little of his will. Tell me, Laertes, 125
Why thou art thus incensed. Let him go, Gertrude.
Speak, man.

LAERTES: Where is my father?

KING: Dead.

QUEEN: But not by him.

KING: Let him demand[5] his fill.

LAERTES: How came he dead? I'll not be juggled with.
To hell allegiance, vows to the blackest devil, 130
Conscience and grace to the profoundest pit!
I dare damnation. To this point I stand,
That both the worlds I give to negligence,[6]
Let come what comes, only I'll be revenged
Most throughly[7] for my father. 135

KING: Who shall stay you?

LAERTES: My will, not all the world's.
And for my means, I'll husband[8] them so well
They shall go far with little.

KING: Good Laertes,
If you desire to know the certainty
Of your dear father, is't writ in your revenge 140
That, swoopstake,[9] you will draw both friend and foe,

---

3. Fear for.
4. See over or through a barrier.
5. Question.
6. That I disregard this world and the next.

7. Thoroughly.
8. Manage.
9. Sweeping the board.

Winner and loser?

LAERTES: None but his enemies.

KING: Will you know them, then?

LAERTES: To his good friends thus wide I'll ope my arms,
   And like the kind life-rend'ring pelican,[1]   145
   Repast them with my blood.

KING: Why, now you speak
   Like a good child and a true gentleman.
   That I am guiltless of your father's death,
   And am most sensibly in grief for it,
   It shall as level[2] to your judgment 'pear   150
   As day does to your eye.
     [*A noise within*: "Let her come in."]

LAERTES: How now? What noise is that?
     [*Enter* OPHELIA.]
   O, heat dry up my brains! tears seven times salt
   Burn out the sense and virtue[3] of mine eye!
   By heaven, thy madness shall be paid with weight   155
   Till our scale turn the beam. O rose of May,
   Dear maid, kind sister, sweet Ophelia!
   O heavens! is't possible a young maid's wits
   Should be as mortal as an old man's life?
   Nature is fine[4] in love, and where 'tis fine   160
   It sends some precious instances of itself
   After the thing it loves.

OPHELIA: [*Sings.*]
     They bore him barefac'd on the bier;
       Hey non nonny, nonny, hey nonny;
     And in his grave rain'd many a tear—   165
   Fare you well, my dove!

LAERTES: Hadst thou thy wits, and didst persuade revenge,
   It could not move thus.

OPHELIA: You must sing "A-down, a-down, and you call him
   a-down-a." O, how the wheel becomes it! It is the false   170
   steward, that stole his master's daughter.

---

1. The pelican was believed to feed her young with her own blood.
2. Plain.
3. The feeling and function.
4. Refined.

LAERTES: This nothing's more than matter.

OPHELIA: There's rosemary, that's for remembrance. Pray you,
love, remember. And there is pansies, that's for thoughts.

LAERTES: A document[5] in madness, thoughts and remem- 175
brance fitted.

OPHELIA: There's fennel for you, and columbines. There's rue
for you, and here's some for me. We may call it herb of
grace a Sundays. O, you must wear your rue with a difference. There's a daisy. I would give you some violets,[6] but 180
they withered all when my father died. They say 'a made a
good end. [*Sings.*]
　　For bonny sweet Robin is all my joy.

LAERTES: Thought and affliction, passion, hell itself,
She turns to favor[7] and to prettiness. 185

OPHELIA: [*Sings.*]
　　And will 'a not come again?
　　And will 'a not come again?
　　　No, no, he is dead,
　　　Go to thy death-bed,
　　He never will come again. 190

　　His beard was as white as snow,
　　All flaxen was his poll;[8]
　　　He is gone, he is gone,
　　　And we cast away moan:
　　God-a-mercy on his soul! 195
And of all Christian souls, I pray God. God b'wi'you.
　　　　　　　　　　　　　　[*Exit.*]

LAERTES: Do you see this, O God?

KING: Laertes, I must commune with your grief,
Or you deny me right. Go but apart,
Make choice of whom your wisest friends you will, 200

---

5. Lesson.

6. Fennel symbolized flattery; columbines, un-
gratefulness; rue, grief; daisies, lies; and violets,
loyalty.

7. Beauty.

8. Head.

And they shall hear and judge 'twixt you and me.
If by direct or by collateral⁹ hand
They find us touched,¹ we will our kingdom give,
Our crown, our life, and all that we call ours,
To you in satisfaction; but if not,   205
Be you content to lend your patience to us,
And we shall jointly labor with your soul
To give it due content.

LAERTES: Let this be so.
His means of death, his obscure funeral—   210
No trophy, sword, nor hatchment,² o'er his bones,
No noble rite nor formal ostentation³—
Cry to be heard, as 'twere from heaven to earth,
That I must call't in question.

KING: So you shall;
And where th' offence is, let the great axe fall.   215
I pray you go with me.   [*Exeunt.*]

Scene 6

Another room in the castle. Enter HORATIO *and a* GENTLEMAN.

HORATIO: What are they that would speak with me?
GENTLEMAN: Sea-faring men, sir. They say they have letters
    for you.
HORATIO: Let them come in.   [*Exit* GENTLEMAN.]
    I do not know from what part of the world   5
    I should be greeted, if not from Lord Hamlet.
        [*Enter* SAILORS.]
SAILOR: God bless you, sir.
HORATIO: Let him bless thee too.
SAILOR: 'A shall, sir, an't please him. There's a letter for you,
    sir—it came from th' ambassador that was bound for   10
    England—if your name be Horatio, as I am let to know⁴
    it is.

9. Indirect.   3. Pomp.
1. By guilt.   4. Informed.
2. Coat of arms.

HORATIO: [*Reads*.] "Horatio, when thou shalt have overlooked this, give these fellows some means[5] to the king. They have letters for him. Ere we were two days old at sea, a pirate of very warlike appointment[6] gave us chase. Finding ourselves too slow of sail, we put on a compelled valor, and in the grapple I boarded them. On the instant they got clear of our ship, so I alone became their prisoner. They have dealt with me like thieves of mercy, but they knew what they did; I am to do a good turn for them. Let the king have the letters I have sent, and repair thou to me with as much speed as thou wouldest fly death. I have words to speak in thine ear will make thee dumb; yet are they much too light for the bore of the matter.[7] These good fellows will bring thee where I am. Rosencrantz and Guildenstern hold their course for England. Of them I have much to tell thee. Farewell. 15 20 25

                        He that thou knowest thine, Hamlet."
Come, I will give you way[8] for these your letters, 30
And do't the speedier that you may direct me
To him from whom you brought them.   [*Exeunt*.]

SCENE 7
Another room in the castle. Enter KING *and* LAERTES.

KING: Now must your conscience my acquittance seal,[9]
  And you must put me in your heart for friend,
  Sith you have heard, and with a knowing ear,
  That he which hath your noble father slain
  Pursued my life.
LAERTES: It well appears. But tell me
  Why you proceeded not against these feats, 5
  So criminal and so capital in nature,

---

5. Access. *Overlooked*: read through.
6. Equipment.
7. A figure from gunnery, referring to shot that is too small for the size of the weapons to be fired.

8. Means of delivery.
9. Grant me innocent.

As by your safety, greatness, wisdom, all things else,
You mainly were stirred up.

KING: O, for two special reasons,
Which may to you, perhaps, seem much unsinewed,[1]   10
But yet to me th' are strong. The queen his mother
Lives almost by his looks, and for myself—
My virtue or my plague, be it either which—
She is so conjunctive[2] to my life and soul
That, as the star moves not but in his sphere,[3]   15
I could not but by her. The other motive,
Why to a public count[4] I might not go,
Is the great love the general gender[5] bear him,
Who, dipping all his faults in their affection,
Work like the spring that turneth wood to stone,[6]   20
Convert his gyves[7] to graces; so that my arrows,
Too slightly timbered[8] for so loud a wind,
Would have reverted to my bow again,
But not where I had aimed them.

LAERTES: And so have I a noble father lost,   25
A sister driven into desp'rate terms,
Whose worth, if praises may go back again,
Stood challenger on mount of all the age
For her perfections.[9] But my revenge will come.

KING: Break not your sleeps for that. You must not think   30
That we are made of stuff so flat and dull
That we can let our beard be shook with danger,
And think it pastime. You shortly shall hear more.
I loved your father, and we love our self,
And that, I hope, will teach you to imagine—   35
     [Enter a MESSENGER with letters.]
How now? What news?

---

1. Weak.
2. Closely joined.
3. A reference to the Ptolemaic cosmology, in which planets and stars were believed to revolve in crystalline spheres concentrically about Earth.
4. Reckoning.
5. Common people.

6. Certain English springs contain so much lime that a lime covering will be deposited on a log that sits in one of them long enough.
7. Shackles, that is, faults.
8. Shafted.
9. Challenged the world to match her perfections.

MESSENGER: Letters, my lord, from Hamlet.
These to your majesty; this to the queen.
KING: From Hamlet! Who brought them?
MESSENGER: Sailors, my lord, they say. I saw them not.
They were given me by Claudio; he received them   40
Of him that brought them.
KING: Laertes, you shall hear them.—
Leave us.   [*Exit* MESSENGER.]
[*Reads.*] "High and mighty, you shall know I am set naked
on your kingdom. Tomorrow shall I beg leave to see your
kingly eyes; when I shall, first asking your pardon there-   45
unto, recount the occasion of my sudden and more strange
return.
Hamlet."
What should this mean? Are all the rest come back?
Or is it some abuse,[1] and no such thing?   50
LAERTES: Know you the hand?
KING: 'Tis Hamlet's character.[2] "Naked"!
And in a postscript here, he says "alone."
Can you devise[3] me?
LAERTES: I am lost in it, my lord. But let him come.   55
It warms the very sickness in my heart
That I shall live and tell him to his teeth
"Thus didest thou."
KING: If it be so, Laertes—
As how should it be so, how otherwise?—
Will you be ruled by me?
LAERTES: Ay, my lord,   60
So you will not o'errule me to a peace.
KING: To thine own peace. If he be now returned,
As checking at[4] his voyage, and that he means
No more to undertake it, I will work him
To an exploit now ripe in my device,   65
Under the which he shall not choose but fall;
And for his death no wind of blame shall breathe

1. Trick.
2. Handwriting.
3. Explain it to.
4. Turning aside from.

But even his mother shall uncharge[5] the practice
And call it accident.

LAERTES: My lord, I will be ruled;
The rather if you could devise it so   70
That I might be the organ.[6]

KING: It falls right.
You have been talked of since your travel much,
And that in Hamlet's hearing, for a quality
Wherein they say you shine. Your sum of parts
Did not together pluck such envy from him   75
As did that one, and that, in my regard,
Of the unworthiest siege.[7]

LAERTES: What part is that, my lord?

KING: A very riband in the cap of youth,
Yet needful too, for youth no less becomes
The light and careless livery that it wears   80
Than settled age his sables and his weeds,[8]
Importing health and graveness. Two months since
Here was a gentleman of Normandy.
I have seen myself, and served against, the French,
And they can[9] well on horseback, but this gallant   85
Had witchcraft in't. He grew unto his seat,
And to such wondrous doing brought his horse,
As had he been incorpsed and demi-natured[1]
With the brave beast. So far he topped my thought
That I, in forgery[2] of shapes and tricks,   90
Come short of what he did.

LAERTES: A Norman was't?

KING: A Norman.

LAERTES: Upon my life, Lamord.

KING: The very same.

LAERTES: I know him well. He is the brooch indeed
And gem of all the nation.   95

---

5. Not find villainy in.
6. Instrument.
7. Rank.
8. Dignified clothing.

9. Perform.
1. Shared a body and a nature.
2. Imagination.

KING: He made confession[3] of you,
    And gave you such a masterly report
    For art and exercise in your defence,[4]
    And for your rapier most especial,
    That he cried out 'twould be a sight indeed   100
    If one could match you. The scrimers[5] of their nation
    He swore had neither motion, guard, nor eye,
    If you opposed them. Sir, this report of his
    Did Hamlet so envenom with his envy
    That he could nothing do but wish and beg   105
    Your sudden coming o'er, to play with you.
    Now out of this—
LAERTES: What out of this, my lord?
KING: Laertes, was your father dear to you?
    Or are you like the painting of a sorrow,
    A face without a heart?
LAERTES: Why ask you this?   110
KING: Not that I think you did not love your father,
    But that I know love is begun by time,
    And that I see in passages of proof,[6]
    Time qualifies the spark and fire of it.
    There lives within the very flame of love   115
    A kind of wick or snuff that will abate it,
    And nothing is at a like goodness still,
    For goodness, growing to a plurisy,[7]
    Dies in his own too much.[8] That we would do,
    We should do when we would; for this "would" changes,   120
    And hath abatements and delays as many
    As there are tongues, are hands, are accidents,
    And then this "should" is like a spendthrift's sigh
    That hurts by easing. But to the quick of th' ulcer—
    Hamlet comes back; what would you undertake   125
    To show yourself in deed your father's son
    More than in words?
LAERTES: To cut his throat i' th' church.

---

3. Gave a report.   6. Tests of experience.
4. Skill in fencing.   7. Fullness.
5. Swordsmen.   8. Excess.

KING: No place indeed should murder sanctuarize;[9]
    Revenge should have no bounds. But, good Laertes,
    Will you do this? Keep close within your chamber.   130
    Hamlet returned shall know you are come home.
    We'll put on those shall praise your excellence,
    And set a double varnish[1] on the fame
    The Frenchman gave you, bring you in fine[2] together,
    And wager on your heads. He, being remiss,[3]   135
    Most generous, and free from all contriving,
    Will not peruse[4] the foils, so that with ease,
    Or with a little shuffling, you may choose
    A sword unbated,[5] and in a pass of practice
    Requite him for your father.
LAERTES: I will do't,   140
    And for that purpose I'll anoint my sword.
    I bought an unction of a mountebank
    So mortal that but dip a knife in it,
    Where it draws blood no cataplasm[6] so rare,
    Collected from all simples[7] that have virtue   145
    Under the moon, can save the thing from death
    That is but scratched withal. I'll touch my point
    With this contagion, that if I gall[8] him slightly,
    It may be death.
KING: Let's further think of this,
    Weigh what convenience both of time and means   150
    May fit us to our shape. If this should fail,
    And that our drift look[9] through our bad performance,
    'Twere better not assayed. Therefore this project
    Should have a back or second that might hold
    If this did blast in proof.[1] Soft, let me see.   155
    We'll make a solemn wager on your cunnings—
    I ha't.

---

9. Provide sanctuary for murder.
1. Gloss.
2. In short.
3. Careless.
4. Examine.
5. Not blunted.

6. Poultice.
7. Herbs.
8. Scratch.
9. Intent become obvious.
1. Fail when tried.

When in your motion you are hot and dry—
As make your bouts more violent to that end—
And that he calls for drink, I'll have prepared him   160
A chalice for the nonce, whereon but sipping,
If he by chance escape your venomed stuck,[2]
Our purpose may hold there.—But stay, what noise?
   [*Enter* QUEEN.]

QUEEN: One woe doth tread upon another's heel,
   So fast they follow. Your sister's drowned, Laertes.   165

LAERTES: Drowned? O, where?

QUEEN: There is a willow grows aslant the brook
   That shows his hoar leaves in the glassy stream.
   Therewith fantastic garlands did she make
   Of crowflowers, nettles, daisies, and long purples   170
   That liberal shepherds give a grosser[3] name,
   But our cold[4] maids do dead men's fingers call them.
   There on the pendent boughs her coronet weeds
   Clamb'ring to hang, an envious[5] sliver broke,
   When down her weedy trophies and herself   175
   Fell in the weeping brook. Her clothes spread wide,
   And mermaid-like awhile they bore her up,
   Which time she chanted snatches of old tunes,
   As one incapable[6] of her own distress,
   Or like a creature native and indued[7]   180
   Unto that element. But long it could not be
   Till that her garments, heavy with their drink,
   Pulled the poor wretch from her melodious lay
   To muddy death.

LAERTES: Alas, then she is drowned?   185

QUEEN: Drowned, drowned.

LAERTES: Too much of water hast thou, poor Ophelia,
   And therefore I forbid my tears; but yet
   It is our trick; nature her custom holds,
   Let shame say what it will. When these[8] are gone,

2. Thrust.
3. Coarser. *Liberal:* vulgar.
4. Chaste.
5. Malicious.

6. Unaware.
7. Habituated.
8. His tears.

The woman will be out. Adieu, my lord.   190
I have a speech o' fire that fain would blaze
But that this folly drowns it.   [*Exit.*]
KING: Let's follow, Gertrude.
How much I had to do to calm his rage!
Now fear I this will give it start again;
Therefore let's follow.   [*Exeunt.*]   195

ACT V
SCENE 1

A churchyard. Enter two CLOWNS.[9]

CLOWN: Is she to be buried in Christian burial when she
wilfully seeks her own salvation?

OTHER: I tell thee she is. Therefore make her grave straight.
The crowner hath sat on her,[1] and finds it Christian
burial.   5

CLOWN: How can that be, unless she drowned herself in her
own defence?

OTHER: Why, 'tis found so.

CLOWN: It must be "se offendendo";[2] it cannot be else. For
here lies the point: if I drown myself wittingly, it argues an   10
act, and an act hath three branches— it is to act, to do, to
perform; argal,[3] she drowned herself wittingly.

OTHER: Nay, but hear you, Goodman Delver.

CLOWN: Give me leave. Here lies the water; good. Here stands
the man; good. If the man go to this water and drown   15
himself, it is, will he, nill he, he goes—mark you that. But
if the water come to him and drown him, he drowns not
himself. Argal, he that is not guilty of his own death short-
ens not his own life.

OTHER: But is this law?   20

CLOWN: Ay, marry, is't; crowner's quest law.

---

9. Rustics.   2. An error for *se defendendo*, "in self-defense."
1. Coroner held an inquest (below, "quest").   3. An error for *ergo*.

OTHER: Will you ha' the truth on't? If this had not been a gentlewoman, she should have been buried out o' Christian burial.

CLOWN: Why, there thou say'st. And the more pity that   25
great folk should have count'nance in this world to drown or hang themselves more than their even-Christen.[4] Come, my spade. There is no ancient gentlemen but gard'ners, ditchers, and grave-makers. They hold up Adam's profession.   30

OTHER: Was he a gentleman?

CLOWN: 'A was the first that ever bore arms.

OTHER: Why, he had none.

CLOWN: What, art a heathen? How dost thou understand the Scripture? The Scripture says Adam digged. Could he dig   35
without arms? I'll put another question to thee. If thou answerest me not to the purpose, confess thyself—

OTHER: Go to.

CLOWN: What is he that builds stronger than either the mason, the shipwright, or the carpenter?   40

OTHER: The gallows-maker, for that frame outlives a thousand tenants.

CLOWN: I like thy wit well, in good faith. The gallows does well. But how does it well? It does well to those that do ill. Now thou dost ill to say the gallows is built stronger than   45
the church. Argal, the gallows may do well to thee. To't again,[5] come.

OTHER: Who builds stronger than a mason, a shipwright, or a carpenter?

CLOWN: Ay tell me that, and unyoke.[6]   50

OTHER: Marry, now I can tell.

CLOWN: To't.

OTHER: Mass, I cannot tell.

CLOWN: Cudgel thy brains no more about it, for your dull ass will not mend his pace with beating. And when you are   55
asked this question next, say "a grave maker." The houses

---

4. Fellow Christians. *Count'nance*: approval.   6. Finish the matter.
5. Guess again.

he makes lasts till doomsday. Go, get thee in, and fetch me a stoup[7] of liquor.   [*Exit* OTHER CLOWN.]
   [*Enter* HAMLET *and* HORATIO *as* CLOWN *digs and sings.*]
   In youth, when I did love, did love,
      Methought it was very sweet,   60
   To contract the time for-a my behove,[8]
      O, methought there-a was nothing-a meet.

HAMLET: Has this fellow no feeling of his business, that 'a sings in grave-making?

HORATIO: Custom hath made it in him a property of easiness.   65

HAMLET: 'Tis e'en so. The band of little employment hath the daintier sense.

CLOWN: [*Sings.*]
   But age, with his stealing steps,
      Hath clawed me in his clutch,
   And hath shipped me into the land,   70
      As if I had never been such. [*Throws up a skull.*]

HAMLET: That skull had a tongue in it, and could sing once. How the knave jowls[9] it to the ground, as if 'twere Cain's jawbone, that did the first murder! This might be the pate of a politician, which this ass now o'erreaches;[1] one that   75 would circumvent God, might it not?

HORATIO: It might, my lord.

HAMLET: Or of a courtier, which could say, "Good morrow, sweet lord! How does thou, sweet lord?" This might be my Lord Such-a-one, that praised my Lord Such-a-one's horse,   80 when 'a meant to beg it, might it not?

HORATIO: Ay, my lord.

HAMLET: Why, e'en so, and now my Lady Worm's, chapless, and knock'd about the mazzard[2] with a sexton's spade. Here's fine revolution, an[3] we had the trick to see't. Did   85 these bones cost no more the breeding but to play at loggets[4] with them? Mine ache to think on't.

---

7. Mug.
8. Advantage. *Contract:* shorten.
9. Hurls.
1. Gets the better of.

2. Head. *Chapless:* lacking a lower jaw.
3. Reversal of fortune, if.
4. Small pieces of wood thrown as part of a game.

CLOWN: [*Sings.*]
> A pick-axe and a spade, a spade,
>> For and a shrouding sheet:
> O, a pit of clay for to be made   90
>> For such a guest is meet. [*Throws up another skull.*]

HAMLET: There's another. Why may not that be the skull of a lawyer? Where be his quiddities now, his quillets, his cases, his tenures, and his tricks?[5] Why does he suffer this mad knave now to knock him about the sconce[6] with a   95 dirty shovel, and will not tell him of his action of battery? Hum! This fellow might be in's time a great buyer of land, with his statutes, his recognizances, his fines, his double vouchers, his recoveries. Is this the fine[7] of his fines, and the recovery of his recoveries, to have his fine pate full of   100 fine dirt? Will his vouchers vouch him no more of his purchases, and double ones too, than the length and breadth of a pair of indentures?[8] The very conveyances of his lands will scarcely lie in this box, and must th' inheritor himself have no more, ha?   105

HORATIO: Not a jot more, my lord.

HAMLET: Is not parchment made of sheepskins?

HORATIO: Ay, my lord, and of calves' skins too.

HAMLET: They are sheep and calves which seek out assurance in that. I will speak to this fellow. Whose grave's this,   110 sirrah?

CLOWN: Mine, sir. [*Sings.*]
> O, a pit of clay for to be made
>> For such a guest is meet.

HAMLET: I think it be thine indeed, for thou liest in't.   115

CLOWN: You lie out on't, sir, and therefore 'tis not yours. For my part, I do not lie in't, yet it is mine.

HAMLET: Thou dost lie in't, to be in't and say it is thine. 'Tis for the dead, not for the quick;[9] therefore thou liest.

CLOWN: 'Tis a quick lie, sir; 'twill away again from me to you.   120

HAMLET: What man dost thou dig it for?

---

5. In this speech Hamlet lists legal terms relating to property transactions.
6. Head.
7. End.
8. Contracts.
9. Living.

CLOWN: For no man, sir.

HAMLET: What woman, then?

CLOWN: For none neither.

HAMLET: Who is to be buried in't? 125

CLOWN: One that was a woman, sir; but, rest her soul, she's dead.

HAMLET: How absolute[1] the knave is! We must speak by the card,[2] or equivocation will undo us. By the Lord, Horatio, this three years I have took note of it, the age is grown so 130 picked that the toe of the peasant comes so near the heel of the courtier, he galls his kibe.[3] How long hast thou been a grave-maker?

CLOWN: Of all the days i' th' year, I came to't that day that our last King Hamlet overcame Fortinbras. 135

HAMLET: How long is that since?

CLOWN: Cannot you tell that? Every fool can tell that. It was that very day that young Hamlet was born—he that is mad, and sent into England.

HAMLET: Ay, marry, why was he sent into England? 140

CLOWN: Why, because 'a was mad. 'A shall recover his wits there; or, if 'a do not, 'tis no great matter there.

HAMLET: Why?

CLOWN: 'Twill not be seen in him there. There the men are as mad as he. 145

HAMLET: How came he mad?

CLOWN: Very strangely, they say.

HAMLET: How strangely?

CLOWN: Faith, e'en with losing his wits.

HAMLET: Upon what ground? 150

CLOWN: Why, here in Denmark. I have been sexton here, man and boy, thirty years.

HAMLET: How long will a man lie i' th' earth ere he rot?

CLOWN: Faith, if 'a be not rotten before 'a die—as we have many pocky[4] corses now-a-days that will scarce hold the 155

---

1. Literal.
2. Exactly.

3. Rubs a blister on his heel. *Picked:* refined.
4. Riddled with pox (syphilis).

laying in—'a will last you some eight year or nine year. A tanner will last you nine year.

HAMLET: Why he more than another?

CLOWN: Why, sir, his hide is so tanned with his trade that 'a will keep out water a great while; and your water is a sore decayer of your whoreson[5] dead body. Here's a skull now hath lien[6] you i' th' earth three and twenty years. 160

HAMLET: Whose was it?

CLOWN: A whoreson mad fellow's it was. Whose do you think it was? 165

HAMLET: Nay, I know not.

CLOWN: A pestilence on him for a mad rogue! 'A poured a flagon of Rhenish on my head once. This same skull, sir, was, sir, Yorick's skull, the king's jester.

HAMLET: [*Takes the skull.*] This? 170

CLOWN: E'en that.

HAMLET: Alas, poor Yorick! I knew him, Horatio—a fellow of infinite jest, of most excellent fancy. He hath bore me on his back a thousand times, and now how abhorred in my imagination it is! My gorge[7] rises at it. Here hung those lips 175 that I have kissed I know not how oft. Where be your gibes now, your gambols, your songs, your flashes of merriment that were wont to set the table on a roar? Not one now to mock your own grinning? Quite chap-fall'n?[8] Now get you to my lady's chamber, and tell her, let her paint an inch 180 thick, to this favor[9] she must come. Make her laugh at that. Prithee, Horatio, tell me one thing.

HORATIO: What's that, my lord?

HAMLET: Dost thou think Alexander looked o' this fashion i' th' earth? 185

HORATIO: E'en so.

HAMLET: And smelt so? Pah! [*Throws down the skull.*]

HORATIO: E'en so, my lord.

HAMLET: To what base uses we may return, Horatio! Why may not imagination trace the noble dust of Alexander till 190 'a find it stopping a bung-hole?

5. Bastard (figuratively).
6. Lain.
7. Throat.

8. Lacking a lower jaw.
9. Appearance.

HORATIO: 'Twere to consider too curiously[1] to consider so.

HAMLET: No, faith, not a jot, but to follow him thither with
modesty[2] enough, and likelihood to lead it. Alexander
died, Alexander was buried, Alexander returneth to dust;   195
the dust is earth; of earth we make loam; and why of that
loam whereto he was converted might they not stop a beer-
barrel?

    Imperious Cæsar, dead and turned to clay,
    Might stop a hole to keep the wind away.   200
    O, that that earth which kept the world in awe
    Should patch a wall t'expel the winter's flaw![3]
But soft, but soft awhile! Here comes the king,
The queen, the courtiers.
    [*Enter* KING, QUEEN, LAERTES, *and the Corpse with a*
    PRIEST *and* LORDS *attendant.*]
                    Who is this they follow?
And with such maiméd[4] rites? This doth betoken   205
The corse they follow did with desperate hand
Fordo its own life. 'Twas of some estate.[5]
Couch we[6] awhile and mark. [*Retires with* HORATIO.]

LAERTES: What ceremony else?[7]

HAMLET: That is Laertes, a very noble youth. Mark.   210

LAERTES: What ceremony else?

PRIEST: Her obsequies have been as far enlarged[8]
    As we have warranty. Her death was doubtful,
    And but that great command o'ersways the order,[9]
    She should in ground unsanctified been lodged   215
    Till the last trumpet. For charitable prayers,
    Shards, flints, and pebbles, should be thrown on her.
    Yet here she is allowed her virgin crants,[1]
    Her maiden strewments,[2] and the bringing home
    Of bell and burial.   220

LAERTES: Must there no more be done?

---

1. Precisely.
2. Moderation.
3. Gusty wind.
4. Abbreviated.
5. Rank. *Fordo:* destroy.
6. Conceal ourselves.

7. More.
8. Extended.
9. Usual rules.
1. Wreaths.
2. Flowers strewn on the grave.

PRIEST: No more be done.
  We should profane the service of the dead
  To sing a requiem and such rest to her
  As to peace-parted souls.
LAERTES: Lay her i' th' earth,
  And from her fair and unpolluted flesh   225
  May violets spring! I tell thee, churlish priest,
  A minist'ring angel shall my sister be
  When thou liest howling.[3]
HAMLET: What, the fair Ophelia!
QUEEN: Sweets to the sweet. Farewell! [*Scatters flowers.*]
  I hoped thou shouldst have been my Hamlet's wife.   230
  I thought thy bride-bed to have decked, sweet maid,
  And not t' have strewed thy grave.
LAERTES: O, treble woe
  Fall ten times treble on that cursèd head
  Whose wicked deed thy most ingenious sense[4]
  Deprived thee of! Hold off the earth awhile,   235
  Till I have caught her once more in mine arms. [*Leaps into
    the grave.*]
  Now pile your dust upon the quick and dead,
  Till of this flat a mountain you have made
  T' o'er-top old Pelion or the skyish head
  Of blue Olympus.[5]   240
HAMLET: [*Coming forward.*] What is he whose grief
  Bears such an emphasis, whose phrase of sorrow
  Conjures[6] the wand'ring stars, and makes them stand
  Like wonder-wounded hearers? This is I,
  Hamlet the Dane. [HAMLET *leaps into the grave and they*   245
    grapple.]
LAERTES: The devil take thy soul!
HAMLET: Thou pray'st not well.
  I prithee take thy fingers from my throat,
  For though I am not splenitive[7] and rash,
  Yet have I in me something dangerous,

3. In Hell.   6. Casts a spell on.
4. Lively mind.   7. Hot-tempered.
5. Like Pelion, mountain in Greece.

Which let thy wisdom fear. Hold off thy hand. 250
KING: Pluck them asunder.
QUEEN: Hamlet! Hamlet!
ALL: Gentlemen!
HORATIO: Good my lord, be quiet.
    [*The* ATTENDANTS *part them, and they come out of the grave.*]
HAMLET: Why, I will fight with him upon this theme 255
    Until my eyelids will no longer wag.[8]
QUEEN: O my son, what theme?
HAMLET: I loved Ophelia. Forty thousand brothers
    Could not with all their quantity of love
    Make up my sum. What wilt thou do for her? 260
KING: O, he is mad, Laertes.
QUEEN: For love of God, forbear[9] him.
HAMLET: 'Swounds, show me what th'owt do.
    Woo't[1] weep, woo't fight, woo't fast, woo't tear thyself,
    Woo't drink up eisel,[2] eat a crocodile? 265
    I'll do't. Dost come here to whine?
    To outface[3] me with leaping in her grave?
    Be buried quick with her, and so will I.
    And if thou prate of mountains, let them throw
    Millions of acres on us, till our ground, 270
    Singeing his pate against the burning zone,[4]
    Make Ossa[5] like a wart! Nay, an thou'lt mouth,
    I'll rant as well as thou.
QUEEN   This is mere madness;
    And thus awhile the fit will work on him.
    Anon, as patient as the female dove 275
    When that her golden couplets[6] are disclosed,
    His silence will sit drooping.
HAMLET: Hear you, sir.
    What is the reason that you use me thus?
    I loved you ever. But it is no matter. 280
    Let Hercules himself do what he may,

8. Move.
9. Bear with.
1. Will you.
2. Vinegar.

3. Get the best of.
4. Sky in the torrid zone.
5. Mountain in Greece.
6. Pair of eggs.

The cat will mew, and dog will have his day.   [*Exit.*]
KING: I pray thee, good Horatio, wait upon⁷ him.

                                                [*Exit* HORATIO.]

[*To* LAERTES.] Strengthen your patience in our last night's
    speech.
We'll put the matter to the present push.⁸—
Good Gertrude, set some watch over your son.—   285
This grave shall have a living monument.
An hour of quiet shortly shall we see;
Till then in patience our proceeding be.   [*Exeunt.*]

SCENE 2
A hall or public room. Enter HAMLET *and* HORATIO.

HAMLET: So much for this, sir; now shall you see the other.
    You do remember all the circumstance?
HORATIO: Remember it, my lord!
HAMLET: Sir, in my heart there was a kind of fighting
    That would not let me sleep. Methought I lay   5
    Worse than the mutines in the bilboes.⁹ Rashly,
    And praised be rashness for it—let us know,
    Our indiscretion sometime serves us well,
    When our deep plots do pall; and that should learn¹ us
    There's a divinity that shapes our ends,   10
    Rough-hew them how we will—
HORATIO: That is most certain.
HAMLET: Up from my cabin,
    My sea-gown scarfed² about me, in the dark
    Groped I to find out them,³ had my desire,
    Fingered their packet, and in fine⁴ withdrew   15
    To mine own room again, making so bold,
    My fears forgetting manners, to unseal
    Their grand commission; where I found, Horatio—
    Ah, royal knavery!—an exact command,

7. Attend.
8. Immediate trial.
9. Mutineers in the stocks.
1. Teach. *Pall:* weaken and die.

2. Wrapped.
3. That is, Rosencrantz and Guildenstern.
4. Quickly. *Fingered:* stole.

Larded[5] with many several sorts of reasons,   20
Importing Denmark's health, and England's too,
With, ho! such bugs and goblins in my life,[6]
That on the supervise, no leisure bated,[7]
No, not to stay the grinding of the axe,
My head should be struck off.

HORATIO: Is't possible?   25

HAMLET: Here's the commission; read it at more leisure.
But wilt thou hear now how I did proceed?

HORATIO: I beseech you.

HAMLET: Being thus benetted round with villainies,
Ere I could make a prologue to my brains,   30
They had begun the play. I sat me down,
Devised a new commission, wrote it fair.[8]
I once did hold it, as our statists[9] do,
A baseness to write fair, and labored much
How to forget that learning; but sir, now   35
It did me yeoman's service. Wilt thou know
Th' effect[1] of what I wrote?

HORATIO: Ay, good my lord.

HAMLET: An earnest conjuration[2] from the king,
As England was his faithful tributary,
As love between them like the palm might flourish,   40
As peace should still her wheaten garland wear
And stand a comma 'tween their amities[3]
And many such like as's of great charge,[4]
That on the view and knowing of these contents,
Without debatement further more or less,   45
He should those bearers put to sudden death,
Not shriving-time allowed.[5]

HORATIO: How was this sealed?

HAMLET: Why, even in that was heaven ordinant,[6]

5. Garnished.
6. Such dangers if I remained alive.
7. As soon as the commission was read, no pause allowed.
8. Legibly. *Devised:* made.
9. Politicians.
1. Contents.

2. Appeal.
3. And link their friendships.
4. Important clauses beginning with "as"; also, asses bearing heavy burdens.
5. Without time for confession.
6. Operative.

I had my father's signet in my purse,
Which was the model of that Danish seal,   50
Folded the writ up in the form of th' other,
Subscribed it, gave't th' impression,[7] placed it safely,
The changeling[8] never known. Now, the next day
Was our sea-fight, and what to this was sequent[9]
Thou knowest already.   55

HORATIO: So Guildenstern and Rosencrantz go to't.

HAMLET: Why, man, they did make love to this employment.
They are not near my conscience; their defeat[1]
Does by their own insinuation grow.
'Tis dangerous when the baser nature comes   60
Between the pass and fell incensèd points[2]
Of mighty opposites.

HORATIO: Why, what a king is this!

HAMLET: Does it not, think thee, stand me now upon—
He that hath killed my king and whored my mother,
Popped in between th' election and my hopes,[3]   65
Thrown out his angle[4] for my proper life,
And with such coz'nage[5]—is't not perfect conscience
To quit[6] him with this arm? And is't not to be damned
To let this canker of our nature come
In further evil?   70

HORATIO: It must be shortly known to him from England
What is the issue of the business there.

HAMLET: It will be short; the interim is mine.
And a man's life's no more than to say "one."
But I am very sorry, good Horatio,   75
That to Laertes I forgot myself;
For by the image of my cause I see
The portraiture of his. I'll court his favors.
But sure the bravery[7] of his grief did put me

---

7. Of the seal.
8. Alteration.
9. Followed.
1. Death. *Are not near:* do not touch.
2. That is, amidst dangerous swordplay.
3. Between the selection of the next king and

Hamlet's desire for the throne.
4. Fishhook.
5. Trickery.
6. Repay.
7. Exaggerated display.

Into a tow'ring passion.

HORATIO: Peace; who comes here?   80

   [*Enter* OSRIC.]

OSRIC: Your lordship is right welcome back to Denmark.

HAMLET: I humbly thank you, sir. [*Aside to* HORATIO.] Dost
  know this water-fly?

HORATIO: [*Aside to* HAMLET.] No, my good lord.

HAMLET: [*Aside to* HORATIO.] Thy state is the more gracious,   85
  for 'tis a vice to know him. He hath much land, and fertile.
  Let a beast be lord of beasts, and his crib shall stand at the
  king's mess. 'Tis a chough,⁸ but as I say, spacious in the
  possession of dirt.

OSRIC: Sweet lord, if your lordship were at leisure, I should   90
  impart a thing to you from his majesty.

HAMLET: I will receive it, sir, with all diligence of spirit. Put
  your bonnet to his right use. 'Tis for the head.

OSRIC: I thank your lordship, it is very hot.

HAMLET: No, believe me, 'tis very cold; the wind is northerly.   95

OSRIC: It is indifferent⁹ cold, my lord, indeed.

HAMLET: But yet methinks it is very sultry and hot for my
  complexion.¹

OSRIC: Exceedingly, my lord; it is very sultry, as 'twere—I cannot tell how. My lord, his majesty bade me signify to you   100
  that 'a has laid a great wager on your head. Sir, this is the
  matter—

HAMLET: I beseech you, remember. [*Moves him to put on his
  hat.*]

OSRIC: Nay, good my lord; for my ease, in good faith. Sir,
  here is newly come to court Laertes; believe me, an abso-   105
  lute gentleman, full of most excellent differences, of very
  soft society and great showing.² Indeed, to speak feelingly
  of him, he is the card or calendar of gentry, for you shall
  find in him the continent³ of what part a gentleman would
  see.   110

---

8. Jackdaw, a bird.   2. Good manners. *Differences:* qualities.
9. Moderately.   3. Sum total. *Calendar:* measure.
1. Temperament.

HAMLET: Sir, his definement suffers no perdition in you, though I know to divide him inventorially would dozy[4] th' arithmetic of memory, and yet but yaw[5] neither in respect of his quick sail. But in the verity of extolment, I take him to be a soul of great article, and his infusion[6] of such dearth and rareness as, to make true diction of him, his semblage[7] is his mirror, and who else would trace him, his umbrage,[8] nothing more.

OSRIC: Your lordship speaks most infallibly of him.

HAMLET: The concernancy,[9] sir? Why do we wrap the gentleman in our more rawer breath?[1]

OSRIC: Sir?

HORATIO: Is't not possible to understand in another tongue? You will to't, sir, really.

HAMLET: What imports the nomination[2] of this gentleman?

OSRIC: Of Laertes?

HORATIO: [*Aside.*] His purse is empty already. All's golden words are spent.

HAMLET: Of him, sir.

OSRIC: I know you are not ignorant—

HAMLET: I would you did, sir; yet, in faith, if you did, it would not much approve me. Well, sir.

OSRIC: You are not ignorant of what excellence Laertes is—

HAMLET: I dare not confess that, lest I should compare[3] with him in excellence; but to know a man well were to know himself.

OSRIC: I mean, sir, for his weapon; but in the imputation laid on him by them, in his meed he's unfellowed.[4]

HAMLET: What's his weapon?

OSRIC: Rapier and dagger.

HAMLET: That's two of his weapons—but well.

---

4. To examine him bit by bit would daze. *Definement:* description.

5. Steer wildly.

6. Great scope, and his nature.

7. To speak truly about him, his likeness.

8. Would keep pace with him, his shadow.

9. Meaning.

1. Cruder words.

2. Naming.

3. I.e., compare myself.

4. Unequaled in his excellence. *Imputation:* reputation.

OSRIC: The king, sir, hath wagered with him six Barbary horses, against the which he has impawned, as I take it, six French rapiers and poniards, with their assigns, as girdle, hangers,[5] and so. Three of the carriages, in faith, are very dear to fancy, very responsive to the hilts, most delicate carriages, and of very liberal conceit.[6]

HAMLET: What call you the carriages?

HORATIO: [*Aside to* HAMLET.] I knew you must be edified by the margent[7] ere you had done.

OSRIC: The carriages, sir, are the hangers.

HAMLET: The phrase would be more germane to the matter if we could carry a cannon by our sides. I would it might be hangers till then. But on! Six Barbary horses against six French swords, their assigns, and three liberal conceited carriages; that's the French bet against the Danish. Why is this all impawned, as you call it?

OSRIC: The king, sir, hath laid, sir, that in a dozen passes between yourself and him he shall not exceed you three hits; he hath laid on twelve for nine, and it would come to immediate trial if your lordship would vouchsafe the answer.

HAMLET: How if I answer no?

OSRIC: I mean, my lord, the opposition of your person in trial.[8]

HAMLET: Sir, I will walk here in the hall. If it please his majesty, it is the breathing time[9] of day with me. Let the foils be brought, the gentleman willing, and the king hold his purpose; I will win for him an I can. If not, I will gain nothing but my shame and the odd hits.

OSRIC: Shall I deliver you so?

HAMLET: To this effect, sir, after what flourish your nature will.

OSRIC: I commend my duty to your lordship.

HAMLET: Yours, yours. [*Exit* OSRIC.] He does well to commend it himself; there are no tongues else for's turn.

---

5. Belts from which swords hang. *Impawned:* staked. *Assigns:* accessories.

6. Intricately decorated. *Fancy:* finely designed. *Delicate:* well adjusted.

7. Marginal gloss.

8. Your participation in the contest.

9. Time for exercise.

HORATIO: This lapwing runs away with the shell on his head.[1]   175

HAMLET: 'A did comply, sir, with his dug[2] before 'a sucked it. Thus has he, and many more of the same bevy that I know the drossy age dotes on, only got the tune of the time; and out of an habit of encounter, a king of yesty[3] collection which carries them through and through the most fanned   180 and winnowed opinions; and do but blow them to their trial, the bubbles are out.

[*Enter a* LORD.]

LORD: My lord, his majesty commended him to you by young Osric, who brings back to him that you attend him in the hall. He sends to know if your pleasure hold to play with   185 Laertes, or that you will take longer time.

HAMLET: I am constant to my purposes; they follow the king's pleasure. If his fitness speaks, mine is ready; now or whensoever, provided I be so able as now.

LORD: The king and queen and all are coming down.   190

HAMLET: In happy time.

LORD: The queen desires you to use some gentle entertainment[4] to Laertes before you fall to play.

HAMLET: She well instructs me.   [*Exit* LORD.]

HORATIO: You will lose this wager, my lord.   195

HAMLET: I do not think so. Since he went into France I have been in continual practice. I shall win at the odds. But thou wouldst not think how ill[5] all's here about my heart. But it's no matter.

HORATIO: Nay, good my lord—   200

HAMLET: It is but foolery, but it is such a kind of gaingiving[6] as would perhaps trouble a woman.

HORATIO: If your mind dislike anything, obey it. I will forestall their repair[7] hither, and say you are not fit.

HAMLET: Not a whit, we defy augury. There is special provi-   205 dence in the fall of a sparrow. If it be now, 'tis not to come;

---

1. The lapwing was thought to be so precocious that it could run immediately after being hatched, even, as here, with bits of the shell still on its head.

2. Deal formally . . . with his mother's breast.

3. Yeasty.

4. Cordiality.

5. Uneasy.

6. Misgiving.

7. Coming.

if it be not to come, it will be now; if it be not now, yet it
will come. The readiness is all. Since no man of aught he
leaves knows, what is't to leave betimes? Let be.

[*A table prepared. Enter* TRUMPETS, DRUMS, *and* OFFICERS
with cushions; KING, QUEEN, OSRIC *and* ATTENDANTS *with
foils, daggers, and* LAERTES.]

KING: Come, Hamlet, come and take this hand from me. [*The*   210
KING *puts* LAERTES' *hand into* HAMLET'S.]

HAMLET: Give me your pardon, sir. I have done you wrong,
But pardon 't as you are a gentleman.
This presence[8] knows, and you must needs have heard,
How I am punished with a sore distraction.
What I have done   215
That might your nature, honor, and exception[9]
Roughly awake, I here proclaim was madness.
Was't Hamlet wronged Laertes? Never Hamlet.
If Hamlet from himself be ta'en away,
And when he's not himself does wrong Laertes,   220
Then Hamlet does it not, Hamlet denies it.
Who does it then? His madness. If't be so,
Hamlet is of the faction that is wronged;
His madness is poor Hamlet's enemy.
Sir, in this audience,   225
Let my disclaiming from[1] a purposed evil
Free[2] me so far in your most generous thoughts
That I have shot my arrow o'er the house
And hurt my brother.

LAERTES: I am satisfied in nature,
Whose motive in this case should stir me most   230
To my revenge. But in my terms of honor
I stand aloof, and will no reconcilement
Till by some elder masters of known honor
I have a voice[3] and precedent of peace.
To keep my name ungored.[4] But till that time   235

___

8. Company.
9. Resentment.
1. Denying of.

2. Absolve.
3. Authority.
4. Unshamed.

I do receive your offered love like love,
And will not wrong it.

HAMLET: I embrace it freely,
And will this brother's wager frankly[5] play.
Give us the foils. Come on.

LAERTES: Come, one for me.

HAMLET: I'll be your foil, Laertes. In mine ignorance   240
Your skill shall, like a star i' th' darkest night,
Stick fiery off[6] indeed.

LAERTES: You mock me, sir.

HAMLET: No, by this hand.

KING: Give them the foils, young Osric. Cousin Hamlet,
You know the wager?

HAMLET: Very well, my lord;   245
Your Grace has laid the odds o' th' weaker side.

KING: I do not fear it, I have seen you both;
But since he is bettered[7] we have therefore odds.

LAERTES: This is too heavy; let me see another.

HAMLET: This likes me well. These foils have all a[8] length?   250
   [*They prepare to play.*]

OSRIC: Ay, my good lord.

KING: Set me the stoups of wine upon that table.
If Hamlet give the first or second hit,
Or quit in answer of[9] the third exchange,
Let all the battlements their ordnance fire.   255
The king shall drink to Hamlet's better breath,
And in the cup an union[1] shall he throw,
Richer than that which four successive kings
In Denmark's crown have worn. Give me the cups,
And let the kettle[2] to the trumpet speak,   260
The trumpet to the cannoneer without,
The cannons to the heavens, the heaven to earth,
"Now the king drinks to Hamlet." Come, begin—
   [*Trumpets the while.*]

---

5. Without rancor.   9. Or repay.
6. Shine brightly.   1. Pearl.
7. Reported better.   2. Kettledrum.
8. The same. *Likes:* suits.

And you, the judges, bear a wary eye.

HAMLET: Come on, sir.

LAERTES: Come, my lord.

    [*They play.*]

HAMLET: One.

LAERTES: No.

HAMLET: Judgment?   265

OSRIC: A hit, a very palpable hit.

    [*Drums, trumpets, and shot. Flourish; a piece goes off.*]

LAERTES: Well, again.

KING: Stay, give me drink. Hamlet, this pearl is thine.

    Here's to thy health. Give him the cup.

HAMLET: I'll play this bout first; set it by awhile.   270

    Come.

      [*They play.*]

    Another hit; what say you?

LAERTES: A touch, a touch, I do confess't.

KING: Our son shall win.

QUEEN: He's fat,[3] and scant of breath.

    Here, Hamlet, take my napkin, rub thy brows.   275

    The queen carouses to thy fortune, Hamlet.

HAMLET: Good madam!

KING: Gertrude, do not drink.

QUEEN: I will, my lord; I pray you pardon me.

KING: [*Aside.*] It is the poisoned cup; it is too late.   280

HAMLET: I dare not drink yet, madam; by and by.

QUEEN: Come, let me wipe thy face.

LAERTES: My lord, I'll hit him now.

KING: I do not think't.

LAERTES: [*Aside.*] And yet it is almost against my conscience.

HAMLET: Come, for the third, Laertes. You do but dally.   285

    I pray you pass[4] with your best violence;

    I am afeard you make a wanton of me.[5]

LAERTES: Say you so? Come on.

    [*They play.*]

---

3. Out of shape.   5. Trifle with me.
4. Attack.

OSRIC: Nothing, neither way.

LAERTES: Have at you now!   290

    [LAERTES *wounds* HAMLET: *then, in scuffling, they change*
    rapiers, and HAMLET *wounds* LAERTES.]

KING: Part them. They are incensed.

HAMLET: Nay, come again.

    [*The* QUEEN *falls*.]

OSRIC: Look to the queen there, ho!

HORATIO: They bleed on both sides. How is it, my lord?

OSRIC: How is't, Laertes?   295

LAERTES: Why, as a woodcock to mine own springe,[6] Osric.

    I am justly killed with mine own treachery.

HAMLET: How does the queen?

KING: She swoons to see them bleed.

QUEEN: No, no, the drink, the drink! O my dear Hamlet!

    The drink, the drink! I am poisoned. [*Dies*.]   300

HAMLET: O, villainy! Ho! let the door be locked.

    Treachery! seek it out.

LAERTES: It is here, Hamlet. Hamlet, thou art slain;

    No med'cine in the world can do thee good.

    In thee there is not half an hour's life.   305

    The treacherous instrument is in thy hand,

    Unbated[7] and envenomed. The foul practice

    Hath turned itself on me. Lo, here I lie,

    Never to rise again. Thy mother's poisoned.

    I can no more. The king, the king's to blame.   310

HAMLET: The point envenomed too?

    Then, venom, to thy work. [*Hurts the* KING.]

ALL: Treason! treason!

KING: O, yet defend me, friends. I am but hurt.[8]

HAMLET: Here, thou incestuous, murd'rous, damnéd Dane,   315

    Drink off this potion. Is thy union here?

    Follow my mother.

    [*The* KING *dies*.]

LAERTES: He is justly served.

    It is a poison tempered[9] by himself.

---

6. Snare.   8. Wounded.
7. Unblunted.   9. Mixed.

Exchange forgiveness with me, noble Hamlet.
Mine and my father's death come not upon thee,   320
Nor thine on me! [*Dies.*]
HAMLET: Heaven make thee free of it! I follow thee.
I am dead, Horatio. Wretched queen, adieu!
You that look pale and tremble at this chance,[1]
That are but mutes or audience to this act,   325
Had I but time, as this fell sergeant Death
Is strict in his arrest,[2] O, I could tell you—
But let it be. Horatio, I am dead:
Thou livest; report me and my cause aright
To the unsatisfied.[3]
HORATIO: Never believe it.   330
I am more an antique Roman than a Dane.[4]
Here's yet some liquor left.
HAMLET: As th'art a man,
Give me the cup. Let go. By heaven; I'll ha't.
O God, Horatio, what a wounded name,
Things standing thus unknown, shall live behind me!   335
If thou didst ever hold me in thy heart,
Absent thee from felicity awhile,
And in this harsh world draw thy breath in pain,
To tell my story.
    [*A march afar off.*]
             What warlike noise is this?
OSRIC: Young Fortinbras, with conquest come from Poland,   340
To th' ambassadors of England gives
This warlike volley.
HAMLET: O, I die, Horatio!
The potent poison quite o'er-crows[5] my spirit.
I cannot live to hear the news from England,
But I do prophesy th' election lights   345
On Fortinbras. He has my dying voice.[6]

1. Circumstance.
2. Summons to court.
3. Uninformed.
4. Horatio proposes to kill himself, as an ancient
Roman might in similar circumstances.
5. Overcomes.
6. Support.

So tell him, with th' occurrents,[7] more and less,
Which have solicited[8]—the rest is silence. [*Dies.*]

HORATIO: Now cracks a noble heart. Good night, sweet
  prince,
And flights of angels sing thee to thy rest!
  [*March within.*]   350
Why does the drum come hither?
  [*Enter* FORTINBRAS, *with the* AMBASSADORS *and with drum,*
  colors, and ATTENDANTS.]

FORTINBRAS: Where is this sight?

HORATIO: What is it you would see?
If aught of woe or wonder, cease your search.

FORTINBRAS: This quarry cries on havoc.[9] O proud death,
What feast is toward[1] in thine eternal cell   355
That thou so many princes at a shot
So bloodily hast struck?

AMBASSADORS: The sight is dismal;
And our affairs from England come too late.
The ears are senseless[2] that should give us hearing
To tell him his commandment is fulfilled,   360
That Rosencrantz and Guildenstern are dead.
Where should we have our thanks?

HORATIO: Not from his[3] mouth,
Had it th' ability of life to thank you.
He never gave commandment for their death.
But since, so jump[4] upon this bloody question,   365
You from the Polack wars, and you from England,
Are here arrived, give orders that these bodies
High on a stage be placéd to the view,
And let me speak to th' yet unknowing world
How these things came about. So shall you hear   370
Of carnal, bloody, and unnatural acts;
Of accidental judgments, casual[5] slaughters;

---

7. Circumstances.
8. Brought about this scene.
9. The game killed in the hunt proclaims a
slaughter.
  1. In preparation.

2. Without sense of hearing.
3. I.e., Claudius's.
4. Exactly.
5. Brought about by apparent accident.

Of deaths put on by cunning and forced cause;
And, in this upshot,[6] purposes mistook
Fall'n on th' inventors' heads. All this can I   375
Truly deliver.

FORTINBRAS: Let us haste to hear it,
And call the noblest to the audience.[7]
For me, with sorrow I embrace my fortune.
I have some rights of memory[8] in this kingdom,
Which now to claim my vantage[9] doth invite me.   380

HORATIO: Of that I shall have also cause to speak,
And from his mouth whose voice will draw on more.
But let this same be presently performed,
Even while men's minds are wild, lest more mischance
On plots and errors happen.

FORTINBRAS: Let four captains   385
Bear Hamlet like a soldier to the stage,
For he was likely, had he been put on,[1]
To have proved most royal; and for his passage
The soldier's music and the rite of war
Speak loudly for him.   390
Take up the bodies. Such a sight as this
Becomes the field, but here shows much amiss.
Go, bid the soldiers shoot.

           [*Exeunt marching. A peal of ordinance shot off.*]

                                                    c. 1600

---

6. Result.   9. Position.
7. Hearing.   1. Elected king.
8. Succession.

Henrik Ibsen
1828–1906

A DOLL'S HOUSE

Ibsen's early plays, beginning in 1850, were poetic, mythic, and romantic. But in the late 1860s he began writing in plain language about the struggles of ordinary, middle-class people. Theatergoers saw on the stage for the first time people just like themselves, who talked as they did, dealt with the same issues they dealt with, and lived the same kinds of lives. The people in the audience became the subjects of the stories dramatized on stage. These plays are sometimes called "social dramas" because they tend to reveal defects in society and the ways those defects hindered the individual's personal growth. The route to the individual's full and unchained growth became Ibsen's most persistent theme, and A Doll's House *represented the centerpiece of his realistic period.*

The rise of the middle class during this time intensified the subjection of women. Women of all classes exercised no political power in the European democracies until they gained the vote in the twentieth century. They had unequal rights in marriage: a husband owned what today would be joint property, and a wife surrendered property she owned even before marriage to her husband's absolute control. Women had unequal rights to divorce and risked losing their children if they pressed for a separation from even an abusive husband. And mainstream attitudes—often based on scientific mistakes, like the comparison of brain sizes between men and women— took for granted that women were mentally inferior to men.

Such attitudes, coupled with the middle class's fetish for home life, left few roles for women other than wife and mother and domestic ornament. Not until late in the nineteenth century could women attend university, and even then they rarely did so. They were systematically excluded from the professions, like medicine and law. Married middle-class women seldom worked outside their homes, so as not to embarrass their husbands. Unmarried middle-class women had very narrow career choices. Middle-class women generally were trained to perform subservient roles, learning, for example, to converse, to entertain, to play a musical instrument, to sketch (but not to paint with oils), to read French or Italian (but not Latin or Greek, the languages that prepared one for the professions), and so on.

As you might expect, many people, men and women alike, were dissatisfied with these conditions, so the "woman question" became a vital social issue. In 1869, John Stuart Mill's revolutionary book The Subjection of Women, *which argued that society ought to extend equal rights to women, was translated into German. Ibsen read the translation, and though he continued to believe that women were mentally inferior to men, he began to realize that both sexes held the right to individualism. And he recognized that Victorian society's compulsory domestication of women made it especially hard for them to fully realize their potential.*

Ironically, Ibsen did not consider himself a feminist. He saw his plays as chronicling the struggles of the individual—any individual, man or woman, artist or schoolteacher, mythic hero or housewife—against the forces of banality, mediocrity, and philistinism. Nora Helmer's story, in A Doll's House, *is one of these chronicles.*

Nora is based on someone Ibsen knew. In 1869, by then a famous playwright in his forties, he became a mentor to a twenty-year-old writer named Laura Peterson, who lived in Copenhagen. Taken by her personality, Ibsen called her "lark" and "songbird," and their friendship grew even after Peterson married a poor schoolteacher in Denmark. The husband fell ill and was advised to travel south to warmer climates; Peterson secretly borrowed the money for the trip, could not pay off the loan, and resorted to forging a note. She confided in Ibsen, who indignantly advised her to confess to her husband. But when she did confess, her husband, enraged, divorced her. This cruel treatment broke the woman, who ended up in an asylum. Laura Peterson's story—and the poor role he played in it—affected Ibsen deeply.

In the summer of 1878, he sent A Doll's House *to Copenhagen, where it was first produced. An immediate success, the play quickly swept through Scandinavia, Germany, Finland, Poland, Russia, Italy, and England. Audiences were attracted to Nora; some sympathized with her, and others were revolted by her. The play constituted the biggest literary controversy of its generation, inspiring ardent defenders and troubled detractors.*

It also reinvented the theater. Realistic social drama would remain on the European stage for generations. In England, the great playwright George Bernard Shaw considered himself the direct descendant of Ibsen, and Shaw's social dramas dominated

London's theatrical tastes well into the twentieth century. To get a feel for this "realism," you might contrast Ibsen's domestic drama with the plays by Sophocles and Shakespeare, comparing the characters, the scope of the stories, and the uses of language.

A good way to engage yourself in this play is to debate Nora's choice. Did she do the right thing? What else might she have done? Can you envision a marriage like hers today? You shouldn't need much imagination to recognize similar cruxes in contemporary lives—struggles between people's obligations to others, the impulse to conform to middle-class standards of behavior, and individuals' duties to themselves.

A Doll's House*

CHARACTERS

TORVALD HELMER, *a lawyer*

NORA, *his wife*

DR. RANK

MRS. LINDE

NILS KROGSTAD, *a bank clerk*

THE HELMERS' THREE SMALL
    CHILDREN

ANNE-MARIE, *their nurse*

HELENE, *a maid*

A DELIVERY BOY

The action takes place in HELMER'*s residence.*

ACT 1

A comfortable room, tastefully but not expensively furnished. A door to the right in the back wall leads to the entryway; another to the left leads to HELMER'S *study. Between these doors, a piano. Midway in the left-hand wall a door, and farther down a window. Near the window a round table with an armchair and a small sofa. In the right-hand wall, toward the rear, a door, and nearer the foreground a porcelain stove with two armchairs and a rocking chair beside it. Between the stove and the side door, a small table. Engravings on the walls. An* etagère[1] *with china figures and other small art objects; a small bookcase with richly bound books; the floor carpeted; a fire burning in the stove. It is a winter day.*

---

*Translated by Rolf Fjelde.

1. Small piece of furniture with shelves for displaying small articles.

A bell rings in the entryway; shortly after we hear the door being unlocked. NORA *comes into the room, humming happily to herself; she is wearing street clothes and carries an armload of packages, which she puts down on the table to the right. She has left the hall door open; and through it a* DELIVERY BOY *is seen, holding a Christmas tree and a basket, which he gives to the* MAID *who let them in.*

HER 1ST WORD IS "HIDE"

NORA: Hide the tree well, Helene. The children mustn't get a glimpse of it till this evening, after it's trimmed. [*To the* DELIVERY BOY, *taking out her purse.*] How much?

DELIVERY BOY: Fifty, ma'am.

NORA: There's a crown. No, keep the change. [*The* BOY *thanks her and leaves.* NORA *shuts the door. She laughs softly to herself while taking off her street things. Drawing a bag of macaroons from her pocket, she eats a couple, then steals over and listens at her husband's study door.*] Yes, he's home. [*Hums again as she moves to the table right.*]

HELMER: [*From the study.*] Is that my little lark twittering out there?

NORA: [*Busy opening some packages.*] Yes, it is.

HELMER: Is that my squirrel rummaging around?

NORA: Yes!

HELMER: When did my squirrel get in?

NORA: Just now. [*Putting the macaroon bag in her pocket and wiping her mouth.*] Do come in, Torvald, and see what I've bought.

HELMER: Can't be disturbed. [*After a moment he opens the door and peers in, pen in hand.*] Bought, you say? All that there? Has the little spendthrift been out throwing money around again?

NORA: Oh, but Torvald, this year we really should let ourselves go a bit. It's the first Christmas we haven't had to economize.

HELMER: But you know we can't go squandering.

NORA: Oh yes, Torvald, we can squander a little now. Can't we? Just a tiny, wee bit. Now that you've got a big salary and are going to make piles and piles of money.

HELMER: Yes—starting New Year's. But then it's a full three months till the raise comes through.

NORA: Pooh! We can borrow that long.

HELMER: Nora! [*Goes over and playfully takes her by the ear.*] Are your scatterbrains off again? What if today I borrowed a thousand crowns, and you squandered them over Christmas week, and then on New Year's Eve a roof tile fell on my head, and I lay there—

HIDE   BOUGHT   BORROWED)

NORA: [*Putting her hand on his mouth.*] Oh! Don't say such things!

HELMER: Yes, but what if it happened—then what?

NORA: If anything so awful happened, then it just wouldn't matter if I had debts or not.

HELMER: Well, but the people I'd borrowed from?

NORA: Them? Who cares about them! They're strangers.

HELMER: Nora, Nora, how like a woman! No, but seriously, Nora, you know what I think about that. No debts! Never borrow! Something of freedom's lost—and something of beauty, too— from a home that's founded on borrowing and debt. We've made a brave stand up to now, the two of us; and we'll go right on like that the little while we have to.

NORA: [*Going toward the stove.*] Yes, whatever you say, Torvald.

HELMER: [*Following her.*] Now, now, the little lark's wings mustn't droop. Come on, don't be a sulky squirrel. [*Taking out his wallet.*] Nora, guess what I have here.

NORA: [*Turning quickly.*] Money!

HELMER: There, see. [*Hands her some notes.*] Good grief, I know how costs go up in a house at Christmastime.

NORA: Ten—twenty—thirty—forty. Oh, thank you, Torvald; I can manage no end on this.

HELMER: You really will have to.

NORA: Oh yes, I promise I will! But come here so I can show you everything I bought. And so cheap! Look, new clothes for Ivar here—and a sword. Here a horse and a trumpet for Bob. And a doll and a doll's bed here for Emmy; they're nothing much, but she'll tear them to bits in no time anyway. And here I have dress material and handkerchiefs for the maids. Old Anne-Marie really deserves something more.

HELMER: And what's in that package there?

NORA: [*With a cry.*] Torvald, no! You can't see that till tonight!

HELMER: I see. But tell me now, you little prodigal, what have you thought of for yourself?

NORA: For myself? Oh, I don't want anything at all.

HELMER: Of course you do. Tell me just what—within reason— you'd most like to have.

NORA: I honestly don't know. Oh, listen, Torvald—

HELMER: Well?

NORA: [*Fumbling at his coat buttons, without looking at him.*] If you want to give me something, then maybe you could—you could—

HELMER: Come on, out with it.

NORA: [*Hurriedly.*] You could give me money, Torvald. No more than you think you can spare; then one of these days I'll buy something with it.

HELMER: But Nora—

NORA: Oh, please, Torvald darling, do that! I beg you, please. Then I could hang the bills in pretty gilt paper on the Christmas tree. Wouldn't that be fun?

HELMER: What are those little birds called that always fly through their fortunes?

NORA: Oh yes, spendthrifts; I know all that. But let's do as I say, Torvald; then I'll have time to decide what I really need most. That's very sensible, isn't it?

HELMER: [*Smiling.*] Yes, very—that is, if you actually hung onto the money I give you, and you actually used it to buy yourself something. But it goes for the house and for all sorts of foolish things, and then I only have to lay out some more.

NORA: Oh, but Torvald—

HELMER: Don't deny it, my dear little Nora. [*Putting his arm around her waist.*] Spendthrifts are sweet, but they use up a frightful amount of money. It's incredible what it costs a man to feed such birds.

NORA: Oh, how can you say that! Really, I save everything I can.

HELMER: [*Laughing.*] Yes, that's the truth. Everything you can. But that's nothing at all.

NORA: [*Humming, with a smile of quiet satisfaction.*] Hm, if you only knew what expenses we larks and squirrels have, Torvald.

HELMER: You're an odd little one. Exactly the way your father was. You're never at a loss for scaring up money; but the moment you have it, it runs right out through your fingers; you never know what you've done with it. Well, one takes you as you are. It's deep in your blood. Yes, these things are hereditary, Nora. **✳**

NORA: Ah, I could wish I'd inherited many of Papa's qualities.

HELMER: And I couldn't wish you anything but just what you are, my sweet little lark. But wait; it seems to me you have a very— what should I call it?—a very suspicious look today— — VIRTUE —

✗ TORVALD WILL APPLY AN ASSUMPTION OF THE TIME THAT CHARACTER WAS HEREDITARY AS WELL — → BAD CHARACTER COULD BE PASSED DOWN

NORA: I do?

HELMER: You certainly do. Look me straight in the eye.

NORA: [*Looking at him.*] Well?

HELMER: [*Shaking an admonitory finger.*] Surely my sweet tooth hasn't been running riot in town today, has she?

NORA: No. Why do you imagine that?

HELMER: My sweet tooth really didn't make a little detour through the confectioner's?

NORA: No, I assure you, Torvald—

HELMER: Hasn't nibbled some pastry?

NORA: No, not at all.

HELMER: Not even munched a macaroon or two?

NORA: No, Torvald, I assure you, really—

HELMER: There, there now. Of course I'm only joking.

NORA: [*Going to the table, right.*] You know I could never think of going against you.   ⟨ SHE IS EXPOSED AS A FIBBER ⟩

HELMER: No, I understand that; and you *have* given me your word. [*Going over to her.*] Well, you keep your little Christmas secrets to yourself, Nora darling. I expect they'll come to light this evening, when the tree is lit.

NORA: Did you remember to ask Dr. Rank?

HELMER: No. But there's no need for that; it's assumed he'll be dining with us. All the same, I'll ask him when he stops by here this morning. I've ordered some fine wine. Nora, you can't imagine how I'm looking forward to this evening.

NORA: So am I. And what fun for the children, Torvald!

HELMER: Ah, it's so gratifying to know that one's gotten a safe, secure job, and with a comfortable salary. It's a great satisfaction, isn't it?

NORA: Oh, it's wonderful!

HELMER: Remember last Christmas? Three whole weeks before, you shut yourself in every evening till long after midnight, making flowers for the Christmas tree, and all the other decorations to surprise us. Ugh, that was the dullest time I've ever lived through.

NORA: It wasn't at all dull for me.

HELMER: [*Smiling.*] But the outcome *was* pretty sorry, Nora.

NORA: Oh, don't tease me with that again. How could I help it that the cat came in and tore everything to shreds.

HELMER: No, poor thing, you certainly couldn't. You wanted so much to please us all, and that's what counts. But it's just as well that the hard times are past.

NORA: Yes, it's really wonderful.

HELMER: Now I don't have to sit here alone, boring myself, and you don't have to tire your precious eyes and your fair little delicate hands—

NORA: [*Clapping her hands.*] No, is it really true, Torvald, I don't have to? Oh, how wonderfully lovely to hear! [*Taking his arm.*] Now I'll tell you just how I've thought we should plan things. Right after Christmas— [*The doorbell rings.*] Oh, the bell. [*Straightening the room up a bit.*] Somebody would have to come. What a bore!

HELMER: I'm not at home to visitors, don't forget.

MAID: [*From the hall doorway.*] Ma'am, a lady to see you—

NORA: All right, let her come in.

MAID: [*To* HELMER.] And the doctor's just come too.

HELMER: Did he go right to my study?

MAID: Yes, he did.

[HELMER *goes into his room. The* MAID *shows in* MRS. LINDE, *dressed in traveling clothes, and shuts the door after her.*]

MRS. LINDE: [*In a dispirited and somewhat hesitant voice.*] Hello, Nora.

NORA: [*Uncertain.*] Hello—

MRS. LINDE: You don't recognize me.

NORA: No, I don't know—but wait, I think— [*Exclaiming.*] What! Kristine! Is it really you?

MRS. LINDE: Yes, it's me.

NORA: Kristine! To think I didn't recognize you. But then, how could I? [*More quietly.*] How you've changed, Kristine!

MRS. LINDE: Yes, no doubt I have. In nine—ten long years.

NORA: Is it so long since we met! Yes, it's all of that. Oh, these last eight years have been a happy time, believe me. And so now you've come in to town, too. Made the long trip in the winter. That took courage.

MRS. LINDE: I just got here by ship this morning.

NORA: To enjoy yourself over Christmas, of course. Oh, how lovely! Yes, enjoy ourselves, we'll do that. But take your coat off. You're not still cold? [*Helping her.*] There now, let's get cozy here by the stove. No, the easy chair there! I'll take the rocker here. [*Seizing her hands.*] Yes, now you have your old look again; it was only in that first moment. You're a bit more pale, Kristine—and maybe a bit thinner.

MRS. LINDE: And much, much older, Nora.

NORA: Yes, perhaps a bit older; a tiny, tiny bit; not much at all. [*Stopping short; suddenly serious.*] Oh, but thoughtless me, to sit here, chattering away. Sweet, good Kristine, can you forgive me?

MRS. LINDE: What do you mean, Nora?

NORA: [*Softly.*] Poor Kristine, you've become a widow.

MRS. LINDE: Yes, three years ago.

NORA: Oh, I knew it, of course; I read it in the papers. Oh, Kristine, you must believe me; I often thought of writing you then, but I kept postponing it, and something always interfered.

MRS. LINDE: Nora dear, I understand completely.

NORA: No, it was awful of me, Kristine. You poor thing, how much you must have gone through. And he left you nothing?

MRS. LINDE: No.

NORA: And no children?

MRS. LINDE: No.

NORA: Nothing at all, then?

MRS. LINDE: Not even a sense of loss to feed on. *ouch!*

NORA: [*Looking incredulously at her.*] But Kristine, how could that be?

MRS. LINDE: [*Smiling wearily and smoothing her hair.*] Oh, sometimes it happens, Nora.

NORA: So completely alone. How terribly hard that must be for you. I have three lovely children. You can't see them now; they're out with the maid. But now you must tell me everything—

MRS. LINDE: No, no, no, tell me about yourself.

NORA: No, you begin. Today I don't want to be selfish. I want to think only of you today. But there *is* something I must tell you. Did you hear of the wonderful luck we had recently?

MRS. LINDE: No, what's that?

NORA: My husband's been made manager in the bank, just think!

MRS. LINDE: Your husband? How marvelous!

NORA: Isn't it? Being a lawyer is such an uncertain living, you know, especially if one won't touch any cases that aren't clean and decent.

HE'S HIGHLY PRINCIPLED

And of course Torvald would never do that, and I'm with him completely there. Oh, we're simply delighted, believe me! He'll join the bank right after New Year's and start getting a huge salary and lots of commissions. From now on we can live quite differently— just as we want. Oh, Kristine, I feel so light and happy! Won't it be lovely to have stacks of money and not a care in the world?

MRS. LINDE: Well, anyway, it would be lovely to have enough for necessities.

NORA: No, not just for necessities, but stacks and stacks of money!

MRS. LINDE: [*Smiling.*] Nora, Nora, aren't you sensible yet? Back in school you were such a free spender.

NORA: [*With a quiet laugh.*] Yes, that's what Torvald still says. [*Shaking her finger.*] But "Nora, Nora" isn't as silly as you all think. Really, we've been in no position for me to go squandering. We've had to work, both of us.

MRS. LINDE: You too?

NORA: Yes, at odd jobs—needlework, crocheting, embroidery, and such—[*Casually.*] and other things too. You remember that Torvald left the department when we were married? There was no chance of promotion in his office, and of course he needed to earn more money. But that first year he drove himself terribly. He took on all kinds of extra work that kept him going morning and night. It wore him down, and then he fell deathly ill. The doctors said it was essential for him to travel south.

MRS. LINDE: Yes, didn't you spend a whole year in Italy?

NORA: That's right. It wasn't easy to get away, you know. Ivar had just been born. But of course we had to go. Oh, that was a beautiful trip, and it saved Torvald's life. But it cost a frightful sum, Kristine.

MRS. LINDE: I can well imagine.

NORA: Four thousand, eight hundred crowns it cost. That's really a lot of money.

MRS. LINDE: But it's lucky you had it when you needed it.

NORA: Well, as it was, we got it from Papa.

MRS. LINDE: I see. It was just about the time your father died.

NORA: Yes, just about then. And, you know, I couldn't make that trip out to nurse him. I had to stay here, expecting Ivar any moment, and with my poor sick Torvald to care for. Dearest

SOME DETAILS THAT WILL
COME UP LATER

Papa, I never saw him again, Kristine. Oh, that was the worst time I've known in all my marriage.

MRS. LINDE: I know how you loved him. And then you went off to Italy?

NORA: Yes. We had the means now, and the doctors urged us. So we left a month after.

MRS. LINDE: And your husband came back completely cured?

NORA: Sound as a drum!

MRS. LINDE: But—the doctor?

NORA: Who?

MRS. LINDE: I thought the maid said he was a doctor, the man who came in with me.

NORA: Yes, that was Dr. Rank—but he's not making a sick call. He's our closest friend, and he stops by at least once a day. No, Torvald hasn't had a sick moment since, and the children are fit and strong, and I am, too. [*Jumping up and clapping her hands.*] Oh, dear God, Kristine, what a lovely thing to live and be happy! But how disgusting of me—I'm talking of nothing but my own affairs. [*Sits on a stool close by* KRISTINE, *arms resting across her knees.*] Oh, don't be angry with me! Tell me, is it really true that you weren't in love with your husband? Why did you marry him, then?

MRS. LINDE: My mother was still alive, but bedridden and helpless—and I had my two younger brothers to look after. In all conscience, I didn't think I could turn him down.

NORA: No, you were right there. But was he rich at the time?

MRS. LINDE: He was very well off, I'd say. But the business was shaky, Nora. When he died, it all fell apart, and nothing was left.

NORA: And, then—?

MRS. LINDE: Yes, so I had to scrape up a living with a little shop and a little teaching and whatever else I could find. The last three years have been like one endless workday without a rest for me. Now it's over, Nora. My poor mother doesn't need me, for she's passed on. Nor the boys, either; they're working now and can take care of themselves.

NORA: How free you must feel—

MRS. LINDE: No—only unspeakably empty. Nothing to live for now. [*Standing up anxiously.*] That's why I couldn't take it any longer out in that desolate hole. Maybe here it'll be easier to find something to do and keep my mind occupied. If I could only be lucky enough to get a steady job, some office work—

NORA: Oh, but Kristine, that's so dreadfully tiring, and you already look so tired. It would be much better for you if you could go off to a bathing resort.

MRS. LINDE: [*Going toward the window.*] I have no father to give me travel money, Nora.

NORA: [*Rising.*] Oh, don't be angry with me.

MRS. LINDE: [*Going to her.*] Nora dear, don't you be angry with me. The worst of my kind of situation is all the bitterness that's stored away. No one to work for, and yet you're always having to snap up your opportunities. You have to live; and so you grow selfish. When you told me the happy change in your lot, do you know I was delighted less for your sakes than for mine?

NORA: How so? Oh, I see. You think maybe Torvald could do something for you.

MRS. LINDE: Yes, that's what I thought.

NORA: And he will, Kristine! Just leave it to me; I'll bring it up so delicately—find something attractive to humor him with. Oh, I'm so eager to help you.

MRS. LINDE: How very kind of you, Nora, to be so concerned over me—doubly kind, considering you really know so little of life's burdens yourself.

NORA: I—? I know so little—?

MRS. LINDE: [*Smiling.*] Well, my heavens—a little needlework and such—Nora, you're just a child.

NORA: [*Tossing her head and pacing the floor.*] You don't have to act so superior.

MRS. LINDE: Oh?

NORA: You're just like the others. You all think I'm incapable of anything serious—

MRS. LINDE: Come now—

NORA: That I've never had to face the raw world.

MRS. LINDE: Nora dear, you've just been telling me all your troubles.

NORA: Hm! Trivia! [*Quietly.*] I haven't told you the big thing.

MRS. LINDE: Big thing? What do you mean?

NORA: You look down on me so, Kristine, but you shouldn't. You're proud that you worked so long and hard for your mother.

MRS. LINDE: I don't look down on a soul. But it *is* true: I'm proud—and happy, too—to think it was given to me to make my mother's last days almost free of care.

NORA: And you're also proud thinking of what you've done for your brothers.

MRS. LINDE: I feel I've a right to be.

NORA: I agree. But listen to this, Kristine—I've also got something to be proud and happy for.

MRS. LINDE: I don't doubt it. But whatever do you mean?

NORA: Not so loud. What if Torvald heard! He mustn't, not for anything in the world. Nobody must know, Kristine. No one but you.

MRS. LINDE: But what is it, then?

NORA: Come here. [*Drawing her down beside her on the sofa.*] It's true—I've also got something to be proud and happy for. I'm the one who saved Torvald's life.

MRS. LINDE: Saved—? Saved how?

NORA: I told you about the trip to Italy. Torvald never would have lived if he hadn't gone south—

MRS. LINDE: Of course; your father gave you the means—

NORA: [*Smiling.*] That's what Torvald and all the rest think, but—

MRS. LINDE: But—?

NORA: Papa didn't give us a pin. I was the one who raised the money.

MRS. LINDE: You? That whole amount?

NORA: Four thousand, eight hundred crowns. What do you say to that?

MRS. LINDE: But Nora, how was it possible? Did you win the lottery?

NORA: [*Disdainfully.*] The lottery? Pooh! No art to that.

MRS. LINDE: But where did you get it from then?

NORA: [*Humming, with a mysterious smile.*] Hmm, tra-la-la-la.

MRS. LINDE: Because you couldn't have borrowed it.

NORA: No? Why not?

MRS. LINDE: A wife can't borrow without her husband's consent.

NORA: [*Tossing her head.*] Oh, but a wife with a little business sense, a wife who knows how to manage—

MRS. LINDE: Nora, I simply don't understand—

NORA: You don't have to. Whoever said I *borrowed* the money? I could have gotten it other ways. [*Throwing herself back on the sofa.*] I could have gotten it from some admirer or other. After all, a girl with my ravishing appeal—

MRS. LINDE: You lunatic.

NORA: I'll bet you're eaten up with curiosity, Kristine.

MRS. LINDE: Now listen here, Nora—you haven't done something indiscreet?

NORA: [*Sitting up again.*] Is it indiscreet to save your husband's life?

MRS. LINDE: I think it's indiscreet that without his knowledge you—

NORA: But that's the point: he mustn't know! My Lord, can't you understand? He mustn't ever know the close call he had. It was to *me* the doctors came to say his life was in danger—that nothing could save him but a stay in the south. Didn't I try strategy then! I began talking about how lovely it would be for me to travel abroad like other young wives; I begged and I cried; I told him please to remember my condition, to be kind and indulge me; and then I dropped a hint that he could easily take out a loan. But at that, Kristine, he nearly exploded. He said I was frivolous, and it was his duty as man of the house not to indulge me in whims and fancies—as I think he called them. Aha, I thought, now you'll just have to be saved—and that's when I saw my chance.

MRS. LINDE: And your father never told Torvald the money wasn't from him?

NORA: No, never. Papa died right about then. I'd considered bringing him into my secret and begging him never to tell. But he was too sick at the time—and then, sadly, it didn't matter.

MRS. LINDE: And you've never confided in your husband since?

NORA: For heaven's sake, no! Are you serious? He's so strict on that subject. Besides—Torvald, with all his masculine pride—how painfully humiliating for him if he ever found out he was in debt to me. That would just ruin our relationship. Our beautiful, happy home would never be the same.

MRS. LINDE: Won't you ever tell him?

NORA: [*Thoughtfully, half smiling.*] Yes—maybe sometime, years from now, when I'm no longer so attractive. Don't laugh! I only mean when Torvald loves me less than now, when he stops enjoying my dancing and dressing up and reciting for him. Then it might be wise to have something in reserve—[*Breaking off.*]

How ridiculous! That'll never happen—Well, Kristine, what do you think of my big secret? I'm capable of something too, hm? You can imagine, of course, how this thing hangs over me. It really hasn't been easy meeting the payments on time. In the business world there's what they call quarterly interest and what they call amortization, and these are always so terribly hard to manage. I've had to skimp a little here and there, wherever I could, you know. I could hardly spare anything from my house allowance, because Torvald has to live well. I couldn't let the children go poorly dressed; whatever I got for them, I felt I had to use up completely—the darlings!

MRS. LINDE: Poor Nora, so it had to come out of your own budget, then?

NORA: Yes, of course. But I was the one most responsible, too. Every time Torvald gave me money for new clothes and such, I never used more than half; always bought the simplest, cheapest outfits. It was a godsend that everything looks so well on me that Torvald never noticed. But it did weigh me down at times, Kristine. It *is* such a joy to wear fine things. You understand.

MRS. LINDE: Oh, of course.

NORA: And then I found other ways of making money. Last winter I was lucky enough to get a lot of copying to do. I locked myself in and sat writing every evening till late in the night. Ah, I was tired so often, dead tired. But still it was wonderful fun, sitting and working like that, earning money. It was almost like being a man.

MRS. LINDE: But how much have you paid off this way so far?

NORA: That's hard to say, exactly. These accounts, you know, aren't easy to figure. I only know that I've paid out all I could scrape together. Time and again I haven't known where to turn. [*Smiling.*] Then I'd sit here dreaming of a rich old gentleman who had fallen in love with me—

MRS. LINDE: What! Who is he?

NORA: Oh, really! And that he'd died, and when his will was opened, there in big letters it said, "All my fortune shall be paid over in cash, immediately, to that enchanting Mrs. Nora Helmer."

MRS. LINDE: But Nora dear—who *was* this gentleman?

NORA: Good grief, can't you understand? The old man never existed; that was only something I'd dream up time and again whenever I was at my wits' end for money. But it makes no difference now; the old fossil can go where he pleases for all I care; I don't need him or his will—because now I'm free. [*Jumping up.*] Oh, how lovely to think of that, Kristine! Carefree! To know you're carefree, utterly carefree; to be able to romp and play with the children, and to keep up a beautiful, charming home—everything just the way Torvald likes it! And think, spring is coming, with big blue skies. Maybe we can travel a little then. Maybe I'll see the ocean again. Oh yes, it *is* so marvelous to live and be happy!

[*The front doorbell rings.*]

MRS. LINDE: [*Rising.*] There's the bell. It's probably best that I go.

NORA: No, stay. No one's expected. It must be for Torvald.

MAID: [*From the hall doorway.*] Excuse me, ma'am—there's a gentleman here to see Mr. Helmer, but I didn't know—since the doctor's with him—

NORA: Who is the gentleman?

KROGSTAD: [*From the doorway.*] It's me, Mrs. Helmer.

[MRS. LINDE *starts and turns away toward the window.*]

NORA: [*Stepping toward him, tense, her voice a whisper.*] You? What is it? Why do you want to speak to my husband?

KROGSTAD: Bank business—after a fashion. I have a small job in the investment bank, and I hear now your husband is going to be our chief—

NORA: In other words, it's—

KROGSTAD: Just dry business, Mrs. Helmer. Nothing but that.

NORA: Yes, then please be good enough to step into the study. [*She nods indifferently as she sees him out by the hall door, then returns and begins stirring up the stove.*]

MRS. LINDE: Nora—who was that man?

NORA: That was a Mr. Krogstad—a lawyer.

MRS. LINDE: Then it really was him.

NORA: Do you know that person?

MRS. LINDE: I did once—many years ago. For a time he was a law clerk in our town.

NORA: Yes, he's been that.

MRS. LINDE: How he's changed.

NORA: I understand he had a very unhappy marriage.

MRS. LINDE: He's a widower now.

NORA: With a number of children. There now, it's burning. [*She closes the stove door and moves the rocker a bit to one side.*]

MRS. LINDE: They say he has a hand in all kinds of business.

NORA: Oh? That may be true; I wouldn't know. But let's not think about business. It's so dull.

[DR. RANK *enters from* HELMER'S *study.*]

RANK: [*Still in the doorway.*] No, no, really—I don't want to intrude, I'd just as soon talk a little while with your wife. [*Shuts the door, then notices* MRS. LINDE.] Oh, beg pardon. I'm intruding here too.

NORA: No, not at all. [*Introducing him.*] Dr. Rank, Mrs. Linde.

RANK: Well now, that's a name much heard in this house. I believe I passed the lady on the stairs as I came.

MRS. LINDE: Yes, I take the stairs very slowly. They're rather hard on me.

RANK: Uh-hm, some touch of internal weakness?

MRS. LINDE: More overexertion, I'd say.

RANK: Nothing else? Then you're probably here in town to rest up in a round of parties?

MRS. LINDE: I'm here to look for work.

RANK: Is that the best cure for overexertion?

MRS. LINDE: One has to live, Doctor.

RANK: Yes, there's a common prejudice to that effect.

NORA: Oh, come on, Dr. Rank—you really do want to live yourself.

RANK: Yes, I really do. Wretched as I am, I'll gladly prolong my torment indefinitely. All my patients feel like that. And it's quite the same, too, with the morally sick. Right at this moment there's one of those moral invalids in there with Helmer—

MRS. LINDE: [*Softly.*] Ah!

NORA: Who do you mean?

RANK: Oh, it's a lawyer, Krogstad, a type you wouldn't know. His character is rotten to the root—but even he began chattering all-importantly about how he had to *live*.

NORA: Oh? What did he want to talk to Torvald about?

RANK: I really don't know. I only heard something about the bank.

SHE KNOWS HIM —

NORA: I didn't know that Krog—that this man Krogstad had anything to do with the bank.

RANK: Yes, he's gotten some kind of berth down there. [*To*
MRS. LINDE.] I don't know if you also have, in your neck of the
woods, a type of person who scuttles about breathlessly, sniffing
EXTORTS — out hints of moral corruption, and then maneuvers his victim
THE — into some sort of key position where he can keep an eye on him.
WEAK — It's the healthy these days that are out in the cold. AFFECTION FOR
NORA MRS. LINDE: All the same, it's the sick who most need to be taken in. KROG.

RANK: [*With a shrug.*] Yes, there we have it. That's the concept that's
turning society into a sanatorium.

> [NORA, *lost in her thoughts, breaks out into quiet laughter and
> claps her hands.*]

RANK: Why do you laugh at that? Do you have any real idea of what
society is?

NORA: What do I care about dreary old society? I was laughing at something quite different—something terribly funny. Tell me, Doctor—
is everyone who works in the bank dependent now on Torvald?

RANK: Is that what you find so terribly funny?

NORA: [*Smiling and humming.*] Never mind, never mind! [*Pacing
the floor.*] Yes, that's really immensely amusing: that we—
that Torvald has so much power now over all those people.
[*Taking the bag out of her pocket.*] Dr. Rank, a little macaroon
on that?

RANK: See here, macaroons! I thought they were contraband here.

NORA: Yes, but these are some that Kristine gave me.

MRS. LINDE: What? I—?

NORA: Now, now, don't be afraid. You couldn't possibly know that
Torvald had forbidden them. You see, he's worried they'll ruin
my teeth. But hmp! Just this once! Isn't that so, Dr. Rank? Help
yourself! [*Puts a macaroon in his mouth.*] And you too, Kristine.
And I'll also have one, only a little one—or two, at the most.
[*Walking about again.*] Now I'm really tremendously happy.
Now there's just one last thing in the world that I have an enor-
mous desire to do.

RANK: Well! And what's that?

NORA: It's something I have such a consuming desire to say so
Torvald could hear.

RANK: And why can't you say it?

NORA: I don't dare. It's quite shocking.

MRS. LINDE: Shocking?

RANK: Well, then it isn't advisable. But in front of us you certainly can. What do you have such a desire to say so Torvald could hear?

NORA: I have such a huge desire to say—to hell and be damned!

RANK: Are you crazy?

MRS. LINDE: My goodness, Nora!

RANK: Go on, say it. Here he is.

NORA: [*Hiding the macaroon bag.*] Shh, shh, shh!

[HELMER *comes in from his study, hat in hand, overcoat over his arm.*]

NORA: [*Going toward him.*] Well, Torvald dear, are you through with him?

HELMER: Yes, he just left.

NORA: Let me introduce you—this is Kristine, who's arrived here in town.

HELMER: Kristine—? I'm sorry, but I don't know—

NORA: Mrs. Linde, Torvald dear. Mrs. Kristine Linde.

HELMER: Of course. A childhood friend of my wife's, no doubt?

MRS. LINDE: Yes, we knew each other in those days.

NORA: And just think, she made the long trip down here in order to talk with you.

HELMER: What's this?

MRS. LINDE: Well, not exactly—

NORA: You see, Kristine is remarkably clever in office work, and so she's terribly eager to come under a capable man's supervision and add more to what she already knows—

HELMER: Very wise, Mrs. Linde.

NORA: And then when she heard that you'd become a bank manager—the story was wired out to the papers—then she came in as fast as she could and— Really, Torvald, for my sake you can do a little something for Kristine, can't you?

HELMER: Yes, it's not at all impossible. Mrs. Linde, I suppose you're a widow?

MRS. LINDE: Yes.

HELMER: Any experience in office work?

MRS. LINDE: Yes, a good deal.

HELMER: Well, it's quite likely that I can make an opening for you—

NORA: [*Clapping her hands.*] You see, you see!

HELMER: You've come at a lucky moment, Mrs. Linde.

MRS. LINDE: Oh, how can I thank you?

HELMER: Not necessary. [*Putting his overcoat on.*] But today you'll have to excuse me—

RANK: Wait, I'll go with you. [*He fetches his coat from the hall and warms it at the stove.*]

NORA: Don't stay out long, dear.

HELMER: An hour; no more.

NORA: Are you going too, Kristine?

MRS. LINDE: [*Putting on her winter garments.*] Yes, I have to see about a room now.

HELMER: Then perhaps we can all walk together.

NORA: [*Helping her.*] What a shame we're so cramped here, but it's quite impossible for us to—

MRS. LINDE: Oh, don't even think of it! Good-bye, Nora dear, and thanks for everything.

NORA: Good-bye for now. Of course you'll be back this evening. And you too, Dr. Rank. What? If you're well enough? Oh, you've got to be! Wrap up tight now.

[*In a ripple of small talk the company moves out into the hall; children's voices are heard outside on the steps.*]

NORA: There they are! There they are! [*She runs to open the door. The children come in with their nurse,* ANNE-MARIE.] Come in, come in! [*Bends down and kisses them.*] Oh, you darlings—! Look at them, Kristine. Aren't they lovely!

RANK: No loitering in the draft here.

HELMER: Come, Mrs. Linde—this place is unbearable now for anyone but mothers.

[DR. RANK, HELMER, *and* MRS. LINDE *go down the stairs.* ANNE-MARIE *goes into the living room with the children.* NORA *follows, after closing the hall door.*]

NORA: How fresh and strong you look. Oh, such red cheeks you have! Like apples and roses. [*The children interrupt her throughout the following.*] And it was so much fun? That's wonderful. Really? You pulled both Emmy and Bob on the sled?

[handwritten annotations:] ATTITUDE TOWARD CHILDREN

* THINK OF HOW HE COULD CONSIDER NORA "UNBEARABLE" IF HE THOUGHT OF HER AS A CHILD—.

Imagine, all together! Yes, you're a clever boy, Ivar. Oh, let me hold her a bit, Anne-Marie. My sweet little doll baby! [*Takes the smallest from the nurse and dances with her.*] Yes, yes, Mama will dance with Bob as well. What? Did you throw snowballs? Oh, if I'd only been there! No, don't bother, Anne-Marie—I'll undress them myself. Oh yes, let me. It's such fun. Go in and rest; you look half frozen. There's hot coffee waiting for you on the stove. [*The nurse goes into the room to the left.* NORA *takes the children's winter things off, throwing them about, while the children talk to her all at once.*] Is that so? A big dog chased you? But it didn't bite? No, dogs never bite little, lovely doll babies. Don't peek in the packages, Ivar! What is it? Yes, wouldn't you like to know. No, no, it's an ugly something. Well? Shall we play? What shall we play? Hide-and-seek? Yes, let's play hide-and-seek. Bob must hide first. I must? Yes, let me hide first. [*Laughing and shouting, she and the children play in and out of the living room and the adjoining room to the right. At last* NORA *hides under the table. The children come storming in, search, but cannot find her, then hear her muffled laughter, dash over to the table, lift the cloth up and find her. Wild shouting. She creeps forward as if to scare them. More shouts. Meanwhile, a knock at the hall door; no one has noticed it. Now the door half opens, and* KROGSTAD *appears. He waits a moment; the game goes on.*]

KROGSTAD: Beg pardon, Mrs. Helmer—

NORA: [*With a strangled cry, turning and scrambling to her knees.*] Oh! What do you want?

KROGSTAD: Excuse me. The outer door was ajar; it must be someone forgot to shut it—

NORA: [*Rising.*] My husband isn't home, Mr. Krogstad.

KROGSTAD: I know that.

NORA: Yes—then what do you want here?

KROGSTAD: A word with you.

NORA: With—? [*To the children, quietly.*] Go in to Anne-Marie. What? No, the strange man won't hurt Mama. When he's gone, we'll play some more. [*She leads the children into the room to the left and shuts the door after them. Then, tense and nervous.*] You want to speak to me?

KROGSTAD: Yes, I want to.

PAYMENT DUE

NORA: Today? But it's not yet the first of the month—

KROGSTAD: No, it's Christmas Eve. It's going to be up to you how merry a Christmas you have.

NORA: What is it you want? Today I absolutely can't—

KROGSTAD: We won't talk about that till later. This is something else. You do have a moment to spare, I suppose?

NORA: Oh yes, of course—I do, except—

KROGSTAD: Good. I was sitting over at Olsen's Restaurant when I saw your husband go down the street—

NORA: Yes?

KROGSTAD: With a lady.

NORA: Yes. So?

KROGSTAD: If you'll pardon my asking: wasn't that lady a Mrs. Linde?

NORA: Yes.

KROGSTAD: Just now come into town?

NORA: Yes, today.

KROGSTAD: She's a good friend of yours?

NORA: Yes, she is. But I don't see—

KROGSTAD: I also knew her once.

NORA: I'm aware of that.

KROGSTAD: Oh? You know all about it. I thought so. Well, then let me ask you short and sweet: is Mrs. Linde getting a job in the bank?

NORA: What makes you think you can cross-examine me, Mr. Krogstad—you, one of my husband's employees? But since you ask, you might as well know—yes, Mrs. Linde's going to be taken on at the bank. And I'm the one who spoke for her, Mr. Krogstad. Now you know.

KROGSTAD: So I guessed right.

NORA: [*Pacing up and down.*] Oh, one does have a tiny bit of influence, I should hope. Just because I am a woman, don't think it means that—When one has a subordinate position, Mr. Krogstad, one really ought to be careful about pushing somebody who—hm—

KROGSTAD: Who has influence?

NORA: That's right.

KROGSTAD: [*In a different tone.*] Mrs. Helmer, would you be good enough to use your influence on my behalf?

NOTE HOW QUICKLY AND EASILY THIS CAN REVERSE —

— WHO REALLY HAS INFLUENCE — FINANCIAL AND REPUTATIONAL INFLUENCE —

NORA: What? What do you mean?

KROGSTAD: Would you please make sure that I keep my subordinate position in the bank?

NORA: What does that mean? Who's thinking of taking away your position?

KROGSTAD: Oh, don't play the innocent with me. I'm quite aware that your friend would hardly relish the chance of running into me again; and I'm also aware now whom I can thank for being turned out.

NORA: But I promise you—

KROGSTAD: Yes, yes, yes, to the point: there's still time, and I'm advising you to use your influence to prevent it.

NORA: But Mr. Krogstad, I have absolutely no influence.

KROGSTAD: You haven't? I thought you were just saying—

NORA: You shouldn't take me so literally. I! How can you believe that I have any such influence over my husband?

KROGSTAD: Oh, I've known your husband from our student days. I don't think the great bank manager's more steadfast than any other married man.

NORA: You speak insolently about my husband, and I'll show you the door.

KROGSTAD: The lady has spirit.

NORA: I'm not afraid of you any longer. After New Year's, I'll soon be done with the whole business.

KROGSTAD: [*Restraining himself.*] Now listen to me, Mrs. Helmer. If necessary, I'll fight for my little job in the bank as if it were life itself.

NORA: Yes, so it seems.

KROGSTAD: It's not just a matter of income; that's the least of it. It's something else— All right, out with it! Look, this is the thing. You know, just like all the others, of course, that once, a good many years ago, I did something rather rash.

NORA: I've heard rumors to that effect.

KROGSTAD: The case never got into court; but all the same, every door was closed in my face from then on. So I took up those various activities you know about. I had to grab hold somewhere; and I dare say I haven't been among the worst. But now I want to drop all that. My boys are growing up. For their sakes, I'll have to win back as much respect as possible here in town. That job in the bank was like the first rung in my ladder. And now your husband wants to kick me right back down in the mud again.

NORA: But for heaven's sake, Mr. Krogstad, it's simply not in my power to help you.

KROGSTAD: That's because you haven't the will to—but I have the means to make you.

NORA: You certainly won't tell my husband that I owe you money?

KROGSTAD: Hm—what if I told him that?

NORA: That would be shameful of you. [*Nearly in tears.*] This secret—my joy and my pride—that he should learn it in such a crude and disgusting way—learn it from you. You'd expose me to the most horrible unpleasantness—

KROGSTAD: Only unpleasantness?

NORA: [*Vehemently.*] But go on and try. It'll turn out the worse for you, because then my husband will really see what a crook you are, and then you'll *never* be able to hold your job.

KROGSTAD: I asked if it was just domestic unpleasantness you were afraid of?

NORA: If my husband finds out, then of course he'll pay what I owe at once, and then we'd be through with you for good.

KROGSTAD: [*A step closer.*] Listen, Mrs. Helmer—you've either got a very bad memory, or else no head at all for business. I'd better put you a little more in touch with the facts.

NORA: What do you mean?

KROGSTAD: When your husband was sick, you came to me for a loan of four thousand, eight hundred crowns.

NORA: Where else could I go?

KROGSTAD: I promised to get you that sum—

NORA: And you got it.

KROGSTAD: I promised to get you that sum, on certain conditions. You were so involved in your husband's illness, and so eager to finance your trip, that I guess you didn't think out all the details. It might just be a good idea to remind you. I promised you the money on the strength of a note I drew up.

NORA: Yes, and that I signed.

KROGSTAD: Right. But at the bottom I added some lines for your father to guarantee the loan. He was supposed to sign down there.

NORA: Supposed to? He did sign.

KROGSTAD: I left the date blank. In other words, your father would have dated his signature himself. Do you remember that?

NORA: Yes, I think—

KROGSTAD: Then I gave you the note for you to mail to your father. Isn't that so?

NORA: Yes.

KROGSTAD: And naturally you sent it at once—because only some five, six days later you brought me the note, properly signed. And with that, the money was yours.

NORA: Well, then; I've made my payments regularly, haven't I?

KROGSTAD: More or less. But—getting back to the point—those were hard times for you then, Mrs. Helmer.

NORA: Yes, they were.

KROGSTAD: Your father was very ill, I believe.

NORA: He was near the end.

KROGSTAD: He died soon after?

NORA: Yes.

KROGSTAD: Tell me, Mrs. Helmer, do you happen to recall the date of your father's death? The day of the month, I mean.

NORA: Papa died the twenty-ninth of September.

KROGSTAD: That's quite correct; I've already looked into that. And now we come to a curious thing—[*Taking out a paper.*] which I simply cannot comprehend.

NORA: Curious thing? I don't know—

KROGSTAD: This is the curious thing: that your father co-signed the note for your loan three days after his death.

NORA: How—? I don't understand.

KROGSTAD: Your father died the twenty-ninth of September. But look. Here your father dated his signature October second. Isn't that curious, Mrs. Helmer? [NORA *is silent.*] Can you explain it to me? [NORA *remains silent.*] It's also remarkable that the words "October second" and the year aren't written in your father's hand, but rather in one that I think I know. Well, it's easy to understand. Your father forgot perhaps to date his signature, and then someone or other added it, a bit sloppily, before anyone knew of his death. There's nothing wrong in that. It all comes down to the signature. And there's no question about *that,*

Mrs. Helmer. It really *was* your father who signed his own name here, wasn't it?

NORA: [*After a short silence, throwing her head back and looking squarely at him.*] No, it wasn't. *I* signed Papa's name.

KROGSTAD: Wait, now—are you fully aware that this is a dangerous confession?

NORA: Why? You'll soon get your money.

KROGSTAD: Let me ask you a question—why didn't you send the paper to your father?

NORA: That was impossible. Papa was so sick. If I'd asked him for his signature, I also would have had to tell him what the money was for. But I couldn't tell him, sick as he was, that my husband's life was in danger. That was just impossible.

KROGSTAD: Then it would have been better if you'd given up the trip abroad.

NORA: I couldn't possibly. The trip was to save my husband's life. I couldn't give that up.

KROGSTAD: But didn't you ever consider that this was a fraud against me?

NORA: I couldn't let myself be bothered by that. You weren't any concern of mine. I couldn't stand you, with all those cold complications you made, even though you knew how badly off my husband was.

KROGSTAD: Mrs. Helmer, obviously you haven't the vaguest idea of what you've involved yourself in. But I can tell you this: it was nothing more and nothing worse that I once did—and it wrecked my whole reputation.

NORA: You? Do you expect me to believe that you ever acted bravely to save your wife's life?

KROGSTAD: Laws don't inquire into motives.

NORA: Then they must be very poor laws.

KROGSTAD: Poor or not—if I introduce this paper in court, you'll be judged according to law.

NORA: This I refuse to believe. A daughter hasn't a right to protect her dying father from anxiety and care? A wife hasn't a right to save her husband's life? I don't know much about laws, but I'm sure that somewhere in the books these things are allowed. And you don't know anything about it—you who practice the law? You must be an awful lawyer, Mr. Krogstad.

KROGSTAD: Could be. But business—the kind of business we two are mixed up in—don't you think I know about that? All right. Do what you want now. But I'm telling you *this*: if I get shoved down a second time, you're going to keep me company. [*He bows and goes out through the hall.*]

NORA: [*Pensive for a moment, then tossing her head.*] Oh, really! Trying to frighten me! I'm not so silly as all that. [*Begins gathering up the children's clothes, but soon stops.*] But—? No, but that's impossible! I did it out of love.

THE CHILDREN: [*In the doorway, left.*] Mama, that strange man's gone out the door.

NORA: Yes, yes, I know it. But don't tell anyone about the strange man. Do you hear? Not even Papa!

THE CHILDREN: No, Mama. But now will you play again?

NORA: No, not now.

THE CHILDREN: Oh, but Mama, you promised.

NORA: Yes, but I can't now. Go inside; I have too much to do. Go in, go in, my sweet darlings. [*She herds them gently back in the room and shuts the door after them. Settling on the sofa, she takes up a piece of embroidery and makes some stitches, but soon stops abruptly.*] No! [*Throws the work aside, rises, goes to the hall door and calls out.*] Helene! Let me have the tree in here. [*Goes to the table, left, opens the table drawer, and stops again.*] No, but that's utterly impossible!

MAID: [*With the Christmas tree.*] Where should I put it, ma'am?

NORA: There. The middle of the floor.

MAID: Should I bring anything else?

NORA: No, thanks. I have what I need.

[*The MAID, who has set the tree down, goes out.*]

NORA: [*Absorbed in trimming the tree.*] Candles here—and flowers here. That terrible creature! Talk, talk, talk! There's nothing to it at all. The tree's going to be lovely. I'll do anything to please you, Torvald. I'll sing for you, dance for you—

[*HELMER comes in from the hall, with a sheaf of papers under his arm.*]

NORA: Oh! You're back so soon?

HELMER: Yes. Has anyone been here?

NORA: Here? No.

HELMER: That's odd. I saw Krogstad leaving the front door.

NORA: So? Oh yes, that's true. Krogstad was here a moment.

HELMER: Nora, I can see by your face that he's been here, begging you to put in a good word for him.

NORA: Yes.

HELMER: And it was supposed to seem like your own idea? You were to hide it from me that he'd been here. He asked you that, too, didn't he?

NORA: Yes, Torvald, but—

HELMER: Nora, Nora, and you could fall for that? Talk with that sort of person and promise him anything? And then in the bargain, tell me an untruth.

NORA: An untruth—?

HELMER: Didn't you say that no one had been here? [*Wagging his finger.*] My little songbird must never do that again. A songbird needs a clean beak to warble with. No false notes. [*Putting his arm about her waist.*] That's the way it should be, isn't it? Yes, I'm sure of it. [*Releasing her.*] And so, enough of that. [*Sitting by the stove.*] Ah, how snug and cozy it is here. [*Leafing among his papers.*]

NORA: [*Busy with the tree, after a short pause.*] Torvald!

HELMER: Yes.

NORA: I'm so much looking forward to the Stenborgs' costume party, day after tomorrow.

HELMER: And I can't wait to see what you'll surprise me with.

NORA: Oh, that stupid business!

HELMER: What?

NORA: I can't find anything that's right. Everything seems so ridiculous, so inane.

HELMER: So my little Nora's come to *that* recognition?

NORA: [*Going behind his chair, her arms resting on its back.*] Are you very busy, Torvald?

HELMER: Oh—

NORA: What papers are those?

HELMER: Bank matters.

NORA: Already?

HELMER: I've gotten full authority from the retiring management to make all necessary changes in personnel and procedure. I'll need

Christmas week for that. I want to have everything in order by New Year's.

NORA: So that was the reason this poor Krogstad—

HELMER: Hm.

NORA: [*Still leaning on the chair and slowly stroking the nape of his neck.*] If you weren't so very busy, I would have asked you an enormous favor, Torvald.

HELMER: Let's hear. What is it?

NORA: You know, there isn't anyone who has your good taste— and I want so much to look well at the costume party. Torvald, couldn't you take over and decide what I should be and plan my costume?

HELMER: Ah, is my stubborn little creature calling for a lifeguard?

NORA: Yes, Torvald, I can't get anywhere without your help.

HELMER: All right—I'll think it over. We'll hit on something.

NORA: Oh, how sweet of you. [*Goes to the tree again. Pause.*] Aren't the red flowers pretty—? But tell me, was it really such a crime that this Krogstad committed?

HELMER: Forgery. Do you have any idea what that means?

NORA: Couldn't he have done it out of need?

HELMER: Yes, or thoughtlessness, like so many others. I'm not so heartless that I'd condemn a man categorically for just one mistake.

NORA: No, of course not, Torvald!

HELMER: Plenty of men have redeemed themselves by openly confessing their crimes and taking their punishment.

NORA: Punishment—?

HELMER: But now Krogstad didn't go that way. He got himself out by sharp practices, and that's the real cause of his moral breakdown.

NORA: Do you really think that would—?

HELMER: Just imagine how a man with that sort of guilt in him has to lie and cheat and deceive on all sides, has to wear a mask even with the nearest and dearest he has, even with his own wife and children. And with the children, Nora—that's where it's most horrible.

NORA: Why?

HELMER: Because that kind of atmosphere of lies infects the whole life of a home. Every breath the children take in is filled with the germs of something degenerate.

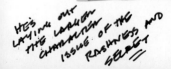

NORA: [*Coming closer behind him.*] Are you sure of that?

HELMER: Oh, I've seen it often enough as a lawyer. Almost everyone who goes bad early in life has a mother who's a chronic liar.

NORA: Why just—the mother?

HELMER: It's usually the mother's influence that's dominant, but the father's works in the same way, of course. Every lawyer is quite familiar with it. And still this Krogstad's been going home year in, year out, poisoning his own children with lies and pretense; that's why I call him morally lost. [*Reaching his hands out toward her.*] So my sweet little Nora must promise me never to plead his cause. Your hand on it. Come, come, what's this? Give me your hand. There, now. All settled. I can tell you it'd be impossible for me to work alongside of him. I literally feel physically revolted when I'm anywhere near such a person.

NORA: [*Withdraws her hand and goes to the other side of the Christmas tree.*] How hot it is here! And I've got so much to do.

HELMER: [*Getting up and gathering his papers.*] Yes, and I have to think about getting some of these read through before dinner. I'll think about your costume, too. And something to hang on the tree in gilt paper, I may even see about that. [*Putting his hand on her head.*] Oh you, my darling little songbird. [*He goes into his study and closes the door after him.*]

NORA: [*Softly, after a silence.*] Oh, really! It isn't so. It's impossible. It must be impossible.

ANNE-MARIE: [*In the doorway, left.*] The children are begging so hard to come in to Mama.

NORA: No, no, no, don't let them in to me! You stay with them, Anne-Marie.

ANNE-MARIE: Of course, ma'am. [*Closes the door.*]

NORA: [*Pale with terror.*] Hurt my children—! Poison my home? [*A moment's pause; then she tosses her head.*] That's not true. Never. Never in all the world.

ACT 2

Same room. Beside the piano the Christmas tree now stands stripped of ornament, burned-down candle stubs on its ragged branches. NORA's street clothes lie on the sofa. NORA, alone in the room, moves restlessly about; at last she stops at the sofa and picks up her coat.

NORA: [*Dropping the coat again.*] Someone's coming! [*Goes toward the door, listens.*] No—there's no one. Of course—nobody's coming today, Christmas Day—or tomorrow, either. But maybe— [*Opens the door and looks out.*] No, nothing in the mailbox. Quite empty. [*Coming forward.*] What nonsense! He won't do anything serious. Nothing terrible could happen. It's impossible. Why, I have three small children.

[ANNE-MARIE, *with a large carton, comes in from the room to the left.*]

ANNE-MARIE: Well, at last I found the box with the masquerade clothes.

NORA: Thanks. Put it on the table.

ANNE-MARIE: [*Does so.*] But they're all pretty much of a mess.

NORA: Ahh! I'd love to rip them in a million pieces!

ANNE-MARIE: Oh, mercy, they can be fixed right up. Just a little patience.

NORA: Yes, I'll go get Mrs. Linde to help me.

ANNE-MARIE: Out again now? In this nasty weather? Miss Nora will catch cold—get sick.

NORA: Oh, worse things could happen— How are the children?

ANNE-MARIE: The poor mites are playing with their Christmas presents, but—

NORA: Do they ask for me much?

ANNE-MARIE: They're so used to having Mama around, you know.

NORA: Yes, but Anne-Marie, I *can't* be together with them as much as I was.

ANNE-MARIE: Well, small children get used to anything.

NORA: You think so? Do you think they'd forget their mother if she was gone for good?

ANNE-MARIE: Oh, mercy—gone for good!

NORA: Wait, tell me, Anne-Marie—I've wondered so often—how could you ever have the heart to give your child over to strangers?

ANNE-MARIE: But I had to, you know, to become little Nora's nurse.

NORA: Yes, but how could you *do* it?

ANNE-MARIE: When I could get such a good place? A girl who's poor and who's gotten in trouble is glad enough for that. Because that slippery fish, he didn't do a thing for me, you know.

NORA: But your daughter's surely forgotten you.

ANNE-MARIE: Oh, she certainly has not. She's written to me, both when she was confirmed and when she was married.

NORA: [*Clasping her about the neck.*] You old Anne-Marie, you were a good mother for me when I was little.

ANNE-MARIE: Poor little Nora, with no other mother but me.

NORA: And if the babies didn't have one, then I know that you'd— What silly talk! [*Opening the carton.*] Go in to them. Now I'll have to— Tomorrow you can see how lovely I'll look.

ANNE-MARIE: Oh, there won't be anyone at the party as lovely as Miss Nora. [*She goes off into the room, left.*]

NORA: [*Begins unpacking the box, but soon throws it aside.*] Oh, if I dared to go out. If only nobody would come. If only nothing would happen here while I'm out. What craziness—nobody's coming. Just don't think. This muff—needs a brushing. Beautiful gloves, beautiful gloves. Let it go. Let it go! One, two, three, four, five, six— [*With a cry.*] Oh, there they are! [*Poises to move toward the door, but remains irresolutely standing.* MRS. LINDE *enters from the hall, where she has removed her street clothes.*]

NORA: Oh, it's you, Kristine. There's no one else out there? How good that you've come.

MRS. LINDE: I hear you were up asking for me.

NORA: Yes, I just stopped by. There's something you really can help me with. Let's get settled on the sofa. Look, there's going to be a costume party tomorrow evening at the Stenborgs' right above us, and now Torvald wants me to go as a Neapolitan peasant girl and dance the tarantella that I learned in Capri.

MRS. LINDE: Really, are you giving a whole performance?

NORA: Torvald says yes, I should. See, here's the dress. Torvald had it made for me down there; but now it's all so tattered that I just don't know—

MRS. LINDE: Oh, we'll fix that up in no time. It's nothing more than the trimmings—they're a bit loose here and there. Needle and thread? Good, now we have what we need.

NORA: Oh, how sweet of you!

MRS. LINDE: [*Sewing.*] So you'll be in disguise tomorrow, Nora. You know what? I'll stop by then for a moment and have a look at you all dressed up. But listen, I've absolutely forgotten to thank you for that pleasant evening yesterday.

NORA: [*Getting up and walking about.*] I don't think it was as pleasant as usual yesterday. You should have come to town a bit sooner,

Kristine—Yes, Torvald really knows how to give a home elegance and charm.

MRS. LINDE: And you do, too, if you ask me. You're not your father's daughter for nothing. But tell me, is Dr. Rank always so down in the mouth as yesterday?

NORA: No, that was quite an exception. But he goes around critically ill all the time—tuberculosis of the spine, poor man. You know, his father was a disgusting thing who kept mistresses and so on—and that's why the son's been sickly from birth.[2]

MRS. LINDE: [*Lets her sewing fall to her lap.*] But my dearest Nora, how do you know about such things?

NORA: [*Walking more jauntily.*] Hmp! When you've had three children, then you've had a few visits from—from women who know something of medicine, and they tell you this and that.

MRS. LINDE: [*Resumes sewing; a short pause.*] Does Dr. Rank come here every day?

NORA: Every blessed day. He's Torvald's best friend from childhood, and *my* good friend, too. Dr. Rank almost belongs to this house.

MRS. LINDE: But tell me—is he quite sincere? I mean, doesn't he rather enjoy flattering people?

NORA: Just the opposite. Why do you think that?

MRS. LINDE: When you introduced us yesterday, he was proclaiming that he'd often heard my name in this house; but later I noticed that your husband hadn't the slightest idea who I really was. So how could Dr. Rank—?

NORA: But it's all true, Kristine. You see, Torvald loves me beyond words, and, as he puts it, he'd like to keep me all to himself. For a long time he'd almost be jealous if I even mentioned any of my old friends back home. So of course I dropped that. But with Dr. Rank I talk a lot about such things, because he likes hearing about them.

MRS. LINDE: Now listen, Nora; in many ways you're still like a child. I'm a good deal older than you, with a little more experience. I'll tell you something: you ought to put an end to all this with Dr. Rank.

NORA: What should I put an end to?

2. Dr. Rank suffers from congenital syphilis.

MRS. LINDE: Both parts of it, I think. Yesterday you said something about a rich admirer who'd provide you with money—

NORA: Yes, one who doesn't exist—worse luck. So?

MRS. LINDE: Is Dr. Rank well off?

NORA: Yes, he is.

MRS. LINDE: With no dependents?

NORA: No, no one. But—

MRS. LINDE: And he's over here every day?

NORA: Yes, I told you that.

MRS. LINDE: How can a man of such refinement be so grasping?

NORA: I don't follow you at all.

MRS. LINDE: Now don't try to hide it, Nora. You think I can't guess who loaned you the forty-eight hundred crowns?

NORA: Are you out of your mind? How could you think such a thing! A friend of ours, who comes here every single day. What an intolerable situation that would have been!   *TRUE ... FOR A SECRET*

MRS. LINDE: Then it really wasn't him.

NORA: No, absolutely not. It never even crossed my mind for a moment— And he had nothing to lend in those days; his inheritance came later.

MRS. LINDE: Well, I think that was a stroke of luck for you, Nora dear.

NORA: No, it never would have occurred to me to ask Dr. Rank— Still, I'm quite sure that if I had asked him—

MRS. LINDE: Which you won't, of course.

NORA: No, of course not. I can't see that I'd ever need to. But I'm quite positive that if I talked to Dr. Rank—

MRS. LINDE: Behind your husband's back?

NORA: I've got to clear up this other thing; *that's* also behind his ✶ back. I've *got* to clear it all up.

MRS. LINDE: Yes, I was saying that yesterday, but—

NORA: [*Pacing up and down.*] A man handles these problems so much better than a woman—

MRS. LINDE: One's husband does, yes.

NORA: Nonsense. [*Stopping.*] When you pay everything you owe, then you get your note back, right?

MRS. LINDE: Yes, naturally.

NORA: And can rip it into a million pieces and burn it up—that filthy scrap of paper!

YES FOR THE NOTE
NOT THE FORGERY —

MRS. LINDE: [*Looking hard at her, laying her sewing aside, and rising slowly.*] Nora, you're hiding something from me.

NORA: You can see it in my face?

MRS. LINDE: Something's happened to you since yesterday morning. Nora, what is it?

NORA: [*Hurrying toward her.*] Kristine! [*Listening.*] Shh! Torvald's home. Look, go in with the children a while. Torvald can't bear all this snipping and stitching. Let Anne-Marie help you.

MRS. LINDE: [*Gathering up some of the things.*] All right, but I'm not leaving here until we've talked this out. [*She disappears into the room, left, as* TORVALD *enters from the hall.*]

NORA: Oh, how I've been waiting for you, Torvald dear.

HELMER: Was that the dressmaker?

NORA: No, that was Kristine. She's helping me fix up my costume. You know, it's going to be quite attractive.

HELMER: Yes, wasn't that a bright idea I had?

NORA: Brilliant! But then wasn't I good as well to give in to you?

HELMER: Good—because you give in to your husband's judgment? All right, you little goose, I know you didn't mean it like that. But I won't disturb you. You'll want to have a fitting, I suppose.

NORA: And you'll be working?

HELMER: Yes. [*Indicating a bundle of papers.*] See. I've been down to the bank. [*Starts toward his study.*]

NORA: Torvald.

HELMER: [*Stops.*] Yes.

NORA: If your little squirrel begged you, with all her heart and soul, for something—?

HELMER: What's that?

NORA: Then would you do it?

HELMER: First, naturally, I'd have to know what it was.

NORA: Your squirrel would scamper about and do tricks, if you'd only be sweet and give in.

HELMER: Out with it.

NORA: Your lark would be singing high and low in every room—

HELMER: Come on, she does that anyway.

NORA: I'd be a wood nymph[3] and dance for you in the moonlight.

---

3. In Greek mythology, a maiden goddess who lives in nature.

HELMER: Nora—don't tell me it's that same business from this morning?

NORA: [*Coming closer.*] Yes, Torvald, I beg you, please!

HELMER: And you actually have the nerve to drag that up again?

NORA: Yes, yes, you've got to give in to me; you *have* to let Krogstad keep his job in the bank.

HELMER: My dear Nora, I've slated his job for Mrs. Linde.

NORA: That's awfully kind of you. But you could just fire another clerk instead of Krogstad.

HELMER: This is the most incredible stubbornness! Because you go and give an impulsive promise to speak up for him, I'm expected to—

NORA: That's not the reason, Torvald. It's for your own sake. That man does writing for the worst papers; you said it yourself. He could do you any amount of harm. I'm scared to death of him—

HELMER: Ah, I understand. It's the old memories haunting you.

NORA: What do you mean by that?

HELMER: Of course, you're thinking about your father.

NORA: Yes, all right. Just remember how those nasty gossips wrote in the papers about Papa and slandered him so cruelly. I think they'd have had him dismissed if the department hadn't sent you up to investigate, and if you hadn't been so kind and open-minded toward him.

HELMER: My dear Nora, there's a notable difference between your father and me. Your father's official career was hardly above reproach. But mine is; and I hope it'll stay that way as long as I hold my position.   PRIDE GOETH BEFORE THE FALL

NORA: Oh, who can ever tell what vicious minds can invent? We could be so snug and happy now in our quiet, carefree home—you and I and the children, Torvald! That's why I'm pleading with you so—

HELMER: And just by pleading for him you make it impossible for me to keep him on. It's already known at the bank that I'm firing Krogstad. What if it's rumored around now that the new bank manager was vetoed by his wife—

NORA: Yes, what then—?

HELMER: Oh yes—as long as our little bundle of stubbornness gets her way—! I should go and make myself ridiculous in front of the whole office—give people the idea I can be swayed by all kinds of outside pressure. Oh, you can bet I'd feel the effects of that soon enough! Besides—there's something that rules Krogstad right out at the bank as long as I'm the manager.

NORA: What's that?

HELMER: His moral failings I could maybe overlook if I had to—

NORA: Yes, Torvald, why not?

HELMER: And I hear he's quite efficient on the job. But he was a crony of mine back in my teens—one of those rash friendships that crop up again and again to embarrass you later in life. Well, I might as well say it straight out: we're on a first-name basis. And that tactless fool makes no effort at all to hide it in front of others. Quite the contrary—he thinks that entitles him to take a familiar air around me, and so every other second he comes booming out with his "Yes, Torvald!" and "Sure thing, Torvald!" I tell you, it's been excruciating for me. He's out to make my place in the bank unbearable.

NORA: Torvald, you can't be serious about all this.

HELMER: Oh no? Why not?

NORA: Because these are such petty considerations.

HELMER: What are you saying? Petty? You think I'm petty!

NORA: No, just the opposite, Torvald dear. That's exactly why—

HELMER: Never mind. You call my motives petty; then I might as well be just that. Petty! All right! We'll put a stop to this for good. [*Goes to the hall door and calls.*] Helene!

NORA: What do you want?

HELMER: [*Searching among his papers.*] A decision. [*The* MAID *comes in.*] Look here; take this letter; go out with it at once. Get hold of a messenger and have him deliver it. Quick now. It's already addressed. Wait, here's some money.

MAID: Yes, sir. [*She leaves with the letter.*]

HELMER: [*Straightening his papers.*] There, now, little Miss Willful.

NORA: [*Breathlessly.*] Torvald, what was that letter?

HELMER: Krogstad's notice.

NORA: Call it back, Torvald! There's still time. Oh, Torvald, call it back! Do it for my sake—for your sake, for the children's sake! Do you hear, Torvald; do it! You don't know how this can harm us.

HELMER: Too late.

NORA: Yes, too late.

HELMER: Nora dear, I can forgive you this panic, even though basically you're insulting me. Yes, you are! Or isn't it an insult to think that *I* should be afraid of a courtroom hack's revenge? But I forgive you anyway, because this shows so beautifully how much you love me. [*Takes her in his arms.*] This is the way it should be, my darling Nora. Whatever comes, you'll see: when it really counts, I have strength and courage enough as a man to take on the whole weight myself.

NORA: [*Terrified.*] What do you mean by that?

[Handwritten note in margin:] ☆ OH WOW! HOW THIS WILL COME BACK TO BITE!

HELMER: The whole weight, I said.

NORA: [*Resolutely.*] No, never in all the world.

HELMER: Good. So we'll share it, Nora, as man and wife. That's as it should be. [*Fondling her.*] Are you happy now? There, there, there—not these frightened dove's eyes. It's nothing at all but empty fantasies— Now you should run through your tarantella and practice your tambourine. I'll go to the inner office and shut both doors, so I won't hear a thing; you can make all the noise you like. [*Turning in the doorway.*] And when Rank comes, just tell him where he can find me. [*He nods to her and goes with his papers into the study, closing the door.*]

NORA: [*Standing as though rooted, dazed with fright, in a whisper.*] He really could do it. He will do it. He'll do it in spite of everything. No, not that, never, never! Anything but that! Escape! A way out— [*The doorbell rings.*] Dr. Rank! Anything but that! *Anything*, whatever it is! [*Her hands pass over her face, smoothing it; she pulls herself together, goes over and opens the hall door.* DR. RANK *stands outside, hanging his fur coat up. During the following scene, it begins getting dark.*]

NORA: Hello, Dr. Rank. I recognized your ring. But you mustn't go in to Torvald yet; I believe he's working.

RANK: And you?

NORA: For you, I always have an hour to spare—you know that. [*He has entered, and she shuts the door after him.*]

RANK: Many thanks. I'll make use of these hours while I can.

NORA: What do you mean by that? While you can?

RANK: Does that disturb you?

NORA: Well, it's such an odd phrase. Is anything going to happen?

RANK: What's going to happen is what I've been expecting so long—but I honestly didn't think it would come so soon.

NORA: [*Gripping his arm.*] What is it you've found out? Dr. Rank, you have to tell me!

RANK: [*Sitting by the stove.*] It's all over with me. There's nothing to be done about it.

NORA: [*Breathing easier.*] Is it you—then—?

RANK: Who else? There's no point in lying to one's self. I'm the most miserable of all my patients, Mrs. Helmer. These past few days I've been auditing my internal accounts. Bankrupt! Within a month I'll probably be laid out and rotting in the churchyard.

NORA: Oh, what a horrible thing to say.

RANK: The thing itself is horrible. But the worst of it is all the other horror before it's over. There's only one final examination left; when I'm finished with that, I'll know about when my disintegration will begin. There's something I want to say. Helmer with his sensitivity has such a sharp distaste for anything ugly. I don't want him near my sickroom.

NORA: Oh, but Dr. Rank—

RANK: I won't have him in there. Under no condition. I'll lock my door to him— As soon as I'm completely sure of the worst, I'll send you my calling card marked with a black cross, and you'll know then the wreck has started to come apart.

NORA: No, today you're completely unreasonable. And I wanted you so much to be in a really good humor.

RANK: With death up my sleeve? And then to suffer this way for somebody else's sins. Is there any justice in that? And in every single family, in some way or another, this inevitable retribution of nature goes on—

NORA: [*Her hands pressed over her ears.*] Oh, stuff! Cheer up! Please—be gay!

RANK: Yes, I'd just as soon laugh at it all. My poor, innocent spine, serving time for my father's gay army days.

NORA: [*By the table, left.*] He was so infatuated with asparagus tips and *pâté de foie gras*, wasn't that it?

RANK: Yes—and with truffles.

NORA: Truffles, yes. And then with oysters, I suppose?

RANK: Yes, tons of oysters, naturally.

NORA: And then the port and champagne to go with it. It's so sad that all these delectable things have to strike at our bones.

RANK: Especially when they strike at the unhappy bones that never shared in the fun.

HMM – A WRY LITTLE REFERENCE

NORA: Ah, that's the saddest of all.

RANK: [*Looks searchingly at her.*] Hm.

NORA: [*After a moment.*] Why did you smile?

RANK: No, it was you who laughed.

ALL THE PLAYFULNESS BETWEEN THEM

NORA: No, it was you who smiled, Dr. Rank!

RANK: [*Getting up.*] You're even a bigger tease than I'd thought.

NORA: I'm full of wild ideas today.

RANK: That's obvious.

NORA: [*Putting both hands on his shoulders.*] Dear, dear Dr. Rank, you'll never die for Torvald and me.

RANK: Oh, that loss you'll easily get over. Those who go away are soon forgotten.

NORA: [*Looks fearfully at him.*] You believe that?

RANK: One makes new connections, and then—

NORA: Who makes new connections?

RANK: Both you and Torvald will when I'm gone. I'd say you're well under way already. What was that Mrs. Linde doing here last evening?

NORA: Oh, come—you can't be jealous of poor Kristine?

RANK: Oh yes, I am. She'll be my successor here in the house. When I'm down under, that woman will probably—

NORA: Shh! Not so loud. She's right in there.

RANK: Today as well. So you see.

NORA: Only to sew on my dress. Good gracious, how unreasonable you are. [*Sitting on the sofa.*] Be nice now, Dr. Rank. Tomorrow you'll see how beautifully I'll dance; and you can imagine then that I'm dancing only for you—yes, and of course for Torvald, too—that's understood. [*Takes various items out of the carton.*] Dr. Rank, sit over here and I'll show you something.

RANK: [*Sitting.*] What's that?

NORA: Look here. Look.

RANK: Silk stockings.

NORA: Flesh-colored. Aren't they lovely? Now it's so dark here, but tomorrow—No, no, no, just look at the feet. Oh well, you might as well look at the rest.

RANK: Hm—

NORA: Why do you look so critical? Don't you believe they'll fit?

RANK: I've never had any chance to form an opinion on that.

NORA: [*Glancing at him a moment.*] Shame on you. [*Hits him lightly on the ear with the stockings.*] That's for you. [*Puts them away again.*]

RANK: And what other splendors am I going to see now?

NORA: Not the least bit more, because you've been naughty. [*She hums a little and rummages among her things.*]

RANK: [*After a short silence.*] When I sit here together with you like this, completely easy and open, then I don't know—I simply can't imagine—whatever would have become of me if I'd never come into this house.

NORA: [*Smiling.*] Yes, I really think you feel completely at ease with us.

RANK: [*More quietly, staring straight ahead.*] And then to have to go away from it all—

NORA: Nonsense, you're not going away.

RANK: [*His voice unchanged.*]—and not even be able to leave some poor show of gratitude behind, scarcely a fleeting regret—no more than a vacant place that anyone can fill.

NORA: And if I asked you now for—? No—

RANK: For what?

NORA: For a great proof of your friendship—

RANK: Yes, yes?

NORA: No, I mean—for an exceptionally big favor—

RANK: Would you really, for once, make me so happy?

NORA: Oh, you haven't the vaguest idea what it is.

RANK: All right, then tell me.

NORA: No, but I can't, Dr. Rank—it's all out of reason. It's advice and help, too—and a favor—

RANK: So much the better. I can't fathom what you're hinting at. Just speak out. Don't you trust me?

NORA: Of course. More than anyone else. You're my best and truest friend, I'm sure. That's why I want to talk to you. All right, then, Dr. Rank: there's something you can help me prevent. You know how deeply, how inexpressibly dearly Torvald loves me; he'd never hesitate a second to give up his life for me.

RANK: [*Leaning close to her.*] Nora—do you think he's the only one—

NORA: [*With a slight start.*] Who—?

RANK: Who'd gladly give up his life for you.

NORA: [*Heavily.*] I see.

RANK: I swore to myself you should know this before I'm gone. I'll never find a better chance. Yes, Nora, now you know. And also you know now that you can trust me beyond anyone else.

NORA: [*Rising, natural and calm.*] Let me by.

RANK: [*Making room for her, but still sitting.*] Nora—

NORA: [*In the hall doorway.*] Helene, bring the lamp in. [*Goes over to the stove.*] Ah, dear Dr. Rank, that was really mean of you.

RANK: [*Getting up.*] That I've loved you just as deeply as somebody else? Was *that* mean?

NORA: No, but that you came out and told me. That was quite unnecessary—

RANK: What do you mean? Have you known—?

[*The* MAID *comes in with the lamp, sets it on the table, and goes out again.*]

RANK: Nora—Mrs. Helmer—I'm asking you: have you known about it?

NORA: Oh, how can I tell what I know or don't know? Really, I don't know what to say— Why did you have to be so clumsy, Dr. Rank! Everything was so good.

RANK: Well, in any case, you now have the knowledge that my body and soul are at your command. So won't you speak out?

NORA: [*Looking at him.*] After that?

RANK: Please, just let me know what it is.

NORA: You can't know anything now.

RANK: I have to. You mustn't punish me like this. Give me the chance to do whatever is humanly possible for you.

NORA: Now there's nothing you can do for me. Besides, actually, I don't need any help. You'll see—it's only my fantasies. That's what it is. Of course! [*Sits in the rocker, looks at him, and smiles.*] What a nice one you are, Dr. Rank. Aren't you a little bit ashamed, now that the lamp is here?

RANK: No, not exactly. But perhaps I'd better go—for good?

NORA: No, you certainly can't do that. You must come here just as you always have. You know Torvald can't do without you.

RANK: Yes, but *you?*

NORA: You know how much I enjoy it when you're here.

RANK: That's precisely what threw me off. You're a mystery to me. So many times I've felt you'd almost rather be with me than with Helmer.

NORA: Yes—you see, there are some people that one loves most and other people that one would almost prefer being with.

RANK: Yes, there's something to that.

NORA: When I was back home, of course I loved Papa most. But I always thought it was so much fun when I could sneak down to the maids' quarters, because they never tried to improve me, and it was always so amusing, the way they talked to each other.

RANK: Aha, so it's *their* place that I've filled.

NORA: [*Jumping up and going to him.*] Oh, dear, sweet Dr. Rank, that's not what I meant at all. But you can understand that with Torvald it's just the same as with Papa—

[*The* MAID *enters from the hall.*]

MAID: Ma'am—please! [*She whispers to* NORA *and hands her a calling card.*]

NORA: [*Glancing at the card.*] Ah! [*Slips it into her pocket.*]

RANK: Anything wrong?

NORA: No, no, not at all. It's only some—it's my new dress—

RANK: Really? But—there's your dress.

NORA: Oh, that. But this is another one—I ordered it—Torvald mustn't know—

RANK: Ah, now we have the big secret.

NORA: That's right. Just go in with him—he's back in the inner study. Keep him there as long as—

RANK: Don't worry. He won't get away. [*Goes into the study.*]

NORA: [*To the* MAID.] And he's standing waiting in the kitchen?

MAID: Yes, he came up by the back stairs.

NORA: But didn't you tell him somebody was here?

MAID: Yes, but that didn't do any good.

NORA: He won't leave?

MAID: No, he won't go till he's talked with you, ma'am.

NORA: Let him come in, then—but quietly. Helene, don't breathe a word about this. It's a surprise for my husband.

MAID: Yes, yes, I understand—[*Goes out.*]

NORA: This horror—it's going to happen. No, no, no, it can't happen, it mustn't. [*She goes and bolts* HELMER'*s door. The* MAID *opens the hall door for* KROGSTAD *and shuts it behind him. He is dressed for travel in a fur coat, boots, and a fur cap.*]

NORA: [*Going toward him.*] Talk softly. My husband's home.

KROGSTAD: Well, good for him.

NORA: What do you want?

KROGSTAD: Some information.

NORA: Hurry up, then. What is it?

KROGSTAD: You know, of course, that I got my notice.

NORA: I couldn't prevent it, Mr. Krogstad. I fought for you to the bitter end, but nothing worked.

KROGSTAD: Does your husband's love for you run so thin? He knows everything I can expose you to, and all the same he dares to—

NORA: How can you imagine he knows anything about this?

KROGSTAD: Ah, no—I can't imagine it either, now. It's not at all like my fine Torvald Helmer to have so much guts—

NORA: Mr. Krogstad, I demand respect for my husband!

KROGSTAD: Why, of course—all due respect. But since the lady's keeping it so carefully hidden, may I presume to ask if you're also a bit better informed than yesterday about what you've actually done?

NORA: More than you ever could teach me.

KROGSTAD: Yes, I *am* such an awful lawyer.

NORA: What is it you want from me?

KROGSTAD: Just a glimpse of how you are, Mrs. Helmer. I've been thinking about you all day long. A cashier, a night-court scribbler, a—well, a type like me also has a little of what they call a heart, you know.

NORA: Then show it. Think of my children.

KROGSTAD: Did you or your husband ever think of mine? But never mind. I simply wanted to tell you that you don't need to take this thing too seriously. For the present, I'm not proceeding with any action.

NORA: Oh no, really! Well—I knew that.

KROGSTAD: Everything can be settled in a friendly spirit. It doesn't have to get around town at all; it can stay just among us three.

NORA: My husband must never know anything of this.

KROGSTAD: How can you manage that? Perhaps you can pay me the balance?

NORA: No, not right now.

KROGSTAD: Or you know some way of raising the money in a day or two?

NORA: No way that I'm willing to use.

KROGSTAD: Well, it wouldn't have done you any good, anyway. If you stood in front of me with a fistful of bills, you still couldn't buy your signature back.

NORA: Then tell me what you're going to do with it.

KROGSTAD: I'll just hold onto it—keep it on file. There's no outsider who'll even get wind of it. So if you've been thinking of taking some desperate step—

NORA: I have.

KROGSTAD: Been thinking of running away from home—

NORA: I have!

KROGSTAD: Or even of something worse—

NORA: How could you guess that?

KROGSTAD: You can drop those thoughts.

NORA: How could you guess I was thinking of *that*?

KROGSTAD: Most of us think about *that* at first. I thought about it too, but I discovered I hadn't the courage—

NORA: [*Lifelessly.*] I don't either.

KROGSTAD: [*Relieved.*] That's true, you haven't the courage? You too?

NORA: I don't have it—I don't have it.

KROGSTAD: It would be terribly stupid, anyway. After that first storm at home blows out, why, then— I have here in my pocket a letter for your husband—

NORA: Telling everything?

KROGSTAD: As charitably as possible.

NORA: [*Quickly.*] He mustn't ever get that letter. Tear it up. I'll find some way to get money.

KROGSTAD: Beg pardon, Mrs. Helmer, but I think I just told you—

NORA: Oh, I don't mean the money I owe you. Let me know how much you want from my husband, and I'll manage it.

KROGSTAD: I don't want any money from your husband.

NORA: What do you want, then?

KROGSTAD: I'll tell you what. I want to recoup, Mrs. Helmer; I want to get on in the world—and there's where your husband can help me. For a year and a half I've kept myself clean of anything disreputable—all that time struggling with the worst conditions; but I was satisfied, working my way up step by step. Now I've been written right off, and I'm just not in the mood to come crawling back. I tell you, I want to move on. I want to get back in the bank—in a better position. Your husband can set up a job for me—

NORA: He'll never do that!

KROGSTAD: He'll do it. I know him. He won't dare breathe a word of protest. And once I'm in there together with him, you just wait and see! Inside of a year, I'll be the manager's right-hand man. It'll be Nils Krogstad, not Torvald Helmer, who runs the bank.

NORA: You'll never see the day!

KROGSTAD: Maybe you think you can—

NORA: I have the courage now—for *that*.

KROGSTAD: Oh, you don't scare me. A smart, spoiled lady like you—

NORA: You'll see; you'll see!

KROGSTAD: Under the ice, maybe? Down in the freezing, coal-black water? There, till you float up in the spring, ugly, unrecognizable, with your hair falling out—

NORA: You don't frighten me.

KROGSTAD: Nor do you frighten me. One doesn't do these things, Mrs. Helmer. Besides, what good would it be? I'd still have him safe in my pocket.

NORA: Afterwards? When I'm no longer—?

KROGSTAD: Are you forgetting that *I'll* be in control then over your final reputation? [NORA *stands speechless, staring at him.*] Good; now I've warned you. Don't do anything stupid. When Helmer's read my letter, I'll be waiting for his reply. And bear in mind that it's your husband himself who's forced me back to my old ways. I'll never forgive him for that. Good-bye, Mrs. Helmer. [*He goes out through the hall.*]

NORA: [*Goes to the hall door, opens it a crack, and listens.*] He's gone. Didn't leave the letter. Oh no, no, that's impossible too! [*Opening the door more and more.*] What's that? He's standing outside—not going downstairs. He's thinking it over? Maybe he'll—? [*A letter falls in the mailbox; then* KROGSTAD'*s footsteps are heard, dying away down a flight of stairs.* NORA *gives a muffled cry and runs over toward the sofa table. A short pause.*] In the mailbox. [*Slips warily over to the hall door.*] It's lying there. Torvald, Torvald—now we're lost!

MRS. LINDE: [*Entering with the costume from the room, left.*] There now, I can't see anything else to mend. Perhaps you'd like to try—

NORA: [*In a hoarse whisper.*] Kristine, come here.

MRS. LINDE: [*Tossing the dress on the sofa.*] What's wrong? You look upset.

NORA: Come here. See that letter? *There! Look*—through the glass in the mailbox.

MRS. LINDE: Yes, yes, I see it.

NORA: That letter's from Krogstad—

MRS. LINDE: Nora—it's Krogstad who loaned you the money!

NORA: Yes, and now Torvald will find out everything.

MRS. LINDE: Believe me, Nora, it's best for both of you.

NORA: There's more you don't know. I forged a name.

MRS. LINDE: But for heaven's sake—?

NORA: I only want to tell you that, Kristine, so that you can be my witness.

MRS. LINDE: Witness? Why should I—?

NORA: If I should go out of my mind—it could easily happen—

MRS. LINDE: Nora!

NORA: Or anything else occurred—so I couldn't be present here—

MRS. LINDE: Nora, Nora, you aren't yourself at all!

NORA: And someone should try to take on the whole weight, all of the guilt, you follow me—

MRS. LINDE: Yes, of course, but why do you think—?

NORA: Then you're the witness that it isn't true, Kristine. I'm very much myself; my mind right now is perfectly clear; and I'm telling you: nobody else has known about this; I alone did everything. Remember that.

MRS. LINDE: I will. But I don't understand all this.

NORA: Oh, how could you ever understand it? It's the miracle now that's going to take place.

MRS. LINDE: The miracle?

NORA: Yes, the miracle. But it's so awful, Kristine. It mustn't take place, not for anything in the world.

MRS. LINDE: I'm going right over and talk with Krogstad.

NORA: Don't go near him; he'll do you some terrible harm!

MRS. LINDE: There was a time once when he'd gladly have done anything for me.

NORA: He?

MRS. LINDE: Where does he live?

NORA: Oh, how do I know? Yes. [*Searches in her pocket.*] Here's his card. But the letter, the letter—!

HELMER: [*From the study, knocking on the door.*] Nora!

NORA: [*With a cry of fear.*] Oh! What is it? What do you want?

HELMER: Now, now, don't be so frightened. We're not coming in. You locked the door—are you trying on the dress?

NORA: Yes, I'm trying it. I'll look just beautiful, Torvald.

MRS. LINDE: [*Who has read the card.*] He's living right around the corner.

NORA: Yes, but what's the use? We're lost. The letter's in the box.

MRS. LINDE: And your husband has the key?

NORA: Yes, always.

MRS. LINDE: Krogstad can ask for his letter back unread; he can find some excuse—

NORA: But it's just this time that Torvald usually—

MRS. LINDE: Stall him. Keep him in there. I'll be back as quick as I can. [*She hurries out through the hall entrance.*]

NORA: [*Goes to* HELMER's *door, opens it, and peers in.*] Torvald!

HELMER: [*From the inner study.*] Well—does one dare set foot in one's own living room at last? Come on, Rank, now we'll get a look— [*In the doorway.*] But what's this?

NORA: What, Torvald dear?

HELMER: Rank had me expecting some grand masquerade.

RANK: [*In the doorway.*] That was my impression, but I must have been wrong.

NORA: No one can admire me in my splendor—not till tomorrow.

HELMER: But Nora dear, you look so exhausted. Have you practiced too hard?

NORA: No, I haven't practiced at all yet.

HELMER: You know, it's necessary—

NORA: Oh, it's absolutely necessary, Torvald. But I can't get anywhere without your help. I've forgotten the whole thing completely.

HELMER: Ah, we'll soon take care of that.

NORA: Yes, take care of me, Torvald, please! Promise me that? Oh, I'm so nervous. That big party— You must give up everything this evening for me. No business—don't even touch your pen. Yes? Dear Torvald, promise?

HELMER: It's a promise. Tonight I'm totally at your service—you little helpless thing. Hm—but first there's one thing I want to— [*Goes toward the hall door.*]

NORA: What are you looking for?

HELMER: Just to see if there's any mail.

NORA: No, no, don't do that, Torvald!

HELMER: Now what?

NORA: Torvald, please. There isn't any.

HELMER: Let me look, though. [*Starts out.* NORA, *at the piano, strikes the first notes of the tarantella.* HELMER, *at the door, stops.*] Aha!

NORA: I can't dance tomorrow if I don't practice with you.

HELMER: [*Going over to her.*] Nora dear, are you really so frightened?

NORA: Yes, so terribly frightened. Let me practice right now; there's still time before dinner. Oh, sit down and play for me, Torvald. Direct me. Teach me, the way you always have.

HELMER: Gladly, if it's what you want. [*Sits at the piano.*]

NORA: [*Snatches the tambourine up from the box, then a long, varicolored shawl, which she throws around herself, whereupon she springs forward and cries out.*] Play for me now! Now I'll dance!
[HELMER *plays and* NORA *dances.* RANK *stands behind* HELMER *at the piano and looks on.*]

HELMER: [*As he plays.*] Slower. Slow down.

NORA: Can't change it.

HELMER: Not so violent, Nora!

NORA: Has to be just like this.

HELMER: [*Stopping.*] No, no, that won't do at all.

NORA: [*Laughing and swinging her tambourine.*] Isn't that what I told you?

RANK: Let me play for her.

HELMER: [*Getting up.*] Yes, go on. I can teach her more easily then. [RANK *sits at the piano and plays*; NORA *dances more and more wildly.* HELMER *has stationed himself by the stove and repeatedly gives her directions; she seems not to hear them; her hair loosens and falls over her shoulders; she does not notice, but goes on dancing.* MRS. LINDE *enters.*]

MRS. LINDE: [*Standing dumbfounded at the door.*] Ah—!

NORA: [*Still dancing.*] See what fun, Kristine!

HELMER: But Nora darling, you dance as if your life were at stake.

NORA: And it is.

HELMER: Rank, stop! This is pure madness. Stop it, I say! [RANK *breaks off playing, and* NORA *halts abruptly.*]

HELMER: [*Going over to her.*] I never would have believed it. You've forgotten everything I taught you.

NORA: [*Throwing away the tambourine.*] You see for yourself.

HELMER: Well, there's certainly room for instruction here.

NORA: Yes, you see how important it is. You've got to teach me to the very last minute. Promise me that, Torvald?

HELMER: You can bet on it.

NORA: You mustn't, either today or tomorrow, think about anything else but me; you mustn't open any letters—or the mailbox—

HELMER: Ah, it's still the fear of that man—

NORA: Oh yes, yes, that too.

HELMER: Nora, it's written all over you—there's already a letter from him out there.

NORA: I don't know. I guess so. But you mustn't read such things now; there mustn't be anything ugly between us before it's all over.

RANK: [*Quietly to* HELMER.] You shouldn't deny her.

HELMER: [*Putting his arm around her.*] The child can have her way. But tomorrow night, after you've danced—

NORA: Then you'll be free.

MAID: [*In the doorway, right.*] Ma'am, dinner is served.

NORA: We'll be wanting champagne, Helene.

MAID: Very good, ma'am. [*Goes out.*]

HELMER: So—a regular banquet, hm?

NORA: Yes, a banquet—champagne till daybreak! [*Calling out.*] And some macaroons, Helene. Heaps of them—just this once.

HELMER: [*Taking her hands.*] Now, now, now—no hysterics. Be my own little lark again.

NORA: Oh, I will soon enough. But go on in—and you, Dr. Rank. Kristine, help me put up my hair.

RANK: [*Whispering, as they go.*] There's nothing wrong—really wrong, is there?

HELMER: Oh, of course not. It's nothing more than this childish anxiety I was telling you about. [*They go out, right.*]

NORA: Well?

MRS. LINDE: Left town.

NORA: I could see by your face.

MRS. LINDE: He'll be home tomorrow evening. I wrote him a note.

NORA: You shouldn't have. Don't try to stop anything now. After all, it's a wonderful joy, this waiting here for the miracle.

MRS. LINDE: What is it you're waiting for?

NORA: Oh, you can't understand that. Go in to them; I'll be along in a moment.

[MRS. LINDE *goes into the dining room.* NORA *stands a short while as if composing herself; then she looks at her watch.*]

NORA: Five. Seven hours to midnight. Twenty-four hours to the midnight after, and then the tarantella's done. Seven and twenty-four? Thirty-one hours to live.

HELMER: [*In the doorway, right.*] What's become of the little lark?

NORA: [*Going toward him with open arms.*] Here's your lark!

ACT 3

Same scene. The table, with chairs around it, has been moved to the center of the room. A lamp on the table is lit. The hall door stands open. Dance music drifts down from the floor above. MRS. LINDE *sits at the table, absently paging through a book, trying to read, but apparently unable to focus her thoughts. Once or twice she pauses, tensely listening for a sound at the outer entrance.*

MRS. LINDE: [*Glancing at her watch.*] Not yet—and there's hardly any time left. If only he's not— [*Listening again.*] Ah, there he is. [*She goes out in the hall and cautiously opens the outer door. Quiet footsteps are heard on the stairs. She whispers.*] Come in. Nobody's here.

KROGSTAD: [*In the doorway.*] I found a note from you at home. What's back of all this?

MRS. LINDE: I just *had* to talk to you.

KROGSTAD: Oh? And it just *had* to be here in this house?

MRS. LINDE: At my place it was impossible; my room hasn't a private entrance. Come in; we're all alone. The maid's asleep, and the Helmers are at the dance upstairs.

KROGSTAD: [*Entering the room.*] Well, well, the Helmers are dancing tonight? Really?

MRS. LINDE: Yes, why not?

KROGSTAD: How true—why not?

MRS. LINDE: All right, Krogstad, let's talk.

KROGSTAD: Do we two have anything more to talk about?

MRS. LINDE: We have a great deal to talk about.

KROGSTAD: I wouldn't have thought so.

MRS. LINDE: No, because you've never understood me, really.

KROGSTAD: Was there anything more to understand—except what's all too common in life? A calculating woman throws over a man the moment a better catch comes by.

MRS. LINDE: You think I'm so thoroughly calculating? You think I broke it off lightly?

KROGSTAD: Didn't you?

MRS. LINDE: Nils—is that what you really thought?

KROGSTAD: If you cared, then why did you write me the way you did?

MRS. LINDE: What else could I do? If I had to break off with you, then it was my job as well to root out everything you felt for me.

KROGSTAD: [*Wringing his hands.*] So that was it. And this—all this, simply for money!

MRS. LINDE: Don't forget I had a helpless mother and two small brothers. We couldn't wait for you, Nils; you had such a long road ahead of you then.

KROGSTAD: That may be; but you still hadn't the right to abandon me for somebody else's sake.

MRS. LINDE: Yes—I don't know. So many, many times I've asked myself if I did have that right.

KROGSTAD: [*More softly.*] When I lost you, it was as if all the solid ground dissolved from under my feet. Look at me; I'm a half-drowned man now, hanging onto a wreck.

MRS. LINDE: Help may be near.

KROGSTAD: It was near—but then you came and blocked it off.

MRS. LINDE: Without my knowing it, Nils. Today for the first time I learned that it's you I'm replacing at the bank.

KROGSTAD: All right—I believe you. But now that you know, will you step aside?

MRS. LINDE: No, because that wouldn't benefit you in the slightest.

KROGSTAD: Not "benefit" me, hm! I'd step aside anyway.

MRS. LINDE: I've learned to be realistic. Life and hard, bitter necessity have taught me that.

KROGSTAD: And life's taught me never to trust fine phrases.

MRS. LINDE: Then life's taught you a very sound thing. But you do have to trust in actions, don't you?

KROGSTAD: What does that mean?

MRS. LINDE: You said you were hanging on like a half-drowned man to a wreck.

KROGSTAD: I've good reason to say that.

MRS. LINDE: I'm also like a half-drowned woman on a wreck. No one to suffer with; no one to care for.

KROGSTAD: You made your choice.

MRS. LINDE: There wasn't any choice then.

KROGSTAD: So—what of it?

MRS. LINDE: Nils, if only we two shipwrecked people could reach across to each other.

KROGSTAD: What are you saying?

MRS. LINDE: Two on one wreck are at least better off than each on his own.

KROGSTAD: Kristine!

MRS. LINDE: Why do you think I came into town?

KROGSTAD: Did you really have some thought of me?

MRS. LINDE: I have to work to go on living. All my born days, as long as I can remember, I've worked, and it's been my best and my only joy. But now I'm completely alone in the world; it frightens me to be so empty and lost. To work for yourself—there's no joy in that. Nils, give me something—someone to work for.

KROGSTAD: I don't believe all this. It's just some hysterical feminine urge to go out and make a noble sacrifice.

MRS. LINDE: Have you ever found me to be hysterical?

This fuss is helpful to see parts of the plot emerge and rescue available — but it also provides counterpoint to hereditary inevitability — can people choose and change?

KROGSTAD: Can you honestly mean this? Tell me—do you know everything about my past?

MRS. LINDE: Yes.

KROGSTAD: And you know what they think I'm worth around here.

MRS. LINDE: From what you were saying before, it would seem that with me you could have been another person.

KROGSTAD: I'm positive of that.

MRS. LINDE: Couldn't it happen still?

KROGSTAD: Kristine—you're saying this in all seriousness? Yes, you are! I can see it in you. And do you really have the courage, then—?

MRS. LINDE: I need to have someone to care for; and your children need a mother. We both need each other. Nils, I have faith that you're good at heart—I'll risk everything together with you.

KROGSTAD: [*Gripping her hands.*] Kristine, thank you, thank you— Now I know I can win back a place in their eyes. Yes—but I forgot—

MRS. LINDE: [*Listening.*] Shh! The tarantella. Go now! Go on!

KROGSTAD: Why? What is it?

MRS. LINDE: Hear the dance up there? When that's over, they'll be coming down.

KROGSTAD: Oh, then I'll go. But—it's all pointless. Of course, you don't know the move I made against the Helmers.

MRS. LINDE: Yes, Nils, I know.

KROGSTAD: And all the same, you have the courage to—?

MRS. LINDE: I know how far despair can drive a man like you.

KROGSTAD: Oh, if I only could take it all back.

MRS. LINDE: You easily could—your letter's still lying in the mailbox.

KROGSTAD: Are you sure of that?

MRS. LINDE: Positive. But—

KROGSTAD: [*Looks at her searchingly.*] Is that the meaning of it, then? You'll save your friend at any price. Tell me straight out. Is that it?

MRS. LINDE: Nils—anyone who's sold herself for somebody else once isn't going to do it again.

KROGSTAD: I'll demand my letter back.

MRS. LINDE: No, no.

KROGSTAD: Yes, of course. I'll stay here till Helmer comes down; I'll tell him to give me my letter again—that it only involves my dismissal—that he shouldn't read it—

MRS. LINDE: No, Nils, don't call the letter back.

KROGSTAD: But wasn't that exactly why you wrote me to come here?

MRS. LINDE: Yes, in that first panic. But it's been a whole day and night since then, and in that time I've seen such incredible things in this house. Helmer's got to learn everything; this dreadful secret has to be aired; those two have to come to a full understanding; all these lies and evasions can't go on.

[handwritten margin note: NOW KRISTINE MAKES A MORAL DECISION FOR ALL, ON WHAT'S BEST]

KROGSTAD: Well, then, if you want to chance it. But at least there's one thing I can do, and do right away—

MRS. LINDE: [*Listening.*] Go now, go, quick! The dance is over. We're not safe another second.

KROGSTAD: I'll wait for you downstairs.

MRS. LINDE: Yes, please do; take me home.

KROGSTAD: I can't believe it; I've never been so happy. [*He leaves by way of the outer door; the door between the room and the hall stays open.*]

MRS. LINDE: [*Straightening up a bit and getting together her street clothes.*] How different now! How different! Someone to work for, to live for—a home to build. Well, it is worth the try! Oh, if they'd only come! [*Listening.*] Ah, there they are. Bundle up. [*She picks up her hat and coat.* NORA's *and* HELMER's *voices can be heard outside; a key turns in the lock, and* HELMER *brings* NORA *into the hall almost by force. She is wearing the Italian costume with a large black shawl about her; he has on evening dress, with a black domino⁴ open over it.*]

NORA: [*Struggling in the doorway.*] No, no, no, not inside! I'm going up again. I don't want to leave so soon.

HELMER: But Nora dear—

NORA: Oh, I beg you, please, Torvald. From the bottom of my heart, *please*—only an hour more!

HELMER: Not a single minute, Nora darling. You know our agreement. Come on, in we go; you'll catch cold out here. [*In spite of her resistance, he gently draws her into the room.*]

---

4. A loose cloak fitted with a mask, used at masquerades.

MRS. LINDE: Good evening.

NORA: Kristine!

HELMER: Why, Mrs. Linde—are you here so late?

MRS. LINDE: Yes, I'm sorry, but I did want to see Nora in costume.

NORA: Have you been sitting here, waiting for me?

MRS. LINDE: Yes. I didn't come early enough; you were all upstairs; and then I thought I really couldn't leave without seeing you.

HELMER: [*Removing* NORA's *shawl.*] Yes, take a good look. She's worth looking at, I can tell you that, Mrs. Linde. Isn't she lovely?

MRS. LINDE: Yes, I should say—

HELMER: A dream of loveliness, isn't she? That's what everyone thought at the party, too. But she's horribly stubborn—this sweet little thing. What's to be done with her? Can you imagine, I almost had to use force to pry her away.

NORA: Oh, Torvald, you're going to regret you didn't indulge me, even for just a half hour more.

HELMER: There, you see. She danced her tarantella and got a tumultuous hand—which was well earned, although the performance may have been a bit too naturalistic—I mean it rather overstepped the proprieties of art. But never mind—what's important is, she made a success, an overwhelming success. You think I could let her stay on after that and spoil the effect? Oh no; I took my lovely little Capri girl—my capricious little Capri girl, I should say—took her under my arm; one quick tour of the ballroom, a curtsy to every side, and then—as they say in novels—the beautiful vision disappeared. An exit should always be effective, Mrs. Linde, but that's what I can't get Nora to grasp. Phew, it's hot in here. [*Flings the domino on a chair and opens the door to his room.*] Why's it dark in here? Oh yes, of course. Excuse me. [*He goes in and lights a couple of candles.*]

NORA: [*In a sharp, breathless whisper.*] So?

MRS. LINDE: [*Quietly.*] I talked with him.

NORA: And—?

MRS. LINDE: Nora—you must tell your husband everything.

NORA: [*Dully.*] I knew it.

MRS. LINDE: You've got nothing to fear from Krogstad, but you have to speak out.

NORA: I won't tell.

MRS. LINDE: Then the letter will.

NORA: Thanks, Kristine. I know now what's to be done. Shh!

HELMER: [*Reentering.*] Well, then, Mrs. Linde—have you admired her?

MRS. LINDE: Yes, and now I'll say good night.

HELMER: Oh, come, so soon? Is this yours, this knitting?

MRS. LINDE: Yes, thanks. I nearly forgot it.

HELMER: Do you knit, then?

MRS. LINDE: Oh yes.

HELMER: You know what? You should embroider instead.

MRS. LINDE: Really? Why?

HELMER: Yes, because it's a lot prettier. See here, one holds the embroidery so, in the left hand, and then one guides the needle with the right—so—in an easy, sweeping curve—right?

MRS. LINDE: Yes, I guess that's—

HELMER: But, on the other hand, knitting—it can never be anything but ugly. Look, see here, the arms tucked in, the knitting needles going up and down—there's something Chinese about it. Ah, that was really a glorious champagne they served.

MRS. LINDE: Yes, good night, Nora, and don't be stubborn anymore.

HELMER: Well put, Mrs. Linde!

MRS. LINDE: Good night, Mr. Helmer.

HELMER: [*Accompanying her to the door.*] Good night, good night. I hope you get home all right. I'd be very happy to—but you don't have far to go. Good night, good night. [*She leaves. He shuts the door after her and returns.*] There, now, at last we got her out the door. She's a deadly bore, that creature.

NORA: Aren't you pretty tired, Torvald?

HELMER: No, not a bit.

NORA: You're not sleepy?

HELMER: Not at all. On the contrary, I'm feeling quite exhilarated. But you? Yes, you really look tired and sleepy.

NORA: Yes, I'm very tired. Soon now I'll sleep.

HELMER: See! You see! I was right all along that we shouldn't stay longer.

NORA: Whatever you do is always right.

HELMER: [*Kissing her brow.*] Now my little lark talks sense. Say, did you notice what a time Rank was having tonight?

NORA: Oh, was he? I didn't get to speak with him.

HELMER: I scarcely did either, but it's a long time since I've seen him in such high spirits. [*Gazes at her a moment, then comes nearer her.*] Hm—it's marvelous, though, to be back home again— to be completely alone with you. Oh, you bewitchingly lovely young woman!

NORA: Torvald, don't look at me like that!

HELMER: Can't I look at my richest treasure? At all that beauty that's mine, mine alone—completely and utterly.

NORA: [*Moving around to the other side of the table.*] You mustn't talk to me that way tonight.

HELMER: [*Following her.*] The tarantella is still in your blood, I can see—and it makes you even more enticing. Listen. The guests are beginning to go. [*Dropping his voice.*] Nora—it'll soon be quiet through this whole house.

NORA: Yes, I hope so.

HELMER: You do, don't you, my love? Do you realize—when I'm out at a party like this with you—do you know why I talk to you so little, and keep such a distance away; just send you a stolen look now and then—you know why I do it? It's because I'm imagining then that you're my secret darling, my secret young bride-to-be, and that no one suspects there's anything between us.

NORA: Yes, yes; oh, yes, I know you're always thinking of me.

HELMER: And then when we leave and I place the shawl over those fine young rounded shoulders—over that wonderful curving neck—then I pretend that you're my young bride, that we're just coming from the wedding, that for the first time I'm bringing you into my house—that for the first time I'm alone with you—completely alone with you, your trembling young beauty! All this evening I've longed for nothing but you. When I saw you turn and sway in the tarantella—my blood was pounding till I couldn't stand it—that's why I brought you down here so early—

NORA: Go away, Torvald! Leave me alone. I don't want all this.

HELMER: What do you mean? Nora, you're teasing me. You will, won't you? Aren't I your husband—?

[*A knock at the outside door.*]

NORA: [*Startled.*] What's that?

HELMER: [*Going toward the hall.*] Who is it?

RANK: [*Outside.*] It's me. May I come in a moment?

HELMER: [*With quiet irritation.*] Oh, what does he want now? [*Aloud.*] Hold on. [*Goes and opens the door.*] Oh, how nice that you didn't just pass us by!

RANK: I thought I heard your voice, and then I wanted so badly to have a look in. [*Lightly glancing about.*] Ah, me, these old familiar haunts. You have it snug and cozy in here, you two.

HELMER: You seemed to be having it pretty cozy upstairs, too.

RANK: Absolutely. Why shouldn't I? Why not take in everything in life? As much as you can, anyway, and as long as you can. The wine was superb—

HELMER: The champagne especially.

RANK: You noticed that too? It's amazing how much I could guzzle down.

NORA: Torvald also drank a lot of champagne this evening.

RANK: Oh?

NORA: Yes, and that always makes him so entertaining.

RANK: Well, why shouldn't one have a pleasant evening after a well-spent day?

HELMER: Well spent? I'm afraid I can't claim that.

RANK: [*Slapping him on the back.*] But I can, you see!

NORA: Dr. Rank, you must have done some scientific research today.

RANK: Quite so.

HELMER: Come now—little Nora talking about scientific research!

NORA: And can I congratulate you on the results?

RANK: Indeed you may.

NORA: Then they were good?

RANK: The best possible for both doctor and patient—certainty.

NORA: [*Quickly and searchingly.*] Certainty?

RANK: Complete certainty. So don't I owe myself a gay evening afterwards?

NORA: Yes, you're right, Dr. Rank.

HELMER: I'm with you—just so long as you don't have to suffer for it in the morning.

RANK: Well, one never gets something for nothing in life.

NORA: Dr. Rank—are you very fond of masquerade parties?

RANK: Yes, if there's a good array of odd disguises—

NORA: Tell me, what should we two go as at the next masquerade?

HELMER: You little featherhead—already thinking of the next!

RANK: We two? I'll tell you what: you must go as Charmed Life—

HELMER: Yes, but find a costume for *that*!

RANK: Your wife can appear just as she looks every day.

HELMER: That was nicely put. But don't you know what you're going to be?

RANK: Yes, Helmer, I've made up my mind.

HELMER: Well?

RANK: At the next masquerade I'm going to be invisible.

HELMER: That's a funny idea.

RANK: They say there's a hat—black, huge—have you never heard of the hat that makes you invisible? You put it on, and then no one on earth can see you.

[handwritten annotation: GRIM / THE REAPER'S CLOAK]

HELMER: [*Suppressing a smile.*] Ah, of course.

RANK: But I'm quite forgetting what I came for. Helmer, give me a cigar, one of the dark Havanas.

HELMER: With the greatest pleasure. [*Holds out his case.*]

RANK: Thanks. [*Takes one and cuts off the tip.*]

NORA: [*Striking a match.*] Let me give you a light.

RANK: Thank you. [*She holds the match for him; he lights the cigar.*] And now good-bye.

HELMER: Good-bye, good-bye, old friend.

NORA: Sleep well, Doctor.

RANK: Thanks for that wish.

NORA: Wish me the same.

RANK: You? All right, if you like—Sleep well. And thanks for the light. [*He nods to them both and leaves.*]

HELMER: [*His voice subdued.*] He's been drinking heavily.

NORA: [*Absently.*] Could be. [HELMER *takes his keys from his pocket and goes out in the hall.*] Torvald—what are you after?

HELMER: Got to empty the mailbox; it's nearly full. There won't be room for the morning papers.

NORA: Are you working tonight?

HELMER: You know I'm not. Why—what's this? Someone's been at the lock.

NORA: At the lock—?

HELMER: Yes, I'm positive. What do you suppose—? I can't imagine one of the maids—? Here's a broken hairpin. Nora, it's yours—

NORA: [*Quickly.*] Then it must be the children—

HELMER: You'd better break them of that. Hm, hm—well, opened it after all. [*Takes the contents out and calls into the kitchen.*] Helene! Helene, would you put out the lamp in the hall. [*He returns to the room, shutting the hall door, then displays the handful of mail.*] Look how it's piled up. [*Sorting through them.*] Now what's this?

NORA: [*At the window.*] The letter! Oh, Torvald, no!

HELMER: Two calling cards—from Rank.

NORA: From Dr. Rank?

HELMER: [*Examining them.*] "Dr. Rank, Consulting Physician." They were on top. He must have dropped them in as he left.

NORA: Is there anything on them?

HELMER: There's a black cross over the name. See? That's a gruesome notion. He could almost be announcing his own death.

NORA: That's just what he's doing.

HELMER: What! You've heard something? Something he's told you?

NORA: Yes. That when those cards came, he'd be taking his leave of us. He'll shut himself in now and die.

HELMER: Ah, my poor friend! Of course I knew he wouldn't be here much longer. But so soon— And then to hide himself away like a wounded animal.

NORA: If it has to happen, then it's best it happens in silence—don't you think so, Torvald?

HELMER: [*Pacing up and down.*] He'd grown right into our lives. I simply can't imagine him gone. He with his suffering and loneliness—like a dark cloud setting off our sunlit happiness. Well, maybe it's best this way. For him, at least. [*Standing still.*] And maybe for us too, Nora. Now we're thrown back on each other, completely. [*Embracing her.*] Oh you, my darling wife, how can I hold you close enough? You know what, Nora—time and again I've wished you were in some terrible danger, just so I could stake my life and soul and everything, for your sake.

NORA: [*Tearing herself away, her voice firm and decisive.*] Now you must read your mail, Torvald.

HELMER: No, no, not tonight. I want to stay with you, dearest.

NORA: With a dying friend on your mind?

HELMER: You're right. We've both had a shock. There's ugliness between us—these thoughts of death and corruption. We'll have to get free of them first. Until then—we'll stay apart.

NORA: [*Clinging about his neck.*] Torvald—good night! Good night!

HELMER: [*Kissing her on the cheek.*] Good night, little songbird. Sleep well, Nora. I'll be reading my mail now. [*He takes the letters into his room and shuts the door after him.*]

NORA: [*With bewildered glances, groping about, seizing* HELMER'*s domino, throwing it around her, and speaking in short, hoarse, broken whispers.*] Never see him again. Never, never. [*Putting her shawl over her head.*] Never see the children either—them, too. Never, never. Oh, the freezing black water! The depths—down—Oh, I wish it were over—He has it now; he's reading it—now. Oh no, no, not yet. Torvald, good-bye, you and the children—[*She starts for the hall; as she does,* HELMER *throws open his door and stands with an open letter in his hand.*]

HELMER: Nora!

NORA: [*Screams.*] Oh—!

HELMER: What is this? You know what's in this letter?

NORA: Yes, I know. Let me go! Let me out!

HELMER: [*Holding her back.*] Where are you going?

NORA: [*Struggling to break loose.*] You can't save me, Torvald!

HELMER: [*Slumping back.*] True! Then it's true what he writes? How horrible! No, no, it's impossible—it can't be true.

NORA: It *is* true. I've loved you more than all this world.

HELMER: Ah, none of your slippery tricks.

NORA: [*Taking one step toward him.*] Torvald—!

HELMER: What *is* this you've blundered into!

NORA: Just let me loose. You're not going to suffer for my sake. You're not going to take on my guilt.

HELMER: No more playacting. [*Locks the hall door.*] You stay right here and give me a reckoning. You understand what you've done? Answer! You understand?

NORA: [*Looking squarely at him, her face hardening.*] Yes. I'm beginning to understand everything now.

HELMER: [*Striding about.*] Oh, what an awful awakening! In all these eight years—she who was my pride and joy—a hypocrite, a liar—

worse, worse—a criminal! How infinitely disgusting it all is! The shame! [NORA *says nothing and goes on looking straight at him. He stops in front of her.*] I should have suspected something of the kind. I should have known. All your father's flimsy values—Be still! All your father's flimsy values have come out in you. No religion, no morals, no sense of duty—Oh, how I'm punished for letting him off! I did it for your sake, and you repay me like this.

NORA: Yes, like this.

HELMER: Now you've wrecked all my happiness—ruined my whole future. Oh, it's awful to think of. I'm in a cheap little grafter's[5] hands; he can do anything he wants with me, ask for anything, play with me like a puppet—and I can't breathe a word. I'll be swept down miserably into the depths on account of a featherbrained woman.

NORA: When I'm gone from this world, you'll be free.

HELMER: Oh, quit posing. Your father had a mess of those speeches too. What good would that ever do me if you were gone from this world, as you say? Not the slightest. He can still make the whole thing known; and if he does, I could be falsely suspected as your accomplice. They might even think that I was behind it—that I put you up to it. And all that I can thank you for—you that I've coddled the whole of our marriage. Can you see now what you've done to me?

NORA: [*Icily calm.*] Yes.

HELMER: It's so incredible, I just can't grasp it. But we'll have to patch up whatever we can. Take off the shawl. I said, take it off! I've got to appease him somehow or other. The thing has to be hushed up at any cost. And as for you and me, it's got to seem like everything between us is just as it was—to the outside world, that is. You'll go right on living in this house, of course. But you can't be allowed to bring up the children; I don't dare trust you with them—Oh, to have to say this to someone I've loved so much, and that I still—! Well, that's done with. From now on happiness doesn't matter; all that matters is saving the bits and pieces, the appearance—[*The doorbell rings.* HELMER *starts.*] What's that? And so late. Maybe the worst—? You think he'd—?

5. Swindler's; in this usage, blackmailer's.

Hide, Nora! Say you're sick. [NORA *remains standing motionless.* HELMER *goes and opens the door.*]

MAID: [*Half dressed, in the hall.*] A letter for Mrs. Helmer.

HELMER: I'll take it. [*Snatches the letter and shuts the door.*] Yes, it's from him. You don't get it; I'm reading it myself.

NORA: Then read it.

HELMER: [*By the lamp.*] I hardly dare. We may be ruined, you and I. But—I've got to know. [*Rips open the letter, skims through a few lines, glances at an enclosure, then cries out joyfully.*] Nora! [NORA *looks inquiringly at him.*] Nora! Wait—better check it again— Yes, yes, it's true. I'm saved. Nora, I'm saved!

NORA: And I?

HELMER: You too, of course. We're both saved, both of us. Look. He's sent back your note. He says he's sorry and ashamed—that a happy development in his life—oh, who cares what he says! Nora, we're saved! No one can hurt you. Oh, Nora, Nora—but first, this ugliness all has to go. Let me see—[*Takes a look at the note.*] No, I don't want to see it; I want the whole thing to fade like a dream. [*Tears the note and both letters to pieces, throws them into the stove and watches them burn.*] There—now there's nothing left—He wrote that since Christmas Eve you—Oh, they must have been three terrible days for you, Nora.

NORA: I fought a hard fight.

HELMER: And suffered pain and saw no escape but— No, we're not going to dwell on anything unpleasant. We'll just be grateful and keep on repeating: it's over now, it's over! You hear me, Nora? You don't seem to realize—it's over. What's it mean—that frozen look? Oh, poor little Nora, I understand. You can't believe I've forgiven you. But I have, Nora; I swear I have. I know that what you did, you did out of love for me.

NORA: That's true.

HELMER: You loved me the way a wife ought to love her husband. It's simply the means that you couldn't judge. But you think I love you any the less for not knowing how to handle your affairs? No, no—just lean on me; I'll guide you and teach you. I wouldn't be a man if this feminine helplessness didn't make you twice as attractive to me. You mustn't mind those sharp words I said—that was all in the first confusion of thinking my world had collapsed. I've forgiven you, Nora; I swear I've forgiven you.

NORA: My thanks for your forgiveness. [*She goes out through the door, right.*]

HELMER: No, wait— [*Peers in.*] What are you doing in there?

NORA: [*Inside.*] Getting out of my costume.

HELMER: [*By the open door.*] Yes, do that. Try to calm yourself and collect your thoughts again, my frightened little songbird. You can rest easy now; I've got wide wings to shelter you with. [*Walking about close by the door.*] How snug and nice our home is, Nora. You're safe here; I'll keep you like a hunted dove I've rescued out of a hawk's claws. I'll bring peace to your poor, shuddering heart. Gradually it'll happen, Nora; you'll see. Tomorrow all this will look different to you; then everything will be as it was. I won't have to go on repeating I forgive you; you'll feel it for yourself. How can you imagine I'd ever conceivably want to disown you—or even blame you in any way? Ah, you don't know a man's heart, Nora. For a man there's something indescribably sweet and satisfying in knowing he's forgiven his wife—and forgiven her out of a full and open heart. It's as if she belongs to him in two ways now: in a sense he's given her fresh into the world again, and she's become his wife and his child as well. From now on that's what you'll be to me—you little, bewildered, helpless thing. Don't be afraid of anything, Nora; just open your heart to me, and I'll be conscience and will to you both— [NORA *enters in her regular clothes.*] What's this? Not in bed? You've changed your dress?

NORA: Yes, Torvald, I've changed my dress.

HELMER: But why now, so late?

NORA: Tonight I'm not sleeping.

HELMER: But Nora dear—

NORA: [*Looking at her watch.*] It's still not so very late. Sit down, Torvald; we have a lot to talk over. [*She sits at one side of the table.*]

HELMER: Nora—what is this? That hard expression—

NORA: Sit down. This'll take some time. I have a lot to say.

HELMER: [*Sitting at the table directly opposite her.*] You worry me, Nora. And I don't understand you.

NORA: No, that's exactly it. You don't understand me. And I've never understood you either—until tonight. No, don't interrupt. You can just listen to what I say. We're closing out accounts, Torvald.

HELMER: How do you mean that?

NORA: [*After a short pause.*] Doesn't anything strike you about our sitting here like this?

HELMER: What's that?

NORA: We've been married now eight years. Doesn't it occur to you that this is the first time we two, you and I, man and wife, have ever talked seriously together?

HELMER: What do you mean—seriously?

NORA: In eight whole years—longer even—right from our first acquaintance, we've never exchanged a serious word on any serious thing.

HELMER: You mean I should constantly go and involve you in problems you couldn't possibly help me with?

NORA: I'm not talking of problems. I'm saying that we've never sat down seriously together and tried to get to the bottom of anything.

HELMER: But dearest, what good would that ever do you?

NORA: That's the point right there: you've never understood me. I've been wronged greatly, Torvald—first by Papa, and then by you.

HELMER: What! By us—the two people who've loved you more than anyone else?

NORA: [*Shaking her head.*] You never loved me. You've thought it fun to be in love with me, that's all.

HELMER: Nora, what a thing to say!

NORA: Yes, it's true now, Torvald. When I lived at home with Papa, he told me all his opinions, so I had the same ones too; or if they were different I hid them, since he wouldn't have cared for that. He used to call me his doll-child, and he played with me the way I played with my dolls. Then I came into your house—

HELMER: How can you speak of our marriage like that?

NORA: [*Unperturbed.*] I mean, then I went from Papa's hands into yours. You arranged everything to your own taste, and so I got the same taste as you—or I pretended to; I can't remember. I guess a little of both, first one, then the other. Now when I look back, it seems as if I'd lived here like a beggar—just from hand to mouth. I've lived by doing tricks for you, Torvald. But that's the way you wanted it. It's a great sin what you and Papa did to me. You're to blame that nothing's become of me.

HELMER: Nora, how unfair and ungrateful you are! Haven't you been happy here?

NORA: No, never. I thought so—but I never have.

HELMER: Not—not happy!

NORA: No, only lighthearted. And you've always been so kind to me. But our home's been nothing but a playpen. I've been your doll-wife here, just as at home I was Papa's doll-child. And in turn the children have been my dolls. I thought it was fun when you played with me, just as they thought it fun when I played with them. That's been our marriage, Torvald.

HELMER: There's some truth in what you're saying—under all the raving exaggeration. But it'll all be different after this. Playtime's over; now for the schooling.

NORA: Whose schooling—mine or the children's?

HELMER: Both yours and the children's, dearest.

NORA: Oh, Torvald, you're not the man to teach me to be a good wife to you.

HELMER: And you can say that?

NORA: And I—how am I equipped to bring up children?

HELMER: Nora!

NORA: Didn't you say a moment ago that that was no job to trust me with?

HELMER: In a flare of temper! Why fasten on that?

NORA: Yes, but you were so very right. I'm not up to the job. There's another job I have to do first. I have to try to educate myself. You can't help me with that. I've got to do it alone. And that's why I'm leaving you now.

HELMER: [*Jumping up.*] What's that?

NORA: I have to stand completely alone, if I'm ever going to discover myself and the world out there. So I can't go on living with you.

HELMER: Nora, Nora!

NORA: I want to leave right away. Kristine should put me up for the night—

HELMER: You're insane! You've no right! I forbid you!

NORA: From here on, there's no use forbidding me anything. I'll take with me whatever is mine. I don't want a thing from you, either now or later.

HELMER: What kind of madness is this!

NORA: Tomorrow I'm going home—I mean, home where I came from. It'll be easier up there to find something to do.

HELMER: Oh, you blind, incompetent child! *[handwritten: IRONIC — A KIND OF MIRROR]*

NORA: I must learn to be competent, Torvald.

HELMER: Abandon your home, your husband, your children! And you're not even thinking what people will say.

NORA: I can't be concerned about that. I only know how essential this is. *[handwritten: ✦]*

HELMER: Oh, it's outrageous. So you'll run out like this on your most sacred vows.

NORA: What do you think are my most sacred vows?

HELMER: And I have to tell you that! Aren't they your duties to your husband and children?

NORA: I have other duties equally sacred.

HELMER: That isn't true. What duties are they?

NORA: Duties to myself.

HELMER: Before all else, you're a wife and a mother.

NORA: I don't believe in that anymore. I believe that, before all else, I'm a human being, no less than you—or anyway, I ought to try to become one. I know the majority thinks you're right, Torvald, and plenty of books agree with you, too. But I can't go on believing what the majority says, or what's written in books. I have to think over these things myself and try to understand them. *[handwritten: ✦]*

HELMER: Why can't you understand your place in your own home? On a point like that, isn't there one everlasting guide you can turn to? Where's your religion?

NORA: Oh, Torvald, I'm really not sure what religion is.

HELMER: What—?

NORA: I only know what the minister said when I was confirmed. He told me religion was this thing and that. When I get clear and away by myself, I'll go into that problem too. I'll see if what the minister said was right, or, in any case, if it's right for me.

HELMER: A young woman your age shouldn't talk like that. If religion can't move you, I can try to rouse your conscience. You do have some moral feeling? Or, tell me—has that gone too?

NORA: It's not easy to answer that, Torvald. I simply don't know.

[handwritten: SINGULAR SELF-DETERMINISM]

[Handwritten margin note: WAS SHE "MARRIED" IN LAW? IN HER WAY LIKE MRS. PETERS IN TRIFLES?]

I'm all confused about these things. I just know I see them so differently from you. I find out, for one thing, that the law's not at all what I'd thought—but I can't get it through my head that the law is fair. A woman hasn't a right to protect her dying father or save her husband's life! I can't believe that.

HELMER: You talk like a child. You don't know anything of the world you live in.

NORA: No, I don't. But now I'll begin to learn for myself. I'll try to discover who's right, the world or I.

HELMER: Nora, you're sick; you've got a fever. I almost think you're out of your head.

NORA: I've never felt more clearheaded and sure in my life.

HELMER: And—clearheaded and sure—you're leaving your husband and children?

NORA: Yes.

HELMER: Then there's only one possible reason.

NORA: What?

HELMER: You no longer love me.

NORA: No. That's exactly it.

HELMER: Nora! You can't be serious!

NORA: Oh, this is so hard, Torvald—you've been so kind to me always. But I can't help it. I don't love you anymore.

HELMER: [*Struggling for composure.*] Are you also clearheaded and sure about that?

NORA: Yes, completely. That's why I can't go on staying here.

HELMER: Can you tell me what I did to lose your love?

NORA: Yes, I can tell you. It was this evening when the miraculous thing didn't come—then I knew you weren't the man I'd imagined.

HELMER: Be more explicit; I don't follow you.

NORA: I've waited now so patiently eight long years—for, my Lord, I know miracles don't come every day. Then this crisis broke over me, and such a certainty filled me: *now* the miraculous event would occur. While Krogstad's letter was lying out there, I never for an instant dreamed that you could give in to his terms. I was so utterly sure you'd say to him: go on, tell your tale to the whole wide world. And when he'd done that—

HELMER: Yes, what then? When I'd delivered my own wife into

shame and disgrace—!

NORA: When he'd done that, I was so utterly sure that you'd step forward, take the blame on yourself and say: I am the guilty one.

HELMER: Nora—!

NORA: You're thinking I'd never accept such a sacrifice from you? No, of course not. But what good would my protests be against you? That was the miracle I was waiting for, in terror and hope. And to stave that off, I would have taken my life.

HELMER: I'd gladly work for you day and night, Nora—and take on pain and deprivation. But there's no one who gives up honor for love.

NORA: Millions of women have done just that.

HELMER: Oh, you think and talk like a silly child.

NORA: Perhaps. But you neither think nor talk like the man I could join myself to. When your big fright was over—and it wasn't from any threat against me, only for what might damage you— when all the danger was past, for you it was just as if nothing had happened. I was exactly the same, your little lark, your doll, that you'd have to handle with double care now that I'd turned out so brittle and frail. [*Gets up.*] Torvald—in that instant it dawned on me that for eight years I've been living here with a stranger, and that I'd even conceived three children—oh, I can't stand the thought of it! I could tear myself to bits.

HELMER: [*Heavily.*] I see. There's a gulf that's opened between us— that's clear. Oh, but Nora, can't we bridge it somehow?

NORA: The way I am now, I'm no wife for you.

HELMER: I have the strength to make myself over.

NORA: Maybe—if your doll gets taken away.

HELMER: But to part! To part from you! No, Nora, no—I can't imagine it.

NORA: [*Going out, right.*] All the more reason why it has to be. [*She reenters with her coat and a small overnight bag, which she puts on a chair by the table.*]

HELMER: Nora, Nora, not now! Wait till tomorrow.

NORA: I can't spend the night in a strange man's room.

HELMER: But couldn't we live here like brother and sister—

NORA: You know very well how long that would last. [*Throws her shawl about her.*] Good-bye, Torvald. I won't look in on the children.

I know they're in better hands than mine. The way I am now, I'm no use to them.

HELMER: But someday, Nora—someday—?

NORA: How can I tell? I haven't the least idea what'll become of me.

HELMER: But you're my wife, now and wherever you go.

NORA: Listen, Torvald—I've heard that when a wife deserts her husband's house just as I'm doing, then the law frees him from all responsibility. In any case, I'm freeing you from being responsible. Don't feel yourself bound, any more than I will. There has to be absolute freedom for us both. Here, take your ring back. Give me mine.

HELMER: That too?

NORA: That too.

HELMER: There it is.

NORA: Good. Well, now it's all over. I'm putting the keys here. The maids know all about keeping up the house—better than I do. Tomorrow, after I've left town, Kristine will stop by to pack up everything that's mine from home. I'd like those things shipped up to me.

HELMER: Over! All over! Nora, won't you ever think about me?

NORA: I'm sure I'll think of you often, and about the children and the house here.

HELMER: May I write you?

NORA: No—never. You're not to do that.

HELMER: Oh, but let me send you—

NORA: Nothing. Nothing.

HELMER: Or help you if you need it.

NORA: No. I accept nothing from strangers.

HELMER: Nora—can I never be more than a stranger to you?

NORA: [*Picking up the overnight bag.*] Ah, Torvald—it would take the greatest miracle of all—

HELMER: Tell me the greatest miracle!

NORA: You and I both would have to transform ourselves to the point that— Oh, Torvald, I've stopped believing in miracles.

HELMER: But I'll believe. Tell me! Transform ourselves to the point that—?

NORA: That our living together could be a true marriage. [*She goes out down the hall.*]

HELMER: [*Sinks down on a chair by the door, face buried in his hands.*]

Nora! Nora! [*Looking about and rising.*] Empty. She's gone.
[*A sudden hope leaps in him.*] The greatest miracle—?
   [*From below, the sound of a door slamming shut.*]   MEH!

1878   1879

Susan Glaspell
1882–1948

TRIFLES

Trifles *is based on a real-life murder. On a cold December night,
in an Iowa farmhouse, John Hossack was sleeping in his bed when
someone struck him in the head with an ax. His wife, Margaret,
claimed she was awakened by the noise of the blows, which sounded
like one block of wood striking another one, but evidence suggested
she was the murderer. Her motive, according to the authorities,
was unhappiness within a bad marriage.*

   Susan Glaspell, a young reporter for the Des Moines Daily
News, *covered the case. At first, she led readers down a familiar,
lurid path of indignation and outrage, appealing to her readers'
prejudices, sensationalizing the crime, and portraying Margaret
Hossack as a monster. But after visiting the Hossacks' kitchen in
the company of investigators, she came to regard the wife not as
a criminal but as a victim, and her newspaper stories began to
describe the horrific life Margaret Hossack suffered during thirty-
three years of marriage to an oppressive and abusive husband.
The trial proved a great public entertainment; the courthouse
was packed to overflowing, with more women in attendance than
men. Although Hossack was convicted of murder and sentenced to
hard labor for life, her lawyers appealed the verdict and won; in a
retrial, the jury couldn't reach a consensus, so Hossack was released.*

   *The story lay dormant in Glaspell's imagination for a dozen
years. When her husband, the writer George Cook, announced to
their friends that Glaspell would provide a new play for the 1916
"season" of the Provincetown Players, a modest theatrical company the couple had co-founded in Provincetown, Massachusetts,
Glaspell, who was really a fiction writer, settled down to write a*

play. In the heat of summer days, she sat in the empty space of the Wharf Theater until, as she put it, the "bare little stage" began to take on the features of Margaret Hossack's kitchen. She wrote the play in two weeks, and it opened on August 8, 1916, with Cook and Glaspell in the roles of Mr. and Mrs. Hale. Some critics have seen features of the young Glaspell, as she was when she reported the Hossack case, in Mrs. Hale.

The play was picked up by New York City's Washington Square Players, a group midway between the Provincetown Players and the mainstream, commercial theaters on Broadway. The New York production gave Glaspell a wider audience, and soon she was a famous figure in the New York theater world, with the New York Times *printing feature stories about her.*

Like her fellow Provincetowners, including playwright Eugene O'Neill, Glaspell sought to give America a serious theater predicated on a repudiation of the melodrama and sentimentality that dominated the popular stage. She did not, however, disdain common theatergoers or think that her proper audience was the elite intellectuals among whom she worked and lived. A socialist, Glaspell wanted her work to affect people beyond her circle, to entertain a popular audience at the same time that it improved Americans' lives.

Within Trifles, *you'll find many insights into relations between men and women in America. If you look carefully, you'll also detect Glaspell's social commentary on class distinctions, in the different characterizations of Mrs. Hale and Mrs. Peters.*

Trifles

CHARACTERS

SHERIFF	MRS. PETERS, *Sheriff's wife*
COUNTY ATTORNEY	MRS. HALE
HALE	

SCENE: *The kitchen in the now abandoned farmhouse of* JOHN WRIGHT, *a gloomy kitchen, and left without having been put in order—unwashed pans under the sink, a loaf of bread outside the breadbox, a dish-towel on the table—other signs of incompleted work. At the rear the outer door opens and the* SHERIFF *comes in followed by the* COUNTY ATTORNEY *and* HALE. *The* SHERIFF *and* HALE *are men in middle life, the* COUNTY ATTORNEY *is a young man; all are much bundled up and go at once to the stove. They are followed by the two women—the* SHERIFF'S *wife first; she is a slight wiry woman, a thin nervous face.* MRS. HALE *is larger and would ordinarily be called more comfortable looking, but she is disturbed now and looks fearfully about as she enters. The women have come in slowly, and stand close together near the door.*

COUNTY ATTORNEY: [*Rubbing his hands.*] This feels good. Come up to the fire, ladies.

MRS. PETERS: [*After taking a step forward.*] I'm not—cold.

SHERIFF: [*Unbuttoning his overcoat and stepping away from the stove as if to mark the beginning of official business.*] Now, Mr. Hale, before we move things about, you explain to Mr. Henderson just what you saw when you came here yesterday morning.

COUNTY ATTORNEY: By the way, has anything been moved? Are things just as you left them yesterday?

SHERIFF: [*Looking about.*] It's just the same. When it dropped below zero last night I thought I'd better send Frank out this morning to make a fire for us—no use getting pneumonia with a big case on, but I told him not to touch anything except the stove—and you know Frank.

COUNTY ATTORNEY: Somebody should have been left here yesterday.

SHERIFF: Oh—yesterday. When I had to send Frank to Morris Center for that man who went crazy—I want you to know I had my hands full yesterday. I knew you could get back from Omaha by today and as long as I went over everything here myself—

COUNTY ATTORNEY: Well, Mr. Hale, tell just what happened when you came here yesterday morning.

HALE: Harry and I had started to town with a load of potatoes. We came along the road from my place and as I got here I said, "I'm going to see if I can't get John Wright to go in with me on a party telephone."[1] I spoke to Wright about it once before and he put me off, saying folks talked too much anyway, and all he asked was peace and quiet—I guess you know about how much he talked himself; but I thought maybe if I went to the house and talked about it before his wife, though I said to Harry that I didn't know

---

1. One telephone line shared by a number of houses.

as what his wife wanted made much difference to John—

COUNTY ATTORNEY: Let's talk about that later, Mr. Hale. I do want to talk about that, but tell now just what happened when you got to the house.

HALE: I didn't hear or see anything; I knocked at the door, and still it was all quiet inside. I knew they must be up, it was past eight o'clock. So I knocked again, and I thought I heard somebody say, "Come in." I wasn't sure, I'm not sure yet, but I opened the door—this door [*Indicating the door by which the two women are still standing.*] and there in that rocker— [*Pointing to it.*] sat Mrs. Wright.

[*They all look at the rocker.*]

COUNTY ATTORNEY: What—was she doing?

HALE: She was rockin' back and forth. She had her apron in her hand and was kind of—pleating it.

COUNTY ATTORNEY: And how did she—look?

HALE: Well, she looked queer.

COUNTY ATTORNEY: How do you mean—queer?

HALE: Well, as if she didn't know what she was going to do next. And kind of done up.

COUNTY ATTORNEY: How did she seem to feel about your coming?

HALE: Why, I don't think she minded—one way or other. She didn't pay much attention. I said, "How do, Mrs. Wright, it's cold, ain't it?" And she said, "Is it?"—and went on kind of pleating at her apron. Well, I was surprised; she didn't ask me to come up to the stove, or to set down, but just sat there, not even looking at me, so I said, "I want to see John." And then she—laughed. I guess you would call it a laugh. I thought of Harry and the team outside, so I said a little sharp: "Can't I see John?" "No," she says, kind o' dull like. "Ain't he home?" says I. "Yes," says she, "he's home." "Then why can't I see him?" I asked her, out of patience. "'Cause he's dead," says she. "*Dead?*" says I. She just nodded her head, not getting a bit excited, but rockin' back and forth. "Why—where is he?" says I, not knowing what to say. She just pointed upstairs— like that. [*Himself pointing to the room above.*] I got up, with the idea of going up there. I walked from there to here—then I says, "Why, what did he die of?" "He died of a rope round his neck," says she, and just went on pleatin' at her apron. Well, I went out and called Harry. I thought I might—need help. We went upstairs and there he was lyin'—

COUNTY ATTORNEY: I think I'd rather have you go into that upstairs, where you can point it all out. Just go on now with the rest of the story.

HALE: Well, my first thought was to get that rope off. It looked . . . [*Stops, his face twitches.*] . . . but Harry, he went up to him, and he said, "No, he's dead all right, and we'd better not touch anything." So we went back down stairs. She was still sitting that same way. "Has anybody been notified?" I asked. "No," says she unconcerned. "Who did this, Mrs. Wright?" said Harry. He said it business-like—and she stopped pleatin' of her apron. "I don't know," she says. "You don't *know?*" says Harry. "No," says she. "Weren't you sleepin' in the bed with him?" says Harry. "Yes," says she, "but I was on the inside." "Somebody slipped a rope round his neck and strangled him and you didn't wake up?" says Harry. "I didn't wake up," she said after him. We must 'a looked as if we didn't see how that could be, for after a minute she said, "I sleep sound." Harry was going to ask her more questions but I said maybe we ought to let her tell her story first to the coroner, or the sheriff, so Harry went fast as he could to Rivers' place, where there's a telephone.

COUNTY ATTORNEY: And what did Mrs. Wright do when she knew that you had gone for the coroner?

HALE: She moved from that chair to this one over here [*Pointing to a small chair in the corner.*] and just sat there with her hands held together and looking down. I got a feeling that I ought to make some conversation, so I said I had come in to see if John wanted to put in a telephone, and at that she started to laugh, and then she stopped and looked at me—scared. [*The* COUNTY ATTORNEY, *who has had his notebook out, makes a note.*] I dunno, maybe it wasn't scared. I wouldn't like to say it was. Soon Harry got back, and then Dr. Lloyd came, and you, Mr. Peters, and so I guess that's all I know that you don't.

COUNTY ATTORNEY: [*Looking around.*] I guess we'll go upstairs first—and then out to the barn and around there. [*To the* SHERIFF.] You're convinced that there was nothing important here—nothing that would point to any motive?

SHERIFF: Nothing here but kitchen things.

[*The* COUNTY ATTORNEY, *after again looking around the kitchen, opens the door of a cupboard closet. He gets up on a chair and looks on a shelf. Pulls his hand away, sticky.*]

COUNTY ATTORNEY: Here's a nice mess.

[*The women draw nearer.*]

MRS. PETERS: [*To the other woman.*] Oh, her fruit; it did freeze. [*To the* LAWYER.] She worried about that when it turned so cold. She said the fire'd go out and her jars would break.

SHERIFF: Well, can you beat the women! Held for murder and worryin' about her preserves.

COUNTY ATTORNEY: I guess before we're through she may have something more serious than preserves to worry about.

HALE: Well, women are used to worrying over trifles.

[*The two women move a little closer together.*]

COUNTY ATTORNEY: [*With the gallantry of a young politician.*] And yet, for all their worries, what would we do without the ladies? [*The women do not unbend. He goes to the sink, takes a dipperful of water from the pail, and pouring it into a basin, washes his hands. Starts to wipe them on the roller-towel, turns it for a cleaner place.*] Dirty towels! [*Kicks his foot against the pans under the sink.*] Not much of a housekeeper, would you say, ladies?

MRS. HALE: [*Stiffly.*] There's a great deal of work to be done on a farm.

COUNTY ATTORNEY: To be sure. And yet [*With a little bow to her.*] I know there are some Dickson county farmhouses which do not have such roller towels. [*He gives it a pull to expose its length again.*]

MRS. HALE: Those towels get dirty awful quick. Men's hands aren't always as clean as they might be.

COUNTY ATTORNEY: Ah, loyal to your sex, I see. But you and Mrs. Wright were neighbors. I suppose you were friends, too.

MRS. HALE: [*Shaking her head.*] I've not seen much of her of late years. I've not been in this house—it's more than a year.

COUNTY ATTORNEY: And why was that? You didn't like her?

MRS. HALE: I liked her all well enough. Farmers' wives have their hands full, Mr. Henderson. And then—

COUNTY ATTORNEY: Yes—?

MRS. HALE: [*Looking about.*] It never seemed a very cheerful place.

COUNTY ATTORNEY: No—it's not cheerful. I shouldn't say she had the homemaking instinct.

MRS. HALE: Well, I don't know as Wright had, either.

COUNTY ATTORNEY: You mean that they didn't get on very well?

MRS. HALE: No, I don't mean anything. But I don't think a place'd be any cheerfuller for John Wright's being in it.

COUNTY ATTORNEY: I'd like to talk more of that a little later. I want to get the lay of things upstairs now. [*He goes to the left, where three steps lead to a stair door.*]

SHERIFF: I suppose anything Mrs. Peters does'll be all right. She was to take in some clothes for her, you know, and a few little things. We left in such a hurry yesterday.

COUNTY ATTORNEY: Yes, but I would like to see what you take, Mrs. Peters, and keep an eye out for anything that might be of use to us.

MRS. PETERS: Yes, Mr. Henderson. [*The women listen to the men's steps on the stairs, then look about the kitchen.*]

MRS. HALE: I'd hate to have men coming into my kitchen, snooping around and criticizing. [*She arranges the pans under sink which the LAWYER had shoved out of place.*]

MRS. PETERS: Of course it's no more than their duty.

MRS. HALE: Duty's all right, but I guess that deputy sheriff that came out to make the fire might have got a little of this on. [*Gives the roller towel a pull.*] Wish I'd thought of that sooner. Seems mean to talk about her for not having things slicked up when she had to come away in such a hurry.

MRS. PETERS: [*Who has gone to a small table in the left rear corner of the room, and lifted one end of a towel that covers a pan.*] She had bread set. [*Stands still.*]

MRS. HALF: [*Eyes fixed on a loaf of bread beside the bread box, which is on a low shelf at the other side of the room. Moves slowly toward it.*] She was going to put this in there. [*Picks up loaf, then abruptly drops it. In a manner of returning to familiar things.*] It's a shame about her fruit. I wonder if it's all gone. [*Gets up on the chair and looks.*] I think there's some here that's all right, Mrs. Peters. Yes—here; [*Holding it toward the window.*] this is cherries, too. [*Looking again.*] I declare I believe that's the only one. [*Gets down, bottle in her hand. Goes to the sink and wipes it off on the outside.*] She'll feel awful bad after all her hard work in the hot weather. I remember the afternoon I put up my cherries last summer. [*She puts the bottle on the big kitchen table, center of the room. With a sigh, is about to sit down in the rocking-chair. Before she is seated realizes what chair it is; with a slow look at it, steps back. The chair, which she has touched, rocks back and forth.*]

MRS. PETERS: Well, I must get those things from the front room closet. [*She goes to the door at the right, but after looking into the other room, steps back.*] You coming with me, Mrs. Hale? You could help me carry them. [*They go in the other room; reappear,* MRS. PETERS *carrying a dress and skirt,* MRS. HALE *following with a pair of shoes.*] My, it's cold in there. [*She puts the clothes on the big table, and hurries to the stove.*]

MRS. HALE: [*Examining the skirt.*] Wright was close. I think maybe that's why she kept so much to herself. She didn't even belong to the Ladies Aid.[2] I suppose she felt she couldn't do her part, and then you don't enjoy things when you feel shabby. She used to wear pretty clothes and be lively, when she was Minnie Foster, one of the town girls singing in the choir. But that—oh, that was thirty years ago. This all you was to take in?

MRS. PETERS: She said she wanted an apron. Funny thing to want, for there isn't much to get you dirty in jail, goodness knows. But I suppose just to make her feel more natural. She said they was in the top drawer in this cupboard. Yes, here. And then her little shawl that always hung behind the door. [*Opens stair door and looks.*] Yes, here it is. [*Quickly shuts door leading upstairs.*]

MRS. HALE: [*Abruptly moving toward her.*] Mrs. Peters?

MRS. PETERS: Yes, Mrs. Hale?

MRS. HALE: Do you think she did it?

MRS. PETERS: [*In a frightened voice.*] Oh, I don't know.

MRS. HALE: Well, I don't think she did. Asking for an apron and her little shawl. Worrying about her fruit.

MRS. PETERS: [*Starts to speak, glances up, where footsteps are heard in the room above. In a low voice.*] Mr. Peters says it looks bad for her. Mr. Henderson is awful sarcastic in a speech and he'll make fun of her sayin' she didn't wake up.

---

2. A volunteer benevolence society.

MRS. HALE: Well, I guess John Wright didn't wake when they was slipping that rope under his neck.

MRS. PETERS: No, it's strange. It must have been done awful crafty and still. They say it was such a—funny way to kill a man, rigging it all up like that.

MRS. HALE: That's just what Mr. Hale said. There was a gun in the house. He says that's what he can't understand.

MRS. PETERS: Mr. Henderson said coming out that what was needed for the case was a motive; something to show anger, or—sudden feeling.

MRS. HALE: [*Who is standing by the table.*] Well, I don't see any signs of anger around here. [*She puts her hand on the dish towel which lies on the table, stands looking down at table, one half of which is clean, the other half messy.*] It's wiped to here. [*Makes a move as if to finish work, then turns and looks at loaf of bread outside the bread box. Drops towel. In that voice of coming back to familiar things.*] Wonder how they are finding things upstairs. I hope she had it a little more red-up[3] up there. You know, it seems kind of *sneaking*. Locking her up in town and then coming out here and trying to get her own house to turn against her!

MRS. PETERS: But Mrs. Hale, the law is the law.

MRS. HALE: I s'pose 'tis. [*Unbuttoning her coat.*] Better loosen up your things, Mrs. Peters. You won't feel them when you go out.
[MRS. PETERS *takes off her fur tippet,[4] goes to hang it on hook at back of room, stands looking at the under part of the small corner table.*]

MRS. PETERS: She was piecing a quilt. [*She brings the large sewing basket and they look at the bright pieces.*]

MRS. HALE: It's log cabin pattern. Pretty, isn't it? I wonder if she was goin' to quilt it or just knot it?[5]
[*Footsteps have been heard coming down the stairs. The* SHERIFF *enters followed by* HALE *and the* COUNTY ATTORNEY.]

SHERIFF: They wonder if she was going to quilt it or just knot it!
[*The men laugh, the women look abashed.*]

---

3. Tidied up.
4. Shoulder covering, like a full scarf.
5. The top of a quilt can be attached to the backing by sewing, which is a laborious process, or by knotting thick yarn, which is much quicker and easier.

COUNTY ATTORNEY: [*Rubbing his hands over the stove.*] Frank's fire didn't do much up there, did it? Well, let's go out to the barn and get that cleared up.

[*The men go outside.*]

MRS. HALE: [*Resentfully.*] I don't know as there's anything so strange, our takin' up our time with little things while we're waiting for them to get the evidence. [*She sits down at the big table smoothing out a block with decision.*] I don't see as it's anything to laugh about.

MRS. PETERS: [*Apologetically.*] Of course they've got awful important things on their minds. [*Pulls up a chair and joins* MRS. HALE *at the table.*]

MRS. HALE: [*Examining another block.*] Mrs. Peters, look at this one. Here, this is the one she was working on, and look at the sewing! All the rest of it has been so nice and even. And look at this! It's all over the place! Why, it looks as if she didn't know what she was about! [*After she has said this they look at each other, then start to glance back at the door. After an instant* MRS. HALE *has pulled at a knot and ripped the sewing.*]

MRS. PETERS: Oh, what are you doing, Mrs. Hale?

MRS. HALE: [*Mildly.*] Just pulling out a stitch or two that's not sewed very good. [*Threading the needle.*] Bad sewing always made me fidgety.

MRS. PETERS: [*Nervously.*] I don't think we ought to touch things.

MRS. HALE: I'll just finish up this end. [*Suddenly stopping and leaning forward.*] Mrs. Peters?

MRS. PETERS: Yes, Mrs. Hale?

MRS. HALE: What do you suppose she was so nervous about?

MRS. PETERS: Oh—I don't know. I don't know as she was nervous. I sometimes sew awful queer when I'm just tired. [MRS. HALE *starts to say something, looks at* MRS. PETERS, *then goes on sewing.*] Well I must get these things wrapped up. They may be through sooner than we think. [*Putting apron and other things together.*] I wonder where I can find a piece of paper, and string.

MRS. HALE: In that cupboard, maybe.

MRS. PETERS: [*Looking in cupboard.*] Why, here's a bird-cage. [*Holds it up.*] Did she have a bird, Mrs. Hale?

MRS. HALE: Why, I don't know whether she did or not—I've not been here for so long. There was a man around last year selling canaries cheap, but I don't know as she took one; maybe she did. She used to sing real pretty herself.

MRS. PETERS: [*Glancing around.*] Seems funny to think of a bird here. But she must have had one, or why would she have a cage? I wonder what happened to it.

MRS. HALE: I s'pose maybe the cat got it.

MRS. PETERS: No, she didn't have a cat. She's got that feeling some people have about cats—being afraid of them. My cat got in her room and she was real upset and asked me to take it out.

MRS. HALE: My sister Bessie was like that. Queer, ain't it?

MRS. PETERS: [*Examining the cage.*] Why, look at this door. It's broke. One hinge is pulled apart.

MRS. HALE: [*Looking too.*] Looks as if someone must have been rough with it.

MRS. PETERS: Why, yes. [*She brings the cage forward and puts it on the table.*]

MRS. HALE: I wish if they're going to find any evidence they'd be about it. I don't like this place.

MRS. PETERS: But I'm awful glad you came with me, Mrs. Hale. It would be lonesome for me sitting here alone.

MRS. HALE: It would, wouldn't it? [*Dropping her sewing.*] But I tell you what I do wish, Mrs. Peters. I wish I had come over sometimes when *she* was here. I—[*Looking around the room.*]—wish I had.

MRS. PETERS: But of course you were awful busy, Mrs. Hale—your house and your children.

MRS. HALE: I could've come. I stayed away because it weren't cheerful—and that's why I ought to have come. I—I've never liked this place. Maybe because it's down in a hollow and you don't see the road. I dunno what it is, but it's a lonesome place and always was. I wish I had come over to see Minnie Foster sometimes. I can see now—[*Shakes her head.*]

MRS. PETERS: Well, you mustn't reproach yourself, Mrs. Hale. Somehow we just don't see how it is with other folks until— something comes up.

MRS. HALE: Not having children makes less work—but it makes a quiet house, and Wright out to work all day, and no company when he did come in. Did you know John Wright, Mrs. Peters?

MRS. PETERS: Not to know him; I've seen him in town. They say he was a good man.

MRS. HALE: Yes—good; he didn't drink, and kept his word as well as most, I guess, and paid his debts. But he was a hard man, Mrs. Peters. Just to pass the time of day with him—[*Shivers.*] Like a raw wind that gets to the bone. [*Pauses, her eye falling on the cage.*] I should think she would 'a wanted a bird. But what do you suppose went with it?

MRS. PETERS: I don't know, unless it got sick and died. [*She reaches over and swings the broken door, swings it again, both women watch it.*]

MRS. HALE: You weren't raised round here, were you? [MRS. PETERS *shakes her head.*] You didn't know—her?

MRS. PETERS: Not till they brought her yesterday.

MRS. HALE: She—come to think of it, she was kind of like a bird herself—real sweet and pretty, but kind of timid and—fluttery. How—she—did—change. [*Silence; then as if struck by a happy thought and relieved to get back to everyday things.*] Tell you what, Mrs. Peters, why don't you take the quilt in with you? It might take up her mind.

MRS. PETERS: Why, I think that's a real nice idea, Mrs. Hale. There couldn't possibly be any objection to it, could there? Now, just what would I take? I wonder if her patches are in here—and her things. [*They look in the sewing basket.*]

MRS. HALE: Here's some red. I expect this has got sewing things in it. [*Brings out a fancy box.*] What a pretty box. Looks like something somebody would give you. Maybe her scissors are in here. [*Opens box. Suddenly puts her hand to her nose.*] Why—[MRS. PETERS *bends nearer, then turns her face away.*] There's something wrapped up in this piece of silk.

MRS. PETERS: Why, this isn't her scissors.

MRS. HALE: [*Lifting the silk.*] Oh, Mrs. Peters—it's—

[MRS. PETERS *bends closer.*]

MRS. PETERS: It's the bird.

MRS. HALE: [*Jumping up.*] But, Mrs. Peters—look at it! Its neck! Look at its neck! It's all—other side *to.*

MRS. PETERS: Somebody—wrung—its—neck.

[*Their eyes meet. A look of growing comprehension, of horror. Steps are heard outside.* MRS. HALE *slips box under quilt pieces, and sinks into her chair. Enter* SHERIFF *and* COUNTY ATTORNEY. MRS. PETERS *rises.*]

COUNTY ATTORNEY: [*As one turning from serious things to little pleasantries.*] Well, ladies, have you decided whether she was going to quilt it or knot it?

MRS. PETERS: We think she was going to—knot it.

COUNTY ATTORNEY: Well, that's interesting, I'm sure. [*Seeing the bird-cage.*] Has the bird flown?

MRS. HALE: [*Putting more quilt pieces over the box.*] We think the—cat got it.

COUNTY ATTORNEY: [*Preoccupied.*] Is there a cat?

[MRS. HALE *glances in a quick covert way at* MRS. PETERS.]

MRS. PETERS: Well, not *now*. They're superstitious, you know. They leave.

COUNTY ATTORNEY: [*To* SHERIFF PETERS, *continuing an interrupted conversation.*] No sign at all of anyone having come from the outside. Their own rope. Now let's go up again and go over it piece by piece. [*They start upstairs.*] It would have to have been someone who knew just the—

[MRS. PETERS *sits down. The two women sit there not looking at one another, but as if peering into something and at the same time holding back. When they talk now it is in the manner of feeling their way over strange ground, as if afraid of what they are saying, but as if they cannot help saying it.*]

MRS. HALE: She liked the bird. She was going to bury it in that pretty box.

MRS. PETERS: [*In a whisper.*] When I was a girl—my kitten—there was a boy took a hatchet, and before my eyes—and before I could get there—[*Covers her face an instant.*] If they hadn't held me back I would have—[*Catches herself, looks upstairs where steps are heard, falters weakly.*]—hurt him.

MRS. HALE: [*With a slow look around her.*] I wonder how it would seem never to have had any children around. [*Pause.*] No, Wright wouldn't like the bird—a thing that sang. She used to sing. He killed that, too.

MRS. PETERS: [*Moving uneasily.*] We don't know who killed the bird.

MRS. HALE: I knew John Wright.

MRS. PETERS: It was an awful thing was done in this house that night, Mrs. Hale. Killing a man while he slept, slipping a rope around his neck that choked the life out of him.

MRS. HALE: His neck. Choked the life out of him. [*Her hand goes out and rests on the bird-cage.*]

MRS. PETERS: [*With rising voice.*] We don't know who killed him. We don't *know.*

MRS. HALE: [*Her own feeling not interrupted.*] If there's been years and years of nothing, then a bird to sing to you, it would be awful—still, after the bird was still.

MRS. PETERS: [*Something within her speaking.*] I know what stillness is. When we homesteaded in Dakota, and my first baby died—after he was two years old, and me with no other then—

MRS. HALE: [*Moving.*] How soon do you suppose they'll be through, looking for the evidence?

MRS. PETERS: I know what stillness is. [*Pulling herself back.*] The law has got to punish crime, Mrs. Hale.

MRS. HALE: [*Not as if answering that.*] I wish you'd seen Minnie Foster when she wore a white dress with blue ribbons and stood up there in the choir and sang. [*A look around the room.*] Oh, I *wish* I'd come over here once in a while! That was a crime! That was a crime! Who's going to punish that?

MRS. PETERS: [*Looking upstairs.*] We mustn't—take on.

MRS. HALE: I might have known she needed help! I know how things can be—for women. I tell you, it's queer, Mrs. Peters. We live close together and we live far apart. We all go through the same things—it's all just a different kind of the same thing. [*Brushes her eyes, noticing the bottle of fruit, reaches out for it.*] If I was you, I wouldn't tell her her fruit was gone. Tell her it *ain't.* Tell her it's all right. Take this in to prove it to her. She—she may never know whether it was broke or not.

MRS. PETERS: [*Takes the bottle, looks about for something to wrap it in; takes petticoat from the clothes brought from the other room, very nervously begins winding this around the bottle. In a false voice.*] My, it's a good thing the men couldn't hear us. Wouldn't they just laugh! Getting all stirred up over a little thing like a—dead canary.

As if that could have anything to do with—with—wouldn't they *laugh!*

[*The men are heard coming down stairs.*]

MRS. HALE: [*Under her breath.*] Maybe they would—maybe they wouldn't.

COUNTY ATTORNEY: No, Peters, it's all perfectly clear except a reason for doing it. But you know juries when it comes to women. If there was some definite thing. Something to show—something to make a story about—a thing that would connect up with this strange way of doing it—

[*The women's eyes meet for an instant. Enter* HALE *from outer door.*]

HALE: Well, I've got the team around. Pretty cold out there.

COUNTY ATTORNEY: I'm going to stay here a while by myself. [*To the* SHERIFF.] You can send Frank out for me, can't you? I want to go over everything. I'm not satisfied that we can't do better.

SHERIFF: Do you want to see what Mrs. Peters is going to take in?

[*The* LAWYER *goes to the table, picks up the apron, laughs.*]

COUNTY ATTORNEY: Oh, I guess they're not very dangerous things the ladies have picked out. [*Moves a few things about, disturbing the quilt pieces which cover the box. Steps back.*] No, Mrs. Peters doesn't need supervising. For that matter, a sheriff's wife is married to the law. Ever think of it that way, Mrs. Peters?

MRS. PETERS: Not—just that way.

SHERIFF: [*Chuckling.*] Married to the law. [*Moves toward the other room.*] I just want you to come in here a minute, George. We ought to take a look at these windows.

COUNTY ATTORNEY: [*Scoffingly.*] Oh, windows!

SHERIFF: We'll be right out, Mr. Hale.

[HALE *goes outside. The* SHERIFF *follows the* COUNTY ATTORNEY *into the other room. Then* MRS. HALE *rises, hands tight together, looking intensely at* MRS. PETERS, *whose eyes make a slow turn, finally meeting* MRS. HALE'*s. A moment* MRS. HALE *holds her, then her own eyes point the way to where the box is concealed. Suddenly* MRS. PETERS *throws back quilt pieces and tries to put the box in the bag she is wearing. It is too big. She opens box, starts to take bird out, cannot touch it, goes to pieces, stands there helpless. Sound of a knob turning in the other room.* MRS. HALE *snatches the box and puts it in the pocket of her big coat. Enter* COUNTY ATTORNEY *and* SHERIFF.]

COUNTY ATTORNEY: [*Facetiously.*] Well, Henry, at least we found out that she was not going to quilt it. She was going to—what is it you call it, ladies?

MRS. HALE: [*Her hand against her pocket.*] We call it—knot it, Mr. Henderson.

[*Curtain.*]

1916   *1920*

Arthur Miller
1915–2005

DEATH OF A SALESMAN

Miller's play melds two types of drama generally thought to be antithetical—realism and Expressionism. Realistic drama, pioneered by playwrights such as Henrik Ibsen in the late nineteenth century, often exposes theatergoers to problems in society, sometimes pointing toward ways to reform. Lorraine Hansberry's A Raisin in the Sun *is a good example of a play written with this social purpose in mind. During the Great Depression, when so many suffered horrible poverty, there was obviously a lot to criticize about Western capitalist countries, and realism dominated not only serious drama but serious literature of all genres. The U.S. involvement in World War II, from 1941 to 1945, is often seen as the turning point in the economic crisis, but even as late as 1949 the prosperity that we now associate with the postwar period was neither secured nor universal. Major strikes revealed problems in the American economy into the early 1950s, and many people decried a corporate heartlessness that treated employees not like human beings but like commodities. According to Miller, Americans in 1949 still had the mentality "of a depression people." In his own memoir, Miller proudly tells the tale of how Bernard Gimbel (of Gimbel's department stores) saw the play and immediately decided to never again fire anyone for being too old. That is the kind of social reform that a realist often intends. Miller saw the play as a "severe" criticism of capitalism, the kind that could not have been written a couple of years later, in the early 1950s, after the "anti-communist tempest," what we often call the Red Scare, had begun.*

A salesman, with his characteristic showmanship and bravura, is an appropriate "Everyman" to put on stage to examine the problems inherent in a modern consumer society. In a consumer economy, products take on symbolic value beyond their functional qualities. We buy things in pursuit of the images and dreams that salesmen teach us to associate with them. Naturally, then, through the years many critics have thought the play criticizes the American Dream that still animates us today.

More recently, historical-minded critics have come to believe that Miller's play is not so universally applicable, that instead the play records a transition in the American economy from an industrial to a postindustrial age. In this view, Willy's problem is that he is a relic of an earlier, less technological age, when his type of selling worked. Whether Miller himself recognized this transition is beside the point. Because realism attempts to reflect real life, we can use plays like this almost the same way a historian examines other types of primary documents. For example, if Miller succeeded in reproducing realistic characters, a feminist approach could detect in the play evidence about the place of women in middle-class American society in the mid-twentieth century, whether or not Miller meant to offer a critique on that topic.

Miller's own theory of realism had another dimension unrelated to social criticism. He thought that realism was the proper format for a "family" drama. During our daily lives, at work and in public spaces, we put on masks or fake versions of ourselves. But at home we are no longer performing, and in the company of our families we have a sense of our real selves. We speak in a revealing, mundane, unadorned, and prosaic language. And the conflicts in our families are battles between psychologically individuated personalities—which can best be depicted in realistic terms. In this sense, Miller's realism does not comment on an economic system so much as it dramatizes the problems and dynamics within a particular American family. It is interesting to note that Miller himself claimed that he never intended any "heavy-handed symbolism" through Willy's surname ("Low-man"). Willy is not a "type," but an individual with as much idiosyncratic, psychological depth as you and me.

Nevertheless, it is impossible to deny the mythic character of the play, and since its first production readers, critics, and audiences have asserted that Death of a Salesman *brilliantly adapts the principles of Greek tragedy, which dealt in myth, to a modern, democratic society. To the degree that the play succeeds as tragedy, it resists the thrust of realism and tends toward Expressionism. In Miller's own words, Expressionism dramatizes "the conflict of either social, religious, ethical, or moral forces per se." In other words, Expressionism deals less with the conflicts between individuals than with the conflicts between "forces." For example,* Antigone *is not so much about an individual person as it is about the human struggle against fate— as the chorus sings, "[W]hat is destined for us, men mortal, there is no escape." You might ask yourself, then, to what degree Miller's play follows Aristotle's description of tragedy (see p. xxiii)? Is anyone "fated" as Creon is? If so, what "force" in twentieth-century America takes the place of the gods in Greek drama? Miller claimed that the pathos of tragedy came easily to him, and he almost regretted how pathetic he made Willy Loman, thinking it nearly ruined his tragic character. But what he meant by "pathetic" is a little different from our common usage. In his "Tragedy and the Common Man," Miller claimed that "the pathetic is achieved when the protagonist is, by virtue of witlessness, his insensitivity or the very air he gives off, incapable of grappling with a much superior force." In that same essay Miller wrote that the so-called tragic flaw "or crack in the character, is really nothing—and need be nothing—but his inherent unwillingness to remain passive in the face of what he conceives to be a challenge to his dignity, his image of his rightful status."*

In the visual arts, such as painting, Expressionists wanted to depict objects not as they "really" are but imbued with the emotional force they aroused in the artist. On the canvas, objects look distorted and unreal, filtered through a dreamlike—often a nightmarish—lens. Vincent Van Gogh's Starry Night *and Edward Munch's* The Scream *are good examples of this style. On the stage, Expressionism sketches mythic characters with little realistic detail. While Expressionist playwrights did intend to revolt against the stifling boundaries imposed by bourgeois, middle-class society, they were not interested in sociological analysis and practical reform. They concerned themselves with timeless, universal themes, like the struggle of youth against age and visions of apocalypse, and they often used the external aspects of stagecraft—lighting, sound, sets—to express internal states of mind. Consequently, Expressionist theater did not look like "real" life. The audience was not looking at the lives of real people through an invisible "fourth wall." Sets are often minimal or distorted. Dialogue makes no attempt to mimic real-life speech. Instead, characters make unrealistic speeches and use poetic constructions. Expressionism flowered in the German theater in the early decades of the twentieth century and had an influence on American playwrights like Eugene O'Neill in the 1920s.*

Ironically, Miller borrowed some of the techniques of Expressionism to convey the inner life of Willy Loman. But those characteristics also lend a mythical atmosphere to the play. Miller expressed his own surprise at how universal the play seems, resonating even in cultures extremely different from our own, such as communist China.

Death of a Salesman

Certain Private Conversations in Two Acts and a Requiem

CHARACTERS

WILLY LOMAN	THE WOMAN	STANLEY
LINDA	CHARLEY	MISS FORSYTHE
BIFF	UNCLE BEN	LETTA
HAPPY	HOWARD WAGNER	
BERNARD	JENNY	

The action takes place in WILLY LOMAN'*s house and yard and in various places he visits in the New York and Boston of today.*[1]

ACT 1

A melody is heard, playing upon a flute. It is small and fine, telling of grass and trees and the horizon. The curtain rises.

Before us is the Salesman's house. We are aware of towering angular shapes behind it, surrounding it on all sides. Only the blue light of

1. Circa 1949.

*the sky falls upon the house and forestage; the surrounding area shows
an angry flow of orange. As more light appears, we see a solid vault of
apartment houses around the small, fragile-seeming home. An air of
the dream clings to the place, a dream rising out of reality. The kitchen
at center seems actual enough, for there is a kitchen table with three
chairs, and a refrigerator. But no other fixtures are seen. At the back of
the kitchen there is a draped entrance, which leads to the living-room.
To the right of the kitchen, on a level raised two feet, is a bedroom
furnished only with a brass bedstead and a straight chair. On a shelf
over the bed a silver athletic trophy stands. A window opens onto the
apartment house at the side.*

*Behind the kitchen, on a level raised six and a half feet, is the boys'
bedroom, at present barely visible. Two beds are dimly seen, and at the
back of the room a dormer window. (This bedroom is above the unseen
living-room.) At the left a stairway curves up to it from the kitchen.*

*The entire setting is wholly or, in some places, partially transparent.
The roof-line of the house is one-dimensional; under and over it we see
the apartment buildings. Before the house lies an apron, curving beyond
the forestage into the orchestra. This forward area serves as the back
yard as well as the locale of all* WILLY*'s imaginings and of his city scenes.
Whenever the action is in the present the actors observe the imaginary
wall-lines, entering the house only through its door at the left. But in
the scenes of the past these boundaries are broken, and characters enter
or leave a room by stepping "through" a wall onto the forestage.*

From the right, WILLY LOMAN, *the Salesman, enters, carrying two
large sample cases. The flute plays on. He hears but is not aware of it.
He is past sixty years of age, dressed quietly. Even as he crosses the stage
to the doorway of the house, his exhaustion is apparent. He unlocks the
door, comes into the kitchen, and thankfully lets his burden down, feeling the soreness of his palms. A word-sigh escapes his lips—it might be
"Oh, boy, oh, boy." He closes the door, then carries his cases out into the
living-room, through the draped kitchen doorway.*

LINDA, *his wife, has stirred in her bed at the right. She gets out and
puts on a robe, listening. Most often jovial, she has developed an iron
repression of her exceptions to* WILLY*'s behavior—she more than loves
him, she admires him, as though his mercurial nature, his temper, his
massive dreams and little cruelties, served her only as sharp reminders of*

*the turbulent longings within him, longings which she shares but lacks
the temperament to utter and follow to their end.*

LINDA: [*Hearing* WILLY *outside the bedroom, calls with some trepidation.*] Willy!

WILLY: It's all right. I came back.

LINDA: Why? What happened`? [*Slight pause.*] Did something happen, Willy?

WILLY: No, nothing happened.

LINDA: You didn't smash the car, did you?

WILLY: [*With casual irritation.*] I said nothing happened. Didn't you hear me?

LINDA: Don't you feel well?

WILLY: I'm tired to the death. [*The flute has faded away. He sits on the bed beside her, a little numb.*] I couldn't make it. I just couldn't make it, Linda.

LINDA: [*Very carefully, delicately.*] Where were you all day? You look terrible.

WILLY: I got as far as a little above Yonkers. I stopped for a cup of coffee. Maybe it was the coffee.

LINDA: What?

WILLY: [*After a pause.*] I suddenly couldn't drive any more. The car kept going off onto the shoulder, y'know?

LINDA: [*Helpfully.*] Oh. Maybe it was the steering again. I don't think Angelo knows the Studebaker.[2]

WILLY: No, it's me, it's me. Suddenly I realize I'm goin' sixty miles an hour and I don't remember the last five minutes. I'm—I can't seem to—keep my mind to it.

LINDA: Maybe it's your glasses. You never went for your new glasses.

WILLY: No, I see everything. I came back ten miles an hour. It took me nearly four hours from Yonkers.

LINDA: [*Resigned.*] Well, you'll just have to take a rest, Willy, you can't continue this way.

WILLY: I just got back from Florida.

LINDA: But you didn't rest your mind. Your mind is overactive, and the mind is what counts, dear.

2. The Studebaker Corporation manufactured cars from 1902 to 1963. It targeted middle-class buyers.

WILLY: I'll start out in the morning. Maybe I'll feel better in the morning. [*She is taking off his shoes.*] These goddam arch supports are killing me.

LINDA: Take an aspirin. Should I get you an aspirin? It'll soothe you.

WILLY: [*With wonder.*] I was driving along, you understand? And I was fine. I was even observing the scenery. You can imagine, me looking at scenery, on the road every week of my life. But it's so beautiful up there, Linda, the trees are so thick, and the sun is warm. I opened the windshield and just let the warm air bathe over me. And then all of a sudden I'm goin' off the road! I'm tellin' ya, I absolutely forgot I was driving. If I'd've gone the other way over the white line I might've killed somebody. So I went on again—and five minutes later I'm dreamin' again, and I nearly—[*He presses two fingers against his eyes.*] I have such thoughts, I have such strange thoughts.

LINDA: Willy, dear. Talk to them again. There's no reason why you can't work in New York.

WILLY: They don't need me in New York. I'm the New England man. I'm vital in New England.

LINDA: But you're sixty years old. They can't expect you to keep traveling every week.

WILLY: I'll have to send a wire[3] to Portland. I'm supposed to see Brown and Morrison tomorrow morning at ten o'clock to show the line. Goddammit, I could sell them! [*He starts putting on his jacket.*]

LINDA: [*Taking the jacket from him.*] Why don't you go down to the place tomorrow and tell Howard you've simply got to work in New York? You're too accommodating, dear.

WILLY: If old man Wagner was alive I'da been in charge of New York now! That man was a prince, he was a masterful man. But that boy of his, that Howard, he don't appreciate. When I went north the first time, the Wagner Company didn't know where New England was!

LINDA: Why don't you tell those things to Howard, dear?

WILLY: [*Encouraged.*] I will, I definitely will. Is there any cheese?

3. Telegram.

LINDA: I'll make you a sandwich.

WILLY: No, go to sleep. I'll take some milk. I'll be up right away. The boys in?

LINDA: They're sleeping. Happy took Biff on a date tonight.

WILLY: [*Interested.*] That so?

LINDA: It was so nice to see them shaving together, one behind the other, in the bathroom. And going out together. You notice? The whole house smells of shaving lotion.

WILLY: Figure it out. Work a lifetime to pay off a house. You finally own it, and there's nobody to live in it.

LINDA: Well, dear, life is a casting off. It's always that way.

WILLY: No, no, some people—some people accomplish something. Did Biff say anything after I went this morning?

LINDA: You shouldn't have criticized him, Willy, especially after he just got off the train. You mustn't lose your temper with him.

WILLY: When the hell did I lose my temper? I simply asked him if he was making any money. Is that a criticism?

LINDA: But, dear, how could he make any money?

WILLY: [*Worried and angered.*] There's such an undercurrent in him. He became a moody man. Did he apologize when I left this morning?

LINDA: He was crestfallen, Willy. You know how he admires you. I think if he finds himself, then you'll both be happier and not fight any more.

WILLY: How can he find himself on a farm? Is that a life? A farmhand? In the beginning, when he was young, I thought, well, a young man, it's good for him to tramp around, take a lot of different jobs. But it's more than ten years now and he has yet to make thirty-five dollars a week!

LINDA: He's finding himself, Willy.

WILLY: Not finding yourself at the age of thirty-four is a disgrace!

LINDA: Shh!

WILLY: The trouble is he's lazy, goddammit!

LINDA: Willy, please!

WILLY: Biff is a lazy bum!

LINDA: They're sleeping. Get something to eat. Go on down.

WILLY: Why did he come home? I would like to know what brought him home.

LINDA: I don't know. I think he's still lost, Willy. I think he's very lost.

WILLY: Biff Loman is lost. In the greatest country in the world a young man with such—personal attractiveness, gets lost. And such a hard worker. There's one thing about Biff—he's not lazy.

LINDA: Never.

WILLY: [*With pity and resolve.*] I'll see him in the morning; I'll have a nice talk with him. I'll get him a job selling. He could be big in no time. My God! Remember how they used to follow him around in high school? When he smiled at one of them their faces lit up. When he walked down the street . . . [*He loses himself in reminiscences.*]

LINDA: [*Trying to bring him out of it.*] Willy, dear, I got a new kind of American-type cheese today. It's whipped.

WILLY: Why do you get American when I like Swiss?

LINDA: I just thought you'd like a change—

WILLY: I don't want a change! I want Swiss cheese. Why am I always being contradicted?

LINDA: [*With a covering laugh.*] I thought it would be a surprise.

WILLY: Why don't you open a window in here, for God's sake?

LINDA: [*With infinite patience.*] They're all open, dear.

WILLY: The way they boxed us in here. Bricks and windows, windows and bricks.

LINDA: We should've bought the land next door.

WILLY: The street is lined with cars. There's not a breath of fresh air in the neighborhood. The grass don't grow any more, you can't raise a carrot in the back yard. They should've had a law against apartment houses. Remember those two beautiful elm trees out there? When I and Biff hung the swing between them?

LINDA: Yeah, like being a million miles from the city.

WILLY: They should've arrested the builder for cutting those down. They massacred the neighborhood. [*Lost.*] More and more I think of those days, Linda. This time of year it was lilac and wisteria. And then the peonies would come out, and the daffodils. What fragrance in this room!

LINDA: Well, after all, people had to move somewhere.

WILLY: No, there's more people now.

LINDA: I don't think there's more people. I think—

WILLY: There's more people! That's what ruining this country! Population is getting out of control. The competition is maddening!

Smell the stink from that apartment house! And another one on the other side . . . How can they whip cheese?

[*On* WILLY'*s last line,* BIFF *and* HAPPY *raise themselves up in their beds, listening.*]

LINDA: Go down, try it. And be quiet.

WILLY: [*Turning to* LINDA, *guiltily.*] You're not worried about me, are you, sweetheart?

BIFF: What's the matter?

HAPPY: Listen!

LINDA: You've got too much on the ball to worry about.

WILLY: You're my foundation and my support, Linda.

LINDA: Just try to relax, dear. You make mountains out of molehills.

WILLY: I won't fight with him anymore. If he wants to go back to Texas, let him go.

LINDA: He'll find his way.

WILLY: Sure. Certain men just don't get started till later in life. Like Thomas Edison, I think. Or B. F. Goodrich. One of them was deaf. [*He starts for the bedroom doorway.*] I'll put my money on Biff.

LINDA: And Willy—if it's warm Sunday we'll drive in the country. And we'll open the windshield, and take lunch.

WILLY: No, the windshields don't open on the new cars.

LINDA: But you opened it today.

WILLY: Me? I didn't. [*He stops.*] Now isn't that peculiar! Isn't that a remarkable—[*He breaks off in amazement and fright as the flute is heard distantly.*]

LINDA: What, darling?

WILLY: That is the most remarkable thing.

LINDA: What, dear?

WILLY: I was thinking of the Chevvy.[4] [*Slight pause.*] Nineteen twenty-eight . . . when I had that red Chevvy—[*Breaks off.*] That funny? I coulda sworn I was driving that Chevvy today.

LINDA: Well, that's nothing. Something must've reminded you.

WILLY: Remarkable. *Ts.*[5] Remember those days? The way Biff used to simonize[6] that car? The dealer refused to believe there was eighty

---

4. Chevrolet, a division of General Motors since 1916, has been making cars since 1911.

5. Between 1908 and 1928, Ford manufac-tured the inexpensive and popular Model T au-tomobile.

6. Polish with Simoniz Paste Wax.

thousand miles on it. [*He shakes his head.*] Heh! [*To* LINDA.] Close your eyes, I'll be right up. [*He walks out of the bedroom.*]

HAPPY: [*To* BIFF.] Jesus, maybe he smashed up the car again!

LINDA: [*Calling after* WILLY.] Be careful on the stairs, dear! The cheese is on the middle shelf! [*She turns, goes over to the bed, takes his jacket, and goes out of the bedroom.*]

[*Light has risen on the boys' room. Unseen,* WILLY *is heard talking to himself, "Eighty thousand miles," and a little laugh.* BIFF *gets out of bed, comes downstage a bit, and stands attentively.* BIFF *is two years older than his brother,* HAPPY, *well built, but in these days bears a worn air and seems less self-assured. He has succeeded less, and his dreams are stronger and less acceptable than* HAPPY*'s.* HAPPY *is tall, powerfully made. Sexuality is like a visible color on him, or a scent that many women have discovered. He, like his brother, is lost, but in a different way, for he has never allowed himself to turn his face toward defeat and is thus more confused and hard-skinned, although seemingly more content.*]

HAPPY: [*Getting out of bed.*] He's going to get his license taken away if he keeps that up. I'm getting nervous about him, y'know, Biff?

BIFF: His eyes are going.

HAPPY: No, I've driven with him. He sees all right. He just doesn't keep his mind on it. I drove into the city with him last week. He stops at a green light and then it turns red and he goes. [*He laughs.*]

BIFF: Maybe he's color-blind.

HAPPY: Pop? Why, he's got the finest eye for color in the business. You know that.

BIFF: [*Sitting down on his bed.*] I'm going to sleep.

HAPPY: You're not still sour on Dad, are you, Biff?

BIFF: He's all right, I guess.

WILLY: [*Underneath them, in the living-room.*] Yes, sir, eighty thousand miles—eighty-two thousand!

BIFF: You smoking?

HAPPY: [*Holding out a pack of cigarettes.*] Want one?

BIFF: [*Taking a cigarette.*] I can never sleep when I smell it.

WILLY: What a simonizing job, heh!

HAPPY: [*With deep sentiment.*] Funny, Biff, y'know? Us sleeping in here again? The old beds. [*He pats his bed affectionately.*] All the talk that went across those two beds, huh? Our whole lives.

BIFF: Yeah. Lotta dreams and plans.

HAPPY: [*With a deep and masculine laugh.*] About five hundred women would like to know what was said in this room.

[*They share a soft laugh.*]

BIFF: Remember that big Betsy something—what the hell was her name—over on Bushwick Avenue?

HAPPY: [*Combing his hair.*] With the collie dog!

BIFF: That's the one. I got you in there, remember?

HAPPY: Yeah, that was my first time—I think. Boy, there was a pig! [*They laugh, almost crudely.*] You taught me everything I know about women. Don't forget that.

BIFF: I bet you forgot how bashful you used to be. Especially with girls.

HAPPY: Oh, I still am, Biff.

BIFF: Oh, go on.

HAPPY: I just control it, that's all. I think I got less bashful and you got more so. What happened, Biff? Where's the old humor, the old confidence? [*He shakes* BIFF*'s knee.* BIFF *gets up and moves restlessly about the room.*] What's the matter?

BIFF: Why does Dad mock me all the time?

HAPPY: He's not mocking you, he—

BIFF: Everything I say there's a twist of mockery on his face. I can't get near him.

HAPPY: He just wants you to make good, that's all. I wanted to talk to you about Dad for a long time, Biff. Something's—happening to him. He—talks to himself.

BIFF: I noticed that this morning. But he always mumbled.

HAPPY: But not so noticeable. It got so embarrassing I sent him to Florida. And you know something? Most of the time he's talking to you.

BIFF: What's he say about me?

HAPPY: I can't make it out.

BIFF: What's he say about me?

HAPPY: I think the fact that you're not settled, that you're still kind of up in the air . . .

BIFF: There's one or two things depressing him, Happy.

HAPPY: What do you mean?

BIFF: Never mind. Just don't lay it all to me.

HAPPY: But I think if you just got started—I mean—is there any future for you out there?

BIFF: I tell ya, Hap, I don't know what the future is. I don't know—what I'm supposed to want.

HAPPY: What do you mean?

BIFF: Well, I spent six or seven years after high school trying to work myself up. Shipping clerk, salesman, business of one kind or another. And it's a measly manner of existence. To get on that subway on the hot mornings in summer. To devote your whole life to keeping stock, or making phone calls, or selling or buying. To suffer fifty weeks of the year for the sake of a two-week vacation, when all you really desire is to be outdoors, with your shirt off. And always to have to get ahead of the next fella. And still—that's how you build a future.

HAPPY: Well, you really enjoy it on a farm? Are you content out there?

BIFF: [*With rising agitation.*] Hap, I've had twenty or thirty different kinds of jobs since I left home before the war, and it always turns out the same. I just realized it lately. In Nebraska when I herded cattle, and the Dakotas, and Arizona, and now in Texas. It's why I came home now, I guess, because I realized it. This farm I work on, it's spring there now, see? And they've got about fifteen new colts. There's nothing more inspiring or—beautiful than the sight of a mare and a new colt. And it's cool there now, see? Texas is cool now, and it's spring. And whenever spring comes to where I am, I suddenly get the feeling, my God, I'm not gettin' anywhere! What the hell am I doing, playing around with horses, twenty-eight dollars a week! I'm thirty-four years old. I oughta be makin' my future. That's when I come running home. And now, I get there, and I don't know what to do with myself. [*After a pause.*] I've always made a point of not wasting my life, and everytime I come back here I know that all I've done is to waste my life.

HAPPY: You're a poet, you know that, Biff? You're a—you're an idealist!

BIFF: No, I'm mixed up very bad. Maybe I oughta get married. Maybe I oughta get stuck into something. Maybe that's my trouble. I'm like a boy. I'm not married. I'm not in business, I just—

I'm like a boy. Are you content, Hap? You're a success, aren't you? Are you content?

HAPPY: Hell, no!

BIFF: Why? You're making money, aren't you?

HAPPY: [*Moving about with energy, expressiveness.*] All I can do now is wait for the merchandise manager to die. And suppose I get to be merchandise manager? He's a good friend of mine, and he just built a terrific estate on Long Island. And he lived there about two months and sold it, and now he's building another one. He can't enjoy it once it's finished. And I know that's just what I would do. I don't know what the hell I'm workin' for. Sometimes I sit in my apartment—all alone. And I think of the rent I'm paying. And it's crazy. But then, it's what I always wanted. My own apartment, a car, and plenty of women. And still, goddammit, I'm lonely.

BIFF: [*With enthusiasm.*] Listen, why don't you come out West with me?

HAPPY: You and I, heh?

BIFF: Sure, maybe we could buy a ranch. Raise cattle, use our muscles. Men built like we are should be working out in the open.

HAPPY: [*Avidly.*] The Loman Brothers, heh?

BIFF: [*With vast affection.*] Sure, we'd be known all over the counties!

HAPPY: [*Enthralled.*] That's what I dream about, Biff. Sometimes I want to just rip my clothes off in the middle of the store and outbox that goddam merchandise manager. I mean I can outbox, outrun, and outlift anybody in that store, and I have to take orders from those common, petty sons-of-bitches till I can't stand it any more.

BIFF: I'm tellin' you, kid, if you were with me I'd be happy out there.

HAPPY: [*Enthused.*] See, Biff, everybody around me is so false that I'm constantly lowering my ideals . . .

BIFF: Baby, together we'd stand up for one another, we'd have someone to trust.

HAPPY: If I were around you—

BIFF: Hap, the trouble is we weren't brought up to grub for money. I don't know how to do it.

HAPPY: Neither can I!

BIFF: Then let's go!

HAPPY: The only thing is—what can you make out there?

BIFF: But look at your friend. Builds an estate and then hasn't the peace of mind to live in it.

HAPPY: Yeah, but when he walks into the store the waves part in front of him. That's fifty-two thousand dollars a year coming through the revolving door, and I got more in my pinky finger than he's got in his head.

BIFF: Yeah, but you just said—

HAPPY: I gotta show some of those pompous, self-important executives over there that Hap Loman can make the grade. I want to walk into the store the way he walks in. Then I'll go with you, Biff. We'll be together yet, I swear. But take those two we had tonight. Now weren't they gorgeous creatures?

BIFF: Yeah, yeah, most gorgeous I've had in years.

HAPPY: I get that any time I want, Biff. Whenever I feel disgusted. The only trouble is, it gets like bowling or something. I just keep knockin' them over and it doesn't mean anything. You still run around a lot?

BIFF: Naa. I'd like to find a girl—steady, somebody with substance.

HAPPY: That's what I long for.

BIFF: Go on! You'd never come home.

HAPPY: I would! Somebody with character, with resistance! Like Mom, y'know? You're gonna call me a bastard when I tell you this. That girl Charlotte I was with tonight is engaged to be married in five weeks. [*He tries on his new hat.*]

BIFF: No kiddin'!

HAPPY: Sure, the guy's in line for the vice-presidency of the store. I don't know what gets into me, maybe I just have an overdeveloped sense of competition or something, but I went and ruined her, and furthermore I can't get rid of her. And he's the third executive I've done that to. Isn't that a crummy characteristic? And to top it all, I go to their weddings! [*Indignantly, but laughing.*] Like I'm not supposed to take bribes. Manufacturers offer me a hundred-dollar bill now and then to throw an order their way. You know how honest I am, but it's like this girl, see. I hate myself for it. Because I don't want the girl, and, still, I take it and—I love it!

BIFF: Let's go to sleep.

HAPPY: I guess we didn't settle anything, heh?

BIFF: I just got one idea that I'm going to try.

HAPPY: What's that?

BIFF: Remember Bill Oliver?

HAPPY: Sure, Oliver is very big now. You want to work for him again?

BIFF: No, but when I quit he said something to me. He put his arm on my shoulder, and he said, "Biff, if you ever need anything, come to me."

HAPPY: I remember that. That sounds good.

BIFF: I think I'll go to see him. If I could get ten thousand or even seven or eight thousand dollars I could buy a beautiful ranch.

HAPPY: I bet he'd back you. 'Cause he thought highly of you, Biff. I mean, they all do. You're well liked, Biff. That's why I say to come back here, and we both have the apartment. And I'm tellin' you, Biff, any babe you want . . .

BIFF: No, with a ranch I could do the work I like and still be something. I just wonder though. I wonder if Oliver still thinks I stole that carton of basketballs.

HAPPY: Oh, he probably forgot that long ago. It's almost ten years. You're too sensitive. Anyway, he didn't really fire you.

BIFF: Well, I think he was going to. I think that's why I quit. I was never sure whether he knew or not. I know he thought the world of me, though. I was the only one he'd let lock up the place.

WILLY: [*Below.*] You gonna wash the engine, Biff?

HAPPY: Shh! [BIFF *looks at* HAPPY, *who is gazing down, listening.* WILLY *is mumbling in the parlor.*] You hear that?

[*They listen.* WILLY *laughs warmly.*]

BIFF: [*Growing angry.*] Doesn't he know Mom can hear that?

WILLY: Don't get your sweater dirty, Biff!

[*A look of pain crosses* BIFF's *face.*]

HAPPY: Isn't that terrible? Don't leave again, will you? You'll find a job here. You gotta stick around. I don't know what to do about him, it's getting embarrassing.

WILLY: What a simonizing job!

BIFF: Mom's hearing that!

WILLY: No kiddin', Biff, you got a date? Wonderful!

HAPPY: Go on to sleep. But talk to him in the morning, will you?

BIFF: [*Reluctantly getting into bed.*] With her in the house. Brother!

HAPPY: [*Getting into bed.*] I wish you'd have a good talk with him.

[*The light on their room begins to fade.*]

BIFF: [*To himself in bed.*] That selfish, stupid . . .

HAPPY: Sh . . . Sleep, Biff.

[*Their light is out. Well before they have finished speaking. WILLY's form is dimly seen below in the darkened kitchen. He opens the refrigerator, searches in there, and takes out a bottle of milk. The apartment houses are fading out, and the entire house and surroundings become covered with leaves. Music insinuates itself as the leaves appear.*]

WILLY: Just wanna be careful with those girls, Biff, that's all. Don't make any promises. No promises of any kind. Because a girl, y'know, they always believe what you tell 'em, and you're very young, Biff, you're too young to be talking seriously to girls. [*Light rises on the kitchen. WILLY, talking, shuts the refrigerator door and comes downstage to the kitchen table. He pours milk into a glass. He is totally immersed in himself, smiling faintly.*] Too young entirely, Biff. You want to watch your schooling first. Then when you're all set, there'll be plenty of girls for a boy like you. [*He smiles broadly at a kitchen chair.*] That so? The girls pay for you? [*He laughs.*] Boy, you must really be makin' a hit. [*WILLY is gradually addressing—physically—a point offstage, speaking through the wall of the kitchen, and his voice has been rising in volume to that of a normal conversation.*] I been wondering why you polish the car so careful. Ha! Don't leave the hubcaps, boys. Get the chamois to the hubcaps. Happy, use newspaper on the windows, it's the easiest thing. Show him how to do it, Biff! You see, Happy? Pad it up, use it like a pad. That's it, that's it, good work. You're doin' all right, Hap. [*He pauses, then nods in approbation for a few seconds, then looks upward.*] Biff, first thing we gotta do when we get time is clip that big branch over the house. Afraid it's gonna fall in a storm and hit the roof. Tell you what. We get a rope and sling her around, and then we climb up there with a couple of saws and take her down. Soon as you finish the car, boys, I wanna see ya. I got a surprise for you, boys.

BIFF: [*Offstage.*] Whatta ya got, Dad?

WILLY: No, you finish first. Never leave a job till you're finished— remember that. [*Looking toward the "big trees."*] Biff, up in Albany I saw a beautiful hammock. I think I'll buy it next trip, and we'll hang it right between those two elms. Wouldn't that be something? Just swingin' there under those branches. Boy, that would be . . .

[YOUNG BIFF *and* YOUNG HAPPY *appear from the direction* WILLY *was addressing.* HAPPY *carries rags and a pail of water.* BIFF, *wearing a sweater with a block "S," carries a football.*]

BIFF: [*Pointing in the direction of the car offstage.*] How's that, Pop, professional?

WILLY: Terrific. Terrific job, boys. Good work, Biff.

HAPPY: Where's the surprise, Pop?

WILLY: In the back seat of the car.

HAPPY: Boy! [*He runs off.*]

BIFF: What is it, Dad? Tell me, what'd you buy?

WILLY: [*Laughing, cuffs him.*] Never mind, something I want you to have.

BIFF: [*Turns and starts off.*] What is it, Hap?

HAPPY: [*Offstage.*] It's a punching bag!

BIFF: Oh, Pop!

WILLY: It's got Gene Tunney's[7] signature on it!

[HAPPY *runs onstage with a punching bag.*]

BIFF: Gee, how'd you know we wanted a punching bag?

WILLY: Well, it's the finest thing for the timing.

HAPPY: [*Lies down on his back and pedals with his feet.*] I'm losing weight, you notice, Pop?

WILLY: [*To* HAPPY.] Jumping rope is good too.

BIFF: Did you see the new football I got?

WILLY: [*Examining the ball.*] Where'd you get a new ball?

BIFF: The coach told me to practice my passing.

WILLY: That so? And he gave you the ball, heh?

BIFF: Well, I borrowed it from the locker room. [*He laughs confidentially.*]

WILLY: [*Laughing with him at the theft.*] I want you to return that.

---

7. James Joseph "Gene" Tunney (1897–1978), skilled and thoughtful heavyweight boxer, defeated Jack Dempsey twice and was champion from 1926 to 1928.

HAPPY: I told you he wouldn't like it!

BIFF: [*Angrily.*] Well, I'm bringing it back!

WILLY: [*Stopping the incipient argument, to* HAPPY.] Sure, he's gotta practice with a regulation ball, doesn't he? [*To* BIFF.] Coach'll probably congratulate you on your initiative!

BIFF: Oh, he keeps congratulating my initiative all the time, Pop.

WILLY: That's because he likes you. If somebody else took that ball there'd be an uproar. So what's the report, boys, what's the report?

BIFF: Where'd you go this time, Dad? Gee, we were lonesome for you.

WILLY: [*Pleased, puts an arm around each boy and they come down to the apron.*] Lonesome, heh?

BIFF: Missed you every minute.

WILLY: Don't say? Tell you a secret, boys. Don't breathe it to a soul. Someday I'll have my own business, and I'll never have to leave home anymore.

HAPPY: Like Uncle Charley, heh?

WILLY: Bigger than Uncle Charley! Because Charley is not—liked. He's liked, but he's not—well liked.

BIFF: Where'd you go this time, Dad?

WILLY: Well, I got on the road, and I went north to Providence. Met the mayor.

BIFF: The mayor of Providence!

WILLY: He was sitting in the hotel lobby.

BIFF: What'd he say?

WILLY: He said, "Morning!" And I said, "You got a fine city here, Mayor." And then he had coffee with me. And then I went to Waterbury. Waterbury is a fine city. Big clock city, the famous Waterbury clock. Sold a nice bill there. And then Boston—Boston is the cradle of the Revolution. A fine city. And a couple of other towns in Mass., and on to Portland and Bangor and straight home!

BIFF: Gee, I'd love to go with you sometime, Dad.

WILLY: Soon as summer comes.

HAPPY: Promise?

WILLY: You and Hap and I, and I'll show you all the towns. America is full of beautiful towns and fine, upstanding people. And they know me, boys, they know me up and down New England.

The finest people. And when I bring you fellas up, there'll be open sesame for all of us, 'cause one thing, boys: I have friends. I can park my car in any street in New England, and the cops protect it like their own. This summer, heh?

BIFF and HAPPY: [*Together.*] Yeah! You bet!

WILLY: We'll take our bathing suits.

HAPPY: We'll carry your bags, Pop!

WILLY: Oh, won't that be something! Me comin' into the Boston stores with you boys carryin' my bags. What a sensation! [BIFF *is prancing around, practicing passing the ball.*] You nervous, Biff, about the game?

BIFF: Not if you're gonna be there.

WILLY: What do they say about you in school, now that they made you captain?

HAPPY: There's a crowd of girls behind him everytime the classes change.

BIFF: [*Taking* WILLY'*s hand.*] This Saturday, Pop, this Saturday— just for you, I'm going to break through for a touchdown.

HAPPY: You're supposed to pass.

BIFF: I'm takin' one play for Pop. You watch me, Pop, and when I take off my helmet, that means I'm breakin' out. Then you watch me crash through that line!

WILLY: [*Kisses* BIFF.] Oh, wait'll I tell this in Boston!

[BERNARD *enters in knickers. He is younger than* BIFF, *earnest and loyal, a worried boy.*]

BERNARD: Biff, where are you? You're supposed to study with me today.

WILLY: Hey, looka Bernard. What're you lookin' so anemic about, Bernard?

BERNARD: He's gotta study, Uncle Willy. He's got Regents[8] next week.

HAPPY: [*Tauntingly, spinning* BERNARD *around.*] Let's box, Bernard!

BERNARD: Biff! [*He gets away from* HAPPY.] Listen, Biff, I heard Mr. Birnbaum say that if you don't start studyin' math he's gonna flunk you, and you won't graduate. I heard him!

8. Exams given under the authority of the Board of Regents to high school students in New York State. To earn a Regents diploma, students must pass not only their classes but the Regents exam in each subject area.

WILLY: You better study with him, Biff. Go ahead now.

BERNARD: I heard him!

BIFF: Oh, Pop, you didn't see my sneakers! [*He holds up a foot for* WILLY *to look at.*]

WILLY: Hey, that's a beautiful job of printing!

BERNARD: [*Wiping his glasses.*] Just because he printed University of Virginia on his sneakers doesn't mean they've got to graduate him, Uncle Willy!

WILLY: [*Angrily.*] What're you talking about? With scholarships to three universities they're gonna flunk him?

BERNARD: But I heard Mr. Birnbaum say—

WILLY: Don't be a pest, Bernard! [*To his boys.*] What an anemic!

BERNARD: Okay, I'm waiting for you in my house, Biff.

[BERNARD *goes off. The* LOMANS *laugh.*]

WILLY: Bernard is not well liked, is he?

BIFF: He's liked, but he's not well liked.

HAPPY: That's right, Pop.

WILLY: That's just what I mean. Bernard can get the best marks in school, y'understand, but when he gets out in the business world, y'understand, you are going to be five times ahead of him. That's why I thank Almighty God you're both built like Adonises. Because the man who makes an appearance in the business world, the man who creates personal interest, is the man who gets ahead. Be liked and you will never want. You take me, for instance. I never have to wait in line to see a buyer. "Willy Loman is here!" That's all they have to know, and I go right through.

BIFF: Did you knock them dead, Pop?

WILLY: Knocked 'em cold in Providence, slaughtered 'em in Boston.

HAPPY: [*On his back, pedaling again.*] I'm losing weight, you notice, Pop?

[LINDA *enters, as of old, a ribbon in her hair, carrying a basket of washing.*]

LINDA: [*With youthful energy.*] Hello, dear!

WILLY: Sweetheart!

LINDA: How'd the Chevvy run?

WILLY: Chevrolet, Linda, is the greatest car ever built. [*To the boys.*] Since when do you let your mother carry wash up the stairs?

BIFF: Grab hold there, boy!

HAPPY: Where to, Mom?

LINDA: Hang them up on the line. And you better go down to your friends, Biff. The cellar is full of boys. They don't know what to do with themselves.

BIFF: Ah, when Pop comes home they can wait!

WILLY: [*Laughs appreciatively.*] You better go down and tell them what to do, Biff.

BIFF: I think I'll have them sweep out the furnace room.

WILLY: Good work, Biff.

BIFF: [*Goes through wall-line of kitchen to doorway at back and calls down.*] Fellas! Everybody sweep out the furnace room! I'll be right down!

VOICES: All right! Okay, Biff.

BIFF: George and Sam and Frank, come out back! We're hangin' up the wash! Come on, Hap, on the double!

[*He and* HAPPY *carry out the basket.*]

LINDA: The way they obey him!

WILLY: Well, that training, the training. I'm tellin' you, I was sellin' thousands and thousands, but I had to come home.

LINDA: Oh, the whole block'll be at that game. Did you sell anything?

WILLY: I did five hundred gross in Providence and seven hundred gross in Boston.

LINDA: No! Wait a minute, I've got a pencil. [*She pulls pencil and paper out of her apron pocket.*] That makes your commission . . . Two hundred—my God! Two hundred and twelve dollars!

WILLY: Well, I didn't figure it yet, but . . .

LINDA: How much did you do?

WILLY: Well, I—I did—about a hundred and eighty gross in Providence. Well, no—it came to—roughly two hundred gross on the whole trip.

LINDA: [*Without hesitation.*] Two hundred gross. That's . . . [*She figures.*]

WILLY: The trouble was that three of the stores were half closed for inventory in Boston. Otherwise I woulda broke records.

LINDA: Well, it makes seventy dollars and some pennies. That's very good.

WILLY: What do we owe?

LINDA: Well, on the first there's sixteen dollars on the refrigerator—

WILLY: Why sixteen?

LINDA: Well, the fan belt broke, so it was a dollar eighty.

WILLY: But it's brand new.

LINDA: Well, the man said that's the way it is. Till they work themselves in, y'know.

[*They move through the wall-line into the kitchen.*]

WILLY: I hope we didn't get stuck on that machine.

LINDA: They got the biggest ads of any of them!

WILLY: I know, it's a fine machine. What else?

LINDA: Well, there's nine-sixty for the washing machine. And for the vacuum cleaner there's three and a half due on the fifteenth. Then the roof, you got twenty-one dollars remaining.

WILLY: It don't leak, does it?

LINDA: No, they did a wonderful job. Then you owe Frank for the carburetor.

WILLY: I'm not going to pay that man! That goddam Chevrolet, they ought to prohibit the manufacture of that car!

LINDA: Well, you owe him three and a half. And odds and ends, comes to around a hundred and twenty dollars by the fifteenth.

WILLY: A hundred and twenty dollars! My God, if business don't pick up I don't know what I'm gonna do!

LINDA: Well, next week you'll do better.

WILLY: Oh, I'll knock 'em dead next week. I'll go to Hartford. I'm very well liked in Hartford. You know, the trouble is, Linda, people don't seem to take to me.

[*They move onto the forestage.*]

LINDA: Oh, don't be foolish.

WILLY: I know it when I walk in. They seem to laugh at me.

LINDA: Why? Why would they laugh at you? Don't talk that way, Willy.

[WILLY *moves to the edge of the stage.* LINDA *goes into the kitchen and starts to darn stockings.*]

WILLY: I don't know the reason for it, but they just pass me by. I'm not noticed.

LINDA: But you're doing wonderful, dear. You're making seventy to a hundred dollars a week.

WILLY: But I gotta be at it ten, twelve hours a day. Other men— I don't know—they do it easier. I don't know why—I can't stop myself—I talk too much. A man oughta come in with a few words. One thing about Charley. He's a man of few words, and they respect him.

LINDA: You don't talk too much, you're just lively.

WILLY: [*Smiling.*] Well, I figure, what the hell, life is short, a couple of jokes. [*To himself.*] I joke too much! [*The smile goes.*]

LINDA: Why? You're—

WILLY: I'm fat. I'm very—foolish to look at, Linda. I didn't tell you, but Christmas time I happened to be calling on F. H. Stewarts, and a salesman I know, as I was going in to see the buyer I heard him say something about—walrus. And I—I cracked him right across the face. I won't take that. I simply will not take that. But they do laugh at me. I know that.

LINDA: Darling . . .

WILLY: I gotta overcome it. I know I gotta overcome it. I'm not dressing to advantage, maybe.

LINDA: Willy, darling, you're the handsomest man in the world—

WILLY: Oh, no, Linda.

LINDA: To me you are. [*Slight pause.*] The handsomest. [*From the darkness is heard the laughter of a woman.* WILLY *doesn't turn to it, but it continues through* LINDA'*s lines.*] And the boys, Willy. Few men are idolized by their children the way you are.

   [*Music is heard as behind a scrim, to the left of the house,* THE WOMAN, *dimly seen, is dressing.*]

WILLY: [*With great feeling.*] You're the best there is, Linda, you're a pal, you know that? On the road—on the road I want to grab you sometimes and just kiss the life outa you. [*The laughter is loud now, and he moves into a brightening area at the left, where* THE WOMAN *has come from behind the scrim and is standing, putting on her hat, looking into a "mirror" and laughing.*] 'Cause I get so lonely—especially when business is bad and there's nobody to talk to. I get the feeling that I'll never sell anything again, that I won't make a living for you, or a business, a business for the boys. [*He talks through* THE WOMAN'*s subsiding laughter.* THE WOMAN *primps at the "mirror."*] There's so much I want to make for—

THE WOMAN: Me? You didn't make me, Willy. I picked you.

WILLY: [*Pleased.*] You picked me?

THE WOMAN: [*Who is quite proper-looking,* WILLY'*s age.*] I did. I've been sitting at that desk watching all the salesmen go by, day in, day out. But you've got such a sense of humor, and we do have such a good time together, don't we?

WILLY: Sure, sure. [*He takes her in his arms.*] Why do you have to go now?

THE WOMAN: It's two o'clock . . .

WILLY: No, come on in! [*He pulls her.*]

THE WOMAN: . . . my sisters'll be scandalized. When'll you be back?

WILLY: Oh, two weeks about. Will you come up again?

THE WOMAN: Sure thing. You do make me laugh. It's good for me. [*She squeezes his arm, kisses him.*] And I think you're a wonderful man.

WILLY: You picked me, heh?

THE WOMAN: Sure. Because you're so sweet. And such a kidder.

WILLY: Well, I'll see you next time I'm in Boston.

THE WOMAN: I'll put you right through to the buyers.

WILLY: [*Slapping her bottom.*] Right. Well, bottoms up!

THE WOMAN: [*Slaps him gently and laughs.*] You just kill me, Willy. [*He suddenly grabs her and kisses her roughly.*] You kill me. And thanks for the stockings. I love a lot of stockings. Well, good night.

WILLY: Good night. And keep your pores open!

THE WOMAN: Oh, Willy!

[THE WOMAN *bursts out laughing, and* LINDA'*s laughter blends in.* THE WOMAN *disappears into the dark. Now the area at the kitchen table brightens.* LINDA *is sitting where she was at the kitchen table, but now is mending a pair of her silk stockings.*]

LINDA: You are, Willy. The handsomest man. You've got no reason to feel that—

WILLY: [*Coming out of* THE WOMAN'*s dimming area and going over to* LINDA.] I'll make it all up to you, Linda. I'll—

LINDA: There's nothing to make up, dear. You're doing fine, better than—

WILLY: [*Noticing her mending.*] What's that?

LINDA: Just mending my stockings. They're so expensive—

WILLY: [*Angrily, taking them from her.*] I won't have you mending stockings in this house! Now throw them out!

[LINDA *puts the stockings in her pocket.*]

BERNARD: [*Entering on the run.*] Where is he? If he doesn't study!

WILLY: [*Moving to the forestage, with great agitation.*] You'll give him the answers!

BERNARD: I do, but I can't on a Regents! That's a state exam! They're liable to arrest me!

WILLY: Where is he? I'll whip him, I'll whip him!

LINDA: And he'd better give back that football, Willy, it's not nice.

WILLY: Biff! Where is he? Why is he taking everything?

LINDA: He's too rough with the girls, Willy. All the mothers are afraid of him!

WILLY: I'll whip him!

BERNARD: He's driving the car without a license!

[THE WOMAN'*s laugh is heard.*]

WILLY: Shut up!

LINDA: All the mothers—

WILLY: Shut up!

BERNARD: [*Backing quietly away and out.*] Mr. Birnbaum says he's stuck up.

WILLY: Get outa here!

BERNARD: If he doesn't buckle down he'll flunk math! [*He goes off.*]

LINDA: He's right, Willy, you've gotta—

WILLY: [*Exploding at her.*] There's nothing the matter with him! You want him to be a worm like Bernard? He's got spirit, personality . . . [*As he speaks,* LINDA, *almost in tears, exits into the living room.* WILLY *is alone in the kitchen, wilting and staring. The leaves are gone. It is night again, and the apartment houses look down from behind.*] Loaded with it. Loaded! What is he stealing? He's giving it back, isn't he? Why is he stealing? What did I tell him? I never in my life told him anything but decent things.

[HAPPY *in pajamas has come down the stairs;* WILLY *suddenly becomes aware of* HAPPY'*s presence.*]

HAPPY: Let's go now, come on.

WILLY: [*Sitting down at the kitchen table.*] Huh! Why did she have to wax the floors herself? Everytime she waxes the floors she keels over. She knows that!

HAPPY: Shh! Take it easy. What brought you back tonight?

WILLY: I got an awful scare. Nearly hit a kid in Yonkers. God! Why didn't I go to Alaska with my brother Ben that time! Ben! That man was a genius, that man was success incarnate! What a mistake! He begged me to go.

HAPPY: Well, there's no use in—

WILLY: You guys! There was a man started with the clothes on his back and ended up with diamond mines!

HAPPY: Boy, someday I'd like to know how he did it.

WILLY: What's the mystery? The man knew what he wanted and went out and got it! Walked into a jungle, and comes out, the age of twenty-one, and he's rich! The world is an oyster, but you don't crack it open on a mattress!

HAPPY: Pop, I told you I'm gonna retire you for life.

WILLY: You'll retire me for life on seventy goddam dollars a week? And your women and your car and your apartment, and you'll retire me for life! Christ's sake, I couldn't get past Yonkers today! Where are you guys, where are you? The woods are burning! I can't drive a car!

[CHARLEY *has appeared in the doorway. He is a large man, slow of speech, laconic, immovable. In all he says, despite what he says, there is pity, and now, trepidation. He has a robe over pajamas, slippers on his feet. He enters the kitchen.*]

CHARLEY: Everything all right?

HAPPY: Yeah, Charley, everything's . . .

WILLY: What's the matter?

CHARLEY: I heard some noise. I thought something happened. Can't we do something about the walls? You sneeze in here, and in my house hats blow off.

HAPPY: Let's go to bed, Dad. Come on.

[CHARLEY *signals to* HAPPY *to go.*]

WILLY: You go ahead, I'm not tired at the moment.

HAPPY: [*To* WILLY.] Take it easy, huh? [*He exits.*]

WILLY: What're you doin' up?

CHARLEY: [*Sitting down at the kitchen table opposite* WILLY.] Couldn't sleep good. I had a heartburn.

WILLY: Well, you don't know how to eat.

CHARLEY: I eat with my mouth.

WILLY: No, you're ignorant. You gotta know about vitamins and things like that.

CHARLEY: Come on, let's shoot. Tire you out a little.

WILLY: [*Hesitantly.*] All right. You got cards?

CHARLEY: [*Taking a deck from his pocket.*] Yeah, I got them. Someplace. What is it with those vitamins?

WILLY: [*Dealing.*] They build up your bones. Chemistry.

CHARLEY: Yeah, but there's no bones in a heartburn.

WILLY: What are you talkin' about? Do you know the first thing about it?

CHARLEY: Don't get insulted.

WILLY: Don't talk about something you don't know anything about. [*They are playing. Pause.*]

CHARLEY: What're you doin' home?

WILLY: A little trouble with the car.

CHARLEY: Oh. [*Pause.*] I'd like to take a trip to California.

WILLY: Don't say.

CHARLEY: You want a job?

WILLY: I got a job, I told you that. [*After a slight pause.*] What the hell are you offering me a job for?

CHARLEY: Don't get insulted.

WILLY: Don't insult me.

CHARLEY: I don't see no sense in it. You don't have to go on this way.

WILLY: I got a good job. [*Slight pause.*] What do you keep comin' in here for?

CHARLEY: You want me to go?

WILLY: [*After a pause, withering.*] I can't understand it. He's going back to Texas again. What the hell is that?

CHARLEY: Let him go.

WILLY: I got nothin' to give him, Charley, I'm clean, I'm clean.

CHARLEY: He won't starve. None a them starve. Forget about him.

WILLY: Then what have I got to remember?

CHARLEY: You take it too hard. To hell with it. When a deposit bottle is broken you don't get your nickel back.

WILLY: That's easy enough for you to say.

CHARLEY: That ain't easy for me to say.

WILLY: Did you see the ceiling I put up in the living-room?

CHARLEY: Yeah, that's a piece of work. To put up a ceiling is a mystery to me. How do you do it?

WILLY: What's the difference?

CHARLEY: Well, talk about it.

WILLY: You gonna put up a ceiling?

CHARLEY: How could I put up a ceiling?

WILLY: Then what the hell are you bothering me for?

CHARLEY: You're insulted again.

WILLY: A man who can't handle tools is not a man. You're disgusting.

CHARLEY: Don't call me disgusting, Willy.

> [UNCLE BEN, *carrying a valise and an umbrella, enters the fore-stage from around the right corner of the house. He is a stolid man, in his sixties, with a mustache and an authoritative air. He is utterly certain of his destiny, and there is an aura of far places about him. He enters exactly as* WILLY *speaks.*]

WILLY: I'm getting awfully tired, Ben.

> [BEN's *music is heard.* BEN *looks around at everything.*]

CHARLEY: Good, keep playing; you'll sleep better. Did you call me Ben?

> [BEN *looks at his watch.*]

WILLY: That's funny. For a second there you reminded me of my brother Ben.

BEN: I only have a few minutes. [*He strolls, inspecting the place.* WILLY *and* CHARLEY *continue playing.*]

CHARLEY: You never heard from him again, heh? Since that time?

WILLY: Didn't Linda tell you? Couple of weeks ago we got a letter from his wife in Africa. He died.

CHARLEY: That so.

BEN: [*Chuckling.*] So this is Brooklyn, eh?

CHARLEY: Maybe you're in for some of his money.

WILLY: Naa, he had seven sons. There's just one opportunity I had with that man . . .

BEN: I must make a train, William. There are several properties I'm looking at in Alaska.

WILLY: Sure, sure! If I'd gone with him to Alaska that time, everything would've been totally different.

CHARLEY: Go on, you'da froze to death up there.

WILLY: What're you talking about?

BEN: Opportunity is tremendous in Alaska, William. Surprised you're not up there.

WILLY: Sure, tremendous.

CHARLEY: Heh?

WILLY: There was the only man I ever met who knew the answers.

CHARLEY: Who?

BEN: How are you all?

WILLY: [*Taking a pot, smiling.*] Fine, fine.

CHARLEY: Pretty sharp tonight.

BEN: Is Mother living with you?

WILLY: No, she died a long time ago.

CHARLEY: Who?

BEN: That's too bad. Fine specimen of a lady, Mother.

WILLY: [*To* CHARLEY.] Heh?

BEN: I'd hoped to see the old girl.

CHARLEY: Who died?

BEN: Heard anything from Father, have you?

WILLY: [*Unnerved.*] What do you mean, who died?

CHARLEY: [*Taking a pot.*] What're you talkin' about?

BEN: [*Looking at his watch.*] William, it's half-past eight!

WILLY: [*As though to dispel his confusion he angrily stops* CHARLEY's *hand.*] That's my build!

CHARLEY: I put the ace—

WILLY: If you don't know how to play the game I'm not gonna throw my money away on you!

CHARLEY: [*Rising.*] It was my ace, for God's sake!

WILLY: I'm through, I'm through!

BEN: When did Mother die?

WILLY: Long ago. Since the beginning you never knew how to play cards.

CHARLEY: [*Picks up the cards and goes to the door.*] All right! Next time I'll bring a deck with five aces.

WILLY: I don't play that kind of game!

CHARLEY: [*Turning to him.*] You ought to be ashamed of yourself!

WILLY: Yeah?

CHARLEY: Yeah! [*He goes out.*]

WILLY: [*Slamming the door after him.*] Ignoramus!

BEN: [*As* WILLY *comes toward him through the wall-line of the kitchen.*] So you're William.

WILLY: [*Shaking* BEN's *hand.*] Ben! I've been waiting for you so long! What's the answer? How did you do it?

BEN: Oh, there's a story in that.

[LINDA *enters the forestage, as of old, carrying the wash basket.*]

LINDA: Is this Ben?

BEN: [*Gallantly.*] How do you do, my dear.

LINDA: Where've you been all these years? Willy's always wondered why you—

WILLY: [*Pulling* BEN *away from her impatiently.*] Where is Dad? Didn't you follow him? How did you get started?

BEN: Well, I don't know how much you remember.

WILLY: Well, I was just a baby, of course, only three or four years old—

BEN: Three years and eleven months.

WILLY: What a memory, Ben!

BEN: I have many enterprises, William, and I have never kept books.

WILLY: I remember I was sitting under the wagon in—was it Nebraska?

BEN: It was South Dakota, and I gave you a bunch of wild flowers.

WILLY: I remember you walking away down some open road.

BEN: [*Laughing.*] I was going to find Father in Alaska.

WILLY: Where is he?

BEN: At that age I had a very faulty view of geography, William. I discovered after a few days that I was heading due south, so instead of Alaska, I ended up in Africa.

LINDA: Africa!

WILLY: The Gold Coast!

BEN: Principally diamond mines.

LINDA: Diamond mines!

BEN: Yes, my dear. But I've only a few minutes—

WILLY: No! Boys! Boys! [*Young* BIFF *and* HAPPY *appear.*] Listen to this. This is your Uncle Ben, a great man! Tell my boys, Ben!

BEN: Why, boys, when I was seventeen I walked into the jungle, and when I was twenty-one I walked out. [*He laughs.*] And by God I was rich.

WILLY: [*To the boys.*] You see what I been talking about? The greatest things can happen!

BEN: [*Glancing at his watch.*] I have an appointment in Ketchikan Tuesday week.

WILLY: No, Ben! Please tell about Dad. I want my boys to hear. I want them to know the kind of stock they spring from. All I remember is a man with a big beard, and I was in Mamma's lap, sitting around a fire, and some kind of high music.

BEN: His flute. He played the flute.

WILLY: Sure, the flute, that's right!

[*New music is heard, a high, rollicking tune.*]

BEN: Father was a very great and a very wild-hearted man. We would start in Boston, and he'd toss the whole family into the wagon, and then he'd drive the team right across the country; through Ohio, and Indiana, Michigan, Illinois, and all the Western states. And we'd stop in the towns and sell the flutes that he'd made on the way. Great inventor, Father. With one gadget he made more in a week than a man like you could make in a lifetime.

WILLY: That's just the way I'm bringing them up, Ben—rugged, well liked, all-around.

BEN: Yeah? [*To* BIFF.] Hit that, boy—hard as you can. [*He pounds his stomach.*]

BIFF: Oh, no, sir!

BEN: [*Taking boxing stance.*] Come on, get to me! [*He laughs.*]

WILLY: Go to it, Biff! Go ahead, show him!

BIFF: Okay! [*He cocks his fist and starts in.*]

LINDA: [*To* WILLY.] Why must he fight, dear?

BEN: [*Sparring with* BIFF.] Good boy! Good boy!

WILLY: How's that, Ben, heh?

HAPPY: Give him the left, Biff!

LINDA: Why are you fighting?

BEN: Good boy! [*Suddenly comes in, trips* BIFF, *and stands over him, the point of his umbrella poised over* BIFF's *eye.*]

LINDA: Look out, Biff!

BIFF: Gee!

BEN: [*Patting* BIFF's *knee.*] Never fight fair with a stranger, boy. You'll never get out of the jungle that way. [*Taking* LINDA's *hand and bowing.*] It was an honor and a pleasure to meet you, Linda.

LINDA: [*Withdrawing her hand coldly, frightened.*] Have a nice—trip.

BEN: [*To* WILLY.] And good luck with your—what do you do?

WILLY: Selling.

BEN: Yes. Well . . . [*He raises his hand in farewell to all.*]

WILLY: No, Ben, I don't want you to think . . . [*He takes* BEN's *arm to show him.*] It's Brooklyn, I know, but we hunt too.

BEN: Really, now.

WILLY: Oh, sure, there's snakes and rabbits and—that's why I moved out here. Why, Biff can fell any one of these trees in no time! Boys! Go right over to where they're building the apartment house and get some sand. We're gonna rebuild the entire front stoop right now! Watch this, Ben!

BIFF: Yes, sir! On the double, Hap!

HAPPY: [*As he and* BIFF *run off.*] I lost weight, Pop, you notice?

[CHARLEY *enters in knickers, even before the boys are gone.*]

CHARLEY: Listen, if they steal any more from that building the watchman'll put the cops on them!

LINDA: [*To* WILLY.] Don't let Biff . . .

[BEN *laughs lustily.*]

WILLY: You shoulda seen the lumber they brought home last week. At least a dozen six-by-tens worth all kinds a money.

CHARLEY: Listen, if that watchman—

WILLY: I gave them hell, understand. But I got a couple of fearless characters there.

CHARLEY: Willy, the jails are full of fearless characters.

BEN: [*Clapping* WILLY *on the back, with a laugh at* CHARLEY.] And the stock exchange, friend!

WILLY: [*Joining in* BEN'*s laughter.*] Where are the rest of your pants?

CHARLEY: My wife bought them.

WILLY: Now all you need is a golf club and you can go upstairs and go to sleep. [*To* BEN.] Great athlete! Between him and his son Bernard they can't hammer a nail!

BERNARD: [*Rushing in.*] The watchman's chasing Biff!

WILLY: [*Angrily.*] Shut up! He's not stealing anything!

LINDA: [*Alarmed, hurrying off left.*] Where is he? Biff, dear! [*She exits.*]

WILLY: [*Moving toward the left, away from* BEN.] There's nothing wrong. What's the matter with you?

BEN: Nervy boy. Good!

WILLY: [*Laughing.*] Oh, nerves of iron, that Biff!

CHARLEY: Don't know what it is. My New England man comes back and he's bleedin', they murdered him up there.

WILLY: It's contacts, Charley, I got important contacts!

CHARLEY: [*Sarcastically.*] Glad to hear it, Willy. Come in later, we'll shoot a little casino. I'll take some of your Portland money. [*He laughs at* WILLY *and exits.*]

WILLY: [*Turning to* BEN.] Business is bad, it's murderous. But not for me, of course.

BEN: I'll stop by on my way back to Africa.

WILLY: [*Longingly.*] Can't you stay a few days? You're just what I need, Ben, because I—I have a fine position here, but I—well, Dad left when I was such a baby and I never had a chance to talk to him and I still feel—kind of temporary about myself.

BEN: I'll be late for my train.

[*They are at opposite ends of the stage.*]

WILLY: Ben, my boys—can't we talk? They'd go into the jaws of hell for me, see, but I—

BEN: William, you're being first-rate with your boys. Outstanding, manly chaps!

WILLY: [*Hanging on to his words.*] Oh, Ben, that's good to hear! Because sometimes I'm afraid that I'm not teaching them the right kind of—Ben, how should I teach them?

BEN: [*Giving great weight to each word, and with a certain vicious audacity.*] William, when I walked into the jungle, I was seventeen. When I walked out I was twenty-one. And, by God, I was rich! [*He goes off into darkness around the right corner of the house.*]

WILLY: . . . was rich! That's just the spirit I want to imbue them with! To walk into a jungle! I was right! I was right! I was right!

[BEN *is gone, but* WILLY *is still speaking to him as* LINDA, *in nightgown and robe, enters the kitchen, glances around for* WILLY, *then goes to the door of the house, looks out and sees him. Comes down to his left. He looks at her.*]

LINDA: Willy, dear? Willy?

WILLY: I was right!

LINDA: Did you have some cheese? [*He can't answer.*] It's very late, darling. Come to bed, heh?

WILLY: [*Looking straight up.*] Gotta break your neck to see a star in this yard.

LINDA: You coming in?

WILLY: Whatever happened to that diamond watch fob? Remember? When Ben came from Africa that time? Didn't he give me a watch fob with a diamond in it?

LINDA: You pawned it, dear. Twelve, thirteen years ago. For Biff's radio correspondence course.

WILLY: Gee, that was a beautiful thing. I'll take a walk.

LINDA: But you're in your slippers.

WILLY: [*Starting to go around the house at the left.*] I was right! I was! [*Half to* LINDA, *as he goes, shaking his head.*] What a man! There was a man worth talking to. I was right!

LINDA: [*Calling after* WILLY.] But in your slippers, Willy!

[WILLY *is almost gone when* BIFF, *in his pajamas, comes down the stairs and enters the kitchen.*]

BIFF: What is he doing out there?

LINDA: Sh!

BIFF: God Almighty, Mom, how long has he been doing this?

LINDA: Don't, he'll hear you.

BIFF: What the hell is the matter with him?

LINDA: It'll pass by morning.

BIFF: Shouldn't we do anything?

LINDA: Oh, my dear, you should do a lot of things, but there's nothing to do, so go to sleep.

[HAPPY *comes down the stairs and sits on the steps.*]

HAPPY: I never heard him so loud, Mom.

LINDA: Well, come around more often; you'll hear him. [*She sits down at the table and mends the lining of* WILLY'*s jacket.*]

BIFF: Why didn't you ever write me about this, Mom?

LINDA: How would I write to you? For over three months you had no address.

BIFF: I was on the move. But you know I thought of you all the time. You know that, don't you, pal?

LINDA: I know, dear, I know. But he likes to have a letter. Just to know that there's still a possibility for better things.

BIFF: He's not like this all the time, is he?

LINDA: It's when you come home he's always the worst.

BIFF: When I come home?

LINDA: When you write you're coming, he's all smiles, and talks about the future, and—he's just wonderful. And then the closer you seem to come, the more shaky he gets, and then, by the time you get here, he's arguing, and he seems angry at you. I think it's just that maybe he can't bring himself to—to open up to you. Why are you so hateful to each other? Why is that?

BIFF: [*Evasively.*] I'm not hateful, Mom.

LINDA: But you no sooner come in the door than you're fighting!

BIFF: I don't know why. I mean to change. I'm tryin', Mom, you understand?

LINDA: Are you home to stay now?

BIFF: I don't know. I want to look around, see what's doin'.

LINDA: Biff, you can't look around all your life, can you?

BIFF: I just can't take hold, Mom. I can't take hold of some kind of a life.

LINDA: Biff, a man is not a bird, to come and go with the springtime.

BIFF: Your hair . . . [*He touches her hair.*] Your hair got so gray.

LINDA: Oh, it's been gray since you were in high school. I just stopped dyeing it, that's all.

BIFF: Dye it again, will ya? I don't want my pal looking old. [*He smiles.*]

LINDA: You're such a boy! You think you can go away for a year and . . . You've got to get it into your head now that one day you'll knock on this door and there'll be strange people here—

BIFF: What are you talking about? You're not even sixty, Mom.

LINDA: But what about your father?

BIFF: [*Lamely.*] Well, I meant him too.

HAPPY: He admires Pop.

LINDA: Biff, dear, if you don't have any feeling for him, then you can't have any feeling for me.

BIFF: Sure I can, Mom.

LINDA: No. You can't just come to see me, because I love him. [*With a threat, but only a threat, of tears.*] He's the dearest man in the world to me, and I won't have anyone making him feel unwanted and low and blue. You've got to make up your mind now, darling, there's no leeway anymore. Either he's your father and you pay him that respect, or else you're not to come here. I know he's not easy to get along with—nobody knows that better than me—but . . .

WILLY: [*From the left, with a laugh.*] Hey, hey, Biffo!

BIFF: [*Starting to go out after* WILLY.] What the hell is the matter with him? [HAPPY *stops him.*]

LINDA: Don't—don't go near him!

BIFF: Stop making excuses for him! He always, always wiped the floor with you. Never had an ounce of respect for you.

HAPPY: He's always had respect for—

BIFF: What the hell do you know about it?

HAPPY: [*Surlily.*] Just don't call him crazy!

BIFF: He's got no character—Charley wouldn't do this. Not in his own house—spewing out that vomit from his mind.

HAPPY: Charley never had to cope with what he's got to.

BIFF: People are worse off than Willy Loman. Believe me, I've seen them!

LINDA: Then make Charley your father, Biff. You can't do that, can you? I don't say he's a great man. Willy Loman never made a lot of money. His name was never in the paper. He's not the finest character that ever lived. But he's a human being, and a terrible thing is happening to him. So attention must be paid. He's not to be allowed to fall into his grave like an old dog. Attention, attention must be finally paid to such a person. You called him crazy—

BIFF: I didn't mean—

LINDA: No, a lot of people think he's lost his—balance. But you don't have to be very smart to know what his trouble is. The man is exhausted.

HAPPY: Sure!

LINDA: A small man can be just as exhausted as a great man. He works for a company thirty-six years this March, opens up unheard-of territories to their trademark, and now in his old age they take his salary away.

HAPPY: [*Indignantly.*] I didn't know that, Mom.

LINDA: You never asked, my dear! Now that you get your spending money someplace else you don't trouble your mind with him.

HAPPY: But I gave you money last—

LINDA: Christmas time, fifty dollars! To fix the hot water it cost ninety-seven fifty! For five weeks he's been on straight commission, like a beginner, an unknown!

BIFF: Those ungrateful bastards!

LINDA: Are they any worse than his sons? When he brought them business, when he was young, they were glad to see him. But now his old friends, the old buyers that loved him so and always found some order to hand him in a pinch—they're all dead, retired. He used to be able to make six, seven calls a day in

Boston. Now he takes his valises out of the car and puts them back and takes them out again and he's exhausted. Instead of walking he talks now. He drives seven hundred miles, and when he gets there no one knows him anymore, no one welcomes him. And what goes through a man's mind, driving seven hundred miles home without having earned a cent? Why shouldn't he talk to himself? Why? When he has to go to Charley and borrow fifty dollars a week and pretend to me that it's his pay? How long can that go on? How long? You see what I'm sitting here and waiting for? And you tell me he has no character? The man who never worked a day but for your benefit? When does he get the medal for that? Is this his reward—to turn around at the age of sixty-three and find his sons, who he loved better than his life, one a philandering bum—

HAPPY: Mom!

LINDA: That's all you are, my baby! [*To* BIFF.] And you! What happened to the love you had for him? You were such pals! How you used to talk to him on the phone every night! How lonely he was till he could come home to you!

BIFF: All right, Mom. I'll live here in my room, and I'll get a job. I'll keep away from him, that's all.

LINDA: No, Biff. You can't stay here and fight all the time.

BIFF: He threw me out of this house, remember that.

LINDA: Why did he do that? I never knew why.

BIFF: Because I know he's a fake and he doesn't like anybody around who knows!

LINDA: Why a fake? In what way? What do you mean?

BIFF: Just don't lay it all at my feet. It's between me and him— that's all I have to say. I'll chip in from now on. He'll settle for half my paycheck. He'll be all right. I'm going to bed. [*He starts for the stairs.*]

LINDA: He won't be all right.

BIFF: [*Turning on the stairs, furiously.*] I hate this city and I'll stay here. Now what do you want?

LINDA: He's dying, BIFF.

[HAPPY *turns quickly to her, shocked.*]

BIFF: [*After a pause.*] Why is he dying?

LINDA: He's been trying to kill himself.

BIFF: [*With great horror.*] How?

LINDA: I live from day to day.

BIFF: What're you talking about?

LINDA: Remember I wrote you that he smashed up the car again? In February?

BIFF: Well?

LINDA: The insurance inspector came. He said that they have evidence. That all these accidents in the last year—weren't—weren't—accidents.

HAPPY: How can they tell that? That's a lie.

LINDA: It seems there's a woman . . . [*She takes a breath as. . . .*]

⎰ BIFF: [*Sharply but contained.*] What woman?
⎱ LINDA: [*Simultaneously.*] . . . and this woman . . .

LINDA: What?

BIFF: Nothing. Go ahead.

LINDA: What did you say?

BIFF: Nothing. I just said what woman?

HAPPY: What about her?

LINDA: Well, it seems she was walking down the road and saw his car. She says that he wasn't driving fast at all, and that he didn't skid. She says he came to that little bridge, and then deliberately smashed into the railing, and it was only the shallowness of the water that saved him.

BIFF: Oh, no, he probably just fell asleep again.

LINDA: I don't think he fell asleep.

BIFF: Why not?

LINDA: Last month . . . [*With great difficulty.*] Oh, boys, it's so hard to say a thing like this! He's just a big stupid man to you, but I tell you there's more good in him than in many other people. [*She chokes, wipes her eyes.*] I was looking for a fuse. The lights blew out, and I went down the cellar. And behind the fuse box—it happened to fall out—was a length of rubber pipe—just short.

HAPPY: No kidding?

LINDA: There's a little attachment on the end of it. I knew right away. And sure enough, on the bottom of the water heater there's a new little nipple on the gas pipe.

HAPPY: [*Angrily.*] That—jerk.

BIFF: Did you have it taken off?

LINDA: I'm—I'm ashamed to. How can I mention it to him? Every day I go down and take away that little rubber pipe. But, when he comes home, I put it back where it was. How can I insult him that way? I don't know what to do. I live from day to day, boys. I tell you, I know every thought in his mind. It sounds so old-fashioned and silly, but I tell you he put his whole life into you and you've turned your backs on him. [*She is bent over in the chair, weeping, her face in her hands.*] Biff, I swear to God! Biff, his life is in your hands!

HAPPY: [*To* BIFF.] How do you like that damned fool!

BIFF: [*Kissing her.*] All right, pal, all right. It's all settled now. I've been remiss. I know that, Mom. But now I'll stay, and I swear to you, I'll apply myself. [*Kneeling in front of her, in a fever of self-reproach.*] It's just—you see, Mom, I don't fit in business. Not that I won't try. I'll try, and I'll make good.

HAPPY: Sure you will. The trouble with you in business was you never tried to please people.

BIFF: I know, I—

HAPPY: Like when you worked for Harrison's. Bob Harrison said you were tops, and then you go and do some damn fool thing like whistling whole songs in the elevator like a comedian.

BIFF: [*Against* HAPPY.] So what? I like to whistle sometimes.

HAPPY: You don't raise a guy to a responsible job who whistles in the elevator!

LINDA: Well, don't argue about it now.

HAPPY: Like when you'd go off and swim in the middle of the day instead of taking the line around.

BIFF: [*His resentment rising.*] Well, don't you run off? You take off sometimes, don't you? On a nice summer day?

HAPPY: Yeah, but I cover myself!

LINDA: Boys!

HAPPY: If I'm going to take a fade the boss can call any number where I'm supposed to be and they'll swear to him that I just left. I'll tell you something that I hate to say, Biff, but in the business world some of them think you're crazy.

BIFF: [*Angered.*] Screw the business world!

HAPPY: All right, screw it! Great, but cover yourself!

LINDA: Hap, Hap!

BIFF: I don't care what they think! They've laughed at Dad for years, and you know why? Because we don't belong in this nuthouse of a city! We should be mixing cement on some open plain, or— or carpenters. A carpenter is allowed to whistle!

[WILLY *walks in from the entrance of the house, at left.*]

WILLY: Even your grandfather was better than a carpenter. [*Pause. They watch him.*] You never grew up. Bernard does not whistle in the elevator, I assure you.

BIFF: [*As though to laugh* WILLY *out of it.*] Yeah, but you do, Pop.

WILLY: I never in my life whistled in an elevator! And who in the business world thinks I'm crazy?

BIFF: I didn't mean it like that, Pop. Now don't make a whole thing out of it, will ya?

WILLY: Go back to the West! Be a carpenter, a cowboy, enjoy yourself!

LINDA: Willy, he was just saying—

WILLY: I heard what he said!

HAPPY: [*Trying to quiet* WILLY.] Hey, Pop, come on now. . .

WILLY: [*Continuing over* HAPPY's *line.*] They laugh at me, heh? Go to Filene's, go to the Hub, go to Slattery's Boston. Call out the name Willy Loman and see what happens! Big shot!

BIFF: All right, Pop.

WILLY: Big!

BIFF: All right!

WILLY: Why do you always insult me?

BIFF: I didn't say a word. [*To* LINDA.] Did I say a word?

LINDA: He didn't say anything, Willy.

WILLY: [*Going to the doorway of the living-room.*] All right, good night, good night.

LINDA: Willy, dear, he just decided. . .

WILLY: [*To* BIFF.] If you get tired hanging around tomorrow, paint the ceiling I put up in the living-room.

BIFF: I'm leaving early tomorrow.

HAPPY: He's going to see Bill Oliver, Pop.

WILLY: [*Interestedly.*] Oliver? For what?

BIFF: [*With reserve, but trying, trying.*] He always said he'd stake me. I'd like to go into business, so maybe I can take him up on it.

LINDA: Isn't that wonderful?

WILLY: Don't interrupt. What's wonderful about it? There's fifty men in the City of New York who'd stake him. [*To* BIFF.] Sporting goods?

BIFF: I guess so. I know something about it and—

WILLY: He knows something about it! You know sporting goods better than Spalding,[9] for God's sake! How much is he giving you?

BIFF: I don't know, I didn't even see him yet, but—

WILLY: Then what're you talkin' about?

BIFF: [*Getting angry.*] Well, all I said was I'm gonna see him, that's all!

WILLY: [*Turning away.*] Ah, you're counting your chickens again.

BIFF: [*Starting left for the stairs.*] Oh, Jesus, I'm going to sleep!

WILLY: [*Calling after him.*] Don't curse in this house!

BIFF: [*Turning.*] Since when did you get so clean?

HAPPY: [*Trying to stop them.*] Wait a. . .

WILLY: Don't use that language to me! I won't have it!

HAPPY: [*Grabbing* BIFF, *shouts.*] Wait a minute! I got an idea. I got a feasible idea. Come here, Biff, let's talk this over now, let's talk some sense here. When I was down in Florida last time, I thought of a great idea to sell sporting goods. It just came back to me. You and I, Biff—we have a line, the Loman Line. We train a couple of weeks, and put on a couple of exhibitions, see?

WILLY: That's an idea!

HAPPY: Wait! We form two basketball teams, see? Two water-polo teams. We play each other. It's a million dollars' worth of publicity. Two brothers, see? The Loman Brothers. Displays in the Royal Palms—all the hotels. And banners over the ring and the basketball court: "Loman Brothers." Baby, we could sell sporting goods!

WILLY: That is a one-million-dollar idea!

LINDA: Marvelous!

BIFF: I'm in great shape as far as that's concerned.

HAPPY: And the beauty of it is, Biff, it wouldn't be like a business. We'd be out playin' ball again . . .

BIFF: [*Enthused.*] Yeah, that's. . .

WILLY: Million-dollar . . .

HAPPY: And you wouldn't get fed up with it, Biff. It'd be the family again. There'd be the old honor, and comradeship, and if you

---

9. Sporting goods manufacturer best known for standardizing baseballs and basketballs.

wanted to go off for a swim or somethin'—well, you'd do it! Without some smart cooky gettin' up ahead of you!

WILLY: Lick the world! You guys together could absolutely lick the civilized world.

BIFF: I'll see Oliver tomorrow. Hap, if we could work that out . . .

LINDA: Maybe things are beginning to—

WILLY: [*Wildly enthused, to* LINDA.] Stop interrupting! [*To* BIFF.] But don't wear sport jacket and slacks when you see Oliver.

BIFF: No, I'll—

WILLY: A business suit, and talk as little as possible, and don't crack any jokes.

BIFF: He did like me. Always liked me.

LINDA: He loved you!

WILLY: [*To* LINDA.] Will you stop! [*To* BIFF.] Walk in very serious. You are not applying for a boy's job. Money is to pass. Be quiet, fine, and serious. Everybody likes a kidder, but nobody lends him money.

HAPPY: I'll try to get some myself, Biff. I'm sure I can.

WILLY: I see great things for you kids, I think your troubles are over. But remember, start big and you'll end big. Ask for fifteen. How much you gonna ask for?

BIFF: Gee, I don't know—

WILLY: And don't say "Gee." "Gee" is a boy's word. A man walking in for fifteen thousand dollars does not say "Gee!"

BIFF: Ten, I think, would be top though.

WILLY: Don't be so modest. You always started too low. Walk in with a big laugh. Don't look worried. Start off with a couple of your good stories to lighten things up. It's not what you say, it's how you say it—because personality always wins the day.

LINDA: Oliver always thought the highest of him—

WILLY: Will you let me talk?

BIFF: Don't yell at her, Pop, will ya?

WILLY: [*Angrily.*] I was talking, wasn't I?

BIFF: I don't like you yelling at her all the time, and I'm tellin' you, that's all.

WILLY: What're you, takin' over this house?

LINDA: Willy—

WILLY: [*Turning on her.*] Don't take his side all the time, goddammit!

BIFF: [*Furiously.*] Stop yelling at her!

WILLY: [*Suddenly pulling on his cheek, beaten down, guilt ridden.*] Give my best to Bill Oliver—he may remember me. [*He exits through the living-room doorway.*]

LINDA: [*Her voice subdued.*] What'd you have to start that for? [BIFF *turns away.*] You see how sweet he was as soon as you talked hopefully? [*She goes over to* BIFF.] Come up and say good night to him. Don't let him go to bed that way.

HAPPY: Come on, Biff, let's buck him up.

LINDA: Please, dear. Just say good night. It takes so little to make him happy. Come. [*She goes through the living-room doorway, calling upstairs from within the living-room.*] Your pajamas are hanging in the bathroom, Willy!

HAPPY: [*Looking toward where* LINDA *went out.*] What a woman! They broke the mold when they made her. You know that, Biff?

BIFF: He's off salary. My God, working on commission!

HAPPY: Well, let's face it: he's no hot-shot selling man. Except that sometimes, you have to admit, he's a sweet personality.

BIFF: [*Deciding.*] Lend me ten bucks, will ya? I want to buy some new ties.

HAPPY: I'll take you to a place I know. Beautiful stuff. Wear one of my striped shirts tomorrow.

BIFF: She got gray. Mom got awful old. Gee, I'm gonna go in to Oliver tomorrow and knock him for a—

HAPPY: Come on up. Tell that to Dad. Let's give him a whirl. Come on.

BIFF: [*Steamed up.*] You know, with ten thousand bucks, boy!

HAPPY: [*As they go into the living-room.*] That's the talk, Biff, that's the first time I've heard the old confidence out of you! [*From within the living-room, fading off.*] You're gonna live with me, kid, and any babe you want just say the word . . .

[*The last lines are hardly heard. They are mounting the stairs to their parents' bedroom.*]

LINDA: [*Entering her bedroom and addressing* WILLY, *who is in the bathroom. She is straightening the bed for him.*] Can you do anything about the shower? It drips.

WILLY: [*From the bathroom.*] All of a sudden everything falls to pieces! Goddam plumbing, oughta be sued, those people. I hardly finished putting it in and the thing . . . [*His words rumble off.*]

LINDA: I'm just wondering if Oliver will remember him. You think he might?

WILLY: [*Coming out of the bathroom in his pajamas.*] Remember him? What's the matter with you, you crazy? If he'd've stayed with Oliver he'd be on top by now! Wait'll Oliver gets a look at him. You don't know the average caliber anymore. The average young man today—[*He is getting into bed.*]—is got a caliber of zero. Greatest thing in the world for him was to bum around. [BIFF *and* HAPPY *enter the bedroom. Slight pause.* WILLY *stops short, looking at* BIFF.] Glad to hear it, boy.

HAPPY: He wanted to say good night to you, sport.

WILLY: [*To* BIFF.] Yeah. Knock him dead, boy. What'd you want to tell me?

BIFF: Just take it easy, Pop. Good night. [*He turns to go.*]

WILLY: [*Unable to resist.*] And if anything falls off the desk while you're talking to him—like a package or something—don't you pick it up. They have office boys for that.

LINDA: I'll make a big breakfast—

WILLY: Will you let me finish? [*To* BIFF.] Tell him you were in the business in the West. Not farm work.

BIFF: All right, Dad.

LINDA: I think everything—

WILLY: [*Going right through her speech.*] And don't undersell yourself. No less than fifteen thousand dollars.

BIFF: [*Unable to bear him.*] Okay. Good night, Mom. [*He starts moving.*]

WILLY: Because you got a greatness in you, Biff, remember that. You got all kinds of greatness . . . [*He lies back, exhausted.* BIFF *walks out.*]

LINDA: [*Calling after* BIFF.] Sleep well, darling!

HAPPY: I'm gonna get married, Mom. I wanted to tell you.

LINDA: Go to sleep, dear.

HAPPY: [*Going.*] I just wanted to tell you.

WILLY: Keep up the good work. [HAPPY *exits.*] God . . . remember that Ebbets Field[1] game? The championship of the city?

LINDA: Just rest. Should I sing to you?

---

1. Home stadium of the Brooklyn Dodgers from 1913 to 1957. Football games were also played there.

WILLY: Yeah. Sing to me. [LINDA *hums a soft lullaby.*] When that team came out—he was the tallest, remember?

LINDA: Oh, yes. And in gold.

[BIFF *enters the darkened kitchen, takes a cigarette, and leaves the house. He comes downstage into a golden pool of light. He smokes, staring at the night.*]

WILLY: Like a young god. Hercules—something like that. And the sun, the sun all around him. Remember how he waved to me? Right up from the field, with the representatives of three colleges standing by? And the buyers I brought, and the cheers when he came out—Loman, Loman, Loman! God Almighty, he'll be great yet. A star like that, magnificent, can never really fade away!

[*The light on* WILLY *is fading. The gas heater begins to glow through the kitchen wall, near the stairs, a blue flame beneath red coils.*]

LINDA: [*Timidly.*] Willy dear, what has he got against you?

WILLY: I'm so tired. Don't talk anymore.

[BIFF *slowly returns to the kitchen. He stops, stares toward the heater.*]

LINDA: Will you ask Howard to let you work in New York?

WILLY: First thing in the morning. Everything'll be all right.

[BIFF *reaches behind the heater and draws out a length of rubber tubing. He is horrified and turns his head toward* WILLY's *room, still dimly lit, from which the strains of* LINDA's *desperate but monotonous humming rise.*]

WILLY: [*Staring through the window into the moonlight.*] Gee, look at the moon moving between the buildings!

[BIFF *wraps the tubing around his hand and quickly goes up the stairs.*]

[*CURTAIN.*]

ACT 2

Music is heard, gay and bright. The curtain rises as the music fades away. WILLY, *in shirt sleeves, is sitting at the kitchen table, sipping coffee, his hat in his lap.* LINDA *is filling his cup when she can.*

WILLY: Wonderful coffee. Meal in itself.

LINDA: Can I make you some eggs?

WILLY: No. Take a breath.

LINDA: You look so rested, dear.

WILLY: I slept like a dead one. First time in months. Imagine, sleeping till ten on a Tuesday morning. Boys left nice and early, heh?

LINDA: They were out of here by eight o'clock.

WILLY: Good work!

LINDA: It was so thrilling to see them leaving together. I can't get over the shaving lotion in this house!

WILLY: [*Smiling.*] Mmm—

LINDA: Biff was very changed this morning. His whole attitude seemed to be hopeful. He couldn't wait to get downtown to see Oliver.

WILLY: He's heading for a change. There's no question, there simply are certain men that take longer to get—solidified. How did he dress?

LINDA: His blue suit. He's so handsome in that suit. He could be a—anything in that suit!

[WILLY *gets up from the table.* LINDA *holds his jacket for him.*]

WILLY: There's no question, no question at all. Gee, on the way home tonight I'd like to buy some seeds.

LINDA: [*Laughing.*] That'd be wonderful. But not enough sun gets back there. Nothing'll grow any more.

WILLY: You wait, kid, before it's all over we're gonna get a little place out in the country, and I'll raise some vegetables, a couple of chickens . . .

LINDA: You'll do it yet, dear.

[WILLY *walks out of his jacket.* LINDA *follows him.*]

WILLY: And they'll get married, and come for a weekend. I'd build a little guest house. 'Cause I got so many fine tools, all I'd need would be a little lumber and some peace of mind.

LINDA: [*Joyfully.*] I sewed the lining . . .

WILLY: I could build two guest houses, so they'd both come. Did he decide how much he's going to ask Oliver for?

LINDA: [*Getting him into the jacket.*] He didn't mention it, but I imagine ten or fifteen thousand. You going to talk to Howard today?

WILLY: Yeah. I'll put it to him straight and simple. He'll just have to take me off the road.

LINDA: And Willy, don't forget to ask for a little advance, because we've got the insurance premium. It's the grace period now.

WILLY: That's a hundred . . . ?

LINDA: A hundred and eight, sixty-eight. Because we're a little short again.

WILLY: Why are we short?

LINDA: Well, you had the motor job on the car . . .

WILLY: That goddam Studebaker!

LINDA: And you got one more payment on the refrigerator . . .

WILLY: But it just broke again!

LINDA: Well, it's old, dear.

WILLY: I told you we should've bought a well-advertised machine. Charley bought a General Electric and it's twenty years old and it's still good, that son-of-a-bitch.

LINDA: But, Willy—

WILLY: Whoever heard of a Hastings refrigerator? Once in my life I would like to own something outright before it's broken! I'm always in a race with the junkyard! I just finished paying for the car and it's on its last legs. The refrigerator consumes belts like a god-dam maniac. They time those things. They time them so when you finally paid for them, they're used up.

LINDA: [*Buttoning up his jacket as he unbuttons it.*] All told, about two hundred dollars would carry us, dear. But that includes the last payment on the mortgage. After this payment, Willy, the house belongs to us.

WILLY: It's twenty-five years!

LINDA: Biff was nine years old when we bought it.

WILLY: Well, that's a great thing. To weather a twenty-five-year mortgage is—

LINDA: It's an accomplishment.

WILLY: All the cement, the lumber, the reconstruction I put in this house! There ain't a crack to be found in it anymore.

LINDA: Well, it served its purpose.

WILLY: What purpose? Some stranger'll come along, move in, and that's that. If only Biff would take this house, and raise a family . . . [*He starts to go.*] Good-bye, I'm late.

LINDA: [*Suddenly remembering.*] Oh, I forgot! You're supposed to meet them for dinner.

WILLY: Me?

LINDA: At Frank's Chop House on Forty-eighth near Sixth Avenue.

WILLY: Is that so! How about you?

LINDA: No, just the three of you. They're gonna blow you to a big meal!

WILLY: Don't say! Who thought of that?

LINDA: Biff came to me this morning, Willy, and he said, "Tell Dad, we want to blow him to a big meal." Be there six o'clock. You and your two boys are going to have dinner.

WILLY: Gee whiz! That's really somethin'. I'm gonna knock Howard for a loop, kid. I'll get an advance, and I'll come home with a New York job. Goddammit, now I'm gonna do it!

LINDA: Oh, that's the spirit, Willy!

WILLY: I will never get behind a wheel the rest of my life!

LINDA: It's changing, Willy, I can feel it changing!

WILLY: Beyond a question. G'bye, I'm late. [*He starts to go again.*]

LINDA: [*Calling after him as she runs to the kitchen table for a handkerchief.*] You got your glasses?

WILLY: [*Feels for them, then comes back in.*] Yeah, yeah, got my glasses.

LINDA: [*Giving him the handkerchief.*] And a handkerchief.

WILLY: Yeah, handkerchief.

LINDA: And your saccharine?[2]

WILLY: Yeah, my saccharine.

LINDA: Be careful on the subway stairs.

[*She kisses him, and a silk stocking is seen hanging from her hand.* WILLY *notices it.*]

WILLY: Will you stop mending stockings? At least while I'm in the house. It gets me nervous. I can't tell you. Please.

[LINDA *hides the stocking in her hand as she follows* WILLY *across the forestage in front of the house.*]

LINDA: Remember, Frank's Chop House.

WILLY: [*Passing the apron.*] Maybe beets would grow out there.

LINDA: [*Laughing.*] But you tried so many times.

WILLY: Yeah. Well, don't work hard today. [*He disappears around the right corner of the house.*]

2. A low-calorie sweetener often substituted for sugar.

LINDA: Be careful! [*As* WILLY *vanishes,* LINDA *waves to him. Suddenly the phone rings. She runs across the stage and into the kitchen and lifts it.*] Hello? Oh, Biff! I'm so glad you called, I just . . . Yes, sure, I just told him. Yes, he'll be there for dinner at six o'clock, I didn't forget. Listen, I was just dying to tell you. You know that little rubber pipe I told you about? That he connected to the gas heater? I finally decided to go down the cellar this morning and take it away and destroy it. But it's gone! Imagine? He took it away himself, it isn't there! [*She listens.*] When? Oh, then you took it. Oh—nothing, it's just that I'd hoped he'd taken it away himself. Oh, I'm not worried, darling, because this morning he left in such high spirits, it was like the old days! I'm not afraid anymore. Did Mr. Oliver see you? . . . Well, you wait there then. And make a nice impression on him, darling. Just don't perspire too much before you see him. And have a nice time with Dad. He may have big news too! . . . That's right, a New York job. And be sweet to him tonight, dear. Be loving to him. Because he's only a little boat looking for a harbor. [*She is trembling with sorrow and joy.*] Oh, that's wonderful, Biff, you'll save his life. Thanks, darling. Just put your arm around him when he comes into the restaurant. Give him a smile. That's the boy . . . Goodbye, dear . . . You got your comb? . . . That's fine. Good-bye, Biff dear.

[*In the middle of her speech,* HOWARD WAGNER, *thirty-six, wheels on a small typewriter table on which is a wire-recording machine and proceeds to plug it in. This is on the left forestage. Light slowly fades on* LINDA *as it rises on* HOWARD. HOWARD *is intent on threading the machine and only glances over his shoulder as* WILLY *appears.*]

WILLY: Pst! Pst!

HOWARD: Hello, Willy, come in.

WILLY: Like to have a little talk with you, Howard.

HOWARD: Sorry to keep you waiting. I'll be with you in a minute.

WILLY: What's that, Howard?

HOWARD: Didn't you ever see one of these? Wire recorder.

WILLY: Oh. Can we talk a minute?

HOWARD: Records things. Just got delivery yesterday. Been driving me crazy, the most terrific machine I ever saw in my life. I was up all night with it.

WILLY: What do you do with it?

HOWARD: I bought it for dictation, but you can do anything with it. Listen to this. I had it home last night. Listen to what I picked up. The first one is my daughter. Get this. [*He flicks the switch and "Roll out the Barrel" is heard being whistled.*] Listen to that kid whistle.

WILLY: That is lifelike, isn't it?

HOWARD: Seven years old. Get that tone.

WILLY: Ts, ts. Like to ask a little favor if you . . .

[*The whistling breaks off, and the voice of* HOWARD's *daughter is heard.*]

HIS DAUGHTER: "Now you, Daddy."

HOWARD: She's crazy for me! [*Again the same song is whistled.*] That's me! Ha! [*He winks.*]

WILLY: You're very good!

[*The whistling breaks off again. The machine runs silent for a moment.*]

HOWARD: Sh! Get this now, this is my son.

HIS SON: "The capital of Alabama is Montgomery; the capital of Arizona is Phoenix; the capital of Arkansas is Little Rock; the capital of California is Sacramento . . ." [*And on, and on.*]

HOWARD: [*Holding up five fingers.*] Five years old, Willy!

WILLY: He'll make an announcer some day!

HIS SON: [*Continuing.*] "The capital . . ."

HOWARD: Get that—alphabetical order! [*The machine breaks off suddenly.*] Wait a minute. The maid kicked the plug out.

WILLY: It certainly is a—

HOWARD: Sh, for God's sake!

HIS SON: "It's nine o'clock, Bulova watch time.[3] So I have to go to sleep."

WILLY: That really is—

HOWARD: Wait a minute! The next is my wife.

[*They wait.*]

HOWARD's VOICE: "Go on, say something." [*Pause.*] "Well, you gonna talk?"

HIS WIFE: "I can't think of anything."

HOWARD's VOICE: "Well, talk—it's turning."

---

3. Commercial slogan of the Bulova Watch Company often heard on the radio.

HIS WIFE: [*Shyly, beaten.*] "Hello." [*Silence.*] "Oh, Howard, I can't talk into this . . ."

HOWARD: [*Snapping the machine off.*] That was my wife.

WILLY: That is a wonderful machine. Can we—

HOWARD: I tell you, Willy, I'm gonna take my camera, and my bandsaw, and all my hobbies, and out they go. This is the most fascinating relaxation I ever found.

WILLY: I think I'll get one myself.

HOWARD: Sure, they're only a hundred and a half. You can't do without it. Supposing you wanna hear Jack Benny,[4] see? But you can't be at home at that hour. So you tell the maid to turn the radio on when Jack Benny comes on, and this automatically goes on with the radio . . .

WILLY: And when you come home you . . .

HOWARD: You can come home twelve o'clock, one o'clock, any time you like, and you get yourself a Coke and sit yourself down, throw the switch, and there's Jack Benny's program in the middle of the night!

WILLY: I'm definitely going to get one. Because lots of time I'm on the road, and I think to myself, what I must be missing on the radio!

HOWARD: Don't you have a radio in the car?

WILLY: Well, yeah, but who ever thinks of turning it on?

HOWARD: Say, aren't you supposed to be in Boston?

WILLY: That's what I want to talk to you about, Howard. You got a minute? [*He draws a chair in from the wing.*]

HOWARD: What happened? What're you doing here?

WILLY: Well . . .

HOWARD: You didn't crack up again, did you?

WILLY: Oh, no. No . . .

HOWARD: Geez, you had me worried there for a minute. What's the trouble?

WILLY: Well, tell you the truth, Howard. I've come to the decision that I'd rather not travel anymore.

HOWARD: Not travel! Well, what'll you do?

---

4. Jack Benny (1894–1974) starred in the popular weekly radio show, *The Jack Benny Program*, from 1932 to 1955.

WILLY: Remember, Christmas time, when you had the party here? You said you'd try to think of some spot for me here in town.

HOWARD: With us?

WILLY: Well, sure.

HOWARD: Oh, yeah, yeah. I remember. Well, I couldn't think of anything for you, Willy.

WILLY: I tell ya, Howard. The kids are all grown up, y'know. I don't need much anymore. If I could take home—well, sixty-five dollars a week, I could swing it.

HOWARD: Yeah, but Willy, see I—

WILLY: I tell ya why, Howard. Speaking frankly and between the two of us, y'know—I'm just a little tired.

HOWARD: Oh, I could understand that, Willy. But you're a road man, Willy, and we do a road business. We've only got a half-dozen salesmen on the floor here.

WILLY: God knows, Howard, I never asked a favor of any man. But I was with the firm when your father used to carry you in here in his arms.

HOWARD: I know that, Willy, but—

WILLY: Your father came to me the day you were born and asked me what I thought of the name of Howard, may he rest in peace.

HOWARD: I appreciate that, Willy, but there just is no spot here for you. If I had a spot I'd slam you right in, but I just don't have a single solitary spot.

[*He looks for his lighter.* WILLY *has picked it up and gives it to him. Pause.*]

WILLY: [*With increasing anger.*] Howard, all I need to set my table is fifty dollars a week.

HOWARD: But where am I going to put you, kid?

WILLY: Look, it isn't a question of whether I can sell merchandise, is it?

HOWARD: No, but it's a business, kid, and everybody's gotta pull his own weight.

WILLY: [*Desperately.*] Just let me tell you a story, Howard—

HOWARD: 'Cause you gotta admit, business is business.

WILLY: [*Angrily.*] Business is definitely business, but just listen for a minute. You don't understand this. When I was a boy—eighteen, nineteen—I was already on the road. And there was a question in my mind as to whether selling had a future for me. Because in those days I had a yearning to go to Alaska. See, there were three gold strikes in one month in Alaska, and I felt like going out. Just for the ride, you might say.

HOWARD: [*Barely interested.*] Don't say.

WILLY: Oh, yeah, my father lived many years in Alaska. He was an adventurous man. We've got quite a little streak of self-reliance in our family. I thought I'd go out with my older brother and try to locate him, and maybe settle in the North with the old man. And I was almost decided to go, when I met a salesman in the Parker House. His name was Dave Singleman. And he was eighty-four years old, and he'd drummed merchandise in thirty-one states. And old Dave, he'd go up to his room, y'understand, put on his green velvet slippers—I'll never forget—and pick up his phone and call the buyers, and without ever leaving his room, at the age of eighty-four, he made a living. And when I saw that, I realized that selling was the greatest career a man could want. 'Cause what could be more satisfying than to be able to go, at the age of eighty-four, into twenty or thirty different cities, and pick up his phone and be remembered and loved and helped by so many different people? Do you know? when he died—and by the way he died the death of a salesman, in his green velvet slippers in the smoker of the New York, New Haven and Hartford, going into Boston[5]—when he died, hundreds of salesmen and buyers were at his funeral. Things were sad on a lotta trains for months after that. [*He stands up.* HOWARD *has not looked at him.*] In those days there was personality in it, Howard. There was respect, and comradeship, and gratitude in it. Today, it's all cut and dried, and there's no chance for bringing friendship to bear—or personality. You see what I mean? They don't know me anymore.

HOWARD: [*Moving away, toward the right.*] That's just the thing, Willy.

WILLY: If I had forty dollars a week—that's all I'd need. Forty dollars, Howard.

HOWARD: Kid, I can't take blood from a stone, I—

5. Smoking lounge on a train running from New York to Boston.

WILLY: [*Desperation is on him now.*] Howard, the year Al Smith[6] was nominated, your father came to me and—

HOWARD: [*Starting to go off.*] I've got to see some people, kid.

WILLY: [*Stopping him.*] I'm talking about your father! There were promises made across this desk! You mustn't tell me you've got people to see—I put thirty-four years into this firm, Howard, and now I can't pay my insurance! You can't eat the orange and throw the peel away—a man is not a piece of fruit! [*After a pause.*] Now pay attention. Your father—in 1928 I had a big year. I averaged a hundred and seventy dollars a week in commissions.

HOWARD: [*Impatiently.*] Now, Willy, you never averaged—

WILLY: [*Banging his hand on the desk.*] I averaged a hundred and seventy dollars a week in the year of 1928! And your father came to me—or rather, I was in the office here—it was right over this desk—and he put his hand on my shoulder—

HOWARD: [*Getting up.*] You'll have to excuse me, Willy, I gotta see some people. Pull yourself together. [*Going out.*] I'll be back in a little while.

[*On* HOWARD's *exit, the light on his chair grows very bright and strange.*]

WILLY: Pull myself together! What the hell did I say to him? My God, I was yelling at him! How could I! [WILLY *breaks off, staring at the light, which occupies the chair, animating it. He approaches this chair, standing across the desk from it.*] Frank, Frank, don't you remember what you told me that time? How you put your hand on my shoulder, and Frank . . . [*He leans on the desk and as he speaks the dead man's name he accidentally switches on the recorder, and instantly.*]

HOWARD'S SON: ". . . of New York is Albany. The capital of Ohio is Cincinnati, the capital of Rhode Island is . . ." [*The recitation continues.*]

WILLY: [*Leaping away with fright, shouting.*] Ha! Howard! Howard! Howard!

HOWARD: [*Rushing in.*] What happened?

---

6. In 1928, New Yorker Alfred E. Smith (1873–1944) was the Democratic candidate for president. He lost to Herbert Hoover.

WILLY: [*Pointing at the machine, which continues nasally, childishly, with the capital cities.*] Shut it off! Shut it off!

HOWARD: [*Pulling the plug out.*] Look, Willy . . .

WILLY: [*Pressing his hands to his eyes.*] I gotta get myself some coffee. I'll get some coffee . . .

[WILLY *starts to walk out.* HOWARD *stops him.*]

HOWARD: [*Rolling up the cord.*] Willy, look . . .

WILLY: I'll go to Boston.

HOWARD: Willy, you can't go to Boston for us.

WILLY: Why can't I go?

HOWARD: I don't want you to represent us. I've been meaning to tell you for a long time now.

WILLY: Howard, are you firing me?

HOWARD: I think you need a good long rest, Willy.

WILLY: Howard—

HOWARD: And when you feel better, come back, and we'll see if we can work something out.

WILLY: But I gotta earn money, Howard. I'm in no position to—

HOWARD: Where are your sons? Why don't your sons give you a hand?

WILLY: They're working on a very big deal.

HOWARD: This is no time for false pride, Willy. You go to your sons and you tell them that you're tired. You've got two great boys, haven't you?

WILLY: Oh, no question, no question, but in the meantime . . .

HOWARD: Then that's that, heh?

WILLY: All right, I'll go to Boston tomorrow.

HOWARD: No, no.

WILLY: I can't throw myself on my sons. I'm not a cripple!

HOWARD: Look, kid, I'm busy, I'm busy this morning.

WILLY: [*Grasping* HOWARD*'s arm.*] Howard, you've got to let me go to Boston!

HOWARD: [*Hard, keeping himself under control.*] I've got a line of people to see this morning. Sit down, take five minutes, and pull yourself together, and then go home, will ya? I need the office, Willy. [*He starts to go, turns, remembering the recorder, starts to push off the table holding the recorder.*] Oh, yeah. Whenever you can this week, stop by and drop off the samples. You'll feel better,

Willy, and then come back and we'll talk. Pull yourself together, kid, there's people outside.

[HOWARD *exits, pushing the table off left.* WILLY *stares into space, exhausted. Now the music is heard*—BEN's *music—first distantly, then closer, closer. As* WILLY *speaks,* BEN *enters from the right. He carries valise and umbrella.*]

WILLY: Oh, Ben, how did you do it? What is the answer? Did you wind up the Alaska deal already?

BEN: Doesn't take much time if you know what you're doing. Just a short business trip. Boarding ship in an hour. Wanted to say good-by.

WILLY: Ben, I've got to talk to you.

BEN: [*Glancing at his watch.*] Haven't the time, William.

WILLY: [*Crossing the apron to* BEN.] Ben, nothing's working out. I don't know what to do.

BEN: Now, look here, William. I've bought timberland in Alaska and I need a man to look after things for me.

WILLY: God, timberland! Me and my boys in those grand outdoors!

BEN: You've a new continent at your doorstep, William. Get out of these cities, they're full of talk and time payments and courts of law. Screw on your fists and you can fight for a fortune up there.

WILLY: Yes, yes! Linda, Linda!

[LINDA *enters as of old, with the wash.*]

LINDA: Oh, you're back?

BEN: I haven't much time.

WILLY: No, wait! Linda, he's got a proposition for me in Alaska.

LINDA: But you've got—[*To* BEN.] He's got a beautiful job here.

WILLY: But in Alaska, kid, I could—

LINDA: You're doing well enough, Willy!

BEN: [*To* LINDA.] Enough for what, my dear?

LINDA: [*Frightened of* BEN *and angry at him.*] Don't say those things to him! Enough to be happy right here, right now. [*To* WILLY, *while* BEN *laughs.*] Why must everybody conquer the world? You're well liked, and the boys love you, and someday—[*To* BEN.]—why, old man Wagner told him just the other day that if he keeps it up he'll be a member of the firm, didn't he, Willy?

WILLY: Sure, sure. I am building something with this firm, Ben, and if a man is building something he must be on the right track, mustn't he?

BEN: What are you building? Lay your hand on it. Where is it?

WILLY: [*Hesitantly.*] That's true, Linda, there's nothing.

LINDA: Why? [*To* BEN.] There's a man eighty-four years old—

WILLY: That's right, Ben, that's right. When I look at that man I say, what is there to worry about?

BEN: Bah!

WILLY: It's true, Ben. All he has to do is go into any city, pick up the phone, and he's making his living and you know why?

BEN: [*Picking up his valise.*] I've got to go.

WILLY: [*Holding* BEN *back.*] Look at this boy! [BIFF, *in his high school sweater, enters carrying suitcase.* HAPPY *carries* BIFF's *shoulder guards, gold helmet, and football pants.*] Without a penny to his name, three great universities are begging for him, and from there the sky's the limit, because it's not what you do, Ben. It's who you know and the smile on your face! It's contacts, Ben, contacts! The whole wealth of Alaska passes over the lunch table at the Commodore Hotel, and that's the wonder, the wonder of this country, that a man can end with diamonds here on the basis of being liked! [*He turns to* BIFF.] And that's why when you get out on that field today it's important. Because thousands of people will be rooting for you and loving you. [*To* BEN, *who has again begun to leave.*] And Ben! when he walks into a business office his name will sound out like a bell and all the doors will open to him! I've seen it, Ben, I've seen it a thousand times! You can't feel it with your hand like timber, but it's there!

BEN: Good-by, William.

WILLY: Ben, am I right? Don't you think I'm right? I value your advice.

BEN: There's a new continent at your doorstep, William. You could walk out rich. Rich! [*He is gone.*]

WILLY: We'll do it here, Ben! You hear me? We're gonna do it here!
[*Young* BERNARD *rushes in. The gay music of the Boys is heard.*]

BERNARD: Oh, gee, I was afraid you left already!

WILLY: Why? What time is it?

BERNARD: It's half-past one!

WILLY: Well, come on, everybody! Ebbets Field next stop! Where's the pennants? [*He rushes through the wall-line of the kitchen and out into the living room.*]

LINDA: [*To* BIFF.] Did you pack fresh underwear?

BIFF: [*Who has been limbering up.*] I want to go!

BERNARD: Biff, I'm carrying your helmet, ain't I?

HAPPY: No, I'm carrying the helmet.

BERNARD: Oh, Biff, you promised me.

HAPPY: I'm carrying the helmet.

BERNARD: How am I going to get in the locker room?

LINDA: Let him carry the shoulder guards. [*She puts her coat and hat on in the kitchen.*]

BERNARD: Can I, Biff? 'Cause I told everybody I'm going to be in the locker room.

HAPPY: In Ebbets Field it's the clubhouse.

BERNARD: I meant the clubhouse, Biff!

HAPPY: Biff!

BIFF: [*Grandly, after a slight pause.*] Let him carry the shoulder guards.

HAPPY: [*As he gives* BERNARD *the shoulder guards.*] Stay close to us now.

[WILLY *rushes in with the pennants.*]

WILLY: [*Handing them out.*] Everybody wave when Biff comes out on the field. [HAPPY *and* BERNARD *run off.*] You set now, boy?

[*The music has died away.*]

BIFF: Ready to go, Pop. Every muscle is ready.

WILLY: [*At the edge of the apron.*] You realize what this means?

BIFF: That's right, Pop.

WILLY: [*Feeling* BIFF'*s muscles.*] You're comin' home this afternoon captain of the All-Scholastic Championship Team of the City of New York.

BIFF: I got it, Pop. And remember, pal, when I take off my helmet, that touchdown is for you.

WILLY: Let's go! [*He is starting out, with his arm around* BIFF, *when* CHARLEY *enters, as of old, in knickers.*] I got no room for you, Charley.

CHARLEY: Room? For what?

WILLY: In the car.

CHARLEY: You goin' for a ride? I wanted to shoot some casino.

WILLY: [*Furiously.*] Casino! [*Incredulously.*] Don't you realize what today is?

LINDA: Oh, he knows, Willy. He's just kidding you.

WILLY: That's nothing to kid about!

CHARLEY: No, Linda, what's goin' on?

LINDA: He's playing in Ebbets Field.

CHARLEY: Baseball in this weather?

WILLY: Don't talk to him. Come on, come on! [*He is pushing them out.*]

CHARLEY: Wait a minute, didn't you hear the news?

WILLY: What?

CHARLEY: Don't you listen to the radio? Ebbets Field just blew up.

WILLY: You go to hell! [CHARLEY *laughs. Pushing them out.*] Come on, come on! We're late.

CHARLEY: [*As they go.*] Knock a homer, Biff, knock a homer!

WILLY: [*The last to leave, turning to* CHARLEY.] I don't think that was funny, Charley. This is the greatest day of my life.

CHARLEY: Willy, when are you going to grow up?

WILLY: Yeah, heh? When this game is over, Charley, you'll be laughing out of the other side of your face. They'll be calling him another Red Grange.[7] Twenty-five thousand a year.

CHARLEY: [*Kidding.*] Is that so?

WILLY: Yeah, that's so.

CHARLEY: Well, then, I'm sorry, Willy. But tell me something.

WILLY: What?

CHARLEY: Who is Red Grange?

WILLY: Put up your hands. Goddam you, put up your hands! [CHARLEY, *chuckling, shakes his head and walks away, around the left corner of the stage.* WILLY *follows him. The music rises to a mocking frenzy.*] Who the hell do you think you are, better than everybody else? You don't know everything, you big, ignorant, stupid . . . Put up your hands!

[*Light rises, on the right side of the forestage, on a small table in the reception room of* CHARLEY's *office. Traffic sounds are heard.* BERNARD, *now mature, sits whistling to himself. A pair of tennis rackets and an overnight bag are on the floor beside him.*]

WILLY: [*Offstage.*] What are you walking away for? Don't walk away! If you're going to say something say it to my face! I know you

7. Harold Edward Grange (1903–1991), a college and professional football hall-of-famer, played half-back at the University of Illinois from 1923 to 1925.

laugh at me behind my back. You'll laugh out of the other side of your goddam face after this game. Touchdown! Touchdown! Eighty thousand people! Touchdown! Right between the goal posts.

[BERNARD *is a quiet, earnest, but self-assured young man.* WILLY'*s voice is coming from right upstage now.* BERNARD *lowers his feet off the table and listens.* JENNY, *his father's secretary, enters.*]

JENNY: [*Distressed.*] Say, Bernard, will you go out in the hall?

BERNARD: What is that noise? Who is it?

JENNY: Mr. Loman. He just got off the elevator.

BERNARD: [*Getting up.*] Who's he arguing with?

JENNY: Nobody. There's nobody with him. I can't deal with him anymore, and your father gets all upset everytime he comes. I've got a lot of typing to do, and your father's waiting to sign it. Will you see him?

WILLY: [*Entering.*] Touchdown! Touch—[*He sees* JENNY.] Jenny, Jenny, good to see you. How're ya? Workin'? Or still honest?

JENNY: Fine. How've you been feeling?

WILLY: Not much anymore, Jenny. Ha, ha! [*He is surprised to see the rackets.*]

BERNARD: Hello, Uncle Willy.

WILLY: [*Almost shocked.*] Bernard! Well, look who's here! [*He comes quickly, guiltily to* BERNARD *and warmly shakes his hand.*]

BERNARD: How are you? Good to see you.

WILLY: What are you doing here?

BERNARD: Oh, just stopped by to see Pop. Get off my feet till my train leaves. I'm going to Washington in a few minutes.

WILLY: Is he in?

BERNARD: Yes, he's in his office with the accountant. Sit down.

WILLY: [*Sitting down.*] What're you going to do in Washington?

BERNARD: Oh, just a case I've got there, Willy.

WILLY: That so? [*Indicating the rackets.*] You going to play tennis there?

BERNARD: I'm staying with a friend who's got a court.

WILLY: Don't say. His own tennis court. Must be fine people, I bet.

BERNARD: They are, very nice. Dad tells me Biff's in town.

WILLY: [*With a big smile.*] Yeah, Biff's in. Working on a very big deal, Bernard.

BERNARD: What's Biff doing?

WILLY: Well, he's been doing very big things in the West. But he decided to establish himself here. Very big. We're having dinner. Did I hear your wife had a boy?

BERNARD: That's right. Our second.

WILLY: Two boys! What do you know!

BERNARD: What kind of a deal has Biff got?

WILLY: Well, Bill Oliver—very big sporting-goods man—he wants Biff very badly. Called him in from the West. Long distance, carte blanche, special deliveries. Your friends have their own private tennis court?

BERNARD: You still with the old firm, Willy?

WILLY: [*After a pause.*] I'm—I'm overjoyed to see how you made the grade, Bernard, overjoyed. It's an encouraging thing to see a young man really—really—Looks very good for Biff—very—[*He breaks off, then.*] Bernard—[*He is so full of emotion, he breaks off again.*]

BERNARD: What is it, Willy?

WILLY: [*Small and alone.*] What—what's the secret?

BERNARD: What secret?

WILLY: How—how did you? Why didn't he ever catch on?

BERNARD: I wouldn't know that, Willy.

WILLY: [*Confidentially, desperately.*] You were his friend, his boyhood friend. There's something I don't understand about it. His life ended after that Ebbets Field game. From the age of seventeen nothing good ever happened to him.

BERNARD: He never trained himself for anything.

WILLY: But he did, he did. After high school he took so many correspondence courses. Radio mechanics; television; God knows what, and never made the slightest mark.

BERNARD: [*Taking off his glasses.*] Willy, do you want to talk candidly?

WILLY: [*Rising, faces* BERNARD.] I regard you as a very brilliant man, Bernard. I value your advice.

BERNARD: Oh, the hell with the advice, Willy. I couldn't advise you. There's just one thing I've always wanted to ask you. When he was supposed to graduate, and the math teacher flunked him—

WILLY: Oh, that son-of-a-bitch ruined his life.

BERNARD: Yeah, but, Willy, all he had to do was go to summer school and make up that subject.

WILLY: That's right, that's right.

BERNARD: Did you tell him not to go to summer school?

WILLY: Me? I begged him to go. I ordered him to go!

BERNARD: Then why wouldn't he go?

WILLY: Why? Why! Bernard, that question has been trailing me like a ghost for the last fifteen years. He flunked the subject, and laid down and died like a hammer hit him!

BERNARD: Take it easy, kid.

WILLY: Let me talk to you—I got nobody to talk to. Bernard, Bernard, was it my fault? Y'see? It keeps going around in my mind, maybe I did something to him. I got nothing to give him.

BERNARD: Don't take it so hard.

WILLY: Why did he lay down? What is the story there? You were his friend!

BERNARD: Willy, I remember, it was June, and our grades came out. And he'd flunked math.

WILLY: That son-of-a-bitch!

BERNARD: No, it wasn't right then. Biff just got very angry, I remember, and he was ready to enroll in summer school.

WILLY: [Surprised.] He was?

BERNARD: He wasn't beaten by it at all. But then, Willy, he disappeared from the block for almost a month. And I got the idea that he'd gone up to New England to see you. Did he have a talk with you then? [WILLY stares in silence.] Willy?

WILLY: [With a strong edge of resentment in his voice.] Yeah, he came to Boston. What about it?

BERNARD: Well, just that when he came back—I'll never forget this, it always mystifies me. Because I'd thought so well of Biff, even though he'd always taken advantage of me. I loved him, Willy, y'know? And he came back after that month and took his sneakers—remember those sneakers with "University of Virginia" printed on them? He was so proud of those, wore them every day. And he took them down in the cellar, and burned them up in the furnace. We had a fist fight. It lasted at least half an hour. Just the two of us, punching each other down the cellar, and crying right through it. I've often thought of how strange it was that

I knew he'd given up his life. What happened in Boston, Willy? [WILLY *looks at him as at an intruder.*] I just bring it up because you asked me.

WILLY: [*Angrily.*] Nothing. What do you mean, "What happened?" What's that got to do with anything?

BERNARD: Well, don't get sore.

WILLY: What are you trying to do, blame it on me? If a boy lays down is that my fault?

BERNARD: Now, Willy, don't get—

WILLY: Well, don't—don't talk to me that way! What does that mean, "What happened?"

[CHARLEY *enters. He is in his vest, and he carries a bottle of bourbon.*]

CHARLEY: Hey, you're going to miss that train. [*He waves the bottle.*]

BERNARD: Yeah, I'm going. [*He takes the bottle.*] Thanks, Pop. [*He picks up his rackets and bag.*] Good-bye, Willy, and don't worry about it. You know, "If at first you don't succeed . . ."

WILLY: Yes, I believe in that.

BERNARD: But sometimes, Willy, it's better for a man just to walk away.

WILLY: Walk away?

BERNARD: That's right.

WILLY: But if you can't walk away?

BERNARD: [*After a slight pause.*] I guess that's when it's tough. [*Extending his hand.*] Good-bye, Willy.

WILLY: [*Shaking* BERNARD'*s hand.*] Good-bye, boy.

CHARLEY: [*An arm on* BERNARD'*s shoulder.*] How do you like this kid? Gonna argue a case in front of the Supreme Court.

BERNARD: [*Protesting.*] Pop!

WILLY: [*Genuinely shocked, pained, and happy.*] No! The Supreme Court!

BERNARD: I gotta run. 'Bye, Dad!

CHARLEY: Knock 'em dead, Bernard!

[BERNARD *goes off.*]

WILLY: [*As* CHARLEY *takes out his wallet.*] The Supreme Court! And he didn't even mention it!

CHARLEY: [*Counting out money on the desk.*] He don't have to—he's gonna do it.

WILLY: And you never told him what to do, did you? You never took any interest in him.

CHARLEY: My salvation is that I never took any interest in anything. There's some money—fifty dollars. I got an accountant inside.

WILLY: Charley, look . . . [*With difficulty.*] I got my insurance to pay. If you can manage it—I need a hundred and ten dollars. [CHARLEY *doesn't reply for a moment; merely stops moving.*] I'd draw it from my bank but Linda would know, and I . . .

CHARLEY: Sit down, Willy.

WILLY: [*Moving toward the chair.*] I'm keeping an account of everything, remember. I'll pay every penny back. [*He sits.*]

CHARLEY: Now listen to me, Willy.

WILLY: I want you to know I appreciate . . .

CHARLEY: [*Sitting down on the table.*] Willy, what're you doin'? What the hell is goin' on in your head?

WILLY: Why? I'm simply . . .

CHARLEY: I offered you a job. You can make fifty dollars a week. And I won't send you on the road.

WILLY: I've got a job.

CHARLEY: Without pay? What kind of job is a job without pay? [*He rises.*] Now, look kid, enough is enough. I'm no genius but I know when I'm being insulted.

WILLY: Insulted!

CHARLEY: Why don't you want to work for me?

WILLY: What's the matter with you? I've got a job.

CHARLEY: Then what're you walkin' in here every week for?

WILLY: [*Getting up.*] Well, if you don't want me to walk in here—

CHARLEY: I am offering you a job!

WILLY: I don't want your goddam job!

CHARLEY: When the hell are you going to grow up?

WILLY: [*Furiously.*] You big ignoramus, if you say that to me again I'll rap you one! I don't care how big you are! [*He's ready to fight. Pause.*]

CHARLEY: [*Kindly, going to him.*] How much do you need, Willy?

WILLY: Charley, I'm strapped, I'm strapped. I don't know what to do. I was just fired.

CHARLEY: Howard fired you?

WILLY: That snotnose. Imagine that? I named him. I named him Howard.

CHARLEY: Willy, when're you gonna realize that them things don't mean anything? You named him Howard, but you can't sell that. The only thing you got in this world is what you can sell. And the funny thing is that you're a salesman, and you don't know that.

WILLY: I've always tried to think otherwise, I guess. I always felt that if a man was impressive, and well liked, that nothing—

CHARLEY: Why must everybody like you? Who liked J. P. Morgan?[8] Was he impressive? In a Turkish bath he'd look like a butcher. But with his pockets on he was very well liked. Now listen, Willy, I know you don't like me, and nobody can say I'm in love with you, but I'll give you a job because—just for the hell of it, put it that way. Now what do you say?

WILLY: I—I just can't work for you, Charley.

CHARLEY: What're you, jealous of me?

WILLY: I can't work for you, that's all, don't ask me why.

CHARLEY: [Angered, takes out more bills.] You been jealous of me all your life, you damned fool! Here, pay your insurance. [He puts the money in WILLY's hand.]

WILLY: I'm keeping strict accounts.

CHARLEY: I've got some work to do. Take care of yourself. And pay your insurance.

WILLY: [Moving to the right.] Funny, y'know? After all the highways and the trains, and the appointments, and the years, you end up worth more dead than alive.

CHARLEY: Willy, nobody's worth nothin' dead. [After a slight pause.] Did you hear what I said? [WILLY stands still, dreaming.] Willy!

WILLY: Apologize to Bernard for me when you see him. I didn't mean to argue with him. He's a fine boy. They're all fine boys, and they'll end up big—all of them. Someday they'll all play tennis together. Wish me luck, Charley. He saw Bill Oliver today.

CHARLEY: Good luck.

WILLY: [On the verge of tears.] Charley, you're the only friend I got. Isn't that a remarkable thing? [He goes out.]

---

8. John Pierpont Morgan (1837–1913), financier who created U.S. Steel, among other companies.

CHARLEY: Jesus!

[CHARLEY *stares after him a moment and follows. All light blacks out. Suddenly raucous music is heard, and a red glow rises behind the screen at right.* STANLEY, *a young waiter, appears, carrying a table, followed by* HAPPY, *who is carrying two chairs.*]

STANLEY: [*Putting the table down.*] That's all right, Mr. Loman, I can handle it myself. [*He turns and takes the chairs from* HAPPY *and places them at the table.*]

HAPPY: [*Glancing around.*] Oh, this is better.

STANLEY: Sure, in the front there you're in the middle of all kinds a noise. Whenever you got a party, Mr. Loman, you just tell me and I'll put you back here. Y'know, there's a lotta people they don't like it private, because when they go out they like to see a lotta action around them because they're sick and tired to stay in the house by theirself. But I know you, you ain't from Hackensack.[9] You know what I mean?

HAPPY: [*Sitting down.*] So how's it coming, Stanley?

STANLEY: Ah, it's a dog life. I only wish during the war they'd a took me in the Army. I coulda been dead by now.

HAPPY: My brother's back, Stanley.

STANLEY: Oh, he come back, heh? From the Far West.

HAPPY: Yeah, big cattle man, my brother, so treat him right. And my father's coming too.

STANLEY: Oh, your father too!

HAPPY: You got a couple of nice lobsters?

STANLEY: Hundred per cent, big.

HAPPY: I want them with the claws.

STANLEY: Don't worry, I don't give you no mice. [HAPPY *laughs.*] How about some wine? It'll put a head on the meal.

HAPPY: No. You remember, Stanley, that recipe I brought you from overseas? With the champagne in it?

STANLEY: Oh, yeah, sure. I still got it tacked up yet in the kitchen. But that'll have to cost a buck apiece anyways.

HAPPY: That's all right.

STANLEY: What'd you, hit a number or somethin'?

HAPPY: No, it's a little celebration. My brother is—I think he pulled off a big deal today. I think we're going into business together.

9. New Jersey city about seven miles west of New York City.

STANLEY: Great! That's the best for you. Because a family business, you know what I mean?—that's the best.

HAPPY: That's what I think.

STANLEY: 'Cause what's the difference? Somebody steals? It's in the family. Know what I mean? [*Sotto voce.*] Like this bartender here. The boss is goin' crazy what kinda leak he's got in the cash register. You put it in but it don't come out.

HAPPY: [*Raising his head.*] Sh!

STANLEY: What?

HAPPY: You notice I wasn't lookin' right or left, was I?

STANLEY: No.

HAPPY: And my eyes are closed.

STANLEY: So what's the—?

HAPPY: Strudel's comin.

STANLEY: [*Catching on, looks around.*] Ah, no, there's no—[*He breaks off as a furred, lavishly dressed* GIRL *enters and sits at the next table. Both follow her with their eyes.*] Geez, how'd ya know?

HAPPY: I got radar or something. [*Staring directly at her profile.*] Oooooooo . . . Stanley.

STANLEY: I think, that's for you, Mr. Loman.

HAPPY: Look at that mouth. Oh, God. And the binoculars.

STANLEY: Geez, you got a life, Mr. Loman.

HAPPY: Wait on her.

STANLEY: [*Going to the* GIRL'*s table.*] Would you like a menu, ma'am?

GIRL: I'm expecting someone, but I'd like a—

HAPPY: Why don't you bring her—excuse me, miss, do you mind? I sell champagne, and I'd like you to try my brand. Bring her a champagne, Stanley.

GIRL: That's awfully nice of you.

HAPPY: Don't mention it. It's all company money. [*He laughs.*]

GIRL: That's a charming product to be selling, isn't it?

HAPPY: Oh, gets to be like everything else. Selling is selling, y'know.

GIRL: I suppose.

HAPPY: You don't happen to sell, do you?

GIRL: No, I don't sell.

HAPPY: Would you object to a compliment from a stranger? You ought to be on a magazine cover.

GIRL: [*Looking at him a little archly.*] I have been.

[STANLEY *comes in with a glass of champagne.*]

HAPPY: What'd I say before, Stanley? You see? She's a cover girl.

STANLEY: Oh, I could see, I could see.

HAPPY: [*To the* GIRL.] What magazine?

GIRL: Oh, a lot of them. [*She takes the drink.*] Thank you.

HAPPY: You know what they say in France, don't you? "Champagne
is the drink of the complexion"—Hya, Biff!

[BIFF *has entered and sits with* HAPPY.]

BIFF: Hello, kid. Sorry I'm late.

HAPPY: I just got here. Uh, Miss—?

GIRL: Forsythe.

HAPPY: Miss Forsythe, this is my brother.

BIFF: Is Dad here?

HAPPY: His name is Biff. You might've heard of him. Great football
player.

GIRL: Really? What team?

HAPPY: Are you familiar with football?

GIRL: No, I'm afraid I'm not.

HAPPY: Biff is quarterback with the New York Giants.

GIRL: Well, that's nice, isn't it? [*She drinks.*]

HAPPY: Good health.

GIRL: I'm happy to meet you.

HAPPY: That's my name, Hap. It's really Harold, but at West Point
they called me Happy.

GIRL: [*Now really impressed.*] Oh, I see. How do you do? [*She turns
her profile.*]

BIFF: Isn't Dad coming?

HAPPY: You want her?

BIFF: Oh, I could never make that.

HAPPY: I remember the time that idea would never come into your
head. Where's the old confidence, Biff?

BIFF: I just saw Oliver—

HAPPY: Wait a minute. I've got to see that old confidence again.
Do you want her? She's on call.

BIFF: Oh, no. [*He turns to look at the* GIRL.]

HAPPY: I'm telling you. Watch this. [*Turning to see the* GIRL.]
Honey? [*She turns to him.*] Are you busy?

GIRL: Well, I am . . . but I could make a phone call.

HAPPY: Do that, will you, honey? And see if you can get a friend. We'll be here for a while. Biff is one of the greatest football players in the country.

GIRL: [*Standing up.*] Well, I'm certainly happy to meet you.

HAPPY: Come back soon.

GIRL: I'll try.

HAPPY: Don't try, honey, try hard. [*The* GIRL *exits.* STANLEY *follows, shaking his head in bewildered admiration.*] Isn't that a shame now? A beautiful girl like that? That's why I can't get married. There's not a good woman in a thousand. New York is loaded with them, kid!

BIFF: Hap, look—

HAPPY: I told you she was on call!

BIFF: [*Strangely unnerved.*] Cut it out, will ya? I want to say something to you.

HAPPY: Did you see Oliver?

BIFF: I saw him all right. Now look, I want to tell Dad a couple of things and I want you to help me.

HAPPY: What? Is he going to back you?

BIFF: Are you crazy? You're out of your goddam head, you know that?

HAPPY: Why? What happened?

BIFF: [*Breathlessly.*] I did a terrible thing today, Hap. It's been the strangest day I ever went through. I'm all numb, I swear.

HAPPY: You mean he wouldn't see you?

BIFF: Well, I waited six hours for him, see? All day. Kept sending my name in. Even tried to date his secretary so she'd get me to him, but no soap.

HAPPY: Because you're not showin' the old confidence, Biff. He remembered you, didn't he?

BIFF: [*Stopping* HAPPY *with a gesture.*] Finally, about five o'clock, he comes out. Didn't remember who I was or anything. I felt like such an idiot, Hap.

HAPPY: Did you tell him my Florida idea?

BIFF: He walked away. I saw him for one minute. I got so mad I could've torn the walls down! How the hell did I ever get the idea I was a salesman there? I even believed myself that I'd been a salesman for him! And then he gave me one look and—I realized what a ridiculous lie my whole life has been! We've been talking in a dream for fifteen years. I was a shipping clerk.

HAPPY: What'd you do?

BIFF: [*With great tension and wonder.*] Well, he left, see. And the secretary went out. I was all alone in the waiting-room. I don't know what came over me, Hap. The next thing I know I'm in his office—paneled walls, everything. I can't explain it. I—Hap, I took his fountain pen.

HAPPY: Geez, did he catch you?

BIFF: I ran out. I ran down all eleven flights. I ran and ran and ran.

HAPPY: That was an awful dumb—what'd you do that for?

BIFF: [*Agonized.*] I don't know, I just—wanted to take something, I don't know. You gotta help me, Hap, I'm gonna tell Pop.

HAPPY: You crazy? What for?

BIFF: Hap, he's got to understand that I'm not the man somebody lends that kind of money to. He thinks I've been spiting him all these years and it's eating him up.

HAPPY: That's just it. You tell him something nice.

BIFF: I can't.

HAPPY: Say you got a lunch date with Oliver tomorrow.

BIFF: So what do I do tomorrow?

HAPPY: You leave the house tomorrow and come back at night and say Oliver is thinking it over. And he thinks it over for a couple of weeks, and gradually it fades away and nobody's the worse.

BIFF: But it'll go on forever!

HAPPY: Dad is never so happy as when he's looking forward to something! [WILLY *enters.*] Hello, scout!

WILLY: Gee, I haven't been here in years!

[STANLEY *has followed* WILLY *in and sets a chair for him.* STANLEY *starts off but* HAPPY *stops him.*]

HAPPY: Stanley!

[STANLEY *stands by, waiting for an order.*]

BIFF: [*Going to* WILLY *with guilt, as to an invalid.*] Sit down, Pop. You want a drink?

WILLY: Sure, I don't mind.

BIFF: Let's get a load on.

WILLY: You look worried.

BIFF: N-no. [*To* STANLEY.] Scotch all around. Make it doubles.

STANLEY: Doubles, right. [*He goes.*]

WILLY: You had a couple already, didn't you?

BIFF: Just a couple, yeah.

WILLY: Well, what happened, boy? [*Nodding affirmatively, with a smile.*] Everything go all right?

BIFF: [*Takes a breath, then reaches out and grasps* WILLY'*s hand.*] Pal . . . [*He is smiling bravely, and* WILLY *is smiling too.*] I had an experience today.

HAPPY: Terrific, Pop.

WILLY: That so? What happened?

BIFF: [*High, slightly alcoholic, above the earth.*] I'm going to tell you everything from first to last. It's been a strange day. [*Silence. He looks around, composes himself as best he can, but his breath keeps breaking the rhythm of his voice.*] I had to wait quite a while for him, and—

WILLY: Oliver?

BIFF: Yeah, Oliver. All day, as a matter of cold fact. And a lot of— instances—facts, Pop, facts about my life came back to me. Who was it, Pop? Who ever said I was a salesman with Oliver?

WILLY: Well, you were.

BIFF: No, Dad, I was a shipping clerk.

WILLY: But you were practically—

BIFF: [*With determination.*] Dad, I don't know who said it first, but I was never a salesman for Bill Oliver.

WILLY: What're you talking about?

BIFF: Let's hold on to the facts tonight, Pop. We're not going to get anywhere bullin' around. I was a shipping clerk.

WILLY: [*Angrily.*] All right, now listen to me—

BIFF: Why don't you let me finish?

WILLY: I'm not interested in stories about the past or any crap of that kind because the woods are burning, boys, you understand? There's a big blaze going on all around. I was fired today.

BIFF: [*Shocked.*] How could you be?

WILLY: I was fired, and I'm looking for a little good news to tell your mother, because the woman has waited and the woman has suffered. The gist of it is that I haven't got a story left in my head, Biff. So don't give me a lecture about facts and aspects. I am not interested.

Now what've you got to say to me? [STANLEY *enters with three drinks. They wait until he leaves.*] Did you see Oliver?

BIFF: Jesus, Dad!

WILLY: You mean you didn't go up there?

HAPPY: Sure he went up there.

BIFF: I did. I—saw him. How could they fire you?

WILLY: [*On the edge of his chair.*] What kind of a welcome did he give you?

BIFF: He won't even let you work on commission?

WILLY: I'm out. [*Driving.*] So tell me, he gave you a warm welcome?

HAPPY: Sure, Pop, sure!

BIFF: [*Driven.*] Well, it was kind of—

WILLY: I was wondering if he'd remember you. [*To* HAPPY.] Imagine, man doesn't see him for ten, twelve years and gives him that kind of a welcome!

HAPPY: Damn right!

BIFF: [*Trying to return to the offensive.*] Pop, look—

WILLY: You know why he remembered you, don't you? Because you impressed him in those days.

BIFF: Let's talk quietly and get this down to the facts, huh?

WILLY: [*As though* BIFF *had been interrupting.*] Well, what happened? It's great news, Biff. Did he take you into his office or'd you talk in the waiting-room?

BIFF: Well, he came in, see, and—

WILLY: [*With a big smile.*] What'd he say? Betcha he threw his arm around you.

BIFF: Well, he kinda—

WILLY: He's a fine man. [*To* HAPPY.] Very hard man to see, y'know.

HAPPY: [*Agreeing.*] Oh, I know.

WILLY: [*To* BIFF.] Is that where you had the drinks?

BIFF: Yeah, he gave me a couple of—no, no!

HAPPY: [*Cutting in.*] He told him my Florida idea.

WILLY: Don't interrupt. [*To* BIFF.] How'd he react to the Florida idea?

BIFF: Dad, will you give me a minute to explain?

WILLY: I've been waiting for you to explain since I sat down here! What happened? He took you into his office and what?

BIFF: Well—I talked. And—he listened, see.

WILLY: Famous for the way he listens, y'know. What was his answer?

BIFF: His answer was—[*He breaks off, suddenly angry.*] Dad, you're not letting me tell you what I want to tell you!

WILLY: [*Accusing, angered.*] You didn't see him, did you?

BIFF: I did see him!

WILLY: What'd you insult him or something? You insulted him, didn't you?

BIFF: Listen, will you let me out of it, will you just let me out of it!

HAPPY: What the hell!

WILLY: Tell me what happened!

BIFF: [*To* HAPPY.] I can't talk to him!

[*A single trumpet note jars the ear. The light of green leaves stains the house, which holds the air of night and a dream.* YOUNG BERNARD *enters and knocks on the door of the house.*]

YOUNG BERNARD: [*Frantically.*] Mrs. Loman, Mrs. Loman!

HAPPY: Tell him what happened!

BIFF: [*To* HAPPY.] Shut up and leave me alone!

WILLY: No, no. You had to go and flunk math!

BIFF: What math? What're you talking about?

YOUNG BERNARD: Mrs. Loman, Mrs. Loman!

[LINDA *appears in the house, as of old.*]

WILLY: [*Wildly.*] Math, math, math!

BIFF: Take it easy, Pop!

YOUNG BERNARD: Mrs. Loman!

WILLY: [*Furiously.*] If you hadn't flunked you'd've been set by now!

BIFF: Now, look, I'm gonna tell you what happened, and you're going to listen to me.

YOUNG BERNARD: Mrs. Loman!

BIFF: I waited six hours—

HAPPY: What the hell are you saying?

BIFF: I kept sending in my name but he wouldn't see me. So finally he . . . [*He continues unheard as light fades low on the restaurant.*]

YOUNG BERNARD: Biff flunked math!

LINDA: No!

YOUNG BERNARD: Birnbaum flunked him! They won't graduate him!

LINDA: But they have to. He's gotta go to the university. Where is he? Biff! Biff!

YOUNG BERNARD: No, he left. He went to Grand Central.

LINDA: Grand—You mean he went to Boston!

YOUNG BERNARD: Is Uncle Willy in Boston?

LINDA: Oh, maybe Willy can talk to the teacher. Oh, the poor, poor boy!

[*Light on house area snaps out.*]

BIFF: [*At the table, now audible, holding up a gold fountain pen.*] . . . so I'm washed up with Oliver, you understand? Are you listening to me?

WILLY: [*At a loss.*] Yeah, sure. If you hadn't flunked—

BIFF: Flunked what? What're you talking about?

WILLY: Don't blame everything on me! I didn't flunk math—you did! What pen?

HAPPY: That was awful dumb, Biff, a pen like that is worth—

WILLY: [*Seeing the pen for the first time.*] You took Oliver's pen?

BIFF: [*Weakening.*] Dad, I just explained it to you.

WILLY: You stole Bill Oliver's fountain pen!

BIFF: I didn't exactly steal it! That's just what I've been explaining to you!

HAPPY: He had it in his hand and just then Oliver walked in, so he got nervous and stuck it in his pocket!

WILLY: My God, Biff!

BIFF: I never intended to do it, Dad!

OPERATOR'S VOICE: Standish Arms, good evening!

WILLY: [*Shouting.*] I'm not in my room!

BIFF: [*Frightened.*] Dad, what's the matter? [*He and* HAPPY *stand up.*]

OPERATOR: Ringing Mr. Loman for you!

BIFF: [*Horrified, gets down on one knee before* WILLY.] Dad, I'll make good, I'll make good. [WILLY *tries to get to his feet.* BIFF *holds him down.*] Sit down now.

WILLY: No, you're no good, you're no good for anything.

BIFF: I am, Dad, I'll find something else, you understand? Now don't worry about anything. [*He holds up* WILLY's *face.*] Talk to me, Dad.

OPERATOR: Mr. Loman does not answer. Shall I page him?

WILLY: [*Attempting to stand, as though to rush and silence the* OPERATOR.] No, no, no!

HAPPY: He'll strike something, Pop.

WILLY: No, no . . .

BIFF: [*Desperately, standing over* WILLY.] Pop, listen! Listen to me! I'm telling you something good. Oliver talked to his partner about the Florida idea. You listening? He—he talked to his partner, and he came to me . . . I'm going to be all right, you hear? Dad, listen to me, he said it was just a question of the amount!

WILLY; Then you . , . got it?

HAPPY: He's gonna be terrific, Pop!

WILLY: [*Trying to stand.*] Then you got it, haven't you? You got it! You got it!

BIFF: [*Agonized, holds* WILLY *down.*] No, no. Look, Pop. I'm supposed to have lunch with them tomorrow. I'm just telling you this so you'll know that I can still make an impression, Pop. And I'll make good somewhere, but I can't go tomorrow, see?

WILLY: Why not? You simply—

BIFF: But the pen, Pop!

WILLY: You give it to him and tell him it was an oversight!

HAPPY: Sure, have lunch tomorrow!

BIFF: I can't say that—

WILLY: You were doing a crossword puzzle and accidentally used his pen!

BIFF: Listen, kid, I took those balls years ago, now I walk in with his fountain pen? That clinches it, don't you see? I can't face him like that! I'll try elsewhere.

PAGE'S VOICE: Paging Mr. Loman!

WILLY: Don't you want to be anything?

BIFF: Pop, how can I go back?

WILLY: You don't want to be anything, is that what's behind it?

BIFF: [*Now angry at* WILLY *for not crediting his sympathy.*] Don't take it that way! You think it was easy walking into that office after what I'd done to him? A team of horses couldn't have dragged me back to Bill Oliver!

WILLY: Then why'd you go?

BIFF: Why did I go? Why did I go! Look at you! Look at what's become of you!

[*Off left,* THE WOMAN *laughs.*]

WILLY: Biff, you're going to go to that lunch tomorrow, or—

BIFF: I can't go. I've got an appointment!

HAPPY: Biff, for . . . !

WILLY: Are you spiting me?

BIFF: Don't take it that way! Goddammit!

WILLY: [*Strikes* BIFF *and falters away from the table.*] You rotten little louse! Are you spiting me?

THE WOMAN: Someone's at the door, Willy!

BIFF: I'm no good, can't you see what I am?

HAPPY: [*Separating them.*] Hey, you're in a restaurant! Now cut it out, both of you! [*The* GIRLS *enter.*] Hello, girls, sit down.

[THE WOMAN *laughs, off left.*]

MISS FORSYTHE: I guess we might as well. This is Letta.

THE WOMAN: Willy, are you going to wake up?

BIFF: [*Ignoring* WILLY.] How're ya, miss, sit down. What do you drink?

MISS FORSYTHE: Letta might not be able to stay long.

LETTA: I gotta get up early tomorrow. I got jury duty. I'm so excited! Were you fellows ever on a jury?

BIFF: No, but I been in front of them! [*The* GIRLS *laugh.*] This is my father.

LETTA: Isn't he cute? Sit down with us, Pop.

HAPPY: Sit him down, Biff!

BIFF: [*Going to him.*] Come on, slugger, drink us under the table. To hell with it! Come on, sit down, pal.

[*On* BIFF's *last insistence,* WILLY *is about to sit.*]

THE WOMAN: [*Now urgently.*] Willy, are you going to answer the door!

[THE WOMAN's *call pulls* WILLY *back. He starts right, befuddled.*]

BIFF: Hey, where are you going?

WILLY: Open the door.

BIFF: The door?

WILLY: The washroom . . . the door . . . where's the door?

BIFF: [*Leading* WILLY *to the left.*] Just go straight down.

[WILLY *moves left.*]

THE WOMAN: Willy, Willy, are you going to get up, get up, get up, get up?

[WILLY *exits left.*]

LETTA: I think it's sweet you bring your daddy along.

MISS FORSYTHE: Oh, he isn't really your father!

BIFF: [*At left, turning to her resentfully.*] Miss Forsythe, you've just seen a prince walk by. A fine, troubled prince. A hardworking, unappreciated prince. A pal, you understand? A good companion. Always for his boys.

LETTA: That's so sweet.

HAPPY: Well, girls, what's the program? We're wasting time. Come on, Biff. Gather round. Where would you like to go?

BIFF: Why don't you do something for him?

HAPPY: Me!

BIFF: Don't you give a damn for him, Hap?

HAPPY: What're you talking about? I'm the one who—

BIFF: I sense it, you don't give a good goddam about him. [*He takes the rolled-up hose from his pocket and puts it on the table in front of* HAPPY.] Look what I found in the cellar, for Christ's sake. How can you bear to let it go on?

HAPPY: Me? Who goes away? Who runs off and—

BIFF: Yeah, but he doesn't mean anything to you. You could help him—I can't! Don't you understand what I'm talking about? He's going to kill himself, don't you know that?

HAPPY: Don't I know it! Me!

BIFF: Hap, help him! Jesus . . . help him . . . Help me, help me, I can't bear to look at his face! [*Ready to weep, he hurries out, up right.*]

HAPPY: [*Starting after him.*] Where are you going?

MISS FORSYTHE: What's he so mad about?

HAPPY: Come on, girls, we'll catch up with him.

MISS FORSYTHE: [*As* HAPPY *pushes her out.*] Say, I don't like that temper of his!

HAPPY: He's just a little overstrung, he'll be all right!

WILLY: [*Off left, as* THE WOMAN *laughs.*] Don't answer! Don't answer!

LETTA: Don't you want to tell your father—

HAPPY: No, that's not my father. He's just a guy. Come on, we'll catch Biff, and, honey, we're going to paint this town! Stanley, where's the check! Hey, Stanley!

[*They exit.* STANLEY *looks toward left.*]

STANLEY: [*Calling to* HAPPY *indignantly.*] Mr. Loman! Mr. Loman!

[STANLEY *picks up a chair and follows them off. Knocking is heard off left.* THE WOMAN *enters, laughing.* WILLY *follows her. She is in a black slip; he is buttoning his shirt. Raw, sensuous music accompanies their speech.*]

WILLY: Will you stop laughing? Will you stop?

THE WOMAN: Aren't you going to answer the door? He'll wake the whole hotel.

WILLY: I'm not expecting anybody.

THE WOMAN: Whyn't you have another drink, honey, and stop being so damn self-centered?

WILLY: I'm so lonely.

THE WOMAN: You know you ruined me, Willy? From now on, whenever you come to the office, I'll see that you go right through to the buyers. No waiting at my desk anymore, Willy. You ruined me.

WILLY: That's nice of you to say that.

THE WOMAN: Gee, you are self-centered! Why so sad? You are the saddest, self-centeredest soul I ever did see-saw. [*She laughs. He kisses her.*] Come on inside, drummer boy. It's silly to be dressing in the middle of the night. [*As knocking is heard.*] Aren't you going to answer the door?

WILLY: They're knocking on the wrong door.

THE WOMAN: But I felt the knocking. And he heard us talking in here. Maybe the hotel's on fire!

WILLY: [*His terror rising.*] It's a mistake.

THE WOMAN: Then tell them to go away!

WILLY: There's nobody there.

THE WOMAN: It's getting on my nerves, Willy. There's somebody standing out there and it's getting on my nerves!

WILLY: [*Pushing her away from him.*] All right, stay in the bathroom here, and don't come out. I think there's a law in Massachusetts about it, so don't come out. It may be that new room clerk. He looked very mean. So don't come out. It's a mistake, there's no fire.

> [*The knocking is heard again. He takes a few steps away from her, and she vanishes into the wing. The light follows him, and now he is facing* YOUNG BIFF, *who carries a suitcase.* BIFF *steps toward him. The music is gone.*]

BIFF: Why didn't you answer?

WILLY: Biff! What are you doing in Boston?

BIFF: Why didn't you answer? I've been knocking for five minutes, I called you on the phone—

WILLY: I just heard you. I was in the bathroom and had the door shut. Did anything happen home?

BIFF: Dad—I let you down.

WILLY: What do you mean?

BIFF: Dad . . .

WILLY: Biffo, what's this about? [*Putting his arm around* BIFF.] Come on, let's go downstairs and get you a malted.

BIFF: Dad, I flunked math.

WILLY: Not for the term?

BIFF: The term. I haven't got enough credits to graduate.

WILLY: You mean to say Bernard wouldn't give you the answers?

BIFF: He did, he tried, but I only got a sixty-one.

WILLY: And they wouldn't give you four points?

BIFF: Birnbaum refused absolutely. I begged him, Pop, but he won't give me those points. You gotta talk to him before they close the school. Because if he saw the kind of man you are, and you just talked to him in your way, I'm sure he'd come through for me. The class came right before practice, see, and I didn't go enough. Would you talk to him? He'd like you, Pop. You know the way you could talk.

WILLY: You're on. We'll drive right back.

BIFF: Oh, Dad, good work! I'm sure he'll change for you!

WILLY: Go downstairs and tell the clerk I'm checkin' out. Go right down.

BIFF: Yes, sir! See, the reason he hates me, Pop—one day he was late for class so I got up at the blackboard and imitated him. I crossed my eyes and talked with a lithp.

WILLY: [*Laughing.*] You did? The kids like it?

BIFF: They nearly died laughing!

WILLY: Yeah? What'd you do?

BIFF: The thquare root of thixthy twee is . . . [WILLY *bursts out laughing;* BIFF *joins him.*] And in the middle of it he walked in!

[WILLY *laughs and* THE WOMAN *joins in offstage.*]

WILLY: [*Without hesitation.*] Hurry downstairs and—

BIFF: Somebody in there?

WILLY: No, that was next door.

[THE WOMAN *laughs offstage.*]

BIFF: Somebody got in your bathroom!

WILLY: No, it's the next room, there's a party—

THE WOMAN: [*Enters laughing. She lisps this.*] Can I come in? There's something in the bathtub, Willy, and it's moving!

[WILLY *looks at* BIFF, *who is staring open-mouthed and horrified at* THE WOMAN.]

WILLY: Ah—you better go back to your room. They must be finished painting by now. They're painting her room so I let her take a shower here. Go back, go back . . . [*He pushes her.*]

THE WOMAN: [*Resisting.*] But I've got to get dressed, Willy, I can't—

WILLY: Get out of here! Go back, go back . . . [*Suddenly striving for the ordinary.*] This is Miss Francis, Biff, she's a buyer. They're painting her room. Go back, Miss Francis, go back . . .

THE WOMAN: But my clothes, I can't go out naked in the hall!

WILLY: [*Pushing her offstage.*] Get outa here! Go back, go back!

[BIFF *slowly sits down on his suitcase as the argument continues offstage.*]

THE WOMAN: Where's my stockings? You promised me stockings, Willy!

WILLY: I have no stockings here!

THE WOMAN: You had two boxes of size nine sheers for me, and I want them!

WILLY: Here, for God's sake, will you get outa here!

THE WOMAN: [*Enters holding a box of stockings.*] I just hope there's nobody in the hall. That's all I hope. [*To* BIFF.] Are you football or baseball?

BIFF: Football.

THE WOMAN: [*Angry, humiliated.*] That's me too. G'night. [*She snatches her clothes from* WILLY, *and walks out.*]

WILLY: [*After a pause.*] Well, better get going. I want to get to the school first thing in the morning. Get my suits out of the closet. I'll get my valise. [BIFF *doesn't move.*] What's the matter? [BIFF *remains motionless, tears falling.*] She's a buyer. Buys for J. H. Simmons. She lives down the hall—they're painting. You don't imagine—[*He breaks off. After a pause.*] Now listen, pal, she's just a buyer. She sees merchandise in her room and they have to keep it looking just so . . . [*Pause. Assuming command.*] All right, get my suits. [BIFF *doesn't move.*] Now stop crying and do as I say. I gave you an order. Biff, I gave you an order! Is that what you do when I give you an order? How dare you cry! [*Putting his arm around* BIFF.] Now look, Biff, when you grow up you'll understand about these things. You mustn't—you mustn't overemphasize a thing like this. I'll see Birnbaum first thing in the morning.

BIFF: Never mind.

WILLY: [*Getting down beside* BIFF.] Never mind! He's going to give you those points. I'll see to it.

BIFF: He wouldn't listen to you.

WILLY: He certainly will listen to me. You need those points for the U. of Virginia.

BIFF: I'm not going there.

WILLY: Heh? If I can't get him to change that mark you'll make it up in summer school. You've got all summer to—

BIFF: [*His weeping breaking from him.*] Dad . . .

WILLY: [*Infected by it.*] Oh, my boy . . .

BIFF: Dad . . .

WILLY: She's nothing to me, Biff. I was lonely, I was terribly lonely.

BIFF: You—you gave her Mama's stockings! [*His tears break through and he rises to go.*]

WILLY: [*Grabbing for* BIFF.] I gave you an order!

BIFF: Don't touch me, you—liar!

WILLY: Apologize for that!

BIFF: You fake! You phony little fake! You fake!

[*Overcome, he turns quickly and weeping fully goes out with his suitcase.* WILLY *is left on the floor on his knees.*]

WILLY: I gave you an order! Biff, come back here or I'll beat you! Come back here! I'll whip you! [STANLEY *comes quickly in from the right and stands in front of* WILLY. WILLY *shouts at* STANLEY.] I gave you an order . . .

STANLEY: Hey, let's pick it up, pick it up, Mr. Loman. [*He helps* WILLY *to his feet.*] Your boys left with the chippies. They said they'll see you home.

[*A* SECOND WAITER *watches some distance away.*]

WILLY: But we were supposed to have dinner together.

[*Music is heard,* WILLY'*s theme.*]

STANLEY: Can you make it?

WILLY: I'll—sure, I can make it. [*Suddenly concerned about his clothes.*] Do I—I look all right?

STANLEY: Sure, you look all right. [*He flicks a speck off* WILLY'*s lapel.*]

WILLY: Here—here's a dollar.

STANLEY: Oh, your son paid me. It's all right.

WILLY: [*Putting it in* STANLEY'*s hand.*] No, take it. You're a good boy.

STANLEY: Oh, no, you don't have to . . .

WILLY: Here—here's some more, I don't need it anymore. [*After a slight pause.*] Tell me—is there a seed store in the neighborhood?

STANLEY: Seeds? You mean like to plant?

> [*As* WILLY *turns,* STANLEY *slips the money back into his jacket pocket.*]

WILLY: Yes. Carrots, peas . . .

STANLEY: Well, there's hardware stores on Sixth Avenue, but it may be too late now.

WILLY: [*Anxiously.*] Oh, I'd better hurry. I've got to get some seeds. [*He starts off to the right.*] I've got to get some seeds, right away. Nothing's planted. I don't have a thing in the ground.

> [WILLY *hurries out as the light goes down.* STANLEY *moves over to the right after him, watches him off. The other* WAITER *has been staring at* WILLY.]

STANLEY: [*To the* WAITER.] Well, whatta you looking at?

> [*The* WAITER *picks up the chairs and moves off right.* STANLEY *takes the table and follows him. The light fades on this area. There is a long pause, the sound of the flute coming over. The light gradually rises on the kitchen, which is empty.* HAPPY *appears at the door of the house, followed by* BIFF. HAPPY *is carrying a large bunch of long-stemmed roses. He enters the kitchen, looks around for* LINDA. *Not seeing her, he turns to* BIFF, *who is just outside the house door, and makes a gesture with his hands, indicating "Not here, I guess." He looks into the living-room and freezes. Inside,* LINDA, *unseen, is seated,* WILLY'*s coat on her lap. She rises ominously and quietly and moves toward* HAPPY, *who backs up into the kitchen, afraid.*]

HAPPY: Hey, what're you doing up? [LINDA *says nothing but moves toward him implacably.*] Where's Pop? [*He keeps backing to the right, and now* LINDA *is in full view in the doorway to the living-room.*] Is he sleeping?

LINDA: Where were you?

HAPPY: [*Trying to laugh it off.*] We met two girls, Mom, very fine types. Here, we brought you some flowers. [*Offering them to her.*]

Put them in your room, Ma. [*She knocks them to the floor at* BIFF'*s feet. He has now come inside and closed the door behind him. She stares at* BIFF, *silent.*] Now what'd you do that for? Mom, I want you to have some flowers—

LINDA: [*Cutting* HAPPY *off, violently to* BIFF.] Don't you care whether he lives or dies?

HAPPY: [*Going to the stairs.*] Come upstairs, Biff.

BIFF: [*With a flare of disgust, to* HAPPY.] Go away from me! [*To* LINDA.] What do you mean, lives or dies? Nobody's dying around here, pal.

LINDA: Get out of my sight! Get out of here!

BIFF: I wanna see the boss.

LINDA: You're not going near him!

BIFF: Where is he? [*He moves into the living-room and* LINDA *follows.*]

LINDA: [*Shouting after* BIFF.] You invite him for dinner. He looks forward to it all day—[BIFF *appears in his parents' bedroom, looks around and exits.*]—and then you desert him there. There's no stranger you'd do that to!

HAPPY: Why? He had a swell time with us. Listen, when I—[LINDA *comes back into the kitchen.*]—desert him I hope I don't outlive the day!

LINDA: Get out of here!

HAPPY: Now look, Mom . . .

LINDA: Did you have to go to women tonight? You and your lousy rotten whores!

[BIFF *re-enters the kitchen.*]

HAPPY: Mom, all we did was follow Biff around trying to cheer him up! [*To* BIFF.] Boy, what a night you gave me!

LINDA: Get out of here, both of you, and don't come back! I don't want you tormenting him anymore. Go on now, get your things together! [*To* BIFF.] You can sleep in his apartment. [*She starts to pick up the flowers and stops herself.*] Pick up this stuff, I'm not your maid anymore. Pick it up, you bum, you! [HAPPY *turns his back to her in refusal.* BIFF *slowly moves over and gets down on his knees, picking up the flowers.*] You're a pair of animals! Not one, not another living soul would have had the cruelty to walk out on that man in a restaurant!

BIFF: [*Not looking at her.*] Is that what he said?

LINDA: He didn't have to say anything. He was so humiliated he nearly limped when he came in.

HAPPY: But, Mom, he had a great time with us—

BIFF: [*Cutting him off violently.*] Shut up!

[*Without another word,* HAPPY *goes upstairs.*]

LINDA: You! You didn't even go in to see if he was all right!

BIFF: [*Still on the floor in front of* LINDA, *the flowers in his hand; with self-loathing.*] No. Didn't. Didn't do a damned thing. How do you like that, heh? Left him babbling in a toilet.

LINDA: You louse. You . . .

BIFF: Now you hit it on the nose! [*He gets up, throws the flowers in the wastebasket.*] The scum of the earth, and you're looking at him!

LINDA: Get out of here!

BIFF: I gotta talk to the boss, Mom. Where is he?

LINDA: You're not going near him. Get out of this house!

BIFF: [*With absolute assurance, determination.*] No. We're gonna have an abrupt conversation, him and me.

LINDA: You're not talking to him! [*Hammering is heard from outside the house, off right.* BIFF *turns toward the noise. Suddenly pleading.*] Will you please leave him alone?

BIFF: What's he doing out there?

LINDA: He's planting the garden!

BIFF: [*Quietly.*] Now? Oh, my God!

[BIFF *moves outside,* LINDA *following. The light dies down on them and comes up on the center of the apron as* WILLY *walks into it. He is carrying a flashlight, a hoe, and a handful of seed packets. He raps the top of the hoe sharply to fix it firmly, and then moves to the left, measuring off the distance with his foot. He holds the flashlight to look at the seed packets, reading off the instructions. He is in the blue of night.*]

WILLY: Carrots . . . quarter-inch apart. Rows . . . one-foot rows. [*He measures it off.*] One foot. [*He puts down a package and measures off.*] Beets. [*He puts down another package and measures again.*] Lettuce. [*He reads the package, puts it down.*] One foot—[*He breaks off as* BEN *appears at the right and moves slowly down to him.*] What a proposition, ts, ts. Terrific, terrific. 'Cause she's suffered, Ben, the woman has suffered. You understand me? A man can't go out the way he came in, Ben, a man has got to add up to something. You can't, you can't— [BEN *moves toward him as though to interrupt.*] You gotta consider, now. Don't answer so quick. Remember, it's a guaranteed twenty-thousand-dollar proposition. Now look, Ben, I want you to go through the ins and outs of this thing with me. I've got nobody to talk to, Ben, and the woman has suffered, you hear me?

BEN: [*Standing still, considering.*] What's the proposition?

WILLY: It's twenty thousand dollars on the barrelhead. Guaranteed, gilt-edged, you understand?

BEN: You don't want to make a fool of yourself. They might not honor the policy.

WILLY: How can they dare refuse? Didn't I work like a coolie to meet every premium on the nose? And now they don't pay off! Impossible!

BEN: It's called a cowardly thing, William.

WILLY: Why? Does it take more guts to stand here the rest of my life ringing up a zero?

BEN: [*Yielding.*] That's a point, William. [*He moves, thinking, turns.*] And twenty thousand—that *is* something one can feel with the hand, it is there.

WILLY: [*Now assured, with rising power.*] Oh, Ben, that's the whole beauty of it! I see it like a diamond, shining in the dark, hard and rough, that I can pick up and touch in my hand. Not like—like an appointment! This would not be another damned-fool appointment, Ben, and it changes all the aspects. Because he thinks I'm nothing, see, and so he spites me. But the funeral— [*Straightening up.*] Ben, that funeral will be massive! They'll come from Maine, Massachusetts, Vermont, New Hampshire! All the old-timers with the strange license plates—that boy will be thunderstruck, Ben, because he never realized—I am known! Rhode Island, New York, New Jersey—I am known, Ben, and he'll see it with his eyes once and for all. He'll see what I am, Ben! He's in for a shock, that boy!

BEN: [*Coming down to the edge of the garden.*] He'll call you a coward.

WILLY: [*Suddenly fearful.*] No, that would be terrible.

BEN: Yes. And a damned fool.

WILLY: No, no, he mustn't, I won't have that! [*He is broken and desperate.*]

BEN: He'll hate you, William.

[*The gay music of the Boys is heard.*]

WILLY: Oh, Ben, how do we get back to all the great times? Used to be so full of light, and comradeship, the sleigh-riding in winter, and the ruddiness on his cheeks. And always some kind of good news coming up, always something nice coming up ahead. And never even let me carry the valises in the house, and simonizing, simonizing that little red car! Why, why can't I give him something and not have him hate me?

BEN: Let me think about it. [*He glances at his watch.*] I still have a little time. Remarkable proposition, but you've got to be sure you're not making a fool of yourself.

[BEN *drifts off upstage and goes out of sight.* BIFF *comes down from the left.*]

WILLY: [*Suddenly conscious of* BIFF, *turns and looks up at him, then begins picking up the packages of seeds in confusion.*] Where the hell is that seed? [*Indignantly.*] You can't see nothing out here! They boxed in the whole goddam neighborhood!

BIFF: There are people all around here. Don't you realize that?

WILLY: I'm busy. Don't bother me.

BIFF: [*Taking the hoe from* WILLY.] I'm saying good-bye to you, Pop. [WILLY *looks at him, silent, unable to move.*] I'm not coming back anymore.

WILLY: You're not going to see Oliver tomorrow?

BIFF: I've got no appointment, Dad.

WILLY: He put his arm around you, and you've got no appointment?

BIFF: Pop, get this now, will you? Everytime I've left it's been a fight that sent me out of here. Today I realized something about myself and I tried to explain it to you and I—I think I'm just not smart enough to make any sense out of it for you. To hell with whose fault it is or anything like that. [*He takes* WILLY's *arm.*] Let's just wrap it up, heh? Come on in, we'll tell Mom. [*He gently tries to pull* WILLY *to left.*]

WILLY: [*Frozen, immobile, with guilt in his voice.*] No, I don't want to see her.

BIFF: Come on! [*He pulls again, and* WILLY *tries to pull away.*]

WILLY: [*Highly nervous.*] No, no, I don't want to see her.

BIFF: [*Tries to look into* WILLY's *face, as if to find the answer there.*] Why don't you want to see her?

WILLY: [*More harshly now.*] Don't bother me, will you?

BIFF: What do you mean, you don't want to see her? You don't want them calling you yellow, do you? This isn't your fault; it's me, I'm a bum. Now come inside! [WILLY *strains to get away.*] Did you hear what I said to you?

[WILLY *pulls away and quickly goes by himself into the house.* BIFF *follows.*]

LINDA: [*To* WILLY.] Did you plant, dear?

BIFF: [*At the door, to* LINDA.] All right, we had it out. I'm going and I'm not writing anymore.

LINDA: [*Going to* WILLY *in the kitchen.*] I think that's the best way, dear. 'Cause there's no use drawing it out, you'll just never get along.

[WILLY *doesn't respond.*]

BIFF: People ask where I am and what I'm doing, you don't know, and you don't care. That way it'll be off your mind and you can start brightening up again. All right? That clears it, doesn't it? [WILLY *is silent, and* BIFF *goes to him.*] You gonna wish me luck, scout? [*He extends his hand.*] What do you say?

LINDA: Shake his hand, Willy.

WILLY: [*Turning to her, seething with hurt.*] There's no necessity to mention the pen at all, y'know.

BIFF: [*Gently.*] I've got no appointment, Dad.

WILLY: [*Erupting fiercely.*] He put his arm around . . . ?

BIFF: Dad, you're never going to see what I am, so what's the use of arguing? If I strike oil I'll send you a check. Meantime forget I'm alive.

WILLY: [*To* LINDA.] Spite, see?

BIFF: Shake hands, Dad.

WILLY: Not my hand.

BIFF: I was hoping not to go this way.

WILLY: Well, this is the way you're going. Good-bye. [BIFF *looks at him a moment, then turns sharply and goes to the stairs.* WILLY *stops him with.*] May you rot in hell if you leave this house!

BIFF: [*Turning.*] Exactly what is it that you want from me?

WILLY: I want you to know, on the train, in the mountains, in the valleys, wherever you go, that you cut down your life for spite!

BIFF: No, no.

WILLY: Spite, spite, is the word of your undoing! And when you're down and out, remember what did it. When you're rotting somewhere beside the railroad tracks, remember, and don't you dare blame it on me!

BIFF: I'm not blaming it on you!

WILLY: I won't take the rap for this, you hear?

[HAPPY *comes down the stairs and stands on the bottom step, watching.*]

BIFF: That's just what I'm telling you!

WILLY: [*Sinking into a chair at the table, with full accusation.*] You're trying to put a knife in me—don't think I don't know what you're doing!

BIFF: All right, phony! Then let's lay it on the line. [*He whips the rubber tube out of his pocket and puts it on the table.*]

HAPPY: You crazy—

LINDA: Biff!

[*She moves to grab the hose, but* BIFF *holds it down with his hand.*]

BIFF: Leave it there! Don't move it!

WILLY: [*Not looking at it.*] What is that?

BIFF: You know goddam well what that is.

WILLY: [*Caged, wanting to escape.*] I never saw that.

BIFF: You saw it. The mice didn't bring it into the cellar! What is this supposed to do, make a hero out of you? This supposed to make me sorry for you?

WILLY: Never heard of it.

BIFF: There'll be no pity for you, you hear it? No pity!

WILLY: [*To* LINDA.] You hear the spite!

BIFF: No, you're going to hear the truth—what you are and what I am!

LINDA: Stop it!

WILLY: Spite!

HAPPY: [*Coming down toward* BIFF.] You cut it now!

BIFF: [*To* HAPPY.] The man don't know who we are! The man is gonna know! [*To* WILLY.] We never told the truth for ten minutes in this house!

HAPPY: We always told the truth!

BIFF: [*Turning on him.*] You big blow, are you the assistant buyer? You're one of the two assistants to the assistant, aren't you?

HAPPY: Well, I'm practically—

BIFF: You're practically full of it! We all are! And I'm through with it. [*To* WILLY.] Now hear this, Willy, this is me.

WILLY: I know you!

BIFF: You know why I had no address for three months? I stole a suit in Kansas City and I was in jail. [*To* LINDA, *who is sobbing.*] Stop crying. I'm through with it.

[LINDA *turns away from them, her hands covering her face.*]

WILLY: I suppose that's my fault!

BIFF: I stole myself out of every good job since high school!

WILLY: And whose fault is that?

BIFF: And I never got anywhere because you blew me so full of hot air I could never stand taking orders from anybody! That's whose fault it is!

WILLY: I hear that!

LINDA: Don't, Biff!

BIFF: It's goddam time you heard that! I had to be boss big shot in two weeks, and I'm through with it!

WILLY: Then hang yourself! For spite, hang yourself!

BIFF: No! Nobody's hanging himself, Willy! I ran down eleven flights with a pen in my hand today. And suddenly I stopped, you hear me? And in the middle of that office building, do you hear this? I stopped in the middle of that building and I saw—the sky. I saw the things that I love in this world. The work and the food and time to sit and smoke. And I looked at the pen and said to myself, what the hell am I grabbing this for? Why am I trying to become what I don't want to be? What am I doing in an office, making a contemptuous, begging fool of myself, when all I want is out there, waiting for me the minute I say I know who I am! Why can't I say that, Willy? [*He tries to make* WILLY *face him, but* WILLY *pulls away and moves to the left.*]

WILLY: [*With hatred, threateningly.*] The door of your life is wide open!

BIFF: Pop! I'm a dime a dozen, and so are you!

WILLY: [*Turning on him now in an uncontrolled outburst.*] I am not a dime a dozen! I am Willy Loman, and you are Biff Loman!

[BIFF *starts for* WILLY, *but is blocked by* HAPPY. *In his fury,* BIFF *seems on the verge of attacking his father.*]

BIFF: I am not a leader of men, Willy, and neither are you. You were never anything but a hard-working drummer who landed in the ash can like all the rest of them! I'm one dollar an hour, Willy![1] I tried seven states and couldn't raise it. A buck an hour! Do you gather my meaning? I'm not bringing home any prizes anymore, and you're going to stop waiting for me to bring them home!

WILLY: [*Directly to* BIFF.] You vengeful, spiteful mutt!

[BIFF *breaks from* HAPPY. WILLY, *in fright, starts up the stairs.* BIFF *grabs him.*]

BIFF: [*At the peak of his fury.*] Pop, I'm nothing! I'm nothing, Pop. Can't you understand that? There's no spite in it anymore. I'm just what I am, that's all.

[BIFF*'s fury has spent itself, and he breaks down, sobbing, holding on to* WILLY, *who dumbly fumbles for* BIFF*'s face.*]

WILLY: [*Astonished.*] What're you doing? What're you doing? [*To* LINDA.] Why is he crying?

BIFF: [*Crying, broken.*] Will you let me go, for Christ's sake? Will you take that phony dream and burn it before something happens? [*Struggling to contain himself, he pulls away and moves to the stairs.*] I'll go in the morning. Put him—put him to bed. [*Exhausted,* BIFF *moves up the stairs to his room.*]

WILLY: [*After a long pause, astonished, elevated.*] Isn't that—isn't that remarkable? Biff—he likes me!

LINDA: He loves you, Willy!

HAPPY: [*Deeply moved.*] Always did, Pop.

WILLY: Oh, Biff! [*Staring wildly.*] He cried! Cried to me. [*He is choking with his love, and now cries out his promise.*] That boy—that boy is going to be magnificent!

[BEN *appears in the light just outside the kitchen.*]

BEN: Yes, outstanding, with twenty thousand behind him.

LINDA: [*Sensing the racing of his mind, fearfully, carefully.*] Now come to bed, Willy. It's all settled now.

---

1. In 1949, Congress raised the minimum wage from forty to seventy-five cents per hour.

WILLY: [*Finding it difficult not to rush out of the house.*] Yes, we'll sleep. Come on. Go to sleep, Hap.

BEN: And it does take a great kind of man to crack the jungle.

[*In accents of dread,* BEN's *idyllic music starts up.*]

HAPPY: [*His arm around* LINDA.] I'm getting married, Pop, don't forget it. I'm changing everything. I'm gonna run that department before the year is up. You'll see, Mom. [*He kisses her.*]

BEN: The jungle is dark but full of diamonds, Willy.

[WILLY *turns, moves, listening to* BEN.]

LINDA: Be good. You're both good boys, just act that way, that's all.

HAPPY: 'Night, Pop. [*He goes upstairs.*]

LINDA: [*To* WILLY.] Come, dear.

BEN: [*With greater force.*] One must go in to fetch a diamond out.

WILLY: [*To* LINDA, *as he moves slowly along the edge of the kitchen, toward the door.*] I just want to get settled down, Linda. Let me sit alone for a little.

LINDA: [*Almost uttering her fear.*] I want you upstairs.

WILLY: [*Taking her in his arms.*] In a few minutes, Linda. I couldn't sleep right now. Go on, you look awful tired. [*He kisses her.*]

BEN: Not like an appointment at all. A diamond is rough and hard to the touch.

WILLY: Go on now. I'll be right up.

LINDA: I think this is the only way, Willy.

WILLY: Sure, it's the best thing.

BEN: Best thing!

WILLY: The only way. Everything is gonna be—go on, kid, get to bed. You look so tired.

LINDA: Come right up.

WILLY: Two minutes. [LINDA *goes into the living-room, then reappears in her bedroom.* WILLY *moves just outside the kitchen door.*] Loves me. [*Wonderingly.*] Always loved me. Isn't that a remarkable thing? Ben, he'll worship me for it!

BEN: [*With promise.*] It's dark there, but full of diamonds.

WILLY: Can you imagine that magnificence with twenty thousand dollars in his pocket?

LINDA: [*Calling from her room.*] Willy! Come up!

WILLY: [*Calling into the kitchen.*] Yes! Yes. Coming! It's very smart, you realize that, don't you, sweetheart? Even Ben sees it. I gotta go, baby. 'Bye! 'Bye! [*Going over to* BEN, *almost dancing.*] Imagine? When the mail comes he'll be ahead of Bernard again!

BEN: A perfect proposition all around.

WILLY: Did you see how he cried to me? Oh, if I could kiss him, Ben!

BEN: Time, William, time!

WILLY: Oh, Ben, I always knew one way or another we were gonna make it, Biff and I!

BEN: [*Looking at his watch.*] The boat. We'll be late. [*He moves slowly off into the darkness.*]

WILLY: [*Elegiacally, turning to the house.*] Now when you kick off, boy, I want a seventy-yard boot, and get right down the field under the ball, and when you hit, hit low and hit hard, because it's important, boy. [*He swings around and faces the audience.*] There's all kinds of important people in the stands, and the first thing you know . . . [*Suddenly realizing he is alone.*] Ben! Ben, where do I . . . ? [*He makes a sudden movement of search.*] Ben, how do I . . . ?

LINDA: [*Calling.*] Willy, you coming up?

WILLY: [*Uttering a gasp of fear, whirling about as if to quiet her.*] Sh! [*He turns around as if to find his way; sounds, faces, voices, seem to be swarming in upon him and he flicks at them, crying!*] Sh! Sh! [*Suddenly music, faint and high, stops him. It rises in intensity, almost to an unbearable scream. He goes up and down on his toes, and rushes off around the house.*] Shhh!

LINDA: Willy? [*There is no answer.* LINDA *waits.* BIFF *gets up off his bed. He is still in his clothes.* HAPPY *sits up.* BIFF *stands listening.*] [*With real fear.*] Willy, answer me! Willy! [*There is the sound of a car starting and moving away at full speed.*] No!

BIFF: [*Rushing down the stairs.*] Pop!

[*As the car speeds off, the music crashes down in a frenzy of sound, which becomes the soft pulsation of a single cello string.* BIFF *slowly returns to his bedroom. He and* HAPPY *gravely don their jackets.* LINDA *slowly walks out of her room. The music has developed into a dead march. The leaves of day are appearing over everything.*

CHARLEY *and* BERNARD, *somberly dressed, appear and knock on the kitchen door.* BIFF *and* HAPPY *slowly descend the stairs to the kitchen as* CHARLEY *and* BERNARD *enter. All stop a moment when* LINDA, *in clothes of mourning, bearing a little bunch of roses, comes through the draped doorway into the kitchen. She goes to* CHARLEY *and takes his arm. Now all move toward the audience, through the wall-line of the kitchen. At the limit of the apron,* LINDA *lays down the flowers, kneels, and sits back on her heels. All stare down at the grave.*]

REQUIEM

CHARLEY: It's getting dark, Linda.

[LINDA *doesn't react. She stares at the grave.*]

BIFF: How about it, Mom? Better get some rest, heh? They'll be closing the gate soon.

[LINDA *makes no move. Pause.*]

HAPPY: [*Deeply angered.*] He had no right to do that. There was no necessity for it. We would've helped him.

CHARLEY: [*Grunting.*] Hmmm.

BIFF: Come along, Mom.

LINDA: Why didn't anybody come?

CHARLEY: It was a very nice funeral.

LINDA: But where are all the people he knew? Maybe they blame him.

CHARLEY: Naa. It's a rough world, Linda. They wouldn't blame him.

LINDA: I can't understand it. At this time especially. First time in thirty-five years we were just about free and clear. He only needed a little salary. He was even finished with the dentist.

CHARLEY: No man only needs a little salary.

LINDA: I can't understand it.

BIFF: There were a lot of nice days. When he'd come home from a trip; or on Sundays, making the stoop; finishing the cellar; putting on the new porch; when he built the extra bathroom; and put up the garage. You know something, Charley, there's more of him in that front stoop than in all the sales he ever made.

CHARLEY: Yeah. He was a happy man with a batch of cement.

LINDA: He was so wonderful with his hands.

BIFF: He had the wrong dreams. All, all, wrong.

HAPPY: [*Almost ready to fight* BIFF.] Don't say that!

BIFF: He never knew who he was.

CHARLEY: [*Stopping* HAPPY's *movement and reply. To* BIFF.] Nobody dast blame this man. You don't understand: Willy was a salesman. And for a salesman, there is no rock bottom to the life. He don't put a bolt to a nut, he don't tell you the law or give you medicine. He's a man way out there in the blue, riding on a smile and a shoeshine. And when they start not smiling back— that's an earthquake. And then you get yourself a couple of spots on your hat, and you're finished. Nobody dast blame this man. A salesman is got to dream, boy. It comes with the territory.

BIFF: Charley, the man didn't know who he was.

HAPPY: [*Infuriated.*] Don't say that!

BIFF: Why don't you come with me, Happy?

HAPPY: I'm not licked that easily. I'm staying right in this city, and I'm gonna beat this racket! [*He looks at* BIFF, *his chin set.*] The Loman Brothers!

BIFF: I know who I am, kid.

HAPPY: All right, boy. I'm gonna show you and everybody else that Willy Loman did not die in vain. He had a good dream. It's the only dream you can have—to come out number-one-man. He fought it out here, and this is where I'm gonna win it for him.

BIFF: [*With a hopeless glance at* HAPPY, *bends towards his mother.*] Let's go, Mom.

LINDA: I'll be with you in a minute. Go on, Charley. [*He hesitates.*] I want to, just for a minute. I never had a chance to say goodbye. [CHARLEY *moves away, followed by* HAPPY. BIFF *remains a slight distance up and left of* LINDA. *She sits there, summoning herself. The flute begins, not far away, playing behind her speech.*] Forgive me, dear. I can't cry. I don't know what it is, but I can't cry. I don't understand it. Why did you ever do that? Help me, Willy, I can't cry. It seems to me that you're just on another trip. I keep expecting you. Willy, dear, I can't cry. Why did you do it? I search and search and I search, and I can't understand it, Willy. I made the last payment on the house today. Today, dear. And there'll be nobody home. [*A sob rises in her throat.*] We're free and clear. [*Sobbing more fully, released.*] We're free. [BIFF *comes slowly toward her.*] We're free . . . We're free . . . [BIFF *lifts her to her feet and moves out up right with her in his arms.* LINDA *sobs quietly.* BERNARD *and* CHARLEY *come together and follow them, followed by* HAPPY. *Only the music of the flute is left on the darkening stage as over the house the hard towers of the apartment buildings rise into sharp focus.*]

[*CURTAIN.*]

1949

Lorraine Hansberry
1930–1965

A RAISIN IN THE SUN

This play takes its title from a line in a Langston Hughes poem that asks, "What happens to a dream deferred?" In the 1950s, many African Americans felt their claim on the American dream had been deferred because "separate but equal," the dominant ideology governing race relations in the United States at that time, was really a formula for white supremacy. Hughes wrote his poem in 1951, when Hansberry was just twenty-one, a student who left college at University of Wisconsin, Madison, to launch her career as a writer in New York.

The play draws on Hansberry's personal experiences. For example, in 1938, Lorraine's father, Carl, decided to fight segregation by moving his family into an all-white community in Chicago. At the time, restrictive residential covenants made such actions illegal, but the Hansberry family fought the law all the way to the U.S. Supreme Court, where they won a landmark decision. Along the way, the eight-year-old Lorraine witnessed an angry white mob gathering outside their house and was nearly hit by a piece of concrete thrown through their window. Nevertheless, Hansberry's own circumstances provided better prospects than those of the Younger family in the play. Her father, successful in real estate, was a member of the NAACP and was politically active, once running (unsuccessfully) for Congress. Her mother was a progressive committee woman in their neighborhood ward. And an uncle, a professor of African American history at Howard University, often brought African visitors, like Joseph Asagai in the play, to the Hansberrys' Chicago home. In addition, many prominent African Americans visited their home, including Paul Robeson, Jesse Owens, and Joe Louis. When she came to New York in 1950, Hansberry went to work for Robeson's newspaper, Freedom.

Not long after the publication of Hughes's poem, Rosa Parks committed her famous act of civil disobedience, sparking the Montgomery bus boycott and the modern civil rights movement; and the U.S. Supreme Court struck down segregated schools in Brown v. the Board of Education. *Hansberry participated in this active challenging of American segregation, often taking part in demonstrations herself. She wrote in an age of greater promise than that of her parents' generation, and her play might be considered a cultural parallel to legal and extra-legal methods of social reform. Her work belongs in the tradition of realists, initiated by Henrik Ibsen, who wrote "problem" plays. It is certainly logical to think of* A Raisin in the Sun *as a descendant of* A Doll's House, *not only stylistically but also thematically. Though more attention has been paid—not only by audiences but also by Hansberry herself—to the racial issues in the play, it is also about women in American society and the special burdens put upon women of color.*

Hansberry was unknown as a creative writer in 1957 when a friend, Philip Rose, read the script of Raisin *and announced he wanted to produce it on Broadway. He secured Sidney Poitier for the role of Walter, and they toured New Haven, Philadelphia, and Chicago before opening on Broadway in March 1959 to excellent reviews. Though the play conformed to many of the conventions of realistic theater, the fact that it portrayed a black family made it revolutionary. It revolutionized audiences as well, drawing more African Americans to Broadway theater than ever before. Most literary historians credit the play with launching African American theater in the United States, as have several generations of black writers, actors, directors, and producers. A few did dissent from the general praise, however. According to these critics, the Youngers aspired to nothing more than the crass materialistic prosperity that white Americans enjoyed, which was a rather shallow goal.*

Today we view the civil rights movement mostly through the lens of Martin Luther King Jr.'s dream of an integrated society, but in the 1950s it was not at all clear that this would be the goal of reform. While the play obviously advocates the better treatment of African Americans, it also participates in a debate among reform-minded African Americans that can be exemplified by the contrast between Martin Luther King Jr. and Malcolm X. The latter advocated an anti-assimilationist black "nationalism." This alternative to integration celebrated black culture, often looking to Africa for a cultural inspiration unashamedly different from mainstream white culture.

If the 1950s were dynamic years for race relations in the United States, they were revolutionary in Africa. In the twenty years between 1950 and 1970, nearly forty African nations gained their independence from European powers. Most of these changes came within a few years of the first production of A Raisin in the Sun *in 1959. As is typical in any decolonization, these independence movements spurred revivals of native culture—in dress, music, and the arts. But also typical of decolonization are internal conflicts that often lead to bloodshed. For example, Nigeria won its independence from Great Britain in 1960, but over the next ten years a million people would die in civil war. Though such consequences are alluded to in the play, in 1959 they were still mostly a dark cloud below the horizon of independence.*

A Raisin in the Sun

What happens to a dream deferred?

Does it dry up
Like a raisin in the sun?
Or fester like a sore—
And then run?
Does it stink like rotten meat?
Or crust and sugar over—
Like a syrupy sweet?
Maybe it just sags
Like a heavy load.

Or does it explode?
—LANGSTON HUGHES[1]

1. The title of this 1951 poem is "Harlem (A Dream Deferred)."

CHARACTERS

RUTH YOUNGER

TRAVIS YOUNGER

WALTER LEE YOUNGER (BROTHER)

BENEATHA YOUNGER

LENA YOUNGER (MAMA)

JOSEPH ASAGAI

GEORGE MURCHISON

KARL LINDNER

BOBO

MOVING MEN

The action of the play is set in Chicago's South Side, sometime between World War II and the present.

ACT 1
SCENE 1

The Younger living room would be a comfortable and well-ordered room if it were not for a number of indestructible contradictions to this state of being. Its furnishings are typical and undistinguished and their primary feature now is that they have clearly had to accommodate the living of too many people for too many years—and they are tired. Still, we can see that at some time, a time probably no longer remembered by the family (except perhaps for MAMA*), the furnishings of this room were actually selected with care and love and even hope—and brought to this apartment and arranged with taste and pride.*

That was a long time ago. Now the once loved pattern of the couch upholstery has to fight to show itself from under acres of crocheted doilies and couch covers which have themselves finally come to be more important than the upholstery. And here a table or a chair has been moved to disguise the worn places in the carpet; but the carpet has fought back by showing its weariness, with depressing uniformity, elsewhere on its surface.

Weariness has, in fact, won in this room. Everything has been polished, washed, sat on, used, scrubbed too often. All pretenses but living itself have long since vanished from the very atmosphere of this room.

Moreover, a section of this room, for it is not really a room unto itself, though the landlord's lease would make it seem so, slopes backward to provide a small kitchen area, where the family prepares the meals that are eaten in the living room proper, which must also serve as dining room. The single window that has been provided for these "two" rooms is located in this kitchen area. The sole natural light the family may enjoy in the course of a day is only that which fights its way through this little window.

At left, a door leads to a bedroom which is shared by MAMA and her daughter, BENEATHA. At right, opposite, is a second room (which in the beginning of the life of this apartment was probably a breakfast room) which serves as a bedroom for WALTER and his wife, RUTH.

Time: Sometime between World War II and the present.[2]

Place: Chicago's South Side.

At Rise: It is morning dark in the living room. TRAVIS is asleep on the make-down bed at center. An alarm clock sounds from within the bedroom at right, and presently RUTH enters from that room and closes the door behind her. She crosses sleepily toward the window. As she passes her sleeping son she reaches down and shakes him a little. At the window she raises the shade and a dusky Southside morning light comes in feebly. She fills a pot with water and puts it on to boil. She calls to the boy, between yawns, in a slightly muffled voice.

RUTH is about thirty. We can see that she was a pretty girl, even exceptionally so, but now it is apparent that life has been little that she expected, and disappointment has already begun to hang in her face. In a few years, before thirty-five even, she will be known among her people as a "settled woman."

She crosses to her son and gives him a good, final, rousing shake.

RUTH: Come on now, boy, it's seven thirty! [*Her son sits up at last, in a stupor of sleepiness.*] I say hurry up, Travis! You ain't the only person in the world got to use a bathroom! [*The child, a sturdy, handsome little boy of ten or eleven, drags himself out of the bed and almost blindly takes his towels and "today's clothes" from drawers and a closet and goes out to the bathroom, which is in an outside hall and which is shared by another family or families on the same floor. RUTH crosses to the bedroom door at right and opens it and calls in to her husband.*] Walter Lee! . . . It's after seven thirty! Lemme see you do some waking up in there now! [*She waits.*] You better

2. Meaning 1959.

get up from there, man! It's after seven thirty I tell you. [*She waits again.*] All right, you just go ahead and lay there and next thing you know Travis be finished and Mr. Johnson'll be in there and you'll be fussing and cussing round here like a mad man! And be late too! [*She waits, at the end of patience.*] Walter Lee—it's time for you to get up!

> [*She waits another second and then starts to go into the bedroom, but is apparently satisfied that her husband has begun to get up. She stops, pulls the door to, and returns to the kitchen area. She wipes her face with a moist cloth and runs her fingers through her sleep-disheveled hair in a vain effort and ties an apron around her housecoat. The bedroom door at right opens and her husband stands in the doorway in his pajamas, which are rumpled and mismated. He is a lean, intense young man in his middle thirties, inclined to quick nervous movements and erratic speech habits— and always in his voice there is a quality of indictment.*]

WALTER: Is he out yet?

RUTH: What you mean *out*? He ain't hardly got in there good yet.

WALTER: [*Wandering in, still more oriented to sleep than to a new day.*] Well, what was you doing all that yelling for if I can't even get in there yet? [*Stopping and thinking.*] Check coming today?

RUTH: They *said* Saturday and this is just Friday and I hopes to God you ain't going to get up here first thing this morning and start talking to me 'bout no money—'cause I 'bout don't want to hear it.

WALTER: Something the matter with you this morning?

RUTH: No—I'm just sleepy as the devil. What kind of eggs you want?

WALTER: Not scrambled. [RUTH *starts to scramble eggs.*] Paper come?
  [RUTH *points impatiently to the rolled up* Tribune *on the table, and he gets it and spreads it out and vaguely reads the front page.*]
  Set off another bomb yesterday.

RUTH: [*Maximum indifference.*] Did they?

WALTER: [*Looking up.*] What's the matter with you?

RUTH: Ain't nothing the matter with me. And don't keep asking me that this morning.

WALTER: Ain't nobody bothering you. [*Reading the news of the day absently again.*] Say Colonel McCormick³ is sick.

RUTH: [*Affecting tea-party interest.*] Is he now? Poor thing.

WALTER: [*Sighing and looking at his watch.*] Oh, me. [*He waits.*] Now what is that boy doing in that bathroom all this time? He just going to have to start getting up earlier. I can't be late to work on account of him fooling around in there.

RUTH: [*Turning on him.*] Oh, no he ain't going to be getting up no earlier no such thing! It ain't his fault that he can't get to bed no earlier nights 'cause he got a bunch of crazy good-for-nothing clowns sitting up running their mouths in what is supposed to be his bedroom after ten o'clock at night . . .

WALTER: That's what you mad about, ain't it? The things I want to talk about with my friends just couldn't be important in your mind, could they?

[*He rises and finds a cigarette in her handbag on the table and crosses to the little window and looks out, smoking and deeply enjoying this first one.*]

RUTH: [*Almost matter of factly, a complaint too automatic to deserve emphasis.*] Why you always got to smoke before you eat in the morning?

WALTER: [*At the window.*] Just look at 'em down there . . . Running and racing to work . . . [*He turns and faces his wife and watches her a moment at the stove, and then, suddenly.*] You look young this morning, baby.

RUTH: [*Indifferently.*] Yeah?

WALTER: Just for a second—stirring them eggs. It's gone now—just for a second it was—you looked real young again. [*Then, drily.*] It's gone now—you look like yourself again.

RUTH: Man, if you don't shut up and leave me alone.

WALTER: [*Looking out to the street again.*] First thing a man ought to learn in life is not to make love to no colored woman first thing in the morning. You all some evil people at eight o'clock in the morning.

[TRAVIS *appears in the hall doorway, almost fully dressed and quite wide awake now, his towels and pajamas across his shoulders. He opens the door and signals for his father to make the bathroom in a hurry.*]

---

3. Robert Rutherford McCormick (1880–1955), long-time publisher, editor, and owner of the *Chicago Tribune*. He championed conservative causes his whole life.

TRAVIS: [*Watching the bathroom.*] Daddy, come on!

[WALTER *gets his bathroom utensils and flies out to the bathroom.*]

RUTH: Sit down and have your breakfast, Travis.

TRAVIS: Mama, this is Friday. [*Gleefully.*] Check coming tomorrow, huh?

RUTH: You get your mind off money and eat your breakfast.

TRAVIS: [*Eating.*] This is the morning we supposed to bring the fifty cents to school.

RUTH: Well, I ain't got no fifty cents this morning.

TRAVIS: Teacher say we have to.

RUTH: I don't care what teacher say. I ain't got it. Eat your breakfast, Travis.

TRAVIS: I *am* eating.

RUTH: Hush up now and just eat!

[*The boy gives her an exasperated look for her lack of understanding, and eats grudgingly.*]

TRAVIS: You think Grandmama would have it?

RUTH: No! And I want you to stop asking your grandmother for money, you hear me?

TRAVIS: [*Outraged.*] Gaaaleee! I don't ask her, she just gimme it sometimes!

RUTH: Travis Willard Younger—I got too much on me this morning to be—

TRAVIS: Maybe Daddy—

RUTH: *Travis!*

[*The boy hushes abruptly. They are both quiet and tense for several seconds.*]

TRAVIS: [*Presently.*] Could I maybe go carry some groceries in front of the supermarket for a little while after school then?

RUTH: Just hush, I said. [TRAVIS *jabs his spoon into his cereal bowl viciously, and rests his head in anger upon his fists.*] If you through eating, you can get over there and make up your bed.

[*The boy obeys stiffly and crosses the room, almost mechanically, to the bed and more or less carefully folds the covering. He carries the bedding into his mother's room and returns with his books and cap.*]

TRAVIS: [*Sulking and standing apart from her unnaturally.*] I'm gone.

RUTH: [*Looking up from the stove to inspect him automatically.*] Come here. [*He crosses to her and she studies his head.*] If you don't take this comb and fix this here head, you better! [TRAVIS *puts down his books with a great sigh of oppression, and crosses to the mirror. His mother mutters under her breath about his "slub-bornness."*] 'Bout to march out of here with that head looking just like chickens slept in it! I just don't know where you get your slub-born ways . . . And get your jacket, too. Looks chilly out this morning.

TRAVIS: [*With conspicuously brushed hair and jacket.*] I'm gone.

RUTH: Get carfare and milk money—[*Waving one finger.*]—and not a single penny for no caps, you hear me?

TRAVIS: [*With sullen politeness.*] Yes'm.

[*He turns in outrage to leave. His mother watches after him as in his frustration he approaches the door almost comically. When she speaks to him, her voice has become a very gentle tease.*]

RUTH: [*Mocking; as she thinks he would say it.*] Oh, Mama makes me so mad sometimes, I don't know what to do! [*She waits and continues to his back as he stands stock-still in front of the door.*] I wouldn't kiss that woman good-bye for nothing in this world this morning! [*The boy finally turns around and rolls his eyes at her, knowing the mood has changed and he is vindicated; he does not, however, move toward her yet.*] Not for nothing in this world! [*She finally laughs aloud at him and holds out her arms to him and we see that it is a way between them, very old and practiced. He crosses to her and allows her to embrace him warmly but keeps his face fixed with masculine rigidity. She holds him back from her presently and looks at him and runs her fingers over the features of his face. With utter gentleness—*] Now—whose little old angry man are you?

TRAVIS: [*The masculinity and gruffness start to fade at last.*] Aw gaalee—Mama . . .

RUTH: [*Mimicking.*] Aw—gaaaaalleeeee, Mama! [*She pushes him, with rough playfulness and finality, toward the door.*] Get on out of here or you going to be late.

TRAVIS: [*In the face of love, new aggressiveness.*] Mama, could I *please* go carry groceries?

RUTH: Honey, it's starting to get so cold evenings.

WALTER: [*Coming in from the bathroom and drawing a make-believe gun from a make-believe holster and shooting at his son.*] What is it he wants to do?

RUTH: Go carry groceries after school at the supermarket.

WALTER: Well, let him go . . .

TRAVIS: [*Quickly, to the ally.*] I *have* to—she won't gimme the fifty cents . . .

WALTER: [*To his wife only.*] Why not?

RUTH: [*Simply, and with flavor.*] 'Cause we don't have it.

WALTER: [*To* RUTH *only.*] What you tell the boy things like that for? [*Reaching down into his pants with a rather important gesture.*] Here, son—
[*He hands the boy the coin, but his eyes are directed to his wife's.* TRAVIS *takes the money happily.*]

TRAVIS: Thanks, Daddy.
[*He starts out.* RUTH *watches both of them with murder in her eyes.* WALTER *stands and stares back at her with defiance, and suddenly reaches into his pocket again on an afterthought.*]

WALTER: [*Without even looking at his son, still staring hard at his wife.*] In fact, here's another fifty cents . . . Buy yourself some fruit today—or take a taxicab to school or something!

TRAVIS: Whoopee—
[*He leaps up and clasps his father around the middle with his legs, and they face each other in mutual appreciation; slowly* WALTER LEE *peeks around the boy to catch the violent rays from his wife's eyes and draws his head back as if shot.*]

WALTER: You better get down now—and get to school, man.

TRAVIS: [*At the door.*] O.K. Good-bye.
[*He exits.*]

WALTER: [*After him, pointing with pride.*] That's *my* boy. [*She looks at him in disgust and turns back to her work.*] You know what I was thinking 'bout in the bathroom this morning?

RUTH: No.

WALTER: How come you always try to be so pleasant!

RUTH: What is there to be pleasant 'bout!

WALTER: You want to know what I was thinking 'bout in the bathroom or not!

RUTH: I know what you thinking 'bout.

WALTER: [*Ignoring her.*] 'Bout what me and Willy Harris was talking about last night.

RUTH: [*Immediately—a refrain.*] Willy Harris is a good-for-nothing loud mouth.

WALTER: Anybody who talks to me has got to be a good-for-nothing loud mouth, ain't he? And what you know about who is just a good-for-nothing loud mouth? Charlie Atkins was just a "good-for-nothing loud mouth" too, wasn't he! When he wanted me to go in the dry-cleaning business with him. And now—he's grossing a hundred thousand a year. A hundred thousand dollars a year! You still call *him* a loud mouth!

RUTH: [*Bitterly.*] Oh, Walter Lee . . .

[*She folds her head on her arms over the table.*]

WALTER: [*Rising and coming to her and standing over her.*] You tired, ain't you? Tired of everything. Me, the boy, the way we live—this beat-up hole—everything. Ain't you? [*She doesn't look up, doesn't answer.*] So tired—moaning and groaning all the time, but you wouldn't do nothing to help, would you? You couldn't be on my side that long for nothing, could you?

RUTH: Walter, please leave me alone.

WALTER: A man needs for a woman to back him up . . .

RUTH: Walter—

WALTER: Mama would listen to you. You know she listen to you more than she do me and Bennie. She think more of you. All you have to do is just sit down with her when you drinking your coffee one morning and talking 'bout things like you do and—[*He sits down beside her and demonstrates graphically what he thinks her methods and tone should be.*]—you just sip your coffee, see, and say easy like that you been thinking 'bout that deal Walter Lee is so interested in, 'bout the store and all, and sip some more coffee, like what you saying ain't really that important to you—And the next thing you know, she be listening good and asking you questions and when I come home—I can tell her the details. This ain't no fly-by-night proposition, baby. I mean we figured it out, me and Willy and Bobo.

RUTH: [*With a frown.*] Bobo?

WALTER: Yeah. You see, this little liquor store we got in mind cost seventy-five thousand and we figured the initial investment on the place be 'bout thirty thousand, see. That be ten thousand each. Course, there's a couple of hundred you got to pay so's you don't spend your life just waiting for them clowns to let your license get approved—

RUTH: You mean graft?

WALTER: [*Frowning impatiently.*] Don't call it that. See there, that just goes to show you what women understand about the world. Baby, don't *nothing* happen for you in this world 'less you pay *somebody* off!

RUTH: Walter, leave me alone! [*She raises her head and stares at him vigorously—then says, more quietly.*] Eat your eggs, they gonna be cold.

WALTER: [*Straightening up from her and looking off.*] That's it. There you are. Man say to his woman: I got me a dream. His woman say: Eat your eggs. [*Sadly, but gaining in power.*] Man say: I got to take hold of this here world, baby! And a woman will say: Eat your eggs and go to work. [*Passionately now.*] Man say: I got to change my life, I'm choking to death, baby! And his woman say—[*In utter anguish as he brings his fists down on his thighs.*]— Your eggs is getting cold!

RUTH: [*Softly.*] Walter, that ain't none of our money.

WALTER: [*Not listening at all or even looking at her.*] This morning, I was lookin' in the mirror and thinking about it . . . I'm thirty-five years old; I been married eleven years and I got a boy who sleeps in the living room—[*Very, very quietly.*]—and all I got to give him is stories about how rich white people live . . .

RUTH: Eat your eggs, Walter.

WALTER: *Damn my eggs . . . damn all the eggs that ever was!*

RUTH: Then go to work.

WALTER: [*Looking up at her.*] See—I'm trying to talk to you 'bout myself—[*Shaking his head with the repetition.*]—and all you can say is eat them eggs and go to work.

RUTH: [*Wearily.*] Honey, you never say nothing new. I listen to you every day, every night and every morning, and you never say nothing new. [*Shrugging.*] So you would rather *be* Mr. Arnold than be his chauffeur. So—I would *rather* be living in Buckingham Palace.[4]

4. The lavish London residence of British royalty.

WALTER: That is just what is wrong with the colored woman in this world . . . Don't understand about building their men up and making 'em feel like they somebody. Like they can do something.

RUTH: [*Drily, but to hurt.*] There *are* colored men who do things.

WALTER: No thanks to the colored woman.

RUTH: Well, being a colored woman, I guess I can't help myself none.
[*She rises and gets the ironing board and sets it up and attacks a huge pile of rough-dried clothes, sprinkling them in preparation for the ironing and then rolling them into tight fat balls.*]

WALTER: [*Mumbling.*] We one group of men tied to a race of women with small minds.

[*His sister* BENEATHA *enters. She is about twenty, as slim and intense as her brother. She is not as pretty as her sister-in-law, but her lean, almost intellectual face has a handsomeness of its own. She wears a bright-red flannel nightie, and her thick hair stands wildly about her head. Her speech is a mixture of many things; it is different from the rest of the family's insofar as education has permeated her sense of English—and perhaps the Midwest rather than the South has finally—at last—won out in her inflection; but not altogether, because over all of it is a soft slurring and transformed use of vowels which is the decided influence of the South Side. She passes through the room without looking at either* RUTH *or* WALTER *and goes to the outside door and looks, a little blindly, out to the bathroom. She sees that it has been lost to the Johnsons. She closes the door with a sleepy vengeance and crosses to the table and sits down a little defeated.*]

BENEATHA: I am going to start timing those people.

WALTER: You should get up earlier.

BENEATHA: [*Her face in her hands. She is still fighting the urge to go back to bed.*] Really—would you suggest dawn? Where's the paper?

WALTER: [*Pushing the paper across the table to her as he studies her almost clinically, as though he has never seen her before.*] You a horrible-looking chick at this hour.

BENEATHA: [*Drily.*] Good morning, everybody.

WALTER: [*Senselessly.*] How is school coming?

BENEATHA: [*In the same spirit.*] Lovely. Lovely. And you know, biology is the greatest. [*Looking up at him.*] I dissected something that looked just like you yesterday.

WALTER: I just wondered if you've made up your mind and everything.

BENEATHA: [*Gaining in sharpness and impatience.*] And what did I answer yesterday morning—and the day before that?

RUTH: [*From the ironing board, like someone disinterested and old.*] Don't be so nasty, Bennie.

BENEATHA: [*Still to her brother.*] And the day before that and the day before that!

WALTER: [*Defensively.*] I'm interested in you. Something wrong with that? Ain't many girls who decide—

WALTER AND BENEATHA: [*In unison.*]—"to be a doctor."

[*Silence.*]

WALTER: Have we figured out yet just exactly how much medical school is going to cost?

RUTH: Walter Lee, why don't you leave that girl alone and get out of here to work?

BENEATHA: [*Exits to the bathroom and bangs on the door.*] Come on out of there, please!

[*She comes back into the room.*]

WALTER: [*Looking at his sister intently.*] You know the check is coming tomorrow.

BENEATHA: [*Turning on him with a sharpness all her own.*] That money belongs to Mama, Walter, and it's for her to decide how she wants to use it. I don't care if she wants to buy a house or a rocket ship or just nail it up somewhere and look at it. It's hers. Not ours—*hers.*

WALTER: [*Bitterly.*] Now ain't that fine! You just got your mother's interest at heart, ain't you, girl? You such a nice girl—but if Mama got that money she can always take a few thousand and help you through school too—can't she?

BENEATHA: I have never asked anyone around here to do anything for me.

WALTER: No! And the line between asking and just accepting when the time comes is big and wide—ain't it!

BENEATHA: [*With fury.*] What do you want from me, Brother—that I quit school or just drop dead, which!

WALTER: I don't want nothing but for you to stop acting holy 'round here. Me and Ruth done made some sacrifices for you— why can't you do something for the family?

RUTH: Walter, don't be dragging me in it.

WALTER: You are in it—Don't you get up and go work in some-body's kitchen for the last three years to help put clothes on her back?

RUTH: Oh, Walter—that's not fair . . .

WALTER: It ain't that nobody expects you to get on your knees and say thank you, Brother; thank you, Ruth; thank you, Mama—and thank you, Travis, for wearing the same pair of shoes for two semesters—

BENEATHA: [*Dropping to her knees.*] Well—I *do*—all right?—thank everybody . . . and forgive me for ever wanting to be anything at all . . . forgive me, forgive me!

RUTH: Please stop it! Your mama'll hear you.

WALTER: Who the hell told you you had to be a doctor? If you so crazy 'bout messing 'round with sick people—then go be a nurse like other women—or just get married and be quiet . . .

BENEATHA: Well—you finally got it said . . . it took you three years but you finally got it said. Walter, give up; leave me alone—it's Mama's money.

WALTER: *He was my father, too!*

BENEATHA: So what? He was mine, too—and Travis' grandfather—but the insurance money belongs to Mama. Picking on me is not going to make her give it to you to invest in any liquor stores—[*Underbreath, dropping into a chair.*]—and I for one say, God bless Mama for that!

WALTER: [*To* RUTH.] See—did you hear? Did you hear!

RUTH: Honey, please go to work.

WALTER: Nobody in this house is ever going to understand me.

BENEATHA: Because you're a nut.

WALTER: Who's a nut?

BENEATHA: You—you are a nut. Thee is mad, boy.

WALTER: [*Looking at his wife and his sister from the door, very sadly.*] The world's most backward race of people, and that's a fact.

BENEATHA: [*Turning slowly in her chair.*] And then there are all those prophets who would lead us out of the wilderness—[WAL-TER *slams out of the house.*]—into the swamps!

RUTH: Bennie, why you always gotta be pickin' on your brother? Can't you be a little sweeter sometimes? [*Door opens.* WALTER *walks in.*]

WALTER: [*To* RUTH.] I need some money for carfare.

RUTH: [*Looks at him, then warms; teasing, but tenderly.*] Fifty cents?
[*She goes to her bag and gets money.*] Here, take a taxi.

> [WALTER *exits.* MAMA *enters. She is a woman in her early sixties, full-bodied and strong. She is one of those women of a certain grace and beauty who wear it so unobtrusively that it takes a while to notice. Her dark-brown face is surrounded by the total whiteness of her hair, and, being a woman who has adjusted to many things in life and overcome many more, her face is full of strength. She has, we can see, wit and faith of a kind that keep her eyes lit and full of interest and expectancy. She is, in a word, a beautiful woman. Her bearing is perhaps most like the noble bearing of the women of the Hereros of Southwest Africa—rather as if she imagines that as she walks she still bears a basket or a vessel upon her head. Her speech, on the other hand, is as careless as her carriage is precise—she is inclined to slur everything—but her voice is perhaps not so much quiet as simply soft.*]

MAMA: Who that 'round here slamming doors at this hour?
> [*She crosses through the room, goes to the window, opens it, and brings in a feeble little plant growing doggedly in a small pot on the window sill. She feels the dirt and puts it back out.*]

RUTH: That was Walter Lee. He and Bennie was at it again.

MAMA: My children and they tempers. Lord, if this little old plant don't get more sun than it's been getting it ain't never going to see spring again. [*She turns from the window.*] What's the matter with you this morning, Ruth? You looks right peaked. You aiming to iron all them things? Leave some for me. I'll get to 'em this afternoon. Bennie honey, it's too drafty for you to be sitting 'round half dressed. Where's your robe?

BENEATHA: In the cleaners.

MAMA: Well, go get mine and put it on.

BENEATHA: I'm not cold, Mama, honest.

MAMA: I know—but you so thin . . .

BENEATHA: [*Irritably.*] Mama, I'm not cold.

MAMA: [*Seeing the make-down bed as* TRAVIS *has left it.*] Lord have mercy, look at that poor bed. Bless his heart—he tries, don't he?
> [*She moves to the bed* TRAVIS *has sloppily made up.*]

RUTH: No—he don't half try at all 'cause he knows you going to come along behind him and fix everything. That's just how come he don't know how to do nothing right now—you done spoiled that boy so.

MAMA: Well—he's a little boy. Ain't supposed to know 'bout house-keeping. My baby, that's what he is. What you fix for his break-fast this morning?

RUTH: [*Angrily.*] I feed my son, Lena!

MAMA: I ain't meddling—[*Underbreath; busy-bodyish.*] I just noticed all last week he had cold cereal, and when it starts getting this chilly in the fall a child ought to have some hot grits or some-thing when he goes out in the cold—

RUTH: [*Furious.*] I gave him hot oats—is that all right!

MAMA: I ain't meddling. [*Pause.*] Put a lot of nice butter on it? [RUTH *shoots her an angry look and does not reply.*] He likes lots of butter.

RUTH: [*Exasperated.*] Lena—

MAMA: [*To* BENEATHA. MAMA *is inclined to wander conversationally sometimes.*] What was you and your brother fussing 'bout this morning?

BENEATHA: It's not important, Mama.

[*She gets up and goes to look out at the bathroom, which is appar-ently free, and she picks up her towels and rushes out.*]

MAMA: What was they fighting about?

RUTH: Now you know as well as I do.

MAMA: [*Shaking her head.*] Brother still worrying hisself sick about that money?

RUTH: You know he is.

MAMA: You had breakfast?

RUTH: Some coffee.

MAMA: Girl, you better start eating and looking after yourself better. You almost thin as Travis.

RUTH: Lena—

MAMA: Un-hunh?

RUTH: What are you going to do with it?

MAMA: Now don't you start, child. It's too early in the morning to be talking about money. It ain't Christian.

RUTH: It's just that he got his heart set on that store—

MAMA: You mean that liquor store that Willy Harris want him to invest in?

RUTH: Yes—

MAMA: We ain't no business people, Ruth. We just plain working folks.

RUTH: Ain't nobody business people till they go into business. Walter Lee say colored people ain't never going to start getting ahead till they start gambling on some different kinds of things in the world—investments and things.

MAMA: What done got into you, girl? Walter Lee done finally sold you on investing.

RUTH: No. Mama, something is happening between Walter and me. I don't know what it is—but he needs something—something I can't give him anymore. He needs this chance, Lena.

MAMA: [*Frowning deeply.*] But liquor, honey—

RUTH: Well—like Walter say—I spec people going to always be drinking themselves some liquor.

MAMA: Well—whether they drinks it or not ain't none of my business. But whether I go into business selling it to 'em *is,* and I don't want that on my ledger this late in life. [*Stopping suddenly and studying her daughter-in-law.*] Ruth Younger, what's the matter with you today? You look like you could fall over right there.

RUTH: I'm tired.

MAMA: Then you better stay home from work today.

RUTH: I can't stay home. She'd be calling up the agency and screaming at them, "My girl didn't come in today—send me somebody! My girl didn't come in!" Oh, she just have a fit . . .

MAMA: Well, let her have it. I'll just call her up and say you got the flu—

RUTH: [*Laughing.*] Why the flu?

MAMA: 'Cause it sounds respectable to 'em. Something white people get, too. They know 'bout the flu. Otherwise they think you been cut up or something when you tell 'em you sick.

RUTH: I got to go in. We need the money.

MAMA: Somebody would of thought my children done all but starved to death the way they talk about money here late. Child, we got a great big old check coming tomorrow.

RUTH: [*Sincerely, but also self-righteously.*] Now that's your money. It ain't got nothing to do with me. We all feel like that—Walter and Bennie and me—even Travis.

MAMA: [*Thoughtfully, and suddenly very far away.*] Ten thousand dollars—

RUTH: Sure is wonderful.

MAMA: Ten thousand dollars.

RUTH: You know what you should do, Miss Lena? You should take yourself a trip somewhere. To Europe or South America or someplace—

MAMA: [*Throwing up her hands at the thought.*] Oh, child!

RUTH: I'm serious. Just pack up and leave! Go on away and enjoy yourself some. Forget about the family and have yourself a ball for once in your life—

MAMA: [*Drily.*] You sound like I'm just about ready to die. Who'd go with me? What I look like wandering 'round Europe by myself?

RUTH: Shoot—these here rich white women do it all the time. They don't think nothing of packing up they suitcases and piling on one of them big steamships and—swoosh!—they gone, child.

MAMA: Something always told me I wasn't no rich white woman.

RUTH: Well—what are you going to do with it then?

MAMA: I ain't rightly decided. [*Thinking. She speaks now with emphasis.*] Some of it got to be put away for Beneatha and her schoolin'— and ain't nothing going to touch that part of it. Nothing. [*She waits several seconds, trying to make up her mind about something, and looks at* RUTH *a little tentatively before going on.*] Been thinking that we maybe could meet the notes on a little old two-story somewhere, with a yard where Travis could play in the summertime, if we use part of the insurance for a down payment and everybody kind of pitch in. I could maybe take on a little day work again, few days a week—

RUTH: [*Studying her mother-in-law furtively and concentrating on her ironing, anxious to encourage without seeming to.*] Well, Lord knows, we've put enough rent into this here rat trap to pay for four houses by now . . .

MAMA: [*Looking up at the words "rat trap" and then looking around and leaning back and sighing—in a suddenly reflective mood—*] "Rat trap"—yes, that's all it is. [*Smiling.*] I remember just as well the day me and Big Walter moved in here. Hadn't been married but two weeks and wasn't planning on living here no more than a year. [*She shakes her head at the dissolved dream.*] We was going to set away, little by little, don't you know, and buy a little place out in Morgan Park.⁵ We had even picked out the house. [*Chuckling a little.*] Looks right dumpy today. But Lord, child, you should know all the dreams I had 'bout buying that house and fixing it up and making me a little garden in the back—[*She waits and stops smiling.*] And didn't none of it happen.

[*Dropping her hands in a futile gesture.*]

RUTH: [*Keeps her head down, ironing.*] Yes, life can be a barrel of disappointments, sometimes.

MAMA: Honey, Big Walter would come in here some nights back then and slump down on that couch there and just look at the rug, and look at me and look at the rug and then back at me—and I'd know he was down then . . . really down. [*After a second very long and thoughtful pause; she is seeing back to times that only she can see.*] And then, Lord, when I lost that baby—little Claude—I almost thought I was going to lose Big Walter too. Oh, that man grieved hisself ! He was one man to love his children.

RUTH: Ain't nothin' can tear at you like losin' your baby.

MAMA: I guess that's how come that man finally worked hisself to death like he done. Like he was fighting his own war with this here world that took his baby from him.

RUTH: He sure was a fine man, all right. I always liked Mr. Younger.

MAMA: Crazy 'bout his children! God knows there was plenty wrong with Walter Younger—hard-headed, mean, kind of wild with women—plenty wrong with him. But he sure loved his children. Always wanted them to have something—be something. That's where Brother gets all these notions, I reckon. Big Walter used to say, he'd get right wet in the eyes sometimes, lean his head back with the water standing in his eyes and say, "Seem like God didn't see fit to give the black man nothing but dreams—but He did give us children to make them dreams seem worthwhile." [*She smiles.*] He could talk like that, don't you know.

RUTH: Yes, he sure could. He was a good man, Mr. Younger.

MAMA: Yes, a fine man—just couldn't never catch up with his dreams, that's all.

5. Respectable neighborhood on the extreme southside of Chicago, largely populated with Irish and African Americans.

[BENEATHA *comes in, brushing her hair and looking up to the ceiling, where the sound of a vacuum cleaner has started up.*]

BENEATHA: What could be so dirty on that woman's rugs that she has to vacuum them every single day?

RUTH: I wish certain young women 'round here who I could name would take inspiration about certain rugs in a certain apartment I could also mention.

BENEATHA: [*Shrugging.*] How much cleaning can a house need, for Christ's sakes.

MAMA: [*Not liking the Lord's name used thus.*] Bennie!

RUTH: Just listen to her—just listen!

BENEATHA: Oh, God!

MAMA: If you use the Lord's name just one more time—

BENEATHA: [*A bit of a whine.*] Oh, Mama—

RUTH: Fresh—just fresh as salt, this girl!

BENEATHA: [*Drily.*] Well—if the salt loses its savor[6]—

MAMA: Now that will do. I just ain't going to have you 'round here reciting the scriptures in vain—you hear me?

BENEATHA: How did I manage to get on everybody's wrong side by just walking into a room?

RUTH: If you weren't so fresh—

BENEATHA: Ruth, I'm twenty years old.

MAMA: What time you be home from school today?

BENEATHA: Kind of late. [*With enthusiasm.*] Madeline is going to start my guitar lessons today.

[MAMA *and* RUTH *look up with the same expression.*]

MAMA: Your *what* kind of lessons?

BENEATHA: Guitar.

RUTH: Oh, Father!

MAMA: How come you done taken it in your mind to learn to play the guitar?

BENEATHA: I just want to, that's all.

MAMA: [*Smiling.*] Lord, child, don't you know what to do with yourself? How long it going to be before you get tired of this now—

6. See Matthew 5:13: "Ye are the salt of the earth: but if the salt have lost his savour, wherewith shall it be salted? it is thenceforth good for nothing, but to be cast out, and to be trodden under foot of men."

like you got tired of that little play-acting group you joined last year? [*Looking at* RUTH.] And what was it the year before that?

RUTH: The horseback-riding club for which she bought that fifty-five-dollar riding habit that's been hanging in the closet ever since!

MAMA: [*To* BENEATHA.] Why you got to flit so from one thing to another, baby?

BENEATHA: [*Sharply.*] I just want to learn to play the guitar. Is there anything wrong with that?

MAMA: Ain't nobody trying to stop you. I just wonders sometimes why you has to flit so from one thing to another all the time. You ain't never done nothing with all that camera equipment you brought home—

BENEATHA: I don't flit! I—I experiment with different forms of expression—

RUTH: Like riding a horse?

BENEATHA:—People have to express themselves one way or another.

MAMA: What is it you want to express?

BENEATHA: [*Angrily.*] Me! [MAMA *and* RUTH *look at each other and burst into raucous laughter.*] Don't worry—I don't expect you to understand.

MAMA: [*To change the subject.*] Who you going out with tomorrow night?

BENEATHA: [*With displeasure.*] George Murchison again.

MAMA: [*Pleased.*] Oh—you getting a little sweet on him?

RUTH: You ask me, this child ain't sweet on nobody but herself— [*Underbreath.*] Express herself!

[*They laugh.*]

BENEATHA: Oh—I like George all right, Mama. I mean I like him enough to go out with him and stuff, but—

RUTH: [*For devilment.*] What does *and stuff* mean?

BENEATHA: Mind your own business.

MAMA: Stop picking at her now, Ruth. [*A thoughtful pause, and then a suspicious sudden look at her daughter as she turns in her chair for emphasis.*] What *does* it mean?

BENEATHA: [*Wearily.*] Oh, I just mean I couldn't ever really be serious about George. He's—he's so shallow.

RUTH: Shallow—what do you mean he's shallow? He's *rich!*

MAMA: Hush, Ruth.

BENEATHA: I know he's rich. He knows he's rich, too.

RUTH: Well—what other qualities a man got to have to satisfy you, little girl?

BENEATHA: You wouldn't even begin to understand. Anybody who married Walter could not possibly understand.

MAMA: [*Outraged.*] What kind of way is that to talk about your brother?

BENEATHA: Brother is a flip—let's face it.

MAMA: [*To* RUTH, *helplessly.*] What's a flip?

RUTH: [*Glad to add kindling.*] She's saying he's crazy.

BENEATHA: Not crazy. Brother isn't really crazy yet—he—he's an elaborate neurotic.

MAMA: Hush your mouth!

BENEATHA: As for George. Well. George looks good—he's got a beautiful car and he takes me to nice places and, as my sister-in-law says, he is probably the richest boy I will ever get to know and I even like him sometimes—but if the Youngers are sitting around waiting to see if their little Bennie is going to tie up the family with the Murchisons, they are wasting their time.

RUTH: You mean you wouldn't marry George Murchison if he asked you someday? That pretty, rich thing? Honey, I knew you was odd—

BENEATHA: No I would not marry him if all I felt for him was what I feel now. Besides, George's family wouldn't really like it.

MAMA: Why not?

BENEATHA: Oh, Mama—The Murchisons are honest-to-God-real-*live*-rich colored people, and the only people in the world who are more snobbish than rich white people are rich colored people. I thought everybody knew that. I've met Mrs. Murchison. She's a scene!

MAMA: You must not dislike people 'cause they well off, honey.

BENEATHA: Why not? It makes just as much sense as disliking people 'cause they are poor, and lots of people do that.

RUTH: [*A wisdom-of-the-ages manner. To* MAMA.] Well, she'll get over some of this—

BENEATHA: Get over it? What are you talking about, Ruth? Listen, I'm going to be a doctor. I'm not worried about who I'm going to marry yet—if I ever get married.

MAMA *and* RUTH: *If!*

MAMA: Now, Bennie—

BENEATHA: Oh, I probably will . . . but first I'm going to be a doctor, and George, for one, still thinks that's pretty funny. I couldn't be bothered with that. I am going to be a doctor and everybody around here better understand that!

MAMA: [*Kindly.*] 'Course you going to be a doctor, honey, God willing.

BENEATHA: [*Drily.*] God hasn't got a thing to do with it.

MAMA: Beneatha—that just wasn't necessary.

BENEATHA: Well—neither is God. I get sick of hearing about God.

MAMA: Beneatha!

BENEATHA: I mean it! I'm just tired of hearing about God all the time. What has He got to do with anything? Does He pay tuition?

MAMA: You 'bout to get your fresh little jaw slapped!

RUTH: That's just what she needs, all right!

BENEATHA: Why? Why can't I say what I want to around here, like everybody else?

MAMA: It don't sound nice for a young girl to say things like that— you wasn't brought up that way. Me and your father went to trouble to get you and Brother to church every Sunday.

BENEATHA: Mama, you don't understand. It's all a matter of ideas, and God is just one idea I don't accept. It's not important. I am not going out and be immoral or commit crimes because I don't believe in God. I don't even think about it. It's just that I get tired of Him getting credit for all the things the human race achieves through its own stubborn effort. There simply is no blasted God—there is only man and it is he who makes miracles!

[MAMA *absorbs this speech, studies her daughter and rises slowly and crosses to* BENEATHA *and slaps her powerfully across the face. After, there is only silence and the daughter drops her eyes from her mother's face, and* MAMA *is very tall before her.*]

MAMA: Now—you say after me, in my mother's house there is still God. [*There is a long pause and* BENEATHA *stares at the floor wordlessly.* MAMA *repeats the phrase with precision and cool emotion.*] In my mother's house there is still God.

BENEATHA: In my mother's house there is still God.

[*A long pause.*]

MAMA: [*Walking away from* BENEATHA, *too disturbed for triumphant posture. Stopping and turning back to her daughter.*] There are some ideas we ain't going to have in this house. Not long as I am at the head of this family.

BENEATHA: Yes, ma'am.

[MAMA *walks out of the room.*]

RUTH: [*Almost gently, with profound understanding.*] You think you a woman, Bennie—but you still a little girl. What you did was childish—so you got treated like a child.

BENEATHA: I see. [*Quietly.*] I also see that everybody thinks it's all right for Mama to be a tyrant. But all the tyranny in the world will never put a God in the heavens!

[*She picks up her books and goes out.*]

RUTH: [*Goes to* MAMA'*s door.*] She said she was sorry.

MAMA: [*Coming out, going to her plant.*] They frightens me, Ruth. My children.

RUTH: You got good children, Lena. They just a little off sometimes— but they're good.

MAMA: No—there's something come down between me and them that don't let us understand each other and I don't know what it is. One done almost lost his mind thinking 'bout money all the time and the other done commence to talk about things I can't seem to understand in no form or fashion. What is it that's changing, Ruth?

RUTH: [*Soothingly, older than her years.*] Now . . . you taking it all too seriously. You just got strong-willed children and it takes a strong woman like you to keep 'em in hand.

MAMA: [*Looking at her plant and sprinkling a little water on it.*] They spirited all right, my children. Got to admit they got spirit— Bennie and Walter. Like this little old plant that ain't never had enough sunshine or nothing—and look at it . . .

[*She has her back to* RUTH, *who has had to stop ironing and lean against something and put the back of her hand to her forehead.*]

RUTH: [*Trying to keep* MAMA *from noticing.*] You . . . sure . . . loves that little old thing, don't you? . . .

MAMA: Well, I always wanted me a garden like I used to see some- times at the back of the houses down home. This plant is close as I ever got to having one. [*She looks out of the window as she replaces the plant.*] Lord, ain't nothing as dreary as the view from this window on a dreary day, is there? Why ain't you singing this morning, Ruth? Sing that "No Ways Tired."[7] That song always lifts me up so—[*She turns at last to see that* RUTH *has slipped quietly into a chair, in a state of semiconsciousness.*] Ruth! Ruth honey—what's the matter with you . . . Ruth!

[*Curtain.*]

SCENE 2

It is the following morning; a Saturday morning, and house cleaning is in progress at the Youngers. Furniture has been shoved hither and yon and MAMA *is giving the kitchen-area walls a washing down.* BENEATHA, *in dungarees, with a handkerchief tied around her face, is spraying insecticide into the cracks in the walls. As they work, the radio is on and a South Side disk-jockey program is inappropriately filling the house with a rather exotic saxophone blues.* TRAVIS, *the sole idle one, is leaning on his arms, looking out of the window.*

TRAVIS: Grandmama, that stuff Bennie is using smells awful. Can I go downstairs, please?

MAMA: Did you get all them chores done already? I ain't seen you doing much.

TRAVIS: Yes'm—finished early. Where did Mama go this morning?

MAMA: [*Looking at* BENEATHA.] She had to go on a little errand.

TRAVIS: Where?

MAMA: To tend to her business.

TRAVIS: Can I go outside then?

MAMA: Oh, I guess so. You better stay right in front of the house, though . . . and keep a good lookout for the postman.

TRAVIS: Yes'm. [*He starts out and decides to give his aunt* BENEATHA *a good swat on the legs as he passes her.*] Leave them poor little old cockroaches alone, they ain't bothering you none.

[*He runs as she swings the spray gun at him both viciously and playfully.* WALTER *enters from the bedroom and goes to the phone.*]

MAMA: Look out there, girl, before you be spilling some of that stuff on that child!

---

7. "I Don't Feel No Ways Tired," a gospel song by the Reverend James Cleveland (1931–1991).

TRAVIS: [*Teasing.*] That's right—look out now!

[*He exits.*]

BENEATHA: [*Drily.*] I can't imagine that it would hurt him—it has never hurt the roaches.

MAMA: Well, little boys' hides ain't as tough as South Side roaches.

WALTER: [*Into phone.*] Hello—Let me talk to Willy Harris.

MAMA: You better get over there behind the bureau. I seen one marching out of there like Napoleon yesterday.

WALTER: Hello, Willy? It ain't come yet. It'll be here in a few minutes. Did the lawyer give you the papers?

BENEATHA: There's really only one way to get rid of them, Mama—

MAMA: How?

BENEATHA: Set fire to this building.

WALTER: Good. Good. I'll be right over.

BENEATHA: Where did Ruth go, Walter?

WALTER: I don't know.

[*He exits abruptly.*]

BENEATHA: Mama, where did Ruth go?

MAMA: [*Looking at her with meaning.*] To the doctor, I think.

BENEATHA: The doctor? What's the matter? [*They exchange glances.*] You don't think—

MAMA: [*With her sense of drama.*] Now I ain't saying what I think. But I ain't never been wrong 'bout a woman neither.

[*The phone rings.*]

BENEATHA: [*At the phone.*] Hay-lo . . . [*Pause, and a moment of recognition.*] Well—when did you get back! . . . And how was it? . . . Of course I've missed you—in my way . . . This morning? No . . . house cleaning and all that and Mama hates it if I let people come over when the house is like this . . . You *have?* Well, that's different . . . What is it—Oh, what the hell, come on over . . . Right, see you then.

[*She hangs up.*]

MAMA: [*Who has listened vigorously, as is her habit.*] Who is that you inviting over here with this house looking like this? You ain't got the pride you was born with!

BENEATHA: Asagai doesn't care how houses look, Mama—he's an intellectual.

MAMA: *Who?*

BENEATHA: Asagai—Joseph Asagai. He's an African boy I met on campus. He's been studying in Canada all summer.

MAMA: What's his name?

BENEATHA: Asagai, Joseph. Ah-sah-guy . . . He's from Nigeria.

MAMA: Oh, that's the little country that was founded by slaves way back . . .

BENEATHA: No, Mama—that's Liberia.

MAMA: I don't think I never met no African before.

BENEATHA: Well, do me a favor and don't ask him a whole lot of ignorant questions about Africans. I mean, do they wear clothes and all that—

MAMA: Well, now, I guess if you think we so ignorant 'round here maybe you shouldn't bring your friends here—

BENEATHA: It's just that people ask such crazy things. All anyone seems to know about when it comes to Africa is Tarzan—

MAMA: [*Indignantly.*] Why should I know anything about Africa?

BENEATHA: Why do you give money at church for the missionary work?

MAMA: Well, that's to help save people.

BENEATHA: You mean save them from *heathenism*—

MAMA: [*Innocently.*] Yes.

BENEATHA: I'm afraid they need more salvation from the British and the French.[8]

[RUTH *comes in forlornly and pulls off her coat with dejection. They both turn to look at her.*]

RUTH: [*Dispiritedly.*] Well, I guess from all the happy faces—everybody knows.

BENEATHA: You pregnant?

MAMA: Lord have mercy, I sure hope it's a little old girl. Travis ought to have a sister.

[BENEATHA *and* RUTH *give her a hopeless look for this grandmotherly enthusiasm.*]

BENEATHA: How far along are you?

RUTH: Two months.

---

8. In the 1950s, seven African nations won their independence from European colonizers. In 1959, over forty other countries were still controlled by foreign powers, mostly France and the United Kingdom.

BENEATHA: Did you mean to? I mean did you plan it or was it an accident?

MAMA: What do you know about planning or not planning?

BENEATHA: Oh, Mama.

RUTH: [*Wearily.*] She's twenty years old, Lena.

BENEATHA: Did you plan it, Ruth?

RUTH: Mind your own business.

BENEATHA: It is my business—where is he going to live, on the roof? [*There is silence following the remark as the three women react to the sense of it.*] Gee—I didn't mean that, Ruth, honest. Gee, I don't feel like that at all. I—I think it is wonderful.

RUTH: [*Dully.*] Wonderful.

BENEATHA: Yes—really.

MAMA: [*Looking at* RUTH, *worried.*] Doctor say everything going to be all right?

RUTH: [*Far away.*] Yes—she says everything is going to be fine . . .

MAMA: [*Immediately suspicious.*] "She"—What doctor you went to?
[RUTH *folds over, near hysteria.*]

MAMA: [*Worriedly hovering over* RUTH.] Ruth honey—what's the matter with you—you sick?
[RUTH *has her fists clenched on her thighs and is fighting hard to suppress a scream that seems to be rising in her.*]

BENEATHA: What's the matter with her, Mama?

MAMA: [*Working her fingers in* RUTH's *shoulder to relax her.*] She be all right. Women gets right depressed sometimes when they get her way. [*Speaking softly, expertly, rapidly.*] Now you just relax. That's right . . . just lean back, don't think 'bout nothing at all . . . nothing at all—

RUTH: I'm all right . . .
[*The glassy-eyed look melts and then she collapses into a fit of heavy sobbing. The bell rings.*]

BENEATHA: Oh, my God—that must be Asagai.

MAMA: [*To* RUTH.] Come on now, honey. You need to lie down and rest awhile . . . then have some nice hot food.
[*They exit,* RUTH's *weight on her mother-in-law.* BENEATHA, *herself profoundly disturbed, opens the door to admit a rather dramatic-looking young man with a large package.*]

ASAGAI: Hello, Alaiyo—

BENEATHA: [*Holding the door open and regarding him with pleasure.*] Hello . . . [*Long pause.*] Well—come in. And please excuse everything. My mother was very upset about my letting anyone come here with the place like this.

ASAGAI: [*Coming into the room.*] You look disturbed too . . . Is something wrong?

BENEATHA: [*Still at the door, absently.*] Yes . . . we've all got acute ghettoitus. [*She smiles and comes toward him, finding a cigarette and sitting.*] So—sit down! How was Canada?

ASAGAI: [*A sophisticate.*] Canadian.

BENEATHA: [*Looking at him.*] I'm very glad you are back.

ASAGAI: [*Looking back at her in turn.*] Are you really?

BENEATHA: Yes—very.

ASAGAI: Why—you were quite glad when I went away. What happened?

BENEATHA: You went away.

ASAGAI: Ahhhhhhhh.

BENEATHA: Before—you wanted to be so serious before there was time.

ASAGAI: How much time must there be before one knows what one feels?

BENEATHA: [*Stalling this particular conversation. Her hands pressed together, in a deliberately childish gesture.*] What did you bring me?

ASAGAI: [*Handing her the package.*] Open it and see.

BENEATHA: [*Eagerly opening the package and drawing out some records and the colorful robes of a Nigerian woman.*] Oh, Asagai! . . . You got them for me! . . . How beautiful . . . and the records too! [*She lifts out the robes and runs to the mirror with them and holds the drapery up in front of herself.*]

ASAGAI: [*Coming to her at the mirror.*] I shall have to teach you how to drape it properly. [*He flings the material about her for the moment and stands back to look at her.*] Ah—*Oh-pay-gay-day, oh-gbah-mu-shay.* [*A Yoruba exclamation for admiration.*] You wear it well . . . very well . . . mutilated hair and all.

BENEATHA: [*Turning suddenly.*] My hair—what's wrong with my hair?

ASAGAI: [*Shrugging.*] Were you born with it like that?

BENEATHA: [*Reaching up to touch it.*] No . . . of course not.

[*She looks back to the mirror, disturbed.*]

ASAGAI: [*Smiling.*] How then?

BENEATHA: You know perfectly well how . . . as crinkly as yours . . . that's how.

ASAGAI: And it is ugly to you that way?

BENEATHA: [*Quickly.*] Oh, no—not ugly . . . [*More slowly, apologetically.*] But it's so hard to manage when it's, well—raw.

ASAGAI: And so to accommodate that—you mutilate it every week?

BENEATHA: It's not mutilation!

ASAGAI: [*Laughing aloud at her seriousness.*] Oh . . . please! I am only teasing you because you are so very serious about these things. [*He stands back from her and folds his arms across his chest as he watches her pulling at her hair and frowning in the mirror.*] Do you remember the first time you met me at school? . . . [*He laughs.*] You came up to me and you said—and I thought you were the most serious little thing I had ever seen—you said: [*He imitates her.*] "Mr. Asagai—I want very much to talk with you. About Africa. You see, Mr. Asagai, I am looking for my *identity!*" [*He laughs.*]

BENEATHA: [*Turning to him, not laughing.*] Yes—
[*Her face is quizzical, profoundly disturbed.*]

ASAGAI: [*Still teasing and reaching out and taking her face in his hands and turning her profile to him.*] Well . . . it is true that this is not so much a profile of a Hollywood queen as perhaps a queen of the Nile—[*A mock dismissal of the importance of the question.*] But what does it matter? Assimilationism[9] is so popular in your country.

BENEATHA: [*Wheeling, passionately, sharply.*] I am not an assimilationist!

ASAGAI: [*The protest hangs in the room for a moment and* ASAGAI *studies her, his laughter fading.*] Such a serious one. [*There is a pause.*] So—you like the robes? You must take excellent care of them—they are from my sister's personal wardrobe.

BENEATHA: [*With incredulity.*] You—you sent all the way home—for me?

ASAGAI: [*With charm.*] For you—I would do much more . . . Well, that is what I came for. I must go.

BENEATHA: Will you call me Monday?

---

9. A minority or marginalized culture molding itself into the majority or mainstream culture.

ASAGAI: Yes . . . We have a great deal to talk about. I mean about identity and time and all that.

BENEATHA: Time?

ASAGAI: Yes. About how much time one needs to know what one feels.

BENEATHA: You never understood that there is more than one kind of feeling which can exist between a man and a woman—or, at least, there should be.

ASAGAI: [Shaking his head negatively but gently.] No. Between a man and a woman there need be only one kind of feeling. I have that for you . . . Now even . . . right this moment . . .

BENEATHA: I know—and by itself—it won't do. I can find that any-where.

ASAGAI: For a woman it should be enough.

BENEATHA: I know—because that's what it says in all the novels that men write. But it isn't. Go ahead and laugh—but I'm not interested in being someone's little episode in America or—[With feminine vengeance.]—one of them! [ASAGAI has burst into laughter again.] That's funny as hell, huh!

ASAGAI: It's just that every American girl I have known has said that to me. White—black—in this you are all the same. And the same speech, too!

BENEATHA: [Angrily.] Yuk, yuk, yuk!

ASAGAI: It's how you can be sure that the world's most liberated women are not liberated at all. You all talk about it too much!

[MAMA enters and is immediately all social charm because of the presence of a guest.]

BENEATHA: Oh—Mama—this is Mr. Asagai.

MAMA: How do you do?

ASAGAI: [Total politeness to an elder.] How do you do, Mrs. Younger. Please forgive me for coming at such an outrageous hour on a Saturday.

MAMA: Well, you are quite welcome. I just hope you understand that our house don't always look like this. [Chatterish.] You must come again. I would love to hear all about—[Not sure of the name.]—your country. I think it's so sad the way our American Negroes don't know nothing about Africa 'cept Tarzan and all that. And all that money they pour into these churches when they ought to be helping you people over there drive out them French and Englishmen done taken away your land.

[*The mother flashes a slightly superior look at her daughter upon completion of the recitation.*]

ASAGAI: [*Taken aback by this sudden and acutely unrelated expression of sympathy.*] Yes . . . yes . . .

MAMA: [*Smiling at him suddenly and relaxing and looking him over.*] How many miles is it from here to where you come from?

ASAGAI: Many thousands.

MAMA: [*Looking at him as she would* WALTER.] I bet you don't half look after yourself, being away from your mama either. I spec you better come 'round here from time to time and get yourself some decent home-cooked meals . . .

ASAGAI: [*Moved.*] Thank you. Thank you very much. [*They are all quiet, then*—] Well . . . I must go. I will call you Monday, Alaiyo.

MAMA: What's that he call you?

ASAGAI: Oh—"Alaiyo." I hope you don't mind. It is what you would call a nickname, I think. It is a Yoruba word. I am a Yoruba.

MAMA: [*Looking at* BENEATHA.] I—I thought he was from—

ASAGAI: [*Understanding.*] Nigeria is my country. Yoruba is my tribal origin—

BENEATHA: You didn't tell us what Alaiyo means . . . for all I know, you might be calling me Little Idiot or something . . .

ASAGAI: Well . . . let me see . . . I do not know how just to explain it . . . The sense of a thing can be so different when it changes languages.

BENEATHA: You're evading.

ASAGAI: No—really it is difficult . . . [*Thinking.*] It means . . . it means One for Whom Bread—Food—Is Not Enough. [*He looks at her.*] Is that all right?

BENEATHA: [*Understanding, softly.*] Thank you.

MAMA: [*Looking from one to the other and not understanding any of it.*] Well . . . that's nice . . . You must come see us again—Mr.—

ASAGAI: Ah-sah-guy . . .

MAMA: Yes . . . Do come again.

ASAGAI: Good-bye.

[*He exits.*]

MAMA: [*After him.*] Lord, that's a pretty thing just went out here! [*Insinuatingly, to her daughter.*] Yes, I guess I see why we done commence to get so interested in Africa 'round here. Missionaries my aunt Jenny!

[*She exits.*]

BENEATHA: Oh, Mama! . . .

[*She picks up the Nigerian dress and holds it up to her in front of the mirror again. She sets the headdress on haphazardly and then notices her hair again and clutches at it and then replaces the headdress and frowns at herself. Then she starts to wriggle in front of the mirror as she thinks a Nigerian woman might.* TRAVIS *enters and regards her.*]

TRAVIS: You cracking up?

BENEATHA: Shut up.

[*She pulls the headdress off and looks at herself in the mirror and clutches at her hair again and squinches her eyes as if trying to imagine something. Then, suddenly, she gets her raincoat and kerchief and hurriedly prepares for going out.*]

MAMA: [*Coming back into the room.*] She's resting now. Travis, baby, run next door and ask Miss Johnson to please let me have a little kitchen cleanser. This here can is empty as Jacob's kettle.

TRAVIS: I just came in.

MAMA: Do as you told. [*He exits and she looks at her daughter.*] Where you going?

BENEATHA: [*Halting at the door.*] To become a queen of the Nile!

[*She exits in a breathless blaze of glory.* RUTH *appears in the bedroom doorway.*]

MAMA: Who told you to get up?

RUTH: Ain't nothing wrong with me to be lying in no bed for. Where did Bennie go?

MAMA: [*Drumming her fingers.*] Far as I could make out—to Egypt. [RUTH *just looks at her.*] What time is it getting to?

RUTH: Ten twenty. And the mailman going to ring that bell this morning just like he done every morning for the last umpteen years.

[TRAVIS *comes in with the cleanser can.*]

TRAVIS: She say to tell you that she don't have much.

MAMA: [*Angrily.*] Lord, some people I could name sure is tightfisted! [*Directing her grandson.*] Mark two cans of cleanser down on the list there. If she that hard up for kitchen cleanser, I sure don't want to forget to get her none!

RUTH: Lena—maybe the woman is just short on cleanser—

MAMA: [*Not listening.*]—Much baking powder as she done borrowed from me all these years, she could of done gone into the baking business!

[*The bell sounds suddenly and sharply and all three are stunned—serious and silent—mid-speech. In spite of all the other conversations and distractions of the morning, this is what they have been waiting for, even* TRAVIS, *who looks helplessly from his mother to his grandmother.* RUTH *is the first to come to life again.*]

RUTH: [*To* TRAVIS.] *Get down them steps, boy!*

[TRAVIS *snaps to life and flies out to get the mail.*]

MAMA: [*Her eyes wide, her hand to her breast.*] You mean it done really come?

RUTH: [*Excited.*] Oh, Miss Lena!

MAMA: [*Collecting herself.*] Well . . . I don't know what we all so excited about 'round here for. We known it was coming for months.

RUTH: That's a whole lot different from having it come and being able to hold it in your hands . . . a piece of paper worth ten thousand dollars . . . [TRAVIS *bursts back into the room. He holds the envelope high above his head, like a little dancer, his face is radiant and he is breathless. He moves to his grandmother with sudden slow ceremony and puts the envelope into her hands. She accepts it, and then merely holds it and looks at it.*] Come on! Open it . . . Lord have mercy, I wish Walter Lee was here!

TRAVIS: Open it, Grandmama!

MAMA: [*Staring at it.*] Now you all be quiet. It's just a check.

RUTH: Open it . . .

MAMA: [*Still staring at it.*] Now don't act silly . . . We ain't never been no people to act silly 'bout no money—

RUTH: [*Swiftly.*] We ain't never had none before—*open it!*

[MAMA *finally makes a good strong tear and pulls out the thin blue slice of paper and inspects it closely. The boy and his mother study it raptly over* MAMA'*s shoulders.*]

MAMA: *Travis!* [*She is counting off with doubt.*] Is that the right number of zeros.

TRAVIS: Yes'm . . . ten thousand dollars. Gaalee, Grandmama, you rich.

MAMA: [*She holds the check away from her, still looking at it. Slowly her face sobers into a mask of unhappiness.*] Ten thousand dollars. [*She hands it to* RUTH.] Put it away somewhere, Ruth. [*She does not look at* RUTH; *her eyes seem to be seeing something somewhere very far off.*] Ten thousand dollars they give you. Ten thousand dollars.

TRAVIS: [*To his mother, sincerely.*] What's the matter with Grand-mama—don't she want to be rich?

RUTH: [*Distractedly.*] You go on out and play now, baby. [TRAVIS *exits.* MAMA *starts wiping dishes absently, humming intently to herself.* RUTH *turns to her, with kind exasperation.*] You've gone and got yourself upset.

MAMA: [*Not looking at her.*] I spec if it wasn't for you all . . . I would just put that money away or give it to the church or something.

RUTH: Now what kind of talk is that. Mr. Younger would just be plain mad if he could hear you talking foolish like that.

MAMA: [*Stopping and staring off.*] Yes . . . he sure would. [*Sighing.*] We got enough to do with that money, all right. [*She halts then, and turns and looks at her daughter-in-law hard;* RUTH *avoids her eyes and* MAMA *wipes her hands with finality and starts to speak firmly to* RUTH.] Where did you go today, girl?

RUTH: To the doctor.

MAMA: [*Impatiently.*] Now, Ruth . . . you know better than that. Old Doctor Jones is strange enough in his way but there ain't nothing 'bout him make somebody slip and call him "she"—like you done this morning.

RUTH: Well, that's what happened—my tongue slipped.

MAMA: You went to see that woman, didn't you?

RUTH: [*Defensively, giving herself away.*] What woman you talking about?

MAMA: [*Angrily.*] That woman who—
    [WALTER *enters in great excitement.*]

WALTER: Did it come?

MAMA: [*Quietly.*] Can't you give people a Christian greeting before you start asking about money?

WALTER: [*To* RUTH.] Did it come? [RUTH *unfolds the check and lays it quietly before him, watching him intently with thoughts of her own.* WALTER *sits down and grasps it close and counts off the zeros.*]

Ten thousand dollars—[*He turns suddenly, frantically to his mother and draws some papers out of his breast pocket.*] Mama—look. Old Willy Harris put everything on paper—

MAMA: Son—I think you ought to talk to your wife . . . I'll go on out and leave you alone if you want—

WALTER: I can talk to her later—Mama, look—

MAMA: Son—

WALTER: WILL SOMEBODY PLEASE LISTEN TO ME TODAY!

MAMA: [*Quietly.*] I don't 'low no yellin' in this house, Walter Lee, and you know it—[WALTER *stares at them in frustration and starts to speak several times.*] And there ain't going to be no investing in no liquor stores. I don't aim to have to speak on that again.

   [*A long pause.*]

WALTER: Oh—so you don't aim to have to speak on that again? So you have decided . . . [*Crumpling his papers.*] Well, *you* tell that to my boy tonight when you put him to sleep on the living-room couch . . . [*Turning to* MAMA *and speaking directly to her.*] Yeah—and tell it to my wife, Mama, tomorrow when she has to go out of here to look after somebody else's kids. And tell it to *me*, Mama, every time we need a new pair of curtains and I have to watch *you* go out and work in somebody's kitchen. Yeah, you tell me then!

   [WALTER *starts out.*]

RUTH: Where you going?

WALTER: I'm going out!

RUTH: Where?

WALTER: Just out of this house somewhere—

RUTH: [*Getting her coat.*] I'll come too.

WALTER: I don't want you to come!

RUTH: I got something to talk to you about, Walter.

WALTER: That's too bad.

MAMA: [*Still quietly.*] Walter Lee—[*She waits and he finally turns and looks at her.*] Sit down.

WALTER: I'm a grown man, Mama.

MAMA: Ain't nobody said you wasn't grown. But you still in my house and my presence. And as long as you are—you'll talk to your wife civil. Now sit down.

RUTH: [*Suddenly.*] Oh, let him go on out and drink himself to death! He makes me sick to my stomach! [*She flings her coat against him.*]

WALTER: [*Violently.*] And you turn mine too, baby! [RUTH *goes into their bedroom and slams the door behind her.*] That was my greatest mistake—

MAMA: [*Still quietly.*] Walter, what is the matter with you?

WALTER: Matter with me? Ain't nothing the matter with *me*!

MAMA: Yes there is. Something eating you up like a crazy man. Something more than me not giving you this money. The past few years I been watching it happen to you. You get all nervous acting and kind of wild in the eyes—[WALTER *jumps up impatiently at her words.*] I said sit there now, I'm talking to you!

WALTER: Mama—I don't need no nagging at me today.

MAMA: Seem like you getting to a place where you always tied up in some kind of knot about something. But if anybody ask you 'bout it you just yell at 'em and bust out the house and go out and drink somewheres. Walter Lee, people can't live with that. Ruth's a good, patient girl in her way—but you getting to be too much. Boy, don't make the mistake of driving that girl away from you.

WALTER: Why—what she do for me?

MAMA: She loves you.

WALTER: Mama—I'm going out. I want to go off somewhere and be by myself for a while.

MAMA: I'm sorry 'bout your liquor store, son. It just wasn't the thing for us to do. That's what I want to tell you about—

WALTER: I got to go out, Mama—
    [*He rises.*]

MAMA: It's dangerous, son.

WALTER: What's dangerous?

MAMA: When a man goes outside his home to look for peace.

WALTER: [*Beseechingly.*] Then why can't there never be no peace in this house then?

MAMA: You done found it in some other house?

WALTER: No—there ain't no woman! Why do women always think there's a woman somewhere when a man gets restless. [*Coming to her.*] Mama—Mama—I want so many things . . .

MAMA: Yes, son—

WALTER: I want so many things that they are driving me kind of crazy . . . Mama—look at me.

MAMA: I'm looking at you. You a good-looking boy. You got a job, a nice wife, a fine boy and—

WALTER: A job. [*Looks at her.*] Mama, a job? I open and close car doors all day long. I drive a man around in his limousine and I say, "Yes, sir; no, sir; very good, sir; shall I take the Drive, sir?" Mama, that ain't no kind of job . . . that ain't nothing at all. [*Very quietly.*] Mama, I don't know if I can make you understand.

MAMA: Understand what, baby?

WALTER: [*Quietly.*] Sometimes it's like I can see the future stretched out in front of me—just plain as day. The future, Mama. Hanging over there at the edge of my days. Just waiting for me—a big, looming blank space—full of *nothing*. Just waiting for *me*. [*Pause.*] Mama—sometimes when I'm downtown and I pass them cool, quiet-looking restaurants where them white boys are sitting back and talking 'bout things . . . sitting there turning deals worth millions of dollars . . . sometimes I see guys don't look much older than me—

MAMA: Son—how come you talk so much 'bout money?

WALTER: [*With immense passion.*] Because it is life, Mama!

MAMA: [*Quietly.*]Oh—[*Very quietly.*] So now it's life. Money is life. Once upon a time freedom used to be life—now it's money. I guess the world really do change . . .

WALTER: No—it was always money, Mama. We just didn't know about it.

MAMA: No . . . something has changed. [*She looks at him.*] You something new, boy. In my time we was worried about not being lynched and getting to the North if we could and how to stay alive and still have a pinch of dignity too . . . Now here come you and Beneatha—talking 'bout things we ain't never even thought about hardly, me and your daddy. You ain't satisfied or proud of nothing we done. I mean that you had a home; that we kept you out of trouble till you was grown; that you don't have to ride to work on the back of nobody's streetcar—You my children—but how different we done become.

WALTER: You just don't understand, Mama, you just don't understand.

MAMA: Son—do you know your wife is expecting another baby? [WALTER *stands, stunned, and absorbs what his mother has said.*] That's what she wanted to talk to you about. [WALTER *sinks down into a chair.*] This ain't for me to be telling—but you ought to know. [*She waits.*] I think Ruth is thinking 'bout getting rid of that child.[1]

WALTER: [*Slowly understanding.*] No—no—Ruth wouldn't do that.

MAMA: When the world gets ugly enough—a woman will do anything for her family. *The part that's already living.*

WALTER: You don't know Ruth, Mama, if you think she would do that.

[RUTH *opens the bedroom door and stands there a little limp.*]

RUTH: [*Beaten.*] Yes I would too, Walter. [*Pause.*] I gave her a five-dollar down payment.

[*There is total silence as the man stares at his wife and the mother stares at her son.*]

MAMA: [*Presently.*] Well—[*Tightly.*] Well—son, I'm waiting to hear you say something . . . I'm waiting to hear how you be your father's son. Be the man he was . . . [*Pause.*] Your wife say she going to destroy your child. And I'm waiting to hear you talk like him and say we a people who give children life, not who destroys them—[*She rises.*] I'm waiting to see you stand up and look like your daddy and say we done give up one baby to poverty and that we ain't going to give up nary another one . . . I'm waiting.

WALTER: Ruth—

MAMA: If you a son of mine, tell her! [WALTER *turns, looks at her and can say nothing. She continues, bitterly.*] You . . . you are a disgrace to your father's memory. Somebody get me my hat.

[*Curtain.*]

ACT 2
SCENE 1

Time: Later the same day.

At rise: RUTH *is ironing again. She has the radio going. Presently* BENEATHA's *bedroom door opens and* RUTH's *mouth falls and she puts down the iron in fascination.*

1. Though abortions were readily available in the 1940s and 1950s, the procedure was illegal and often dangerous.

RUTH: What have we got on tonight!

BENEATHA: [*Emerging grandly from the doorway so that we can see her thoroughly robed in the costume* ASAGAI *brought.*] You are looking at what a well-dressed Nigerian woman wears—[*She parades for* RUTH, *her hair completely hidden by the headdress; she is coquettishly fanning herself with an ornate oriental fan, mistakenly more like Butterfly*[2] *than any Nigerian that ever was.*] Isn't it beautiful? [*She promenades to the radio and, with an arrogant flourish, turns off the good loud blues that is playing.*] Enough of this assimilationist junk! [RUTH *follows her with her eyes as she goes to the phonograph and puts on a record and turns and waits ceremoniously for the music to come up. Then, with a shout*—] OCOMOGOSIAY!

[RUTH *jumps. The music comes up, a lovely Nigerian melody.* BENEATHA *listens, enraptured, her eyes far away*—"*back to the past.*" *She begins to dance.* RUTH *is dumbfounded.*]

RUTH: What kind of dance is that?

BENEATHA: A folk dance.

RUTH: [*Pearl Bailey.*][3] What kind of folks do that, honey?

BENEATHA: It's from Nigeria. It's a dance of welcome.

RUTH: Who you welcoming?

BENEATHA: The men back to the village.

RUTH: Where they been?

BENEATHA: How should I know—out hunting or something. Anyway, they are coming back now . . .

RUTH: Well, that's good.

BENEATHA: [*With the record.*]

Alundi, alundi
Alundi alunya
Jop pu a jeepua
Ang gu sooooooooooo

2. Perhaps Madame Butterfly, the titular heroine and tragic victim of Giacomo Puccini's 1907 opera about a love affair between a Japanese woman and an American naval officer. Or Butterfly McQueen (1911–1995), the African American actor most famous for her role as Prissy in the 1938 *Gone with the Wind*. Prissy speaks the notorious line, "I don't know nuthin' 'bout birthin' babies," a line that came to exemplify Hollywood's stereotyping of African Americans.

3. In other words, in imitation of the singer and actor Pearl Bailey (1918–1990).

Ai yai yae . . .
Ayehaye—alundi . . .

[WALTER *comes in during this performance; he has obviously been drinking. He leans against the door heavily and watches his sister, at first with distaste. Then his eyes look off—"back to the past"— as he lifts both his fists to the roof, screaming.*]

WALTER: YEAH . . . AND ETHIOPIA STRETCH FORTH HER HANDS AGAIN!⁴ . . .

RUTH: [*Drily, looking at him.*] Yes—and Africa sure is claiming her own tonight. [*She gives them both up and starts ironing again.*]

WALTER: [*All in a drunken, dramatic shout.*] Shut up! . . . I'm digging them drums . . . them drums move me! . . . [*He makes his weaving way to his wife's face and leans in close to her.*] In my *heart of hearts*—[*He thumps his chest.*]—I am much warrior!

RUTH: [*Without even looking up.*] In your heart of hearts you are much drunkard.

WALTER: [*Coming away from her and starting to wander around the room, shouting.*] Me and Jomo . . . [*Intently, in his sister's face. She has stopped dancing to watch him in this unknown mood.*] That's my man, Kenyatta.⁵ [*Shouting and thumping his chest.*] FLAMING SPEAR! HOT DAMN! [*He is suddenly in possession of an imaginary spear and actively spearing enemies all over the room.*] OCOMOGOSIAY . . . THE LION IS WAKING . . . OWIMOWEH!⁶ [*He pulls his shirt open and leaps up on a table and gestures with his spear. The bell rings.* RUTH *goes to answer.*]

4. A loose translation of Psalm 68, these lines were often invoked as a hopeful prediction of the restoration of independence to black nations. Ethiopia, which largely resisted European colonization, was unique among African nations and therefore enjoyed a special point of pride in the black cultural movement.

5. Jomo Kenyatta (1893–1978) would become the first president of the independent nation of Kenya (1964–78). In the late 1940s, he was a leader in the independence movement. The British incarcerated him on trumped-up charges in 1952, and he was still in prison when this play was written.

6. Walter and Beneatha are making up words that have plausible African sounds. "THE LION IS WAKING" might reference the song "Wimoweh" or "The Lion Sleeps Tonight." Pete Seeger popularized this song, a bastardization of a 1930s Zulu song, in the 1950s. According to Seeger, the song is about Chaka the Lion, who did not die but went to sleep when Europeans took over South Africa.

BENEATHA: [*To encourage* WALTER, *thoroughly caught up with this side of him.*] OCOMOGOSIAY, FLAMING SPEAR!

WALTER: [*On the table, very far gone, his eyes pure glass sheets. He sees what we cannot, that he is a leader of his people, a great chief, a descendant of Chaka,*[7] *and that the hour to march has come.*] Listen, my black brothers—

BENEATHA: OCOMOGOSIAY!

WALTER:—Do you hear the waters rushing against the shores of the coastlands—

BENEATHA: OCOMOGOSIAY!

WALTER:—Do you hear the screeching of the cocks in yonder hills beyond where the chiefs meet in council for the coming of the mighty war—

BENEATHA: OCOMOGOSIAY!

WALTER:—Do you hear the beating of the wings of the birds flying low over the mountains and the low places of our land—

[RUTH *opens the door.* GEORGE MURCHISON *enters.*]

BENEATHA: OCOMOGOSIAY!

WALTER:—Do you hear the singing of the women, singing the war songs of our fathers to the babies in the great houses . . . singing the sweet war songs? OH, DO YOU HEAR, MY BLACK BROTHERS!

BENEATHA: [*Completely gone.*] We hear you, Flaming Spear—

WALTER: Telling us to prepare for the greatness of the time—[*To* GEORGE.] Black Brother!

[*He extends his hand for the fraternal clasp.*]

GEORGE: Black Brother, hell!

RUTH: [*Having had enough, and embarrassed for the family.*] Beneatha, you got company—what's the matter with you? Walter Lee Younger, get down off that table and stop acting like a fool . . .

[WALTER *comes down off the table suddenly and makes a quick exit to the bathroom.*]

RUTH: He's had a little to drink . . . I don't know what her excuse is.

GEORGE: [*To* BENEATHA.] Look honey, we're going *to* the theatre— we're not going to be *in* it . . . so go change, huh?

---

7. Chaka or Shaka (1786–1828) was also a Zulu chief, known as the Black Napoleon. He was widely credited with revolutionizing African warfare and organizing a number of tribes into a nation. The British did not conquer the Zulus until 1879.

RUTH: You expect this boy to go out with you looking like that?

BENEATHA: [*Looking at* GEORGE.] That's up to George. If he's ashamed of his heritage—

GEORGE: Oh, don't be so proud of yourself, Bennie—just because you look eccentric.

BENEATHA: How can something that's natural be eccentric?

GEORGE: That's what being eccentric means—being natural. Get dressed.

BENEATHA: I don't like that, George.

RUTH: Why must you and your brother make an argument out of everything people say?

BENEATHA: Because I hate assimilationist Negroes!

RUTH: Will somebody please tell me what assimila-who-ever means!

GEORGE: Oh, it's just a college girl's way of calling people Uncle Toms[8]—but that isn't what it means at all.

RUTH: Well, what does it mean?

BENEATHA: [*Cutting* GEORGE *off and staring at him as she replies to* RUTH.] It means someone who is willing to give up his own culture and submerge himself completely in the dominant, and in this case, *oppressive* culture!

GEORGE: Oh, dear, dear, dear! Here we go! A lecture on the African past! On our Great West African Heritage! In one second we will hear all about the great Ashanti empires; the great Songhay civilizations; and the great sculpture of Bénin—and then some poetry in the Bantu—and the whole monologue will end with the word *heritage*![9] [*Nastily.*] Let's face it, baby, your heritage is nothing but a bunch of raggedy-assed spirituals and some grass huts!

BENEATHA: *Grass huts!* [RUTH *crosses to her and forcibly pushes her toward the bedroom.*] See there . . . you are standing there in your splendid ignorance talking about people who were the first to

---

8. The black hero of Harriet Beecher Stowe's 1852 *Uncle Tom's Cabin.* Though the novel was anti-slavery, the character Uncle Tom became synonymous with docile acceptance of white supremacy.

9. The Ashanti Empire was a West African nation in what is today Ghana; the British conquered and colonized the country in 1896. The Songhay or Songhai Empire flourished in West Africa in the fifteenth and sixteenth centuries. Bénin, an empire from 1440 to 1897 and located in modern-day Nigeria, is famed for its sculptures in bronze, ivory, and iron. *Bantu:* a linguistic and ethnic grouping of peoples in central, eastern, and south Africa. There are over five hundred languages in the Bantu grouping.

smelt iron on the face of the earth! [RUTH *is pushing her through the door.*] The Ashanti were performing surgical operations when the English—[RUTH *pulls the door to, with* BENEATHA *on the other side, and smiles graciously at* GEORGE. BENEATHA *opens the door and shouts the end of the sentence defiantly at* GEORGE.]—were still tattooing themselves with blue dragons . . . [*She goes back inside.*]

RUTH: Have a seat, George. [*They both sit.* RUTH *folds her hands rather primly on her lap, determined to demonstrate the civilization of the family.*] Warm, ain't it? I mean for September. [*Pause.*] Just like they always say about Chicago weather: If it's too hot or cold for you, just wait a minute and it'll change. [*She smiles happily at this cliché of clichés.*] Everybody say it's got to do with them bombs and things they keep setting off.[1] [*Pause.*] Would you like a nice cold beer?

GEORGE: No, thank you. I don't care for beer. [*He looks at his watch.*] I hope she hurries up.

RUTH: What time is the show?

GEORGE: It's an eight-thirty curtain. That's just Chicago, though. In New York standard curtain time is eight-forty.

[*He is rather proud of this knowledge.*]

RUTH: [*Properly appreciating it.*] You get to New York a lot?

GEORGE: [*Offhand.*] Few times a year.

RUTH: Oh—that's nice. I've never been to New York.

[WALTER *enters. We feel he has relieved himself, but the edge of unreality is still with him.*]

WALTER: New York ain't got nothing Chicago ain't. Just a bunch of hustling people all squeezed up together—being "Eastern."

[*He turns his face into a screw of displeasure.*]

GEORGE: Oh—you've been?

WALTER: *Plenty* of times.

RUTH: [*Shocked at the lie.*] Walter Lee Younger!

WALTER: [*Staring her down.*] Plenty! [*Pause.*] What we got to drink in this house? Why don't you offer this man some refreshment. [*To* GEORGE.] They don't know how to entertain people in this house, man.

GEORGE: Thank you—I don't really care for anything.

---

1. It was not uncommon in the 1950s to attribute weather anomalies to nuclear weapons testing.

WALTER: [*Feeling his head; sobriety coming.*] Where's Mama?

RUTH: She ain't come back yet.

WALTER: [*Looking* MURCHISON *over from head to toe, scrutinizing his carefully casual tweed sports jacket over cashmere V-neck sweater over soft eyelet shirt and tie, and soft slacks, finished off with white buckskin shoes.*] Why all you college boys wear them fairyish-looking white shoes?

RUTH: Walter Lee!

[GEORGE MURCHISON *ignores the remark.*]

WALTER: [*To* RUTH.] Well, they look crazy as hell—white shoes, cold as it is.

RUTH: [*Crushed.*] You have to excuse him—

WALTER: No he don't! Excuse me for what? What you always excusing me for! I'll excuse myself when I needs to be excused! [*A pause.*] They look as funny as them black knee socks Beneatha wears out of here all the time.

RUTH: It's the college *style*, Walter.

WALTER: Style, hell, she looks like she got burnt legs or something!

RUTH: Oh, Walter—

WALTER: [*An irritable mimic.*] Oh, Walter! Oh, Walter! [*To* MURCHISON.] How's your old man making out? I understand you all going to buy that big hotel on the Drive?[2] [*He finds a beer in the refrigerator, wanders over to* MURCHISON, *sipping and wiping his lips with the back of his hand, and straddling a chair backwards to talk to the other man.*] Shrewd move. Your old man is all right, man. [*Tapping his head and half winking for emphasis.*] I mean he knows how to operate. I mean he thinks *big*, you know what I mean, I mean for a *home*, you know? But I think he's kind of running out of ideas now. I'd like to talk to him. Listen, man, I got some plans that could turn this city upside down. I mean I think like he does. *Big*. Invest big, gamble big, hell, lose *big* if you have to, you know what I mean. It's hard to find a man on this whole South-side who understands my kind of thinking—you dig? [*He scrutinizes* MURCHISON *again, drinks his beer, squints his eyes and leans in close, confidential, man to man.*] Me and you ought to sit down and talk sometimes, man. Man, I got me some ideas . . .

---

2. Lake Shore Drive, a fashionable street along the shore of Lake Michigan.

GEORGE: [*With boredom.*] Yeah—sometimes we'll have to do that, Walter.

WALTER: [*Understanding the indifference, and offended.*] Yeah—well, when you get the time, man. I know you a busy little boy.

RUTH: Walter, please—

WALTER: [*Bitterly, hurt.*] I know ain't nothing in this world as busy as you colored college boys with your fraternity pins and white shoes . . .

RUTH: [*Covering her face with humiliation.*] Oh, Walter Lee—

WALTER: I see you all the time—with the books tucked under your arms—going to your [*British A—a mimic.*] "clahsses." And for what! What the hell you learning over there? Filling up your heads—[*Counting off on his fingers.*]—with the sociology and the psychology—but they teaching you how to be a man? How to take over and run the world? They teaching you how to run a rubber plantation or a steel mill? Naw—just to talk proper and read books and wear white shoes . . .

GEORGE: [*Looking at him with distaste, a little above it all.*] You're all wacked up with bitterness, man.

WALTER: [*Intently, almost quietly, between the teeth, glaring at the boy.*] And you—ain't you bitter, man? Ain't you just about had it yet? Don't you see no stars gleaming that you can't reach out and grab? You happy?—You contented son-of-a-bitch—you happy? You got it made? Bitter? Man, I'm a volcano. Bitter? Here I am a giant—surrounded by ants! Ants who can't even understand what it is the giant is talking about.

RUTH: [*Passionately and suddenly.*] Oh, Walter—ain't you with nobody!

WALTER: [*Violently.*] No! 'Cause ain't nobody with me! Not even my own mother!

RUTH: Walter, that's a terrible thing to say!

[BENEATHA *enters, dressed for the evening in a cocktail dress and earrings.*]

GEORGE: Well—hey, you look great.

BENEATHA: Let's go, George. See you all later.

RUTH: Have a nice time.

GEORGE: Thanks. Good night. [*To* WALTER, *sarcastically.*] Good night, *Prometheus.*[3]

[BENEATHA *and* GEORGE *exit.*]

---

3. Greek god associated with human aspirations and civilization. He gave humanity the gift of fire.

WALTER: [*To* RUTH.] Who is Prometheus?

RUTH: I don't know. Don't worry about it.

WALTER: [*In fury, pointing after* GEORGE.] See there—they get to a point where they can't insult you man to man—they got to go talk about something ain't nobody never heard of!

RUTH: How do you know it was an insult? [*To humor him.*] Maybe Prometheus is a nice fellow.

WALTER: Prometheus! I bet there ain't even no such thing! I bet that simpleminded clown—

RUTH: Walter—

[*She stops what she is doing and looks at him.*]

WALTER: [*Yelling.*] Don't start!

RUTH: Start what?

WALTER: Your nagging! Where was I? Who was I with? How much money did I spend?

RUTH: [*Plaintively.*] Walter Lee—why don't we just try to talk about it . . .

WALTER: [*Not listening.*] I been out talking with people who understand me. People who care about the things I got on my mind.

RUTH: [*Wearily.*] I guess that means people like Willy Harris.

WALTER: Yes, people like Willy Harris.

RUTH: [*With a sudden flash of impatience.*] Why don't you all just hurry up and go into the banking business and stop talking about it!

WALTER: Why? You want to know why? 'Cause we all tied up in a race of people that don't know how to do nothing but moan, pray and have babies!

[*The line is too bitter even for him and he looks at her and sits down.*]

RUTH: Oh, Walter . . . [*Softly.*] Honey, why can't you stop fighting me?

WALTER: [*Without thinking.*] Who's fighting you? Who even cares about you?

[*This line begins the retardation of his mood.*]

RUTH: Well—[*She waits a long time, and then with resignation starts to put away her things.*] I guess I might as well go on to bed . . . [*More or less to herself.*] I don't know where we lost it . . . but we have . . . [*Then, to him.*] I—I'm sorry about this new baby, Walter. I guess maybe I better go on and do what I started . . . I guess

I just didn't realize how bad things was with us . . . I guess I just
didn't really realize—[*She starts out to the bedroom and stops.*] You
want some hot milk?

WALTER: Hot milk?

RUTH: Yes—hot milk.

WALTER: Why hot milk?

RUTH: 'Cause after all that liquor you come home with you ought
to have something hot in your stomach.

WALTER: I don't want no milk.

RUTH: You want some coffee then?

WALTER: No, I don't want no coffee. I don't want nothing hot to
drink. [*Almost plaintively.*] Why you always trying to give me
something to eat?

RUTH: [*Standing and looking at him helplessly.*] What else can I give
you, Walter Lee Younger?

[*She stands and looks at him and presently turns to go out again.
He lifts his head and watches her going away from him in a new
mood which began to emerge when he asked her "Who cares about
you?"*]

WALTER: It's been rough, ain't it, baby? [*She hears and stops but does
not turn around and he continues to her back.*] I guess between two
people there ain't never as much understood as folks generally
thinks there is. I mean like between me and you—[*She turns to
face him.*] How we gets to the place where we scared to talk soft-
ness to each other. [*He waits, thinking hard himself.*] Why you
think it got to be like that? [*He is thoughtful, almost as a child
would be.*] Ruth, what is it gets into people ought to be close?

RUTH: I don't know, honey. I think about it a lot.

WALTER: On account of you and me, you mean? The way things are
with us. The way something done come down between us.

RUTH: There ain't so much between us, Walter . . . Not when you
come to me and try to talk to me. Try to be with me . . . a little
even.

WALTER: [*Total honesty.*] Sometimes . . . sometimes . . . I don't even
know how to try.

RUTH: Walter—

WALTER: Yes?

RUTH: [*Coming to him, gently and with misgiving, but coming to
him.*] Honey . . . life don't have to be like this. I mean sometimes

people can do things so that things are better . . . You remember how we used to talk when Travis was born . . . about the way we were going to live . . . the kind of house . . . [*She is stroking his head.*] Well, it's all starting to slip away from us . . .

[MAMA *enters, and* WALTER *jumps up and shouts at her.*]

WALTER: Mama, where have you been?

MAMA: My—them steps is longer than they used to be. Whew! [*She sits down and ignores him.*] How you feeling this evening, Ruth?

[RUTH *shrugs, disturbed some at having been prematurely interrupted and watching her husband knowingly.*]

WALTER: Mama, where have you been all day?

MAMA: [*Still ignoring him and leaning on the table and changing to more comfortable shoes.*] Where's Travis?

RUTH: I let him go out earlier and he ain't come back yet. Boy, is he going to get it!

WALTER: Mama!

MAMA: [*As if she has heard him for the first time.*] Yes, son?

WALTER: Where did you go this afternoon?

MAMA: I went downtown to tend to some business that I had to tend to.

WALTER: What kind of business?

MAMA: You know better than to question me like a child, Brother.

WALTER: [*Rising and bending over the table.*] Where were you, Mama? [*Bringing his fists down and shouting.*] Mama, you didn't go do something with that insurance money, something crazy?

[*The front door opens slowly, interrupting him, and* TRAVIS *peeks his head in, less than hopefully.*]

TRAVIS: [*To his mother.*] Mama, I—

RUTH: "Mama I" nothing! You're going to get it, boy! Get on in that bedroom and get yourself ready!

TRAVIS: But I—

MAMA: Why don't you all never let the child explain hisself.

RUTH: Keep out of it now, Lena.

[MAMA *clamps her lips together, and* RUTH *advances toward her son menacingly.*]

RUTH: A thousand times I have told you not to go off like that—

MAMA: [*Holding out her arms to her grandson.*] Well—at least let me tell him something. I want him to be the first one to hear . . .

Come here, Travis. [*The boy obeys, gladly.*] Travis—[*She takes him by the shoulder and looks into his face.*]—you know that money we got in the mail this morning?

TRAVIS: Yes'm—

MAMA: Well—what you think your grandmama gone and done with that money?

TRAVIS: I don't know, Grandmama.

MAMA: [*Putting her finger on his nose for emphasis.*] She went out and she bought you a house! [*The explosion comes from* WALTER *at the end of the revelation and he jumps up and turns away from all of them in a fury.* MAMA *continues, to* TRAVIS.] You glad about the house? It's going to be yours when you get to be a man.

TRAVIS: Yeah—I always wanted to live in a house.

MAMA: All right, gimme some sugar then—[TRAVIS *puts his arms around her neck as she watches her son over the boy's shoulder. Then, to* TRAVIS, *after the embrace.*] Now when you say your prayers tonight, you thank God and your grandfather—'cause it was him who give you the house—in his way.

RUTH: [*Taking the boy from* MAMA *and pushing him toward the bedroom.*] Now you get out of here and get ready for your beating.

TRAVIS: Aw, Mama—

RUTH: Get on in there—[*Closing the door behind him and turning radiantly to her mother-in-law.*] So you went and did it!

MAMA: [*Quietly, looking at her son with pain.*] Yes, I did.

RUTH: [*Raising both arms classically.*] Praise God! [*Looks at* WALTER *a moment, who says nothing. She crosses rapidly to her husband.*] Please, honey—let me be glad . . . you be glad too. [*She has laid her hands on his shoulders, but he shakes himself free of her roughly, without turning to face her.*] Oh, Walter . . . a home . . . *a home.* [*She comes back to* MAMA.] Well—where is it? How big is it? How much it going to cost?

MAMA: Well—

RUTH: When we moving?

MAMA: [*Smiling at her.*] First of the month.

RUTH: [*Throwing back her head with jubilance.*] Praise God!

MAMA: [*Tentatively, still looking at her son's back turned against her and* RUTH.] It's—it's a nice house too . . . [*She cannot help speaking directly to him. An imploring quality in her voice, her manner, makes her almost like a girl now.*] Three bedrooms—nice big one for you and Ruth . . . Me and Beneatha still have to share our room, but Travis have one of his own—and [*With difficulty.*] I figure if the—new baby—is a boy, we could get one of them double-decker outfits . . . And there's a yard with a little patch of dirt where I could maybe get to grow me a few flowers . . . And a nice big basement . . .

RUTH: Walter honey, be glad—

MAMA: [*Still to his back, fingering things on the table.*] 'Course I don't want to make it sound fancier than it is . . . It's just a plain little old house—but it's made good and solid—and it will be *ours.* Walter Lee—it makes a difference in a man when he can walk on floors that belong to *him* . . .

RUTH: Where is it?

MAMA: [*Frightened at this telling.*] Well—well—it's out there in Clybourne Park[4]—

[RUTH's *radiance fades abruptly, and* WALTER *finally turns slowly to face his mother with incredulity and hostility.*]

RUTH: Where?

MAMA: [*Matter-of-factly.*] Four o six Clybourne Street, Clybourne Park.

RUTH: Clybourne Park? Mama, there ain't no colored people living in Clybourne Park.

MAMA: [*Almost idiotically.*] Well, I guess there's going to be some now.

WALTER: [*Bitterly.*] So that's the peace and comfort you went out and bought for us today!

MAMA: [*Raising her eyes to meet his finally.*] Son—I just tried to find the nicest place for the least amount of money for my family.

RUTH: [*Trying to recover from the shock.*] Well—well—'course I ain't one never been 'fraid of no crackers[5] mind you—but—well, wasn't there no other houses nowhere?

MAMA: Them houses they put up for colored in them areas way out all seem to cost twice as much as other houses. I did the best I could.

---

4. Neighborhood in the Lincoln Park section of Chicago.
5. Insulting term for poor whites.

RUTH: [*Struck senseless with the news, in its various degrees of goodness and trouble, she sits a moment, her fists propping her chin in thought, and then she starts to rise, bringing her fists down with vigor, the radiance spreading from cheek to cheek again.*] Well—well!—All I can say is—if this is my time in life—*my time*—to say good-bye—[*And she builds with momentum as she starts to circle the room with an exuberant, almost tearfully happy release.*]—to these Goddamned cracking walls!—[*She pounds the walls.*]—and these marching roaches!—[*She wipes at an imaginary army of marching roaches.*]—and this cramped little closet which ain't now or never was no kitchen! . . . then I say it loud and good, *Hallelujah! and good-bye misery . . . I don't never want to see your ugly face again!* [*She laughs joyously, having practically destroyed the apartment, and flings her arms up and lets them come down happily, slowly, reflectively, over her abdomen, aware for the first time perhaps that the life therein pulses with happiness and not despair.*] Lena?

MAMA: [*Moved, watching her happiness.*] Yes, honey?

RUTH: [*Looking off.*] Is there—is there a whole lot of sunlight?

MAMA: [*Understanding.*] Yes, child, there's a whole lot of sunlight.

[*Long pause.*]

RUTH: [*Collecting herself and going to the door of the room* TRAVIS *is in.*] Well—I guess I better see 'bout Travis. [*To* MAMA.] Lord, I sure don't feel like whipping nobody today!

[*She exits.*]

MAMA: [*The mother and son are left alone now and the mother waits a long time, considering deeply, before she speaks.*] Son—you—you understand what I done, don't you? [WALTER *is silent and sullen.*] I—I just seen my family falling apart today . . . just falling to pieces in front of my eyes . . . We couldn't of gone on like we was today. We was going backwards 'stead of forwards—talking 'bout killing babies and wishing each other was dead . . . When it gets like that in life—you just got to do something different, push on out and do something bigger . . . [*She waits.*] I wish you say something, son . . . I wish you'd say how deep inside you you think I done the right thing—

WALTER: [*Crossing slowly to his bedroom door and finally turning there and speaking measuredly.*] What you need me to say you done right for? *You* the head of this family. You run our lives like you want to.

It was your money and you did what you wanted with it. So what you need for me to say it was all right for? [*Bitterly, to hurt her as deeply as he knows is possible.*] So you butchered up a dream of mine—you—who always talking 'bout your children's dreams . . .

MAMA: Walter Lee—

[*He just closes the door behind him.* MAMA *sits alone, thinking heavily.*]

[*Curtain.*]

SCENE 2

Time: Friday night. A few weeks later.

At rise: Packing crates mark the intention of the family to move. BENEATHA *and* GEORGE *come in, presumably from an evening out again.*

GEORGE: O.K. . . . O.K., whatever you say . . . [*They both sit on the couch. He tries to kiss her. She moves away.*] Look, we've had a nice evening; let's not spoil it, huh? . . .

[*He again turns her head and tries to nuzzle in and she turns away from him, not with distaste but with momentary lack of interest; in a mood to pursue what they were talking about.*]

BENEATHA: I'm *trying* to talk to you.

GEORGE: We always talk.

BENEATHA: Yes—and I love to talk.

GEORGE: [*Exasperated; rising.*] I know it and I don't mind it some-times . . . I want you to cut it out, see—The moody stuff, I mean. I don't like it. You're a nice-looking girl . . . all over. That's all you need, honey, forget the atmosphere. Guys aren't going to go for the atmosphere—they're going to go for what they see. Be glad for that. Drop the Garbo[6] routine. It doesn't go with you. As for myself, I want a nice—[*Groping.*]—simple [*Thought-fully.*]—sophisticated girl . . . not a poet—O.K.?

[*She rebuffs him again and he starts to leave.*]

BENEATHA: Why are you angry?

---

6. Greta Garbo (1905–1990), American movie star, sex symbol, celebrity noted for her moodiness.

GEORGE: Because this is stupid! I don't go out with you to discuss the nature of "quiet desperation"[7] or to hear all about your thoughts—because the world will go on thinking what it thinks regardless—

BENEATHA: Then why read books? Why go to school?

GEORGE: [*With artificial patience, counting on his fingers.*] It's simple. You read books—to learn facts—to get grades—to pass the course—to get a degree. That's all—it has nothing to do with thoughts.

[*A long pause.*]

BENEATHA: I see. [*A longer pause as she looks at him.*] Good night, George.
[GEORGE *looks at her a little oddly, and starts to exit. He meets* MAMA *coming in.*]

GEORGE: Oh—hello, Mrs. Younger.

MAMA: Hello, George, how you feeling?

GEORGE: Fine—fine, how are you?

MAMA: Oh, a little tired. You know them steps can get you after a day's work. You all have a nice time tonight?

GEORGE: Yes—a fine time. Well, good night.

MAMA: Good night. [*He exits.* MAMA *closes the door behind her.*] Hello, honey. What you sitting like that for?

BENEATHA: I'm just sitting.

MAMA: Didn't you have a nice time?

BENEATHA: No.

MAMA: No? What's the matter?

BENEATHA: Mama, George is a fool—honest. [*She rises.*]

MAMA: [*Hustling around unloading the packages she has entered with. She stops.*] Is he, baby?

BENEATHA: Yes.

[BENEATHA *makes up* TRAVIS' *bed as she talks.*]

MAMA: You sure?

BENEATHA: Yes.

MAMA: Well—I guess you better not waste your time with no fools.
[BENEATHA *looks up at her mother, watching her put groceries in the refrigerator. Finally she gathers up her things and starts into the bedroom. At the door she stops and looks back at her mother.*]

---

7. Part of Henry David Thoreau's famous line from *Walden* (1852): "the mass of men lead lives of quiet desperation."

BENEATHA: Mama—

MAMA: Yes, baby—

BENEATHA: Thank you.

MAMA: For what?

BENEATHA: For understanding me this time.

> [*She exits quickly and the mother stands, smiling a little, looking at the place where* BENEATHA *just stood.* RUTH *enters.*]

RUTH: Now don't you fool with any of this stuff, Lena—

MAMA: Oh, I just thought I'd sort a few things out.

> [*The phone rings.* RUTH *answers.*]

RUTH: [*At the phone.*] Hello—Just a minute. [*Goes to door.*] Walter, it's Mrs. Arnold. [*Waits. Goes back to the phone. Tense.*] Hello. Yes, this is his wife speaking . . . He's lying down now. Yes . . . well, he'll be in tomorrow. He's been very sick. Yes—I know we should have called, but we were so sure he'd be able to come in today. Yes—yes, I'm very sorry. Yes . . . Thank you very much. [*She hangs up.* WALTER *is standing in the doorway of the bedroom behind her.*] That was Mrs. Arnold.

WALTER: [*Indifferently.*] Was it?

RUTH: She said if you don't come in tomorrow that they are getting a new man . . .

WALTER: Ain't that sad—ain't that crying sad.

RUTH: She said Mr. Arnold has had to take a cab for three days . . . Walter, you ain't been to work for three days! [*This is a revelation to her.*] Where you been, Walter Lee Younger? [WALTER *looks at her and starts to laugh.*] You're going to lose your job.

WALTER: That's right . . .

RUTH: Oh, Walter, and with your mother working like a dog every day—

WALTER: That's sad too—Everything is sad.

MAMA: What you been doing for these three days, son?

WALTER: Mama—you don't know all the things a man what got leisure can find to do in this city . . . What's this—Friday night? Well—Wednesday I borrowed Willy Harris' car and I went for a drive . . . just me and myself and I drove and drove . . . Way out . . . way past South Chicago, and I parked the car and I sat and looked at the steel mills all day long. I just sat in the car and looked at them big black chimneys for hours. Then I drove back

and I went to the Green Hat. [*Pause.*] And Thursday—Thursday
I borrowed the car again and I got in it and I pointed it the other
way and I drove the other way—for hours—way, way up to
Wisconsin, and I looked at the farms. I just drove and looked at
the farms. Then I drove back and I went to the Green Hat. [*Pause.*]
And today—today I didn't get the car. Today I just walked. All
over the South Side. And I looked at the Negroes and they looked
at me and finally I just sat down on the curb at Thirty-ninth and
South Parkway and I just sat there and watched the Negroes go by.
And then I went to the Green Hat. You all sad? You all depressed?
And you know where I am going right now—

[RUTH *goes out quietly.*]

MAMA: Oh, Big Walter, is this the harvest of our days?

WALTER: You know what I like about the Green Hat? [*He turns the
radio on and a steamy, deep blues pours into the room.*] I like this
little cat they got there who blows a sax . . . He blows. He talks
to me. He ain't but 'bout five feet tall and he's got a conked
head[8] and his eyes is always closed and he's all music—

MAMA: [*Rising and getting some papers out of her handbag.*] Walter—

WALTER: And there's this other guy who plays the piano . . . and
they got a sound. I mean they can work on some music . . . They
got the best little combo in the world in the Green Hat . . . You
can just sit there and drink and listen to them three men play
and you realize that don't nothing matter worth a damn, but just
being there—

MAMA: I've helped do it to you, haven't I, son? Walter, I been wrong.

WALTER: Naw—you ain't never been wrong about nothing, Mama.

MAMA: Listen to me, now. I say I been wrong, son. That I been doing
to you what the rest of the world been doing to you. [*She stops and
he looks up slowly at her and she meets his eyes pleadingly.*] Walter—
what you ain't never understood is that I ain't got nothing, don't
own nothing, ain't never really wanted nothing that wasn't for
you. There ain't nothing as precious to me . . . There ain't nothing
worth holding on to, money, dreams, nothing else—if it means—
if it means it's going to destroy my boy. [*She puts her papers in front
of him and he watches her without speaking or moving.*] I paid the

---

8. Straightened hair popular with African American musicians in the mid-twentieth century.

man thirty-five hundred dollars down on the house. That leaves sixty-five hundred dollars. Monday morning I want you to take this money and take three thousand dollars and put it in a savings account for Beneatha's medical schooling. The rest you put in a checking account—with your name on it. And from now on any penny that come out of it or that go in it is for you to look after. For you to decide. [*She drops her hands a little helplessly.*] It ain't much, but it's all I got in the world and I'm putting it in your hands. I'm telling you to be the head of this family from now on like you supposed to be.

WALTER: [*Stares at the money.*] You trust me like that, Mama?

MAMA: I ain't never stop trusting you. Like I ain't never stop loving you.

> [*She goes out, and* WALTER *sits looking at the money on the table as the music continues in its idiom, pulsing in the room. Finally, in a decisive gesture, he gets up, and, in mingled joy and desperation, picks up the money. At the same moment,* TRAVIS *enters for bed.*]

TRAVIS: What's the matter, Daddy? You drunk?

WALTER: [*Sweetly, more sweetly than we have ever known him.*] No, Daddy ain't drunk. Daddy ain't going to never be drunk again. . . .

TRAVIS: Well, good night, Daddy.

> [*The father has come from behind the couch and leans over, embracing his son.*]

WALTER: Son, I feel like talking to you tonight.

TRAVIS: About what?

WALTER: Oh, about a lot of things. About you and what kind of man you going to be when you grow up . . . Son—son, what do you want to be when you grow up?

TRAVIS: A bus driver.

WALTER: [*Laughing a little.*] A what? Man, that ain't nothing to want to be!

TRAVIS: Why not?

WALTER: 'Cause, man—it ain't big enough—you know what I mean.

TRAVIS: I don't know then. I can't make up my mind. Sometimes Mama asks me that too. And sometimes when I tell you I just want to be like you—she says she don't want me to be like that and sometimes she says she does . . .

WALTER: [*Gathering him up in his arms.*] You know what, Travis? In seven years you going to be seventeen years old. And things is going to be very different with us in seven years, Travis . . . One day when you are seventeen I'll come home—home from my office downtown somewhere—

TRAVIS: You don't work in no office, Daddy.

WALTER: No—but after tonight. After what your daddy gonna do tonight, there's going to be offices—a whole lot of offices . . .

TRAVIS: What you gonna do tonight, Daddy?

WALTER: You wouldn't understand yet, son, but your daddy's gonna make a transaction . . . a business transaction that's going to change our lives . . . That's how come one day when you 'bout seventeen years old I'll come home and I'll be pretty tired, you know what I mean, after a day of conferences and secretaries getting things wrong the way they do . . . 'cause an executive's life is hell, man— [*The more he talks the farther away he gets.*] And I'll pull the car up on the driveway . . . just a plain black Chrysler, I think, with white walls—no—black tires. More elegant. Rich people don't have to be flashy . . . though I'll have to get something a little sportier for Ruth—maybe a Cadillac convertible to do her shopping in . . . And I'll come up the steps to the house and the gardener will be clipping away at the hedges and he'll say, "Good evening, Mr. Younger." And I'll say, "Hello, Jefferson, how are you this evening?" And I'll go inside and Ruth will come downstairs and meet me at the door and we'll kiss each other and she'll take my arm and we'll go up to your room to see you sitting on the floor with the catalogues of all the great schools in America around you . . . All the great schools in the world. And—and I'll say, all right son—it's your seventeenth birthday, what is it you've decided? . . . Just tell me where you want to go to school and you'll *go*. Just tell me, what it is you want to be—and you'll *be* it . . . Whatever you want to be—Yessir! [*He holds his arms open for* TRAVIS.] You just name it, son . . . [TRAVIS *leaps into them.*] and I hand you the world! [WALTER*'s voice has risen in pitch and hysterical promise and on the last line he lifts* TRAVIS *high.*]

[*BLACKOUT.*]

SCENE 3

Time: Saturday, moving day, one week later.

Before the curtain rises, RUTH's voice, a strident, dramatic church alto, cuts through the silence.

It is, in the darkness, a triumphant surge, a penetrating statement of expectation: "Oh, Lord, I don't feel no ways tired! Children, oh, glory hallelujah!"

As the curtain rises we see that RUTH is alone in the living room, finishing up the family's packing. It is moving day. She is nailing crates and tying cartons. BENEATHA enters, carrying a guitar case, and watches her exuberant sister-in-law.

RUTH: Hey!

BENEATHA: [*Putting away the case.*] Hi.

RUTH: [*Pointing at a package.*] Honey—look in that package there and see what I found on sale this morning at the South Center. [RUTH *gets up and moves to the package and draws out some curtains.*] Lookahere—hand-turned hems!

BENEATHA: How do you know the window size out there?

RUTH: [*Who hadn't thought of that.*] Oh—Well, they bound to fit something in the whole house. Anyhow, they was too good a bargain to pass up. [RUTH *slaps her head, suddenly remembering something.*] Oh, Bennie—I meant to put a special note on that carton over there. That's your mama's good china and she wants 'em to be very careful with it.

BENEATHA: I'll do it.

[BENEATHA *finds a piece of paper and starts to draw large letters on it.*]

RUTH: You know what I'm going to do soon as I get in that new house?

BENEATHA: What?

RUTH: Honey—I'm going to run me a tub of water up to here . . . [*With her fingers practically up to her nostrils.*] And I'm going to get in it—and I am going to sit . . . and sit . . . and sit in that hot water and the first person who knocks to tell *me* to hurry up and come out—

BENEATHA: Gets shot at sunrise.

RUTH: [*Laughing happily.*] You said it, sister! [*Noticing how large
BENEATHA is absentmindedly making the note.*] Honey, they ain't
going to read that from no airplane.

BENEATHA: [*Laughing herself.*] I guess I always think things have
more emphasis if they are big, somehow.

RUTH: [*Looking up at her and smiling.*] You and your brother seem to
have that as a philosophy of life. Lord, that man—done changed
so 'round here. You know—you know what we did last night?
Me and Walter Lee?

BENEATHA: What?

RUTH: [*Smiling to herself.*] We went to the movies. [*Looking at
BENEATHA to see if she understands.*] We went to the movies. You
know the last time me and Walter went to the movies together?

BENEATHA: No.

RUTH: Me neither. That's how long it been. [*Smiling again.*] But we
went last night. The picture wasn't much good, but that didn't
seem to matter. We went—and we held hands.

BENEATHA: Oh, Lord!

RUTH: We held hands—and you know what?

BENEATHA: What?

RUTH: When we come out of the show it was late and dark and all
the stores and things was closed up . . . and it was kind of chilly
and there wasn't many people on the streets . . . and we was still
holding hands, me and Walter.

BENEATHA: You're killing me.

[WALTER *enters with a large package. His happiness is deep in
him; he cannot keep still with his new-found exuberance. He is
singing and wiggling and snapping his fingers. He puts his package in a corner and puts a phonograph record, which he has
brought in with him, on the record player. As the music comes
up he dances over to* RUTH *and tries to get her to dance with
him. She gives in at last to his raunchiness and in a fit of giggling
allows herself to be drawn into his mood and together they deliberately burlesque an old social dance of their youth.*]

BENEATHA: [*Regarding them a long time as they dance, then drawing in
her breath for a deeply exaggerated comment which she does not particularly mean.*] Talk about—olddddddddddd-fashionedddddddd—
Negroes!

WALTER: [*Stopping momentarily.*] What kind of Negroes?

[*He says this in fun. He is not angry with her today, nor with anyone. He starts to dance with his wife again.*]

BENEATHA: Old-fashioned.

WALTER: [*As he dances with* RUTH.] You know, when these *New Negroes* have their convention—[*Pointing at his sister.*]—that is going to be the chairman of the Committee on Unending Agitation. [*He goes on dancing, then stops.*] Race, race, race! . . . Girl, I do believe you are the first person in the history of the entire human race to successfully brainwash yourself. [BENEATHA *breaks up and he goes on dancing. He stops again, enjoying his tease.*] Damn, even the N double A C P[9] *takes a holiday sometimes!* [BENEATHA *and* RUTH *laugh. He dances with* RUTH *some more and starts to laugh and stops and pantomimes someone over an operating table.*] I can just see that chick someday looking down at some poor cat on an operating table before she starts to slice him, saying . . . [*Pulling his sleeves back maliciously.*] "By the way, what are your views on civil rights down there? . . . "

[*He laughs at her again and starts to dance happily. The bell sounds.*]

BENEATHA: Sticks and stones may break my bones but . . . words will never hurt me!

[BENEATHA *goes to the door and opens it as* WALTER *and* RUTH *go on with the clowning.* BENEATHA *is somewhat surprised to see a quiet-looking middle-aged white man in a business suit holding his hat and a briefcase in his hand and consulting a small piece of paper.*]

MAN: Uh—how do you do, miss. I am looking for a Mrs.—[*He looks at the slip of paper.*] Mrs. Lena Younger?

BENEATHA: [*Smoothing her hair with slight embarrassment.*] Oh— yes, that's my mother. Excuse me [*She closes the door and turns to quiet the other two.*] Ruth! Brother! Somebody's here. [*Then she opens the door. The* MAN *casts a curious quick glance at all of them.*] Uh—come in please.

MAN: [*Coming in.*] Thank you.

9. National Association for the Advancement of Colored People, civil rights organization founded in 1909. In 1955, Rosa Parks, a member of the NAACP, sparked the modern civil rights movement by refusing to go to the back of the bus in Montgomery, Alabama.

BENEATHA: My mother isn't here just now. Is it business?

MAN: Yes . . . well, of a sort.

WALTER: [*Freely, the Man of the House.*] Have a seat. I'm Mrs. Younger's son. I look after most of her business matters.

    [RUTH *and* BENEATHA *exchange amused glances.*]

MAN: [*Regarding* WALTER, *and sitting.*] Well—My name is Karl Lindner . . .

WALTER: [*Stretching out his hand.*] Walter Younger. This is my wife—[RUTH *nods politely.*]—and my sister.

LINDNER: How do you do.

WALTER: [*Amiably, as he sits himself easily on a chair, leaning with interest forward on his knees and looking expectantly into the newcomer's face.*] What can we do for you, Mr. Lindner!

LINDNER: [*Some minor shuffling of the hat and briefcase on his knees.*] Well—I am a representative of the Clybourne Park Improvement Association—

WALTER: [*Pointing.*] Why don't you sit your things on the floor?

LINDNER: Oh—yes. Thank you. [*He slides the briefcase and hat under the chair.*] And as I was saying—I am from the Clybourne Park Improvement Association and we have had it brought to our attention at the last meeting that you people—or at least your mother—has bought a piece of residential property at—[*He digs for the slip of paper again.*]—four o six Clybourne Street . . .

WALTER: That's right. Care for something to drink? Ruth, get Mr. Lindner a beer.

LINDNER: [*Upset for some reason.*] Oh—no, really. I mean thank you very much, but no thank you.

RUTH: [*Innocently.*] Some coffee?

LINDNER: Thank you, nothing at all.

    [BENEATHA *is watching the man carefully.*]

LINDNER: Well, I don't know how much you folks know about our organization. [*He is a gentle man; thoughtful and somewhat labored in his manner.*] It is one of these community organizations set up to look after—oh, you know, things like block upkeep and special projects and we also have what we call our New Neighbors Orientation Committee . . .

BENEATHA: [*Drily.*] Yes—and what do they do?

LINDNER: [*Turning a little to her and then returning the main force to* WALTER.] Well—it's what you might call a sort of welcoming committee, I guess. I mean they, we, I'm the chairman of the committee—go around and see the new people who move into the neighborhood and sort of give them the lowdown on the way we do things out in Clybourne Park.

BENEATHA: [*With appreciation of the two meanings, which escape* RUTH *and* WALTER.] Un-huh.

LINDNER: And we also have the category of what the association calls— [*He looks elsewhere.*]—uh—special community problems . . .

BENEATHA: Yes—and what are some of those?

WALTER: Girl, let the man talk.

LINDNER: [*With understated relief.*] Thank you. I would sort of like to explain this thing in my own way. I mean I want to explain to you in a certain way.

WALTER: Go ahead.

LINDNER: Yes. Well. I'm going to try to get right to the point. I'm sure we'll all appreciate that in the long run.

BENEATHA: Yes.

WALTER: Be still now!

LINDNER: Well—

RUTH: [*Still innocently.*] Would you like another chair—you don't look comfortable.

LINDNER: [*More frustrated than annoyed.*] No, thank you very much. Please. Well—to get right to the point I—[*A great breath, and he is off at last.*] I am sure you people must be aware of some of the incidents which have happened in various parts of the city when colored people have moved into certain areas—[BENEATHA *exhales heavily and starts tossing a piece of fruit up and down in the air.*] Well—because we have what I think is going to be a unique type of organization in American community life—not only do we deplore that kind of thing—but we are trying to do something about it. [BENEATHA *stops tossing and turns with a new and quizzical interest to the man.*] We feel—[*Gaining confidence in his mission because of the interest in the faces of the people he is talking to.*]—we feel that most of the trouble in this world, when you come right down to it—[*He hits his knee for emphasis.*]—most of the trouble exists because people just don't sit down and talk to each other.

RUTH: [*Nodding as she might in church, pleased with the remark.*] You can say that again, mister.

LINDNER: [*More encouraged by such affirmation.*] That we don't try hard enough in this world to understand the other fellow's problem. The other guy's point of view.

RUTH: Now that's right.

[BENEATHA *and* WALTER *merely watch and listen with genuine interest.*]

LINDNER: Yes—that's the way we feel out in Clybourne Park. And that's why I was elected to come here this afternoon and talk to you people. Friendly like, you know, the way people should talk to each other and see if we couldn't find some way to work this thing out. As I say, the whole business is a matter of *caring* about the other fellow. Anybody can see that you are a nice family of folks, hard working and honest I'm sure. [BENEATHA *frowns slightly, quizzically, her head tilted regarding him.*] Today everybody knows what it means to be on the outside of something. And of course, there is always somebody who is out to take the advantage of people who don't always understand.

WALTER: What do you mean?

LINDNER: Well—you see our community is made up of people who've worked hard as the dickens for years to build up that little community. They're not rich and fancy people; just hard-working, honest people who don't really have much but those little homes and a dream of the kind of community they want to raise their children in. Now, I don't say we are perfect and there is a lot wrong in some of the things they want. But you've got to admit that a man, right or wrong, has the right to want to have the neighborhood he lives in a certain kind of way. And at the moment the overwhelming majority of our people out there feel that people get along better, take more of a common interest in the life of the community, when they share a common background. I want you to believe me when I tell you that race prejudice simply doesn't enter into it. It is a matter of the people of Clybourne Park believing, rightly or wrongly, as I say, that for the happiness of all concerned that our Negro families are happier when they live in their *own* communities.

BENEATHA: [*With a grand and bitter gesture.*] This, friends, is the Welcoming Committee!

WALTER: [*Dumbfounded, looking at* LINDNER.] Is this what you came marching all the way over here to tell us?

LINDNER: Well, now we've been having a fine conversation. I hope you'll hear me all the way through.

WALTER: [*Tightly.*] Go ahead, man.

LINDNER: You see—in the face of all things I have said, we are prepared to make your family a very generous offer . . .

BENEATHA: Thirty pieces and not a coin less![1]

WALTER: Yeah?

LINDNER: [*Putting on his glasses and drawing a form out of the briefcase.*] Our association is prepared, through the collective effort of our people, to buy the house from you at a financial gain to your family.

RUTH: Lord have mercy, ain't this the living gall!

WALTER: All right, you through?

LINDNER: Well, I want to give you the exact terms of the financial arrangement—

WALTER: We don't want to hear no exact terms of no arrangements. I want to know if you got any more to tell us 'bout getting together?

LINDNER: [*Taking off his glasses.*] Well—I don't suppose that you feel . . .

WALTER: Never mind how I feel—you got any more to say 'bout how people ought to sit down and talk to each other? . . . Get out of my house, man.

[*He turns his back and walks to the door.*]

LINDNER: [*Looking around at the hostile faces and reaching and assembling his hat and briefcase.*] Well—I don't understand why you people are reacting this way. What do you think you are going to gain by moving into a neighborhood where you just aren't wanted and where some elements—well—people can get awful worked up when they feel that their whole way of life and everything they've ever worked for is threatened.

WALTER: Get out.

---

1. Judas was paid thirty pieces of silver after he betrayed Jesus. Matthew 26:15.

LINDNER: [*At the door, holding a small card.*] Well—I'm sorry it went like this.

WALTER: Get out.

LINDNER: [*Almost sadly regarding* WALTER.] You just can't force people to change their hearts, son.

[*He turns and put his card on a table and exits.* WALTER *pushes the door to with stinging hatred, and stands looking at it.* RUTH *just sits and* BENEATHA *just stands. They say nothing.* MAMA *and* TRAVIS *enter.*]

MAMA: Well—this all the packing got done since I left out of here this morning. I testify before God that my children got all the energy of the dead. What time the moving men due?

BENEATHA: Four o'clock. You had a caller, Mama.

[*She is smiling, teasingly.*]

MAMA: Sure enough—who?

BENEATHA: [*Her arms folded saucily.*] The Welcoming Committee.

[WALTER *and* RUTH *giggle.*]

MAMA: [*Innocently.*] Who?

BENEATHA: The Welcoming Committee. They said they're sure going to be glad to see you when you get there.

WALTER: [*Devilishly.*] Yeah, they said they can't hardly wait to see your face.

[*Laughter.*]

MAMA: [*Sensing their facetiousness.*] What's the matter with you all?

WALTER: Ain't nothing the matter with us. We just telling you 'bout the gentleman who came to see you this afternoon. From the Clybourne Park Improvement Association.

MAMA: What he want?

RUTH: [*In the same mood as* BENEATHA *and* WALTER.] To welcome you, honey.

WALTER: He said they can't hardly wait. He said the one thing they don't have, that they just *dying* to have out there is a fine family of colored people! [*To* RUTH *and* BENEATHA.] Ain't that right!

RUTH AND BENEATHA: [*Mockingly.*] Yeah! He left his card in case—

[*They indicate the card, and* MAMA *picks it up and throws it on the floor—understanding and looking off as she draws her chair up to the table on which she has put her plant and some sticks and some cord.*]

MAMA: Father, give us strength. [*Knowingly—and without fun.*] Did he threaten us?

BENEATHA: Oh—Mama—they don't do it like that anymore. He talked Brotherhood. He said everybody ought to learn how to sit down and hate each other with good Christian fellowship.

[*She and* WALTER *shake hands to ridicule the remark.*]

MAMA: [*Sadly.*] Lord, protect us . . .

RUTH: You should hear the money those folks raised to buy the house from us. All we paid and then some.

BENEATHA: What they think we going to do—eat 'em?

RUTH: No, honey, marry 'em.

MAMA: [*Shaking her head.*] Lord, Lord, Lord . . .

RUTH: Well—that's the way the crackers crumble. Joke.

BENEATHA: [*Laughingly noticing what her mother is doing.*] Mama, what are you doing?

MAMA: Fixing my plant so it won't get hurt none on the way . . .

BENEATHA: Mama, you going to take *that* to the new house?

MAMA: Un-huh—

BENEATHA: That raggedy-looking old thing?

MAMA: [*Stopping and looking at her.*] It expresses *me.*

RUTH: [*With delight, to* BENEATHA.] So there, Miss Thing!

[WALTER *comes to* MAMA *suddenly and bends down behind her and squeezes her in his arms with all his strength. She is overwhelmed by the suddenness of it and, though delighted, her manner is like that of* RUTH *with* TRAVIS.]

MAMA: Look out now, boy! You make me mess up my thing here!

WALTER: [*His face lit, he slips down on his knees beside her, his arms still about her.*] Mama . . . you know what it means to climb up in the chariot?

MAMA: [*Gruffly, very happy.*] Get on away from me now . . .

RUTH: [*Near the gift-wrapped package, trying to catch* WALTER's *eye.*] Psst—

WALTER: What the old song say, Mama . . .

RUTH: Walter—Now?

[*She is pointing at the package.*]

WALTER: [*Speaking the lines, sweetly, playfully, in his mother's face.*]

I got wings . . . you got wings . . .
All God's Children got wings . . .

MAMA: Boy—get out of my face and do some work . . .

WALTER:
> When I get to heaven gonna put on my wings,
> Gonna fly all over God's heaven[2] . . .

BENEATHA: [*Teasingly, from across the room.*] Everybody talking 'bout heaven ain't going there!

WALTER: [*To* RUTH, *who is carrying the box across to them.*] I don't know, you think we ought to give her that . . . Seems to me she ain't been very appreciative around here.

MAMA: [*Eying the box, which is obviously a gift.*] What is that?

WALTER: [*Taking it from* RUTH *and putting it on the table in front of* MAMA.] Well—what you all think? Should we give it to her?

RUTH: Oh—she was pretty good today.

MAMA: I'll good you—
[*She turns her eyes to the box again.*]

BENEATHA: Open it, Mama.
[*She stands up, looks at it, turns and looks at all of them, and then presses her hands together and does not open the package.*]

WALTER: [*Sweetly.*] Open it, Mama. It's for you. [MAMA *looks in his eyes. It is the first present in her life without its being Christmas. Slowly she opens her package and lifts out, one by one, a brand-new sparkling set of gardening tools.* WALTER *continues, prodding.*] Ruth made up the note—read it . . .

MAMA: [*Picking up the card and adjusting her glasses.*] "To our own Mrs. Miniver[3]—Love from Brother, Ruth and Beneatha." Ain't that lovely . . .

TRAVIS: [*Tugging at his father's sleeve.*] Daddy, can I give her mine now?

WALTER: All right, son. [TRAVIS *flies to get his gift.*] Travis didn't want to go in with the rest of us, Mama. He got his own. [*Somewhat amused.*] We don't know what it is . . .

TRAVIS: [*Racing back in the room with a large hatbox and putting it in front of his grandmother.*] Here!

---

2. Lines from "I Got Shoes," an African American spiritual.

3. Mrs. Miniver is the titular heroine of a popular 1942 film credited with helping to swing American sentiment toward war against Nazi Germany. Mrs. Miniver is a plucky suburban London housewife whose adventures include disarming a Nazi pilot who parachutes into her garden.

MAMA: Lord have mercy, baby. You done gone and bought your grandmother a hat?

TRAVIS: [*Very proud.*] Open it!

[*She does and lifts out an elaborate, but very elaborate, wide gardening hat, and all the adults break up at the sight of it.*]

RUTH: Travis, honey, what is that?

TRAVIS: [*Who thinks it is beautiful and appropriate.*] It's a gardening hat! Like the ladies always have on in the magazines when they work in their gardens.

BENEATHA: [*Giggling fiercely.*] Travis—we were trying to make Mama Mrs. Miniver—not Scarlett O'Hara![4]

MAMA: [*Indignantly.*] What's the matter with you all! This here is a beautiful hat! [*Absurdly.*] I always wanted me one just like it!

[*She pops it on her head to prove it to her grandson, and the hat is ludicrous and considerably oversized.*]

RUTH: Hot dog! Go, Mama!

WALTER: [*Doubled over with laughter.*] I'm sorry, Mama—but you look like you ready to go out and chop you some cotton sure enough!

[*They all laugh except* MAMA, *out of deference to* TRAVIS' *feelings.*]

MAMA: [*Gathering the boy up to her.*] Bless your heart—this is the prettiest hat I ever owned—[WALTER, RUTH *and* BENEATHA *chime in—noisily, festively and insincerely congratulating* TRAVIS *on his gift.*] What are we all standing around here for? We ain't finished packin' yet. Bennie, you ain't packed one book.

[*The bell rings.*]

BENEATHA: That couldn't be the movers . . . it's not hardly two good yet—

[BENEATHA *goes into her room.* MAMA *starts for door.*]

WALTER: [*Turning, stiffening.*] Wait—wait—I'll get it.

[*He stands and looks at the door.*]

MAMA: You expecting company, son?

WALTER: [*Just looking at the door.*] Yeah—yeah . . .

[MAMA *looks at* RUTH, *and they exchange innocent and unfrightened glances.*]

---

4. Scarlett O'Hara is the heroine of *Gone with the Wind*, the popular 1939 movie whose romantic depictions of the South promoted the Ku Klux Klan and perpetuated gross racial stereotypes. Scarlett is a self-serving, vain, ingenious survivor, the heiress of a plantation ruined by the Civil War.

MAMA: [*Not understanding.*] Well, let them in, son.

BENEATHA: [*From her room.*] We need some more string.

MAMA: Travis—you run to the hardware and get me some string cord.

[MAMA *goes out and* WALTER *turns and looks at* RUTH. TRAVIS *goes to a dish for money.*]

RUTH: Why don't you answer the door, man?

WALTER: [*Suddenly bounding across the floor to her.*] 'Cause sometimes it hard to let the future begin! [*Stooping down in her face.*]

I got wings! You got wings!
All God's children got wings!

[*He crosses to the door and throws it open. Standing there is a very slight little man in a not too prosperous business suit and with haunted frightened eyes and a hat pulled down tightly, brim up, around his forehead.* TRAVIS *passes between the men and exits.* WALTER *leans deep in the man's face, still in his jubilance.*]

When I get to heaven gonna put on my wings,
Gonna fly all over God's heaven . . .

[*The little man just stares at him.*]

Heaven—

[*Suddenly he stops and looks past the little man into the empty hallway.*] Where's Willy, man?

BOBO: He ain't with me.

WALTER: [*Not disturbed.*] Oh—come on in. You know my wife.

BOBO: [*Dumbly, taking off his hat.*] Yes—h'you, Miss Ruth.

RUTH: [*Quietly, a mood apart from her husband already, seeing* BOBO.] Hello, Bobo.

WALTER: You right on time today . . . Right on time. That's the way! [*He slaps* BOBO *on his back.*] Sit down . . . lemme hear.

[RUTH *stands stiffly and quietly in back of them, as though somehow she senses death, her eyes fixed on her husband.*]

BOBO: [*His frightened eyes on the floor, his hat in his hands.*] Could I please get a drink of water, before I tell you about it, Walter Lee? [WALTER *does not take his eyes off the man.* RUTH *goes blindly to the tap and gets a glass of water and brings it to* BOBO.]

WALTER: There ain't nothing wrong, is there?

BOBO: Lemme tell you—

WALTER: Man—didn't nothing go wrong?

BOBO: Lemme tell you—Walter Lee. [*Looking at* RUTH *and talking to her more than to* WALTER.] You know how it was. I got to tell you how it was. I mean first I got to tell you how it was all the way . . . I mean about the money I put in, Walter Lee . . .

WALTER: [*With taut agitation now.*] What about the money you put in?

BOBO: Well—it wasn't much as we told you—me and Willy—[*He stops.*] I'm sorry, Walter. I got a bad feeling about it. I got a real bad feeling about it . . .

WALTER: Man, what you telling me about all this for? . . . Tell me what happened in Springfield . . .

BOBO: Springfield.

RUTH: [*Like a dead woman.*] What was supposed to happen in Springfield?

BOBO: [*To her.*] This deal that me and Walter went into with Willy—Me and Willy was going to go down to Springfield and spread some money 'round so's we wouldn't have to wait so long for the liquor license . . . That's what we were going to do. Everybody said that was the way you had to do, you understand, Miss Ruth?

WALTER: Man—what happened down there?

BOBO: [*A pitiful man, near tears.*] I'm trying to tell you, Walter.

WALTER: [*Screaming at him suddenly.*] THEN TELL ME, GOD DAMMIT . . . WHAT'S THE MATTER WITH YOU?

BOBO: Man . . . I didn't go to no Springfield, yesterday.

WALTER: [*Halted, life hanging in the moment.*] Why not?

BOBO: [*The long way, the hard way to tell.*] 'Cause I didn't have no reasons to . . .

WALTER: Man, what are you talking about!

BOBO: I'm talking about the fact that when I got to the train station yesterday morning—eight o'clock like we planned . . . Man— *Willy didn't never show up.*

WALTER: Why . . . where was he . . . where is he?

BOBO: That's what I'm trying to tell you . . . I don't know . . . I waited six hours . . . I called his house . . . and I waited . . . six hours . . . I waited in that train station six hours . . . [*Breaking into tears.*] That was all the extra money I had in the world . . . [*Looking up at* WALTER *with the tears running down his face.*] Man, *Willy is gone.*

WALTER: Gone, what you mean Willy is gone? Gone where? You mean he went by himself. You mean he went off to Springfield by himself—to take care of getting the license—[*Turns and looks anxiously at* RUTH.] You mean maybe he didn't want too many people in on the business down there? [*Looks to* RUTH *again, as before.*] You know Willy got his own ways. [*Looks back to* BOBO.] Maybe you was late yesterday and he just went on down there without you. Maybe—maybe—he's been callin' you at home tryin' to tell you what happened or something. Maybe—maybe—he just got sick. He's somewhere—he's got to be somewhere. We just got to find him—me and you got to find him. [*Grabs* BOBO *senselessly by the collar and starts to shake him.*] We got to!

BOBO: [*In sudden angry, frightened agony.*] What's the matter with you, Walter! *When a cat take off with your money he don't leave you no maps!*

WALTER: [*Turning madly, as though he is looking for* WILLY *in the very room.*] Willy! . . . Willy . . . don't do it . . . Please don't do it . . . Man, not with that money . . . Man, please, not with that money . . . Oh, God . . . Don't let it be true . . . [*He is wandering around, crying out for* WILLY *and looking for him or perhaps for help from God.*] Man . . . I trusted you . . . Man, I put my life in your hands . . . [*He starts to crumple down on the floor as* RUTH *just covers her face in horror.* MAMA *opens the door and comes into the room, with* BENEATHA *behind her.*] Man . . . [*He starts to pound the floor with his fists, sobbing wildly.*] That money is made out of my father's flesh . . .

BOBO: [*Standing over him helplessly.*] I'm sorry, Walter . . . [*Only* WALTER's *sobs reply.* BOBO *puts on his hat.*] I had my life staked on this deal, too . . .

[*He exits.*]

MAMA: [*To* WALTER.] Son—[*She goes to him, bends down to him, talks to his bent head.*] Son . . . Is it gone? Son, I gave you sixty-five hundred dollars. Is it gone? All of it? Beneatha's money too?

WALTER: [*Lifting his head slowly.*] Mama . . . I never . . . went to the bank at all . . .

MAMA: [*Not wanting to believe him.*] You mean . . . your sister's school money . . . you used that too . . . Walter? . . .

WALTER: Yessss! . . . All of it . . . It's all gone . . . [*There is total silence.* RUTH *stands with her face covered with her hands;* BENEATHA *leans forlornly against a wall, fingering a piece of red ribbon from the mother's gift.* MAMA *stops and looks at her son without recognition and then, quite without thinking about it, starts to beat him senselessly in the face.* BENEATHA *goes to them and stops it.*]

BENEATHA: Mama!

[MAMA *stops and looks at both of her children and rises slowly and wanders vaguely, aimlessly away from them.*]

MAMA: I seen . . . him . . . night after night . . . come in . . . and look at that rug . . . and then look at me . . . the red showing in his eyes . . . the veins moving in his head . . . I seen him grow thin and old before he was forty . . . working and working and working like somebody's old horse . . . killing himself . . . and you—you give it all away in a day . . .

BENEATHA: Mama—

MAMA: Oh, God . . . [*She looks up to Him.*] Look down here—and show me the strength.

BENEATHA: Mama—

MAMA: [*Folding over.*] Strength . . .

BENEATHA: [*Plaintively.*] Mama . . .

MAMA: Strength!

[*Curtain.*]

ACT 3

An hour later.

At curtain, there is a sullen light of gloom in the living room, gray light not unlike that which began the first scene of Act I. At left we can see WALTER *within his room, alone with himself. He is stretched out on the bed, his shirt out and open, his arms under his head. He does not smoke, he does not cry out, he merely lies there, looking up at the ceiling, much as if he were alone in the world.*

In the living room BENEATHA *sits at the table, still surrounded by the now almost ominous packing crates. She sits looking off. We feel that this is a mood struck perhaps an hour before, and it lingers now, full of the empty sound of profound disappointment. We see on a line from her brother's bedroom the sameness of their attitudes. Presently the bell rings and* BENEATHA *rises without ambition or interest in answering. It is* ASAGAI, *smiling broadly, striding into the room with energy and happy expectation and conversation.*

ASAGAI: I came over . . . I had some free time. I thought I might help with the packing. Ah, I like the look of packing crates! A household in preparation for a journey! It depresses some people . . . but for me . . . it is another feeling. Something full of the flow of life, do you understand? Movement, progress . . . It makes me think of Africa.

BENEATHA: Africa!

ASAGAI: What kind of a mood is this? Have I told you how deeply you move me?

BENEATHA: He gave away the money, Asagai . . .

ASAGAI: Who gave away what money?

BENEATHA: The insurance money. My brother gave it away.

ASAGAI: Gave it away?

BENEATHA: He made an investment! With a man even Travis wouldn't have trusted.

ASAGAI: And it's gone?

BENEATHA: Gone!

ASAGAI: I'm very sorry . . . And you, now?

BENEATHA: Me? . . . Me? . . . Me, I'm nothing . . . Me. When I was very small . . . we used to take our sleds out in the wintertime and the only hills we had were the ice-covered stone steps of some houses down the street. And we used to fill them in with snow and make them smooth and slide down them all day . . . and it was very dangerous you know . . . far too steep . . . and sure enough one day a kid named Rufus came down too fast and hit the sidewalk . . . and we saw his face just split open right there in front of us . . . And I remember standing there looking at his bloody open face thinking that was the end of Rufus. But the ambulance came and they took him to the hospital and they fixed the broken bones and they sewed it all up . . . and the next time I saw Rufus he just had a little line down the middle of his face . . . I never got over that . . .

[WALTER *sits up, listening on the bed. Throughout this scene it is important that we feel his reaction at all times, that he visibly respond to the words of his sister and* ASAGAI.]

ASAGAI: What?

BENEATHA: That that was what one person could do for another, fix him up—sew up the problem, make him all right again. That was the most marvelous thing in the world . . . I wanted to do that. I always thought it was the one concrete thing in the world that a human being could do. Fix up the sick, you know—and make them whole again. This was truly being God . . .

ASAGAI: You wanted to be God?

BENEATHA: No—I wanted to cure. It used to be so important to me. I wanted to cure. It used to matter. I used to care. I mean about people and how their bodies hurt . . .

ASAGAI: And you've stopped caring?

BENEATHA: Yes—I think so.

ASAGAI: Why?

[WALTER *rises, goes to the door of his room and is about to open it, then stops and stands listening, leaning on the door jamb.*]

BENEATHA: Because it doesn't seem deep enough, close enough to what ails mankind—I mean this thing of sewing up bodies or administering drugs. Don't you understand? It was a child's reaction to the world. I thought that doctors had the secret to all the hurts . . . That's the way a child sees things—or an idealist.

ASAGAI: Children see things very well sometimes—and idealists even better.

BENEATHA: I know that's what you think. Because you are still where I left off—you still care. This is what you see for the world, for Africa. You with the dreams of the future will patch up all Africa—you are going to cure the Great Sore of colonialism with Independence——

ASAGAI: Yes!

BENEATHA: Yes—and you think that one word is the penicillin of the human spirit: "Independence!" But then what?

ASAGAI: That will be the problem for another time. First we must get there.

BENEATHA: And where does it end?

ASAGAI: End? Who even spoke of an end? To life? To living?

BENEATHA: An end to misery!

ASAGAI: [*Smiling.*] You sound like a French intellectual.

BENEATHA: No! I sound like a human being who just had her future taken right out of her hands! While I was sleeping in my bed in there, things were happening in this world that directly concerned me—and nobody asked me, consulted me—they just went out and did things—and changed my life. Don't you see there isn't any real progress, Asagai, there is only one large circle that we march in, around and around, each of us with our own little picture—in front of us—our own little mirage that we think is the future.

ASAGAI: That is the mistake.

BENEATHA: What?

ASAGAI: What you just said—about the circle. It isn't a circle—it is simply a long line—as in geometry, you know, one that reaches into infinity. And because we cannot see the end—we also cannot see how it changes. And it is very odd but those who see the changes are called "idealists"—and those who cannot, or refuse to think, they are the "realists." It is very strange, and amusing too, I think.

BENEATHA: You—you are almost religious.

ASAGAI: Yes . . . I think I have the religion of doing what is necessary in the world—and of worshipping man—because he is so marvelous, you see.

BENEATHA: Man is foul! And the human race deserves its misery!

ASAGAI: You see: *you* have become the religious one in the old sense. Already, and after such a small defeat, you are worshipping despair.

BENEATHA: From now on, I worship the truth—and the truth is that people are puny, small and selfish . . .

ASAGAI: Truth? Why is it that you despairing ones always think that only you have the truth? I never thought to see *you* like that. You! Your brother made a stupid, childish mistake—and you are grateful to him. So that now you can give up the ailing human race on account of it. You talk about what good is struggle; what good is anything? Where are we all going? And why are we bothering?

BENEATHA: *And you cannot answer it!* All your talk and dreams about Africa and Independence. Independence and then what? What about all the crooks and petty thieves and just plain idiots who will come into power to steal and plunder the same as before— only now they will be black and do it in the name of the new Independence—You cannot answer that.

ASAGAI: [*Shouting over her.*] *I live the answer!* [*Pause.*] In my village at home it is the exceptional man who can even read a newspaper . . . or who ever *sees* a book at all. I will go home and much of what I will have to say will seem strange to the people of my village . . . But I will teach and work and things will happen, slowly and swiftly. At times it will seem that nothing changes at all . . . and then again . . . the sudden dramatic events which make history leap into the future. And then quiet again. Retrogression even. Guns, murder, revolution. And I even will have moments when I wonder if the quiet was not better than all that death and hatred. But I will look about my village at the illiteracy and disease and ignorance and I will not wonder long. And perhaps . . . perhaps I will be a great man . . . I mean perhaps I will hold on to the substance of truth and find my way always with the right course . . . and perhaps for it I will be butchered in my bed some night by the servants of empire . . .

BENEATHA: *The martyr!*

ASAGAI: . . . or perhaps I shall live to be a very old man, respected and esteemed in my new nation . . . And perhaps I shall hold office and this is what I'm trying to tell you, Alaiyo; perhaps the things I believe now for my country will be wrong and outmoded, and I will not understand and do terrible things to have things my way or merely to keep my power. Don't you see that there will be young men and women, not British soldiers then, but my own black countrymen . . . to step out of the shadows some evening and slit my then useless throat? Don't you see they have always been there . . . that they always will be. And that such a thing as my own death will be an advance? They who might kill me even . . . actually replenish me!

BENEATHA: Oh, Asagai, I know all that.

ASAGAI: Good! Then stop moaning and groaning and tell me what you plan to do.

BENEATHA: Do?

ASAGAI: I have a bit of a suggestion.

BENEATHA: What?

ASAGAI: [*Rather quietly for him.*] That when it is all over—that you come home with me—

BENEATHA: [*Slapping herself on the forehead with exasperation born of misunderstanding.*] Oh—Asagai—at this moment you decide to be romantic!

ASAGAI: [*Quickly understanding the misunderstanding.*] My dear, young creature of the New World—I do not mean across the city—I mean across the ocean; home—to Africa.

BENEATHA: [*Slowly understanding and turning to him with murmured amazement.*] To—to Nigeria?

ASAGAI: Yes! . . . [*Smiling and lifting his arms playfully.*] Three hundred years later the African Prince rose up out of the seas and swept the maiden back across the middle passage over which her ancestors had come—

BENEATHA: [*Unable to play.*] Nigeria?

ASAGAI: Nigeria. Home. [*Coming to her with genuine romantic flippancy.*] I will show you our mountains and our stars; and give you cool drinks from gourds and teach you the old songs and the ways of our people—and, in time, we will pretend that—[*Very softly.*]—you have only been away for a day—

[*She turns her back to him, thinking. He swings her around and takes her full in his arms in a long embrace which proceeds to passion.*]

BENEATHA: [*Pulling away.*] You're getting me all mixed up—

ASAGAI: Why?

BENEATHA: Too many things—too many things have happened today. I must sit down and think. I don't know what I feel about anything right this minute.

[*She promptly sits down and props her chin on her fist.*]

ASAGAI: [*Charmed.*] All right, I shall leave you. No—don't get up. [*Touching her, gently, sweetly.*] Just sit awhile and think . . . Never be afraid to sit awhile and think. [*He goes to door and looks at her.*]

How often I have looked at you and said, "Ah—so this is what the New World hath finally wrought . . . "

[*He exits.* BENEATHA *sits on alone. Presently* WALTER *enters from his room and starts to rummage through things, feverishly looking for something. She looks up and turns in her seat.*]

BENEATHA: [*Hissingly.*] Yes—just look at what the New World hath wrought! . . . Just look! [*She gestures with bitter disgust.*] There he is! *Monsieur le petit bourgeois noir*—himself! There he is—Symbol of a Rising Class! Entrepreneur! Titan of the system! [WALTER *ignores her completely and continues frantically and destructively looking for something and hurling things to the floor and tearing things out of their place in his search.* BENEATHA *ignores the eccentricity of his actions and goes on with the monologue of insult.*] Did you dream of yachts on Lake Michigan, Brother? Did you see yourself on that Great Day sitting down at the Conference Table, surrounded by all the mighty bald-headed men in America? All halted, waiting, breathless, waiting for your pronouncements on industry? Waiting for you—Chairman of the Board? [WALTER *finds what he is looking for—a small piece of white paper—and pushes it in his pocket and puts on his coat and rushes out without ever having looked at her. She shouts after him.*] I look at you and I see the final triumph of stupidity in the world!

[*The door slams and she returns to just sitting again.* RUTH *comes quickly out of* MAMA's *room.*]

RUTH: Who was that?

BENEATHA: Your husband.

RUTH: Where did he go?

BENEATHA: Who knows—maybe he has an appointment at U.S. Steel.

RUTH: [*Anxiously, with frightened eyes.*] You didn't say nothing bad to him, did you?

BENEATHA: Bad? Say anything bad to him? No—I told him he was a sweet boy and full of dreams and everything is strictly peachy keen, as the ofay[5] kids say!

---

5. White.

[MAMA *enters from her bedroom. She is lost, vague, trying to catch hold, to make some sense of her former command of the world, but it still eludes her. A sense of waste overwhelms her gait; a measure of apology rides on her shoulders. She goes to her plant, which has remained on the table, looks at it, picks it up and takes it to the window sill and sits it outside, and she stands and looks at it a long moment. Then she closes the window, straightens her body with effort and turns around to her children.*]

MAMA: Well—ain't it a mess in here, though? [*A false cheerfulness, a beginning of something.*] I guess we all better stop moping around and get some work done. All this unpacking and everything we got to do. [RUTH *raises her head slowly in response to the sense of the line; and* BENEATHA *in similar manner turns very slowly to look at her mother.*] One of you all better call the moving people and tell 'em not to come.

RUTH: Tell 'em not to come?

MAMA: Of course, baby. Ain't no need in 'em coming all the way here and having to go back. They charges for that too. [*She sits down, fingers to her brow, thinking.*] Lord, ever since I was a little girl, I always remembers people saying, "Lena—Lena Eggleston, you aims too high all the time. You needs to slow down and see life a little more like it is. Just slow down some." That's what they always used to say down home—"Lord, that Lena Eggleston is a high-minded thing. She'll get her due one day!"

RUTH: No, Lena . . .

MAMA: Me and Big Walter just didn't never learn right.

RUTH: Lena, no! We gotta go. Bennie—tell her . . . [*She rises and crosses to* BENEATHA *with her arms outstretched.* BENEATHA *doesn't respond.*] Tell her we can still move . . . the notes ain't but a hundred and twenty-five a month. We got four grown people in this house—we can work . . .

MAMA: [*To herself.*] Just aimed too high all the time—

RUTH: [*Turning and going to* MAMA *fast—the words pouring out with urgency and desperation.*] Lena—I'll work . . . I'll work twenty hours a day in all the kitchens in Chicago . . . I'll strap my baby on my back if I have to and scrub all the floors in America and wash all the sheets in America if I have to—but we got to move . . . We got to get out of here . . .

[MAMA *reaches out absently and pats* RUTH's *hand.*]

MAMA: No—I sees things differently now. Been thinking 'bout some of the things we could do to fix this place up some. I seen a second-hand bureau over on Maxwell Street just the other day that could fit right there. [*She points to where the new furniture might go.* RUTH *wanders away from her.*] Would need some new handles on it and then a little varnish and then it look like something brand-new. And—we can put up them new curtains in the kitchen . . . Why this place be looking fine. Cheer us all up so that we forget trouble ever came . . . [*To* RUTH.] And you could get some nice screens to put up in your room round the baby's bassinet . . . [*She looks at both of them, pleadingly.*] Sometimes you just got to know when to give up some things . . . and hold on to what you got.

[WALTER *enters from the outside, looking spent and leaning against the door, his coat hanging from him.*]

MAMA: Where you been, son?

WALTER: [*Breathing hard.*] Made a call.

MAMA: To who, son?

WALTER: To The Man.

MAMA: What man, baby?

WALTER: The Man, Mama. Don't you know who The Man is?

RUTH: Walter Lee?

WALTER: *The Man.* Like the guys in the streets say—The Man. Captain Boss—Mistuh Charley . . . Old Captain Please Mr. Bossman . . .

BENEATHA: [*Suddenly.*] Lindner!

WALTER: That's right! That's good. I told him to come right over.

BENEATHA: [*Fiercely, understanding.*] For what? What do you want to see him for!

WALTER: [*Looking at his sister.*] We going to do business with him.

MAMA: What you talking 'bout, son?

WALTER: Talking 'bout life, Mama. You all always telling me to see life like it is. Well—I laid in there on my back today . . . and I figured it out. Life just like it is. Who gets and who don't get.

[*He sits down with his coat on and laughs.*] Mama, you know it's all divided up. Life is. Sure enough. Between the takers and the "tooken." [*He laughs.*] I've figured it out finally. [*He looks around at them.*] Yeah. Some of us always getting "tooken." [*He laughs.*] People like Willy Harris, they don't never get "tooken." And you know why the rest of us do? 'Cause we all mixed up. Mixed up bad. We get to looking 'round for the right and the wrong, and we worry about it and cry about it and stay up nights trying to figure out 'bout the wrong and the right of things all the time . . . And all the time, man, them takers is out there operating, just taking and taking. Willy Harris? Shoot—Willy Harris don't even count. He don't even count in the big scheme of things. But I'll say one thing for old Willy Harris . . . he's taught me something. He's taught me to keep my eye on what counts in this world. Yeah—[*Shouting out a little.*] Thanks, Willy!

RUTH: What did you call that man for, Walter Lee?

WALTER: Called him to tell him to come on over to the show. Gonna put on a show for the man. Just what he wants to see. You see, Mama, the man came here today and he told us that them people out there where you want us to move—well they so upset they willing to pay us not to move out there. [*He laughs again.*] And—and oh, Mama—you would of been proud of the way me and Ruth and Bennie acted. We told him to get out . . . Lord have mercy! We told the man to get out. Oh, we was some proud folks this afternoon, yeah. [*He lights a cigarette.*] We were still full of that old-time stuff . . .

RUTH: [*Coming toward him slowly.*] You talking 'bout taking them people's money to keep us from moving in that house?

WALTER: I ain't just talking 'bout it, baby—I'm telling you that's what's going to happen.

BENEATHA: Oh, God! Where is the bottom! Where is the real honest-to-God bottom so he can't go any farther!

WALTER: See—that's the old stuff. You and that boy that was here today. You all want everybody to carry a flag and a spear and sing some marching songs, huh? You wanna spend your life looking into things and trying to find the right and the wrong part, huh? Yeah. You know what's going to happen to that boy someday—he'll find himself sitting in a dungeon, locked in forever—and the takers will have the key! Forget it, baby! There ain't no causes—there ain't nothing but taking in this world, and he who takes most is smartest—and it don't make a damn bit of difference *how*.

MAMA: You making something inside me cry, son. Some awful pain inside me.

WALTER: Don't cry, Mama. Understand. That white man is going to walk in that door able to write checks for more money than we ever had. It's important to him and I'm going to help him . . . I'm going to put on the show, Mama.

MAMA: Son—I come from five generations of people who was slaves and share-croppers—but ain't nobody in my family never let nobody pay 'em no money that was a way of telling us we wasn't fit to walk the earth. We ain't never been that poor. [*Raising her eyes and looking at him.*] We ain't never been that dead inside.

BENEATHA: Well—we are dead now. All the talk about dreams and sunlight that goes on in this house. All dead.

WALTER: What's the matter with you all! I didn't make this world! It was give to me this way! Hell, yes, I want me some yachts someday! Yes, I want to hang some real pearls 'round my wife's neck. Ain't she supposed to wear no pearls? Somebody tell me—tell me, who decides which women is suppose to wear pearls in this world. I tell you I am a *man*—and I think my wife should wear some pearls in this world!

[*This last line hangs a good while and* WALTER *begins to move about the room. The word "Man" has penetrated his consciousness; he mumbles it to himself repeatedly between strange agitated pauses as he moves about.*]

MAMA: Baby, how you going to feel on the inside?

WALTER: Fine! . . . Going to feel fine . . . a man . . .

MAMA: You won't have nothing left then, Walter Lee.

WALTER: [*Coming to her.*] I'm going to feel fine, Mama. I'm going to look that son-of-a-bitch in the eyes and say—[*He falters.*]—and say, "All right, Mr. Lindner—[*He falters even more.*]—that's your neighborhood out there. You got the right to keep it like you want. You got the right to have it like you want. Just write the check and—the house is yours." And, and I am going to say—[*His voice almost breaks.*] And you—you people just put the money in my hand and you won't have to live next to this bunch of stinking niggers! . . . [*He straightens up and moves away from his mother, walking around the room.*] Maybe—maybe I'll just get down on my black knees . . . [*He does so;* RUTH *and* BENNIE *and* MAMA *watch him in frozen horror.*] Captain, Mistuh, Bossman. [*He starts crying.*] A-hee-hee-hee! [*Wringing his hands in profoundly anguished imitation.*] Yassss-suh! Great White Father, just gi' ussen de money, fo' God's sake, and we's ain't gwine come out deh and dirty up yo' white folks neighborhood . . .

[*He breaks down completely, then gets up and goes into the bedroom.*]

BENEATHA: That is not a man. That is nothing but a toothless rat.

MAMA: Yes—death done come in this here house. [*She is nodding, slowly, reflectively.*] Done come walking in my house. On the lips of my children. You what supposed to be my beginning again. You—what supposed to be my harvest. [*To* BENEATHA.] You— you mourning your brother?

BENEATHA: He's no brother of mine.

MAMA: What you say?

BENEATHA: I said that that individual in that room is no brother of mine.

MAMA: That's what I thought you said. You feeling like you better than he is today? [BENEATHA *does not answer.*] Yes? What you tell him a minute ago? That he wasn't a man? Yes? You give him up for me? You done wrote his epitaph too—like the rest of the world? Well, who give you the privilege?

BENEATHA: Be on my side for once! You saw what he just did, Mama! You saw him—down on his knees. Wasn't it you who taught me—to despise any man who would do that. Do what he's going to do.

MAMA: Yes—I taught you that. Me and your daddy. But I thought I taught you something else too . . . I thought I taught you to love him.

BENEATHA: Love him? There is nothing left to love.

MAMA: There is always something left to love. And if you ain't learned that, you ain't learned nothing. [*Looking at her.*] Have you cried for that boy today? I don't mean for yourself and for the family 'cause we lost the money. I mean for him; what he been through and what it done to him. Child, when do you think is the time to love somebody the most; when they done good and made things easy for everybody? Well then, you ain't through learning—because that ain't the time at all. It's when he's at his lowest and can't believe in hisself 'cause the world done whipped him so. When you starts measuring somebody, measure him right, child, measure him right. Make sure you done taken into account what hills and valleys he come through before he got to wherever he is.

[TRAVIS *bursts into the room at the end of the speech, leaving the door open.*]

TRAVIS: Grandmama—the moving men are downstairs! The truck just pulled up.

MAMA: [*Turning and looking at him.*] Are they, baby? They downstairs?

[*She sighs and sits.* LINDNER *appears in the doorway. He peers in and knocks lightly, to gain attention, and comes in. All turn to look at him.*]

LINDNER: [*Hat and briefcase in hand.*] Uh—hello . . .

[RUTH *crosses mechanically to the bedroom door and opens it and lets it swing open freely and slowly as the lights come up on* WAL-TER *within, still in his coat, sitting at the far corner of the room. He looks up and out through the room to* LINDNER.]

RUTH: He's here.

[*A long minute passes and* WALTER *slowly gets up.*]

LINDNER: [*Coming to the table with efficiency, putting his briefcase on the table and starting to unfold papers and unscrew fountain pens.*] Well, I certainly was glad to hear from you people. [WALTER *has begun the trek out of the room, slowly and awkwardly, rather like a small boy, passing the back of his sleeve across his mouth from time to time.*] Life can really be so much simpler than people let it be most of the time. Well—with whom do I negotiate? You, Mrs. Younger, or your son here? [MAMA *sits with her hands folded on her lap and her eyes closed as* WALTER *advances.* TRAVIS *goes close to* LINDNER *and looks at the papers curiously.*] Just some official papers, sonny.

RUTH: Travis, you go downstairs.

MAMA: [*Opening her eyes and looking into* WALTER'*s.*] No. Travis, you stay right here. And you make him understand what you doing, Walter Lee. You teach him good. Like Willy Harris taught you. You show where our five generations done come to. Go ahead, son—

WALTER: [*Looks down into his boy's eyes.* TRAVIS *grins at him merrily and* WALTER *draws him beside him with his arm lightly around his shoulders.*] Well, Mr. Lindner. [BENEATHA *turns away.*] We called you—[*There is a profound, simple groping quality in his speech.*]— because, well, me and my family [*He looks around and shifts from one foot to the other.*] Well—we are very plain people . . .

LINDNER: Yes—

WALTER: I mean—I have worked as a chauffeur most of my life— and my wife here, she does domestic work in people's kitchens. So does my mother. I mean—we are plain people . . .

LINDNER: Yes, Mr. Younger—

WALTER: [*Really like a small boy, looking down at his shoes and then up at the man.*] And—uh—well, my father, well, he was a laborer most of his life.

LINDNER: [*Absolutely confused.*] Uh, yes—

WALTER: [*Looking down at his toes once again.*] My father almost beat a man to death once because this man called him a bad name or something, you know what I mean?

LINDNER: No, I'm afraid I don't.

WALTER: [*Finally straightening up.*] Well, what I mean is that we come from people who had a lot of pride. I mean—we are very proud people. And that's my sister over there and she's going to be a doctor—and we are very proud—

LINDNER: Well—I am sure that is very nice, but—

WALTER: [*Starting to cry and facing the man eye to eye.*] What I am telling you is that we called you over here to tell you that we are very proud and that this is—this is my son, who makes the sixth generation of our family in this country, and that we have all thought about your offer and we have decided to move into our house because my father—my father—he earned it. [MAMA *has her eyes closed and is rocking back and forth as though she were in church, with her head nodding the amen yes.*] We don't want to make no trouble for nobody or fight no causes—but we will try to be good neighbors. That's all we got to say. [*He looks the man absolutely in the eyes.*] We don't want your money.

[*He turns and walks away from the man.*]

LINDNER: [*Looking around at all of them.*] I take it then that you have decided to occupy.

BENEATHA: That's what the man said.

LINDNER: [*To* MAMA *in her reverie.*] Then I would like to appeal to you, Mrs. Younger. You are older and wiser and understand things better I am sure . . .

MAMA: [*Rising.*] I am afraid you don't understand. My son said we was going to move and there ain't nothing left for me to say. [*Shaking her head with double meaning.*] You know how these young folks is nowadays, mister. Can't do a thing with 'em. Good-bye.

LINDNER: [*Folding up his materials.*] Well—if you are that final about it . . . There is nothing left for me to say. [*He finishes. He is almost ignored by the family, who are concentrating on* WALTER LEE. *At the door* LINDNER *halts and looks around.*] I sure hope you people know what you're doing.

[*He shakes his head and exits.*]

RUTH: [*Looking around and coming to life.*] Well, for God's sake—if the moving men are here—LET'S GET THE HELL OUT OF HERE!

MAMA: [*Into action.*] Ain't it the truth! Look at all this here mess. Ruth, put Travis' good jacket on him . . . Walter Lee, fix your tie and tuck your shirt in, you look just like somebody's hoodlum. Lord have mercy, where is my plant? [*She flies to get it amid the general bustling of the family, who are deliberately try-ing to ignore the nobility of the past moment.*] You all start on down . . . Travis child, don't go empty-handed . . . Ruth, where did I put that box with my skillets in it? I want to be in charge of it myself . . . I'm going to make us the biggest dinner we ever ate tonight . . . Beneatha, what's the matter with them stockings?

Pull them things up, girl . . .

[*The family starts to file out as two moving men appear and begin to carry out the heavier pieces of furniture, bumping into the family as they move about.*]

BENEATHA: Mama, Asagai—asked me to marry him today and go to Africa—

MAMA: [*In the middle of her getting-ready activity.*] He did? You ain't old enough to marry nobody—[*Seeing the moving men lifting one of her chairs precariously.*] Darling, that ain't no bale of cotton, please handle it so we can sit in it again. I had that chair twenty-five years . . .

[*The movers sigh with exasperation and go on with their work.*]

BENEATHA: [*Girlishly and unreasonably trying to pursue the conversation.*] To go to Africa, Mama—be a doctor in Africa . . .

MAMA: [*Distracted.*] Yes, baby—

WALTER: Africa! What he want you to go to Africa for?

BENEATHA: To practice there . . .

WALTER: Girl, if you don't get all them silly ideas out your head! You better marry yourself a man with some loot . . .

BENEATHA: [*Angrily, precisely as in the first scene of the play.*] What have you got to do with who I marry!

WALTER: Plenty. Now I think George Murchison—

[*He and* BENEATHA *go out yelling at each other vigorously;* BENEATHA *is heard saying that she would not marry* GEORGE MURCHISON *if he were Adam and she were Eve, etc. The anger is loud and real till their voices diminish.* RUTH *stands at the door and turns to* MAMA *and smiles knowingly.*]

MAMA: [*Fixing her hat at last.*] Yeah—they something all right, my children . . .

RUTH: Yeah—they're something. Let's go, Lena.

MAMA: [*Stalling, starting to look around at the house.*] Yes—I'm coming. Ruth—

RUTH: Yes?

MAMA: [*Quietly, woman to woman.*] He finally come into his manhood today, didn't he? Kind of like a rainbow after the rain . . .

RUTH: [*Biting her lip lest her own pride explode in front of* MAMA.] Yes, Lena.

[WALTER's *voice calls for them raucously.*]

MAMA: [*Waving* RUTH *out vaguely.*] All right, honey—go on down. I be down directly.

> [RUTH *hesitates, then exits.* MAMA *stands, at last alone in the living room, her plant on the table before her as the lights start to come down. She looks around at all the walls and ceilings and suddenly, despite herself, while the children call below, a great heaving thing rises in her and she puts her fist to her mouth, takes a final desperate look, pulls her coat about her, pats her hat and goes out. The lights dim down. The door opens and she comes back in, grabs her plant, and goes out for the last time.*]

[*CURTAIN.*]

1959

August Wilson
1945–2005

FENCES

> *All of August Wilson's plays dramatize the experiences of African Americans in a racist society. Most of them focus on life in an African American neighborhood of Pittsburgh, the "Hill," during particular decades of the twentieth century.* Fences, *the second play in this historical cycle, takes place during the 1950s and derives partly from Wilson's family history. Like the play's main character, Troy Maxson, Wilson's stepfather, David Bedford, had been an exceptional high school athlete in the 1930s. He was poor, however, and at that time few colleges would offer a scholarship to a black man. Bedford turned to crime, and in a robbery gone wrong he killed someone. He served over two decades in prison before he was released and married Wilson's mother.*
>
> *While he drew on Bedford for some details of Maxson's biography, Wilson's portrait of a proud soul battered by racism needed no model other than himself. As an African American growing up in a largely white suburb, he saw and experienced the*

effects of an environment hostile to its inhabitants' success, especially to their intellectual success. In response, Wilson later affiliated himself with the Nation of Islam, especially with the civil rights leader Malcolm X and his message of black self-reliance and independence.

Another model for Troy Maxson is the baseball legend Josh Gibson. Born in Georgia in 1911, Gibson moved with his family to Pittsburgh, Pennsylvania, in the early 1920s. He studied to be an electrician, but had to drop out of school after the ninth grade to work in a factory. He started playing for a Negro League baseball team, the Pittsburgh Crawfords, in 1929, and for the next seventeen years he played for the Crawfords, for the Homestead Grays (also in Pittsburgh), and in the Mexican League. He was a prodigious slugger, the black Babe Ruth (as many called him, though it might have been more accurate to call Ruth the white Josh Gibson). His accomplishments are incredible: 962 home runs, a lifetime batting average of .354, and an amazing 84 home runs in one season in 1936. In the mid-1940s, the Washington Senators (a Major League team) flirted with the idea of signing Gibson, but the owner, Clark Griffith, lacked the courage to break the color barrier. Gibson's last season was 1946. He died of a stroke in early 1947. His health had been declining for four years, and he was always a hard drinker, but legend contends that he died of a broken heart, for by 1946, Jackie Robinson was headed for the Major Leagues and Gibson knew that he was too old to join him. Though Gibson made decent money in the Negro Leagues and even more in the Mexican League, he was so poor when he died that donations had to be collected to pay for his funeral. You might consider Troy Maxson to be a portrait of Josh Gibson had he lived another ten years.

Maxson's experience as a garbage man, especially his fights with the sanitation workers' union, reflects Wilson's interest in the rise of the American labor movement. Of all American cities, Pittsburgh probably has been the most important to the political cause of labor, and Homestead, on the outskirts of the city, was the battleground of the most notorious assault on workers in American history. In 1892, industrialist Andrew Carnegie assiduously denied steel workers the right to unionize and refused them a decent wage, triggering a long and bloody battle between labor and capital.

Until fairly recently, however, unions were just as racist as the rest of American society. Though all laborers had the same interest in wresting decent pay and humane working conditions from corporations, whites typically refused to close ranks with their black coworkers. African Americans had to fight for equal treatment by the labor movement just as they fought for equal treatment by the law. In fact, Martin Luther King Jr. was helping black sanitation workers unionize when he was assassinated in Memphis in 1968.

As he chronicles such changes, Wilson also notes what the black communities lost when America integrated. Though few people today would argue for the ghettoizing of any single race of Americans, such enforced isolation fostered a sense of community and allowed for an economic independence that integration undermined. For example, integrating the Major Leagues destroyed the Negro Leagues, and with the Negro Leagues went the only black-owned ball clubs in America. Only now, more than half a century after Jackie Robinson started to play for the Dodgers, are African Americans breaking into the upper ranks of management and ownership in the Major Leagues.

The first generation of integrated minorities must experience a sense of loss even as it gains so much. Wilson was accused of sentimentalizing that loss and even of supporting separatism, the belief that African Americans must sustain their own communities and cultural institutions apart from the white-dominated mainstream. Certainly, he worked to improve opportunities for black actors, black theaters, and black directors, staunchly supporting regional theaters that cater to black audiences. Indeed, Paramount Pictures' plans to make a movie out of Fences *stalled because of Wilson's insistence on using a black director.*

Even as you read the play in light of these issues, however, don't forget that it is also about family—about fathers and sons, wives and husbands. Like the best "problem" plays in the Ibsen tradition, Fences *can stand as well outside as it stands inside its historical and cultural context.*

Fences

CHARACTERS

TROY MAXSON

JIM BONO, *Troy's friend*

ROSE, *Troy's wife*

LYONS, *Troy's oldest son by previous marriage*

GABRIEL, *Troy's brother*

CORY, *Troy and Rose's son*

RAYNELL, *Troy's daughter*

SETTING

The setting is the yard which fronts the only entrance to the MAX-SON household, an ancient two-story brick house set back off a small alley in a big-city neighborhood. The entrance to the house is gained by two or three steps leading to a wooden porch badly in need of paint.

A relatively recent addition to the house and running its full width, the porch lacks congruence. It is a sturdy porch with a flat roof. One or two chairs of dubious value sit at one end where the kitchen window opens onto the porch. An old-fashioned icebox stands silent guard at the opposite end.

The yard is a small dirt yard, partially fenced, except for the last scene, with a wooden sawhorse, a pile of lumber, and other fence-building equipment set off to the side. Opposite is a tree from which hangs a ball made of rags. A baseball bat leans against the tree. Two oil drums serve as garbage receptacles and sit near the house at right to complete the setting.

THE PLAY

Near the turn of the century, the destitute of Europe sprang on the city with tenacious claws and an honest and solid dream. The city devoured them. They swelled its belly until it burst into a thousand furnaces and sewing machines, a thousand butcher shops and bakers' ovens, a thousand churches and hospitals and funeral parlors and moneylenders. The city grew. It nourished itself and offered each man a partnership limited only by his talent, his guile, and his willingness and capacity for hard work. For the immigrants of Europe, a dream dared and won true.

The descendants of African slaves were offered no such welcome or participation. They came from places called the Carolinas and the Virginias, Georgia, Alabama, Mississippi, and Tennessee. They came strong, eager, searching. The city rejected them and they fled and settled along the riverbanks and under bridges in shallow, ramshackle houses made of sticks and tar-paper. They collected rags and wood. They sold the use of their muscles and their bodies. They cleaned houses and washed clothes, they shined shoes, and in quiet desperation and vengeful pride, they stole, and lived in pursuit of their own dream. That they could breathe free, finally, and stand to meet life with the force of dignity and whatever eloquence the heart could call upon.

By 1957, the hard-won victories of the European immigrants had solidified the industrial might of America. War had been confronted and won with new energies that used loyalty and patriotism as its fuel. Life was rich, full, and flourishing. The Milwaukee Braves won the World Series, and the hot winds of change that would make the sixties a turbulent, racing, dangerous, and provocative decade had not yet begun to blow full.

ACT 1
SCENE 1

It is 1957. TROY *and* BONO *enter the yard, engaged in conversation.* TROY *is fifty-three years old, a large man with thick, heavy hands; it is this largeness that he strives to fill out and make an accommodation with. Together with his blackness, his largeness informs his sensibilities and the choices he has made in his life.*

Of the two men, BONO *is obviously the follower. His commitment to their friendship of thirty-odd years is rooted in his admiration of* TROY'*s honesty, capacity for hard work, and strength, which* BONO *seeks to emulate.*

It is Friday night, payday, and the one night of the week the two men engage in a ritual of talk and drink. TROY *is usually the most talkative and at times he can be crude and almost vulgar, though he is capable of rising to profound heights of expression. The men carry lunch buckets and wear or carry burlap aprons and are dressed in clothes suitable to their jobs as garbage collectors.*

BONO: Troy, you ought to stop that lying!
TROY: I ain't lying! The nigger had a watermelon this big. [*He*

indicates with his hands.] Talking about . . . "What watermelon, Mr. Rand?" I liked to fell out! "What watermelon, Mr. Rand?" . . . And it sitting there big as life.

BONO: What did Mr. Rand say?

TROY: Ain't said nothing. Figure if the nigger too dumb to know he carrying a watermelon, he wasn't gonna get much sense out of him. Trying to hide that great big old watermelon under his coat. Afraid to let the white man see him carry it home.

BONO: I'm like you. . . . I ain't got no time for them kind of people.

TROY: Now what he look like getting mad cause he see the man from the union talking to Mr. Rand?

BONO: He come to me talking about . . . "Maxson gonna get us fired." I told him to get away from me with that. He walked away from me calling you a troublemaker. What Mr. Rand say?

TROY: Ain't said nothing. He told me to go down the Commissioner's office next Friday. They called me down there to see them.

BONO: Well, as long as you got your complaint filed, they can't fire you. That's what one of them white fellows tell me.

TROY: I ain't worried about them firing me. They gonna fire me cause I asked a question? That's all I did. I went to Mr. Rand and asked him, "Why? Why you got the white mens driving and the colored lifting?" Told him, "What's the matter, don't I count? You think only white fellows got sense enough to drive a truck. That ain't no paper job! Hell, anybody can drive a truck. How come you got all whites driving and the colored lifting? He told me "take it to the union." Well, hell, that's what I done! Now they wanna come up with this pack of lies.

BONO: I told Brownie if the man come and ask him any questions . . . just tell the truth! It ain't nothing but something they done trumped up on you cause you filed a complaint on them.

TROY: Brownie don't understand nothing. All I want them to do is change the job description. Give everybody a chance to drive the truck. Brownie can't see that. He ain't got that much sense.

BONO: How you figure he be making out with that gal be up at Taylors' all the time . . . that Alberta gal?

TROY: Same as you and me. Getting just as much as we is. Which is to say, nothing.

BONO: It is, huh? I figure you doing a little better than me . . . and I ain't saying what I'm doing.

TROY: Aw, nigger, look here . . . I know you. If you had got anywhere near that gal, twenty minutes later you be looking to tell somebody. And the first one you gonna tell . . . that you gonna want to brag to . . . is gonna be me.

BONO: I ain't saying that. I see where you be eyeing her.

TROY: I eye all the women. I don't miss nothing. Don't never let nobody tell you Troy Maxson don't eye the women.

BONO: You been doing more than eyeing her. You done bought her a drink or two.

TROY: Hell yeah, I bought her a drink! What that mean? I bought you one, too. What that mean cause I buy her a drink? I'm just being polite.

BONO: It's alright to buy her one drink. That's what you call being polite. But when you wanna be buying two or three . . . that's what you call eyeing her.

TROY: Look here, as long as you known me . . . you ever known me to chase after women?

BONO: Hell yeah! Long as I done known you. You forgetting I knew you when.

TROY: Naw, I'm talking about since I been married to Rose?

BONO: Oh, not since you been married to Rose. Now, that's the truth, there. I can say that.

TROY: Alright then! Case closed.

BONO: I see you be walking up around Alberta's house. You supposed to be at Taylors' and you be walking up around there.

TROY: What you watching where I'm walking for? I ain't watching after you.

BONO: I seen you walking around there more than once.

TROY: Hell, you liable to see me walking anywhere! That don't mean nothing cause you see me walking around there.

BONO: Where she come from anyway? She just kinda showed up one day.

TROY: Tallahassee. You can look at her and tell she one of them Florida gals. They got some big healthy women down there. Grow them right up out the ground. Got a little bit of Indian in her. Most of them niggers down in Florida got some Indian in them.

BONO: I don't know about that Indian part. But she damn sure big and healthy. Woman wear some big stockings. Got them great big old legs and hips as wide as the Mississippi River.

TROY: Legs don't mean nothing. You don't do nothing but push them out of the way. But them hips cushion the ride!

BONO: Troy, you ain't got no sense.

TROY: It's the truth! Like you riding on Goodyears!

[ROSE *enters from the house. She is ten years younger than* TROY, *her devotion to him stems from her recognition of the possibilities of her life without him: a succession of abusive men and their babies, a life of partying and running the streets, the Church, or aloneness with its attendant pain and frustration. She recognizes* TROY*'s spirit as a fine and illuminating one and she either ignores or forgives his faults, only some of which she recognizes. Though she doesn't drink, her presence is an integral part of the Friday night rituals. She alternates between the porch and the kitchen, where supper preparations are under way.*]

ROSE: What you all out here getting into?

TROY: What you worried about what we getting into for? This is men talk, woman.

ROSE: What I care what you all talking about? Bono, you gonna stay for supper?

BONO: No, I thank you, Rose. But Lucille say she cooking up a pot of pigfeet.

TROY: Pigfeet! Hell, I'm going home with you! Might even stay the night if you got some pigfeet. You got something in there to top them pigfeet, Rose?

ROSE: I'm cooking up some chicken. I got some chicken and collard greens.

TROY: Well, go on back in the house and let me and Bono finish what we was talking about. This is men talk. I got some talk for you later. You know what kind of talk I mean. You go on and powder it up.

ROSE: Troy Maxson, don't you start that now!

TROY: [*Puts his arm around her.*] Aw, woman . . . come here. Look here, Bono . . . when I met this woman . . . I got out that place, say, "Hitch up my pony, saddle up my mare . . . there's a woman out there for me somewhere. I looked here. Looked there. Saw Rose and latched on to her." I latched on to her and told her— I'm gonna tell you the truth—I told her, "Baby, I don't wanna marry, I just wanna be your man." Rose told me . . . tell him what you told me, Rose.

ROSE: I told him if he wasn't the marrying kind, then move out the way so the marrying kind could find me.

TROY: That's what she told me. "Nigger, you in my way. You blocking the view! Move out the way so I can find me a husband." I thought it over two or three days. Come back—

ROSE: Ain't no two or three days nothing. You was back the same night.

TROY: Come back, told her . . . "Okay, baby . . . but I'm gonna buy me a banty rooster and put him out there in the backyard . . . and when he see a stranger come, he'll flap his wings and crow . . ." Look here, Bono, I could watch the front door by myself . . . it was that back door I was worried about.

ROSE: Troy, you ought not talk like that. Troy ain't doing nothing but telling a lie.

TROY: Only thing is . . . when we first got married . . . forget the rooster . . . we ain't had no yard!

BONO: I hear you tell it. Me and Lucille was staying down there on Logan Street. Had two rooms with the outhouse in the back. I ain't mind the outhouse none. But when that goddamn wind blow through there in the winter . . . that's what I'm talking about! To this day I wonder why in the hell I ever stayed down there for six long years. But see, I didn't know I could do no better. I thought only white folks had inside toilets and things.

ROSE: There's a lot of people don't know they can do no better than they doing now. That's just something you got to learn. A lot of folks still shop at Bella's.

TROY: Ain't nothing wrong with shopping at Bella's. She got fresh food.

ROSE: I ain't said nothing about if she got fresh food. I'm talking about what she charge. She charge ten cents more than the A&P.

TROY: The A&P ain't never done nothing for me. I spends my money where I'm treated right. I go down to Bella, say, "I need a loaf of bread, I'll pay you Friday." She give it to me. What sense that make when I got money to go and spend it somewhere else and ignore the person who done right by me? That ain't in the Bible.

ROSE: We ain't talking about what's in the Bible. What sense it make to shop there when she overcharge?

TROY: You shop where you want to. I'll do my shopping where the people been good to me.

ROSE: Well, I don't think it's right for her to overcharge. That's all I was saying.

BONO: Look here . . . I got to get on. Lucille going be raising all kind of hell.

TROY: Where you going, nigger? We ain't finished this pint. Come here, finish this pint.

BONO: Well, hell, I am . . . if you ever turn the bottle loose.

TROY: [*Hands him the bottle.*] The only thing I say about the A&P is I'm glad Cory got that job down there. Help him take care of his school clothes and things. Gabe done moved out and things getting tight around here. He got that job. . . . He can start to look out for himself.

ROSE: Cory done went and got recruited by a college football team.

TROY: I told that boy about that football stuff. The white man ain't gonna let him get nowhere with that football. I told him when he first come to me with it. Now you come telling me he done went and got more tied up in it. He ought to go and get recruited in how to fix cars or something where he can make a living.

ROSE: He ain't talking about making no living playing football. It's just something the boys in school do. They gonna send a recruiter by to talk to you. He'll tell you he ain't talking about making no living playing football. It's a honor to be recruited.

TROY: It ain't gonna get him nowhere. Bono'll tell you that.

BONO: If he be like you in the sports . . . he's gonna be alright. Ain't but two men ever played baseball as good as you. That's Babe Ruth and Josh Gibson.[1] Them's the only two men ever hit more home runs than you.

TROY: What it ever get me? Ain't got a pot to piss in or a window to throw it out of.

ROSE: Times have changed since you was playing baseball, Troy. That was before the war.[2] Times have changed a lot since then.

TROY: How in hell they done changed?

ROSE: They got lots of colored boys playing ball now. Baseball and football.

1. See headnote (p. 445) for a discussion of Josh Gibson.   2. World War II, which ended in 1945.

BONO: You right about that, Rose. Times have changed, Troy. You just come along too early.

TROY: There ought not never have been no time called too early! Now you take that fellow . . . what's that fellow they had playing right field for the Yankees back then? You know who I'm talking about, Bono. Used to play right field for the Yankees.

ROSE: Selkirk?

TROY: Selkirk! That's it! Man batting .269, understand? .269. What kind of sense that make? I was hitting .432 with thirty-seven home runs! Man batting .269 and playing right field for the Yankees! I saw Josh Gibson's daughter yesterday. She walking around with raggedy shoes on her feet. Now I bet you Selkirk's daughter ain't walking around with raggedy shoes on her feet! I bet you that!

ROSE: They got a lot of colored baseball players now. Jackie Robinson was the first. Folks had to wait for Jackie Robinson.

TROY: I done seen a hundred niggers play baseball better than Jackie Robinson. Hell, I know some teams Jackie Robinson couldn't even make! What you talking about Jackie Robinson. Jackie Robinson wasn't nobody. I'm talking about if you could play ball then they ought to have let you play. Don't care what color you were. Come telling me I come along too early. If you could play . . . then they ought to have let you play. [TROY *takes a long drink from the bottle.*]

ROSE: You gonna drink yourself to death. You don't need to be drinking like that.

TROY: Death ain't nothing. I done seen him. Done wrassled with him. You can't tell me nothing about death. Death ain't nothing but a fastball on the outside corner. And you know what I'll do to that! Lookee here, Bono . . . am I lying? You get one of them fastballs, about waist high, over the outside corner of the plate where you can get the meat of the bat on it . . . and good God! You can kiss it goodbye. Now, am I lying?

BONO: Naw, you telling the truth there. I seen you do it.

TROY: If I'm lying . . . that 450 feet worth of lying! [*Pause.*] That's all death is to me. A fastball on the outside corner.

ROSE: I don't know why you want to get on talking about death.

TROY: Ain't nothing wrong with talking about death. That's part of life. Everybody gonna die. You gonna die, I'm gonna die. Bono's gonna die. Hell, we all gonna die.

ROSE: But you ain't got to talk about it. I don't like to talk about it.

TROY: You the one brought it up. Me and Bono was talking about baseball . . . you tell me I'm gonna drink myself to death. Ain't that right, Bono? You know I don't drink this but one night out of the week. That's Friday night. I'm gonna drink just enough to where I can handle it. Then I cuts it loose. I leave it alone. So don't you worry about me drinking myself to death. 'Cause I ain't worried about Death. I done seen him. I done wrestled with him.

Look here, Bono . . . I looked up one day and Death was marching straight at me. Like Soldiers on Parade! The Army of Death was marching straight at me. The middle of July, 1941. It got real cold just like it be winter. It seem like Death himself reached out and touched me on the shoulder. He touch me just like I touch you. I got cold as ice and Death standing there grinning at me.

ROSE: Troy, why don't you hush that talk.

TROY: I say . . . What you want, Mr. Death? You be wanting me? You done brought your army to be getting me? I looked him dead in the eye. I wasn't fearing nothing. I was ready to tangle. Just like I'm ready to tangle now. The Bible say be ever vigilant. That's why I don't get but so drunk. I got to keep watch.

ROSE: Troy was right down there in Mercy Hospital. You remember he had pneumonia? Laying there with a fever talking plumb out of his head.

TROY: Death standing there staring at me . . . carrying that sickle in his hand. Finally he say, "You want bound over for another year?" See, just like that . . . "You want bound over for another year?" I told him, "Bound over hell! Let's settle this now!"

It seem like he kinda fell back when I said that, and all the cold went out of me. I reached down and grabbed that sickle and threw it just as far as I could throw it . . . and me and him commenced to wrestling.

We wrestled for three days and three nights. I can't say where I found the strength from. Every time it seemed like he was gonna get the best of me, I'd reach way down deep inside myself and find the strength to do him one better.

ROSE: Every time Troy tell that story he find different ways to tell it. Different things to make up about it.

TROY: I ain't making up nothing. I'm telling you the facts of what happened. I wrestled with Death for three days and three nights and I'm standing here to tell you about it. [*Pause.*] Alright. At the end of the third night we done weakened each other to where we can't hardly move. Death stood up, throwed on his robe . . . had him a white robe with a hood on it. He throwed on that robe and went off to look for his sickle. Say, "I'll be back." Just like that. "I'll be back." I told him, say, "Yeah, but . . . you gonna have to find me!" I wasn't no fool. I wasn't going looking for him. Death ain't nothing to play with. And I know he's gonna get me. I know I got to join his army . . . his camp followers. But as long as I keep my strength and see him coming . . . as long as I keep up my vigilance . . . he's gonna have to fight to get me. I ain't going easy.

BONO: Well, look here, since you got to keep up your vigilance . . . let me have the bottle.

TROY: Aw hell, I shouldn't have told you that part. I should have left out that part.

ROSE: Troy be talking that stuff and half the time don't even know what he be talking about.

TROY: Bono know me better than that.

BONO: That's right. I know you. I know you got some Uncle Remus[3] in your blood. You got more stories than the devil got sinners.

TROY: Aw hell, I done seen him too! Done talked with the devil.

ROSE: Troy, don't nobody wanna be hearing all that stuff.

[LYONS *enters the yard from the street. Thirty-four years old,* TROY's *son by a previous marriage, he sports a neatly trimmed goatee, sport coat, white shirt, tieless and buttoned at the collar. Though he fancies himself a musician, he is more caught up in the rituals and "idea" of being a musician than in the actual practice of the music. He has come to borrow money from* TROY, *and while he knows he will be successful, he is uncertain as to what extent his lifestyle will be held up to scrutiny and ridicule.*]

LYONS: Hey, Pop.

TROY: What you come "Hey, Popping" me for?

LYONS: How you doing, Rose? [*He kisses her.*] Mr. Bono. How you doing?

3. The wise, old, black narrator of a series of stories about Brer Rabbit and Brer Fox, written by Joel Chandler Harris (1848–1908).

BONO: Hey, Lyons . . . how you been?

TROY: He must have been doing alright. I ain't seen him around here last week.

ROSE: Troy, leave your boy alone. He come by to see you and you wanna start all that nonsense.

TROY: I ain't bothering Lyons. [*Offers him the bottle.*] Here . . . get you a drink. We got an understanding. I know why he come by to see me and he know I know.

LYONS: Come on, Pop . . . I just stopped by to say hi . . . see how you was doing.

TROY: You ain't stopped by yesterday.

ROSE: You gonna stay for supper, Lyons? I got some chicken cooking in the oven.

LYONS: No, Rose . . . thanks. I was just in the neighborhood and thought I'd stop by for a minute.

TROY: You was in the neighborhood alright, nigger. You telling the truth there. You was in the neighborhood cause it's my payday.

LYONS: Well, hell, since you mentioned it . . . let me have ten dollars.

TROY: I'll be damned! I'll die and go to hell and play blackjack with the devil before I give you ten dollars.

BONO: That's what I wanna know about . . . that devil you done seen.

LYONS: What . . . Pop done seen the devil? You too much, Pops.

TROY: Yeah, I done seen him. Talked to him too!

ROSE: You ain't seen no devil. I done told you that man ain't had nothing to do with the devil. Anything you can't understand, you want to call it the devil.

TROY: Look here, Bono . . . I went down to see Hertzberger about some furniture. Got three rooms for two-ninety-eight. That what it say on the radio. "Three rooms . . . two-ninety-eight." Even made up a little song about it. Go down there . . . man tell me I can't get no credit. I'm working every day and can't get no credit. What to do? I got an empty house with some raggedy furniture in it. Cory ain't got no bed. He's sleeping on a pile of rags on the floor. Working every day and can't get no credit. Come back here—Rose'll tell you—madder than hell. Sit down . . . try to figure what I'm gonna do. Come a knock on the door. Ain't been living here but three days. Who know I'm here? Open the door . . .

devil standing there bigger than life. White fellow . . . got on good clothes and everything. Standing there with a clipboard in his hand. I ain't had to say nothing. First words come out of his mouth was . . . "I understand you need some furniture and can't get no credit." I liked to fell over. He say "I'll give you all the credit you want, but you got to pay the interest on it." I told him, "Give me three rooms' worth and charge whatever you want." Next day a truck pulled up here and two men unloaded them three rooms. Man what drove the truck give me a book. Say send ten dollars, first of every month to the address in the book and everything will be alright. Say if I miss a payment the devil was coming back and it'll be hell to pay. That was fifteen years ago. To this day . . . the first of the month I send my ten dollars, Rose'll tell you.

ROSE: Troy lying.

TROY: I ain't never seen that man since. Now you tell me who else that could have been but the devil? I ain't sold my soul or nothing like that, you understand. Naw, I wouldn't have truck with the devil about nothing like that. I got my furniture and pays my ten dollars the first of the month just like clockwork.

BONO: How long you say you been paying this ten dollars a month?

TROY: Fifteen years!

BONO: Hell, ain't you finished paying for it yet? How much the man done charged you.

TROY: Aw hell, I done paid for it. I done paid for it ten times over! The fact is I'm scared to stop paying it.

ROSE: Troy lying. We got that furniture from Mr. Glickman. He ain't paying no ten dollars a month to nobody.

TROY: Aw hell, woman. Bono know I ain't that big a fool.

LYONS: I was just getting ready to say . . . I know where there's a bridge for sale.

TROY: Look here, I'll tell you this . . . it don't matter to me if he was the devil. It don't matter if the devil give credit. Somebody has got to give it.

ROSE: It ought to matter. You going around talking about having truck with the devil . . . God's the one you gonna have to answer to. He's the one gonna be at the Judgment.

LYONS: Yeah, well, look here, Pop . . . let me have that ten dollars. I'll give it back to you. Bonnie got a job working at the hospital.

TROY: What I tell you, Bono? The only time I see this nigger is when he wants something. That's the only time I see him.

LYONS: Come on, Pop, Mr. Bono don't want to hear all that. Let me have the ten dollars. I told you Bonnie working.

TROY: What that mean to me? "Bonnie working." I don't care if she working. Go ask her for the ten dollars if she working. Talking about "Bonnie working." Why ain't you working?

LYONS: Aw, Pop, you know I can't find no decent job. Where am I gonna get a job at? You know I can't get no job.

TROY: I told you I know some people down there. I can get you on the rubbish if you want to work. I told you that the last time you came by here asking me for something.

LYONS: Naw, Pop . . . thanks. That ain't for me. I don't wanna be carrying nobody's rubbish. I don't wanna be punching nobody's time clock.

TROY: What's the matter, you too good to carry people's rubbish? Where you think that ten dollars you talking about come from? I'm just supposed to haul people's rubbish and give my money to you cause you too lazy to work. You too lazy to work and wanna know why you ain't got what I got.

ROSE: What hospital Bonnie working at? Mercy?

LYONS: She's down at Passavant working in the laundry.

TROY: I ain't got nothing as it is. I give you that ten dollars and I got to eat beans the rest of the week. Naw . . . you ain't getting no ten dollars here.

LYONS: You ain't got to be eating no beans. I don't know why you wanna say that.

TROY: I ain't got no extra money. Gabe done moved over to Miss Pearl's paying her the rent and things done got tight around here. I can't afford to be giving you every payday.

LYONS: I ain't asked you to give me nothing. I asked you to loan me ten dollars. I know you got ten dollars.

TROY: Yeah, I got it. You know why I got it? Cause I don't throw my money away out there in the streets. You living the fast life . . . wanna be a musician . . . running around in them clubs and things . . . then, you learn to take care of yourself. You ain't gonna find me going and asking nobody for nothing. I done spent too many years without.

LYONS: You and me is two different people, Pop.

TROY: I done learned my mistake and learned to do what's right by it. You still trying to get something for nothing. Life don't owe you nothing. You owe it to yourself. Ask Bono. He'll tell you I'm right.

LYONS: You got your way of dealing with the world . . . I got mine. The only thing that matters to me is the music.

TROY: Yeah, I can see that! It don't matter how you gonna eat . . . where your next dollar is coming from. You telling the truth there.

LYONS: I know I got to eat. But I got to live too. I need something that gonna help me to get out of the bed in the morning. Make me feel like I belong in the world. I don't bother nobody. I just stay with my music cause that's the only way I can find to live in the world. Otherwise there ain't no telling what I might do. Now I don't come criticizing you and how you live. I just come by to ask you for ten dollars. I don't wanna hear all that about how I live.

TROY: Boy, your mama did a hell of a job raising you.

LYONS: You can't change me, Pop. I'm thirty-four years old. If you wanted to change me, you should have been there when I was growing up. I come by to see you . . . ask for ten dollars and you want to talk about how I was raised. You don't know nothing about how I was raised.

ROSE: Let the boy have ten dollars, Troy.

TROY: [*To* LYONS.] What the hell you looking at me for? I ain't got no ten dollars. You know what I do with my money. [*To* ROSE.] Give him ten dollars if you want him to have it.

ROSE: I will. Just as soon as you turn it loose.

TROY: [*Handing* ROSE *the money.*] There it is. Seventy-six dollars and forty-two cents. You see this, Bono? Now, I ain't gonna get but six of that back.

ROSE: You ought to stop telling that lie. Here, Lyons. [*She hands him the money.*]

LYONS: Thanks, Rose. Look . . . I got to run. . . . I'll see you later.

TROY: Wait a minute. You gonna say, "Thanks, Rose" and ain't gonna look to see where she got that ten dollars from? See how they do me, Bono?

LYONS: I know she got it from you, Pop. Thanks. I'll give it back to you.

TROY: There he go telling another lie. Time I see that ten dollars . . . he'll be owing me thirty more.

LYONS: See you, Mr. Bono.

BONO: Take care, Lyons!

LYONS: Thanks, Pop. I'll see you again. [LYONS *exits the yard.*]

TROY: I don't know why he don't go and get him a decent job and take care of that woman he got.

BONO: He'll be alright, Troy. The boy is still young.

TROY: The *boy* is thirty-four years old.

ROSE: Let's not get off into all that.

BONO: Look here . . . I got to be going. I got to be getting on. Lucille gonna be waiting.

TROY: [*Puts his arm around* ROSE.] See this woman, Bono? I love this woman. I love this woman so much it hurts. I love her so much . . . I done run out of ways of loving her. So I got to go back to basics. Don't you come by my house Monday morning talking about time to go to work . . . 'cause I'm still gonna be stroking!

ROSE: Troy! Stop it now!

BONO: I ain't paying him no mind, Rose. That ain't nothing but gintalk. Go on, Troy. I'll see you Monday.

TROY: Don't you come by my house, nigger! I done told you what I'm gonna be doing.

[*The lights go down to black.*]

SCENE 2

The lights come up on ROSE *hanging up clothes. She hums and sings softly to herself. It is the following morning.*

ROSE: [*Sings.*] Jesus, be a fence all around me every day.
  Jesus, I want you to protect me as I travel on my way.
  Jesus, be a fence all around me every day.
  [TROY *enters from the house.*]
  Jesus, I want you to protect me
  As I travel on my way.
[*To* TROY.] 'Morning. You ready for breakfast? I can fix it soon as I finish hanging up these clothes.

TROY: I got the coffee on. That'll be alright. I'll just drink some of that this morning.

ROSE: That 651 hit yesterday. That's the second time this month. Miss Pearl hit for a dollar . . . seem like those that need the least always get lucky. Poor folks can't get nothing.

TROY: Them numbers don't know nobody. I don't know why you fool with them. You and Lyons both.

ROSE: It's something to do.

TROY: You ain't doing nothing but throwing your money away.

ROSE: Troy, you know I don't play foolishly. I just play a nickel here and a nickel there.

TROY: That's two nickels you done thrown away.

ROSE: Now I hit sometimes . . . that makes up for it. It always comes in handy when I do hit. I don't hear you complaining then.

TROY: I ain't complaining now. I just say it's foolish. Trying to guess out of six hundred ways which way the number gonna come. If I had all the money niggers, these Negroes, throw away on numbers for one week—just one week—I'd be a rich man.

ROSE: Well, you wishing and calling it foolish ain't gonna stop folks from playing numbers. That's one thing for sure. Besides . . . some good things come from playing numbers. Look where Pope done bought him that restaurant off of numbers.

TROY: I can't stand niggers like that. Man ain't had two dimes to rub together. He walking around with his shoes all run over bumming money for cigarettes. Alright. Got lucky there and hit the numbers. . . .

ROSE: Troy, I know all about it.

TROY: Had good sense, I'll say that for him. He ain't throwed his money away. I seen niggers hit the numbers and go through two thousand dollars in four days. Man brought him that restaurant down there . . . fixed it up real nice . . . and then didn't want nobody to come in it! A Negro go in there and can't get no kind of service. I seen a white fellow come in there and order a bowl of stew. Pope picked all the meat out the pot for him. Man ain't had nothing but a bowl of meat! Negro come behind him and ain't got nothing but the potatoes and carrots. Talking about what numbers do for people, you picked a wrong example. Ain't done nothing but make a worser fool out of him than he was before.

ROSE: Troy, you ought to stop worrying about what happened at work yesterday.

TROY: I ain't worried. Just told me to be down there at the Commissioner's office on Friday. Everybody think they gonna fire me. I ain't worried about them firing me. You ain't got to worry about that. [*Pause.*] Where's Cory? Cory in the house? [*Calls.*] Cory?

ROSE: He gone out.

TROY: Out, huh? He gone out 'cause he know I want him to help me with this fence. I know how he is. That boy scared of work. [GABRIEL *enters. He comes halfway down the alley and, hearing* TROY's *voice, stops.*] He ain't done a lick of work in his life.

ROSE: He had to go to football practice. Coach wanted them to get in a little extra practice before the season start.

TROY: I got his practice . . . running out of here before he get his chores done.

ROSE: Troy, what is wrong with you this morning? Don't nothing set right with you. Go on back in there and go to bed . . . get up on the other side.

TROY: Why something got to be wrong with me? I ain't said nothing wrong with me.

ROSE: You got something to say about everything. First it's the numbers . . . then it's the way the man runs his restaurant . . . then you done got on Cory. What's it gonna be next? Take a look up there and see if the weather suits you . . . or is it gonna be how you gonna put up the fence with the clothes hanging in the yard.

TROY: You hit the nail on the head then.

ROSE: I know you like I know the back of my hand. Go on in there and get you some coffee . . . see if that straighten you up. 'Cause you ain't right this morning.

[TROY *starts into the house and sees* GABRIEL. GABRIEL *starts singing.* TROY's *brother, he is seven years younger than* TROY. *Injured in World War II, he has a metal plate in his head. He carries an old trumpet tied around his waist and believes with every fiber of his being that he is the Archangel Gabriel.*[4] *He carries a chipped basket with an assortment of discarded fruits*

---

4. In Christianity, God's messenger who announced the births of John the Baptist and Jesus.

and vegetables he has picked up in the strip district and which he attempts to sell.]

GABRIEL: [*Singing.*] Yes, ma'am, I got plums
You ask me how I sell them
Oh ten cents apiece
Three for a quarter
Come and buy now
'Cause I'm here today
And tomorrow I'll be gone
[GABRIEL *enters.*] Hey, Rose!

ROSE: How you doing, Gabe?

GABRIEL: There's Troy. . . . Hey, Troy!

TROY: Hey, Gabe. [*Exit into kitchen.*]

ROSE: [*To* GABRIEL.] What you got there?

GABRIEL: You know what I got, Rose. I got fruits and vegetables.

ROSE: [*Looking in basket.*] Where's all these plums you talking about?

GABRIEL: I ain't got no plums today, Rose. I was just singing that. Have some tomorrow. Put me in a big order for plums. Have enough plums tomorrow for St. Peter and everybody.

[TROY *reenters from kitchen, crosses to steps.*]

[*To* ROSE.] Troy's mad at me.

TROY: I ain't mad at you. What I got to be mad at you about? You ain't done nothing to me.

GABRIEL: I just moved over to Miss Pearl's to keep out from in your way. I ain't mean no harm by it.

TROY: Who said anything about that? I ain't said anything about that.

GABRIEL: You ain't mad at me, is you?

TROY: Naw . . . I ain't mad at you, Gabe. If I was mad at you I'd tell you about it.

GABRIEL: Got me two rooms. In the basement. Got my own door too. Wanna see my key? [*He holds up a key.*] That's my own key! Ain't nobody else got a key like that. That's my key! My two rooms!

TROY: Well, that's good, Gabe. You got your own key . . . that's good.

ROSE: You hungry, Gabe? I was just fixing to cook Troy his breakfast.

GABRIEL: I'll take some biscuits. You got some biscuits? Did you know when I was in heaven . . . every morning me and St. Peter would sit down by the gate and eat some big fat biscuits?

Oh, yeah! We had us a good time. We'd sit there and eat us them biscuits and then St. Peter would go off to sleep and tell me to wake him up when it's time to open the gates for the judgment.

ROSE: Well, come on . . . I'll make up a batch of biscuits. [ROSE *exits into the house.*]

GABRIEL: Troy . . . St. Peter got your name in the book. I seen it. It say . . . Troy Maxson. I say . . . I know him! He got the same name like what I got. That's my brother!

TROY: How many times you gonna tell me that, Gabe?

GABRIEL: Ain't got my name in the book. Don't have to have my name. I done died and went to heaven. He got your name though. One morning St. Peter was looking at his book . . . marking it up for the judgment . . . and he let me see your name. Got it in there under M. Got Rose's name. . . . I ain't seen it like I seen yours . . . but I know it's in there. He got a great big book. Got everybody's name what was ever been born. That's what he told me. But I seen your name. Seen it with my own eyes.

TROY: Go on in the house there. Rose going to fix you something to eat.

GABRIEL: Oh, I ain't hungry. I done had breakfast with Aunt Jemimah. She come by and cooked me up a whole mess of flapjacks. Remember how we used to eat them flapjacks?

TROY: Go on in the house and get you something to eat now.

GABRIEL: I got to go sell my plums. I done sold some tomatoes. Got me two quarters. Wanna see? [*He shows* TROY *his quarters.*] I'm gonna save them and buy me a new horn so St. Peter can hear me when it's time to open the gates. [GABRIEL *stops suddenly. Listens.*] Hear that? That's the hellhounds. I got to chase them out of here. Go on get out of here! Get out! [GABRIEL *exits singing.*]

> Better get ready for the judgment
> Better get ready for the judgment
> My Lord is coming down
> [ROSE *enters from the house.*]

TROY: He gone off somewhere.

GABRIEL: [*Offstage.*] Better get ready for the judgment
> Better get ready for the judgment morning
> Better get ready for the judgment
> My God is coming down

ROSE: He ain't eating right. Miss Pearl say she can't get him to eat nothing.

TROY: What you want me to do about it, Rose? I done did everything I can for the man. I can't make him get well. Man got half his head blown away . . . what you expect?

ROSE: Seem like something ought to be done to help him.

TROY: Man don't bother nobody. He just mixed up from that metal plate he got in his head. Ain't no sense for him to go back into the hospital.

ROSE: Least he be eating right. They can help him take care of himself.

TROY: Don't nobody wanna be locked up, Rose. What you wanna lock him up for? Man go over there and fight the war . . . messin' around with them Japs, get half his head blown off . . . and they give him a lousy three thousand dollars. And I had to swoop down on that.

ROSE: Is you fixing to go into that again?

TROY: That's the only way I got a roof over my head . . . 'cause of that metal plate.

ROSE: Ain't no sense you blaming yourself for nothing. Gabe wasn't in no condition to manage that money. You done what was right by him. Can't nobody say you ain't done what was right by him. Look how long you took care of him . . . till he wanted to have his own place and moved over there with Miss Pearl.

TROY: That ain't what I'm saying, woman! I'm just stating the facts. If my brother didn't have that metal plate in his head . . . I wouldn't have a pot to piss in or a window to throw it out of. And I'm fifty-three years old. Now see if you can understand that! [TROY *gets up from the porch and starts to exit the yard.*]

ROSE: Where you going off to? You been running out of here every Saturday for weeks. I thought you was gonna work on this fence?

TROY: I'm gonna walk down to Taylors'. Listen to the ball game. I'll be back in a bit. I'll work on it when I get back. [*He exits the yard. The lights go to black.*]

SCENE 3

The lights come up on the yard. It is four hours later. ROSE *is taking down the clothes from the line.* CORY *enters carrying his football equipment.*

ROSE: Your daddy like to had a fit with you running out of here this morning without doing your chores.

CORY: I told you I had to go to practice.

ROSE: He say you were supposed to help him with this fence.

CORY: He been saying that the last four or five Saturdays, and then he don't never do nothing, but go down to Taylors'. Did you tell him about the recruiter?

ROSE: Yeah, I told him.

CORY: What he say?

ROSE: He ain't said nothing too much. You get in there and get started on your chores before he gets back. Go on and scrub down them steps before he gets back here hollering and carrying on.

CORY: I'm hungry. What you got to eat, Mama?

ROSE: Go on and get started on your chores. I got some meat loaf in there. Go on and make you a sandwich . . . and don't leave no mess in there. [CORY *exits into the house.* ROSE *continues to take down the clothes.* TROY *enters the yard and sneaks up and grabs her from behind.*] Troy! Go on, now. You liked to scared me to death. What was the score of the game? Lucille had me on the phone and I couldn't keep up with it.

TROY: What I care about the game? Come here, woman. [*He tries to kiss her.*]

ROSE: I thought you went down Taylors' to listen to the game. Go on, Troy! You supposed to be putting up this fence.

TROY: [*Attempting to kiss her again.*] I'll put it up when I finish with what is at hand.

ROSE: Go on, Troy. I ain't studying you.

TROY: [*Chasing after her.*] I'm studying you . . . fixing to do my homework!

ROSE: Troy, you better leave me alone.

TROY: Where's Cory? That boy brought his butt home yet?

ROSE: He's in the house doing his chores.

TROY: [*Calling.*] Cory! Get your butt out here, boy!

[ROSE *exits into the house with the laundry.* TROY *goes over to the pile of wood, picks up a board, and starts sawing.* CORY *enters from the house.*]

TROY: You just now coming in here from leaving this morning?

CORY: Yeah, I had to go to football practice.

TROY: Yeah, what?

CORY: Yes sir.

TROY: I ain't but two seconds off you noway. The garbage sitting in there overflowing . . . you ain't done none of your chores . . . and you come in here talking about "Yeah."

CORY: I was just getting ready to do my chores now, Pop. . . .

TROY: Your first chore is to help me with this fence on Saturday. Everything else come after that. Now get that saw and cut them boards.

[CORY *takes the saw and begins cutting the boards.* TROY *continues working. There is a long pause.*]

CORY: Hey, Pop . . . why don't you buy a TV?

TROY: What I want with a TV? What I want one of them for?

CORY: Everybody got one. Earl, Ba Bra . . . Jesse!

TROY: I ain't asked you who had one. I say what I want with one?

CORY: So you can watch it. They got lots of things on TV. Baseball games and everything. We could watch the World Series.

TROY: Yeah . . . and how much this TV cost?

CORY: I don't know. They got them on sale for around two hundred dollars.

TROY: Two hundred dollars, huh?

CORY: That ain't that much, Pop.

TROY: Naw, it's just two hundred dollars. See that roof you got over your head at night? Let me tell you something about that roof. It's been over ten years since that roof was last tarred. See now . . . the snow come this winter and sit up there on that roof like it is . . . and it's gonna seep inside. It's just gonna be a little bit . . . ain't gonna hardly notice it. Then the next thing you know, it's gonna be leaking all over the house. Then the wood rot from all that water and you gonna need a whole new roof. Now, how much you think it cost to get that roof tarred?

CORY: I don't know.

TROY: Two hundred and sixty-four dollars . . . cash money. While you thinking about a TV, I got to be thinking about the roof . . . and whatever else go wrong around here. Now if you had two hundred dollars, what would you do . . . fix the roof or buy a TV?

CORY: I'd buy a TV. Then when the roof started to leak . . . when it needed fixing . . . I'd fix it.

TROY: Where you gonna get the money from? You done spent it for a TV. You gonna sit up and watch the water run all over your brand new TV.

CORY: Aw, Pop. You got money. I know you do.

TROY: Where I got it at, huh?

CORY: You got it in the bank.

TROY: You wanna see my bankbook? You wanna see that seventy-three dollars and twenty-two cents I got sitting up in there.

CORY: You ain't got to pay for it all at one time. You can put a down payment on it and carry it on home with you.

TROY: Not me. I ain't gonna owe nobody nothing if I can help it. Miss a payment and they come and snatch it right out your house. Then what you got? Now, soon as I get two hundred dollars clear, then I'll buy a TV. Right now, as soon as I get two hundred and sixty-four dollars, I'm gonna have this roof tarred.

CORY: Aw . . . Pop!

TROY: You go on and get you two hundred dollars and buy one if ya want it. I got better things to do with my money.

CORY: I can't get no two hundred dollars. I ain't never seen two hundred dollars.

TROY: I'll tell you what . . . you get you a hundred dollars and I'll put the other hundred with it.

CORY: Alright, I'm gonna show you.

TROY: You gonna show me how you can cut them boards right now.

[CORY *begins to cut the boards. There is a long pause.*]

CORY: The Pirates won today. That makes five in a row.

TROY: I ain't thinking about the Pirates. Got an all-white team. Got that boy . . . that Puerto Rican boy . . . Clemente.[5] Don't even half-play him. That boy could be something if they give him a chance. Play him one day and sit him on the bench the next.

CORY: He gets a lot of chances to play.

TROY: I'm talking about playing regular. Playing every day so you can get your timing. That's what I'm talking about.

---

5. Roberto Clemente (1934–1972), Hall of Fame right fielder for the Pittsburgh Pirates from 1955 until his death, in a plane crash en route to Nicaragua, where he intended to help victims of an earthquake.

CORY: They got some white guys on the team that don't play every day. You can't play everybody at the same time.

TROY: If they got a white fellow sitting on the bench . . . you can bet your last dollar he can't play! The colored guy got to be twice as good before he get on the team. That's why I don't want you to get all tied up in them sports. Man on the team and what it get him? They got colored on the team and don't use them. Same as not having them. All them teams the same.

CORY: The Braves got Hank Aaron and Wes Covington.[6] Hank Aaron hit two home runs today. That makes forty-three.

TROY: Hank Aaron ain't nobody. That's what you supposed to do. That's how you supposed to play the game. Ain't nothing to it. It's just a matter of timing . . . getting the right follow-through. Hell, I can hit forty-three home runs right now!

CORY: Not off no major-league pitching, you couldn't.

TROY: We had better pitching in the Negro leagues. I hit seven home runs off of Satchel Paige.[7] You can't get no better than that!

CORY: Sandy Koufax.[8] He's leading the league in strikeouts.

TROY: I ain't thinking of no Sandy Koufax.

CORY: You got Warren Spahn and Lew Burdette.[9] I bet you couldn't hit no home runs off of Warren Spahn.

TROY: I'm through with it now. You go on and cut them boards. [*Pause.*] Your mama tell me you done got recruited by a college football team? Is that right?

CORY: Yeah. Coach Zellman say the recruiter gonna be coming by to talk to you. Get you to sign the permission papers.

TROY: I thought you supposed to be working down there at the A&P. Ain't you suppose to be working down there after school?

CORY: Mr. Stawicki say he gonna hold my job for me until after the football season. Say starting next week I can work weekends.

6. John Wesley Covington (1932–1956), out-fielder, and Henry Louis Aaron (b. 1934), infielder and outfielder, helped the Milwau-kee Braves win the World Series in 1957. Aaron held the all-time home-run record until it was broken by Barry Bonds in 2007.

7. Leroy Robert Paige (1906?–1982), consid-ered by many the best pitcher in baseball history, played in the Negro Leagues for over twenty years before the Cleveland Indians hired him in 1948.

8. Sanford Koufax (b. 1935) pitched for the Brooklyn Dodgers in 1957.

9. Selva Lewis Burdette Jr. (1926–2007) and Warren Edward Spahn (1921–2003) were star pitchers for the Braves in 1957.

TROY: I thought we had an understanding about this football stuff? You suppose to keep up with your chores and hold that job down at the A&P. Ain't been around here all day on a Saturday. Ain't none of your chores done . . . and now you telling me you done quit your job.

CORY: I'm gonna be working weekends.

TROY: You damn right you are! And ain't no need for nobody coming around here to talk to me about signing nothing.

CORY: Hey, Pop . . . you can't do that. He's coming all the way from North Carolina.

TROY: I don't care where he coming from. The white man ain't gonna let you get nowhere with that football noway. You go on and get your book-learning so you can work yourself up in that A&P or learn how to fix cars or build houses or something, get you a trade. That way you have something can't nobody take away from you. You go on and learn how to put your hands to some good use. Besides hauling people's garbage.

CORY: I get good grades, Pop. That's why the recruiter wants to talk with you. You got to keep up your grades to get recruited. This way I'll be going to college. I'll get a chance. . . .

TROY: First you gonna get your butt down there to the A&P and get your job back.

CORY: Mr. Stawicki done already hired somebody else 'cause I told him I was playing football.

TROY: You a bigger fool than I thought . . . to let somebody take away your job so you can play some football. Where you gonna get your money to take out your girlfriend and whatnot? What kind of foolishness is that to let somebody take away your job?

CORY: I'm still gonna be working weekends.

TROY: Naw . . . naw. You getting your butt out of here and finding you another job.

CORY: Come on, Pop! I got to practice. I can't work after school and play football too. The team needs me. That's what Coach Zellman say. . . .

TROY: I don't care what nobody else say. I'm the boss . . . you understand? I'm the boss around here. I do the only saying what counts.

CORY: Come on, Pop!

TROY: I asked you . . . did you understand?

CORY: Yeah . . .

TROY: What?!

CORY: Yessir.

TROY: You go on down there to that A&P and see if you can get your job back. If you can't do both . . . then you quit the football team. You've got to take the crookeds with the straights.

CORY: Yessir. [*Pause.*] Can I ask you a question?

TROY: What the hell you wanna ask me? Mr. Stawicki the one you got the questions for.

CORY: How come you ain't never liked me?

TROY: Liked you? Who the hell say I got to like you? What law is there say I got to like you? Wanna stand up in my face and ask a damn fool-ass question like that. Talking about liking somebody. Come here, boy, when I talk to you. [CORY *comes over to where* TROY *is working. He stands slouched over and* TROY *shoves him on his shoulder.*] Straighten up, goddammit! I asked you a question . . . what law is there say I got to like you?

CORY: None.

TROY: Well, alright then! Don't you eat every day? [*Pause.*] Answer me when I talk to you! Don't you eat every day?

CORY: Yeah.

TROY: Nigger, as long as you in my house, you put that sir on the end of it when you talk to me!

CORY: Yes . . . sir.

TROY: You eat every day.

CORY: Yessir!

TROY: Got a roof over your head.

CORY: Yessir!

TROY: Got clothes on your back.

CORY: Yessir.

TROY: Why you think that is?

CORY: 'Cause of you.

TROY: Aw, hell I know it's 'cause of me . . . but why do you think that is?

CORY: [*Hesitant.*] 'Cause you like me.

TROY: Like you? I go out of here every morning . . . bust my butt . . . putting up with them crackers every day . . . cause I like you? You about the biggest fool I ever saw. [*Pause.*] It's my job.

It's my responsibility! You understand that? A man got to take care of his family. You live in my house . . . sleep you behind on my bedclothes . . . fill you belly up with my food . . . 'cause you my son. You my flesh and blood. Not 'cause I like you! 'Cause it's my duty to take care of you. I owe a responsibility to you!

Let's get this straight right here . . . before it go along any further. . . . I ain't got to like you. Mr. Rand don't give me my money come payday cause he likes me. He gives me cause he owe me. I done give you everything I had to give you. I gave you your life! Me and your mama worked that out between us. And liking your black ass wasn't part of the bargain. Don't you try and go through life worrying about if somebody like you or not. You best be making sure they doing right by you. You understand what I'm saying, boy?

CORY: Yessir.

TROY: Then get the hell out of my face, and get on down to that A&P.

[ROSE *has been standing behind the screen door for much of the scene. She enters as* CORY *exits.*]

ROSE: Why don't you let the boy go ahead and play football, Troy? Ain't no harm in that. He's just trying to be like you with the sports.

TROY: I don't want him to be like me! I want him to move as far away from my life as he can get. You the only decent thing that ever happened to me. I wish him that. But I don't wish him a thing else from my life. I decided seventeen years ago that boy wasn't getting involved in no sports. Not after what they did to me in the sports.

ROSE: Troy, why don't you admit you was too old to play in the major leagues? For once . . . why don't you admit that?

TROY: What do you mean too old? Don't come telling me I was too old. I just wasn't the right color. Hell, I'm fifty-three years old and can do better than Selkirk's .269 right now!

ROSE: How's was you gonna play ball when you were over forty? Sometimes I can't get no sense out of you.

TROY: I got good sense, woman. I got sense enough not to let my boy get hurt over playing no sports. You been mothering that boy too much. Worried about if people like him.

ROSE: Everything that boy do . . . he do for you. He wants you to say "Good job, son." That's all.

TROY: Rose, I ain't got time for that. He's alive. He's healthy. He's got to make his own way. I made mine. Ain't nobody gonna hold his hand when he get out there in that world.

ROSE: Times have changed from when you was young, Troy. People change. The world's changing around you and you can't even see it.

TROY: [*Slow, methodical.*] Woman . . . I do the best I can do. I come in here every Friday. I carry a sack of potatoes and a bucket of lard. You all line up at the door with your hands out. I give you the lint from my pockets. I give you my sweat and my blood. I ain't got no tears. I done spent them. We go upstairs in that room at night . . . and I fall down on you and try to blast a hole into forever. I get up Monday morning . . . find my lunch on the table. I go out. Make my way. Find my strength to carry me through to the next Friday. [*Pause.*] That's all I got, Rose. That's all I got to give. I can't give nothing else. [TROY *exits into the house. The lights go down to black.*]

SCENE 4

It is Friday. Two weeks later. CORY *starts out of the house with his football equipment. The phone rings.*

CORY: [*Calling.*] I got it! [*He answers the phone and stands in the screen door talking.*] Hello? Hey, Jesse. Naw . . . I was just getting ready to leave now.

ROSE: [*Calling.*] Cory!

CORY: I told you, man, them spikes is all tore up. You can use them if you want, but they ain't no good. Earl got some spikes.

ROSE: [*Calling.*] Cory!

CORY: [*Calling to* ROSE.] Mam? I'm talking to Jesse. [*Into phone.*] When she say that? [*Pause.*] Aw, you lying, man. I'm gonna tell her you said that.

ROSE: [*Calling.*] Cory, don't you go nowhere!

CORY: I got to go to the game, Ma! [*Into the phone.*] Yeah, hey, look, I'll talk to you later. Yeah, I'll meet you over Earl's house. Later. Bye, Ma. [CORY *exits the house and starts out the yard.*]

ROSE: Cory, where you going off to? You got that stuff all pulled out and thrown all over your room.

CORY: [*In the yard.*] I was looking for my spikes. Jesse wanted to borrow my spikes.

ROSE: Get up there and get that cleaned up before your daddy get back in here.

CORY: I got to go to the game! I'll clean it up when I get back. [CORY *exits.*]

ROSE: That's all he need to do is see that room all messed up.

    [ROSE *exits into the house.* TROY *and* BONO *enter the yard.* TROY *is dressed in clothes other than his work clothes.*]

BONO: He told him the same thing he told you. Take it to the union.

TROY: Brownie ain't got that much sense. Man wasn't thinking about nothing. He wait until I confront them on it . . . then he wanna come crying seniority. [*Calls.*] Hey, Rose!

BONO: I wish I could have seen Mr. Rand's face when he told you.

TROY: He couldn't get it out of his mouth! Liked to bit his tongue! When they called me down there to the Commissioner's office . . . he thought they was gonna fire me. Like everybody else.

BONO: I didn't think they was gonna fire you. I thought they was gonna put you on the warning paper.

TROY: Hey, Rose! [*To* BONO.] Yeah, Mr. Rand like to bit his tongue.

    [TROY *breaks the seal on the bottle, takes a drink, and hands it to* BONO.]

BONO: I see you run right down to Taylors' and told that Alberta gal.

TROY: [*Calling.*] Hey, Rose! [*To* BONO.] I told everybody. Hey, Rose! I went down there to cash my check.

ROSE: [*Entering from the house.*] Hush all that hollering, man! I know you out here. What they say down there at the Commissioner's office?

TROY: You supposed to come when I call you, woman. Bono'll tell you that. [*To* BONO.] Don't Lucille come when you call her?

ROSE: Man, hush your mouth. I ain't no dog . . . talk about "come when you call me."

TROY: [*Puts his arm around* ROSE.] You hear this, Bono? I had me an old dog used to get uppity like that. You say, "C'mere, Blue!" . . . and he just lay there and look at you. End up getting a stick and chasing him away trying to make him come.

ROSE: I ain't studying you and your dog. I remember you used to sing that old song.

TROY: [*He sings.*] Hear it ring! Hear it ring!

I had a dog his name was Blue.

ROSE: Don't nobody wanna hear you sing that old song.

TROY: [*Sings.*] You know Blue was mighty true.

ROSE: Used to have Cory running around here singing that song.

BONO: Hell, I remember that song myself.

TROY: [*Sings.*] You know Blue was a good old dog.

Blue treed a possum in a hollow log.

That was my daddy's song. My daddy made up that song.

ROSE: I don't care who made it up. Don't nobody wanna hear you sing it.

TROY: [*Makes a song like calling a dog.*] Come here, woman.

ROSE: You come in here carrying on, I reckon they ain't fired you. What they say down there at the Commissioner's office?

TROY: Look here, Rose . . . Mr. Rand called me into his office today when I got back from talking to them people down there . . . it come from up top . . . he called me in and told me they was making me a driver.

ROSE: Troy, you kidding!

TROY: No I ain't. Ask Bono.

ROSE: Well, that's great, Troy. Now you don't have to hassle them people no more.

[LYONS *enters from the street.*]

TROY: Aw hell, I wasn't looking to see you today. I thought you was in jail. Got it all over the front page of the *Courier* about them raiding Sefus' place . . . where you be hanging out with all them thugs.

LYONS: Hey, Pop . . . that ain't got nothing to do with me. I don't go down there gambling. I go down there to sit in with the band. I ain't got nothing to do with the gambling part. They got some good music down there.

TROY: They got some rogues . . . is what they got.

LYONS: How you been, Mr. Bono? Hi, Rose.

BONO: I see where you playing down at the Crawford Grill tonight.

ROSE: How come you ain't brought Bonnie like I told you. You should have brought Bonnie with you, she ain't been over in a month of Sundays.

LYONS: I was just in the neighborhood . . . thought I'd stop by.

TROY: Here he come. . . .

BONO: Your daddy got a promotion on the rubbish. He's gonna be the first colored driver. Ain't got to do nothing but sit up there and read the paper like them white fellows.

LYONS: Hey, Pop . . . if you knew how to read you'd be alright.

BONO: Naw . . . naw . . . you mean if the nigger knew how to *drive* he'd be all right. Been fighting with them people about driving and ain't even got a license. Mr. Rand know you ain't got no driver's license?

TROY: Driving ain't nothing. All you do is point the truck where you want it to go. Driving ain't nothing.

BONO: Do Mr. Rand know you ain't got no driver's license? That's what I'm talking about. I ain't asked if driving was easy. I asked if Mr. Rand know you ain't got no driver's license.

TROY: He ain't got to know. The man ain't got to know my business. Time he find out, I have two or three driver's licenses.

LYONS: [*Going into his pocket.*] Say, look here, Pop . . .

TROY: I knew it was coming. Didn't I tell you, Bono? I know what kind of "Look here, Pop" that was. The nigger fixing to ask me for some money. It's Friday night. It's my payday. All them rogues down there on the avenue . . . the ones that ain't in jail . . . and Lyons is hopping in his shoes to get down there with them.

LYONS: See, Pop . . . if you give somebody else a chance to talk sometime, you'd see that I was fixing to pay you back your ten dollars like I told you. Here . . . I told you I'd pay you when Bonnie got paid.

TROY: Naw . . . you go ahead and keep that ten dollars. Put it in the bank. The next time you feel like you wanna come by here and ask me for something . . . you go on down there and get that.

LYONS: Here's your ten dollars, Pop. I told you I don't want you to give me nothing. I just wanted to borrow ten dollars.

TROY: Naw . . . you go on and keep that for the next time you want to ask me.

LYONS: Come on, Pop . . . here go your ten dollars.

ROSE: Why don't you go on and let the boy pay you back, Troy?

LYONS: Here you go, Rose. If you don't take it I'm gonna have to hear about it for the next six months. [*He hands her the money.*]

ROSE: You can hand yours over here too, Troy.

TROY: You see this, Bono. You see how they do me.

BONO: Yeah, Lucille do me the same way.

[GABRIEL *is heard singing offstage. He enters.*]

GABRIEL: Better get ready for the Judgment! Better get ready for . . . Hey! . . . Hey! . . . There's Troy's boy!

LYONS: How you doing, Uncle Gabe?

GABRIEL: Lyons . . . The King of the Jungle! Rose . . . hey, Rose. Got a flower for you. [*He takes a rose from his pocket.*] Picked it myself. That's the same rose like you is!

ROSE: That's right nice of you, Gabe.

LYONS: What you been doing, Uncle Gabe?

GABRIEL: Oh, I been chasing hellhounds and waiting on the time to tell St. Peter to open the gates.

LYONS: You been chasing hellhounds, huh? Well . . . you doing the right thing, Uncle Gabe. Somebody got to chase them.

GABRIEL: Oh, yeah . . . I know it. The devil's strong. The devil ain't no pushover. Hellhounds snipping at everybody's heels. But I got my trumpet waiting on the judgment time.

LYONS: Waiting on the Battle of Armageddon, huh?

GABRIEL: Ain't gonna be too much of a battle when God get to waving that Judgment sword. But the people's gonna have a hell of a time trying to get into heaven if them gates ain't open.

LYONS: [*Putting his arm around* GABRIEL.] You hear this, Pop. Uncle Gabe, you alright!

GABRIEL: [*Laughing with* LYONS.] Lyons! King of the Jungle.

ROSE: You gonna stay for supper, Gabe. Want me to fix you a plate?

GABRIEL: I'll take a sandwich, Rose. Don't want no plate. Just wanna eat with my hands. I'll take a sandwich.

ROSE: How about you, Lyons? You staying? Got some short ribs cooking.

LYONS: Naw, I won't eat nothing till after we finished playing. [*Pause.*] You ought to come down and listen to me play, Pop.

TROY: I don't like that Chinese music. All that noise.

ROSE: Go on in the house and wash up, Gabe. . . . I'll fix you a sandwich.

GABRIEL: [*To* LYONS, *as he exits.*] Troy's mad at me.

LYONS: What you mad at Uncle Gabe for, Pop.

ROSE: He thinks Troy's mad at him cause he moved over to Miss Pearl's.

TROY: I ain't mad at the man. He can live where he want to live at.

LYONS: What he move over there for? Miss Pearl don't like nobody.

ROSE: She don't mind him none. She treats him real nice. She just don't allow all that singing.

TROY: She don't mind that rent he be paying . . . that's what she don't mind.

ROSE: Troy, I ain't going through that with you no more. He's over there cause he want to have his own place. He can come and go as he please.

TROY: Hell, he could come and go as he please here. I wasn't stopping him. I ain't put no rules on him.

ROSE: It ain't the same thing, Troy. And you know it. [GABRIEL *comes to the door.*] Now, that's the last I wanna hear about that. I don't wanna hear nothing else about Gabe and Miss Pearl. And next week . . .

GABRIEL: I'm ready for my sandwich, Rose.

ROSE: And next week . . . when that recruiter come from that school . . . I want you to sign that paper and go on and let Cory play football. Then that'll be the last I have to hear about that.

TROY: [*To* ROSE *as she exits into the house.*] I ain't thinking about Cory nothing.

LYONS: What . . . Cory got recruited? What school he going to?

TROY: That boy walking around here smelling his piss . . . thinking he's grown. Thinking he's gonna do what he want, irrespective of what I say. Look here, Bono . . . I left the Commissioner's office and went down to the A&P . . . that boy ain't working down there. He lying to me. Telling me he got his job back . . . telling me he working weekends . . . telling me he working after school. . . . Mr. Stawicki tell me he ain't working down there at all!

LYONS: Cory just growing up. He's just busting at the seams trying to fill out your shoes.

TROY: I don't care what he's doing. When he get to the point where he wanna disobey me . . . then it's time for him to move on. Bono'll tell you that. I bet he ain't never disobeyed his daddy without paying the consequences.

BONO: I ain't never had a chance. My daddy came on through . . . but I ain't never knew him to see him . . . or what he had on his mind or where he went. Just moving on through. Searching out the New Land. That's what the old folks used to call it. See a fellow moving around from place to place . . . woman to woman . . . called it searching out the New Land. I can't say if he ever found it. I come along, didn't want no kids. Didn't know if I was gonna be in one place long enough to fix on them right as their daddy. I figured I was going searching too. As it turned out I been hooked up with Lucille near about as long as your daddy been with Rose. Going on sixteen years.

TROY: Sometimes I wish I hadn't known my daddy. He ain't cared nothing about no kids. A kid to him wasn't nothing. All he wanted was for you to learn how to walk so he could start you to working. When it come time for eating . . . he ate first. If there was anything left over, that's what you got. Man would sit down and eat two chickens and give you the wing.

LYONS: You ought to stop that, Pop. Everybody feed their kids. No matter how hard times is . . . everybody care about their kids. Make sure they have something to eat.

TROY: The only thing my daddy cared about was getting them bales of cotton in to Mr. Lubin. That's the only thing that mattered to him. Sometimes I used to wonder why he was living. Wonder why the devil hadn't come and got him. "Get them bales of cotton in to Mr. Lubin" and find out he owe him money. . . .

LYONS: He should have just went on and left when he saw he couldn't get nowhere. That's what I would have done.

TROY: How he gonna leave with eleven kids? And where he gonna go? He ain't knew how to do nothing but farm. No, he was trapped and I think he knew it. But I'll say this for him . . . he felt a responsibility toward us. Maybe he ain't treated us the way I felt he should have . . . but without that responsibility he could have walked off and left us . . . made his own way.

BONO: A lot of them did. Back in those days what you talking about . . . they walk out their front door and just take on down one road or another and keep on walking.

LYONS: There you go! That's what I'm talking about.

BONO: Just keep on walking till you come to something else. Ain't you never heard of nobody having the walking blues? Well, that's what you call it when you just take off like that.

TROY: My daddy ain't had them walking blues! What you talking about? He stayed right there with his family. But he was just as evil as he could be. My mama couldn't stand him. Couldn't stand that evilness. She run off when I was about eight. She sneaked off one night after he had gone to sleep. Told me she was coming back for me. I ain't never seen her no more. All his women run off and left him. He wasn't good for nobody.

When my turn come to head out, I was fourteen and got to sniffing around Joe Canewell's daughter. Had us an old mule we called Greyboy. My daddy sent me out to do some plowing and I tied up Greyboy and went to fooling around with Joe Canewell's daughter. We done found us a nice little spot, got real cozy with each other. She about thirteen and we done figured we was grown anyway . . . so we down there enjoying ourselves . . . ain't thinking about nothing. We didn't know Greyboy had got loose and wandered back to the house and my daddy was looking for me. We down there by the creek enjoying ourselves when my daddy come up on us. Surprised us. He had them leather straps off the mule and commenced to whupping me like there was no tomorrow. I jumped up, mad and embarrassed. I was scared of my daddy. When he commenced to whupping on me . . . quite naturally I run to get out of the way. [*Pause.*]

Now I thought he was mad cause I ain't done my work. But I see where he was chasing me off so he could have the gal for himself. When I see what the matter of it was, I lost all fear of my daddy. Right there is where I become a man . . . at fourteen years of age. [*Pause.*]

Now it was my turn to run him off. I picked up them same reins that he had used on me. I picked up them reins and commenced to whupping on him. The gal jumped up and run off . . . and when my daddy turned to face me, I could see why the devil had never come to get him . . . 'cause he was the devil himself. I don't know what happened. When I woke up, I was laying right there by the creek, and Blue . . . this old dog we had . . . was licking my face. I thought I was blind. I couldn't see nothing.

Both my eyes were swollen shut. I layed there and cried. I didn't know what I was gonna do. The only thing I knew was the time had come for me to leave my daddy's house. And right there the world suddenly got big. And it was a long time before I could cut it down to where I could handle it.

Part of that cutting down was when I got to the place where I could feel him kicking in my blood and knew that the only thing that separated us was the matter of a few years.

[GABRIEL *enters from the house with a sandwich.*]

LYONS: What you got there, Uncle Gabe?

GABRIEL: Got me a ham sandwich. Rose gave me a ham sandwich.

TROY: I don't know what happened to him. I done lost touch with everybody except Gabriel. But I hope he's dead. I hope he found some peace.

LYONS: That's a heavy story, Pop. I didn't know you left home when you was fourteen.

TROY: And didn't know nothing. The only part of the world I knew was the forty-two acres of Mr. Lubin's land. That's all I knew about life.

LYONS: Fourteen's kinda young to be out on your own. [*Phone rings.*] I don't even think I was ready to be out on my own at fourteen. I don't know what I would have done.

TROY: I got up from the creek and walked on down to Mobile. I was through with farming. Figured I could do better in the city. So I walked the two hundred miles to Mobile.

LYONS: Wait a minute . . . you ain't walked no two hundred miles, Pop. Ain't nobody gonna walk no two hundred miles. You talking about some walking there.

BONO: That's the only way you got anywhere back in them days.

LYONS: Shhh. Damn if I wouldn't have hitched a ride with somebody!

TROY: Who you gonna hitch it with? They ain't had no cars and things like they got now. We talking about 1918.

ROSE: [*Entering.*] What you all out here getting into?

TROY: [*To* ROSE.] I'm telling Lyons how good he got it. He don't know nothing about this I'm talking.

ROSE: Lyons, that was Bonnie on the phone. She say you supposed to pick her up.

LYONS: Yeah, okay, Rose.

TROY: I walked on down to Mobile and hitched up with some of them fellows that was heading this way. Got up here and found out . . . not only couldn't you get a job . . . you couldn't find no place to live. I thought I was in freedom. Shhh. Colored folks living down there on the riverbanks in whatever kind of shelter they could find for themselves. Right down there under the Brady Street Bridge. Living in shacks made of sticks and tarpaper. Messed around there and went from bad to worse. Started stealing. First it was food. Then I figured, hell, if I steal money I can buy me some food. Buy me some shoes too! One thing led to another. Met your mama. I was young and anxious to be a man. Met your mama and had you. What I do that for? Now I got to worry about feeding you and her. Got to steal three times as much. Went out one day looking for somebody to rob . . . that's what I was, a robber. I'll tell you the truth. I'm ashamed of it today. But it's the truth. Went to rob this fellow . . . pulled out my knife . . . and he pulled out a gun. Shot me in the chest. It felt just like somebody had taken a hot branding iron and laid it on me. When he shot me I jumped at him with my knife. They told me I killed him and they put me in the penitentiary and locked me up for fifteen years. That's where I met Bono. That's where I learned how to play baseball. Got out that place and your mama had taken you and went on to make life without me. Fifteen years was a long time for her to wait. But that fifteen years cured me of that robbing stuff. Rose'll tell you. She asked me when I met her if I had gotten all that foolishness out of my system. And I told her, "Baby, it's you and baseball all what count with me." You hear me, Bono? I meant it too. She say, "Which one comes first?" I told her, "Baby, ain't no doubt it's baseball . . . but you stick and get old with me and we'll both outlive this baseball." Am I right, Rose? And it's true.

ROSE: Man, hush your mouth. You ain't said no such thing. Talking about, "Baby, you know you'll always be number one with me." That's what you was talking.

TROY: You hear that, Bono. That's why I love her.

BONO: Rose'll keep you straight. You get off the track, she'll straighten you up.

ROSE: Lyons, you better get on up and get Bonnie. She waiting on you.

LYONS: [*Gets up to go.*] Hey, Pop, why don't you come on down to the Grill and hear me play?

TROY: I ain't going down there. I'm too old to be sitting around in them clubs.

BONO: You got to be good to play down at the Grill.

LYONS: Come on, Pop . . .

TROY: I got to get up in the morning.

LYONS: You ain't got to stay long.

TROY: Naw, I'm gonna get my supper and go on to bed.

LYONS: Well, I got to go. I'll see you again.

TROY: Don't you come around my house on my payday.

ROSE: Pick up the phone and let somebody know you coming. And bring Bonnie with you. You know I'm always glad to see her.

LYONS: Yeah, I'll do that, Rose. You take care now. See you, Pop. See you, Mr. Bono. See you, Uncle Gabe.

GABRIEL: Lyons! King of the Jungle!

    [LYONS *exits.*]

TROY: Is supper ready, woman? Me and you got some business to take care of. I'm gonna tear it up too.

ROSE: Troy, I done told you now!

TROY: [*Puts his arm around* BONO.] Aw hell, woman . . . this is Bono. Bono like family. I done known this nigger since . . . how long I done know you?

BONO: It's been a long time.

TROY: I done known this nigger since Skippy was a pup. Me and him done been through some times.

BONO: You sure right about that.

TROY: Hell, I done know him longer than I known you. And we still standing shoulder to shoulder. Hey, look here, Bono . . . a man can't ask for no more than that. [*Drinks to him.*] I love you, nigger.

BONO: Hell, I love you too . . . but I got to get home see my woman. You got yours in hand. I got to go get mine.

    [BONO *starts to exit as* CORY *enters the yard, dressed in his football uniform. He gives* TROY *a hard, uncompromising look.*]

CORY: What you do that for, Pop? [*He throws his helmet down in the direction of* TROY.]

ROSE: What's the matter? Cory . . . what's the matter?

CORY: Papa done went up to the school and told Coach Zellman

I can't play football no more. Wouldn't even let me play the game. Told him to tell the recruiter not to come.

ROSE: Troy . . .

TROY: What you Troying me for. Yeah, I did it. And the boy know why I did it.

CORY: Why you wanna do that to me? That was the one chance I had.

ROSE: Ain't nothing wrong with Cory playing football, Troy.

TROY: The boy lied to me. I told the nigger if he wanna play football . . . to keep up his chores and hold down that job at the A&P. That was the conditions. Stopped down there to see Mr. Stawicki . . .

CORY: I can't work after school during the football season, Pop! I tried to tell you that Mr. Stawicki's holding my job for me. You don't never want to listen to nobody. And then you wanna go and do this to me!

TROY: I ain't done nothing to you. You done it to yourself.

CORY: Just cause you didn't have a chance! You just scared I'm gonna be better than you, that's all.

TROY: Come here.

ROSE: Troy . . .

[CORY *reluctantly crosses over to* TROY.]

TROY: Alright! See. You done made a mistake.

CORY: I didn't even do nothing!

TROY: I'm gonna tell you what your mistake was. See . . . you swung at the ball and didn't hit it. That's strike one. See, you in the batter's box now. You swung and you missed. That's strike one. Don't you strike out!

[*Lights fade to black.*]

ACT 2
SCENE 1

The following morning. CORY *is at the tree hitting the ball with the bat. He tries to mimic* TROY, *but his swing is awkward, less sure.* ROSE *enters from the house.*

ROSE: Cory, I want you to help me with this cupboard.

CORY: I ain't quitting the team. I don't care what Poppa say.

ROSE: I'll talk to him when he gets back. He had to go see about your Uncle Gabe. The police done arrested him. Say he was disturbing the peace. He'll be back directly. Come on in here and help me clean out the top of this cupboard. [CORY *exits into the house.* ROSE *sees* TROY *and* BONO *coming down the alley.*] Troy . . . what they say down there?

TROY: Ain't said nothing. I give them fifty dollars and they let him go. I'll talk to you about it. Where's Cory?

ROSE: He's in there helping me clean out these cupboards.

TROY: Tell him to get his butt out here.

> [TROY *and* BONO *go over to the pile of wood.* BONO *picks up the saw and begins sawing.*]

TROY: [*To* BONO.] All they want is the money. That makes six or seven times I done went down there and got him. See me coming they stick out their *hands.*

BONO: Yeah. I know what you mean. That's all they care about . . . that money. They don't care about what's right. [*Pause.*] Nigger, why you got to go and get some hard wood? You ain't doing nothing but building a little old fence. Get you some soft pine wood. That's all you need.

TROY: I know what I'm doing. This is outside wood. You put pine wood inside the house. Pine wood is inside wood. This here is outside wood. Now you tell me where the fence is gonna be?

BONO: You don't need this wood. You can put it up with pine wood and it'll stand as long as you gonna be here looking at it.

TROY: How you know how long I'm gonna be here, nigger? Hell, I might just live forever. Live longer than old man Horsely.

BONO: That's what Magee used to say.

TROY: Magee's a damn fool. Now you tell me who you ever heard of gonna pull their own teeth with a pair of rusty pliers.

BONO: The old folks . . . my granddaddy used to pull his teeth with pliers. They ain't had no dentists for the colored folks back then.

TROY: Get clean pliers! You understand? Clean pliers! Sterilize them! Besides we ain't living back then. All Magee had to do was walk over to Doc Goldblums.

BONO: I see where you and that Tallahassee gal . . . that Alberta . . . I see where you all done got tight.

TROY: What you mean "got tight"?

BONO: I see where you be laughing and joking with her all the time.

TROY: I laughs and jokes with all of them, Bono. You know me.

BONO: That ain't the kind of laughing and joking I'm talking about.

[CORY *enters from the house.*]

CORY: How you doing, Mr. Bono?

TROY: Cory? Get that saw from Bono and cut some wood. He talking about the wood's too hard to cut. Stand back there, Jim, and let that young boy show you how it's done.

BONO: He's sure welcome to it. [CORY *takes the saw and begins to cut the wood.*] Whew-e-e! Look at that. Big old strong boy. Look like Joe Louis.[1] Hell, must be getting old the way I'm watching that boy whip through that wood.

CORY: I don't see why Mama want a fence around the yard noways.

TROY: Damn if I know either. What the hell she keeping out with it? She ain't got nothing nobody want.

BONO: Some people build fences to keep people out . . . and other people build fences to keep people in. Rose wants to hold on to you all. She loves you.

TROY: Hell, nigger, I don't need nobody to tell me my wife loves me, Cory . . . go on in the house and see if you can find that other saw.

CORY: Where's it at?

TROY: I said find it! Look for it till you find it! [CORY *exits into the house.*] What's that supposed to mean? Wanna keep us in?

BONO: Troy . . . I done known you seem like damn near my whole life. You and Rose both. I done know both of you all for a long time. I remember when you met Rose. When you was hitting them baseball out the park. A lot of them old gals was after you then. You had the pick of the litter. When you picked Rose, I was happy for you. That was the first time I knew you had any sense. I said . . . My man Troy knows what he's doing . . . I'm gonna follow this nigger . . . he might take me somewhere. I been following you too. I done learned a whole heap of things about life watching you. I done learned how to tell where the shit lies. How to tell it from the alfalfa.

---

1. Boxer (1914–1981), heavyweight champion of the world from 1937 to 1949.

You done learned me a lot of things. You showed me how to not make the same mistakes . . . to take life as it comes along and keep putting one foot in front of the other. [*Pause.*] Rose a good woman, Troy.

TROY: Hell, nigger, I know she a good woman. I been married to her for eighteen years. What you got on your mind, Bono?

BONO: I just say she a good woman. Just like I say anything. I ain't got to have nothing on my mind.

TROY: You just gonna say she a good woman and leave it hanging out there like that? Why you telling me she a good woman?

BONO: She loves you, Troy. Rose loves you.

TROY: You saying I don't measure up. That's what you trying to say. I don't measure up cause I'm seeing this other gal. I know what you trying to say.

BONO: I know what Rose means to you, Troy. I'm just trying to say I don't want to see you mess up.

TROY: Yeah, I appreciate that, Bono. If you was messing around on Lucille I'd be telling you the same thing.

BONO: Well, that's all I got to say. I just say that because I love you both.

TROY: Hell, you know me. . . . I wasn't out there looking for nothing. You can't find a better woman than Rose. I know that. But seems like this woman just stuck onto me where I can't shake her loose. I done wrestled with it, tried to throw her off me . . . but she just stuck on tighter. Now she's stuck on for good.

BONO: You's in control . . . that's what you tell me all the time. You responsible for what you do.

TROY: I ain't ducking the responsibility of it. As long as it sets right in my heart . . . then I'm okay. 'Cause that's all I listen to. It'll tell me right from wrong every time. And I ain't talking about doing Rose no bad turn. I love Rose. She done carried me a long ways and I love and respect her for that.

BONO: I know you do. That's why I don't want to see you hurt her. But what you gonna do when she find out? What you got then? If you try and juggle both of them . . . sooner or later you gonna drop one of them. That's common sense.

TROY: Yeah, I hear what you saying, Bono. I been trying to figure a way to work it out.

BONO: Work it out right, Troy. I don't want to be getting all up between you and Rose's business . . . but work it so it come out right.

TROY: Aw hell, I get all up between you and Lucille's business. When you gonna get that woman that refrigerator she been wanting? Don't tell me you ain't got no money now. I know who your banker is. Mellon don't need that money bad as Lucille want that refrigerator. I'll tell you that.

BONO: Tell you what I'll do . . . when you finish building this fence for Rose . . . I'll buy Lucille that refrigerator.

TROY: You done stuck your foot in your mouth now! [TROY *grabs up a board and begins to saw.* BONO *starts to walk out the yard.*] Hey, nigger . . . where you going?

BONO: I'm going home. I know you don't expect me to help you now. I'm protecting my money. I wanna see you put that fence up by yourself. That's what I want to see. You'll be here another six months without me.

TROY: Nigger, you ain't right.

BONO: When it comes to my money . . . I'm right as fireworks on the Fourth of July.

TROY: Alright, we gonna see now. You better get out your bankbook. [BONO *exits, and* TROY *continues to work.* ROSE *enters from the house.*]

ROSE: What they say down there? What's happening with Gabe?

TROY: I went down there and got him out. Cost me fifty dollars. Say he was disturbing the peace. Judge set up a hearing for him in three weeks. Say to show cause why he shouldn't be recommitted.

ROSE: What was he doing that cause them to arrest him?

TROY: Some kids was teasing him and he run them off home. Say he was howling and carrying on. Some folks seen him and called the police. That's all it was.

ROSE: Well, what's you say? What'd you tell the judge?

TROY: Told him I'd look after him. It didn't make no sense to recommit the man. He stuck out his big greasy palm and told me to give him fifty dollars and take him on home.

ROSE: Where's he at now? Where'd he go off to?

TROY: He's gone on about his business. He don't need nobody to hold his hand.

ROSE: Well, I don't know. Seem like that would be the best place for him if they did put him into the hospital. I know what you're gonna say. But that's what I think would be best.

TROY: The man done had his life ruined fighting for what? And they wanna take and lock him up. Let him be free. He don't bother nobody.

ROSE: Well, everybody got their own way of looking at it, I guess. Come on and get your lunch. I got a bowl of lima beans and some cornbread in the oven. Come on get something to eat. Ain't no sense you fretting over Gabe. [ROSE *turns to go into the house.*]

TROY: Rose . . . got something to tell you.

ROSE: Well, come on . . . wait till I get this food on the table.

TROY: Rose! [*She stops and turns around.*] I don't know how to say this. [*Pause.*] I can't explain it none. It just sort of grows on you till it gets out of hand. It starts out like a little bush . . . and the next think you know it's a whole forest.

ROSE: Troy . . . what is you talking about?

TROY: I'm talking, woman, let me talk. I'm trying to find a way to tell you . . . I'm gonna be a daddy. I'm gonna be somebody's daddy.

ROSE: Troy . . . you're not telling me this? You're gonna be . . . what?

TROY: Rose . . . now . . . see . . .

ROSE: You telling me you gonna be somebody's daddy? You telling your *wife* this?

[GABRIEL *enters from the street. He carries a rose in his hand.*]

GABRIEL: Hey, Troy! Hey, Rose!

ROSE: I have to wait eighteen years to hear something like this.

GABRIEL: Hey, Rose . . . I got a flower for you. [*He hands it to her.*] That's a rose. Same rose like you is.

ROSE: Thanks, Gabe.

GABRIEL: Troy, you ain't mad at me, is you? Them bad mens come and put me away. You ain't mad at me, is you?

TROY: Naw, Gabe, I ain't mad at you.

ROSE: Eighteen years and you wanna come with this.

GABRIEL: [*Takes a quarter out of his pocket.*] See what I got? Got a brand new quarter.

TROY: Rose . . . it's just . . .

ROSE: Ain't nothing you can say, Troy. Ain't no way of explaining that.

GABRIEL: Fellow that give me this quarter had a whole mess of them. I'm gonna keep this quarter till it stop shining.

ROSE: Gabe, go on in the house there. I got some watermelon in the frigidaire. Go on and get you a piece.

GABRIEL: Say, Rose . . . you know I was chasing hellhounds and them bad mens come and get me and take me away. Troy helped me. He come down there and told them they better let me go before he beat them up. Yeah, he did!

ROSE: You go on and get you a piece of watermelon, Gabe. Them bad mens is gone now.

GABRIEL: Okay, Rose . . . gonna get me some watermelon. The kind with the stripes on it. [GABRIEL *exits into the house.*]

ROSE: Why, Troy? Why? After all these years to come dragging this in to me now. It don't make no sense at your age. I could have expected this ten or fifteen years ago, but not now.

TROY: Age ain't got nothing to do with it, Rose.

ROSE: I done tried to be everything a wife should be. Everything a wife could be. Been married eighteen years and I got to live to see the day you tell me you been seeing another woman and done fathered a child by her. And you know I ain't never wanted no half nothing in my family. My whole family is half. Everybody got different fathers and mothers . . . my two sisters and my brother. Can't hardly tell who's who. Can't never sit down and talk about Papa and Mama. It's your papa and your mama and my papa and my mama . . .

TROY: Rose . . . stop it now.

ROSE: I ain't never wanted that for none of my children. And now you wanna drag your behind in here and tell me something like this.

TROY: You ought to know. It's time for you to know.

ROSE: Well, I don't want to know, goddamn it!

TROY: I can't just make it go away. It's done now. I can't wish the circumstance of the thing away.

ROSE: And you don't want to either. Maybe you want to wish me and my boy away. Maybe that's what you want? Well, you can't wish us away. I've got eighteen years of my life invested in you. You ought to have stayed upstairs in my bed where you belong.

TROY: Rose . . . now listen to me . . . we can get a handle on this thing. We can talk this out . . . come to an understanding.

ROSE: All of a sudden it's "we." Where was "we" at when you was down there rolling around with some godforsaken woman? "We" should have come to an understanding before you started making a damn fool of yourself. You're a day late and a dollar short when it comes to an understanding with me.

TROY: It's just . . . She gives me a different idea . . . a different understanding about myself. I can step out of this house and get away from the pressures and problems . . . be a different man. I ain't got to wonder how I'm gonna pay the bills or get the roof fixed. I can just be a part of myself that I ain't never been.

ROSE: What I want to know . . . is do you plan to continue seeing her. That's all you can say to me.

TROY: I can sit up in her house and laugh. Do you understand what I'm saying. I can laugh out loud . . . and it feels good. It reaches all the way down to the bottom of my shoes. [*Pause.*] Rose, I can't give that up.

ROSE: Maybe you ought to go on and stay down there with her . . . if she a better woman than me.

TROY: It ain't about nobody being a better woman or nothing. Rose, you ain't the blame. A man couldn't ask for no woman to be a better wife than you've been. I'm responsible for it. I done locked myself into a pattern trying to take care of you all that I forgot about myself.

ROSE: What the hell was I there for? That was my job, not somebody else's.

TROY: Rose, I done tried all my life to live decent . . . to live a clean . . . hard . . . useful life. I tried to be a good husband to you. In every way I knew how. Maybe I come into the world backwards, I don't know. But . . . you born with two strikes on you before you come to the plate. You got to guard it closely . . . always looking for the curve-ball on the inside corner. You can't afford to let none get past you. You can't afford a call strike. If you going down . . . you going down swinging. Everything lined up against you. What you gonna do. I fooled them, Rose. I bunted. When I found you and Cory and a halfway decent job . . . I was safe. Couldn't nothing touch me. I wasn't gonna strike out no more. I wasn't going back to the penitentiary. I wasn't gonna lay in the streets with a bottle of wine. I was safe. I had me a family. A job. I wasn't gonna get that last strike. I was on first looking for one of them boys to knock me in. To get me home.

ROSE: You should have stayed in my bed, Troy.

TROY: Then when I saw that gal . . . she firmed up my backbone. And I got to thinking that if I tried . . . I just might be able to steal second. Do you understand after eighteen years I wanted to steal second.

ROSE: You should have held me tight. You should have grabbed me and held on.

TROY: I stood on first base for eighteen years and I thought . . . well, goddamn it . . . go on for it!

ROSE: We're not talking about baseball! We're talking about you going off to lay in bed with another woman . . . and then bring it home to me. That's what we're talking about. We ain't talking about no baseball.

TROY: Rose, you're not listening to me. I'm trying the best I can to explain it to you. It's not easy for me to admit that I been standing in the same place for eighteen years.

ROSE: I been standing with you! I been right here with you, Troy. I got a life too. I gave eighteen years of my life to stand in the same spot with you. Don't you think I ever wanted other things? Don't you think I had dreams and hopes? What about my life? What about me. Don't you think it ever crossed my mind to want to know other men? That I wanted to lay up somewhere and forget about my responsibilities? That I wanted someone to make me laugh so I could feel good? You not the only one who's got wants and needs. But I held on to you, Troy. I took all my feelings, my wants and needs, my dreams . . . and I buried them inside you. I planted a seed and watched and prayed over it. I planted myself inside you and waited to bloom. And it didn't take me no eighteen years to find out the soil was hard and rocky and it wasn't never gonna bloom.

But I held on to you, Troy. I held you tighter. You was my husband. I owed you everything I had. Every part of me I could find to give you. And upstairs in that room . . . with the darkness falling in on me . . . I gave everything I had to try and erase the doubt that you wasn't the finest man in the world. And wherever you was going . . . I wanted to be there with you. 'Cause you was my husband. 'Cause that's the only way I was gonna survive as your wife. You always talking about what you give . . . and what you don't have to give. But you take too. You take . . . and don't even know nobody's giving!

[ROSE *turns to exit into the house;* TROY *grabs her arm.*]

TROY: You say I take and don't give!

ROSE: Troy! You're hurting me!

TROY: You say I take and don't give.

ROSE: Troy . . . you're hurting my arm! Let go!

TROY: I done give you everything I got. Don't you tell that lie on me.

ROSE: Troy!

TROY: Don't you tell that lie on me!

[CORY *enters from the house.*]

CORY: Mama!

ROSE: Troy. You're hurting me.

TROY: Don't you tell me about no taking and giving.

[CORY *comes up behind* TROY *and grabs him.* TROY, *surprised, is thrown off balance just as* CORY *throws a glancing blow that catches him on the chest and knocks him down.* TROY *is stunned, as is* CORY.]

ROSE: Troy. Troy. No! [TROY *gets to his feet and starts at* CORY.] Troy . . . no. Please! Troy! [ROSE *pulls on* TROY *to hold him back.* TROY *stops himself.*]

TROY: [*To* CORY] Alright. That's strike two. You stay away from around me, boy. Don't you strike out. You living with a full count. Don't you strike out. [TROY *exits out the yard as the lights go down.*]

SCENE 2

It is six months later, early afternoon. TROY *enters from the house and starts to exit the yard.* ROSE *enters from the house.*

ROSE: Troy, I want to talk to you.

TROY: All of a sudden, after all this time, you want to talk to me, huh? You ain't wanted to talk to me for months. You ain't wanted to talk to me last night. You ain't wanted no part of me then. What you wanna talk to me about now?

ROSE: Tomorrow's Friday.

TROY: I know what day tomorrow is. You think I don't know tomorrow's Friday? My whole life I ain't done nothing but look to see Friday coming and you got to tell me it's Friday.

ROSE: I want to know if you're coming home.

TROY: I always come home, Rose. You know that. There ain't never been a night I ain't come home.

ROSE: That ain't what I mean . . . and you know it. I want to know if you're coming straight home after work.

TROY: I figure I'd cash my check . . . hang out at Taylors' with the boys . . . maybe play a game of checkers. . . .

ROSE: Troy, I can't live like this. I won't live like this. You livin' on borrowed time with me. It's been going on six months now you ain't been coming home.

TROY: I be here every night. Every night of the year. That's 365 days.

ROSE: I want you to come home tomorrow after work.

TROY: Rose . . . I don't mess up my pay. You know that now. I take my pay and I give it to you. I don't have no money but what you give me back. I just want to have a little time to myself . . . a little time to enjoy life.

ROSE: What about me? When's my time to enjoy life?

TROY: I don't know what to tell you, Rose. I'm doing the best I can.

ROSE: You ain't been home from work but time enough to change your clothes and run out . . . and you wanna call that the best you can do?

TROY: I'm going over to the hospital to see Alberta. She went into the hospital this afternoon. Look like she might have the baby early. I won't be gone long.

ROSE: Well, you ought to know. They went over to Miss Pearl's and got Gabe today. She said you told them to go ahead and lock him up.

TROY: I ain't said no such thing. Whoever told you that is telling a lie. Pearl ain't doing nothing but telling a big fat lie.

ROSE: She ain't had to tell me. I read it on the papers.

TROY: I ain't told them nothing of the kind.

ROSE: I saw it right there on the papers.

TROY: What it say, huh?

ROSE: It said you told them to take him.

TROY: Then they screwed that up, just the way they screw up everything. I ain't worried about what they got on the paper.

ROSE: Say the government send part of his check to the hospital and the other part to you.

TROY: I ain't got nothing to do with that if that's the way it works. I ain't made up the rules about how it work.

ROSE: You did Gabe just like you did Cory. You wouldn't sign the paper for Cory . . . but you signed for Gabe. You signed that paper.

[*The telephone is heard ringing inside the house.*]

TROY: I told you I ain't signed nothing, woman! The only thing I signed was the release form. Hell, I can't read, I don't know what they had on that paper! I ain't signed nothing about sending Gabe away.

ROSE: I said send him to the hospital . . . you said let him be free . . . now you done went down there and signed him to the hospital for half his money. You went back on yourself, Troy. You gonna have to answer for that.

TROY: See now . . . you been over there talking to Miss Pearl. She done got mad cause she ain't getting Gabe's rent money. That's all it is. She's liable to say anything.

ROSE: Troy, I seen where you signed the paper.

TROY: You ain't seen nothing I signed. What she doing got papers on my brother anyway? Miss Pearl telling a big fat lie. And I'm gonna tell her about it too! You ain't seen nothing I signed. Say . . . you ain't seen nothing I signed.

[ROSE *exits into the house to answer the telephone. Presently she returns.*]

ROSE: Troy . . . that was the hospital. Alberta had the baby.

TROY: What she have? What is it?

ROSE: It's a girl.

TROY: I better get on down to the hospital to see her.

ROSE: Troy . . .

TROY: Rose . . . I got to go see her now. That's only right . . . what's the matter . . . the baby's alright, ain't it?

ROSE: Alberta died having the baby.

TROY: Died . . . you say she's dead? Alberta's dead?

ROSE: They said they done all they could. They couldn't do nothing for her.

TROY: The baby? How's the baby?

ROSE: They say it's healthy. I wonder who's gonna bury her.

TROY: She had family, Rose. She wasn't living in the world by herself.

ROSE: I know she wasn't living in the world by herself.

TROY: Next thing you gonna want to know if she had any insurance.

ROSE: Troy, you ain't got to talk like that.

TROY: That's the first thing that jumped out your mouth. "Who's gonna bury her?" Like I'm fixing to take on that task for myself.

ROSE: I am your wife. Don't push me away.

TROY: I ain't pushing nobody away. Just give me some space. That's all. Just give me some room to breathe.

[ROSE *exits into the house.* TROY *walks about the yard.*]

TROY: [*With a quiet rage that threatens to consume him.*] Alright . . . Mr. Death. See now . . . I'm gonna tell you what I'm gonna do. I'm gonna take and build me a fence around this yard. See? I'm gonna build me a fence around what belongs to me. And then I want you to stay on the other side. See? You stay over there until you're ready for me. Then you come on. Bring your army. Bring your sickle. Bring your wrestling clothes. I ain't gonna fall down on my vigilance this time. You ain't gonna sneak up on me no more. When you ready for me . . . when the top of your list say Troy Maxson . . . that's when you come around here. You come up and knock on the front door. Ain't nobody else got nothing to do with this. This is between you and me. Man to man. You stay on the other side of that fence until you ready for me. Then you come up and knock on the front door. Anytime you want. I'll be ready for you.

[*The lights go down to black.*]

SCENE 3

The lights come up on the porch. It is late evening three days later. ROSE *sits listening to the ball game waiting for* TROY. *The final out of the game is made and* ROSE *switches off the radio.* TROY *enters the yard carrying an infant wrapped in blankets. He stands back from the house and calls.*

[ROSE *enters and stands on the porch. There is a long, awkward silence, the weight of which grows heavier with each passing second.*]

TROY: Rose . . . I'm standing here with my daughter in my arms. She ain't but a wee bittie little old thing. She don't know nothing about grownups' business. She innocent . . . and she ain't got no mama.

ROSE: What you telling me for, Troy? [*She turns and exits into the house.*]

TROY: Well . . . I guess we'll just sit out here on the porch. [*He sits down on the porch. There is an awkward indelicateness about the way he handles the baby. His largeness engulfs and seems to swallow it. He speaks loud enough for* ROSE *to hear.*] A man's got to do what's right for him. I ain't sorry for nothing I done. It felt right in my heart.

[*To the baby.*] What you smiling at? Your daddy's a big man. Got these great big old hands. But sometimes he's scared. And right now your daddy's scared cause we sitting out here and ain't got no home. Oh, I been homeless before. I ain't had no little baby with me. But I been homeless. You just be out on the road by your lonesome and you see one of them trains coming and you just kinda go like this . . .

[*He sings as a lullaby.*]
Please, Mr. Engineer let a man ride the line
Please, Mr. Engineer let a man ride the line
I ain't got no ticket please let me ride the blinds
[ROSE *enters from the house.* TROY, *hearing her steps behind him, stands and faces her.*]
She's my daughter, Rose. My own flesh and blood. I can't deny her no more than I can deny them boys. [*Pause.*] You and them boys is my family. You and them and this child is all I got in the world. So I guess what I'm saying is . . . I'd appreciate it if you'd help me take care of her.

ROSE: Okay, Troy . . . you're right. I'll take care of your baby for you . . . 'cause . . . like you say . . . she's innocent . . . and you can't visit the sins of the father upon the child. A motherless child has got a hard time. [*She takes the baby from him.*] From right now . . . this child got a mother. But you a womanless man.

[ROSE *turns and exits into the house with the baby. Lights go down to black.*]

SCENE 4

It is two months later. LYONS *enters from the street. He knocks on the door and calls.*

LYONS: Hey, Rose! [*Pause.*] Rose!

ROSE: [*From inside the house.*] Stop that yelling. You gonna wake up Raynell. I just got her to sleep.

LYONS: I just stopped by to pay Papa this twenty dollars I owe him. Where's Papa at?

ROSE: He should be here in a minute. I'm getting ready to go down to the church. Sit down and wait on him.

LYONS: I got to go pick up Bonnie over her mother's house.

ROSE: Well, sit it down there on the table. He'll get it.

LYONS: [*Enters the house and sets the money on the table.*] Tell Papa I said thanks. I'll see you again.

ROSE: Alright, Lyons. We'll see you.

[LYONS *starts to exit as* CORY *enters.*]

CORY: Hey, Lyons.

LYONS: What's happening, Cory. Say, man, I'm sorry I missed your graduation. You know I had a gig and couldn't get away. Otherwise, I would have been there, man. So what you doing?

CORY: I'm trying to find a job.

LYONS: Yeah I know how that go, man. It's rough out here. Jobs are scarce.

CORY: Yeah, I know.

LYONS: Look here, I got to run. Talk to Papa . . . he know some people. He'll be able to help get you a job. Talk to him . . . see what he say.

CORY: Yeah . . . alright, Lyons.

LYONS: You take care. I'll talk to you soon. We'll find some time to talk.

[LYONS *exits the yard.* CORY *wanders over to the tree, picks up the bat and assumes a batting stance. He studies an imaginary pitcher and swings. Dissatisfied with the result, he tries again.* TROY *enters. They eye each other for a beat.* CORY *puts the bat down and exits the yard.* TROY *starts into the house as* ROSE *exits with* RAYNELL. *She is carrying a cake.*]

TROY: I'm coming in and everybody's going out.

ROSE: I'm taking this cake down to the church for the bakesale. Lyons was by to see you. He stopped by to pay you your twenty dollars. It's laying in there on the table.

TROY: [*Going into his pocket.*] Well . . . here go this money.

ROSE: Put in there on the table, Troy. I'll get it.

TROY: What time you coming back?

ROSE: Ain't no use in you studying me. It don't matter what time I come back.

TROY: I just asked you a question, woman. What's the matter . . . can't I ask you a question?

ROSE: Troy, I don't want to go into it. Your dinner's in there on the stove. All you got to do is heat it up. And don't you be eating the rest of them cakes in there. I'm coming back for them. We having a bakesale at the church tomorrow.

[ROSE *exits the yard.* TROY *sits down on the steps, takes a pint bottle from his pocket, opens it and drinks. He begins to sing.*]

TROY: Hear it ring! Hear it ring!

    Had an old dog his name was Blue

    You know Blue was mighty true

    You know Blue as a good old dog

    Blue trees a possum in a hollow log

    You know from that he was a good old dog

    [BONO *enters the yard.*]

BONO: Hey, Troy.

TROY: Hey, what's happening, Bono?

BONO: I just thought I'd stop by to see you.

TROY: What you stop by and see me for? You ain't stopped by in a month of Sundays. Hell, I must owe you money or something.

BONO: Since you got your promotion I can't keep up with you. Used to see you everyday. Now I don't even know what route you working.

TROY: They keep switching me around. Got me out in Greentree now . . . hauling white folks' garbage.

BONO: Greentree, huh? You lucky, at least you ain't got to be lifting them barrels. Damn if they ain't getting heavier. I'm gonna put in my two years and call it quits.

TROY: I'm thinking about retiring myself.

BONO: You got it easy. You can *drive* for another five years.

TROY: It ain't the same, Bono. It ain't like working the back of the truck. Ain't got nobody to talk to . . . feel like you working by yourself. Naw, I'm thinking about retiring. How's Lucille?

BONO: She alright. Her arthritis get to acting up on her sometime. Saw Rose on my way in. She going down to the church, huh?

TROY: Yeah, she took up going down there. All them preachers looking for somebody to fatten their pockets. [*Pause.*] Got some gin here.

BONO: Naw, thanks. I just stopped by to say hello.

TROY: Hell, nigger . . . you can take a drink. I ain't never known you to say no to a drink. You ain't got to work tomorrow.

BONO: I just stopped by. I'm fixing to go over to Skinner's. We got us a domino game going over his house every Friday.

TROY: Nigger, you can't play no dominoes. I used to whup you four games out of five.

BONO: Well, that learned me. I'm getting better.

TROY: Yeah? Well, that's alright.

BONO: Look here . . . I got to be getting on. Stop by sometime, huh?

TROY: Yeah, I'll do that, Bono. Lucille told Rose you bought her a new refrigerator.

BONO: Yeah, Rose told Lucille you had finally built your fence . . . so I figured we'd call it even.

TROY: I knew you would.

BONO: Yeah . . . okay. I'll be talking to you.

TROY: Yeah, take care, Bono. Good to see you. I'm gonna stop over.

BONO: Yeah. Okay, Troy. [BONO *exits.* TROY *drinks from the bottle.*]

TROY: Old Blue died and I dig his grave
   Let him down with a golden chain
   Every night when I hear old Blue bark
   I know Blue treed a possum in Noah's Ark.
   Hear it ring! Hear it ring!
   [CORY *enters the yard. They eye each other for a beat.* TROY *is sitting in the middle of the steps.* CORY *walks over.*]

CORY: I got to get by.

TROY: Say what? What's you say?

CORY: You in my way. I got to get by.

TROY: You got to get by where? This is my house. Bought and paid for. In full. Took me fifteen years. And if you wanna go in my house and I'm sitting on the steps . . . you say excuse me. Like your mama taught you.

CORY: Come on, Pop . . . I got to get by.

[CORY *starts to maneuver his way past* TROY. TROY *grabs his leg and shoves him back.*]

TROY: You just gonna walk over top of me?

CORY: I live here too!

TROY: [*Advancing toward him.*] You just gonna walk over top of me in my own house?

CORY: I ain't scared of you.

TROY: I ain't asked if you was scared of me. I asked you if you was fixing to walk over top of me in my own house? That's the question. You ain't gonna say excuse me? You just gonna walk over top of me?

CORY: If you wanna put it like that.

TROY: How else am I gonna put it?

CORY: I was walking by you to go into the house cause you sitting on the steps drunk, singing to yourself. You can put it like that.

TROY: Without saying excuse me??? [CORY *doesn't respond.*] I asked you a question. Without saying excuse me???

CORY: I ain't got to say excuse me to you. You don't count around here no more.

TROY: Oh, I see, . . . I don't count around here no more. You ain't got to say excuse me to your daddy. All of a sudden you done got so grown that your daddy don't count around here no more. . . . Around here in his own house and yard that he done paid for with the sweat of his brow. You done got so grown to where you gonna take over. You gonna take over my house. Is that right? You gonna wear my pants. You gonna go in there and stretch out on my bed. You ain't got to say excuse me cause I don't count around here no more. Is that right?

CORY: That's right. You always talking this dumb stuff. Now, why don't you just get out my way.

TROY: I guess you got someplace to sleep and something to put in your belly. You got that, huh? You got that? That's what you need. You got that, huh?

CORY: You don't know what I got. You ain't got to worry about what I got.

TROY: You right! You one hundred percent right! I done spent the last seventeen years worrying about what you got. Now it's your turn, see? I'll tell you what to do. You grown . . . we done established that. You a man. Now, let's see you act like one. Turn your behind around and walk out this yard. And when you get out there in the alley . . . you can forget about this house. See? 'Cause this is my house. You go on and be a man and get your own house. You can forget about this. 'Cause this is mine. You go on and get yours 'cause I'm through with doing for you.

CORY: You talking about what you did for me . . . what'd you ever give me?

TROY: Them feet and bones! That pumping heart, nigger! I give you more than anybody else is ever gonna give you.

CORY: You ain't never gave me nothing! You ain't never done nothing but hold me back. Afraid I was gonna be better than you. All you ever did was try and make me scared of you. I used to tremble every time you called my name. Every time I heard your footsteps in the house. Wondering all the time . . . what's Papa gonna say if I do this? . . . What's he gonna say if I do that? . . . What's Papa gonna say if I turn on the radio? And Mama, too . . . she tries . . . but she's scared of you.

TROY: You leave your mama out of this. She ain't got nothing to do with this.

CORY: I don't know how she stand you . . . after what you did to her.

TROY: I told you to leave your mama out of this! [*He advances toward* CORY.]

CORY: What you gonna do . . . give me a whupping? You can't whup me no more. You're too old. You just an old man.

TROY: [*Shoves him on his shoulder.*] Nigger! That's what you are. You just another nigger on the street to me!

CORY: You crazy! You know that?

TROY: Go on now! You got the devil in you. Get on away from me!

CORY: You just a crazy old man . . . talking about I got the devil in me.

TROY: Yeah, I'm crazy! If you don't get on the other side of that yard . . . I'm gonna show you how crazy I am! Go on . . . get the hell out of my yard.

CORY: It ain't your yard. You took Uncle Gabe's money he got from the army to buy this house and then you put him out.

TROY: [TROY *advances on* CORY.] Get your black ass out of my yard!
   [TROY*'s advance backs* CORY *up against the tree.* CORY *grabs up the bat.*]

CORY: I ain't going nowhere! Come on . . . put me out! I ain't scared of you.

TROY: That's my bat!

CORY: Come on!

TROY: Put my bat down!

CORY: Come on, put me out. [CORY *swings at* TROY, *who backs across the yard.*] What's the matter? You so bad . . . put me out!
   [TROY *advances toward* CORY.]

CORY: [*Backing up.*] Come on! Come on!

TROY: You're gonna have to use it! You wanna draw that bat back on me . . . you're gonna have to use it.

CORY: Come on! . . . Come on!
   [CORY *swings the bat at* TROY *a second time. He misses.* TROY *continues to advance toward him.*]

TROY: You're gonna have to kill me! You wanna draw that bat back on me. You're gonna have to kill me.
   [CORY, *backed up against the tree, can go no farther.* TROY *taunts him. He sticks out his head and offers him a target.*]
Come on! Come on!
   [CORY *is unable to swing the bat.* TROY *grabs it.*]

TROY: Then I'll show you.
   [CORY *and* TROY *struggle over the bat. The struggle is fierce and fully engaged.* TROY *ultimately is the stronger, and takes the bat from* CORY *and stands over him ready to swing. He stops himself.*]
Go on and get away from around my house.
   [CORY, *stung by his defeat, picks himself up, walks slowly out of the yard and up the alley.*]

CORY: Tell Mama I'll be back for my things.

TROY: They'll be on the other side of that fence.
   [CORY *exits.*]

TROY: I can't taste nothing. Helluljah! I can't taste nothing no more.
   [TROY *assumes a batting posture and begins to taunt Death, the fastball in the outside corner.*] Come on! It's between you and me now!

Come on! Anytime you want! Come on! I be ready for you . . .
but I ain't gonna be easy.

[*The lights go down on the scene.*]

SCENE 5

The time is 1965. The lights come up in the yard. It is the morning
of TROY*'s funeral. A funeral plaque with a light hangs beside the door.*
There is a small garden plot off to the side. There is noise and activity in
the house as ROSE, GABRIEL *and* BONO *have gathered. The door opens*
and RAYNELL, *seven years old, enters dressed in a flannel nightgown.*
She crosses to the garden and pokes around with a stick. ROSE *calls from*
the house.

ROSE: Raynell!
RAYNELL: Mam?
ROSE: What you doing out there?
RAYNELL: Nothing.

[ROSE *comes to the door.*]

ROSE: Girl, get in here and get dressed. What you doing?
RAYNELL: Seeing if my garden growed.
ROSE: I told you it ain't gonna grow overnight. You got to wait.
RAYNELL: It don't look like it never gonna grow. Dag!
ROSE: I told you a watched pot never boils. Get in here and get
    dressed.
RAYNELL: This ain't even no pot, Mama.
ROSE: You just have to give it a chance. It'll grow. Now you come
    on and do what I told you. We got to be getting ready. This ain't
    no morning to be playing around. You hear me?
RAYNELL: Yes, mam.

[ROSE *exits into the house.* RAYNELL *continues to poke at her gar-*
den with a stick. CORY *enters. He is dressed in a Marine corpo-*
ral's uniform, and carries a duffel bag. His posture is that of a
military man, and his speech has a clipped sternness.]

CORY: [*To* RAYNELL.] Hi. [*Pause.*] I bet your name is Raynell.
RAYNELL: Uh huh.
CORY: Is your mama home?

[RAYNELL *runs up on the porch and calls through the screendoor.*]

RAYNELL: Mama . . . there's some man out here. Mama?

[ROSE *comes to the door.*]

ROSE: Cory? Lord have mercy! Look here, you all!

[ROSE *and* CORY *embrace in a tearful reunion as* BONO *and* LYONS *enter from the house dressed in funeral clothes.*]

BONO: Aw, looka here . . .

ROSE: Done got all grown up!

CORY: Don't cry, Mama. What you crying about?

ROSE: I'm just so glad you made it.

CORY: Hey, Lyons. How you doing, Mr. Bono.

[LYONS *goes to embrace* CORY.]

LYONS: Look at you, man. Look at you. Don't he look good, Rose. Got them Corporal stripes.

ROSE: What took you so long.

CORY: You know how the Marines are, Mama. They got to get all their paperwork straight before they let you do anything.

ROSE: Well, I'm sure glad you made it. They let Lyons come. Your Uncle Gabe's still in the hospital. They don't know if they gonna let him out or not. I just talked to them a little while ago.

LYONS: A Corporal in the United States Marines.

BONO: Your daddy knew you had it in you. He used to tell me all the time.

LYONS: Don't he look good, Mr. Bono?

BONO: Yeah, he remind me of Troy when I first met him. [*Pause.*] Say, Rose, Lucille's down at the church with the choir. I'm gonna go down and get the pallbearers lined up. I'll be back to get you all.

ROSE: Thanks, Jim.

CORY: See you, Mr. Bono.

LYONS: [*With his arm around* RAYNELL.] Cory . . . look at Raynell. Ain't she precious? She gonna break a whole lot of hearts.

ROSE: Raynell, come and say hello to your brother. This is your brother, Cory. You remember Cory.

RAYNELL: No, Mam.

CORY: She don't remember me, Mama.

ROSE: Well, we talk about you. She heard us talk about you. [*To* RAYNELL.] This is your brother, Cory. Come on and say hello.

RAYNELL: Hi.

CORY: Hi. So you're Raynell. Mama told me a lot about you.

ROSE: You all come on into the house and let me fix you some breakfast. Keep up your strength.

CORY: I ain't hungry, Mama.

LYONS: You can fix me something, Rose. I'll be in there in a minute.

ROSE: Cory, you sure you don't want nothing. I know they ain't feeding you right.

CORY: No, Mama . . . thanks. I don't feel like eating. I'll get something later.

ROSE: Raynell . . . get on upstairs and get that dress on like I told you.

[ROSE *and* RAYNELL *exit into the house.*]

LYONS: So . . . I hear you thinking about getting married.

CORY: Yeah, I done found the right one, Lyons. It's about time.

LYONS: Me and Bonnie been split up about four years now. About the time Papa retired. I guess she just got tired of all them changes I was putting her through. [*Pause.*] I always knew you was gonna make something out yourself. Your head was always in the right direction. So . . . you gonna stay in . . . make it a career . . . put in your twenty years?

CORY: I don't know. I got six already, I think that's enough.

LYONS: Stick with Uncle Sam and retire early. Ain't nothing out here. I guess Rose told you what happened with me. They got me down the workhouse. I thought I was being slick cashing other people's checks.

CORY: How much time you doing?

LYONS: They give me three years. I got that beat now. I ain't got but nine more months. It ain't so bad. You learn to deal with it like anything else. You got to take the crookeds with the straights. That's what Papa used to say. He used to say that when he struck out. I seen him strike out three times in a row . . . and the next time up he hit the ball over the grandstand. Right out there in Homestead Field. He wasn't satisfied hitting in the seats . . . he want to hit it over everything! After the game he had two hundred people standing around waiting to shake his hand. You got to take the crookeds with the straights. Yeah, Papa was something else.

CORY: You still playing?

LYONS: Cory . . . you know I'm gonna do that. There's some fellows down there we got us a band . . . we gonna try and stay together when we get out . . . but yeah, I'm still playing. It still helps me to get out of bed in the morning. As long as it do that I'm gonna be right there playing and trying to make some sense out of it.

ROSE: [*Calling.*] Lyons, I got these eggs in the pan.

LYONS: Let me go on and get these eggs, man. Get ready to go bury Papa. [*Pause.*] How you doing? You doing alright?

[CORY *nods.* LYONS *touches him on the shoulder and they share a moment of silent grief.* LYONS *exits into the house.* CORY *wanders about the yard.* RAYNELL *enters.*]

RAYNELL: Hi.

CORY: Hi.

RAYNELL: Did you used to sleep in my room?

CORY: Yeah . . . that used to be my room.

RAYNELL: That's what Papa call it. "Cory's room." It got your football in the closet.

[ROSE *comes to the door.*]

ROSE: Raynell, get in there and get them good shoes on.

RAYNELL: Mama, can't I wear these. Them other one hurt my feet.

ROSE: Well, they just gonna have to hurt your feet for a while. You ain't said they hurt your feet when you went down to the store and got them.

RAYNELL: They didn't hurt then. My feet done got bigger.

ROSE: Don't you give me no backtalk now. You get in there and get them shoes on. [RAYNELL *exits into the house.*] Ain't too much changed. He still got that piece of rag tied to that tree. He was out here swinging that bat. I was just ready to go back in the house. He swung that bat and then he just fell over. Seem like he swung it and stood there with this grin on his face . . . and then he just fell over. They carried him on down to the hospital, but I knew there wasn't no need . . . why don't you come on in the house?

CORY: Mama . . . I got something to tell you. I don't know how to tell you this . . . but I've got to tell you . . . I'm not going to Papa's funeral.

ROSE: Boy, hush your mouth. That's your daddy you talking about. I don't want hear that kind of talk this morning. I done raised you to come to this? You standing there all healthy and grown talking about you ain't going to your daddy's funeral?

CORY: Mama . . . listen . . .

ROSE: I don't want to hear it, Cory. You just get that thought out of your head.

CORY: I can't drag Papa with me everywhere I go. I've got to say no to him. One time in my life I've got to say no.

ROSE: Don't nobody have to listen to nothing like that. I know you and your daddy ain't seen eye to eye, but I ain't got to listen to that kind of talk this morning. Whatever was between you and your daddy . . . the time has come to put it aside. Just take it and set it over there on the shelf and forget about it. Disrespecting your daddy ain't gonna make you a man, Cory. You got to find a way to come to that on your own. Not going to your daddy's funeral ain't gonna make you a man.

CORY: The whole time I was growing up . . . living in his house . . . Papa was like a shadow that followed you everywhere. It weighed on you and sunk into your flesh. It would wrap around you and lay there until you couldn't tell which one was you anymore. That shadow digging in your flesh. Trying to crawl in. Trying to live through you. Everywhere I looked, Troy Maxson was staring back at me . . . hiding under the bed . . . in the closet. I'm just saying I've got to find a way to get rid of that shadow, Mama.

ROSE: You just like him. You got him in you good.

CORY: Don't tell me that, Mama.

ROSE: You Troy Maxson all over again.

CORY: I don't want to be Troy Maxson. I want to be me.

ROSE: You can't be nobody but who you are, Cory. That shadow wasn't nothing but you growing into yourself. You either got to grow into it or cut it down to fit you. But that's all you got to make life with. That's all you got to measure yourself against that world out there. Your daddy wanted you to be everything he wasn't . . . and at the same time he tried to make you into everything he was. I don't know if he was right or wrong . . . but I do know he meant to do more good than he meant to do harm. He wasn't always right. Sometimes when he touched he bruised. And sometimes when he took me in his arms he cut.

When I first met your daddy I thought . . . Here is a man I can lay down with and make a baby. That's the first thing I thought when I seen him. I was thirty years old and had done seen my share of men. But when he walked up to me and said, "I can dance a waltz that'll make you dizzy," I thought, Rose Lee, here is a man that you can open yourself up to and be filled to bursting. Here is a man that can fill all them empty spaces you been tipping around the edges of. One of them empty spaces was being somebody's mother.

I married your daddy and settled down to cooking his supper and keeping clean sheets on the bed. When your daddy walked through the house he was so big he filled it up. That was my first mistake. Not to make him leave some room for me. For my part in the matter. But at that time I wanted that. I wanted a house that I could sing in. And that's what your daddy gave me. I didn't know to keep up his strength I had to give up little pieces of mine. I did that. I took on his life as mine and mixed up the pieces so that you couldn't hardly tell which was which anymore. It was my choice. It was my life and I didn't have to live it like that. But that's what life offered me in the way of being a woman and I took it. I grabbed hold of it with both hands.

By the time Raynell came into the house, me and your daddy had done lost touch with one another. I didn't want to make my blessing off of nobody's misfortune . . . but I took on to Raynell like she was all them babies I had wanted and never had. [*The phone rings.*] Like I'd been blessed to relive a part of my life. And if the Lord see fit to keep up my strength . . . I'm gonna do her just like your daddy did you . . . I'm gonna give her the best of what's in me.

RAYNELL: [*Entering, still with her old shoes.*] Mama . . . Reverend Tollivier on the phone.

[ROSE *exits into the house.*]

RAYNELL: Hi.

CORY: Hi.

RAYNELL: You in the Army or the Marines?

CORY: Marines.

RAYNELL: Papa said it was the Army. Did you know Blue?

CORY: Blue? Who's Blue?

RAYNELL: Papa's dog what he sing about all the time.

CORY: [*Singing.*] Hear it ring! Hear it ring!
    I had a dog his name was Blue
    You know Blue was mighty true
    You know Blue was a good old dog
    Blue treed a possum in a hollow log
    You know from that he was a good old dog.
    Hear it ring! Hear it ring!
    [RAYNELL *joins in singing.*]

CORY *and* RAYNELL: Blue treed a possum out on a limb
    Blue looked at me and I looked at him
    Grabbed that possum and put him in a sack
    Blue stayed there till I came back
    Old Blue's feets was big and round
    Never allowed a possum to touch the ground.

    Old Blue died and I dug his grave
    I dug his grave with a silver spade
    Let him down with a golden chain
    And every night I call his name
    Go on Blue, you good dog you
    Go on Blue, you good dog you

RAYNELL: Blue laid down and died like a man
    Blue laid down and died . . .

BOTH: Blue laid down and died like a man
    Now he's treeing possums in the Promised Land
    I'm gonna tell you this to let you know
    Blue's gone where the good dogs go
    When I hear old Blue bark
    When I hear old Blue bark
    Blue treed a possum in Noah's Ark
    Blue treed a possum in Noah's Ark.
    [ROSE *comes to the screen door.*]

ROSE: Cory, we gonna be ready to go in a minute.

CORY: [*To* RAYNELL.] You go on in the house and change them shoes like Mama told you so we can go to Papa's funeral.

RAYNELL: Okay, I'll be back.

[RAYNELL *exits into the house.* CORY *gets up and crosses over to the tree.* ROSE *stands in the screen door watching him.* GABRIEL *enters from the alley.*]

GABRIEL: [*Calling.*] Hey, Rose!

ROSE: Gabe?

GABRIEL: I'm here, Rose. Hey, Rose, I'm here!

[ROSE *enters from the house.*]

ROSE: Lord . . . Look here, Lyons!

LYONS: See, I told you, Rose . . . I told you they'd let him come.

CORY: How you doing, Uncle Gabe?

LYONS: How you doing, Uncle Gabe?

GABRIEL: Hey, Rose. It's time. It's time to tell St. Peter to open the gates. Troy, you ready? You ready, Troy. I'm gonna tell St. Peter to open the gates. You get ready now. [GABRIEL, *with great fanfare, braces himself to blow. The trumpet is without a mouthpiece. He puts the end of it into his mouth and blows with great force, like a man who has been waiting some twenty-odd years for this single moment. No sound comes out of the trumpet. He braces himself and blows again with the same result. A third time he blows. There is a weight of impossible description that falls away and leaves him bare and exposed to a frightful realization. It is a trauma that a sane and normal mind would be unable to withstand. He begins to dance. A slow, strange dance, eerie and lifegiving. A dance of atavistic signature and ritual.* LYONS *attempts to embrace him.* GABRIEL *pushes* LYONS *away. He begins to howl in what is an attempt at song, or perhaps a song turning back into itself in an attempt at speech. He finishes his dance and the gates of heaven stand open as wide as God's closet.*] That's the way that go!

[*Blackout.*]

1983   *1986*

Margaret Edson
b. 1961

Wit *has a remarkable backstory. Though she won the Pulitzer Prize, Edson has written no other play before or since. She's not a playwright, really. She's teaches middle school in Atlanta, far from the New York theater scene, with no desire to live in that world.*

Early in her adult life, she worked as a clerk at a research hospital in Washington, D.C., supporting cancer and AIDS inpatients. She describes her responsibilities as very low level, like a stage manager, making her almost invisible to the doctors, nurses, and patients who constituted the real drama of the unit. Unobserved, she watched the unguarded goings-on of the sick and the professionals.

In the summer of 1991, Edson wrote the first draft of the play, almost as if compelled. In her own words, she "just felt like doing it." She had had no training in drama (she studied history at Smith College), though a close friend from high school, Derek Jones, studied theater in college. Sitting around her kitchen table, Jones and Edson's family members read the script aloud. The play was an hour longer then—revision consisted largely of cutting. Rejected by several theaters, the script finally was accepted in 1995 by the South Coast Repertory theater in Costa Mesa, California. From there, it gradually made its way to off Broadway, where influential New York critics noticed it. In 1999, it won the Pulitzer Prize for drama. Derek Jones was the director; he died of complications from AIDS in 2000.

At first Edson imagined the main character would be a powerful politician, judge, or doctor. She wanted the character to be "skilled in the use of words and skilled in the acquisition of knowledge," while at the same time "very inept and very clumsy in her relations with people," so she settled on the profession of English professor. In her own college days, Edson heard that John Donne was the most difficult of poets to study, and so she made her protagonist a Donne scholar. Edson had little prior knowledge of the poetry of John Donne: she had to study it to write the play, and she found relevant themes of faith, mortality, pride, and humility in his Holy Sonnets. None was published before his death in 1633; perhaps the most authoritative version, the Westmoreland manuscript, dates from 1620 and is housed now in the New York Public Library. Textual scholars do debate issues of minutiae, such as the poems' punctuation, as dramatized in the play.

This play is one of several narratives that, in the late 1990s and early 2000s, explored the experiences of women in what author Barbara Ehrenreich called "the Cancer Industrial Complex: the multinational corporate enterprises that with the one hand doles out carcinogens and disease and, with the other, offers expensive, semi-toxic pharmaceutical treatments." Ehrenreich explains, for example, that AstraZeneca, the company that makes the chemotherapeutic tamoxifen, until 2000 also manufactured carcinogenic pesticides. In the view of some, the cancer-fighting industry—including such feel-good events as the Susan G. Komen Race for the Cure—"serves as an accomplice to global poisoning [by] normalizing cancer, prettying it up, even presenting it, perversely, as a positive and enviable experience." Meanwhile, perhaps 90 percent of breast cancers have environmental causes. However Wit *is interpreted, it certainly enters into these public debates about how to represent cancer treatment, especially that of women's cancer, in contemporary culture.*

Wit

CHARACTERS

VIVIAN BEARING, PH.D., *50; professor of seventeenth-century poetry at the university*

HARVEY KELEKIAN, M.D., *50; chief of medical oncology, University Hospital*

JASON POSNER, M.D., *28; clinical fellow, Medical Oncology Branch*

SUSIE MONAHAN, R.N., B.S.N., *28; primary nurse, Cancer Inpatient Unit*

E. M. ASHFORD, D.PHIL., *80; professor emerita of English literature*
MR. BEARING, *Vivian's father*
LAB TECHNICIANS
CLINICAL FELLOWS
STUDENTS
CODE TEAM

The play may be performed with a cast of nine: the four TECHNICIANS, FELLOWS, STUDENTS, *and* CODE TEAM MEMBERS *should double;* DR. KELEKIAN *and* MR. BEARING *should double.*

NOTES

Most of the action, but not all, takes place in a room of the University Hospital Comprehensive Cancer Center. The stage is empty, and furniture is rolled on and off by the technicians.

Jason and Kelekian wear lab coats, but each has a different shirt and tie every time he enters. Susie wears white jeans, white sneakers, and a different blouse each entrance.

Scenes are indicated by a line space in the script; there is no break in the action between scenes, but there might be a change in lighting. There is no intermission.

Vivian has a central-venous-access catheter over her left breast, so the IV tubing goes there, not into her arm. The IV pole, with a Port-a-Pump attached, rolls easily on wheels. Every time the IV pole reappears, it has a different configuration of bottles.

[VIVIAN BEARING *walks on the empty stage pushing her IV pole. She is fifty, tall and very thin, barefoot, and completely bald. She wears two hospital gowns—one tied in the front and one tied in the back—a baseball cap, and a hospital ID bracelet. The house lights are at half strength.*
VIVIAN *looks out at the audience, sizing them up.*]

VIVIAN: [*In false familiarity, waving and nodding to the audience.*] Hi. How are you feeling today? Great. That's just great. [*In her own professorial tone.*] This is not my standard greeting, I assure you.

I tend toward something a little more formal, a little less inquisitive, such as, say, "Hello."

But it is the standard greeting here.

There is some debate as to the correct response to this salutation. Should one reply "I feel good," using "feel" as a copulative to link the subject, "I," to its subjective complement, "good"; or "I feel well," modifying with an adverb the subject's state of being?

I don't know. I am a professor of seventeenth-century poetry, specializing in the Holy Sonnets of John Donne.[1]

So I just say, "Fine."

Of course it is not very often that I do feel fine.

I have been asked "How are you feeling today?" while I was throwing up into a plastic washbasin. I have been asked as I was emerging from a four-hour operation with a tube in every orifice, "How are you feeling today?"

I am waiting for the moment when someone asks me this question and I am dead.

I'm a little sorry I'll miss that.

It is unfortunate that this remarkable line of inquiry has come to me so late in my career. I could have exploited its feigned solicitude to great advantage: as I was distributing the final examination to the graduate course in seventeenth-century textual criticism—"Hi. How are you feeling today?"

Of course I would not be wearing this costume at the time, so the question's *ironic significance* would not be fully apparent.

As I trust it is now.

Irony is a literary device that will necessarily be deployed to great effect.

I ardently wish this were not so. I would prefer that a play about me be cast in the mythic-heroic-pastoral mode; but the facts, most notably stage-four metastatic ovarian cancer,[2] conspire against that. *The Faerie Queene*[3], this is not.

And I was dismayed to discover that the play would contain elements of . . . *humor*.

---

1. John Donne (1572–1631), British poet. Though later he became an Anglican minister, Donne wrote most of his *Holy Sonnets* in 1609–1610, well before his ordination.

2. At this stage the cancer has spread to the liver or otherwise out of the abdomen. Treatment consists of surgery and chemotherapy; as of the publishing of this anthology, long-term survival rates are only about 10% percent.

3. An epic poem in just such a mode as described; composed between 1590 and 1596 by Edmund Spenser (1552–1599).

I have been, at best, an *unwitting* accomplice. [*She pauses.*] It is not my intention to give away the plot; but I think I die at the end. They've given me less than two hours.

If I were poetically inclined, I might employ a threadbare metaphor—the sands of time slipping through the hourglass, the two-hour glass.

Now our sands are almost run;
More a little, and then dumb.

Shakespeare.[4] I trust the name is familiar.

At the moment, however, I am disinclined to poetry.

I've got less than two hours. Then: curtain.

[*She disconnects herself from the IV pole and shoves it to a crossing* TECHNICIAN. *The house lights go out.*]

VIVIAN: I'll never forget the time I found out I had cancer.

[DR. HARVEY KELEKIAN *enters at a big desk piled high with papers.*]

KELEKIAN: You have cancer.

VIVIAN: [*To audience.*] See? Unforgettable. It was something of a shock. I had to sit down. [*She plops down.*]

KELEKIAN: Please sit down. Miss Bearing, you have advanced metastatic ovarian cancer.

VIVIAN: Go on.

KELEKIAN: You are a professor, Miss Bearing.

VIVIAN: Like yourself, Dr. Kelekian.

KELEKIAN: Well, yes. Now then. You present with a growth that, unfortunately, went undetected in stages one, two, and three. Now it is an insidious adenocarcinoma, which has spread from the primary adnexal mass—

VIVIAN: "Insidious"?

KELEKIAN: "Insidious" means undetectable at an—

VIVIAN: "Insidious" *means* treacherous.

KELEKIAN: Shall I continue?

VIVIAN: By all means.

---

4. William Shakespeare (1564–1616). The lines are from *Pericles, Prince of Tyre,* act 5, scene 2, when the character Gower directly addresses the audience as Vivian does here.

KELEKIAN: Good. In invasive epithelial carcinoma, the most effective treatment modality is a chemotherapeutic agent. We are developing an experimental combination of drugs designed for primary-site ovarian, with a target specificity of stage three-and-beyond administration.

Am I going too fast?

Good.

You will be hospitalized as an in-patient for treatment each cycle. You will be on complete intake-and-output measurement for three days after each treatment to monitor kidney function. After the initial eight cycles, you will have another battery of tests.

The antineoplastic will inevitably affect some healthy cells, including those lining the gastrointestinal tract from lips to the arms and the hair follicles. We will of course be relying on your resolve to withstand some of the more pernicious side effects.

VIVIAN: Insidious. Hmm. Curious word choice.

Cancer. Cancel.

"By cancer nature's changing course untrimmed." No—that's not it.

[*To* KELEKIAN] No.

Must read something about cancer.

Must get some books, articles. Assemble a bibliography.

Is anyone doing research on cancer?

Concentrate.

Antineoplastic. Anti: against. Neo: new. Plastic. To mold. Shaping. Antineoplastic.

Against new shaping.

Hair follicles. My resolve.

"Pernicious." That doesn't seem—

KELEKIAN: Miss Bearing?
VIVIAN: I beg your pardon?
KELEKIAN: Do you have any questions so far?
VIVIAN: Please, go on.

KELEKIAN: Perhaps some of these terms are new. I realize—

VIVIAN: No, no. Ah. You're being very thorough.

KELEKIAN: I make a point of it. And I always emphasize it with my students—

VIVIAN: So do I. "Thoroughness"—I always tell my students, but they are constitutionally averse to painstaking work.

KELEKIAN: Yours, too.

VIVIAN: Oh, it's worse every year.

KELEKIAN: And this is not dermatology, it's medical oncology, for Chrissake.

VIVIAN: My students read through a text once—*once!*—and think it's time for a break.

KELEKIAN: Mine are blind.

VIVIAN: Well, mine are deaf.

KELEKIAN: [*Resigned, but warmly.*] You just have to hope . . .

VIVIAN: [*Not so sure*] I suppose.

[*Pause*]

KELEKIAN: Where were we, Dr. Bearing?

VIVIAN: I believe I was being thoroughly diagnosed.

KELEKIAN: Right. Now. The tumor is spreading very quickly, and this treatment is very aggressive. So far, so good?

VIVIAN: Yes.

KELEKIAN: Better not teach next semester.

VIVIAN: [*Indignant*] Out of the question.

KELEKIAN: The first week of each cycle you'll be hospitalized for chemotherapy; the next week you may feel a little tired; the next two weeks'll be fine, relatively. This cycle will repeat eight times, as I said before.

VIVIAN: Eight months like that?

KELEKIAN: This treatment is the strongest thing we have to offer you. And, as research, it will make a significant contribution to our knowledge.

VIVIAN: Knowledge, yes.

KELEKIAN: [*Giving her a piece of paper*] Here is the informed-consent form. Should you agree, you sign there, at the bottom. Is there a family member you want me to explain this to?

VIVIAN: [*Signing*] That won't be necessary.

KELEKIAN: [*Taking back the paper*] Good. The important thing is for you to take the full dose of chemotherapy. There may be times when you'll wish for a lesser dose, due to the side effects. But we've got to go full-force. The experimental phase has got to have the maximum dose to be of any use. Dr. Bearing—

VIVIAN: Yes?

KELEKIAN: You must be very tough. Do you think you can be very tough?

VIVIAN: You needn't worry.

KELEKIAN: Good. Excellent.

    [KELEKIAN *and the desk exit* as VIVIAN *stands and walks forward.*]

VIVIAN: [*Hesitantly*] I should have asked more questions, because I know there's going to be a test.

    I have cancer, insidious cancer, with pernicious side effects— no, the *treatment* has pernicious side effects.

    I have stage-four metastatic ovarian cancer. There is no stage five. Oh, and I have to be very tough. It appears to be a matter, as the saying goes, of life and death.

    I know all about life and death. I am, after all, a scholar of Donne's Holy Sonnets[4] which explore mortality in greater depth than any other body of work in the English language.

    And I know for a fact that I am tough. A demanding professor. Uncompromising. Never one to turn from a challenge. That is why I chose, while a student of the great E. M. Ashford, to study Donne.

    [PROFESSOR E. M. ASHFORD, *fifty-two, enters, seated at the same desk as* KELEKIAN *was. The scene is twenty-eight years ago.* VIVIAN *suddenly turns twenty-two, eager and intimidated.*]

VIVIAN: Professor Ashford?

E. M.: Do it again.

VIVIAN: [*To audience*] It was something of a shock. I had to sit down. [*She plops down.*]

E. M.: Please sit down. Your essay on Holy Sonnet Six, Miss Bearing, is a melodrama, with a veneer of scholarship unworthy of you— to say nothing of Donne. Do it again.

VIVIAN: I, ah . . .

E. M.: You must begin with a text, Miss Bearing, not with a feeling.

Death be not proud, though some have called thee Mighty and dreadfull, for, thou art not soe.

You have entirely missed the point of the poem, because, I must tell you, you have used an edition of the text that is inauthentically punctuated. In the Gardner edition[5]—

VIVIAN: That edition was checked out of the library—

E. M.: Miss Bearing!

VIVIAN: Sorry.

E. M.: You take this too lightly, Miss Bearing. This is Metaphysical Poetry,[6] not The Modern Novel. The standards of scholarship and critical reading which one would apply to any other text are simply insufficient. The effort must be total for the results to be meaningful. Do you think the punctuation of the last line of this sonnet is merely an insignificant detail?

The sonnet begins with a valiant struggle with death, calling on all the forces of intellect and drama to vanquish the enemy. But it is ultimately about overcoming the seemingly insuperable barriers separating life, death, and eternal life.

In the edition you chose, this profoundly simple meaning is sacrificed to hysterical punctuation:

And Death—*capital D*—shall be no more—*semicolon!*

Death—*capital D—comma*—thou shalt die—*exclamation point!*

If you go in for this sort of thing, I suggest you take up Shakespeare.

5. Probably Helen Gardner, *John Donne: The Divine Poems* (Oxford: Oxford University Press, 1952). Gardner (1908–1986), English literary critic and first woman to hold the position of Oxford University's Merton Professor of English Literature. The text of "If poysonous mineralls" (p. 548) comes from the 2nd edition of 1978.

6. Around the same time he was writing the *Holy Sonnets,* Donne addressed to his wife several poems that employ difficult-to-understand extended metaphors, or conceits, to convey the nature of their romantic love. It is largely in reference to this strange convergence of these intellectual puzzles with erotic subjects that critics later called Donne a metaphysical poet. Metaphysics, a branch of philosophy, concerns itself with the fundamental nature of existence.

Gardner's edition of the Holy Sonnets returns to the Westmoreland manuscript source of 1610—not for sentimental reasons, I assure you, but because Helen Gardner is a *scholar*. It reads:

And death shall be no more, *comma,* Death thou shalt die.

[*As she recites this line, she makes a little gesture at the comma.*]

Nothing but a breath—a comma—separates life from life everlasting. It is very simple really. With the original punctuation restored, death is no longer something to act out on a stage, with exclamation points. It's a comma, a pause.

This way, the *uncompromising* way, one learns something from this poem, wouldn't you say? Life, death. Soul, God. Past, present. Not insuperable barriers, not semicolons, just a comma.

VIVIAN: Life, death. . . I see. [*Standing*] It's a metaphysical conceit. It's wit! I'll go back to the library and rewrite the paper—

E. M: [*Standing emphatically*] It is *not wit,* Miss Bearing. It is truth. [*Walking around the desk to her.*] The paper's not the point.

VIVIAN: It isn't?

E. M.: [*Tenderly*] Vivian. You're a bright young woman. Use your intelligence. Don't go back to the library. Go out. Enjoy yourself with your friends. Hmm?

[VIVIAN *walks away.* E. M. *slides off.*]

VIVIAN: [*As she gradually returns to the hospital*] I, ah, went outside. The sun was very bright. I, ah, walked around, past the . . . There were students on the lawn, talking about nothing, laughing. The insuperable barrier between one thing and another is . . . just a comma? Simple human truth, uncompromising scholarly standards? They *connected?* I just couldn't . . .

I went back to the libary.

Anyway.

All right. Significant contribution to knowledge.

Eight cycles of chemotherapy. Give me the full dose, the full dose every time.

[*In a burst of activity, the hospital scene is created.*]

VIVIAN: The attention was flattering. For the first five minutes. Now I know how poems feel.

[SUSIE MONAHAN, VIVIAN'S *primary nurse, gives* VIVIAN *her chart, then puts her in a wheelchair and takes her to her first appointment: chest x-ray. This and all other diagnostic tests are suggested by light and sound.*]

TECHNICIAN 1: Name.

VIVIAN: My name? Vivian Bearing.

TECHNICIAN 1: Huh?

VIVIAN: Bearing. B-E-A-R-I-N-G. VIVIAN. V-I-V-I-A-N.

TECHNICIAN 1: Doctor.

VIVIAN: Yes, I have a Ph.D.

TECHNICIAN 1: *Your* doctor.

VIVIAN: Oh. Dr. Harvey Kelekian.

[TECHNICIAN 1 *positions her so that she is learning forward and embracing the metal plate, then steps offstage.*]

VIVIAN: I am a doctor of philosophy—

TECHNICIAN 1: [*From offstage.*] Take a deep breath, and hold it. [*Pause, with light and sound*] Okay.

VIVIAN: —a scholar of seventeenth-century poetry.

TECHNICIAN 1: [*From offstage*] Turn sideways, arms behind your head, and hold it. [*Pause*] Okay.

VIVIAN: I have made an immeasurable contribution to the discipline of English literature. [TECHNICIAN 1 *returns and puts her in the wheelchair.*] I am, in short, a force.

[TECHNICIAN 1 *rolls her to upper GI series, where* TECHNICIAN 2 *picks up.*]

TECHNICIAN 2: Name.

VIVIAN: Lucy, Countess of Bedford.

TECHNICIAN 2: [*Checking a printout*] I don't see it here.

VIVIAN: My name is Vivian Bearing. B-E-A-R-I-N-G. Dr. Kelekian is my doctor.

TECHNICIAN 2: Okay. Lie down. [TECHNICIAN 2 *positions her on a stretcher and leaves. Light and sound suggest the filming.*]

VIVIAN: After an outstanding undergraduate career, I studied with Professor E. M. Ashford for three years, during which time I learned by instruction and example what it means to be a scholar of distinction.

As her research fellow, my principal task was the alphabetizing of index cards for Ashford's monumental critical edition of Donne's *Devotions upon Emergent Occasions.*

[*During the procedure, another* TECHNICIAN *takes the wheelchair away.*]

I am thanked in the preface: "Miss Vivian Bearing for her able assistance."

My dissertation, "Ejaculations in Seventeenth-Century Manuscript and Printed Editions of the Holy Sonnets: A Comparison," was revised for publication in the *Journal of English Texts,* a very prestigious venue for a first appearance.

TECHNICIAN 2: Where's your wheelchair?

VIVIAN: I do not know. I was busy just now.

TECHNICIAN 2: Well, how are you going to get out of here?

VIVIAN: Well, I do not know. Perhaps you would like me to stay.

TECHNICIAN 2: I guess I got to go find you a chair.

VIVIAN: [*Sarcastically*] Don't inconvenience yourself on my behalf.

[TECHNICIAN 2 *leaves to get a wheelchair.*]

My second article, a classic explication of Donne's sonnet "Death be not proud," was published in *Critical Discourse.*

The success of the essay prompted the University Press to solicit a volume on the twelve Holy Sonnets in the 1633 edition, which I produced in the remarkably short span of three years. My book, entitled *Made Cunningly,* remains an immense success, in paper as well as cloth.

In it, I devote one chapter to a thorough examination of each sonnet, discussing every word in extensive detail.

[TECHNICIAN 2 *returns with a wheelchair.*]

TECHNICIAN 2: Here.

VIVIAN: I summarize previous critical interpretations of the text and offer my own analysis. It is exhaustive.

[TECHNICIAN 2 *deposits her at CT scan.*]

Bearing. B-E-A-R-I-N-G. Kelekian.

[TECHNICIAN 3 *has* VIVIAN *lie down on a metal stretcher. Light and sound suggest the procedure.*]

TECHNICIAN 3: Here. Hold still.

VIVIAN: For how long?

TECHNICIAN 3: Just a little while. [TECHNICIAN 3 *leaves. Silence*]

VIVIAN: The scholarly study of poetic texts requires a capacity for scrupulously detailed examination, particularly the poetry of John Donne.

The salient characteristic of the poems is wit: "Itchy outbreaks of far-fetched wit," as Donne himself said.

To the common reader—that is to say, the undergraduate with a B-plus or better average—wit provides an invaluable exercise for sharpening the mental faculties, for stimulating the flash of comprehension that can only follow hours of exacting and seemingly pointless scrutiny.

[TECHNICIAN 3 *puts* VIVIAN *back in the wheelchair and wheels her toward the unit. Partway,* TECHNICIAN 3 *gives the chair a shove and* SUSIE MONAHAN, VIVIAN'S *primary nurse, takes over.* SUSIE *rolls* VIVIAN *to the exam room.*]

To the scholar, to the mind comprehensively trained in the subtleties of seventeenth-century vocabulary, versification, and theological, historical, geographical, political, and mythological allusions, Donne's wit is . . . a way to see how good you really are.

After twenty years, I can say with confidence, no one is quite as good as I.

[*By now,* SUSIE *has helped* VIVIAN *sit on the exam table.*

DR. JASON POSNER, *clinical fellow, stands in the doorway.*]

JASON: Ah, Susie?

SUSIE: Oh, hi.

JASON: Ready when you are.

SUSIE: Okay. Go ahead. Ms. Bearing, this is Jason Posner. He's going to do your history, ask you a bunch of questions. He's Dr. Kelekian's fellow.

[SUSIE *is busy in the room, setting up for the exam.*]

JASON: Hi, Professor Bearing. I'm Dr. Posner, clinical fellow in the medical oncology branch, working with Dr. Kelekian.

Professor Bearing. I, ah, I was an undergraduate at the U. I took your course in seventeenth-century poetry.

VIVIAN: You did?

JASON: Yes. I thought it was excellent.

VIVIAN: Thank you. Were you an English major?

JASON: No. Biochemistry. But you can't get into medical school unless you're well-rounded. And I made a bet with myself that I could get an A in the three hardest courses on campus.

SUSIE: Howdjya do, Jace?

JASON: Success.

VIVIAN: [*Doubtful*] Really?

JASON: A minus. It was a very tough course. [*To* SUSIE] I'll call you.

SUSIE: *Okay.* [*She leaves.*]

JASON: I'll just pull this over. [*He gets a little stool on wheels.*] Get the proxemics right here. There. [*Nervously*] Good. Now. I'm going to be taking your history. It's a medical interview, and then I give you an exam.

VIVIAN: I believe Dr Kelekian has already done that.

JASON: Well, I know, but Dr. Kelekian wants *me* to do it, too. Now. I'll be taking a few notes as we go along.

VIVIAN: Very well.

JASON: Okay. Let's get started. How are you feeling today?

VIVIAN: Fine, thank you.

JASON: Good. How is your general health?

VIVIAN: Fine.

JASON: Excellent. Okay. We know you are an academic.

VIVIAN: Yes, we've established that.

JASON: So we don't need to talk about your interesting work.

VIVIAN: No.

[*The following questions and answers go extremely quickly.*]

JASON: How old are you?

VIVIAN: Fifty.

JASON: Are you married?

VIVIAN: No.

JASON: Are your parents living?

VIVIAN: No.

JASON: How and when did they die?

VIVIAN: My father suddenly, when I was twenty, of a heart attack. My mother, slowly, when I was forty-one and forty-two, of cancer. Breast cancer.

JASON: Cancer?

VIVIAN: Breast cancer.

JASON: I see. Any siblings?

VIVIAN: No.

JASON: Do you have any questions so far?

VIVIAN: Not so far.

JASON: Well, that about does it for your life history.

VIVIAN: Yes, that's all there is to my life history.

JASON: Now I'm going to ask you about your past medical history. Have you ever been hospitalized?

VIVIAN: I had my tonsils out when I was eight.

JASON: Have you ever been pregnant?

VIVIAN: No.

JASON: Ever had heart murmurs? High blood pressure?

VIVIAN: No.

JASON: Stomach, liver, kidney problems?

VIVIAN: No.

JASON: Venereal diseases? Uterine infections?

VIVIAN: No.

JASON: Thyroid, diabetes, cancer?

VIVIAN: No—cancer, yes.

JASON: When?

VIVIAN: Now.

JASON: Well, not including now.

VIVIAN: In that case, no.

JASON: Okay. Clinical depression? Nervous breakdowns? Suicide attempts?

VIVIAN: No.

JASON: Do you smoke?

VIVIAN: No.

JASON: Ethanol?

VIVIAN: I'm sorry?

JASON: Alcohol.

VIVIAN: Oh. Ethanol. Yes, I drink wine.

JASON: How much? How often?

VIVIAN: A glass with dinner occasionally. And perhaps a Scotch every now and then.

JASON: Do you use substances?

VIVIAN: Such as.

JASON: Marijuana, cocaine, crack cocaine, PCP, ecstasy, poppers—

VIVIAN: No.

JASON: Do you drink caffeinated beverages?

VIVIAN: Oh, yes!

JASON: Which ones?

VIVIAN: Coffee. A few cups a day.

JASON: How many?

VIVIAN: Two . . . to six. But I really don't think that's immoderate—

JASON: How often do you undergo routine medical checkups?

VIVIAN: Well, not as often as I should, probably, but I've felt fine, I really have.

JASON: So the answer is?

VIVIAN: Every three to . . . five years.

JASON: What do you do for exercise?

VIVIAN: Pace.

JASON: Are you having sexual relations?

VIVIAN: Not at the moment.

JASON: Are you pre- or post-menopausal?

VIVIAN: Pre.

JASON: When was the first day of your last period?

VIVIAN: Ah, ten days—two weeks ago.

JASON: Okay. When did you first notice your present complaint?

VIVIAN: This time, now?

JASON: Yes.

VIVIAN: Oh, about four months ago. I felt a pain in my stomach, in my abdomen, like a cramp, but not the same.

JASON: How did it feel?

VIVIAN: Like a cramp.

JASON: But not the same?

VIVIAN: No, duller, and stronger. I can't describe it.

JASON: What came next?

VIVIAN: Well, I just, I don't know, I started noticing my body, little things. I would be teaching, and feel a sharp pain.

JASON: What kind of pain?

VIVIAN: Sharp, and sudden. Then it would go away. Or I would be tired. Exhausted. I was working on a major project, the article on John Donne for *The Oxford Encyclopedia of English Literature*. It was a great honor. But I had a very strict deadline.

JASON: So you would say you were under stress?

VIVIAN: It wasn't so much more stress than usual, I just couldn't withstand it this time. I don't know.

JASON: So?

VIVIAN: So I went to Dr. Chin, my gynecologist, after I had turned in the article, and explained all this. She examined me, and sent me to Jefferson the internist, and he sent me to Kelekian because he thought I might have a tumor.

JASON: And that's it?

VIVIAN: Till now.

JASON: Hmmm. Well, that's very interesting.

[*Nervous pause*]

Well, I guess I'll start the examination. It'll only take a few minutes. Why don't you, um, sort of lie back, and—oh—relax.

[*He helps her lie back on the table, raises the stirrups out of the table, raises her legs and puts them in the stirrups, and puts a paper sheet over her.*]

Be very relaxed. This won't hurt. Let me get this sheet. Okay. Just stay calm. Okay. Put your feet in these stirrups. Okay. Just. There. Okay? Now. Oh, I have to go get Susie. Got to have a girl here. Some crazy clinical rule. Um. I'll be right back. Don't move.

[JASON *leaves. Long pause. He is seen walking quickly back and forth in the hall, and calling* SUSIE's *name as he goes by.*]

VIVIAN:[*To herself*] I wish I had given him an A. [*Silence*]

Two times one is two.

Two times two is four.

Two times three is six.

Um.

Oh.

Death be not proud, though some have called thee
Mighty and dreadfull, for, thou art not soe,
For, those, whom thou think'st, thou dost overthrow,
Die not, poore death, nor yet canst thou kill mee . . .

JASON: [*In the hallway*] Has anybody seen Susie?

VIVIAN: [*Losing her place for a second*] Ah.

Thou'art slave to Fate, chance, kings, and desperate men,
And dost with poyson, warre, and sicknesse dwell,
And poppie, or charmes can make us sleepe as well,
And better than thy stroake; why swell'st thou then?

JASON: [*In the hallway*] She was here just a minute ago.

VIVIAN:

One short sleepe past, wee wake eternally,
And death shall be no more—*comma*—Death thou shalt die.

[JASON *and* SUSIE *return.*]

JASON: Okay. Here's everything. Okay.

SUSIE: What is this? Why did you leave her—

JASON: [*To* SUSIE] I had to find you. Now, come on. [*To* VIVIAN] We're ready, Professor Bearing. [*To himself, as he puts on exam gloves*] Get these on. Okay. Just lift this up. Ooh. Okay. [*As much to himself as to* her] Just relax. [*He begins the pelvic exam, with one hand on her abdomen and the other inside her, looking blankly at the ceiling as he feels around*] Okay. [*Silence*] Susie, isn't that interesting, that I had Professor Bearing.

SUSIE: Yeah. I wish I had taken some literature. I don't know anything about poetry.

JASON: [*Trying to be casual*] Professor Bearing was very highly regarded on campus. It looked very good on my transcript that I had taken her course. [*Silence*] They even asked me about it in my interview for med school—[*He feels the mass and does a double take.*] Jesus! [*Tense silence. He is amazed and fascinated.*]

SUSIE: What?

VIVIAN: What?

JASON: Um. [*He tries for composure.*] Yeah. I survived Bearing's course. No problem. Heh. [*Silence*] Yeah, John Donne, those metaphysical poets, that metaphysical wit. Hardest poetry in the English department. Like to see *them* try biochemistry. [*Silence*] Okay. We're about done. Okay. That's it. Okay, Professor Bearing. Let's take your feet out there. [*He takes off his gloves and throws them away.*] Okay. I gotta go. I gotta go.

[JASON *quickly leaves.* VIVIAN *slowly gets up from this scene and walks stiffly away.* SUSIE *cleans up the exam room and exits.*]

VIVIAN: [*Walking downstage to audience*] That. . . was. . . hard. That . . . was . . .

One thing can be said for an eight-month course of cancer treatment: it is highly educational. I am learning to suffer.

Yes, it is mildly uncomfortable to have an electrocardiogram, but the . . . agony . . . of a proctosigmoidoscopy[7] sweeps it from memory. Yes, it was embarrassing to have to wear a nightgown

---

7. A procedure in which a physician inserts a lighted instrument into the patient's anus to examine the interior of the rectum and colon.

all day long—two nightgowns!—but that seemed like a positive privilege compared to watching myself go bald. Yes, having a former student give me a pelvic exam was thoroughly *degrading*—and I use the term deliberately—but I could not have imagined the depths of humiliation that—

Oh, God—[VIVIAN *runs across the stage to her hospital room, dives onto the bed, and throws up into a large plastic washbasin.*] Oh, God. Oh. Oh. [*She lies slumped on the bed, fastened to the IV, which now includes a small bottle with a bright orange label.*] Oh, God. It can't be. [*Silence*] Oh, God. Please. Steady. Steady. [*Silence*] Oh—Oh, no! [*She throws up again, moans, and retches in agony.*] Oh, God. What's left? I haven't eaten in two days. What's left to puke?

You may remark that my vocabulary has taken a turn for the Anglo-Saxon.[8]

God, I'm going to barf my brains out.

[*She begins to relax.*] If I actually did barf my brains out, it would be a great loss to my discipline. Of course, not a few of my colleagues would be relieved. To say nothing of my students.

It's not that I'm controversial. Just uncompromising. Ooh—[*She lunges for the basin. Nothing*] Oh. [*Silence*] False alarm. If the word went round that Vivian Bearing had barfed her brains out . . .

Well, first my colleagues, most of whom are my former students, would scramble madly for my position. Then their consciences would flare up, so to honor *my* memory they would put together a collection of *their* essays about John Donne. The volume would begin with a warm introduction, capturing my most endearing qualities. It would be short. But sweet.

Published *and* perished.

Now, watch this. I have to ring the bell [*She presses the button on the bed*] to get someone to come and measure this emesis, and record the amount on a chart of my intake and output. This counts as output.

---

8. Many of the English language's more colorful words derive from Old English or Anglo-Saxon, while many Latinate words, such as *regurgitate* and *vomit*, have a more euphemistic connotation. [*The Oxford English Dictionary* reports that the origin of *puke* is actually unknown and speculates that it derives from Dutch or German.]

[SUSIE *enters.*]

SUSIE: [*Bright*] How you doing, Ms. Bearing? You having some nausea?

VIVIAN: [*Weakly*] Uhh, yes.

SUSIE: Why don't I take that? Here.

VIVIAN: It's about 300 cc's.

SUSIE: That all?

VIVIAN: It was very hard work.

[SUSIE *takes the basin to the bathroom and rinses it.*]

SUSIE: Yup. Three hundred. Good guess. [*She marks the graph.*] Okay. Anything else I can get for you? Some Jell-O or anything?

VIVIAN: Thank you, no.

SUSIE: You okay all by yourself here?

VIVIAN: Yes.

SUSIE: You're not having a lot of visitors, are you?

VIVIAN: [*Correcting*] None, to be precise.

SUSIE: Yeah, I didn't think so. Is there somebody you want me to call for you?

VIVIAN: That won't be necessary.

SUSIE: Well, I'll just pop my head in every once in a while to see how you're coming along. Kelekian and the fellows should be in soon. [*She touches* VIVIAN's *arm.*] If there's anything you need, you just ring.

VIVIAN: [*Uncomfortable with kindness*] Thank you.

SUSIE: Okay. Just call. [SUSIE *disconnects the IV bottle with the orange label and takes it with her as she leaves.* VIVIAN *lies still. Silence*]

VIVIAN: In this dramatic structure you will see the most interesting aspects of my tenure as an in-patient receiving experimental chemotherapy for advanced metastatic ovarian cancer.

But as I am a *scholar* before . . . an impresario, I feel obliged to document what it is like here most of the time, between the dramatic climaxes. Between the spectacles.

In truth, it is like this:

[*She ceremoniously lies back and stares at the ceiling.*]

You cannot imagine how time . . . can be . . . so still.

It hangs. It weighs. And yet there is so little of it.

It goes so slowly, and yet it is so scarce.

If I were writing this scene, it would last a full fifteen minutes. I would lie here, and you would sit there.

[*She looks at the audience, daring them.*]

Not to worry. Brevity is the soul of wit.

But if you think eight months of cancer treatment is tedious for the *audience,* consider how it feels to play my part.

All right. All right. It is Friday morning: Grand Rounds. [*Loudly, giving a cue*] Action.

[KELEKIAN *enters, followed by* JASON *and four other* FELLOWS.]

KELEKIAN: Dr. Bearing.

VIVIAN: Dr. Kelekian.

KELEKIAN: Jason.

[JASON *moves to the front of the group.*]

JASON: Professor Bearing. How are you feeling today?

VIVIAN: Fine.

JASON: That's great. That's just great. [*He takes a sheet and carefully covers her legs and groin, then pulls up her gown to reveal her entire abdomen. He is barely audible, but his gestures are clear.*]

VIVIAN: "Grand Rounds." The term is theirs. Not "Grand" in the traditional sense of sweeping or magnificent. Not "Rounds" as in a musical canon, or a *round* of applause (though either would be refreshing at this point). Here, "Rounds" seems to signify darting *around* the main issue . . . which I suppose would be the struggle for life . . . *my* life . . . with heated discussions of side effects, other complaints, additional treatments.

JASON: Very late detection. Staged as a four upon admission. Hexamethophosphacil with Vinplatin to potentiate. Hex at 300 mg. per meter squared, Vin at 100. Today is cycle two, day three. Both cycles at the *full dose.* [*The* FELLOWS *are impressed.*]

The primary site is—*here* [*He puts his finger on the spot on her abdomen*], behind the left ovary. Metastases are suspected in the peritoneal cavity—here. And—here. [*He touches those spots.*]

Grand Rounds is not
Grand Opera. But compared
to lying here, it is positively
dramatic.

Full of subservience,
hierarchy, gratuitous
displays, sublimated
rivalries—I feel right at
home. It is just like a
graduate seminar.

With one important dif-
ference: in Grand Rounds,
they read *me* like a book.
Once I did the teaching,
now I am taught.

This is much easier. I just
hold still and look cancerous. It
requires less acting every time.

Excellent command of
details.

Full lymphatic
involvement. [*He moves his
hands over her entire body.*]

At the time of first-look
surgery, a significant part of
the tumor was de-bulked,
mostly in this area—*here.*
[*He points to each organ,
poking her abdomen.*] Left,
right ovaries. Fallopian tubes.
Uterus. All out.

Evidence of primary-site
shrinkage. Shrinking in metastatic tumors has not been
documented. Primary mass
frankly palpable in pelvic
exam, all through here—*here.*
[*Some* FELLOWS *reach and
press where he is pointing.*]

KELEKIAN: Excellent command of details.
VIVIAN: [*To herself*] I taught him, you know—
KELEKIAN: Okay. Problem areas with Hex and Vin. [*He addresses all
the* FELLOWS, *but* JASON *answers first and they resent him.*]
FELLOW 1: Myelosu—
JASON: [*Interrupting*] Well, first of course is myelosuppression, a
lowering of blood-cell counts. It goes without saying. With this
combination of agents, nephrotoxicity will be next.
KELEKIAN: Go on.
JASON: The kidneys are designed to filter out impurities in the
bloodstream. In trying to filter the chemotherapeutic agent out
of the bloodstream, the kidneys shut down.

KELEKIAN: Intervention.

JASON: Hydration.

KELEKIAN: Monitoring.

JASON: Full recording of fluid intake and output, as you see here on these graphs, to monitor hydration and kidney function. Totals monitored daily by the clinical fellow, as per the protocol.

KELEKIAN: Anybody else. Side effects.

FELLOW 1: Nausea and vomiting.

KELEKIAN: Jason.

JASON: Routine.

FELLOW 2: Pain while urinating.

JASON: Routine. [*The* FELLOWS *are trying to catch* JASON.]

FELLOW 3: Psychological depression.

JASON: No way.

[*The* FELLOWS *are silent.*]

KELEKIAN: [*Standing by* VIVIAN *at the head of the bed.*] Anything else. Other complaints with Hexamethophosphacil and Vinplatin. Come on. [*Silence.* KELEKIAN *and* VIVIAN *wait together for the correct answer.*]

FELLOW 4: Mouth sores.

JASON: Not yet.

FELLOW 2: [*Timidly*] Skin rash?

JASON: Nope.

KELEKIAN: [*Sharing this with* VIVIAN] Why do we waste our time, Dr. Bearing?

VIVIAN: [*Delighted*] I do not know, Dr. Kelekian.

KELEKIAN: [*To the* FELLOWS] Use your eyes. [*All* FELLOWS *looks closely at* VIVIAN.] Jesus God. Hair loss.

FELLOWS: [All *protesting.* VIVIAN *and* KELEKIAN *are amused.*]
—Come on.
—You can see it.
—It doesn't count.
—No fair.

KELEKIAN: Jason.

JASON: [*Begrudgingly*] Hair loss after first cycle of treatment.

KELEKIAN: That's better. [*To* VIVIAN.] Dr. Bearing. Full dose. Excellent. Keep pushing the fluids.

[*The* FELLOWS *leave,* KELEKIAN *stops* JASON.]

KELEKIAN: Jason.

JASON: Huh?

KELEKIAN: Clinical.

JASON: Oh, right. [*To* VIVIAN] Thank you, Professor Bearing. You've been very cooperative. [*They leave her with her stomach uncovered.*]

VIVIAN: Wasn't that . . . Grand? [*She gets up without the IV pole.*] At times, this obsessively detailed examination, this *scrutiny* seems to me to be a nefarious business. On the other hand, what is the alternative? Ignorance? Ignorance may be . . . bliss; but it is not a very noble goal.

So I play my part.

[*Pause*]

I receive chemotherapy, throw up, am subjected to countless indignities, feel better; go home. Eight cycles. Eight neat little strophes.[9] Oh, there have been the usual variations, subplots, red herrings: hepatotoxicity (liver poison), neuropathy (nerve death).

[*Righteously*] They are medical terms. I look them up.

It has always been my custom to treat words with respect.

I can recall the time—the very hour of the very day—when I knew words would be my life's work.

[*A pile of six little white books appears, with* MR. BEARING, VIVIAN'*s father, seated behind an open newspaper.*]

It was my fifth birthday.

[VIVIAN, *now a child, flops down to the books.*]

I liked that one best.

MR. BEARING: [*Disinterested but tolerant, never distracted from his newspaper*] Read another.

VIVIAN: I think I'll read . . . [*She takes a book from the stack and reads its spine intently.*] The Tale of the Flopsy Bunnies. [*Reading the front cover*] The Tale of the Flopsy Bunnies. It has little bunnies on the front.

[*Opening to the title page.*] The Tale of the Flopsy Bunnies by Beatrix Potter. [*She turns the page and begins to read.*]

---

9. Or stanzas. The word derives from the first stanzaic pattern in an ode (the others are *antistrophe* and *epode*); the chorus in a Greek tragedy would move in harmony with the strophe and then perform a countermovement while chanting the antistrophe.

It is said that the effect of eating too much lettuce is sopor—sop—or—what is that word?

MR. BEARING: Sound it out.

VIVIAN: Sop—or—fic. Sop—or—i—fic. Soporific. What does that mean?

MR. BEARING: Soporific. Causing sleep.

VIVIAN: Causing sleep.

MR. BEARING: Makes you sleepy.

VIVIAN: "Soporific" means "makes you sleepy"?

MR. BEARING: Correct.

VIVIAN: "Soporific" means "makes you sleepy." Soporific.

MR. BEARING: Now use it in a sentence. What has a soporific effect on *you*?

VIVIAN: A soporific effect on me.

MR. BEARING: What makes you sleepy?

VIVIAN: Aahh—nothing.

MR. BEARING: Correct.

VIVIAN: What about you?

MR BEARING: What has a soporific effect on me? Let me think: boring conversation, I suppose, after dinner.

VIVIAN: Me too, boring conversation.

MR. BEARING: Carry on.

VIVIAN: It is said that the effect of eating too much lettuce is soporific.

The little bunnies in the picture are asleep! They're sleeping! Like you said, because of *soporific!*

[*She stands up, and* MR. BEARING *exits.*]

The illustration bore out the meaning of the word, just as he had explained it. At the time, it seemed like magic.

So imagine the effect that the words of John Donne first had on me: ratiocination, concatenation, coruscation, tergiversation.

Medical terms are less evocative. Still, I want to know what the doctors mean when they . . . anatomize me. And I will grant that in this particular field of endeavor they possess a more potent arsenal of terminology than I. My only defense is the acquisition of vocabulary.

[SUSIE *enters and puts her arm around* VIVIAN'S *shoulders to hold her up.* VIVIAN *is shaking, feverish, and weak.*]

VIVIAN: [*All at once*] Fever and neutropenia.[1]

SUSIE: When did it start?

VIVIAN: [*Having difficulty speaking*] I—I was at home—reading—and I—felt so bad. I called. Fever and neutropenia. They said to come in.

SUSIE: You did the right thing to come. Did somebody drive you?

VIVIAN: Cab. I took a taxi.

SUSIE: [*She grabs a wheelchair and helps* VIVIAN *sit. As* SUSIE *speaks, she takes* VIVIAN's *temperature, pulse, and respiration rates.*] Here, why don't you sit? Just sit there a minute. I'll get Jason. He's on call tonight. We'll get him to give you some meds. I'm glad I was here on nights. I'll make sure you get to bed soon, okay? It'll just be a minute. I'll get you some juice, some nice juice with lots of ice.

[SUSIE *leaves quickly.* VIVIAN *sits there, agitated, confused, and very sick.* SUSIE *returns with the juice.*]

VIVIAN: Lights. I left all the lights on at my house.

SUSIE: Don't you worry. It'll be all right.

[JASON *enters, roused from his sleep and not fully awake. He wears surgical scrubs and puts on a lab coat as he enters.*]

JASON: [*Without looking at* VIVIAN] How are you feeling, Professor Bearing?

VIVIAN: My teeth—are chattering.

JASON: Vitals.

SUSIE: [*Giving* VIVIAN *juice and a straw, without looking at* JASON] Temp 39.4. Pulse 120. Respiration 36. Chills and sweating.

JASON: Fever and neutropenia. It's a "shake and bake." Blood cultures and urine, stat. Admit her. Prepare for reverse isolation. Start with acetaminophen.[2] Vitals every four hours. [*He starts to leave.*]

SUSIE: [*Following him*] Jason—I think you need to talk to Kelekian about lowering the dose for the next cycle. It's too much for her like this.

JASON: Lower the dose? No way. Full dose. She's tough. She can take it. Wake me up when the counts come from the lab.

---

1. A condition consisting of lowered effectiveness of white blood cells and hence increased susceptibility to infections.

2. A pain- and fever-reducing drug: a common brand name is Tylenol.

[*He pads off.* SUSIE *wheels* VIVIAN *to her room, and* VIVIAN *collapses on the bed.* SUSIE *connects* VIVIAN's *IV, then wets a washcloth and rubs her face and neck.* VIVIAN *remains delirious.* SUSIE *checks the IV and leaves with the wheelchair.*]

[*After a while,* KELEKIAN *appears in the doorway holding a surgical mask near his face.* JASON *is with him, now dressed and clean-shaven.*]

KELEKIAN: Good morning, Dr. Bearing. Fifth cycle. Full dose. Definite progress. Everything okay.

VIVIAN: [*Weakly*] Yes.

KELEKIAN: You're doing swell. Isolation is no problem. Couple of days. Think of it as a vacation.

VIVIAN: Oh.

[JASON *starts to enter, holding a mask near his face, just like* KELEKIAN.]

KELEKIAN: Jason.

JASON: Oh, Jesus. Okay, okay.

[*He returns to the doorway, where he puts on a paper gown, mask, and gloves.* KELEKIAN *leaves.*]

VIVIAN: [*To audience*] In isolation, I am isolated. For once I can use a term literally. The chemotherapeutic agents eradicating my cancer have also eradicated my immune system. In my present condition, every living thing is a health hazard to me . . .

[JASON *comes in to check the intake-and-output.*]

JASON: [*Complaining to himself*] I really have not got time for this . . .

VIVIAN: . . . particularly health-care professionals.

JASON: [*Going right to the graph on the wall*] Just to look at the I&O sheets for one minute, and it takes me half an hour to do precautions. Four, seven, eleven. Two-fifty twice. Okay. [*Remembering*] Oh, Jeez. Clinical. Professor Bearing. How are you feeling today?

VIVIAN: [*Very sick*] Fine. Just shaking sometimes from the chills.

JASON: IV will kick in anytime now. No problem. Listen, gotta go. Keep pushing the fluids.

[*As he exits, he takes off the gown, mask, and gloves.*]

VIVIAN: [*Getting up from bed with her IV pole and resuming her explanation.*] I am not in isolation because I have cancer, because I have a tumor the size of a grapefruit. No. I am in isolation because I am being treated for cancer. My treatment imperils my health.

Herein lies the paradox. John Donne would revel in it. I would revel in it, if he wrote a poem about it. My students would flounder in it, because paradox is too difficult to understand. Think of it as a puzzle, I would tell them, an intellectual game.

[*She is trapped.*] Or, I *would have* told them. Were it a game. Which it is not.

[*Escaping*] If they were here, if I were lecturing. How I would *perplex* them! I could work my students into a frenzy. Every ambiguity, every shifting awareness. I could draw so much from the poems.

I could be so powerful.

[VIVIAN *stands still, as if conjuring a scene. Now at the height of her powers, she grandly disconnects herself from the IV.* TECHNICIANS *remove the bed and hand her a pointer.*]

VIVIAN: The poetry of the early seventeenth century, what has been called the metaphysical school, considers an intractable mental puzzle by exercising the outstanding human faculty of the era, namely *wit*.

The greatest wit—the greatest English poet, some would say—was John Donne. In the Holy Sonnets, Donne applied his capacious, agile wit to the larger aspects of the human experience: life, death, and God.

In his poems, metaphysical quandaries are addressed, but never resolved. Ingenuity, virtuosity, and a vigorous intellect that jousts with the most exalted concepts: these are the tools of wit.

[*The lights dim. A screen lowers, and the sonnet "If poysonous mineralls" from the Gardner edition, appears on it.* VIVIAN *recites.*]

If poysonous mineralls, and if that tree,
Whose fruit threw death on else immortall us,
If lecherous goats, if serpents envious
Cannot be damn'd; Alas; why should I bee?
Why should intent or reason, borne in mee,
Make sinnes, else equall, in mee, more heinous?
And mercy being easie, and glorious
To God, in his sterne wrath, why threatens hee?
But who am I, that dare dispute with thee?
O God, Oh! of thine onely worthy blood,

And my teares, make a heavenly Lethean flood.
And drowne in it my sinnes blacke memorie.
That thou remember them, some claime as debt,
I thinke it mercy, if thou wilt forget.

[VIVIAN *occasionally whacks the screen with a pointer far emphasis. She moves around as she lectures.*]

Aggressive intellect. Pious melodrama. And a final, fearful point. Donne's Holy Sonnet Five, 1609. From the Ashford edition, based on Gardner.

The speaker of the sonnet has a brilliant mind, and he plays the part convincingly; but in the end he finds God's *forgivensss* hard to believe, so he crawls under a rock to *hide.*

If arsenic and serpents are not damned, then why is he? In asking the question, the speaker turns eternal damnation into an intellectual game. Why would God choose to do what is *hard,* to condemn, rather than what is *easy,* and also *glorious*—to show mercy?

(Several scholars have disputed Ashford's third comma in line six, but none convincingly.)

But. Exception. Limitation. Contrast. The argument shifts from cleverness to melodrama, an unconvincing eruption of piety: "O" "God" "Oh!"

A typical prayer would plead "Remember me, O Lord." (This point is nicely explicated in an article by Richard Strier—a former student of mine who once sat where you do now, although I dare say he was *awake*—in the May 1989 issue of *Modern Philology.*) True believers ask to be *remembered* by God. The speaker of this sonnet asks God to forget. [VIVIAN *moves in front of the screen, and the projection of the poem is cast directly upon her.*] Where is the hyperactive intellect of the first section? Where is the histrionic outpouring of the second? When the speaker considers his own *sins,* and the inevitability of God's *judgment,* he can conceive of but one resolution: to *disappear.* [VIVIAN *moves away from the screen.*] Doctrine assures us that no sinner is denied *forgiveness,* not even one whose sins are overweening *intellect* or overwrought *dramatics.* The speaker does not need to *hide* from God's *judgment,* only to accept God's *forgiveness.* It is very simple. Suspiciously simple.

We want to correct the speaker, to remind him of the assurance of salvation. But it is too late. The poetic encounter is over. We are left to our own consciences. Have we outwitted Donne? Or have we been outwitted?

[SUSIE *comes on.*]

SUSIE: Ms. Bearing?

VIVIAN: [*Continuing*] Will the po—

SUSIE: Ms. Bearing?

VIVIAN: [*Crossly*] What is it?

SUSIE: You have to go down for a test. Jason just called. They want another ultrasound. They're concerned about a bowel obstruction— Is it okay if I come in?

VIVIAN: No. Not now.

SUSIE: I'm sorry, but they want it now.

VIVIAN: Not right now. It's not *supposed* to be now.

SUSIE: Yes, they want to do it now. I've got the chair.

VIVIAN: It should not be now. I am in the middle of—this. I have *this* planned for now, not ultrasound. No more tests. We've covered that.

SUSIE: I know, I know, but they need for it to be now. It won't take long, and it isn't a bad procedure. Why don't you just come along.

VIVIAN: *I do not want to go now!*

SUSIE: Ms. Bearing.

[*Silence.* VIVIAN *raises the screen, walks away from the scene, hooks herself to the IV, and gets in the wheelchair.* SUSIE *wheels* VIVIAN, *and a* TECHNICIAN *takes her.*]

TECHNICIAN: Name.

VIVIAN: B-E-A-R-I-N-G. Kelekian.

TECHNICIAN: It'll just be a minute.

VIVIAN: Time for your break.

TECHNICIAN: Yup.

[*The* TECHNICIAN *leaves.*]

VIVIAN: [*Mordantly*] Take a break!

[VIVIAN *sits weakly in the wheelchair.*]

VIVIAN:

This is my playes last scene, here heavens appoint
My pilgrimages last mile; and my race
Idly, yet quickly runne, hath this last pace,

My spans last inch, my minutes last point,
And gluttonous death will instantly unjoynt
My body, 'and soule

John Donne. 1609.

I have always particularly liked that poem. In the abstract. Now I find the image of "my minute's last point" a little too, shall we say, *pointed.*

I don't mean to complain, but I am becoming very sick. Very, very sick. Ultimately sick, as it were.

In everything I have done, I have been steadfast, resolute— some would say in the extreme. Now, as you can see, I am distinguishing myself in illness.

I have survived eight treatments of Hexamethophosphacil and Vinplatin at the *full* dose, ladies and gentlemen. I have broken the record. I have become something of a celebrity. Kelekian and Jason are simply delighted. I think they foresee celebrity status for themselves upon the appearance of the journal article they will no doubt write about me.

But I flatter myself. The article will not be about *me,* it will be about my ovaries. It will be about my peritoneal cavity, which, despite their best intentions, is now crawling with cancer.

What we have come to think of as *me* is, in fact, just the specimen jar, just the dust jacket, just the white piece of paper that bears the little black marks.

My next line is supposed to be something like this:

"It is such a *relief* to get back to my room after those infernal tests."

This is hardly true.

It would be a *relief* to be a cheerleader on her way to Daytona Beach for Spring Break.

To get back to my room after those infernal tests is just the next thing that happens.

[*She returns to her bed, which now has a commode next to it. She is very sick.*]

Oh, God. It is such a relief to get back to my goddamn room after those goddamn tests.

[JASON *enters.*]

JASON: Professor Bearing. Just want to check the I&O. Four-fifty, six, five. Okay. How are you feeling today? [*He makes notations on his clipboard throughout the scene.*]

VIVIAN: Fine.

JASON: That's great. Just great.

VIVIAN: How are my fluids?

JASON: Pretty good. No kidney involvement yet. That's pretty amazing, with Hex and Vin.

VIVIAN: How will you know when the kidneys are involved?

JASON: Lots of in, not much out.

VIVIAN: That simple.

JASON: Oh, no way. Compromised kidney function is a highly complex reaction. I'm simplifying for you.

VIVIAN: Thank you.

JASON: We're supposed to.

VIVIAN: Bedside manner.

JASON: Yeah, there's a whole course on it in med school. It's required. Colossal waste of time for researchers. [*He turns to go.*]

VIVIAN: I can imagine. [*Trying to ask something important*] Jason?

JASON: Huh?

VIVIAN: [*Not sure of herself*] Ah, what… [*Quickly*] What were you just saying?

JASON: When?

VIVIAN: Never mind.

JASON: Professor Bearing?

VIVIAN: Yes.

JASON: Are you experiencing confusion? Short-term memory loss?

VIVIAN: No.

JASON: Sure?

VIVIAN: Yes. [*Pause*] I was just wondering: why cancer?

JASON: Why cancer?

VIVIAN: Why not open-heart surgery?

JASON: Oh yeah, why not *plumbing*. Why not run a *lube rack,* for all the surgeons know about *Homo sapiens sapiens*. No way. Cancer's the only thing I ever wanted.

VIVIAN: [*Intrigued*] Huh.

JASON: No, really. Cancer is . . . [*Searching*]

VIVIAN: [*Helping*] Awesome.

JASON: [*Pause*] Yeah. Yeah, that's right. It is. It is awesome. How does it do it? The intercellular regulatory mechanisms—especially for proliferation and differentiation—the malignant neoplasia just don't get it. You grow normal cells in tissue culture in the lab, and they replicate just enough to make a nice, confluent mono-layer. They divide twenty times, or fifty times, but eventually they conk out. You grow cancer cells, and they never stop. No contact inhibition whatsoever. They just pile up, just keep replicating for-ever. [*Pause*] That's got a funny name. Know what it is?

VIVIAN: No. What?

JASON: Immortality in culture.

VIVIAN: Sounds like a symposium.

JASON: It's an error in judgment, in a molecular way. But *why?* Even on the protistic level the normal cell–cell interactions are so subtle they'll take your breath away. Golden-brown algae, for instance, the lowest multicellular life form on earth—they're *idiots*—and it's incredible. It's perfect. So what's up with the cancer cells? Smartest guys in the world, with the best labs, funding—they don't know what to make of it.

VIVIAN: What about you?

JASON: Me? Oh, I've got a couple of ideas, things I'm kicking around. Wait till I get a lab of my own. If I can survive this . . . *fellowship.*

VIVIAN: The part with the human beings.

JASON: Everybody's got to go through it. All the great researchers. They want us to be able to converse intelligently with the clini-cians. As though *researchers* were the impediments. The clinicians are such troglodytes. So smarmy. Like we have to hold hands to discuss creatinine clearance. Just cut the crap, I say.

VIVIAN: Are you going to be sorry when I— Do you ever miss people?

JASON: Everybody asks that. Especially girls.

VIVIAN: What do you tell them?

JASON: I tell them yes.

VIVIAN: Are they persuaded?

JASON: Some.

VIVIAN: Some. I see. [*With great difficulty*] And what do you say when a patient is . . . apprehensive . . . frightened.

JASON: Of who?

VIVIAN: I just . . . Never mind.

JASON: Professor Bearing, who is the President of the United States?

VIVIAN: I'm fine, really. It's all right.

JASON: You sure? I could order a test—

VIVIAN: No! No. I'm fine. Just a little tired.

JASON: Okay. Look. Gotta go. Keep pushing the fluids. Try for 2,000 a day, okay?

VIVIAN: Okay. To use your word. Okay.

[JASON *leaves.*]

VIVIAN: [Getting *out of bed, without her IV*] So. The young doctor, like the senior scholar, prefers research to humanity. At the same time the senior scholar, in her pathetic state as a simpering victim, wishes the young doctor would take more interest in personal contact.

Now I suppose we shall see, through a series of flashbacks, how the senior scholar ruthlessly denied her simpering students the touch of human kindness she now seeks.

[STUDENTS *appear, sitting at chairs with writing desks attached to the right arm.*]

VIVIAN: [*Commanding attention*] How then would you characterize [*pointing to a student*]—you.

STUDENT 1: Huh?

VIVIAN: How would you characterize the animating force of this sonnet?

STUDENT 1: Huh?

VIVIAN: In this sonnet, what is the principal poetic device? I'll give you a hint. It has nothing to do with football. What propels this sonnet?

STUDENT 1: Um.

VIVIAN: [*Speaking to the audience*] Did I say [*tenderly*] "You are nineteen years old. You are so young. You don't know a sonnet from a steak sandwich." [*Pause*] By no means.

[*Sharply, to* STUDENT 1] You can come to this class prepared, or you can excuse yourself from this class, this department, and this university. Do not think for a moment that I will tolerate anything in between.

[*To the audience, defensively*] I was teaching him a lesson. [*She walks away from* STUDENT 1, *then turns and addresses the class.*]

So we have another instance of John Donne's agile wit at work not so much *resolving* the issues of life and God as *reveling* in their complexity.

STUDENT 2: But why?

VIVIAN: Why what?

STUDENT 2: Why does Donne make everything so *complicated?* [*The other* STUDENTS *laugh in agreement.*] No, really, *why?*

VIVIAN: [*To the audience*] You know, someone asked me that every year. And it was always one of the smart ones. What could I say? [*To* STUDENT 2] What do you think?

STUDENT 2: I think it's like he's hiding. I think he's really confused, I don't know, maybe he's scared, so he hides behind all this complicated stuff, hides behind this *wit.*

VIVIAN: *Hides* behind *wit?*

STUDENT 2: I mean, if it's really something he's sure of, he can say it more simple—simply. He doesn't have to be such a brain, or such a performer. It doesn't have to be such a big deal.

[*The other* STUDENTS *encourage him.*]

VIVIAN: Perhaps he is suspicious of simplicity.

STUDENT 2: Perhaps, but that's pretty stupid.

VIVIAN: [*To the audience*] That observation, despite its infelicitous phrasing, contained the seed of a perspicacious remark. Such an unlikely occurrence left me with two choices. I could draw it out, or I could allow the brain to rest after that heroic effort. If I pursued, there was the chance of great insight, or the risk of undergraduate banality. I could never predict. [*To* STUDENT 2] Go on.

STUDENT 2: Well, if he's trying to figure out God, and the meaning of life, and big stuff like that, why does he keep running away, you know?

VIVIAN: [*To the audience, moving closer to* STUDENT 2] So far so good, but they can think for themselves only so long before they begin to self-destruct.

STUDENT 2: Um, it's like, the more you hide, the less—no, wait— the more you are getting closer—although you don't know it— and the simple thing is there—you see what I mean?

VIVIAN: [*To the audience, looking at* STUDENT 2, *as suspense collapses*]
Lost it.

[*She walks away and speaks to the audience.*] I distinctly remember an exchange between two students after my lecture on pronun-
ciation and scansion. I overheard them talking on their way out of
class. They were young and bright, gathering their books and laughing at the expense of seventeenth-century poetry, at *my* expense.

[*To the class*] To scan the line properly, we must take advantage of the contemporary flexibility in "i-o-n" endings, as in
"expansion." The quatrain stands:

> Our two souls therefore, which are one,
>> Though I must go, endure not yet
> A breach, but an *ex-pan*-see-on,
>> Like gold to airy thinness beat.
>> Bear this in mind in your reading. That's all for today.

[*The* STUDENTS *get up in a chaotic burst.* STUDENT 3 *and* STUDENT
4 *pass by* VIVIAN *on their way out.*]

STUDENT 3: I hope I can get used to this pronuncia-see-on.

STUDENT 4: I know. I hope I can survive this course and make it to
gradua-see-on.

[*They laugh.* VIVIAN *glowers at them. They fall silent, embarrassed.*]

VIVIAN: [*To the audience*] That was a witty little exchange, I must admit. It
showed the mental acuity I would praise in a poetic text. But I admired
only the studied application of wit, not its spontaneous eruption.

[STUDENT 1 *interrupts.*]

STUDENT 1: Professor Bearing? Can I talk to you for a minute?

VIVIAN: You may.

STUDENT 1: I need to ask for an extension on my paper. I'm really
sorry, and I know your policy, but see—

VIVIAN: Don't tell me. Your grandmother died.

STUDENT 1: You knew.

VIVIAN. It was a guess.

STUDENT 1: I have to go home.

VIVIAN: Do what you will, but the paper is due when it is due.

[*As* STUDENT 1 *leaves and the classroom disappears,* VIVIAN
watches. Pause]

VIVIAN: I don't know. I feel so much—what is the word? I look
back, I see these scenes, and I . . .

[*Long silence.* VIVIAN *walks absently around the stage, trying to think of something. Finally, giving up, she trudges back to bed.*]

VIVIAN: It was late at night, the graveyard shift. Susie was on. I could hear her in the hall.

I wanted her to come and see me. So I had to create a little emergency. Nothing dramatic.

[VIVIAN *pinches the IV tubing. The pump alarm beeps.*]

It worked.

[SUSIE *enters, concerned.*]

SUSIE: Ms. Bearing? Is that you beeping at four in the morning? [*She checks the tubing and presses buttons on the pump. The alarm stops.*] Did that wake you up? I'm sorry. It just gets occluded sometimes.

VIVIAN: I was awake.

SUSIE: You were? What's the trouble, sweetheart?

VIVIAN: [*To the audience, roused*] Do not think for a minute that anyone calls me "Sweetheart." But then . . . I allowed it. [*To* SUSIE] Oh, I don't know.

SUSIE: You can't sleep?

VIVIAN: No. I just keep thinking.

SUSIE: If you do that too much, you can get kind of confused.

VIVIAN: I know. I can't figure things out. I'm in a . . . *quandary,* having these . . . *doubts.*

SUSIE: What you're doing is very hard.

VIVIAN: Hard things are what I like best.

SUSIE: It's not the same. It's like it's out of control, isn't it?

VIVIAN: [*Crying, in spite of herself*] I am scared.

SUSIE: [*Stroking her*] Oh, honey, of course you are.

VIVIAN: I want . . .

SUSIE: I know. It's hard.

VIVIAN: I don't feel sure of myself anymore.

SUSIE: And you used to feel sure.

VIVIAN: [*Crying*] Oh, yes. I used to feel sure.

SUSIE: Vivian. It's all right. I know. It hurts. I know. It's all right. Do you want a tissue? It's all right. [*Silence*] Vivian, would you like a Popsicle?

VIVIAN: [*Like a child*] Yes, please.

SUSIE: I'll get it for you. I'll be right back.

VIVIAN: Thank you.

[SUSIE *leaves.*]

VIVIAN: [*Pulling herself together*] The epithelial cells in my GI tract have been killed by the chemo. The cold Popsicle feels good, it's something I can digest, and it helps keep me hydrated. For your information.

[SUSIE *returns with an orange two-stick Popsicle.* VIVIAN *unwraps it and breaks it in half.*]

VIVIAN: Here.

SUSIE: Sure?

VIVIAN: Yes.

SUSIE: Thanks. [SUSIE *sits on the commode by the bed. Silence*] When I was a kid, we used to get these from a truck. The man would come around and ring his bell and we'd all run over. Then we'd sit on the curb and eat our Popsicles.

Pretty profound, huh?

VIVIAN: It sounds nice.

[*Silence*]

SUSIE: Vivian, there's something we need to talk about, you need to think about.

[*Silence*]

VIVIAN: My cancer is not being cured, is it.

SUSIE: Huh-uh.

VIVIAN: They never expected it to be, did they.

SUSIE: Well, they thought the drugs would make the tumor get smaller, and it has gotten a lot smaller. But the problem is that it started in new places too. They've learned a lot for their research. It was the best thing they had to give you, the strongest drugs. There just isn't a good treatment for what you have yet, for advanced ovarian. I'm sorry. They should have explained this—

VIVIAN: I knew.

SUSIE: You did.

VIVIAN: I read between the lines.

SUSIE: What you have to think about is your "code status." What you want them to do if your heart stops.

VIVIAN: Well.

SUSIE: You can be "full code," which means that if your heart stops, they'll call a Code Blue and the code team will come and resuscitate you and take you to Intensive Care until you stabilize again.

Or you can be "Do Not Resuscitate," so if your heart stops we'll . . . well, we'll just let it. You'll be "DNR." You can think about it, but I wanted to present both choices before Kelekian and Jason talk to you.

VIVIAN: You don't agree about this?

SUSIE: Well, they like to save lives. So anything's okay, as long as life continues. It doesn't matter if you're hooked up to a million machines. Kelekian is a great researcher and everything. And the fellows, like Jason, they're really smart. It's really an honor for them to work with him. But they always . . . want to know more things.

VIVIAN: I always want to know more things. I'm a scholar. Or I was when I had shoes, when I had eyebrows.

SUSIE: Well, okay then. You'll be full code. That's fine.

[*Silence*]

VIVIAN: No, don't complicate the matter.

SUSIE: It's okay. It's up to you—

VIVIAN: Let it stop.

SUSIE: Really?

VIVIAN: Yes.

SUSIE: So if your heart stops beating—

VIVIAN: Just let it stop.

SUSIE: Sure?

VIVIAN: Yes.

SUSIE: Okay. I'll get Kelekian to give the order, and then—

VIVIAN: Susie?

SUSIE: Uh-huh?

VIVIAN: You're still going to take care of me, aren't you?

SUSIE: 'Course, sweetheart. Don't you worry.

[*As* SUSIE *leaves,* VIVIAN *sits upright, full of energy and rage.*]

VIVIAN: That certainly was a *maudlin* display. Popsicles?

"Sweetheart"? I can't believe my life has become so . . . *corny.*

But it can't be helped. I don't see any other way. We are discussing life and death, and not in the abstract, either; we are discussing *my* life and *my* death, and my brain is dulling, and poor Susie's was never very sharp to begin with, and I can't conceive of any other . . . *tone.*

[*Quickly*] Now is not the time for verbal swordplay, for unlikely flights of imagination and wildly shifting perspectives, for metaphysical conceit, for wit.

And nothing would be worse than a detailed scholarly analysis. Erudition. Interpretation. Complication.

[*Slowly*] Now is a time for simplicity. Now is a time for, dare I say it, kindness.

[*Searchingly*] I thought being extremely smart would take care of it. But I see that I have been found out. Ooohhh.

I'm scared. Oh, God. I want . . . I want . . . No. I want to hide. I just want to curl up in a little ball. [*She dives under the covers.*]

[VIVIAN *wakes in horrible pain. She is tense, agitated, fearful. Slowly she calms down and addresses the audience.*]

VIVIAN: [*Trying extremely hard*] I want to tell you how it feels. I want to explain it, to use *my* words. It's as if . . . I can't . . . There aren't . . . I'm like a student and this is the final exam and I don't know what to put down because I don't understand the question and I'm *running out of time.*

The time for extreme measures has come. I am in terrible pain. Susie says that I need to begin aggressive pain management if I am going to stand it.

"It": such a little word. In this case, I think "it" signifies "being alive."

I apologize in advance for what this palliative treatment modality does to the dramatic coherence of my play's last scene. It can't be helped. They have to do something. I'm in terrible pain.

Say it, Vivian. *It hurts like hell. It really does.*

[SUSIE *enters.* VIVIAN *is writhing in pain.*]

Oh, God. Oh, God.

SUSIE: Sshh. It's okay. Sshh. I paged Kelekian up here, and we'll get you some meds.

VIVIAN: Oh, God, it is so painful. So painful. So much pain. So much pain.

SUSIE: I know, I know, it's okay. Sshh. Just try and clear your mind. It's all right. We'll get you a Patient-Controlled Analgesic. It's a little pump, and you push a little button, and you decide how much medication you want. [*Importantly*] It's very simple, and it's up to you.

[KELEKIAN *storms in;* JASON *follows with chart.*]

KELEKIAN: Dr. Bearing. Susie.

SUSIE: Time for Patient-Controlled Analgesic. The pain is killing her.

KELEKIAN: Dr. Bearing, are you in pain? [KELEKIAN *holds out his hand for chart;* JASON *hands it to him. They read.*]

VIVIAN: [*Sitting up, unnoticed by the staff*] Am I in pain? I don't believe this. Yes, I'm in goddamn pain. [*Furious*] I have a fever of 101 spiking to 104. And I have bone metastases in my pelvis and both femurs. *(Screaming)* There is cancer eating away at my goddamn bones, and I did not know there could be such pain on this earth. [*She flops back on the bed and cries audibly to them.*] Oh, God.

KELEKIAN: [*Looking at* VIVIAN *intently*] I want a morphine drip.

SUSIE: What about Patient-Controlled? She could be more alert—

KELEKIAN: [*Teaching*] Ordinarily, yes. But in her case, no.

SUSIE: But—

KELEKIAN: [*To* SUSIE] She's earned a rest. [*To* JASON] Morphine, ten push now, then start at ten on hour [*To* VIVIAN) Dr. Bearing, try to relax. We're going to help you through this, don't worry. Dr. Bearing? Excellent. [*He squeezes* VIVIAN'*s shoulder. They all leave.*]

VIVIAN: [*Weakly, painfully, learning on her IV pole, she moves to address the audience.*] Hi. How are you feeling today?

[*Silence*]

These are my last coherent lines. I'll have to leave the action to the professionals.

It came so quickly, after taking so long. Not even time for a proper conclusion.

[VIVIAN *concentrates with all her might, and she attempts a grand summation, as if trying to conjure her own ending.*]

And Death—*capital D*—shall be no more—semicolon.
Death—*capital D*—thou shalt die—*ex-cla-mation point!*
[*She looks down at herself, looks out at the audience, and sees that the line doesn't work. She shakes her head and exhales with resignation.*]
I'm sorry.

[*She gets back into bed as* SUSIE *injects morphine into the IV tubing.* VIVIAN *lies down and, in a final melodramatic gesture, shuts the lids of her own eyes and folds her arms over her chest.*]

VIVIAN: I trust this will have a soporific effect.

SUSIE: Well, I don't know about that, but it sure makes you sleepy.

[*This strikes* VIVIAN *as delightfully funny. She starts to giggle, then laughs out loud,* SUSIE *doesn't get it.*]

SUSIE: What's so funny? [VIVIAN *keeps laughing*] What?

VIVIAN: Oh! It's that—"Soporific" *means* "makes you sleepy."

SUSIE: It does?

VIVIAN: Yes. [*Another fit of laughter*)

SUSIE: [*Giggling*] Well, that was pretty dumb—

VIVIAN: No! No, no! It was *funny!*

SUSIE: [*Starting to catch on*] Yeah, I guess so. [*laughing*] In a dumb sort of way. [*This sets them both off laughing again.*] I never would have gotten it. I'm glad you explained it.

VIVIAN: [*Simply*] I'm a teacher.

[*They laugh a little together. Slowly the morphine kicks in, and* VIVIAN's *laughs become long sighs. Finally she falls asleep.* SUSIE *checks everything out, then leaves. Long silence*]

[JASON *and* SUSIE *chat as they enter to insert a catheter.*]

JASON: Oh, yeah. She was a great scholar. Wrote tons of books, articles, was the head of everything. [*He checks the I&O sheet.*] Two hundred. Seventy-five. Five-twenty. Let's up the hydration. She won't be drinking anymore. See if we can keep her kidneys from fading. Yeah, I had a lot of respect for her; which is more than I can say for the *entire* biochemistry department.

SUSIE: What do you want? Dextrose?

JASON: Give her saline.

SUSIE: Okay.

JASON: She gave a hell of a lecture. No notes, not a word out of place. It was pretty impressive. A lot of students hated her, though.

SUSIE: Why?

JASON: Well, she wasn't exactly a cupcake.

SUSIE: [*Laughing, fondly*] Well, she hasn't exactly been a cupcake here, either. [*Leaning over* VIVIAN *and talking loudly and slowly in her ear.*] Now, Ms. Bearing, Jason and I are here, and we're going to insert a catheter to collect your urine. It's not going to hurt, don't you worry. [*During the conversation she inserts the catheter.*]

JASON: Like she can hear you.

SUSIE: It's just nice to do.

JASON: Eight cycles of Hex and Vin at the full dose. Kelekian didn't think it was possible. I wish they could all get through it at full throttle. Then we could really have some data.

SUSIE: She's not what I imagined. I thought somebody who studied poetry would be sort of dreamy, you know?

JASON: Oh, not the way she did it. It felt more like boot camp than English class. This guy John Donne was incredibly intense. Like your whole brain had to be in knots before you could get it.

SUSIE: He made it hard on purpose?

JASON: Well, it has to do with the subject. The Holy Sonnets we worked on most, they were mostly about Salvation Anxiety. That's a term I made up in one of my papers, but I think it fits pretty well. Salvation Anxiety. You're this brilliant guy, I mean, brilliant—this guy makes Shakespeare sound like a Hallmark card. And you know you're a sinner. And there's this promise of salvation, the whole religious thing. But you just can't deal with it.

SUSIE: How come?

JASON: It just doesn't stand up to scrutiny. But you can't face life without it either. So you write these screwed-up sonnets. Everything is brilliantly convoluted. Really tricky stuff. Bouncing off the walls. Like a game, to make the puzzle so complicated.

[*The catheter is inserted.* SUSIE *puts things away.*]

SUSIE: But what happens in the end?

JASON: End of what?

SUSIE: To John Donne. Does he ever get it?

JASON: Get what?

SUSIE: His Salvation Anxiety. Does he ever understand?

JASON: Oh, no way. The puzzle takes over. You're not even trying to solve it anymore. Fascinating, really. Great training for lab research. Looking at things in increasing levels of complexity.

SUSIE: Until what?

JASON: What do you mean?

SUSIE: Where does it end? Don't you get to solve the puzzle?

JASON: Nah. When it comes right down to it, research is just trying to quantify the complications of the puzzle.

SUSIE: But you *help* people! You save lives and stuff.

JASON: Oh, yeah, I save some guy's life, and then the poor slob gets hit by a bus!

SUSIE: [*Confused*] Yeah, I guess so. I just don't think of it that way. Guess you can tell I never took a class in poetry.

JASON: Listen, if there's one thing we learned in Seventeenth-Century Poetry, it's that you can forget about that sentimental stuff. *Enzyme Kinetics* was more poetic than Bearing's class. Besides, you can't think about that *meaning-of-life* garbage all the time or you'd go nuts.

SUSIE: Do you believe in it?

JASON: In what?

SUSIE: Umm. I don't know, the meaning-of-life garbage. [*She laughs a little.*]

JASON: What do they *teach* you in nursing school? [*Checking* VIVIAN's *pulse*] She's out of it. Shouldn't be too long. You done here?

SUSIE: Yeah, I'll just . . . tidy up.

JASON: See ya. [*He leaves.*]

SUSIE: Bye, Jace. [*She thinks for a minute, then carefully rubs baby oil on* VIVIAN's *hands. She checks the catheter, then leaves.*]

[*Professor* E. M. ASHFORD, *now eighty, enters.*]

E. M.: Vivian? Vivian? It's Evelyn. Vivian?

VIVIAN: [*Waking, slurred*] Oh, God. [*Surprised*] Professor Ashford. Oh, God.

E. M.: I'm in town visiting my great-grandson, who is celebrating his fifth birthday. I went to see you at your office, and they directed me here. [*She lays her jacket, scarf, and parcel on the bed.*] I have been walking all over town. I had forgotten how early it gets chilly here.

VIVIAN: [*Weakly*] I feel so bad.

E. M.: I know you do. I can see. [VIVIAN *cries.*] Oh, dear, there, there. There, there. [VIVIAN *cries more, letting the tears flow.*] Vivian, Vivian. [E. M. *looks toward the hall, then furtively slips off her shoes and swings up on the bed. She puts her arm around* VIVIAN.] There, there. There, there, Vivian. [*Silence*]

　　It's a windy day. [*Silence*]

　　Don't worry, dear. [*Silence*]

Let's see. Shall I recite to you? Would you like that? I'll recite something by Donne.

VIVIAN: [*Moaning*] Nooooooo.

E. M.: Very well. [*Silence*] Hmmm. [*Silence*] Little Jeffrey is very sweet. Gets into everything.

[*Silence.* E. M. *takes a children's book out of the paper bag and begins reading.* VIVIAN *nestles in, drifting in and out of sleep.*]

Let's see. *The Runaway Bunny.* By Margaret Wise Brown. Pictures by Clement Hurd. Copyright 1942. First Harper Trophy Edition, 1972.

Now then.

Once there was a little bunny who wanted to run away.
So he said to his mother, "I am running away."
"If you run away," said his mother, "I will run after you. For you are my little bunny."
"If you run after me," said the little bunny, "I will become a fish in a trout stream and I will swim away from you."
"If you become a fish in a trout stream," said his mother, "I will become a fisherman and I will fish for you."

[*Thinking out loud*] Look at that. A little allegory of the soul. No matter where it hides, God will find it. See, Vivian?

VIVIAN: [*Meaning*] Uhhhhhh.

E. M.:

"If you become a fisherman," said the little bunny, "I will be a bird and fly away from you."
"If you become a bird and fly away from me," said his mother, "I will be a tree that you come home to."

[*To herself*] Very clever.

"Shucks," said the little bunny, "I might just as well stay where I am and be your little bunny."
And so he did.
"Have a carrot," said the mother bunny.

[*To herself*] Wonderful.

[VIVIAN *is now fast asleep.* E. M. *slowly gets down and gathers her things. She leans over and kisses her.*]

It's time to go. And flights of angels sing thee to thy rest. [*She leaves.*]

[JASON *strides in and goes directly to the I&O sheet without looking at* VIVIAN.]

JASON: Professor Bearing. How are you feeling today? Three p.m. IV hydration totals. Two thousand in. Thirty out. Uh-oh. That's it. Kidneys gone.

[*He looks at* VIVIAN.] Professor Bearing? Highly unresponsive. Wait a second—[*Puts his head down to her mouth and chest to listen for heartbeat and breathing*] Wait a sec—Jesus Christ! [*Yelling*] CALL A CODE!

JASON *throws down the chart, dives over the bed, and lies on top of her body as he reaches for the phone and punches in the numbers.*

[*To himself*] Code: 4-5-7-5. [*To operator*] Code Blue, room 707. Code Blue, room 707. Dr. Posner—P-O-S-N-E-R. Hurry up!

[*He throws down the phone and lowers the head of the bed.*]
Come on, come on, COME ON.

[*He begins CPR, kneeling over* VIVIAN, *alternately pounding frantically and giving mouth-to-mouth resuscitation. Over the loudspeaker in the hall, a droning voice repeats "Code Blue, room 707. Code Blue, room 707."*]

One! Two! Three! Four! Five! [*He breathes in her mouth.*]

[SUSIE, *hearing the announcement, runs into the room.*]

SUSIE: WHAT ARE YOU DOING?

JASON: A GODDAMN CODE. GET OVER HERE!

SUSIE: She's DNR! [*She grabs him.*]

JASON: [*He pushes her away.*] She's Research!

SUSIE: She's NO CODE!

[SUSIE *grabs* JASON *and hurls him off the bed.*]

JASON: Ooowww! Goddamnit, Susie!

SUSIE: She's no code!

JASON: Aaargh!

SUSIE: Kelekian put the order in—you saw it! You were right there, Jason! Oh, God, the code [*She runs to the phone. He struggles to stand.*] 4-5-7-5.

[*The* CODE TEAM *swoops in. Everything changes. Frenzy takes over. They knock* SUSIE *out of the way with their equipment.*]

SUSIE: [*At the phone*] Cancel code, room 707. Sue Monahan, primary nurse. Cancel code. Dr. Posner is here.

JASON: [*In agony*] Oh, God.

CODE TEAM:

> —Get out of the way!
>
> —Unit staff out!
>
> —Get the board!
>
> —Over here!
>
> [*They throw* VIVIAN's *body up at the waist and stick a Board underneath for CPR. In a whirlwind of sterile packaging and barked commands, one team member attaches a respirator, one begins CPR, and one prepares the defibrillator.* SUSIE *and* JASON *try to stop them but are pushed away. The loudspeaker in the hall announces "Cancel code, room 707. Cancel code, 707."*]

CODE TEAM:

> —Bicarb amp!
>
> —I got it! [*To* SUSIE] Get out!
>
> —One, two three, four, five!
>
> —Get ready to shock! *(To* JASON*)* Move it!

SUSIE: [*Running to each person yelling*] STOP! Patient is DNR!

JASON: [*At the same time, to the* CODE TEAM] No, no! Stop doing this. STOP!

CODE TEAM:

> —Keep it going!
>
> —What do you get?
>
> —Bicarb amp!
>
> —No pulse!

SUSIE: She's NO CODE! Order was given—[*She dives for the chart and holds it up as she cries out*] Look! Look at this! DO NOT RESUSCITATE. KELEKIAN.

CODE TEAM: [*As they administer electric shock,* VIVIAN's *body arches and bounces back down.*]

> —Almost ready!
>
> —Hit her!
>
> —CLEAR!
>
> —Pulse? Pulse?

JASON: [*Howling*] I MADE A MISTAKE!

> [*Pause. The* CODE TEAM *looks at him. He collapses on the floor.*]

SUSIE: No code! Patient is no code.

CODE TEAM HEAD: Who the hell are you?

SUSIE: Sue Monahan, primary nurse.

CODE TEAM HEAD: Let me see the goddamn chart.

CHART!

CODE TEAM: [*Slowing down*]

——What's going on?

——Should we stop?

——What's it say?

SUSIE: [*Pushing them away from the bed*] Patient is no code.

Get away from her!

[SUSIE *lifts the blanket.* VIVIAN *steps out of the bed.*

She walks away from the scene, toward a little light.

She is now attentive and eager, moving slowly toward the light.

She takes off her cap and lets it drop.

She slips off her bracelet.

She loosens the ties and the top gown slides to the floor. She lets the second gown fall.

The instant she is naked, and beautiful, reaching for the light—

Lights out.]

CODE TEAM HEAD: [*Reading.*] Do Not Resuscitate. Kelekian. Shit.

[*The* CODE TEAM *stops working.*]

JASON: [*Whispering*] Oh, God.

CODE TEAM HEAD: Order was put in yesterday.

CODE TEAM:

——It's a doctor fuck-up.

——What is he, a resident?

——Got us up here on a DNR.

——Called a code on a no-code.

JASON: Oh, God.

[*The bedside scene fades.*]

1995

Quiara Alegría Hudes

b. 1977

This play premiered in late 2011 before moving to off Broadway in early 2012; it won the Pulitzer Prize for Drama that year, at about the same time that the Iraq War was winding down. The war began in 2003, when U.S. forces invaded Iraq, purportedly to eliminate the imminent threat it posed through its weapons of mass destruction. No such weapons were ever found, but by the peak of U.S. involvement in the country in 2007, about 170,000 troops were deployed there. Almost 4,500 Americans died in that war, and more than 30,000 were wounded. The Marines had particularly difficult fights in the cities of Fallujah and Ramadi, with casualty rates not seen since the Vietnam War. Meanwhile, on the home front, more than forty years after Richard Nixon declared a "War on Drugs," addiction was still widespread and devastating. As late as 2014, more than 4.5 million Americans admitted to using cocaine in the last year. Among people describing themselves as Hispanic or Latino, about 146,000 had used crack cocaine in the previous twelve months, and more than 50,000 in the last thirty days. In that same year, the Department of Veterans Affairs prescribed opiates for 650,000 veterans. Clearly, drugs still pervade our society today.

It is nothing new for plays to connect themselves closely to contemporary issues. Parts of Hamlet, *for instance, join public debates about contemporary issues, even issues as narrow as grudges between theater companies. Ibsen's* A Doll's House *initiated the modern tradition of using drama to diagnose specific social problems, creating the genre of "realistic social drama." Such plays might not offer clear solutions, but they try to dig into problems so we can discover their root causes. Those roots can be found in the soil, the environment that conditions people's experiences. But Hudes pays less attention to the soil (in this case, the barrios of American cities and the battlefields of the Iraq war) than she does to the psychological experiences of people suffering the effects of these problems. The drama humanizes them, eliciting understanding and sympathy rather than cold judgment. Plays like this explode the facile*

political slogans; Water by the Spoonful *makes us feel as if someone in our own family suffers addiction.*

*But the play is not just about drugs and war. In addition to these
topical issues,* Water by the Spoonful *explores perennial themes of
class, race, religion, love, friendship, sin, redemption, family, and
national identity. This play dramatizes the experience of a Puerto
Rican American family in Philadelphia with three generations of
military service (in Korea, Vietnam, and Iraq). Some aspects of
their lives are specific to this background. Nevertheless, all families
feel the binding forces exhibited here, as well as the forces of dissolu-
tion. Living up to our responsibilities to those we love and failing to
do so are universal themes. One way to read this play is to get into
conversation with Hudes: in what ways are your familial experiences similar or dissimilar to those of the Ortiz family?*

Water by the Spoonful

CHARACTERS

ELLIOT ORTIZ, *an Iraq vet with a slight limp, works at Subway sandwich shop, scores an occasional job as a model or actor, Yazmin's
cousin, Odessa's birth son, Puerto Rican, twenty-four.*

YAZMIN ORTIZ, *in her first year as an adjunct professor of music,[1]
Odessa's niece and Elliot's cousin, Puerto Rican, twenty-nine.*

HAIKUMOM, *aka Odessa Ortiz, founder of www.recover-together.com,
works odd janitorial jobs, lives one notch above squalor, Puerto Rican,
thirty-nine.*

FOUNTAINHEAD, *aka John, a computer programmer and entrepreneur,
lives on Philadelphia's Main Line,[2] white, forty-one.*

CHUTES&LADDERS, *lives in San Diego, has worked a low-level job at the
IRS since the Reagan years,[3] his real name is Clayton "Buddy" Wilkie,
African American, fifty-six.*

---

1. Part-time instructor, usually paid by-the-course, often without fringe benefits, rather than salaried, like tenure-track faculty. Generally, adjunct faculty are very poorly paid and have little or no job security.

2. Prestigious, wealthy suburbs along today's Lancaster Avenue, named for its proximity to the old "Main Line" of the suburban railroad serving Philadelphia's commercial center.

3. 1981–1989, the span of Ronald Reagan's presidency.

ORANGUTAN, *a recent community college graduate, her real name is Madeleine Mays and before that Yoshiko Sakai, Japanese by birth, thirty-one.*

A GHOST, *also plays Professor Aman, an Arabic professor at Swarthmore;*[4] *also plays a Policeman in Japan.*

SETTING

2009. Six years after Elliot left for Iraq. Philadelphia, San Diego, Japan and Puerto Rico.

The stage has two worlds. The "real world" is populated with chairs. The chairs are from many locations—living rooms, an office, a seminar room, a church, a diner, internet cafés, etc. They all have the worn-in feel of life. A duct-taped La-Z-Boy. Salvaged trash chairs. A busted-up metal folding chair from a rec center. An Aero chair. An Eames chair.[5] A chair/desk from a college classroom. Diner chairs. A chair from an internet café in Japan. Living room chairs. Library chairs. A church pew. Facing in all different directions.

The "online world" is an empty space. A space that connects the chairs.

MUSIC

Jazz. John Coltrane.[6] The sublime stuff (*A Love Supreme*). And the noise (*Ascension*).

NOTE

Unless specifically noted, when characters are online, don't have actors typing on a keyboard. Treat it like regular conversation rather than the act of writing or typing. They can be doing things people do in the comfort of their home, like eating potato chips, walking around in jammies, cooking, doing dishes, clipping nails, etc.

SCENE 1

Swarthmore College. ELLIOT *and* YAZ *eat breakfast.* ELLIOT *wears a Subway sandwich shop polo shirt.*

---

4. Private liberal arts university southwest of Philadelphia; tuition today is near $50,000 per year.

5. Charles and Ray Eames were designers known best for the molded, plastic, spare, modern-looking chairs ubiquitous now in many commercial settings. *Aero chair*: a modern-style chair with low sides.

6. John Coltrane (1926–1967): celebrated jazz saxophonist. *A Love Supreme* (recorded in 1964, released in 1965) was Coltrane's greatest critical success and is often described as a spiritual album; *Ascension* (recorded in 1965, released in 1966) explored a "freer" style of jazz.

ELLIOT: This guy ain't coming. How do you know him?

YAZ: We're on a committee together.

ELLIOT: My shift starts in fifteen.

YAZ: All right, we'll go.

ELLIOT: Five more minutes. Tonight on the way home, we gotta stop by Whole Foods.[7]

YAZ: Sure, I need toothpaste.

ELLIOT: You gotta help me with my mom, Yaz.

YAZ: You said she had a good morning.

ELLIOT: She cooked breakfast.

YAZ: Progress.

ELLIOT: No. The docs said she can't be eating all that junk, it'll mess with her chemo, so she crawls out of bed for the first time in days and cooks eggs for breakfast. In two inches of pork-chop fat. I'm like, Mom, recycle glass and plastic, not grease. She thinks putting the egg on top of a paper towel after you cook it makes it healthy. I told her, Mom, you gotta cook egg whites. In Pam spray. But it has to be her way. Like, "That's how we ate them in Puerto Rico and we turned out fine." You gotta talk to her. I'm trying to teach her about quinoa. Broccoli rabe. Healthy shit. So I get home the other day, she had made quinoa with bacon. She was like, "It's healthy!"

YAZ: That's Ginny. The more stubborn she's being, the better she's feeling.

ELLIOT: I gave those eggs to the dogs when she went to the bathroom.

YAZ: [*Pulls some papers from her purse*] You wanna be my witness?

ELLIOT: To what?

[YAZ *signs the papers.*]

YAZ: My now-legal failure. I'm divorced.

ELLIOT: Yaz. I don't want to hear that.

YAZ: You've been saying that for months and I've been keeping my mouth closed. I just need a John Hancock.[8]

ELLIOT: What happened to "trial separation"?

YAZ: There was a verdict. William fell out of love with me.

---

7. Chain of grocery stores specializing in organic and healthy foods; they tend to be located in higher-income areas.

8. Signature.

ELLIOT: I've never seen you two argue.

YAZ: We did, we just had smiles on our faces.

ELLIOT: That's bullshit. You don't divorce someone before you even have a fight with them. I'm calling him.

YAZ: Go ahead.

ELLIOT: He was just texting me about going to the Phillies[9] game on Sunday.

YAZ: So, go. He didn't fall out of love with the family, just me.

ELLIOT: I'm going to ask him who he's been screwing behind your back.

YAZ: No one, Elliot.

ELLIOT: You were tappin' some extra on the side?

YAZ: He woke up one day and I was the same as any other person passing by on the street, and life is short, and you can only live in mediocrity so long.

ELLIOT: You two are the dog and the owner that look like each other. Ya'll are the *Cosby Show*.[1] Conundrum, Yaz and William make a funny, end-of episode. You show all us cousins, maybe we can't ever do it ourselves, but it *is* possible.

YAZ: Did I ever say, "It's possible"?

ELLIOT: By example.

YAZ: Did I ever say those words?

[PROFESSOR AMAN *enters.*]

AMAN: Yazmin, forgive me. You must be . . .

ELLIOT: Elliot Ortiz. Nice to meet you, I appreciate it.

AMAN: Professor Aman. [*They shake*] We'll have to make this short and sweet, my lecture begins . . . began . . . well, talk fast.

ELLIOT: Yaz, give us a second?

YAZ: I'll be in the car. [*Exits*]

---

9. Major League Baseball team in Philadelphia.

1. *The Cosby Show* (1984–1992) was a smash-hit situation comedy that aired weekly on NBC. Appealing to a wide range of viewers, it is credited with breaking color barriers in American television, and it helped to discredit racial stereotypes by dramatizing an upper-middle-class African American family, the Huxtables (the father, played by Bill Cosby, was a doctor and the mother, played by Phylicia Rashad, was a lawyer). Until Cosby's sex scandals changed public perception, *The Cosby Show* was synonymous with wholesome American family values. "Conundrum . . ." refers to the formulaic, happy-ending plot of sit-coms.

ELLIOT: I'm late, too, so . . .

AMAN: You need something translated.

ELLIOT: Just a phrase. Thanks, man.

AMAN: Eh, your sister's cute.

ELLIOT: Cousin. I wrote it phonetically. You grow up speaking Arabic?

AMAN: English. What's your native tongue?

ELLIOT: Spanglish. [*Hands* AMAN *a piece of paper*]

AMAN: Mom-ken men fad-luck ted-dini ga-waz saf-far-i. Mom-ken men-fadluck ted-dini gawaz saffari. Am I saying that right?

ELLIOT: [*Spooked*] Spot on.

AMAN: You must have some familiarity with Arabic to remember it so clearly.

ELLIOT: Maybe I heard it on TV or something.

AMAN: An odd phrase.

ELLIOT: It's like a song I can't get out of my head.

AMAN: Yazmin didn't tell me what this is for.

ELLIOT: It's not for anything.

AMAN: Do you mind me asking, what's around your neck?

ELLIOT: Something my girl gave me.

AMAN: Can I see? [ELLIOT *pulls dog tags from under his shirt*] Romantic gift. You were in the army.

ELLIOT: Marines.

AMAN: Iraq?

ELLIOT: For a minute.

AMAN: Were you reluctant to tell me that?

ELLIOT: No.

AMAN: Still in the service?

ELLIOT: Honorable discharge. Leg injury.

AMAN: When?

ELLIOT: A few years ago.

AMAN: This is a long time to have a phrase stuck in your head.

ELLIOT: What is this, man?

AMAN: You tell me.

ELLIOT: It's just a phrase. If you don't want to translate, just say so.

AMAN: A college buddy is making a film about Marines in Iraq. Gritty, documentary-style. He's looking for some veterans to interview. Get an authentic point of view. Maybe I could pass your number onto him.

ELLIOT: Nope. No interviews for this guy.

AMAN: You're asking me for a favor. [*Pause*] Yazmin told me you're an actor. Every actor needs a break, right?

ELLIOT: I did enough Q&As about the service. People manipulate you with the questions.

AMAN: It's not just to interview. He needs a right-hand man, an expert to help him. How do Marines hold a gun? How do they kick in civilian doors, this sort of thing. How do they say "Ooh-rah" in a patriotic manner?

ELLIOT: Are you his headhunter or something?

AMAN: I'm helping with the translations, I have a small stake and I want the movie to be accurate. And you seem not unintelligent. For a maker of sandwiches. [*Hands him a business card*] He's in L.A. In case you want a career change. I give you a cup of sugar, you give me a cup of sugar.

ELLIOT: If I have a minute, I'll dial the digits. [*Takes the business card*] So what's it mean?

AMAN: Momken men-fadluck ted-dini gawaz saffari. Rough translation, "Can I please have my passport back?"

Scene 2

ODESSA's *living room and kitchen. She makes coffee. She goes over to her computer, clicks a button. On a screen we see:*

HAIKUMOM, SITEADMIN
STATUS: ONLINE

HAIKUMOM: Rise and shine, kiddos, the rooster's a-crowin', it's a beautiful day to be sober. [*No response*] Your Thursday morning haiku:[2]

> if you get restless
> buy a hydrangea or rose
> water it, wait, bloom

---

2. Japanese verse form popular with Anglophone poets; it consists of three unrhymed lines, the first and third of which contain five syllables, while the second line must be seven syllables.

[ODESSA *continues making coffee. A computer dings and on another screen we see:*]

ORANGUTAN
STATUS: ONLINE

ORANGUTAN: Ninety-one days. Smiley face.

HAIKUMOM: [*Relieved*] Orangutan! Jesus, I thought my primate friend had disappeared back to the jungle.

ORANGUTAN: Disappeared? Yes. Jungle? Happily, no.

HAIKUMOM: I'm trying to put a high-five emoticon, but my computer is being a capital B. So, high-five!

[*They high-five in the air. Another computer screen lights up:*]

CHUTES&LADDERS
STATUS: ONLINE

CHUTES&LADDERS: Orangutan? I was about to send a search party after your rear end. Kid, *log on.* No news is bad news.

ORANGUTAN: Chutes&Ladders, giving me a hard time as usual. I'd expect nothing less.

CHUTES&LADDERS: Your last post says: "Day One. Packing bags, gotta run," and then you don't log on for three months?

ORANGUTAN: I was going to Japan, I had to figure out what shoes to bring.

HAIKUMOM: The country?

CHUTES&LADDERS: What happened to Maine?

ORANGUTAN: And I quote, "Get a hobby, find a new job, an exciting city, go teach English in a foreign country." Did you guys think I wouldn't take your seasoned advice? I was batting 0 for ten, and for the first time, guys, I feel fucking free.

HAIKUMOM: [*Nonjudgmental*] Censored.

ORANGUTAN: I wake up and I think, What's the world got up its sleeve today? And I look forward to the answer. So, thank you.

CHUTES&LADDERS: We told you so.

ORANGUTAN: [*Playful*] Shut up.

HAIKUMOM: You're welcome.

ORANGUTAN: I gave my parents the URL. My username, my password. They logged on and read every post I've ever put on here and for once they said they understood. They had completely cut me off, but after reading this site they bought me the plane ticket. One way. I teach English in the mornings. I have a class of children, a class of teens, and a class of adults, most of whom are older than me. I am free in the afternoons. I have a paycheck which I use for legal things like ice cream, noodles and socks. I walk around feeling like maybe I *am* normal. Maybe, just possibly, I'm not that different. Or maybe it's just homeland delusions.

CHUTES&LADDERS AND HAIKUMOM: Homeland?

HAIKUMOM: You're Japanese?

ORANGUTAN: I *was*, for the first eight days of my life. Yoshiko Sakai. Then on day nine I was adopted and moved to Cape Lewiston, Maine, where I became Ma—M.M., and where in all my days I have witnessed *one* other Asian. In the Superfresh. Deli counter.

CHUTES&LADDERS: Japan . . . Wow, that little white rock[3] sure doesn't discriminate.

HAIKUMOM: Amen.

ORANGUTAN: Mango Internet Café. I'm sitting in an orange plastic chair, a little view of the Hokkaido[4] waterfront.

HAIKUMOM: Japan has a waterfront?

CHUTES&LADDERS: It's an island.

HAIKUMOM: Really? Are there beaches? Can you go swimming?

ORANGUTAN: The ocean reminds me of Maine. Cold water, very quiet, fisherman, boats, the breeze. I wouldn't try swimming. I'm just a looker. I was never one to actually have an experience.

CHUTES&LADDERS: Ah, the ocean . . . There's only one thing on this planet I'm more scared of than that big blue lady.

HAIKUMOM: Let me guess: landing on a sliding board square?[5]

---

3. Crack cocaine.

4. Second-largest island of Japan, located north of the main island, Honshu.

5. Reference to the game "Chutes & Ladders." Players roll dice to advance horizontally on the board. When they come to a "ladder" square, they skip ahead vertically. When they come to a "chute," they slide down vertically, falling further away from the goal line.

CHUTES&LADDERS: Lol, truer words have never been spoken. You know I was born just a few miles from the Pacific. In the fresh salt air. Back in "those days" I'm at Coronado Beach[6] with a few "friends" doing my "thing" and I get sucked up under this wave. I gasp, I breathe in and my lungs fill with water. I'm like, this is it, I'm going to meet my maker. I had never felt so heavy, not even during my two OD's.[7] I was sinking to the bottom and my head hit the sand like a lead ball. My body just felt like an anvil. The next thing I know there's fingers digging in my ankles. This life-guard pulls me out, I'm throwing up salt water. I say to him, "Hey blondie, you don't know me from Adam but you are my witness: today's the day I start to *live*." And this lifeguard, I mean he was young with these muscles, this kid looks at me like, "Who is this big black dude who can't even doggy paddle?" When I stand up and brush the sand off me, people *applaud*. An old lady touches my cheek and says, "I thought you were done for." I get back to San Diego that night, make one phone call, the next day I'm in my first meeting, sitting in a folding chair, saying the serenity prayer.[8]

ORANGUTAN: I hate to inflate your already swollen ego, but that was a lucid, touching story. By the way, did you get the lifeguard's name? He sounds hot.

HAIKUMOM: Hey Chutes&Ladders, it's never too late to learn. Most YMCAs offer adult swimming classes.

CHUTES&LADDERS: I'll do the world a favor and stay out of a speedo.

ORANGUTAN: Sober air toast. To lifeguards.

CHUTES&LADDERS AND HAIKUMOM: To lifeguards.

ORANGUTAN, CHUTES&LADDERS AND HAIKUMOM: Clink.

HAIKUMOM: Chutes&Ladders, I'm buying you a pair of water wings.

Scene 3

John Coltrane's A Love Supreme *plays. A Subway sandwich shop on Philadelphia's Main Line.* ELLIOT *sits behind the counter. The phone rings. He gets up, hobbles to it—he walks with a limp.*

---

6. Beach in Southern California near San Diego.

7. Overdoses.

8. "God, grant me the serenity to accept the things I cannot change, courage to change the things I can, and the wisdom to know the difference." Penned by American theologian Reinhold Niebuhr, it was adopted by Alcoholics Anonymous. The "meeting" here is an A. A. meeting.

ELLIOT: Subway Main Line. Lar! Laaar, what's it doing for you today? Staying in the shade? I got you, how many you need? Listen, the delivery guy's out and my little sports injury is giving me hell so can you pick up? Cool, sorry for the inconvenience. Let me grab a pen. A'ight, pick a hoagie, any hoagie!

[ELLIOT *begins writing the order.*
Lights rise to a seminar room at Swarthmore College. We find YAZ *mid-class. She hits a button on a stereo and the Coltrane stops playing.*]

YAZ: Coltrane's *A Love Supreme*, 1964. Dissonance is still a gateway to resolution. A B-diminished chord is still resolving to? C-major. A tritone is still resolving up to? The major sixth. Diminished chords, tritones, still didn't have the right to be their own independent thought. In 1965 something changed. The ugliness bore no promise of a happy ending. The ugliness became an end in itself. Coltrane democratized the notes. He said, they're all equal. Freedom. It was called Free Jazz but freedom is a hard thing to express musically without spinning into noise. This is from *Ascension*, 1965.

[*She plays* Ascension. *It sounds uglier than the first sample. In the Subway, a figure comes into view. It is the* GHOST.]

GHOST: Momken men-fadluck ted-dini gawaz saffari?

[ELLIOT *tries to ignore the* GHOST, *reading off the order.*]

ELLIOT: That's three teriyaki onion with chicken. First with hots and onions. Second with everything. Third with extra bacon. Two spicy Italian with American cheese on whole grain. One BMT on flatbread. Good so far?

GHOST: Momken men-fadluck ted-dini gawaz saffari?

ELLIOT: Five chocolate chip cookies, one oatmeal raisin. Three Baked Lay's, three Doritos. Two Sprite Zeros, one Barq's, one Coke, two orange sodas. How'd I do?

GHOST: Momken men-fadluck ted-dini gawaz saffari?

ELLIOT: All right, that'll be ready in fifteen minutes. One sec for your total.

[ELLIOT *gets a text message. He reads it; his entire demeanor shifts.*]

Lar, I just got a text. There's a family emergency, I can't do this order right now.

[ELLIOT *hangs up. He exits, limping away.*]

YAZ: Oh come on, don't make that face. I know it feels academic. You're going to leave here and become R&B hit makers and Sondheim[9] clones and never think about this noise again. But this is Coltrane, people, this is not Schoenberg![1] This is jazz, stuff people listen to *voluntarily.* Shopping period is still on—go sit in one session of "Germans and Noise" down the hall and you'll come running back begging for this muzak.

[YAZ *turns off the music.*]

In fact, change the syllabus. No listening report next week. Instead, I want you to pinpoint the first time you really noticed dissonance. The composer, the piece, the measures. Two pages analyzing the notes and two pages describing the experience personally. This is your creation myth. Before you leave this school you better figure out that story and cling to it for dear life or you'll be a stockbroker within a year.

I was thirteen, I worked in a corrugated box factory all summer, I saved up enough to find my first music teacher—up to that point I was self-taught, playing to the radio. I walked into Don Rappaport's room at Settlement Music School.[2] He was old, he had jowls, he was sitting at the piano and he said, "What do you do?" I said, "I'm a composer, sir." Presumptuous, right? I sat down and played Mr. Rappaport a Yazmin original. He said, "It's pretty, everything goes together. It's like an outfit where your socks are blue and your pants, shirt, hat are all blue." Then he said, "Play an

---

9. Stephen Sondheim (b. 1930); an award-winning composer and lyricist of the American stage and film. *West Side Story* (music by Leonard Bernstein) and *Sweeney Todd* are among his more popular works. *R&B:* rhythm and blues, an African American musical style that laid the foundation for rock & roll.

1. Arnold Schoenberg (1874–1951): Austrian

famed for his modern, atonal musical compositions; the satiric reference to a class in "Germans and Noise" probably includes Schoenberg on its syllabus.

2. Music academy for children founded in 1908 in Philadelphia, and after 1924 a pre-professional conservatory; historically, the Settlement catered to Philadelphia's immigrant populations.

F-sharp major in your left hand." Then he said, "Play a C-major in your right hand." "Now play them together." He asked me, "Does it go together?" I told him, "No, sir." He said, "Now go home and write." My first music lesson was seven minutes long. I had never really heard dissonance before.

[YAZ's *phone vibrates. She sees the caller with concern.*]

Let's take five.

[*As students file out,* YAZ *makes a phone call. Lights up on* ELLIOT *outside the Subway.*]

[*"What's the bad news?"*] You called three times.

ELLIOT: She's still alive.

YAZ: Okay.

ELLIOT: Jefferson Hospital. They admitted her three hours ago. Pop had the courtesy to text me.

YAZ: Are you still at work?

ELLIOT: Just smashed the bathroom mirror all over the floor. Boss sent me out to the parking lot.

YAZ: Wait there. I'm on my way.

ELLIOT: "Your mom is on breathing machine." Who texts that? Who texts that and then doesn't pick up the phone?

YAZ: I'll be there within twenty.

ELLIOT: Why did I come to work today?

YAZ: She had a good morning. You wanted your thing translated.

ELLIOT: She cooked and I wouldn't eat a bite off the fork. There's a Subway hoagies around the corner and I had to work half an hour away.

YAZ: You didn't want your buddies to see you working a normal job.

ELLIOT: Not normal job. Shit job. I'm a butler. A porter of sand-wiches.

YAZ: Ginny's been to Hades and back, stronger each time.

ELLIOT: What is Hades?

YAZ: In Greek mythology, the river through the underworld—

ELLIOT: My mom's on a machine and you're dropping vocab words?!

[*A ding.*]

yaz: Text message, don't hang up. [*She looks at her phone. A moment, then*] You still there?

elliot: It was my dad, wasn't it? Yaz, spit it out.

yaz: It was your dad.

elliot: And? Yaz, I'm about to start walking down Lancaster Avenue for thirty miles till I get back to Philly and I don't care if I snap every wire out my leg and back—I need to get out of here. I need to see Mom, I need to talk to her!

yaz: He said, "Waiting for Elliot till we turn off the machine."

Scene 4

The chat room. A screen lights up:

> [no image]
> fountainhead[3]
> status: online

fountainhead: I've uh, wow, hello there everyone. Delete, delete. Good afternoon. Evening. Delete.

[*Deep breath.*]

Things I am taking:

—My life into my own hands.
—My gorgeous, deserving wife out for our seventh anniversary.
Me: mildly athletic, but work twice as hard. Won state for javelin two years straight. Ran a half marathon last fall. Animated arguer. Two medals for undergrad debate. MBA from Wharton.[4] Beautiful wife, two sons. Built a programming company from the ground up, featured in the *New York Times'* Circuits section, sold it at its peak, bought a yellow Porsche, got a day job to keep myself honest. Salary was 300K, company was run by morons, got laid off, handsome severance, which left me swimming in cash and free time.

---

3. *The Fountainhead* is a 1943 novel by Ayn Rand; today it is associated with an extreme form of individualism that celebrates the supposed positive social effects of greed, self-interest, and disregard for the suffering of others.

4. Now part of the University of Pennsylvania, The Wharton School in Philadelphia claims to be "the world's first business school." *MBA:* a master's in business administration, the educational prerequisite for many careers in business.

Me and crack: long story short, I was at a conference with our CFO and two programmers and a not-unattractive lady in HR.[5] They snorted, invited me to join. A few weeks later that little rock waltzed right into my hand. I've been using off and on since. One eight ball every Saturday, strict rations, portion control. Though the last three or four weeks, it's less like getting high and more like trying to build a time machine. Anything to get back the romance of that virgin smoke.

Last weekend I let myself buy more than my predetermined allotment—I buy in small quantity, because as with my food, I eat what's on my plate. Anyway, I ran over a curb, damaged the underside of my Porsche. Now it's in the shop and I'm driving a rental Mustang. So, not rock bottom but a rental Ford is as close to rock bottom as I'd like to get. Fast forward to tonight. I'm watching my wife's eyelids fall and telling myself, "You are on punishment, Poppa. Daddy's on time out. Do not get out of bed, do not tiptoe down those stairs, do not go down to that basement, do not sit beside that foosball table, do not smoke, and please do not crawl on the carpet looking for one last hit in the fibers."

[*Pause.*]

In kindergarten my son tested into G and T. Gifted and talented. You meet with the school, they tailor the program to the kid. Math, reading, art, whatever the parent chooses. I said, "Teach my son how to learn. How to use a library. How to find original source material, read a map, track down the experts so he becomes an expert." Which gets me to—

You: the experts. It's the first day of school and I'm knocking at your classroom door. I got my No. 2 pencils, I'll sit in the front row, pay attention, and do my homework. No lesson is too basic. Teach me every technique. Any tip so that Saturday doesn't become every day. Any actions that keep you in the driver seat. Healthy habits and rational thoughts to blot out that voice in the back of my head.

---

5. Human resources, the division of a corporation that manages employee benefits, grievances, compliance with legal regulations regarding labor, etc. *CFO*: chief financial officer, usually one of the most important vice presidents in a corporation.

Today, I quit. My wife cannot know, she'd get suspicious if I were at meetings all the time. There can be no medical records, so therapy is out. At least it's not heroin, I'm not facing a physical war. It's a psychological battle and I'm armed with two weapons: willpower and the experts.

I'm taking my wife out tomorrow for our seventh anniversary and little does she know that when we clink glasses, I'll be toasting to Day One.

[ODESSA *is emotional.* CHUTES&LADDERS *and* ORANGUTAN *seem awestruck.*]

ORANGUTAN: [*Clapping*] That was brave.

CHUTES&LADDERS: What. The.

HAIKUMOM: Careful.

CHUTES&LADDERS: Fuck.

HAIKUMOM: Censored.

ORANGUTAN: I'm making popcorn. Oh, this is gonna be fun!

CHUTES&LADDERS: Fountainhead, speaking of experts, I've been meaning to become an asshole. Can you teach me how?

HAIKUMOM: Censored!

ORANGUTAN: "Tips"? This isn't a cooking website. And what is a half marathon?

CHUTES&LADDERS: Maybe it's something like a half crack addict. Or a half husband.

ORANGUTAN: Was that an addiction coming out or an online dating profile? "Married Male Dope Fiend. Smokin' hot."

CHUTES&LADDERS: Fountainhead, you sound like the kind of guy who's read *The 7 Habits of Highly Effective People*[6] cover to cover. Was one of those habits crack? Give the essays a rest and type three words. "I'm. A. Crackhead."

ORANGUTAN: You know, adderall is like totes[7] cool. Us crackheads, we're like yucky and stuff. We're like so nineties. Go try the adderall edge!

---

6. 1989 self-help book by Stephen Covey that purports to reveal the habits of mind and practice that lead to success in business and public life, based on universal principles of natural human behavior.

7. Totally; in this usage, sarcastic slang. *Adderall*: an amphetamine often proscribed for attention deficit hyperactivity disorder; it is often used illegally for its euphoric effects.

HAIKUMOM: Hey.

ORANGUTAN: The guy's a hoax. Twenty bucks says he's pranking. Let's start a new thread.

HAIKUMOM: Hi, Fountainhead, welcome. As the site administrator, I want to honestly congratulate you for accomplishing what so many addicts only hope for: one clean day. Any time you feel like using, log on here instead. It's worked for me. When it comes to junkies, I dug lower than the dungeon. Once upon a time I had a beautiful family, too. Now all I have is six years clean. Don't lose what I lost, what Chutes&Ladders lost.

CHUTES&LADDERS: Excuse me.

HAIKUMOM: Orangutan, I just checked and Fountainhead has no aliases and has never logged onto this site before under a different pseudonym, which are the usual markers of a scam.

ORANGUTAN: I'm just saying. Who toasts to their first day of sobriety?

CHUTES&LADDERS: I hope it's seltzer in that there champagne glass.

ORANGUTAN: Ginger ale, shirley temple.

CHUTES&LADDERS: "A toast, honey. I had that seven-year itch so I became a crackhead."

CHUTES&LADDERS AND ORANGUTAN: Clink.

HAIKUMOM: Hey, kiddos. Your smiley administrator doesn't want to start purging messages. For rules of the forums click on this link. No personal attacks.

ORANGUTAN: We don't come to this site for a pat on the back.

HAIKUMOM: I'm just saying. R-e-s-p-e-c-t.

CHUTES&LADDERS: I will always give *crack* the respect it deserves. Some purebred poodle comes pissing on my tree trunk? Damn straight I'll chase his ass out my forest.

HAIKUMOM: This here is my forest. You two think you were all humble pie when you started out? Check your original posts.

ORANGUTAN: Oh, I know mine. "I-am-scared-I-will-kill-myself-talk-me-off-the-ledge."

HAIKUMOM: So unless someone gets that desperate they don't deserve our noble company? "Suffer like me, or you ain't legit"?

ORANGUTAN: Haikumom's growing claws.

HAIKUMOM: Just don't act entitled because you got so low. [*To* FOUNTAINHEAD] Sorry. Fountainhead, forgive us. We get very passionate because—

CHUTES&LADDERS: Fountainhead, your Porsche has a massive engine. You got bulging marathon muscles. I'm sure your penis is as big as that javelin you used to throw.

HAIKUMOM: Censored.

CHUTES&LADDERS: But none of those things come close to the size of your ego. If you can put that aside, you may, *may* stand a chance. Otherwise, you're fucked, my friend.

HAIKUMOM: Message purged.

ORANGUTAN: OH MY GOD, WE'RE DYING HERE, DO WE HAVE TO BE SO POLITE ABOUT IT?

HAIKUMOM: Censored.

ORANGUTAN: Oh my G-zero-D. Democracy or dictatorship?

CHUTES&LADDERS: Hey Fountainhead, why the silence?

[FOUNTAINHEAD *logs off.*]

HAIKUMOM: Nice work, guys. Congratulations.

CHUTES&LADDERS: You don't suppose he's . . . crawling on the carpet looking for one last rock??

ORANGUTAN: Lordy lord lord, I'm about to go over his house and start looking for one myself!

HAIKUMOM: That's why you're in Japan, little monkey. For now, I'm closing this thread. Fountainhead, if you want to reopen it, email me directly.

SCENE 5

A flower shop in Center City[8] Philadelphia. YAZ *looks over some brochures.* ELLIOT *enters, his limp looking worse.*

YAZ: I was starting to get worried. How you holding?

ELLIOT: Joe's Gym, perfect remedy.

YAZ: You went boxing? Really?

ELLIOT: I had to blow off steam. Women don't get it.

YAZ: Don't be a pig. You've had four leg surgeries, no more boxing.

ELLIOT: Did Odessa call?

YAZ: You know how she is. Shutting herself out from the world.

ELLIOT: We need help this week.

YAZ: And I got your back.

---

8. Central business, commercial, and densely-populated residential district of Philadelphia.

ELLIOT: I'm just saying, pick up the phone and ask, "Do you need anything, Elliot?"

YAZ: I did speak to your dad. Everyone's gathering at the house. People start arriving from PR[9] in a few hours. The next door neighbor brought over two trays of pigs feet.

ELLIOT: I just threw up in my mouth.

YAZ: Apparently a fight broke out over who gets your mom's pocketbooks.

ELLIOT: Those pleather things from the ten-dollar store?

YAZ: Thank you, it's not like she had Gucci purses!

ELLIOT: People just need to manufacture drama.

YAZ: He said they were tearing through Ginny's closets like it was a shopping spree. "I want this necklace!" "I want the photo album!" "Yo, those chancletas[1] are mine!" I'm like, damn, let the woman be buried first.

ELLIOT: Yo, let's spend the day here.

YAZ: [*Handing him some papers*] Brochures. I was being indecisive so the florist went to work on a wedding bouquet. I ruled out seven, you make the final call. Celebration of Life, Blooming Garden, Eternity Wreath.

ELLIOT: All of those have carnations. I don't want a carnation within a block of the church.

YAZ: You told me to eliminate seven. I eliminated seven. Close your eyes and point.

ELLIOT: Am I a particularly demanding person?

YAZ: Yes. What's so wrong with a carnation?

ELLIOT: You know what a carnation says to the world? That they were out of roses at the 7-Eleven. It should look something like Mom's garden.

YAZ: [*In agreement*] Graveside Remembrances? That looks something like it . . . I'm renominating Graveside Remembrances. Putting it back on the table.

ELLIOT: You couldn't find anything tropical? Yaz, you could find a needle in a damn haystack and you couldn't find a bird of paradise or something?

YAZ: He just shoved some brochures in my hand.

9. Puerto Rico.   1. Flip-flops.

ELLIOT: [*Stares her down*] You have an awful poker face.

YAZ: Now, look here.

ELLIOT: You did find something.

YAZ: No. Not exactly.

ELLIOT: How much does it cost? Yaz, this is my mom we're talking about.

YAZ: Five hundred more. Just for the casket piece.

ELLIOT: You can't lie for shit, you never could.

YAZ: Orchid Paradise.

[YAZ *hands him another brochure. They look at it together.*]

ELLIOT: Aw damn. Damn. That looks like her garden.

YAZ: Spitting image.

ELLIOT: [*Pointing*] I think she grew those.

YAZ: Right next to the tomatoes.

ELLIOT: But hers were yellow. Fuck.

YAZ: It's very odd to order flowers when someone dies. Because the flowers are just gonna die, too. "Would you like some death with your death?"

ELLIOT: [*A confession*] I didn't water them.

YAZ: [*Getting it*] What, are you supposed to be a gardener all of a sudden?

ELLIOT: It doesn't rain for a month and do I grab the hose and water Mom's garden one time?

YAZ: You were feeding her. Giving her meds. Bathing her. I could've come over and watered a leaf. A single petal.

ELLIOT: The last four days, she'd wake me up in the middle of the night. "Did you water the flowers?" "Yeah, Mom, just like you told me to yesterday." "Carry me out back, I want to see." "Mom, you're too heavy, I can't carry you down those steps one more time today."

YAZ: Little white lies.

ELLIOT: Can you do the sermon?

YAZ: This is becoming a second career.

ELLIOT: Because you're the only one who doesn't cry.

YAZ: Unlike Julia.

ELLIOT: [*Imitating*] "¡Ay dios mio!² ¡Ay! ¡Ay!"

---

2. "Oh, my God!"

YAZ: I hate public speaking.

ELLIOT: You're a teacher.

YAZ: It's different when it's ideas. Talking about ideas isn't saying something, it's making syllables with your mouth.

ELLIOT: You love ideas. All you ever wanted to do was have ideas.

YAZ: It was an elaborate bait and switch. The ideas don't fill the void, they just help you articulate it.

ELLIOT: You've spoken at city hall. On the radio.

YAZ: You're the face of Main Line Chevrolet. [*Pause*] Can I do it in English?

ELLIOT: You could do it in Russian for all I care. I'll just be in the front row acting like my cheek is itchy so no one sees me crying.

YAZ: The elders want a good Spanish sermon.

ELLIOT: Mami Ginny was it. You're the elder now.

YAZ: I'm twenty-nine.

ELLIOT: But you don't look a day over fifty.

YAZ: You gotta do me a favor in return. I know this is your tragedy but . . . Call William. Ask him not to come to the funeral.

ELLIOT: Oh shit.

YAZ: He saw the obit in the *Daily News.*

ELLIOT: They were close. Mami Ginny loved that blond hair. She was the madrina[3] of your wedding.

YAZ: William relinquished mourning privileges. You fall out of love with me, you lose certain rights. He calls talking about, "I want the condo." Fuck that. Fuck that. Coming from you it won't seem bitter. Wants the fucking condo all for hisself. That I decorated, that I painted. "Oh, and where's the funeral, by the way?" You know, he's been to four funerals in the Ortiz clan and I could feel it, there was a part of him, under it all, that was disgusted. The open casket. The prayers.

ELLIOT: It is disgusting.

YAZ: Sitting in the pew knowing what freaks we are.

ELLIOT: He's good people.

YAZ: I was probably at his side doing the same thing, thinking I'm removed, that I'm somehow different.

ELLIOT: Hey, hey, done.

YAZ: One more condition. I go to Puerto Rico with you. We scatter her ashes together.

3. Godmother.

ELLIOT: Mami Ginny couldn't be buried in Philly. She had to have her ashes thrown at a waterfall in El Yunque,[4] just to be the most Puerto Rican motherfucker around.

YAZ: I saw your Colgate ad.

ELLIOT: Dang, cousin Yaz watches Spanish TV?

YAZ: Shut up.

ELLIOT: I walked into the casting office, flashed my pearly whites, showed them my military ID and I charmed them.

YAZ: Do it.

ELLIOT: Give me a dollar.

YAZ: For that big cheeseburger smile?

[*She gives him a dollar.*]

ELLIOT: [*Smiling*] "Sonrisa,[5] baby!"

[YAZ *cracks up laughing, which devolves into tears.*]

How we gonna pay for Orchid Paradise?

YAZ: They should have a frequent-flower card. They punch a hole. Buy nine funeral bouquets, get the tenth free. We'd be living in a house full of lilies. Look at that guy. Arranging his daisies like little treasures. What do you think it's like to be him? To be normal?

ELLIOT: Normal? A hundred bucks says that dude has a closet full of animal porno at home.

YAZ: I bet in his family, funerals are rare occasions. I bet he's never seen a cousin get arrested. Let alone one under the age of eighteen. I bet he never saw his eight-year-old cousin sipping rum through a twisty straw or . . . I just remembered this time cousin Maria was babysitting me . . .

ELLIOT: Fat Maria or Buck Tooth Maria?

YAZ: Pig.

ELLIOT: Ah, Fat Maria.

YAZ: I was dyeing her hair. I had never dyed hair before so I asked her to read me the next step and she handed me the box and

---

4. Tropical rainforest in the northeast of Puerto Rico, now protected as a National Forest.
5. Smile.

said, "You read it." And I said, "My rubber gloves are covered in toxic goop, I can't really hold that right now." And so she held it in front of my eyes and said, "You gonna have to read it because I sure as hell can't."

ELLIOT: I been knowed that.

YAZ: I said, "But you graduated from high school." She said, "They just pass you, I just stood in the back." I was in fourth grade. *I could read!* [*Pause*] I have a degree written in Latin that I don't even understand. I paid seventeen thousand dollars for my piano.

ELLIOT: Oh shit.

YAZ: I have a mortgage on my piano. Drive two miles north? William told me every time I went to North Philly, I'd come back different. His family has Quaker Oats[6] for DNA. They play Pictionary on New Year's. I'd sit there wishing I could scoop the blood out my veins like you scoop the seeds out a pumpkin and he'd be like, "Whatchu thinking about, honey?" And I'd be like, "Nothing. Let's play some Pictionary."

ELLIOT: Yo, being the scholarship case at an all-white prep school really fucked with your head, didn't it?

YAZ: I should've gone to Edison.

ELLIOT: Public school in el barrio.[7] You wouldn't have survived there for a day.

YAZ: Half our cousins didn't survive there.

ELLIOT: True. But you would've pissed your pants. At least their pants was dry when they went down.

YAZ: You're sick.

ELLIOT: And the ladies love me.

YAZ: I thought abuela[8] dying, that would be the end of us. But Ginny grabbed the torch. Christmas, Easter. Now what? Our family may be fucked-up but we had somewhere to go. A kitchen that connected us. Plastic-covered sofas where we could park our communal asses.

ELLIOT: Pop's selling the house. And the plastic-covered sofas. He's moving back to the Bronx, be with his sisters.

6. A brand of oatmeal; that is, bland, unexciting, perhaps with a reference to the pacifist, strait-laced Quakers who settled Pennsylvania. *North Philly:* a cluster of neighborhoods immediately north of Center City that are segregated by race, dominated largely by African Americans and Hispanics.

7. In the United States, an area of a city with a high concentration of Spanish speakers and often, as here, a concentration of poverty.

8. Grandmother.

YAZ: You going with him? [ELLIOT *shrugs*] Wow. I mean, once that living room is gone, I may never step foot in North Philly again.

ELLIOT: Washed up at age twenty-four. Disabled vet. Motherless chil'. Working at Subway. Soon-to-be homeless.

YAZ: My couch is your couch.

ELLIOT: Until William takes your couch.

YAZ: My cardboard box is your cardboard box.

ELLIOT: I could go out to L.A. and be a movie star.

YAZ: You need a manager? Shoot, I'm coming witchu. Forget Philly.

ELLIOT: Change of scene, baby. Dream team.

YAZ: Probably we should order some flowers first, though. Don'tcha think? [ELLIOT *nods. To the florist*] Sir?

SCENE 6

The chat room. ORANGUTAN *is online, seems upset.*

ORANGUTAN: 2:38 A.M. Tuesday. The witching hour.

    [CHUTES&LADDERS *logs on.*]

CHUTES&LADDERS: 1:38 P.M. Monday. The lunch hour.

ORANGUTAN: I'm in a gay bar slash internet café in the city of Sapporo.[9] Deafening dance music.

CHUTES&LADDERS: Sure you should be in a bar, little monkey?

ORANGUTAN: [*Disappointed*] I flew halfway around the world and guess what? It was still me who got off the plane. [*Taking comfort*] Sapporo is always open. The world turns upside down at night.

CHUTES&LADDERS: You're in a city named after a beer sitting in a bar. Go home.

ORANGUTAN: Everything in this country makes sense but me. The noodles in soup make sense. The woodpecker outside my window every evening? Completely logical. The girls getting out of school in their miniskirts and shy smiles? Perfectly natural. I'm floating. I'm a cloud. My existence is one sustained out-of-body experience. It doesn't matter if I change my shoes, there's not a pair I've ever been able to fill. I'm a baby in a basket on an endless river. Wherever I go I don't make sense there.

CHUTES&LADDERS: Hey, little monkey. How many days you got?

---

9. The capital of Hokkaido.

ORANGUTAN: I think day ninety-six is when the demons really come out to play.

CHUTES&LADDERS: Ninety-six? Girl, hang your hat on that.

ORANGUTAN: I really really really want to smoke crack.

CHUTES&LADDERS: Yeah, well *don't.*

ORANGUTAN: Distract me from myself. What do you really really really want, Chutes&Ladders?

CHUTES&LADDERS: I wouldn't say no to a new car—my Tercel is one sorry sight.

ORANGUTAN: What else?

CHUTES&LADDERS: Tuesday's crossword. On Monday I'm done by the time I sit at my desk. I wish every day could be a Tuesday.

ORANGUTAN: What about your son? Don't you really really really want to call him?

CHUTES&LADDERS: By all accounts, having me be a stranger these ten years has given him the best decade of his life.

ORANGUTAN: I've known you for how long?

CHUTES&LADDERS: Three Christmas Eves. When you logged on you were a stone-cold user. We sang Christmas carols online all night. Now you've got ninety days.

ORANGUTAN: Can I ask you a personal question? What's your day job?

CHUTES&LADDERS: IRS. GS4 paper pusher.

ORANGUTAN: Got any vacation days?

CHUTES&LADDERS: A solid collection. I haven't taken a vacation in ten years.

ORANGUTAN: Do you have money?

CHUTES&LADDERS: Enough to eat steak on Friday nights. Enough to buy pay-per-view boxing.

ORANGUTAN: Yeah, I bet that's all the pay-per-view you buy. [*Pause*] Enough money to fly to Japan?

[*Pause.*]

CHUTES&LADDERS: You should know I'm fifty years old on a good day. I eat three and a half doughnuts for breakfast and save the remaining half for brunch. I have small hands, six toes on my left foot. And my face resembles a corgi.[1]

---

1. A breed of small herding dog originating in Wales.

ORANGUTAN: If I was looking for a hot screw I wouldn't be logging on to this site.

CHUTES&LADDERS: Damn, was it something I said?

ORANGUTAN: [*With honest admiration*] I've been on this planet for thirty-one years and you're the only person I've ever met who's more sarcastic than I am yet still believes in God.

CHUTES&LADDERS: [*Taking the compliment*] Says the agnostic.

ORANGUTAN: The atheist. Who is very envious of believers. My brain is my biggest enemy—always arguing my soul into a corner. [*Pause*] I like you. Come to Japan. We can go get an ice cream. I can show you the countryside.

CHUTES&LADDERS: I don't have a passport. If my Tercel can't drive there, I generally don't go.

ORANGUTAN: Come save me in Japan. Be my knight in shining armor.

CHUTES&LADDERS: I'll admit, I'm a dashing concept. If you saw my flesh and blood, you'd be disappointed.

ORANGUTAN: I see my flesh and blood every day and I've learned to live with the disappointment.

CHUTES&LADDERS: I'm the squarest of the square. I live in a square house on a square block watching a square box eating square-cut fries.

ORANGUTAN: I get it. You were the kid who colored inside the lines.

CHUTES&LADDERS: No, I was the kid who ate the crayons. *Was*. I went clean and all personality left my life. Flew right out the window. I had to take life on life's terms. Messy, disappointing, bad shit happens to good people, coffee stains on my necktie, boring life.

ORANGUTAN: Maybe we could hang out and have a relationship that has very little to do with crack or addiction or history. We could watch DVDs and microwave popcorn and take walks on the waterfront while we gossip about celebrities. It could be the land of the living.

CHUTES&LADDERS: Stay in the box. Keep things in their place. It's a simple, effective recipe for ten clean years.

ORANGUTAN: Forget simple. I want a goddamn challenge.

CHUTES&LADDERS: You're in recovery and work in a foreign country. That's a challenge.

ORANGUTAN: No. No, it's fucking not. Not if I just stay anonymous and alone. Like every day of my shit life so far. A friend, the kind that is nice to you and you are nice to in return. *That* would push the comfort zone. The invitation is open. Come tear my shyness open.

CHUTES&LADDERS: All right, now you're being weird. Can we change the subject?

[HAIKUMOM *appears. She's reading the newspaper.*]

HAIKUMOM: Orangutan, cover your ears.

ORANGUTAN: Big Brother, always watching.

HAIKUMOM: Cover your ears, kiddo.

ORANGUTAN: That doesn't really work online.

HAIKUMOM: Okay, Chutes and Ladders, can we g-chat? One on one?

ORANGUTAN: Come on! No talking behind backs.

HAIKUMOM: Fine. Chutes&Ladders, you listening?

CHUTES&LADDERS: Lord have mercy, spit it out.

HAIKUMOM: Orangutan may be immature . . .

ORANGUTAN: Hey.

HAIKUMOM: She may be annoying at times . . .

ORANGUTAN: What the f?

HAIKUMOM: She may be overbearing and self-obsessed and a little bit of a concern troll and she can type faster than she can think which often leads to diarrhea of the keyboard—

CHUTES&LADDERS: Your point?

HAIKUMOM: But she's telling you, "Be my friend." When's the last time someone opened your closet door, saw all them skeletons, and said, "Wassup?! Can I join the party?"

CHUTES&LADDERS: All right, my wrist is officially slapped. Thank you, oh nagging wives.

HAIKUMOM: Internal Revenue Service, 300 North Los Angeles Street 90012? Is that you?

CHUTES&LADDERS: Need my name, too? It's Wilkie. I'll leave it at that.

HAIKUMOM: I'm sending you a care package. Orangutan, you can uncover your ears now. I love you.

ORANGUTAN: Middle finger.

[FOUNTAINHEAD's *log-on appears.*]

FOUNTAINHEAD: Hey all, thanks for the warm two-by-four to my head.

HAIKUMOM: All right, look who's back.

FOUNTAINHEAD: Knives sharpened? Last night we ran out of butter while my wife was cooking and she sent me to the store and it took every bit of strength I could summon not to make a "wrong turn" to that parking lot I know so well. I got the butter and on the car ride home, I couldn't help it, I drove by the lot, and there was my dealer in the shadows. My brain went on attack. "Use one more time just to prove you won't need another hit tomorrow." I managed to keep on driving and bring the butter home. Major victory. And my wife pulls it out of the plastic bag and says, "This is unsalted. I said salted." Then she feels guilty so she says never mind, never mind, she'll just add a little extra salt to the pie crust but I insist. "No, no, no, my wife deserves the right kind of butter and she's gonna get it!" I mean, I bark it, I'm already halfway out the door, my heart was racing all the way to the parking lot and raced even harder when I sat in the car and smoked. So, Michael Jordan[2] is benched with a broken foot. But he'll come back in the finals.

HAIKUMOM: Thanks for the update, Fountainhead. You may not believe this, but we were missing you and worried about you. Don't beat yourself up about the slip. You had three days clean. This time you'll make it to day four.

FOUNTAINHEAD: Be ambitious. Why not reach for a whopping five?

ORANGUTAN: Maybe you'll make it to day thirty if you tell your wife.

FOUNTAINHEAD: I told you, I have my reasons, I cannot do that. My wife has some emotional issues.

ORANGUTAN: [*Sarcastic*] No!

FOUNTAINHEAD: Listen? Please? Are you capable of that? She's in therapy twice a week. Depression, manic. I don't want to be the

---

2. Professional basketball star for the Chicago Bulls, often described as the best ever to play the game.

reason she goes down a tailspin. I actually have her best interest in mind.

CHUTES&LADDERS: Yawn.

FOUNTAINHEAD: Ah, Chutes&Ladders. I could feel you circling like a vulture. Weigh in, by all means.

CHUTES&LADDERS: And I repeat. Yawn.

FOUNTAINHEAD: Chutes&Ladders, why do I get the feeling you'd be the first in line for tickets to watch me smoke again? That you'd be in the bleachers cheering if I relapse?

CHUTES&LADDERS: How can you relapse when you don't even think you're addicted?

FOUNTAINHEAD: If you read my original post clearly, I wrote that it's a psychological addiction, not like heroin.

CHUTES&LADDERS: Well see then, you're not a junkie after all.

FOUNTAINHEAD: What is this, first-grade recess?

CHUTES&LADDERS: No, this is a site for crackheads trying not to be crackheads anymore. If you're not a crackhead, leave, we don't want you, you are irrelevant, get off my lawn, go.

HAIKUMOM: Chutes&Ladders, please.

CHUTES&LADDERS: I got this.

ORANGUTAN: He's still logged on.

CHUTES&LADDERS: Hey Fountainhead, why did you come to this website?

FOUNTAINHEAD: Because I thoroughly enjoy getting shit on.

HAIKUMOM: Censored.

CHUTES&LADDERS: Why do you want to be here?

FOUNTAINHEAD: Want? The two times I've logged on here I've *wanted* to vomit.

CHUTES&LADDERS: Well? Did you receive some sort of invitation? Did one of us ask you here?

FOUNTAINHEAD: Look, I'm the first to say it. I have a problem.

CHUTES&LADDERS: Adam had problems. Eve had problems. Why are *you here?*

FOUNTAINHEAD: To get information.

CHUTES&LADDERS: Go to Wikipedia. Why are you *here?*

FOUNTAINHEAD: Because I smoke crack.

CHUTES&LADDERS: Go to a dealer. Why are you here?

FOUNTAINHEAD: Because I plan to stop smoking crack.

CHUTES&LADDERS: Fine, when your son has a tummy-ache in the middle of the night and walks in on you tweaking and geeking just tell him, "Don't worry, Junior, Daddy's sucking on a glass dick—"

HAIKUMOM: [*Overlaps*] Hey!

CHUTES&LADDERS: "—but Daddy makes 300K and this is all a part of Daddy's Plan!"

FOUNTAINHEAD: I'M A FUCKING CRACKHEAD.

HAIKUMOM: [*Apologetic*] Censored.

FOUNTAINHEAD: Fuck you, Chutes&Ladders.

HAIKUMOM: Bleep.

FOUNTAINHEAD: Fuck you . . . Don't talk about my sons. Don't fucking talk about my boys.

HAIKUMOM: Bleep again.

FOUNTAINHEAD: Are you happy, Chutes&Ladders?

CHUTES&LADDERS: Absolutely not, my friend. I'm a crackhead, too, and I wouldn't wish it on my worst enemy.

FOUNTAINHEAD: And I *made* 300K, I'm currently unemployed. An unemployed crackhead. At least I still have all my teeth. [*They laugh*] Better than I can say for my dealer.

CHUTES&LADDERS: [*Being a friend*] Ex-dealer, man.

FOUNTAINHEAD: Ex-dealer. Thank you.

HAIKUMOM: Fountainhead, welcome to the dinner party. Granted, it's a party we never wanted to be invited to, but pull up a chair and pass the salt. Some people here may pour it in your wounds. Just like you, we've all crawled on the floor with a flashlight. We've thrown out the brillo and bought some more. But guess what? You had three days. For three days straight, you didn't try to kill yourself on an hourly basis. Please. Talk to your wife about your addiction. You need every supporting resource. You are in for the fight of your life. You mentioned Wharton. I live in Philly. If you're still in the area and you have an emergency or even a craving, email me directly. Any time of night. Don't take it lightly when I say a sober day for you is a sober day for me. I know you can do this but I know you can't do it alone. So stop being a highly functioning isolator and start being a highly dysfunctional *person*. The only way out of it is through it.

ORANGUTAN: [*Nostalgic*] Slogans . . .

HAIKUMOM: Ya'll know I know 'em all.

CHUTES&LADDERS: They saved my life.

ORANGUTAN: Your personal favorite. Go.

HAIKUMOM: "Nothing changes if nothing changes."

[ELLIOT *appears at the boxing gym, punching a bag. The* GHOST *watches him.*]

GHOST: Momken men-fadluck ted-dini gawaz saffari?

ORANGUTAN: "It came to pass, it didn't come to stay."

FOUNTAINHEAD: "I obsessively pursue feeling good, no matter how bad it makes me feel."

CHUTES&LADDERS: Okay, now!

ORANGUTAN: Nice!

HAIKUMOM: Rookie don't play!

GHOST: Momken men-fadluck ted-dini gawaz saffari?

ORANGUTAN: "One hit is too many, one thousand never enough."

HAIKUMOM: "Have an at-ti-tude of gra-ti-tude."

CHUTES&LADDERS: "If you are eating a shit sandwich, chances are you ordered it."

ORANGUTAN: Ding ding ding. We have a winner!

HAIKUMOM: Censored. But good one.

GHOST: Momken men-fadluck ted-dini gawaz saffari?

HAIKUMOM: [*Turning a page in the paper*] Oh shit!

ORANGUTAN: CENSORED!!!!!! YES!!!!!! Whoooooo!

HAIKUMOM: You got me.

ORANGUTAN: [*Victorious*] You know how long I've been waiting to do that?!

HAIKUMOM: My sister Ginny's in the *Daily News*! A nice big picture!

GHOST: Momken men-fadluck ted-dini gawaz saffari?

HAIKUMOM: "Eugenia P. Ortiz, A Force For Good In Philadelphia!" Okay, now!

[ELLIOT *punches harder. His leg is starting to bother him.*]

ELLIOT: Your leg feels great. Your leg feels like a million bucks. No pain. No pain.

HAIKUMOM: "In lieu of flowers contributions may be made to . . ."

> [HAIKUMOM *drops the newspaper.*
> *The* GHOST *blows on* ELLIOT, *knocking him to the floor.*]

GHOST: Momken men-fadluck ted-dini gawaz saffari?

INTERMISSION.

Scene 7
A diner. ODESSA *and* JOHN, *aka* FOUNTAINHEAD, *sit in a booth.*

ODESSA: To lapsed Catholics. [*They clink coffee mugs*] And you thought we had nothing in common.

JOHN: When did you become interested in Buddhism?

ODESSA: My older brother used to terrorize me during mass. He would point to a statue, tell me about the evil spirit hiding behind it. Fangs, claws. I thought Saint Lazarus[3] was gonna come to life and suck my eyes out. Buddhism? Not scary. If there's spirits, they're hiding inside you.

JOHN: Aren't those the scariest kind?

ODESSA: So, how many days do you have? It should be two now.

JOHN: I put my sons' picture on my cell phone so if I get the urge, I can just look at them instead.

ODESSA: How many days?

JOHN: [*Small talk*] I love Puerto Rico. On my honeymoon we stayed at that hotel in Old San Juan, the old convent. [ODESSA *shrugs*] And that Spanish fort at the top of the city? El Morro?

ODESSA: I've always been meaning to make it there.

JOHN: There are these keyholes where the cannons used to fit, and the view of the waves through them, you can practically see the Spanish armada approaching.

ODESSA: I mean, one of these days I've gotta make it to PR.

JOHN: Oh. I just figured . . .

ODESSA: The Jersey Shore. Atlantic City. The Philadelphia airport. Oh, I've been places.

JOHN: On an actual plane?

---

3. In the Gospel of John, Jesus raises Lazarus from his tomb four days after he died.

ODESSA: I only fly first-class, and I'm still saving for that ticket.

[ODESSA's *cell phone rings.*]

JOHN: You're a popular lady.

ODESSA: [*Into her phone, her demeanor completely changing*] What? I told you, the diner on Spring Garden and Third. I'm busy, come in an hour. One hour. Now stop calling me and asking fucking directions. [*She hangs up*]

JOHN: Says the one who censors.

ODESSA: My sister died.

JOHN: Right. You sure you're okay?

ODESSA: She's dead, ain't nothing left to do. People act like the world is going to fall apart.

JOHN: You write very Zen[4] messages. And yet.

ODESSA: My family knows every button to push.

JOHN: My condolences. [*Pause*] You don't strike me as a computer nerd. I used to employ an entire floor of them.

ODESSA: You should've seen me at first, pecking with two fingers. Now I'm like an octopus with ten little tentacles. In my neck of the woods staying clean is like trying to tap-dance on a minefield. The website fills the hours. So how are we gonna fill yours, huh? When was the last time you picked up a javelin?

JOHN: Senior year of high school.

ODESSA: [*Hands him a sheet of paper*] There's a sober softball league. Fairmount Park, games on Sundays. Sober bowling on Thursdays.

JOHN: I lied in my first post. I've been smoking crack for two years. I've tried quitting hundreds of times. Day two? Please, I'm in the seven-hundredth day of hell.

ODESSA: You got it out of your system. Most people lie at one time or another on the site. The good news is, two years in, there's still time. [*Hands him another sheet of paper*] Talbott Recovery Center in Atlanta. It's designed for professionals with addictions. Paradise Recovery in Hawaii. They actually check your income before admitting you. Just for the wealthy. This place in Jersey,

---

4. Aphorisms in the spirit of Zen Buddhism; probably meant here as similar to the Serenity Prayer: the acceptance of imperfection, advocacy of stillness, tranquility and simplicity.

it's right over the bridge, they have an outpatient program for professionals like you.

JOHN: I'm tenacious. I'm driven. I love my parents.

ODESSA: Pitchforks against tanks.

JOHN: I relish in paying my taxes.

ODESSA: And you could be dead tomorrow. [*Pause*] Is your dealer male or female?

JOHN: I had a few. Flushed their numbers down the toilet like you suggested.

ODESSA: Your original connection. The one who got you hooked.

JOHN: Female.

ODESSA: Did you have sex with her?

JOHN: You don't beat around the bush, do you?

ODESSA: I'll take that as a yes. [*No answer*] Do you prefer sex when you're high to sex when you're sober?

JOHN: I've never really analyzed it.

ODESSA: It can be a dangerous cocktail. Some men get off on smoking and fucking.

JOHN: All men get off on fucking.

ODESSA: Are you scared your wife will find out you're addicted to crack? Or are you scared she'll find out what came of your wedding vows?

JOHN: I should go.

ODESSA: We just ordered.

JOHN: I promised my son. There's a science fair tomorrow. Something about dioramas and crazy glue.

ODESSA: Don't talk about them. Get sober for them.

JOHN: Fuck you.

ODESSA: Leave me three bucks for your coffee cuz I ain't got it.

[*He stands, pulls out three dollars. She throws the money back at him.*]

You picked up the phone and called me.

JOHN: [*He sits down again*] I don't know how to do this. I've never done this before.

ODESSA: I have and it usually doesn't end up so good. One in twenty, maybe, hang around. Most people just don't write one day and then thirty days and then you're wondering . . . And sometimes you get the answer. Cuz their wife looks on their computer and sees the website and logs on and writes, "I found him face down in the snow."

JOHN: How many day ones did you have?

ODESSA: Seven years' worth.

JOHN: Do you still crave?

ODESSA: On the good days, only every hour. Would you rather be honest with your wife, or would you rather end up like me? [*Pause*] That wasn't rhetorical.

JOHN: You're not exactly what I wanted to be when I grew up.

ODESSA: Truth. Now we're talking.

[ELLIOT *and* YAZ *enter.*]

YAZ: There she is.

[ELLIOT *and* YAZ *sit down in the booth.*]

ELLIOT: You were supposed to meet us at the flower place.

YAZ: The deposit was due at nine.

ODESSA: My alarm clock didn't go off.

ELLIOT: Were you up on that chat room all night?

ODESSA: [*Ignoring him, to a waiter, off*] Can I get a refill, please?

ELLIOT: Where's the money?

ODESSA: I told you I don't have any money.

ELLIOT: And you think I do? I been paying for Mami Ginny's meds for six months straight—

ODESSA: Well get it from Yaz's mom.

YAZ: My mom put in for the headstone. She got an expensive one.

ODESSA: Headstone? She's getting cremated.

YAZ: She still needs a proper Catholic piece of granite. Right beside abuela, right beside your dad and sister and brother.

ELLIOT: And daughter.

YAZ: Everyone agreed.

ODESSA: No one asked my opinion.

ELLIOT: Everyone who showed up to the family meeting.

ODESSA: I wasn't invited.

YAZ: I texted you twice.

ODESSA: I was out of minutes.

ELLIOT: We just spoke on the phone.

ODESSA: Whatchu want me to do, Elliot, if I say I ain't got no fucking money, I ain't got no money.

JOHN: Hi, I'm John, nice to meet you.

YAZ: Yazmin.

ELLIOT: You one of Mom's rehab buddies?

JOHN: We know each other from work.

ELLIOT: You scrub toilets?

ODESSA: [*To* JOHN] I'm a practitioner of the custodial arts.

ELLIOT: Is she your sponsor?

JOHN: [*To* ODESSA] I thought this was going to be a private meeting.

ELLIOT: I'm her son.

JOHN: [*To* ODESSA] You must have been young.

ELLIOT: But I was raised by my Aunt Ginny and that particular aunt just died. [*To* ODESSA] So now, you got three hours to find some money to pay for one basket of flowers in the funeral of the woman who changed my pampers.

YAZ: We're all supposed to be helping out.

ODESSA: You both know I run out of minutes all the time. No one could be bothered to drive by and tell me face to face?

ELLIOT: Because you always bothered to drive by and say hello to Mami Ginny when you knew she was sick? Because you bothered to hit me up one time this week and say, "Elliot, I'm sorry your mom died."

ODESSA: You still got one mom alive.

ELLIOT: Really? You want to go there?

YAZ: The flower place needs the money today.

ODESSA: She was my sister and you are my son, too.

YAZ: Guys. Two hundred dollars by end of business day.

ODESSA: That's my rent.

ELLIOT: Then fifty.

ODESSA: I just spent fifty getting my phone back on.

ELLIOT: Ten dollars. For the woman who raised your son! Do we hear ten dollars? Going once!

ODESSA: I spent my last ten at the post office.

ELLIOT: Going twice!

[JOHN *goes into his wallet.*]

JOHN: Here's fifty.

[*They all look at him like he's crazy. He pulls out some more money.*]

Two hundred?

[ELLIOT *pushes the money back to* JOHN *with one pointer finger, as if the bills might be contaminated.*]

ELLIOT: No offense, I don't take money from users.
JOHN: I'm not . . . I think that was my cue.
ODESSA: Sit down. My son was just going.
ELLIOT: Did World's Best Mom here tell you about her daughter?
ODESSA: I'm about to throw this coffee in your fucking face.
YAZ: Come on, Elliot, I'll pay for the flowers.

[ELLIOT *doesn't get up.*]

ELLIOT: I looked at that chat room once. The woman I saw there? She's literally not the same person I know. *(To John)* Did she tell you how she became such a saint?
JOHN: We all have skeletons.
ELLIOT: Yeah, well, she's an archaeological dig. Did she tell you about her daughter?
ODESSA: [*Suddenly resigned*] Go ahead, I ain't got no secrets.
YAZ: [*Getting up*] Excuse me.
ELLIOT: Sit here and listen, Yaz. You were born with a silver spoon and you need to know how it was for me.
YAZ: I said I'd pay for the goddamn flowers so LET'S GO. NOW!
ELLIOT: My sister and I had the stomach flu, right? For a whole day we couldn't keep nothing down.
ODESSA: Three days . . . You were vomiting three days straight.
ELLIOT: Medicine, juice, anything we ate, it would come right back up. [*To* JOHN] Your co-worker here took us to Children's Hospital.
ODESSA: Jefferson.
ELLIOT: It was wall-to-wall packed. Every kid in Philly had this bug. ERs were turning kids away. They gave us a flier about stomach flu and sent us home. Bright blue paper. Little cartoon diagrams. It said give your kids a spoonful of water every five minutes.
ODESSA: A teaspoon.
ELLIOT: A small enough amount that they can keep it down. Five minutes. Spoon. Five minutes. Spoon. I remember thinking, Wow, this is it. Family time. Quality time. Just the three of us.

Because it was gentle, the way you said, "Open up." I opened my mouth, you put that little spoon of water into my mouth. That little bit of relief. And then I watched you do the same thing with my little sister. And I remember being like, "Wow, I love you, Mom. My moms is all right." Five minutes. Spoon. Five minutes. Spoon. But you couldn't stick to something simple like that. You couldn't sit still like that. You had to have your thing. That's where I stop remembering.

ODESSA: I left.

ELLIOT: A Department of Human Services report. That's my memory. Six hours later a neighbor kicks in the door. Me and my sister are lying in a pile of laundry. My shorts was all messed up. And what I really don't remember is my sister. Quote: "Female infant, approximately two years, pamper and tear ducts dry, likely cause of death, dehydration." Cuz when you dehydrate you can't form a single tear.

JOHN: [*To* ELLIOT] I'm very sorry . . . [*He puts some money on the table*] For the coffee. [*Exits*]

ELLIOT: That's some friend you got there.

[*Pause.*]

YAZ: Mary Lou. We can at least say her name out loud. Mary Lou. Mary Lou. [*To* ODESSA] One time you came to babysit me, you brought Elliot and Mary Lou—she was still in pampers—and Mary Lou had this soda from 7-Eleven. She didn't want to give me a sip. You yelled at her so bad, you totally cursed her out and I said, "You're not supposed to yell at people like that!" And you said, "No, Yaz, let her cry. She's gotta learn that ya'll are cousins, ya'll are flesh and blood, and we share everything. You hear me, Yaz? In this family we share *everything*." You walked out of the room, came back from the kitchen with four straws in your hand, sat us down on the floor in a circle, pointed to me and said, "You first." I sipped. "Elliot's turn." He sipped. "Mary Lou's turn." She sipped. Then you sipped. You made us do like that, taking turns, going around the circle, till the cup was empty.

[ODESSA *hands* ELLIOT *a key.*]

ODESSA: The pawn shop closes at five. Go into my house. Take my computer. Pawn it. However much you get, put towards a few flowers, okay?

[ODESSA *exits.*]

SCENE 8

Split scene: ODESSA's *living room and the chat room.* CHUTES&LADDERS *holds a phone.*

ORANGUTAN: Did you hit the call button yet?

CHUTES&LADDERS: I'm working on it.

ORANGUTAN: Where are you? Are you at home?

CHUTES&LADDERS: *Jeopardy!*'s on mute.

ORANGUTAN: Dude, turn off the tube. This is serious. Did you even dial?

CHUTES&LADDERS: Yeah, yeah. [*He does*] All right, it's ringing. What am I going to say?

ORANGUTAN: "Hi, Son, it's Dad."

CHUTES&LADDERS: Wendell. That's his name. [*Hangs up*] No answer.

ORANGUTAN: As in, you hung up?

CHUTES&LADDERS: Yes. I hung up.

ORANGUTAN: Dude, way too quick!

CHUTES&LADDERS: What do you have, a stopwatch? Do you know the average time before someone answers a telephone?

ORANGUTAN: 3.2 rings.

CHUTES&LADDERS: According to . . .

ORANGUTAN: I don't reveal my sources.

CHUTES&LADDERS: Look, my son's a grown man with a good life.

ORANGUTAN: Quit moping and dial Wendell's number.

CHUTES&LADDERS: This Japan thing is cramping my style. Different networks, different time zones. No concurrent *Jeopardy!* watching.

ORANGUTAN: Deflection: nostalgia.

CHUTES&LADDERS: Humor me.

ORANGUTAN: [*Humoring him*] How's my little Trebeky[5] doing?

---

5. Alex Trebek (b. 1940), host of the game show *Jeopardy!* since 1984.

CHUTES&LADDERS: He's had work done. Man looks younger than he did twenty years ago.

ORANGUTAN: Needle or knife?

CHUTES&LADDERS: Needle. His eyes are still in the right place.

ORANGUTAN: Well, it's working. Meow. Purrrrr. Any good categories?

CHUTES&LADDERS: Before and After.

ORANGUTAN: I love Before and After! But I'll go with . . . Quit Stalling for two hundred. [*She hums the* Jeopardy! *theme*]

CHUTES&LADDERS: It's ringing.

ORANGUTAN: My stopwatch is running.

CHUTES&LADDERS: Still ringing.

ORANGUTAN: You're going to be great.

CHUTES&LADDERS: It rang again.

ORANGUTAN: You're a brave soul.

[*We hear a man's voice at the other end of the line say, "Hello?"* CHUTES&LADDERS *hangs up.*]

CHUTES&LADDERS: He must not be around.

ORANGUTAN: Leave a voice mail.

CHUTES&LADDERS: Maybe next time.

[CHUTES&LADDERS *logs off.*]

ORANGUTAN: Hey! Don't log off, come on. Chutes&Ladders. Whatever happened to tough love? Log back on, we'll do a crossword. You can't fly before "Final Jeopardy!" Sigh. Anyone else online? Haikumom? I'm still waiting for that daily poem . . . Bueller? Bueller?

[*In* ODESSA's *living room,* ELLIOT *and* YAZ *enter.*]

YAZ: Wow, look at that computer. Stone age.

ELLIOT: Fred Flinstone shit.

YAZ: Positively Dr. Who.[6]

ELLIOT: Dr. Who?

---

6. A sometimes campy science-fiction television program produced by the British Broadcasting Company from 1963 to 1989 and revived in 2005. Characters in the show travel through time.

YAZ: That computer is actually worse than what they give the adjuncts at Swarthmore.

ELLIOT: What does "adjunct" even mean?

YAZ: Exactly. It's the nicest thing she owns.

ELLIOT: Let's not act like this is some heroic sacrifice. Like this makes her the world's martyr.

YAZ: We're not going to get more than fifteen bucks for it.

ELLIOT: Symbols matter, Yaz. This isn't about the money. This is shaking hands. This is tipping your hat. This is holding the door open. This is the bare minimum, the least effort possible to earn the label "person." [*Looks at the screen*] What do you think her password is? [*Types*] "Odessa." Nope. "Odessaortiz." Nope.

YAZ: It's probably Elliot.

[*He types.* HAIKUMOM's *log-on appears.*]

ELLIOT: The irony.

YAZ: I think legally that might be like breaking and entering.

ELLIOT: [*Typing*] Hello? Oh shit, it posted.

ORANGUTAN: Haikumom! Hit me with those seventeen syllables, baby!

YAZ: Haikumom? What the hell is that?

ELLIOT: Her username. She has the whole world thinking she's some Chinese prophet.

YAZ: Haiku are Japanese.

ELLIOT: "Haiku are Japanese." [*Typing*] Hello, Orangutan. How are you?

ORANGUTAN: [*Formal*] I am fine. How are you?

ELLIOT: [*Typing*] So, I guess you like monkeys, huh?

ORANGUTAN: An orangutan is a primate.

YAZ: Elliot.

ELLIOT: Chill.

ORANGUTAN: And this primate has ninety-eight days. That deserves a poem, don't you think?

ELLIOT: [*Typing*] I don't have a poem, but I have a question. What does crack feel like?

ORANGUTAN: What?

YAZ: Elliot, cut it out.

ELLIOT: [*Typing*] Sometimes I'm amazed I don't know firsthand.

ORANGUTAN: Who is this?

ELLIOT: [*Typing*] How does it make your brain feel?

ORANGUTAN: Like it's flooded with dopamine.[7] Listen, cyber-stalker, if you came here for shits and giggles, we are a sadly unfunny bunch.

ELLIOT: [*Typing*] Are you just a smoker or do you inject it right into your eyeballs?

ORANGUTAN: Who the fuck is this?

ELLIOT: [*Typing*] Haikumom.

ORANGUTAN: Bullshit, you didn't censor me. Quit screwing around, hacker, who are you?

YAZ: You think Ginny would want you acting this way?

ELLIOT: I think Mami Ginny would want Mami Odessa to pay for a single flower on her fucking casket.

YAZ: [*Types*] This is not Haikumom. It's her son.

ORANGUTAN: Well, if you're looking for the friends and family thread, you have to go to the home page and create a new log-on. This particular forum is for people actually in recovery. Wait, her son the actor? From the Crest ad?

ELLIOT: [*Typing*] Colgate.

ORANGUTAN: "Sonrisa baby!" I saw that on YouTube! Your teeth are insanely white. Ever worked in Hollywood?

ELLIOT: [*Typing*] Psh. I just had this guy begging me to do a feature film. Gritty, documentary-style, about Marines in Iraq. I just don't want to do anything cheesy.

ORANGUTAN: So you're the war hero . . .

ELLIOT: [*Typing*] Haikumom brags.

ORANGUTAN: How's your recovery going? [*No answer*] This is the crack forum, but there's a really good pain-meds forum on this site, too. Link here.

YAZ: What is she talking about?

ORANGUTAN: There's a few war vets on that forum, just like you. You'd be in good company.

YAZ: Pain meds? Elliot? [*He doesn't respond.* YAZ *types*] What are you talking about?

ORANGUTAN: Haikumom told us about your history.

---

7. A neural transmitter occurring naturally in the brain; many drugs, such as crack cocaine, increase dopamine levels, producing a euphoric feeling.

YAZ: [*Typing*] What history?

ORANGUTAN: Sorry. Maybe she told us in confidence.

ELLIOT: Confidence? They call this shit "world wide" for a reason.

YAZ: [*Typing*] I can search all the threads right now.

ORANGUTAN: That you had a bunch of leg surgeries in Iraq. That if a soldier said they hurt, the docs practically threw pills at them. That you OD'd three times and were in the hospital for it. She was real messed up about it. I guess she had hoped the fruit would fall a little farther from the tree.

YAZ: [*To* ELLIOT] Is this true?

ELLIOT: I wasn't a soldier. I was a Marine. Soldiers is the army.

YAZ: Oh my god.

ELLIOT: [*Takes the keyboard, types*] What I am: sober. What I am not and never will be: a pathetic junkie like you.

> [*He unplugs the computer. He throws the keyboard on the ground. He starts unplugging cables violently.*]

YAZ: Hold on. Just stop it, Elliot! Stop it!

ELLIOT: The one time I ever reached out to her for anything and she made me a story on a website.

YAZ: Why wouldn't you ask me for help? Why would you deal with that alone?

ELLIOT: The opposite of alone. I seen barracks that looked like dope houses. It was four months in my life, it's over. We've chopped up a lot of shit together, Yaz, but we ain't gonna chop this up. This shit stays in the vault. You got me?

YAZ: No!

ELLIOT: Yaz. [*He looks her straight in the eye*] Please. Please.

YAZ: I want to grab the sky and smash it into pieces. Are you clean?

ELLIOT: The only thing I got left from those days is the nightmares. That's when he came, and some days I swear he ain't never gonna leave.

YAZ: Who?

> [ELLIOT *tries to walk away from the conversation, but the* GHOST *is there, blocking his path.*]

> Who?!

ELLIOT: [*Almost like a child*] Please, Yaz. Please end this conversation. Don't make me beg, Yaz.

YAZ: The pawn shop closes in fifteen minutes. I'll get the monitor, you grab the computer.

Scene 9

CHUTES&LADDERS *is at work, on his desk phone. A bundled pile of mail is on his desk. He takes off the rubber band, browses. Junk, mostly.*

CHUTES&LADDERS: [*Into the work phone*] That's right. Three Ws. Dot. Not the word, the punctuation mark. I-R-S. Not "F" like flamingo; "S" like Sam. Dot. Yup, another one. Gov. Grover orange victor.

[ORANGUTAN *appears, online.*]

ORANGUTAN: I'm doing it. I'm almost there. *And* I can chat! Japan is so advanced. Internet cafes are like parking meters here.

CHUTES&LADDERS: Where are you and what are you doing?

ORANGUTAN: Sapporo train station. Just did some research. Get this: in the early eighties, they straightened all the rivers in Hokkaido.

CHUTES&LADDERS: Why?

ORANGUTAN: To create jobs the government straightened the rivers! Huge bodies of water, manual laborers, scientists, engineers, bulldozers, and the rivers became straight! How nuts is that?

CHUTES&LADDERS: People can't leave good enough alone. Why are humans so damn restless?

ORANGUTAN: It's not restlessness. It's ego. Massive, bizarre ego.

CHUTES&LADDERS: Can't let a river be a river. [*Into the phone*] The forms link is on the left.

ORANGUTAN: Now it's the aughts, people keep being born, jobs still need creating, but there's no curves left to straighten, so, drum roll, the government is beginning a new program to put all the original turns back in the rivers!

CHUTES&LADDERS: Well good luck to them, but no amount of engineering can put a wrinkle back in Nicole Kidman's[8] forehead.

ORANGUTAN: Ever heard of Kushiro?

CHUTES&LADDERS: Is that your new boyfriend's name?

---

8. Academy Award-winning actor from Australia; the sense here is that plastic surgery prevents her face from making natural expressions, such as a furrowed brow.

ORANGUTAN: Ha. Ha ha ha. It's home of the hundred-mile-long Kushiro River, which is the pilot project, the first river they're trying to recurve.

CHUTES&LADDERS: Kushiro River. Got it. Burned in the brain. One day I'll win a Trivial Pursuit's[9] wedge with that. [*Into the phone*] You, too, ma'am. [*He hangs up*]

ORANGUTAN: My train to Kushiro leaves in twenty minutes. My heart is pounding.

CHUTES&LADDERS: I don't follow.

ORANGUTAN: Kushiro is the town where I was born. I'm going. I'm doing it.

CHUTES&LADDERS: Hold on, now you're throwing curveballs.

ORANGUTAN: In my hand is a sheet of paper. On the paper is the address of the house where my birth parents once lived. I'm going to knock on their door.

[CHUTES&LADDER'*s desk phone rings.*]

CHUTES&LADDERS: [*Into the phone*] Help desk, please hold. [*To ORANGUTAN*] How long have you had that address for?

ORANGUTAN: It's been burning a hole in my pocket for two days. I hounded my mom before I left Maine. She finally wrote down the name of the adoption agency. The first clue, the first evidence of who I was I ever had. I made a vow to myself, if I could stay sober for three months, I would track my parents down. So a few days ago class ended early, I went to the agency, showed my passport, and thirty minutes later I had an address on a piece of paper. Ask me anything about Kushiro. All I've done the last two days is research it. I'm an expert. Population, 190,000. There's a tech school, there's an airport.

CHUTES&LADDERS: Why are you telling me this? To get my blessing?

ORANGUTAN: I tell you about the things I do.

CHUTES&LADDERS: You don't want my opinion, you want my approval.

ORANGUTAN: Hand it over.

CHUTES&LADDERS: No.

ORANGUTAN: Don't get monosyllabic.

---

9. In the game *Trivial Pursuit,* correct answers are rewarded with a "wedge," which is inserted into a circular, pie-like game piece. Six wedges fill up the game piece.

CHUTES&LADDERS: Take that piece of paper and use it as kindling for a warm winter fire.

ORANGUTAN: Jeez, what did they slip into your Wheaties this morning?

CHUTES&LADDERS: Do a ritual burning and never look back. You have three months. Do you know the worth in gold of three months? Don't give yourself a reason to go back to the shadows.

ORANGUTAN: I'm in recovery. I have no illusions about catharsis. I realize what will most likely happen is nothing. Maybe something tiny. A microscopic butterfly flapping her microscopic wings.

CHUTES&LADDERS: Live in the past, follow your ass.

ORANGUTAN: Don't you have the slightest ambition?

CHUTES&LADDERS: Yes, and I achieve it every day: Don't use and don't hurt anyone. Two things I used to do on a daily basis. I don't do them anymore. Done. Dream realized. No more dreaming.

[*His phone rings again.*]

[*Into the phone*] Continue holding, please.

ORANGUTAN: When was the last time you went out on a limb?

CHUTES&LADDERS: Three odd weeks ago.

ORANGUTAN: Did you try hazelnut instead of french roast? Did you listen to *Soul Mornings* instead of NPR?[1]

CHUTES&LADDERS: There's a new secretary down the hall, she's got a nice smile. I decided to go say hello. We had a little back and forth. I said, let's have lunch, she said maybe but meant no, I turned away, looked down and my tie was floating in my coffee cup.

ORANGUTAN: I waited three months to tell you this, every step of the way, the train ride, what the river looks like. What their front door looks like. [*Pause*] I'm quitting this site. I hate this site. I fucking hate this site.

CHUTES&LADDERS: You're already losing it and you haven't even gotten on the train.

ORANGUTAN: Three days ago I suggested you and I meet face to face and you blew a fucking gasket.

CHUTES&LADDERS: That's what this is about?

---

1. National Public Radio, a fairly staid radio network featuring news and talk shows; by contrast, *Soul Mornings* suggests programming designed to elicit a more emotional response from listeners.

ORANGUTAN: Don't flatter yourself. This is about me wanting relationships. With humans, not ones and zeroes. So we were once junkies. It's superficial. It's not real friendship.

CHUTES&LADDERS: I beg to differ.

ORANGUTAN: Prove me wrong.

CHUTES&LADDERS: Search down that address and a hundred bucks says your heart comes back a shattered light bulb.

ORANGUTAN: You mean, gasp, I'll actually FEEL something?

CHUTES&LADDERS: What are you going to do if the address is wrong? What if the building's been bulldozed? What if some new tenant lives there? What if the woman who gave you birth then gave you away answers the door?

ORANGUTAN: I DON'T KNOW! A concept you clearly avoid at all costs. Learn how to live, that's all I'm goddamn trying to do!

[*His phone rings. He picks up the receiver and hangs it up.*]

CHUTES&LADDERS: I have three grandsons. You know how I know that? Because I rang my son's doorbell one day. Step 9,[2] make amends. And his wife answered, and I don't blame her for hating me. But I saw three little boys in that living room and one of those boys said, "Daddy, who's that man at the door?" And my son said to *my grandson*, "I don't know. He must be lost." My son came outside, closed the door behind him, exchanged a few cordial words and then asked me to go.

ORANGUTAN: So I shouldn't even try.

CHUTES&LADDERS: I had five years sober until that day.

ORANGUTAN: You really believe in your heart of hearts I should not even try. [*Pause*] Coward.

[*His phone rings. He unplugs the phone line.*]

CHUTES&LADDERS: You think it's easy being your friend?

ORANGUTAN: Sissy. You walk the goddamn earth scared of your own shadow, getting smaller and smaller, until you disappear.

CHUTES&LADDERS: You tease me. You insult me. It's like breathing to you.

---

2. One of Alcoholics Anonymous's "Twelve Steps" to addiction recovery. Step 8 directs addicts to make a list of people they have harmed; step 9 is to make amends for those injuries, unless making amends would further harm them or other people.

ORANGUTAN: You fucking idiot. Why do little girls tease little boys on the playground at recess? Why the fuck were cooties invented? You fucking imbecile!

CHUTES&LADDERS: You disappeared for three months. I couldn't sleep for three months!

ORANGUTAN: I wanted to impress you. I wanted to log on and show you I could be better. And I was an idiot because you're just looking for cowards like you. I'm logging off. This is it. It's over.

CHUTES&LADDERS: Orangutan.

ORANGUTAN: Into the abyss I climb, looking for a flesh-and-blood hand to grasp onto.

CHUTES&LADDERS: Little monkey, stop it.

ORANGUTAN: I'm in the station. My train is in five minutes, you gave me all the motivational speech I need, I'm going to the platform, I'm getting on the train, I'm going to see the house where I was born.

[*She logs off.* CHUTES&LADDERS *grabs his phone and hurls it into his wastebasket. He throws his calculator, his mail pile, his pen cup to the ground. Left on his desk is one padded envelope.*]

CHUTES&LADDERS: "To Chutes&Ladders Wilkie." "From Haikumom Ortiz."

[*He rips it open, pulls out a deflated orange water wing, puts it over his hand.*]

Scene 10

Split scene. Lights rise on a church. ELLIOT *and* YAZ *stand at the lectern.*

YAZ: It is time to honor a woman.[3]

ELLIOT: A woman who built her community with a hammer and nails.

YAZ: A woman who knew her nation's history. Its African roots. European roots. Indigenous roots. A woman who refused to be enslaved but lived to serve.

ELLIOT: A carpenter, a nurse, a comedian, a cook.

YAZ: Eugenia Ortiz.

---

3. This eulogy is inspired by and owes much debt to Roger Zepernick's eulogy for Eugenia Burgos [Hudes's note].

ELLIOT: Mami Ginny.

[*Lights rise on* ODESSA'*s house. She sits on her floor. She scoops a spoonful of water from a mug, pours it onto the floor in a slow ribbon.*]

YAZ: She grew vegetables in her garden lot and left the gate open so anyone could walk in and pick dinner off the vine.

ELLIOT: She drank beer and told dirty jokes and even the never-crack-a-smile church ladies would be rolling laughing.

YAZ: She told me every time I visited, "Yaz, you're going to Juilliard."[4]

ELLIOT: Every morning when I left for school, "Elliot, nobody can make you invisible but you."

[*Lights rise on the Sapporo train station.* ORANGUTAN *is on the platform.*]

LOUDSPEAKER: [*An announcement in Japanese*] 3:00 express to Kushiro now boarding on track one. Please have tickets out and ready for inspection.

YAZ: Zero.

ELLIOT: Birth children.

YAZ: One.

ELLIOT: Adopted son.

[ODESSA *pours another spoonful of water on the floor. Again, it creates a slow ribbon.*]

YAZ: Three.

ELLIOT: Years in the army nurse corps.

YAZ: Three.

ELLIOT: Arrests for civil disobedience. I was in Iraq and she was demonstrating for peace.

YAZ: Forty-seven.

ELLIOT: Wheelchair ramps she installed in homes with disabled children or elderly.

[ODESSA *pours another spoonful of water on the floor. A small pool is forming.*]

YAZ: Twelve.

4. Prestigious and highly-competitive music conservatory in New York City.

ELLIOT: Abandoned lots she turned into city-recognized public gardens.

[*Another spoonful.*]

YAZ: Twenty-two.

ELLIOT: Godchildren recognized by this church.

[*Another spoonful.*]

YAZ: One hundred and thirty.

ELLIOT: Abandoned homes she refurbished and sold to young families.

LOUDSPEAKER: [*Another announcement in Japanese*] Final boarding call, 3:00 express to Kushiro, track one.

[ORANGUTAN *is still on the platform. She seems frozen, like she cannot move.*]

YAZ: All while having a fresh pot of rice and beans on the stove every night. For any hungry stranger. And the pilgrims stopped. And they planted roots, because she was here. We are the living, breathing proof.

ELLIOT: I am the . . . Excuse me.

[*He exits.*]

YAZ: Elliot is the standing, walking testimony to a life. She. Was. Here.

[ODESSA *turns the cup upside down. It is empty.*]

Scene 11

CHUTES&LADDERS *at his desk. In front of him: an inflated orange water wing.*

CHUTES&LADDERS: [*On the phone*] Yeah, it's a 1995 Tercel. Midnight blue. It's got a few miles. A hundred and twenty thousand. But like I said, I'll give it to you for three hundred below Kelley Blue Book. Yup, automatic. Just got new brake pads. Cassette deck, mint condition. I'll even throw in a few tapes. Tina Turner and Lionel Richie.[5] Oh, hold on, call-waiting.

[*He presses mute. Sings to himself.*]

---

5. American singers whose popularity peaked in the 1970s and early 1980s.

A tisket, a tasket.
A green and yellow basket.
I bought a basket for my mommy.
On the way I dropped it.
Was it red? No no no no!
Was it brown? No no no no!6

[*Back into the phone*] Sorry about that. I got someone else interested. No, it's all right, I have them on hold. You need to see this thing tonight if you're serious. I put this listing up thirty minutes ago, my phone is ringing off the hook. 6:30? Hey, I didn't mention. Little lady has racing stripes.

Scene 12

Split scene. Lights rise on the Sapporo train station, same as before. ORANGUTAN *has laid down on the platform and fallen asleep, her backpack like a pillow.*

Lights rise on ODESSA's *house, that night. Her phone rings. We hear loud knocking.*

ELLIOT: [*Offstage*] Mami Odessa! Open the door!

[*More ringing.*]

[*Offstage*] Yo, Mom!
YAZ: [*Offstage*] She's not there.
ELLIOT: [*Offstage*] Can't you hear her phone ringing? Move out the way.
YAZ: [*Offstage*] Be careful, your leg!

[*A few kicks and the door bursts open.* YAZ *and* ELLIOT *enter, switch on the lights.* ODESSA *is in a heap, motionless, on the floor.* YAZ *runs and holds* ODESSA *in her arms.*]

Oh shit. Odessa! Odessa! Wake up.

[YAZ *slaps* ODESSA's *face a few times.*]

Her pulse is racing.

[YAZ *opens her cell phone, dials.*
    ELLIOT *finds a spoon on the floor.*]

6. American nursery rhyme with various versions; Ella Fitzgerald (1917–1996) released a popular song version in 1939.

ELLIOT: Oh no. Oh no you fucking didn't! MOM!!! Get up!

YAZ: [*Into the phone*] Hi, I need an ambulance. I have someone un-conscious here. I think it's an overdose, crack cocaine. Yes, she has a pulse. 33 Ontario Street. No, no seizures, she's just a lump. Well, what should we do while we wait? Okay. Yes. [*She hangs up*] They're on their way. Elevate her feet.

ELLIOT: Help me get her to the sofa. One, two, three.

> [ELLIOT *lifts her with* YAZ's *help. They struggle under her weight. In fact they lift the air.* ODESSA *stands up, lucid, and watches the action:* ELLIOT *and* YAZ *struggling under her invisible weight.*]

YAZ: Watch her head.

ELLIOT: Aw, fuck, my leg.

YAZ: Careful.

> [*They set "Odessa" on the sofa, while* ODESSA *watches, unseen, calm.*]

ODESSA: I must be in the terminal. Between flights. The layover.

YAZ: Oh god, not two in one day, please.

ELLIOT: She's been through this shit a million times. She's a survi-vor! WAKE UP! Call your mom. She'll get here before the am-bulance.

> [YAZ *dials.*]

ODESSA: I've been to the airport, one time. My dad flew here from Puerto Rico. First time I met him. We stood by the baggage claim, his flight was late, we waited forever. There was one single, lone suitcase, spinning around a carousel.

YAZ: [*To* ELLIOT] Voice mail. [*Into the phone*] Mom? Call me back immediately, it's an emergency.

ELLIOT: Give me that. [*Grabs the phone*] Titi, Odessa fucking OD'd and she's dying on her living room floor and I can't take this anymore! COME GET US before I walk off and leave her on the sofa! [*He hangs up*]

YAZ: If you need to, go. No guilt. I got this.

ELLIOT: She's my *mom*. Can I be angry? Can you let me be angry?

YAZ: Why is this family plagued? [ELLIOT *moves to go*] Where are you going?

ELLIOT: To find something fragile.

> [*He exits. We hear something shatter.*]

ODESSA: Everyone had cleared away from the carousel. Everyone had their bags. But this one was unclaimed. It could still be there for all I know. Spiraling. Spinning. Looking for an owner. Abandoned.

[*In the Sapporo station, a* POLICEMAN *enters with a bright, beaming flashlight and points it at* ORANGUTAN.

In ODESSA's *house, a radiant white light suddenly pours in from above.* ODESSA *looks up, is overwhelmed. It is beautiful.* YAZ *sees it.*]

YAZ: Dear god, do you see that?

[ELLIOT *enters. Watching* YAZ, *he looks up.*]

ELLIOT: [*Not seeing it*] What?
YAZ: [*To* ODESSA] It's okay, Odessa, go, go, we love you, I love you *Titi,*[7] you are good, you *are* good. Oh my god, she's beautiful.
ELLIOT: What are you talking about?
YAZ: It's okay, it's okay. We love you, Odessa.
POLICEMAN: [*In Japanese*] Miss, miss, are you okay?
ORANGUTAN: [*Waking*] English, please.
POLICEMAN: No sleeping on the floor.
ORANGUTAN: [*Getting up slowly*] Sorry.
POLICEMAN: Are you sick?
ORANGUTAN: No.
POLICEMAN: Are you intoxicated?
ORANGUTAN: No. I'm very sorry. I just got tired. I'll go. I'm going.
POLICEMAN: Please, can I give you a hand?
ORANGUTAN: No. I got it.

[ORANGUTAN *exits. The* POLICEMAN *turns off his flashlight, exits. The sound of an ambulance siren. Suddenly the white light disappears.* ODESSA *crawls onto the couch and slips into* YAZ's *arms, where she's been all along.*]

YAZ: Holy shit . . .
ELLIOT: What's happening, Yaz? What the fuck was that?
YAZ: You've got to forgive her, Elliot. You have to.

7. Auntie.

SCENE 13

The chat room.

CHUTES&LADDERS: Oh nagging wives? Orangutan? Hello? Earth to Orangutan. Come on, three days straight I been worrying about you. I have time-sensitive information. Ground control to Major Orangutan.[8]

ORANGUTAN: Ta-da.

CHUTES&LADDERS: Where you been?

ORANGUTAN: Here. There. Morrissey and Nine Inch Nails[9] on loop.

CHUTES&LADDERS: Is that what the kids like these days?

ORANGUTAN: [*Rolls eyes*] That was me rolling my eyes.

CHUTES&LADDERS: Guess what I did.

ORANGUTAN: [*Shrugs*] That was me shrugging.

CHUTES&LADDERS: Guess.

ORANGUTAN: Guess what I didn't do?

CHUTES&LADDERS: Meet your birth parents?

ORANGUTAN: Board the train.

CHUTES&LADDERS: Sorry.

ORANGUTAN: Don't apologize. You had my number.

CHUTES&LADDERS: Guess what I did.

ORANGUTAN: Told me so. Had my shit pegged.

CHUTES&LADDERS: I sold my Tercel. My plane lands in Narita Airport a week from this Wednesday.

ORANGUTAN: What?

CHUTES&LADDERS: American Airlines Flight 3312. Arriving 10:01 A.M.

ORANGUTAN: You're a dumbass. Tokyo? Do you have any idea how far that is from Hokkaido? And how much a ticket on the train costs? Oy, and how the hell am I going to get out of teaching that day? Oh, you dollface, you ducky!

CHUTES&LADDERS: I'll be wearing a jean jacket and a Padres cap. That's how you'll know me.

---

8. Reference to David Bowie's 1969 song, "Space Oddity," during which Ground Control attempts to contact the astronaut, Major Tom, who is distracted by the beauty of outer space.

9. Stephen Patrick Morrisey (b. 1959), popular British singer with The Smiths in the 1980s and solo artist after that. *Nine Inch Nails*: industrial rock band from Cleveland, popular in the 1990s.

ORANGUTAN: Oh Chutes&Ladders. You old bag of bones, you! You old so-and-so, you mensch,[1] you human being! Why the hell didn't you tell me?

CHUTES&LADDERS: I'm just hoping I have the guts to get on the plane.

ORANGUTAN: Of course you're getting on that damn plane! For me you did this?

[FOUNTAINHEAD *logs on.*]

FOUNTAINHEAD: Hey everyone. I managed to find one computer here at the hospital that works. Odessa asked me to post a message on her behalf. She landed on: "Go." Hit reset on the timer. Back to day one.

ORANGUTAN: Who's Odessa?

FOUNTAINHEAD: Sorry. Haikumom.

ORANGUTAN: What? Do you log on here just to mock us?

CHUTES&LADDERS: Hold on, is she okay?

FOUNTAINHEAD: Cardiac arrest. They said she was one hair from a coma. She hadn't used in six years and her system went nuts.

CHUTES&LADDERS: So she's alive?

FOUNTAINHEAD: And just barely ticking. Tubes in and out of her nose. She's responsive, she mumbled a few words.

ORANGUTAN: You can't be serious.

CHUTES&LADDERS: Why are you there? Were you using with her?

FOUNTAINHEAD: No.

CHUTES&LADDERS: Did you sell her the stuff?

FOUNTAINHEAD: No, Jesus, of course not. She gave them my number, I'm her emergency contact. Why, I have no idea, we're practically strangers. Getting here to the hospital, seeing her like that . . . I don't mean this as an insult, but she looked not human. Bones with skin covering. Mummy-like.

ORANGUTAN: Fuck. You.

FOUNTAINHEAD: I'm being descriptive. I'm being honest. The thought of my boys walking in on me like that. My wife finding me . . .

1. Human being (Yiddish), with a connotation of a trustworthy, honorable, noble person.

ORANGUTAN: That woman is the reason I'm. Oh god, you get complacent for one second! One second! You get comfortable for one minute! Fountainhead, go to the stats page. You'll see. There's thousands of members on this site. People she has saved, people she may yet save some day. I am one of them. You are one of them.

CHUTES&LADDERS: Fountainhead, does she have family there? Has anyone come through her room?

FOUNTAINHEAD: Apparently a son and a niece but they had to catch a flight to San Juan.[2]

CHUTES&LADDERS: No parents? No other children? A friend? A neighbor?

FOUNTAINHEAD: None showed up.

CHUTES&LADDERS: Fountainhead. You have a family, I absolutely understand that, and I mean zero disrespect when I say, when I beg of you this: your job on this earth has just changed. It is not to stay clean. It's not to be a husband or a father or a CEO. It's to stay by that woman's side. Make sure she gets home safe. Bathe her. Feed her. Get her checked into a rehab, inpatient. Do not leave her side for a second. Can you do this?

FOUNTAINHEAD: I have one day clean. I'm not meant to be a saint.

CHUTES&LADDERS: Tell me now, swear on your mother's name, otherwise I'm on the first flight to Philadelphia.

FOUNTAINHEAD: I don't know.

CHUTES&LADDERS: Look man, do you believe in God?

FOUNTAINHEAD: Sure, along with unicorns and the boogeyman.

CHUTES&LADDERS: How about miracles?

FOUNTAINHEAD: When the Phils are winning.

CHUTES&LADDERS: How about actions? I bet you believe in those.

FOUNTAINHEAD: Yeah.

CHUTES&LADDERS: Your lifeboat has just arrived. Get on board or get out of the way.

FOUNTAINHEAD: I'll take care of Odessa. You have my word. My solemn word. [*Pause*] She did manage to say one thing: Someone

2. Capital of Puerto Rico.

has to take over site admin. She doesn't want the chat room full of curse words.

[YAZ *appears. A screen lights up:*]

FREEDOM&NOISE
STATUS: ONLINE

FREEDOM&NOISE: I'm good with computers. I'll throw my hat in the ring.

CHUTES&LADDERS: Freedom&Noise, are you new here?

FREEDOM&NOISE: Yes. Very.

[FOUNTAINHEAD'*s phone rings.*]

FOUNTAINHEAD: Freedom&Noise, email me offline. Link attached. I gotta go.

CHUTES&LADDERS: You gave us your word. Don't be a stranger.

[FOUNTAINHEAD *logs off. Into the phone:*]

FOUNTAINHEAD: Hi, honey, sorry I haven't called sooner. Something came up. Listen, I'm not coming home tonight, just order in. I have a friend who got sick, she's having an emergency. No, it's not a romantic friend. I will tell you about it. When I get home. When I— Honey? Honey . . .

[*The call is over. He writes a text message.*]

Honey, under my bookmarks, click on "Fantasy Football" link. My username is "Fountainhead." My password is "Porsche71." Log on and read. Send.

Scene 14

Puerto Rico. A hotel room. YAZ *is online.*

FREEDOM&NOISE: Hello, I am Freedom&Noise, your interim site manager, currently logging on from the Rainforest B&B in Puerto Rico. I am not a user, I've smoked pot twice, both times when I was thirteen, and am therefore unqualified for this position. There was a young woman I once knew. Let's call her "O." My crazy aunt, a fun babysitter, the baddest hide-and-seek player north of Girard Avenue. We played dress-up, built booby traps and forts, and when I was eight, she disappeared. No explanation, no acknowledgment she had ever existed, the grown-ups in the family had taken a vow of silence, and O. had been erased. My freshman year at college, I returned home for Thanksgiving, and thanks to a snow delay I walked into the middle of turkey dinner itself, and there was O., a plate full of food, chowing down. I hadn't seen her in ten years. After dinner she told me to congratulate her, it was her anniversary. I said, "Did you get married?" She pulled a necklace out from under her shirt and said, "You know what these gold letters mean? The 'N' is for narcotics, the 'A' is for anonymous and today is my two-year anniversary of being clean." [*Pause*] A few days ago I met a new woman: Haikumom. A woman who created a living, breathing ecosystem, and since I've never sown a single seed, let alone planted a garden, the least I can do is censor you, fix glitches—and one other thing . . . Formulating first line. Did Haikumom really do these on the fly? Five-seven-five, right? [*Counting the syllables on her fingers*] Box full of ashes . . .

[ELLIOT *enters from the bathroom, freshly showered, pulling on a shirt*]

ELLIOT: Whatchu looking at, Willis?[3]
YAZ: Sh. I'm counting syllables.

[ELLIOT *looks over* YAZ's *shoulder at the computer.*]

ELLIOT: Hold up. Don't read that shit, Yaz.
YAZ: You know how Odessa got into haiku in the first place?
ELLIOT: For real, close the computer.
YAZ: I went through this Japanese minimalist phase freshman year. Rock Gardens, Zen Buddhism, the works. I gave her a haiku collection for Christmas.
ELLIOT: Yeah, and you gave me a midget tree that died by New Year's.
YAZ: Bonsai. You didn't water it.
ELLIOT: [*Closing* YAZ's *laptop*] For the two days I'm away from Philly, let me be away from Philly?

---

3. Variation on the catch phrase of the child character Arnold, played by Gary Coleman, on the television sit-com *Different Strokes* (1978–1985).

YAZ: You know where I was gonna be by thirty? Two kids. Equal-housework marriage. Tenure, no question. Waaaay tenured, like by the age of twenty-four. Carnegie Hall debuts: Yazmin Ortiz's "Oratorio for Electric Guitar and Children's Choir." I wrote a list on a piece of paper and dug a hole in Fairmount Park[4] and put it in the ground and said, "When I turn thirty, I'll dig it up and cross it all off." And I promise you I'll never have the courage to go to that spot with a shovel and face my list full of crumbs, decoys and bandaids.

ELLIOT: Married with kids, what an awful goal.

YAZ: Odessa's done things.

ELLIOT: Well, when you throw her a parade, don't expect me to come.

YAZ: You've done things.

ELLIOT: I wouldn't come to my own parade, either.

YAZ: Ginny did things. What have I done?

ELLIOT: Second-grade Language Arts. You glued my book report.

YAZ: I couldn't stop your leg from getting chewed up.

ELLIOT: Fairmount little league basketball. You kept score, you brought our equipment.

YAZ: I didn't hold your hand when you were in the desert popping pills trying to make yourself disappear. I didn't keep Odessa away from that needle. I didn't water a single plant in Ginny's garden. We're in PR and I'm gonna dig a new hole and I'm not putting a wish or a list in there, I'm putting a scream in there. And I'm gonna sow it like the ugliest foulest and most necessary seed in the world and it's going to bloom! This time it's going to fucking bloom!

ELLIOT: My eyes just did this weird thing. For a second, it was Mom standing in front of me.

YAZ: Odessa?

ELLIOT: Ginny.

YAZ: Elliot, your birth mother saved your life by giving you away. Tell me I'm wrong.

[ELLIOT *doesn't respond.* YAZ *begins gathering her stuff hastily.*]

Now we got some ashes to throw. El Yunque closes in an hour and a half.

---

4. Popular and scenic park along the Schuylkill river front in downtown Philadelphia.

ELLIOT: Maybe we should do this tomorrow.
YAZ: I gotta make a call. I'll be in the lobby!

[*She exits.*]

ELLIOT: Yaz?

[*The* GHOST *appears. He's probably been there the whole time.*]

Yaz!

GHOST: Momken men-fadluck ted-dini gawaz saffari?

[*The* GHOST *reaches out his hand to touch* ELLIOT.]

Momken men-fadluck ted-dini gawaz saffari?

[*The second they make contact,* ELLIOT *spins on his heels and grabs the* GHOST. *The* GHOST *defends himself, pulling away. They start pushing, grabbing, fighting. The* GHOST *is looking for something—is it* ELLIOT'*s wallet?*]

Momken men-fadluck ted-dini gawaz saffari?

[*The* GHOST *finds* ELLIOT'*s wallet and tears through it, hurling its contents onto the floor.* ELLIOT *attacks again, but this time the* GHOST *reaches out his hand and touches* ELLIOT'*s face.* ELLIOT *freezes, unable to move, as the* GHOST'*s hands glide across his features, considering each one with authority, taking inventory.*]

Momken men-fadluck ted-dini gawaz saffari?

[*The* GHOST *is gone.* ELLIOT *catches his breath, shaken. He reaches into his pocket and pulls out a bottle of pills. He puts one pill in his hand. Then he empties the entire bottle of pills into his hand. He stares at the pills, wanting to throw them away.*]

Scene 15

Split scene. ODESSA'*s bathroom. The bathtub is filled with water.* JOHN *enters, carrying a very weak* ODESSA. ODESSA *is wearing shorts and a bra, a modest outfit for bathing.* JOHN *lowers her gently into the bathtub.*

JOHN: Does that feel okay?

[ODESSA *barely nods.*]

It's not too hot or cold?

[ODESSA *shakes her head.*]

I don't know how to do this. These are things women do. Take care of sick people. Make the wounds go away.

[*He takes a sponge and starts to bathe her.*]

Is this okay?

[*He lifts her arms and washes her armpits. Embarrassed at first, but quickly gets the swing of it.*]

We check you in at 4:30 so we have plenty of time to clean you up and get you in good clothes, okay? You'll go in there looking like a decent woman.

[ODESSA *whispers something inaudible.*]

What was that?

[*She gestures for him to lean in. She whispers into his ear.*]

One more time.

[*She whispers a little louder.*]

Did someone take swimming lessons?

[*She whispers again.*]

Did someone put on water wings?

[*She nods. He continues to bathe her, gently, in silence as:
    Lights rise on Tokyo. Narita Airport.* ORANGUTAN *sits on the floor by the luggage carousel. At her feet is a sign that says* CHUTES&LADDERS. *She throws the sign like a frisbee across the floor and gets up to leave.* CHUTES&LADDERS *enters, rolling a suitcase behind him. He waves to* ORANGUTAN.]

CHUTES&LADDERS: Orangutan?
ORANGUTAN: What the holy hell?
CHUTES&LADDERS: Sorry. Sorry. I tried calling but my cell doesn't work here. I told you I'm no good at this fancy kind of living.
ORANGUTAN: You were supposed to land yesterday, you were too scared to get on the plane. You rebook, you were supposed to

land today, forty-five minutes ago. Everyone got their luggage already. The last person pulled the last suitcase from the carousel half an hour ago. I thought, Wow, this one sure knows how to play a joke on the ladies. I thought you had left me at the fucking altar.

CHUTES&LADDERS: I got sick on the flight. Totally embarrassing. I had a panic attack as the plane landed and I started tossing into the doggy bag right next to this nice old lady. I've been sitting on the bathroom floor emptying my stomach. Then I had to find a toothbrush and toothpaste and mouthwash because I didn't want to greet you with bad breath and all.

[*She looks skeptical. She sniffs his mouth quickly.*]

ORANGUTAN: Minty. [*Pause*] Oh, you dummy, you big old dummy. COME HERE, you San Diego Padre.

[*They hug. A warm and brief greeting.*]

What's your name?

CHUTES&LADDERS: Clay. Clayton "Buddy" Wilkie.

ORANGUTAN: I'm Madeleine Mays.

CHUTES&LADDERS: It's weird, huh?

ORANGUTAN: Totally weird. The land of the living.

[*They hug. They melt into each other's arms. A hug of basic survival and necessary friendship. Then, they exit, rolling* CHUTES&LADDERS'*s suitcase off as lights rise in:
    Puerto Rico. A rock outcropping looking out over a waterfall.* ELLIOT *is there, looking down at the water.*]

ELLIOT: [*Looking down*] Oh shit! Yaz, you gotta see this! Yaz? Fucking Johnny Appleseed of El Yunque.

[YAZ *enters holding a soil-covered flower bulb. She compares the root against a field book.*]

YAZ: I found my spiral ginger! This is going right next to the aloe by the kitchen door, baby!

ELLIOT: Yo, this science experiment ain't getting past security.

YAZ: Experiment my ass. I'm planting these in Ginny's garden.

ELLIOT: Customs gonna sniff that shit from a mile away.

YAZ: [*Putting the bulb in a ziploc baggie full of dirt and bulbs*] China rose . . . Sea grape . . . Some kind of fern . . .

ELLIOT: When they cuff those wrists, I don't know you.

YAZ: I'll hide them in my tampon box.

ELLIOT: That don't work. My first trip to PR, Mami Ginny smuggled a coqui[5] back with her kotex and got arrested. Front page of the *Daily News*.

YAZ: Good shit. [*A dirty little secret*] You know what Grandma did?

ELLIOT: Do I want to?

YAZ: She used to smuggle stuff back, too. She'd tuck it below her boobs. She had storage space under there!

ELLIOT: Yeah after she was sixty and had nursed seven kids. Yo you think if I jumped off this rock right now and dove into that water, I'd survive?

YAZ: Just watch out for the huge boulders and the footbridge.

ELLIOT: It's tempting. That spray. [*His phone beeps*] Reception in the rainforest.

YAZ: Kind of ruins the romance.

ELLIOT: [*Reads a text message*] Damn, that was fast.

YAZ: What?

ELLIOT: Pop sold the house. Did he even put out a listing?

YAZ: Not that I know of.

ELLIOT: That's like a VW bus going from zero to sixty in three seconds. Don't make no sense.

YAZ: Must have been an inside job.

ELLIOT: I guess so.

YAZ: A way way inside job . . .

ELLIOT: Yaz . . .

YAZ: [*Conspiratorially*] Yeeeees?

ELLIOT: What did you do?

YAZ: [*Very conspiratorially*] Nothing . . .

ELLIOT: Holy shit!

YAZ: Put my Steinway[6] on craigslist. Got four responses before you made it down to the lobby. My eighty-eight keys are worth more than Ginny's whole house. Sadly. I'll buy an upright.

5. Species of small frog indigenous to Puerto Rico.   6. A top-of-the-line brand of piano.

ELLIOT: You are one crazy motherfucking adjunct! Yo, I don't know if el barrio is ready for you. I don't know if they can handle you!

YAZ: Oh, they gonna handle me.

ELLIOT: Wait wait wait. You need a title.

YAZ: Yaz will do just fine.

ELLIOT: Hells no. Command respect. I step on those corners, I'm Big El. [*Pause*] "Professor."

YAZ: "Professor."

ELLIOT: You like that, huh?

YAZ: It'll be the Cousins House. We'll renovate the kitchen. You redo the plumbing, I'll hook up a little tile backsplash.

ELLIOT: I watched Bob Vila[7] with Pop, but I ain't no handyman.

YAZ: Just wait, Mr. Home Depot. You're gonna be like, "Fuacata, fuacata, fuacata,"[8] with your power drill and nail gun and vise grips.

ELLIOT: Something like that.

YAZ: Well? Get to it. Toss 'em.

ELLIOT: Me? Why the hell do you think I let you come along?

[*He hands* YAZ *the box.*]

YAZ: Well then say something. Pray.

ELLIOT: I'm all out of prayers.

YAZ: Me, too. Make a toast.

ELLIOT: To LAX. I'm not flying back with you.

YAZ: What do you mean?

ELLIOT: I called from the hotel and changed my flight. One-way ticket. Watch out, Hollywood. [*Pause*] You know how you had to shake me awake last night?

YAZ: [*Demeanor shifting*] You were literally sobbing in your sleep.

ELLIOT: This dream was different than usual. I'm fixing a Subway hoagie, I feel eyes on the back of my neck, I turn around and expect to see him, the first guy I shot down in Iraq. But instead it's Mami Ginny. Standing next to the bread oven, smiling. You know how her eyes smile?

YAZ: Best smile in the world.

---

7. First host of a popular do-it-yourself television show, *This Old House*, on PBS, from 1979 to 1989.

8. Exclamation, such as "bang!" or "wham!" used when people accidentally hurt themselves.

ELLIOT: Looking at me, her son. Coming to say good-bye.

YAZ: That's beautiful.

ELLIOT: She puts on her glasses to see my face even better. She squints and something changes. The moment I come into focus, her eyes widen. Her jaw drops, she starts trembling. Then she starts to cry. Something she's seeing scares her. Then she starts to scream. Loud, like, "Ahhh! Ahhh!" She won't stop looking at me, but she's terrified, horrified by what she sees. And I don't know if my lip is bleeding or there's a gash on my forehead or she's looking through my eyes and seeing straight into my fucking soul.

YAZ: Jesus.

ELLIOT: I wanted Mami Odessa to relapse, Yaz. I wanted her to pick up that needle. I knew precisely what to do, what buttons to push, I engineered that shit, I might as well have pushed the thing into her vein. Because I thought, Why would God take the good one? Yo, take the bad mom instead! I was like, Why wouldn't you take the bad fucking mom? If I stay in Philly, I'm gonna turn into it. I'm gonna become one of them. I'm already halfway there. You've got armor, you've got ideas, but I don't.

YAZ: Go. Go and don't you ever, ever look back.

[*She takes his hand.*]

But if you do, there will be a plastic-covered sofa waiting for you.

[*Below them, in Philadelphia,* JOHN *is done bathing* ODESSA. *He lifts her and holds her like an angel above the bathtub. She is dripping wet and seems almost radiant, and yet deeply, deeply sick.*]

I'm the elder now. I stay home. I hold down the fort.

ELLIOT: I'm walking.

YAZ: On three?

YAZ *and* ELLIOT: One.

Two.

Three.

[*They toss the ashes. Blackout.*]

2011

Biographical Sketches

Margaret Edson (b. 1961) Despite degrees in Renaissance history and English literature from Smith College and Georgetown University, respectively, Margaret Edson has not limited herself to the collegiate classroom. She has sold hot dogs in Iowa City, lived for a year in a convent in Rome, volunteered as an ESL instructor, and worked for a research hospital in Washington, D.C. It was during this last occupation that Edson conceived of what soon became her first, only, and Pulitzer Prize–winning play, *Wit* (1999), about a John Donne professor battling terminal cancer. After her instant success as a playwright, Edson continued teaching kindergarten. She does not have plans to return to playwriting, affirming that she has said what she needed to say; she "could go on, but [she] won't." Edson now teaches sixth-grade social studies and lives with her partner and two sons in Atlanta, Georgia.

Susan Glaspell (1882–1948) Glaspell was born in Davenport, Iowa, earned a bachelor's degree in philosophy from Drake University, and started her writing career as a reporter in Des Moines. After a few years on the job, including a period in graduate school at the University of Chicago, she returned to Davenport and wrote short stories for magazines. In 1913, she and George Cook, a writer from a prominent Davenport family, relocated to New York City's Greenwich Village, where they married and became vital figures in the bohemian, literary scene. Each summer they vacationed in Provincetown, Massachusetts, and there, in 1915, they founded the Provincetown Players. A semiprofessional group distinguished by its association with radicals such as the journalist and communist John Reed and the poet Edna St. Vincent Millay, this company launched not only Glaspell's career as a playwright but also Eugene

O'Neill's, and it enjoyed success in Greenwich Village. Glaspell and Cook had been living in Greece for two years when Cook died in 1924. Glaspell returned to America, where she wrote mostly fiction and a memoir of Cook's life. She died of cancer in Provincetown.

Lorraine Hansberry (1930–1965) Hansberry grew up in Chicago, the daughter of politically active, middle-class African Americans. The household was vibrant, and among the visitors the young Hansberry met were the singer Paul Robeson, the musician Duke Ellington, and the athletes Jesse Owens and Joe Louis. The family had a tradition of attending Howard University, but Hansberry chose to enroll in the University of Wisconsin, though she did not stay long enough to graduate. She moved to New York and began writing for Robeson's newspaper, *Freedom*. She did carry on the family tradition of fighting against racism in American life and law. In 1952, she stood in for Robeson at the Intercontinental Peace Conference in Montevideo, Chile. Robeson could not attend because the State Department had refused to issue him a passport, and Hansberry's trip was undertaken in a surreptitious manner. After a couple of fitful starts, she wrote *A Raisin in the Sun* in 1957 and read it to her husband's friend, Philip Rose, who so liked it that he immediately embarked on a campaign to get it on Broadway, which he succeeded in doing by 1959. The play was a smash hit, winning the New York Drama Critics Circle Award and running for hundreds of performances. Columbia Pictures made it into a movie, and Hansberry enjoyed instant celebrity as a prominent African American intellectual. She continued writing plays and worked actively for the Student Nonviolent Coordinating Committee, even after she was diagnosed with cancer in 1963. Within two years the cancer claimed her life, at the age of thirty-four.

Quiara Alegría Hudes (b. 1977) Hudes grew up in west Philadelphia, where she studied piano at a branch campus of the Settlement Music School. She went on to Yale University to study music and then earned an MFA from Brown University in playwriting. Her 2007 play, *Elliot, a Soldier's Fugue,* was a finalist for the Pulitzer Prize. It was the first in a trilogy, along with *Water by the Spoonful* (2011) and *The Happiest Song Plays Last* (2013). In 2010, she collaborated with Lin-Manuel Miranda on the libretto for *In the Heights,* which earned Hudes a second finalist listing for the Pulitzer. In 2011, *Water by the Spoonful* premiered at the Hartford Stage and did win the Pulitzer Prize for Drama for that year. Hudes is a professor at Wesleyan University and playwright in residence at New York's Signature Theater.

Henrik Ibsen (1828–1906) Ibsen was born to a well-to-do family in a lumber town south of Christiana (later called Oslo), Norway. His father's business crashed when Ibsen was six, and the family experienced the humiliations that follow a financial reversal. At fifteen, Ibsen was apprenticed to a druggist; he went to Christiana six years later and, failing to enter the university there, eventually found work in the theater, as an assistant stage manager in Bergen. Here he wrote the plays of his first "period," romantic, mythological works celebrating Norway's national independence. Frustrated and poor, Ibsen left Norway at thirty-six, partly subsidized by government grants, for the warmer climates of Italy and Germany, where he lived for the next three decades. The production of *The League of Youth* in 1869 began the second of Ibsen's periods, this one of realistic drama exemplified by *A Doll's House*, which he wrote in 1879. His plays during these twelve or so years revolutionized the European stage, and on the strength of this achievement Ibsen is often called the father of modern theater. During his third period, Ibsen's work remained realistic but made increasing use of symbolic metaphor and was preoccupied with the place of the artist in the world. He died after a series of strokes that made him an invalid in his final years, which he spent in Norway.

Arthur Miller (1915–2005) Miller's family lived in Manhattan until the Great Depression reversed their fortunes, and they moved to Brooklyn. There Miller graduated from high school, where he excelled more as an athlete than as a student. His grades were good enough for college, but it took him three years of odd jobs before he got accepted to the University of Michigan, where he began writing plays. By the late 1930s, he was writing for radio shows; his first Broadway play, a failure, premiered in 1944. He wrote a successful novel and then the Ibsen-esque play *All My Sons* in 1947, which beat out a play by Eugene O'Neill for the New York Drama Critics Circle Award. In a six-week burst of creativity, he wrote *Death of a Salesman*, abandoning the strict conventions of realism he had used earlier and experimenting with stage design, lighting, music, and the like. The play was an instant success, running for more than two years on Broadway, inspiring a film, and becoming a favorite of local repertoire theaters across the nation. It also won the Pulitzer Prize. Most notable among Miller's subsequent work was *The Crucible* (1953), a play about the Salem witch hunts that allegorizes Senator Joseph McCarthy's persecution of American communists. Miller himself was persecuted by the Catholic War Veterans and the Committee on Un-American Activities, which brought him before Congress to testify about his involvement with communists. He refused to name other writers who had links to the communists and was convicted of contempt of Congress, though the conviction was overturned on appeal. In 1956, Miller married Marilyn Monroe and wrote a film, *The Misfits*, with her in a leading role, but they divorced in 1961. He continued writing plays into the 1990s and lived on a farm in Connecticut until his death from heart failure in 2005.

William Shakespeare (1564–1616) Shakespeare was born into an upwardly mobile family in the country town of Stratford-on-Avon, England. His father, the son of a tenant farmer, became a leatherworker, a small businessman, and eventually the mayor of Stratford. His mother came from a fairly prosperous farming family. The Shakespeares' oldest son, William probably went to grammar school, where he would have learned rhetoric and read at least some of the Roman playwrights, but not studied the wider field of classical authors that a university man would have read. At eighteen, he married Anne Hathaway, who was twenty-six and apparently pregnant. They had three children. Shakespeare might have taught school for awhile, but no one knows what he did in the years before history finds him, in 1592, away from his family, living in London, acting, writing plays, and perhaps managing a theater company. During the next twenty-five years he wrote thirty-eight plays, becoming the unrivaled king of London theater, growing richer every year (in fact, multiplying his fortune many times over), buying property and fine houses back in Stratford and a coat of arms for his family. In 1599, he bought a ten-percent share in the Globe, a new theater on the south bank of the River Thames. He quit the theater in his late forties and retired to the relative quiet and beauty of Stratford, where he died (legend has it) on his birthday, April 23.

Sophocles (496?–406? B.C.E.) Sophocles was born to a wealthy family in a small town outside Athens, Greece, the age's most industrious and intellectual metropolis. Legend holds that he was handsome and a talented public singer. Famous for his companion-ability, Sophocles held a number of public positions—civic, military, and religious—through his long life. Athens was at the peak of its power and of its culture, and the finest ornaments of that culture were the plays staged in celebration of the annual Dionysian festivals. The playwright Aeschylus had raised the original choral songs and dances to the height of drama, but Sophocles became the master of the Greek stage when, at twenty-eight, he beat Aeschylus in the annual dramatic competition. Over the course of his career he wrote 125 tragedies, including the ever-popular *Antigone*, never finishing worse than second place in the competitions. Only seven of his plays have survived antiquity, and these all come from the third and most mature period in Sophocles' career, spanning the latter fifty years of his life. His last play, *Oedipus at Colonus*, a sequel to *Oedipus the King*, was first performed five years after Sophocles' death.

August Wilson (1945–2005) Wilson was born Frederick August Kittel in "The Hill," the African American community in Pittsburgh, Pennsylvania. His father, a white man, abandoned the family when Wilson was young, and his mother, a black woman whose surname was Wilson, remarried and eventually moved the family to Hazelwood, a predominantly white neighborhood. A teacher's racially motivated accusation of plagiarism led Wilson to leave his Catholic high school, and he largely continued his education on his own. In his twenties, Wilson began writing poetry and founded a theater company, Black Horizons, dedicated to voicing the black experience in America and inspiring audiences to political action. In 1978, he moved to St. Paul, Minnesota, where he wrote, among other things, dramatic pieces for the Science Museum. In 1982, his full-length play *Ma Rainey's Black Bottom* was read at the National Playwrights Conference at the O'Neill Theater Center, in Waterford, Connecticut; a production at Yale University went to Broadway two years later. Wilson's first national success began his series of historical plays, each set in a different decade of the twentieth century. *Fences* was read at the O'Neill Theater Center in 1983, and by 1987 it was on Broadway, breaking box-office records for nonmusical dramas. The play also won the New York Drama Critics Circle Award and the Pulitzer Prize, as well as numerous Tony Awards. *Joe Turner's Come and Gone* (1984), *The Piano Lesson* (1987), and subsequent plays in the series enjoyed critical and commercial success.

Glossary

antagonist   the character against whom the protagonist struggles. For example, Helmer is the antagonist in *A Doll's House*.

atmosphere   the emotional effect or mood produced in an audience, especially by the physical spectacle and the sound of a scene or play: the set, the music, and so on. For example, the atmosphere of *Death of a Salesman* should be claustrophobic or confining.

catharsis   an effect of tragedy in which the emotions of pity and terror are purged from an audience; according to Aristotle, catharsis accounts for viewers' pleasure in viewing the troubling events of tragedy on stage.

character   most generally, any person represented in a play by an actor; more narrowly, the personality of such a person. Aristotle used the term to refer to the moral temperament of a person.

citation   a formal way of directing your readers to a source to which you refer in your own paper. Different disciplines use different conventions for citing sources; most literary journals use the Modern Language Association (MLA) style sheet for citations.

chorus   a conventional element of ancient Greek drama, consisting of a group of singers and dancers who participate in or comment on the action. For example, Sophocles used the chorus to represent crowds, such as the citizens of Thebes in *Antigone*, and to voice what might be considered mainstream attitudes toward the characters' interactions.

climax   the moment within a plot in which the conflict ends; often (though not necessarily), the emotional high point of the drama.

close reading   careful, attentive reading of a work with an eye not just to what happens, but to the literary elements, like setting, metaphor, and symbol, that create meaning in a work.

comedy   a subgenre of drama that generally celebrates the human condition; usually, a comedy is funny.

complication   an event that sets a conflict in motion. For example, in *Hamlet*, the arrival of the ghost is the complication, because he spurs Hamlet to enmity with Claudius.

conflict   the opposition of two people or forces; without this crucial element of plot, there could be no play. For example, in *A Doll's House*, Nora, the protagonist, struggles against social conventions and laws, against Helmer, and against her own internalized patterns of behavior.

conventional symbol   a thing carrying symbolic meaning only within the context of a particular culture. For example, the maple leaf conventionally symbolizes Canada; that meaning is bestowed on the object by Canadians.

cultural context   the nexus of social institutions and beliefs in which a play is produced. For example, the cultural context of *Antigone* is (broadly speaking) democratic Athens and (more narrowly) Athens during a war with Sparta. Although *Fences* is set in 1950s America, its cultural context is the Reagan era, the 1980s, when the play was first produced.

diction   the style of language used by a character, especially his or her vocabulary, which can indicate the character's station in life. For example, in *Hamlet*, Polonius's diction marks him as an educated courtier, while the gravediggers' diction indicates their place among the lower classes.

dramatic convention   any device habitually used in theater. For example, the closing of a curtain to mark the end of a scene is a convention that arose in the nineteenth-century theater; in Shakespeare's day, playwrights often ended scenes with a rhyming couplet; the use of a chorus is a convention of the Greek theater.

dynamic character   a character who changes during the course of the play; usually, the protagonist will be dynamic. For example, Hamlet undergoes mental and physical transformations throughout *Hamlet*.

equilibrium   the state of relative stability that precedes the introduction of a conflict. For example, Hamlet, though he is unhappy, is in a state of equilibrium until his colloquy with his father's ghost.

exposition   the revelation, usually by recitation, of events that occurred before the opening scene in a play.

falling action   the events in a play—a sequence of consequences— that occur after the climax. For example, the funeral scene in *Fences* is part of the falling action.

flashback   a scene interrupting the normal chronological sequence of a play or film; a flashback enacts events that occurred prior to the stage "present."

genre   any category into which similar works of literature, film, and so on are grouped. For example, speaking broadly, drama is a genre; tragedy and comedy are genres within that larger category; satire is a genre within comedy. The hour-long television drama is a genre, and the cop drama and the hospital drama are genres within that larger category. Genres within genres are sometimes called *subgenres*.

groundlings   the poorest members of the audience in the Elizabethan theater; the groundlings stood in the open-air yard surrounding the stage.

heuristics   strategies and techniques of applying problem-solving frameworks to a particular problem or question.

hubris   excessive pride; it is a common characteristic of tragic heroes.

identify   to imagine that you are a particular character on the stage; you identify with a character if the events in a play trigger the same emotions in you (though perhaps less intensely) as they trigger in the character. For example, someone who identifies with Cory in *Fences* will feel frustrated and angry and threatened when Troy triggers those emotions in Cory.

in media res   literally, "in the middle of things"; a story that begins in media res is already beyond the plot's complication, which then must be divulged to the audience through exposition.

literary symbol   a thing carrying symbolic meaning only within a particular work of literature; the same object in another literary work or in real life does not necessarily carry the same symbolic meaning.

meaning   what a play says about its theme(s). The meaning is usually a matter of complex interpretation, and in an interpretive essay it is generally summarized by a thesis statement.

method acting   a style of acting developed by the Russian director Konstantin Stanislavsky (1863–1938) and popularized in the United States by Elia Kazan, who directed the first production of *Death of a Salesman*. A method actor tries to take on the identity of the character, identify with the character psychologically, and "act" according to the character's nature.

orchestra   in ancient Greek theaters, the circular floor where the chorus danced and sang; in contemporary theaters, the space in front of the stage (used by the orchestra) or the forward section of seats on the main floor.

pity   one of the emotions aroused in an audience by tragedy; according to Aristotle, pity comes from feeling that the protagonist's suffering goes beyond what he or she deserves.

plot   the events that constitute the story in a play. The plot begins when a conflict is introduced into a state of equilibrium; the events that intensify the conflict are called the rising action; the conflict is ended at the climax; the events following the climax are called the falling action; and the resolution is the final state of equilibrium.

prop   any material object handled in a play, such as the swords in the final scene of *Hamlet*.

proscenium arch   a decorative arch over the stage separating it from the auditorium in many nineteenth-century and some twentieth-century theaters; often, the curtain descends from behind this arch.

prosperity   in a tragedy, the state of relative success and comfort the protagonist enjoys at the play's beginning.

protagonist   the character that the play is about; its central character. The protagonist usually is dynamic and must always be the focus of the primary conflict. For example, Nora is the protagonist in *A Doll's House*.

recognition   the self-knowledge that a tragic hero gains through the events of the play; usually, this knowledge concerns his or her complicity in the reversal, but it comes too late to mitigate the consequences of that reversal.

recursive   literally, circling back or repeating. In rhetoric, *recursive* refers to the circular nature of the writing process: most writers repeat stages in the process, rewriting (for instance) their thesis several times at different stages of the essay's composition.

resolution in a tragedy, the relatively stable (though often unpleasant) conditions that are the consequence of the working out of the conflict.

revenge tragedy a type of tragedy in which an oath or powerful emotion compels the protagonist to acts of bloody revenge that are often self-destructive; for example, *Hamlet*.

reversal in a tragedy, the moment at which the tragic hero, who has begun the play in a relatively exalted position, falls.

rising action the events that increase the intensity of the conflict.

romantic comedy a drama, usually light and funny, in which the conflict concerns the hindered but eventually successful match of two lovers.

scenery the materials on stage, such as backdrops and structures, that help the audience imagine the setting of a scene or play.

set all the materials, including the scenery, that convey a sense of place to the audience.

spectacle an element in Aristotle's analysis of drama; anything that appeals to the eyes in a play, from costumes to scenery.

static character a character who does not change during the course of the play.

stock character a stereotypical character that reappears in a genre.

symbol a thing that represents something other than itself. The thing might stand for an object or objects, or it might represent an abstraction or a range of abstractions. For example, a backyard barbecue grill might represent a suburb, or it might represent the American dream.

sympathetic character a character with whom the audience sympathizes; a likeable character.

terror in a tragedy, the emotion the audience feels as a consequence of recognizing that they share the tragic hero's fate.

theme what a play is about on an abstract level. For example, love, revenge, friendship, or mortality.

thesis statement a sentence or small group of sentences that summarize what a critic is trying to persuade his or her readers to believe about a work. It must be debatable rather than a point of fact, and it is the main point of a critical essay.

tiring-house the enclosure at the back of the Elizabethan stage; the inside of the tiring-house was out of the audience's view and thus served for costume changes and other business.

tragedy   a genre of drama that traces the fall from prosperity of a heroic, though imperfect, protagonist; for example, *Antigone*.

tragic hero   the protagonist in a tragedy; the tragic hero is generally a larger-than-life character, a leader in his or her community, who falls from a state of prosperity to poverty (either material or metaphoric) over the course of the play.

universal symbol   a thing carrying the same symbolic meaning in various cultures. For example, the setting sun generally represents death or ending.

unsympathetic character   a character with whom the audience does not sympathize; an unlikeable character.

well-made play   a type of play popular in the nineteenth century that drew upon a repertoire of crowd-pleasing plot elements and stock characters; the term became synonymous with superficiality.

*

Thematic Index

Class / Economic Status

Death / Dying

Disability / Illness

Family

Gender / Sexuality

Race

War